W9-BBS-099

The Mammoth Book of

HISTORICAL EROTICA

Also available

The Mammoth Book of Vintage Science Fiction
The Mammoth Book of New Age Science Fiction
The Mammoth Book of Fantastic Science Fiction
The Mammoth Book of Modern Science Fiction
The Mammoth Book of Great Detective Stories
The Mammoth Book of True Murder
The Mammoth Book of Short Horror Novels
The Mammoth Book of True War Stories
The Mammoth Book of Modern War Stories
The Mammoth Book of the Western
The Mammoth Book of Ghost Stories
The Mammoth Book of Ghost Stories 2
The Mammoth Book of the Supernatural
The Mammoth Book of Astounding Puzzles
The Mammoth Book of Terror
The Mammoth Book of Vampires
The Mammoth Book of Killer Women
The Mammoth Book of Historical Whodunnits
The Mammoth Book of Werewolves
The Mammoth Book of Golden Age Detective Stories
The Mammoth Book of Contemporary SF Masters
The Mammoth Book of Erotica
The Mammoth Book of Frankenstein
The Mammoth Book of Battles
The Mammoth Book of Astounding Word Games
The Mammoth Book of Mindbending Puzzles
The Mammoth Book of Historical Detectives
The Mammoth Book of Victorian & Edwardian Ghost Stories
The Mammoth Book of Dreams
The Mammoth Book of Symbols
The Mammoth Book of Brainstorming Puzzles
The Mammoth Book of Great Lives
The Mammoth Book of International Erotica
The Mammoth Book of Pulp Fiction
The Mammoth Book of The West
The Mammoth Book of Love & Sensuality
The Mammoth Book of Chess
The Mammoth Book of Fortune Telling
The Mammoth Puzzle Carnival
The Mammoth Book of Dracula
The Mammoth Book of Gay Short Stories
The Mammoth Book of Fairy Tales
The Mammoth Book of New Sherlock Holmes Adventures
The Mammoth Book of Gay Erotica
The Mammoth Book of the Third Reich at War
The Mammoth Book of Best New Horror
The Mammoth Book of Tasteless Lists
The Mammoth Book of Comic Fantasy
The Mammoth Book of New Erotica
The Mammoth Book of Arthurian Legends
The Mammoth Book of Eye-Witness History
The Mammoth Book of True Crime (New edition)

The Mammoth Book of
HISTORICAL EROTICA

Edited by
Maxim Jakubowski

Carroll & Graf Publishers, Inc.
NEW YORK

Carroll & Graf Publishers, Inc.
19 West 21st Street
Suite 601
New York
NY 10010–6805

ISBN 0-7394-0265-X

CONTENTS

ACKNOWLEDGEMENTS

All individual stories © 1998 by their respective authors and reproduced with their permission, with the exception of:

No Natural Magic by Alice Joanou © Alice Joanou, 1992. First appeared in *Tourniquet*.

Amelia by Valentina Cilescu © Valentina Cilescu, 1994. First appeared in *The Rosebud Sutra*.

Perfect Little Venus by Alizarin Lake © Alizarin Lake, 1991. First appeared in *Festival of Venus*.

INTRODUCTION

WELCOME TO THE fourth volume in the Mammoth Book of Erotica series.

This time we decided to assign a specific theme to all the writers who had previously contributed, as well as to our many talented newcomers. The challenge was to create new stories set in the past, but still dripping with our usual quota of sex, lust, desire, emotions and passions. The past is a different country, as we all know, but it is also a fertile ground for the imagination, offering exotic, alien if familiar landscapes in which relationships between men and women (and other variations) can develop in fascinating ways.

I think the results speak for themselves, and we have ended up with a wonderful collection of erotic stories which in no way lack that magic spark for want of present-day technology or the romance of modern cities.

The stories range imaginatively from the garden of Eden and prehistory to 1940, encompassing varied periods and countries and featuring quite an assortment of actual historical characters, with impudent and innovative slices of secret history which might in some cases actually ring truer to the reality of those past days than the dry and factual tales we all have read in history books time and time again!

The authors here range from far and wide, representing Britain, the USA, Canada and Australia, another graceful demonstration that no passport is required for the charmed domain of erotica, where the senses are in full bloom twenty-four hours a day, seven days a week.

Enjoy this lustful descent into the fires of the past, where every sense is there to be tickled, caressed, licked, touched, and untold delights are on wanton display for your delectation, be you male or female or otherwise inclined.

Some have said that sex only began in the 1960s, or with dear Dr Freud making us aware of the fact of its suppressed existence deep down in our psyche. This book jubilantly offers another thesis, so roll on our cast of thousands, led by Adam and Eve, Cleopatra, Mona Lisa, Scott and Zelda Fitzgerald, kings, queens, princesses, maharajahs, courtesans and vestal virgins, to demonstrate how things have never changed and the delights of sex remain paramount in our unhibited enjoyment of life.

Maxim Jakubowski

The Mammoth Book of

HISTORICAL EROTICA

EVELINA

Louisa Campion

THE SOUND OF a horse galloping up to the house made Lady Evelina Trevaire leap to her feet, the novel she'd been reading falling to her feet unheeded.

"Gerrard!" she gasped, running to the window, thinking it might be her husband, but instead it was her cousin Ivor, astride his chestnut stallion.

She hurried over to the mirror and smoothed her hands over her pale gold ringlets, made a slight adjustment to the neckline of her high-waisted lilac gown, then ran into the hallway. Ivor had already dismounted and was striding through the door, his riding crop tucked under his arm.

"Ivor!" she exclaimed in delight as he enfolded her in his arms, his lean body pressed against hers. She leant against him, breathing in the faint tang of his cologne overlaid with a tantalizing hint of leather, and felt the usual quickening in her sex flesh that his close proximity evoked.

The sound of a door closing on the upper gallery warned Evelina that her detestable mother-in-law was about to descend. Reluctantly she drew back while Ivor raised her hand decorously to his lips and kissed it, sending shivers of lust up her arm.

"You're looking ravishing, Cousin," he drawled. "I see that married life agrees with you."

"I fear that you're sadly mistaken," she informed him in a low voice, then, hearing her mother-in-law on the stairs behind her, added urgently, "I must see you alone."

He nodded in understanding before stepping forward to greet the dowager Lady Trevaire.

"Servant, ma'am," he said, bowing gracefully over her hand. Tall, slim, with blond hair and the face of a fallen angel, Ivor was also possessed of considerable charm. So much so that although Lady Trevaire made it a point to disapprove of everything about Evelina – including her relatives – she didn't glare at him with quite the animosity she might have done had he been less well favoured.

"What are you doing here?" she demanded brusquely.

"I've come to pay my respects to you, ma'am, and my sister has charged me with a message for our cousin," he told her smoothly.

"Hrrmph. Then I suppose you'd better stay for a glass of wine," she snapped, taking the arm he proffered and allowing him to conduct her into the blue sitting room.

Evelina followed, fervently hoping that somehow Ivor's appearance might signal the end to what she considered little better than house arrest in the countryside, with her mother-in-law cast in the role of gaoler.

While Lady Trevaire talked non-stop, Evelina studied her cousin covertly. It was over two months since she'd last set eyes on him – her wedding day, in fact – and his golden good looks seemed to shimmer and shine in the dark, over-furnished room.

He was wearing a beautifully cut navy blue riding coat, with his long legs encased in buff-coloured breeches and glossy black top boots. The sight of him made her mouth go dry, and she pressed her thighs together as a lascivious little flame licked at her sex.

Although she willed Lady Trevaire to excuse herself and leave them alone together, Evelina knew that the chances of her doing so were virtually non-existent and racked her brains for some way of getting rid of the older woman. It would be unbearable if Ivor left without her having the chance to speak to him on his own.

Happily he was equal to the occasion, and when Lady Trevaire paused for breath he put down his wine glass and said, "I wonder if you would permit my cousin to show me the orangery, so I might convey my sister's message to her."

Lady Trevaire stiffened. "You may convey it to her in front of me. In my son's absence, Evelina's affairs are my business."

"Perhaps so, but my sister's affairs are not, and she particularly charged me to deliver her message in confidence." He softened the words with a beguiling smile, then rose to his feet saying to Evelina, "After you, Cousin."

The orangery opened off the blue sitting room, and Evelina could only admire Ivor's strategy. They would be within view, so the question of chaperonage wouldn't arise, but they could at least speak privately.

Once the door was closed behind them she burst out, "Detestable woman! How *dare* she behave as if you had come to see her and not me? And how *could* my husband abandon me here with her for weeks on end?"

Seeing how furious she was, Ivor tucked her hand into his arm and stroked it soothingly, being careful to keep their backs turned to Lady Trevaire, whom he knew was watching them beadily through the glass.

"Calm yourself and tell me what happened. Where *is* Gerrard?"

"I don't have the faintest idea, and I don't believe his mother knows either. After our wedding we spent a week together on his estate in Kent, then he said he had some urgent business to attend to, brought me here and I have heard nothing from him since."

"Did you quarrel?" asked Ivor cautiously.

"Indeed, no. Oh, Ivor, if only I'd been able to marry you as we wished – we get along so well together and you're undoubtedly the most handsome man of my acquaintance."

"There's little point in dwelling on it. With no fortune to either of our names it simply wasn't possible." He glanced down at her, his eyes lingering on the swell of her breasts. "Did he bed you to your satisfaction?"

A dreamy smile curved Evelina's lovely mouth and her grey eyes sparkled with pleasure. "It was ecstasy," she confided, then her expression grew stormy as she continued, "But *he* obviously didn't think so. Perhaps he found my lack of experience not to his taste."

"He could hardly have expected otherwise. Ecstasy, you say?"

"Mmm. He made love to me for hours at a time and did things I could never have imagined in my wildest fantasies." Her cheeks grew warm at the memory, and the sight of her obvious arousal sent spears of lust lancing through Ivor's body.

He drew her to stand behind the waist-high wall encircling the ornamental fountain, so they were facing the blue sitting room. She started when she felt his caressing hand on her bottom over the thin silk of her dress.

"Ivor, you must not – she'll see," Evelina protested.

"Not if we remain in this position, as if admiring that singularly ugly fountain." He stroked her lazily, sending shivers of desire rippling through her slender frame and reminding her of the many times he'd touched her intimately for their mutual pleasure.

Slowly, he raised her skirts at the back and slipped his hand under them, then into her silk pantalettes. She inhaled sharply as his fingers glided down the cleft between her buttocks to make contact with the damp curls of her fleece.

He toyed with the slippery tissues of her sex lips, easing them apart and tracing the hidden valleys with his fingertips until she felt warm moisture gathering and then trickling stealthily downwards.

When he slid two fingers inside her and subjected her to a voluptuous internal examination, she felt her knees trembling and hastily gripped the parapet of the fountain to steady herself.

Her tiny bud tingled under his ministrations, eager for his touch, but he concentrated his attention on her velvet sheath, arousingly probing her to her very core.

She eased her thighs further apart to give him greater access as he said, "We must be seen to be conversing in order not to arouse suspicion."

A wave of shivering heat rose slowly through her body as she gasped, "How can I converse when you're touching me so?"

"Then at least nod and smile from time to time while I talk. If only we were alone, so I could free your rose-tipped breasts from the constraints of your bodice and caress them into hard peaks of desire."

A film of perspiration broke out on Evelina's smooth brow, due only in part to the steamy heat of the orangery. Glancing up at Ivor, she had to admire his self-control, for nothing on his face gave away the fact that he was delving between her thighs, his hand already running with her honeyed juices as he continued, 'I wish you could touch me too, hold my manhood in your hand and then take it in your mouth, slipping it between your luscious lips as far as it would go."

She moaned faintly at the heady carnal images this conjured up, and then bit her lip as he turned his attention to her throbbing bud and began to stroke it deftly. Hot, wanton pleasure lanced through her and turned her limbs to water as he worked her towards the release she craved, still describing lewd scenarios he wished to enact with her.

She gripped the parapet harder, almost losing sight of where they were and the fact they were being observed as she ascended the heady spiral of arousal.

Then, in a sudden surge of erotic sensation, she came, gazing hastily downwards as she struggled not to let her intense pleasure show on her face. Panting and striving for self-control, she kept his hand trapped between her thighs until the last wave died down, then she swallowed and murmured, "Is my mother-in-law still watching us?"

"Thankfully for the last minute or so she has been engaged in directing a servant to build up the fire, but she will turn this way again at any moment." Swiftly, he withdrew his hand, allowing her skirts to flutter back around her ankles.

By the time Lady Trevaire resumed her scrutiny of the couple, they had resumed strolling around the room.

"I won't stay here any longer with Gerrard's hateful mother," Evelina declared. "I'm a married woman now, not a schoolroom miss, and I wish to attend balls and assemblies instead of rotting here in the country. Dearest Ivor, would you ask Pauline if I could come and stay with her in London?"

"I'm certain my sister will be delighted, but are you sure it's wise? Gerrard may not like it."

"Gerrard can go to hell," announced Evelina, tossing her golden ringlets. "I had hoped that after our honeymoon we would reside mostly in London, but if that is not to be, I see no reason why I should not enjoy the pleasures of the capital with my cousins."

Ivor's blue eyes gleamed. "Then at last there will be the

opportunity for us to enjoy the particular delight always denied to us before."

Evelina looked up at him with a smile so imbued with sensual promise that he felt his manhood hardening anew.

"Indeed, previously I had to withhold my virtue in readiness for my husband, but he has taken it, as is a husband's privilege, and now there is nothing to prevent us doing as we please – it will serve him right."

They were interrupted by Lady Trevaire, entering the orangery and marching towards them.

"Pauline will need to collect me for I have no carriage of my own," whispered Evelina.

"She will – I'll see to it," he assured her.

"What have you two been talking of for such an age?" demanded Lady Trevaire.

"The message from my sister was a long one," said Ivor mendaciously. "But now I have delivered it I shall take my leave." He bowed over Lady Trevaire's hand and then sketched a bow to Evelina, before striding from the room.

Three days later Evelina went tripping gaily down the stairs of Pauline's palatial townhouse, feeling deeply grateful to her cousin for having responded so promptly to her cry for help.

Pauline had arrived at Lady Trevaire's house the previous day and announced her intention of carrying Evelina back to London with her. Lady Trevaire had flown into a rage and forbidden it, then, when both women had completely ignored her, her fury had known no bounds. Her threat to immediately write to her son had not shaken their resolve, and Evelina was almost giddy with relief at having escaped.

Pauline, at twenty-six, was eight years older than Evelina, but they'd always been close. She was waiting in the drawing room, attired in a ballgown of the deepest rose-pink silk which set off her glossy dark hair and creamy skin to perfection. Married to a man twenty years her senior and quite prepared to indulge her every whim, Pauline devoted herself to a life of pleasure which she found deeply satisfying.

"That gown becomes you," she greeted Evelina. "Do you not think so, Ivor?"

"She'll cast all the other females into the shade," he said, running an appraising eye over Evelina's dress, which was of almond-green chiffon worn over a slip of a deeper green. With a high waist and scooped *décolletage*, it set off her slender figure to perfection. "The carriage is waiting – shall we go?" he enquired.

The ball was in full swing when they arrived, and Ivor immediately swept Evelina off to dance. The subtle pressure of his hand on her back as they waltzed around the room made her yearn for a more intimate touch.

"When can we be alone?" he asked.

"As soon as it may be arranged," she returned, looking provocatively up at him through her long lashes. She was unprepared to have him lead her from the dance floor and out of the ballroom.

"Where are we going?"

He glanced swiftly over his shoulder to make sure they were not observed, then ushered her into the library.

"I've thought of little but this moment," he muttered, taking her into his arms, his mouth descending on hers. Her lips parted to admit his searching tongue, which found and mated with her own, while she pressed herself avidly against him, aware of his male hardness against her hip. She knew she was behaving rashly, and that at any minute they might be disturbed, but she didn't care.

When Ivor freed her breasts from her bodice, she didn't protest, but gave herself up to his intoxicating caresses. He cupped one alabaster orb, then bent his blond head to take the jutting point of her nipple between his lips. He flicked his tongue wickedly over it, making her sigh with delight, then sucked it gently until it swelled into ruby hardness.

A moist heat grew in her quim, and ripples of sheer erotic sensation suffused her body as he paid equal attention to her other breast before lifting her off her feet and laying her on a sofa. Swiftly, he gathered her skirts up around her waist to reveal her stockings, garters and the delicate silk of her pantalettes.

He drew the flimsy undergarment down her hips as she raised her bottom to assist him. The sight of her golden fleece made him inhale sharply, and he parted her thighs and feasted his eyes on the glistening folds of her labia.

"I have dreamt of this moment for years," he sighed, before kneeling beside her and bending to kiss her full on her inner sex lips. She squirmed with delight as he flicked his tongue over her tiny bud and then swirled it over her folds and valleys, exploring every hidden crevice.

The exquisite feeling of his lips and tongue on her most private parts seared her with sexual heat, and she moaned as he licked rhythmically at her plump nub.

When her breathing had become ragged and her eyes glazed with desire, he withdrew his mouth and cupped her mound for a moment before sliding his hand downwards to delicately massage her vulva. Within moments his palm became slippery with her juices, then he slid two fingers inside her.

"Dripping wet," he breathed, withdrawing them and then ripping open his breeches. His member sprang out, hugely erect, and he knelt between her parted thighs and guided it to the tingling bud of her clit. With his hand encircling the shaft he rubbed the glans teasingly over the plump nub until she felt waves of heat washing over her.

It was the most intoxicating sensation to have him touch her in that way, made all the more intense by the knowledge that at any moment he would sheathe his member inside her up to the hilt. His movements became swifter as he stimulated the swollen sliver of flesh until her spine arched and she cried out as she was assailed by the heady delight of a climax.

He positioned himself above her, then in one smooth thrust he was inside her, filling her completely and making her moan as he commenced a slow, steady thrusting that soon had her ascending the slopes of arousal again.

She clutched his shoulders, oblivious now to the danger of discovery, concerned only with their feverish coupling. Their lips met again in a heart-stopping kiss while his movements quickened. Evelina found herself undulating her pelvis beneath him, while the blood surged through her veins like molten lava.

He groaned, and his thrusts became faster and more staccato, until at last he let out a deep groan and came in a boiling flood which pushed her over the edge into another ecstatic, long drawn-out release.

They lay in each other's arms while their breathing slowed,

then reluctantly Ivor disengaged himself and straightened his clothing.

"Reluctant though I am to say it, we should return to the ballroom," he told her. "It would not do for us to be missed."

Her movements languorous, Evelina picked up her pantalettes and slipped them back on, enjoying the feeling of their mingled juices soaking into the crotch. She straightened her gown and then checked her appearance in the pier glass over the fireplace, before turning back to him.

"I'm ready. Shall we go?"

"We have invitations to two functions tonight," said Pauline, who was reclining on a sofa in the drawing room. "We have a choice between a musical evening or a masked ball – which would you prefer?"

Evelina looked up from the fashion periodical she was flicking through.

"The masked ball sounds most entertaining," she said, thinking it would afford more opportunities for dalliance with Ivor. They had managed to enjoy several more sessions of lovemaking, but the need to be discreet limited the time they could spend alone together.

"I'll have my maid get out masks and dominos for us." There was a pause, then Pauline continued, "Have you still had no word from your husband?"

Evelina's mouth was set in resolute lines as she replied, "No, and quite frankly I neither know nor care where he is. I'm having the most wonderful time without him."

"Nevertheless, it seems strange that he has been gone for so long. I could tell by the way he looked at you that his desire for you ran hotly through his veins."

"Indeed it did, but I can only think his thirst was quickly slaked that he abandoned the bridal bed so soon after our wedding." Not wishing to discuss the subject further, Evelina indicated an illustration in the fashion periodical. "Do you admire this gown? I think I would like one with just those sleeves, but perhaps in blue."

Evelina felt in low spirits as they left for the ball. She was forced to admit to herself that in taking up residence in London she'd thought to bring Gerrard back to her side, but she'd been there two weeks now and she'd heard nothing from him.

In an attempt to lift herself from her despondent mood she drank several glasses of champagne, and, unused to alcohol, swiftly became giddy and exhilarated. With her identity concealed by a mask she found herself flirting recklessly with her partners, including Ivor, who claimed several dances before going off to the card room.

Breathless after a waltz with a red-haired stranger, Evelina succumbed to his suggestion that they take a turn on the terrace. When they stepped outside she was surprised to discover that they were alone, as she'd expected other guests to be taking the air.

"We had better return to the ballroom, sir," she said. "I did not anticipate finding myself alone with you."

"One kiss first," he said in a thickened voice. Allowing Ivor delicious liberties was one thing, but not this stranger. She turned to go back inside, but he dragged her into his arms and pressed unwelcome kisses on her neck, one hand squeezing her breast painfully.

"Let me go this instant!" she exclaimed, outraged by his ungentlemanly treatment of her. Raising a hand, she slapped him hard across the face and then gasped as he thrust her roughly back against the wall, forcing a thigh between hers.

A moment later he was wrenched away from her and sent sprawling on the ground. A tall, shadowy figure in a black domino and mask stepped forward and hauled the red-haired man to his feet.

"Now beg the lady's pardon," he ordered. Her attacker took in the other man's height and the spread of his shoulders, then obviously decided not to argue.

"I beg your pardon," he snarled, and beat a hasty retreat.

"Allow me to escort you back inside," her rescuer said, proffering his arm.

"Thank you, sir," she murmured, taking it but making no move towards the door. There was something familiar about him which made her think they must have met before.

"Do I know you?" she asked.

"I think not." In the moonlight his eyes glittered through the slits in his mask, and she was surprised to feel a strong pull of carnal attraction. Her pulses began to race and she had to fight an urge to wind her arms around his neck. She took a deep breath and tried to clear her head, but the champagne had affected her more than she'd realized, and confused thoughts were whirling around in her mind.

"Will you tell me your name?" she asked.

He shook his head. "Anonymity is a prerequisite of a masked ball. Allow me take you back to your friends."

"At least let me thank you."

Afterwards, Evelina couldn't imagine what had possessed her, but she found herself wrapping her arms around his neck and drawing his head down so she could kiss him. For a moment he didn't respond, then he enfolded her in an unyielding embrace and his mouth came down hard on hers in a kiss so potent that instantly liquid fire began to surge through her veins.

She could feel the hard ridge of his manhood pressing into her belly and rubbed herself wantonly against it, a slave to her own sensuality.

Taking one of his hands, she guided it to her breast and exhaled with pleasure as he subjected it to an intoxicating caress. Long fingers slipped inside the low neck of her gown to toy with the hard point of her nipple, and she moaned softly as she felt her own avid response.

He drew her around the corner of the terrace, where they would be out of sight of anyone coming out of the ballroom. In the grip of a wanton heat, and with dancing flames of lust licking at her female core, she sank to her knees and fumbled to unfasten his breeches.

He groaned as she drew out the throbbing length of his phallus and placed the end between her parted lips. She swirled her tongue over the large plum-like glans, probing the tiny aperture at the end, then sucking hard while clasping the shaft in her hand.

Oblivious to the passage of time, she pleasured him with her lips, taking as much of his member inside her mouth as she could, then allowing it to slip slowly out until only the swollen end remained.

He groaned again, and reached down to help her to her feet, then bent her over the back of a rustic bench. She was aware of him pulling her skirts up to her waist and then he dragged her pantalettes down around her ankles.

Evelina let out a cry as she felt him forging strongly inside her, stretching her velvet membranes to capacity. His rod felt like silk-covered steel as he shafted her with powerful, determined strokes. She clung onto the back of the bench, feeling the chill from it strike through her belly while a molten heat suffused her from within.

She began to push the pert globes of her bottom back at every thrust, inciting him to shaft her yet more vigorously. A kind of madness possessed her and she moaned aloud as his rhythm changed as he speeded up.

His hands were on her breasts, stroking them and teasing her nipples into thimble-hard peaks. She was dimly aware of the strains of music floating outside into the cool night air, and the rattle of carriages passing in the street, but other than that she was numb to everything but the eroticism of the moment.

She felt his hand delving between her thighs from the front, and then he was deftly rubbing her tingling, throbbing nub until she was assailed by a surge of pleasure so strong she almost lost consciousness. A white brilliance flashed before her eyes as wave after wave of sensation washed over her, leaving her weak and breathless.

From a long way away she was aware that he'd speeded up his movements and then, in a surge of boiling fluid, he achieved his own climax.

He leant over her, his hand still inside her bodice, cupping one breast, then the sound of laughter just around the corner made him straighten hastily and ease himself free. In a daze, Evelina smoothed her own clothing and retied the strings of her domino.

Before she could speak, he took her chin in his hand and tipped her face upwards so he could kiss her.

"We'll meet again," he promised, then strode off into the shadows, his black domino floating out around his well-muscled legs.

When she awoke the following morning with a pounding headache, Evelina wondered if she might have dreamt the whole encounter, but a lingering tenderness between her thighs told her it was otherwise. She felt in a dreamy state all day, and even though she upbraided herself for having been so lost to common decency as to couple in a public place she found even the memory arousing.

At dinner that night Pauline announced gaily, "Ivor, I think I may have found you a suitable bride."

"Is she possessed of a handsome fortune?" he asked, taking an appreciative gulp of the fine claret he was drinking.

"She is."

"Is she a beauty?" was his next idle question.

"All young women possessed of large fortunes are considered beauties."

He grimaced. "You mean she's plain."

"I mean that the time for prevaricating is now over. I know only too well the extent of your debts, and a rich wife is your last hope, however much you may dislike the idea. I intend to introduce you to her tomorrow at a musical evening being given by a friend of mine in Hampstead. I advise you to charm her as swiftly as possible, because you won't be the only suitor for her hand."

Evelina was conscious of a faint pang of jealousy at the idea of Ivor marrying, but told herself firmly not to be foolish.

The following evening she felt constrained to keep her distance and to watch him dance attendance on Miss Faversham, once Pauline had performed the introductions.

"You mustn't mind," Pauline said softly, slipping her arm through Evelina's. "People like us are not able to marry where we choose – you know that yourself."

"I know," Evelina murmured, and squeezed Pauline's hand.

It was a warm evening towards midsummer, and as she listened to the music Evelina fanned herself languidly and found herself searching the crowd with her eyes, hoping to see the man who'd pleasured her so thoroughly on the terrace, but he was nowhere to be seen.

She felt restless, and suffused by sexual yearnings which made it difficult to remain still. Finding that she couldn't bear the idea of sitting through two more hours of music, she sought out her cousin.

"Pauline, I find myself a little fatigued. Do you mind

if I take the carriage home now and then send it back for you?"

"Of course not. Get a good night's sleep and tomorrow I shall devise some scheme to raise your flagging spirits."

As the carriage rattled its way across the deserted Heath, Evelina sat back on her seat and allowed herself to daydream about her masked lover. Her fantasies became so arousing that she felt a fine film of perspiration gathering on her cleavage, and of its own volition her hand slid between her thighs and she stimulated herself over the silk of her gown.

But the touch wasn't intimate enough to satisfy her, and she slipped off her pantalettes and arranged her skirts around her waist, her thighs widely parted.

She traced the contours of her sex flesh with a dreamy smile on her face, her eyes half closed, enjoying her own touch as she recalled the stranger's kiss.

Her tissues were slippery with her own juices and the folds of her labia as swollen as if she'd just enjoyed a man's caresses. She slid two fingers inside her slick female core and moved them languidly around, craving something which would fill her more completely.

The realization that the coach had just pulled to a halt jolted her back to reality, but before she could pull her skirts down and look out to see why they'd stopped, the door was flung open, and to her horror a man climbed swiftly in.

Her eyes widened in shock at the unexpected intrusion, and the shaming realization that she'd been caught blatantly pleasuring herself. Dusk was just beginning to fall and, seated directly opposite her as he was, he had a clear view of her exposed vulva with its golden fleece, her own hand buried between her thighs.

She had a glimpse of his mask in the shadow of his tricorne hat, and her first thought was that he was a highwayman, making her freeze with fear.

"I told you we'd meet again." The voice of her masked lover sent shivers down her spine, and she hastily removed her hand from her female delta. She would have wrenched her skirt down, but he grabbed her wrist.

Raising her hand to his lips, he licked her glistening fingers, winding his tongue around them until he'd cleaned them of her juices, then he replaced her hand between her thighs.

"Continue to pleasure yourself," he growled. Like a woman in a trance Evelina let her hand move tentatively over her aching bud, aware of a hungry, tingling itch gathering high up in her inner chamber as she obeyed him.

Such was her sensual haze that she barely noticed that the coach had set off again. He watched her avidly, fuelling the flames of her arousal with his dark, glittering gaze.

She stroked herself harder, feeling herself rapidly ascending the spiral of desire until, with a heartfelt moan, her head fell back on her shoulders and she came with a long, shuddering sigh.

Her eyes fluttered open in time to see him freeing his enormous phallus from the constraints of his breeches, then he reached across and lifted her onto his lap. Clinging to his shoulders, she sat astride him, positioning herself so his member was nudging at the whorled entrance to her quim.

She lowered herself onto it an inch at a time, enjoying the slow penetration, undulating her hips as she impaled herself on his throbbing column which felt hot and ramrod-hard. He kissed her deeply, letting her feel its virile throbbing, then as she began to move slowly on it, using it for an instrument of her own pleasure, he took her by the waist and assisted her.

She rode him gently at first, but then, as a smouldering heat grew high up in her groin, faster and more vigorously, until she was breathless and panting, the jolting of the coach adding impetus to her movements.

She came again in a delirious cresting of a wave of carnality, then cried out as he jammed her down hard on his engorged shaft and achieved his own discharge like a dam breaching its banks.

She rested her head on his shoulder, aware that night had now fallen and that it was dark inside the carriage.

"Where did you come from?" she asked wonderingly. "Or is this a dream?"

"It's no dream," he told her. "I'd just arrived at the party and heard you ordering your carriage. I merely bribed your men to let my own driver and myself take their place, assuring them that the carriage would be returned in time to pick up your cousins. If I'm not very much mistaken you're almost home."

She glanced at the window to see that they were in fact turning into the quiet London square where Pauline's townhouse was located.

The suspicion that had been fermenting in her brain since he'd first rescued her on the terrace prompted her to say, "Won't you unmask for me?"

He laughed softly. "Soon, but not now. I must make haste back to Hampstead. Goodnight and sweet dreams."

"Your spirits seem much improved today," commented Pauline the following morning as she sipped her chocolate with her glossy dark hair spilling becomingly over her shoulders. She was propped up in bed against several downy pillows while Evelina was perched on a chair by the window.

"I do indeed feel much more myself," she replied.

"Then perhaps I could ask you for a favour."

"Indeed, anything – for I'm very grateful to you for having me to stay."

"Use your influence on Ivor to persuade him he must marry Miss Faversham. He is deeply in debt, and although I have bailed him out on several occasions, my husband has forbidden me to do so again. If Ivor does not hasten to fix his interest with her someone else will do so and he may well be ruined. His propensity for gambling needs much deeper pockets than he possesses."

"I had no idea that the situation was desperate," said Evelina in dismay.

"He still hankers after you, and has dragged his feet in proposing to any of the young women I have thrown his way. If you'll persuade him that he'll retain your . . . your affection, even in a married state, he may steel himself to do what is necessary."

"We're going riding in Hyde Park this afternoon. I'll talk to him then," Evelina assured her.

"I shall give an evening party to celebrate your engagement," Pauline announced triumphantly a few days later, after Ivor had informed them that Miss Faversham had accepted his proposal. Pauline kissed him warmly and then hugged Evelina, whispering, "Thank you."

Ivor took a deep drink from his glass of wine and regarded his booted feet with a melancholy expression on his face.

"It will be like being in prison," he said glumly.

"Nonsense. She seems like a tractable girl, and if you exert yourself to charm her I'm sure you may do as you please. Now, I'll leave you two alone and go and consult with my housekeeper. It will be the event of the season and I shall invite absolutely everyone we know."

Pauline left the room in a swirl of amethyst skirts while Evelina went to join Ivor on the sofa.

"You must be kind to Miss Faversham," she said, taking his hand. "If you are sensitive to her needs and discreet about taking your own pleasure elsewhere, I'm sure it will work out very well. Look at me – wedlock has improved my life immeasurably. I have the status and freedom of a married woman, without the drawback of a husband always breathing down my neck." She swallowed as she spoke, for her situation still had the power to hurt her.

He kissed her hand. "And I for one am grateful for Gerrard's continuing absence. You are right, of course, my dear Evelina. I shall marry Miss Faversham and live a life of luxury and ease."

He pulled her down beside him, his hand finding her breast.

It seemed that all of London had accepted invitations to Pauline's party, and the line of carriages waiting to disgorge their occupants stretched for almost a mile.

Evelina felt that her face was beginning to ache from smiling so much as she stood in the receiving line in her ivory and silver gauze gown, greeting their guests.

The party passed in a whirl as she danced and flirted the night away, until late in the evening a desire for a few moments on her own led her to seek the solitude of the morning room.

A single candle flickered on the mantelpiece as she opened the door and slipped inside. She went over to the window and opened it, gratefully breathing in the cool scented air wafting up from the garden. The sound of the door opening made her turn swiftly, just as the candle guttered in the breeze and then went out.

A tall, shadowy figure entered the room, and Evelina felt a hot little spear of lust lancing upwards from her sex.

"You came," she breathed.

"I was invited," he told her, drawing her into his arms and bending to kiss her.

It seemed an eternity since she'd last tasted the delight that his practised caresses could give her, and she rubbed herself against him, cat-like, making no protest when he freed her breasts from the confines of her bodice.

"I mustn't stay long – I'll be missed," she gasped as he fondled the smooth orbs, grazing her nipples with his thumbs.

She was standing by the table and in an unexpected movement he pushed her back onto it and thrust her gauzy skirts around her waist. She was startled when he gripped her embroidered pantalettes with both hands and ripped them from her, tossing the tattered shreds of material to the floor. He spread her thighs, unfastened his fly and plunged into her with no further caresses.

Even though she'd urged haste, Evelina was taken aback, and cried out as he pierced her to her very core. It was only as he commenced a measured thrusting that she began to feel the heat building in her loins.

But before she'd even come close to her own satisfaction, he made several final staccato thrusts and then erupted into her. He withdrew abruptly and straightened his clothing, leaving her frustrated and very much regretting her urge for haste. She slid off the table and shook out her gown, wondering what she was going to do with her torn undergarment.

The door was pushed abruptly open, and in the light spilling in from the hallway Evelina saw Pauline standing on the threshold. Swiftly, her cousin lifted a candelabra from a table in the hall and came in, closing the door behind her.

"Evelina," she said urgently, taking in the scene at once. "I have to warn you – Gerrard is here!"

Evelina smiled at her. "I know," she said, taking her lover's hand and drawing him into the pool of light cast by the candelabra. "He's already found me."

But instead of exhibiting the delight Evelina had expected at seeing the two of them reunited, Pauline looked horrified, and stared at her as if she'd taken leave of her senses. Puzzled, Evelina glanced up at the man by her side, then her hand flew to her throat in shock, the colour draining from her face.

"Y . . . you aren't my husband," she faltered.

He cast her a mocking bow. "I don't recall claiming to be."

Evelina's legs trembled so much they would no longer support her, and she sank into a chair. "Then who are you?" she asked weakly.

"This is Lord Calder," Pauline informed her. "Whom, I might add, is one of the most notorious libertines in London. Had anyone else found you closeted with him, your reputation would have been ruined."

"I . . . I thought he was Gerrard," she explained. "It was too dark to see his face."

It was true that he was around the same height as Gerrard, with a similar lean, well-muscled frame and broad shoulders, but in the light from the candelabra she could now see he was at least ten years older, with much harsher features. His voice, however, sounded virtually indistinguishable.

"I'm wounded to the core," he complained. "I thought it was my chivalry in rescuing you from the oaf on the terrace the night of the masked ball which first attracted you, and that you'd then fallen for my manifold charms. Little did I suspect that you thought me to be your husband."

His expression indicated that he didn't believe her assertion, and, glancing at Pauline, Evelina saw scepticism writ large upon her lovely features too.

"No matter," said Pauline. "There's no time to discuss the whys and wherefores. Lord Calder, I know we can rely on your complete discretion, but now you must leave us."

"Assuredly," he said, kissing first Evelina's limp hand and then Pauline's.

Evelina forced herself to get to her feet and hurried to the mirror over the fireplace to smooth her hair, saying agitatedly, "What if he tells anyone? Gerrard may come to hear."

"He won't."

"How can you be sure?"

"From personal experience," Pauline confessed, picking up the rags of Evelina's pantalettes and stuffing them in her reticule. "Lord Calder has bedded half the women in society – including myself – without a breath of scandal being attached to any woman's name. Are you ready for me to bring your husband to you?"

Her head whirling, Evelina murmured, "Yes."

Pauline vanished, and a minute later the door opened to admit Gerrard. Evelina's heart lurched at the sight of him and she wondered how she could ever have mistaken Lord Calder for him. He was so much more mesmerizingly attractive, with his chiselled features, strong nose and well-shaped mouth.

But somehow, from the moment she'd met Lord Calder, she'd become convinced that he was in truth her husband, playing some erotic game with her. A game she'd found exciting in the extreme.

"Gerrard," she greeted him, not sure what to say. Should she be angry?

"Dearest Evelina, can you ever forgive me for staying away so long? It was not my own desire to leave your side so soon after my wedding, I give you my word." He took her in his arms and kissed her, provoking a hectic response in her loins that made her feel as though an inferno was blazing there.

When at last they drew apart she was on fire for him, but managed to ask, "Where have you been this age, and why did you not write to me?"

He caressed her breast in lazy circles as he replied, "The day I left I received a letter from an old friend whose daughter had been seduced and abandoned in France. His health was too poor to allow him to travel to bring her safely back home so he charged me with that mission. I only meant to be gone a short while, but when I arrived I found her ill with the fever and had to delay my return. Within two days I too had succumbed to it and lay delirious for several weeks. As soon as I could put pen to paper I wrote to you – did you not receive my letter?"

"No," said Evelina slowly, thinking it must have been delivered after she'd left her mother-in-law's house and Lady Trevaire had deliberately withheld it.

He clasped her hand and kissed it. "Forgive me," he begged her. "But my friend's daughter is now restored to him, and I give you my word that nothing will persuade me to leave you again. I should have told you where I was going, but I was entreated to say nothing to anyone. Now I see a man should not have secrets from his wife. Come – show me to your bedchamber or I'll be unable to stop myself from taking you here on the floor."

You could see things from the street projected onto the ceiling, just as he describes.

When I found the journal it became tragically clear that poor old "Fizzy" had completely lost his marbles with the war and overstrain, and had hallucinated some Lamia in his digs. What a mess the poor devil had made of his body!

Mind you, I found it hard to imagine all this mad sexual passion going on in "Fizzy's" head. A less passionate-looking man it was harder to imagine; he was a typical pudding-faced army type, with expressionless eyes behind his steel-rimmed glasses. Still, if I learned one thing from the war it was not to trust to appearances.

By the way, poor old "Fizzy" got his nickname by "fizzing over" his superiors when something got his goat. There was an explosive side to his nature.

I included the journal in my report, but no one had time to read the thing, and it's one of those bits of junk that remains in one's possession. I include it here as a curiosity and an example of what the stress of war can do to the human mind.

THE JOURNAL OF OLIVER ALAN "FIZZY" CHIGWORTH

August 14th 1944

I am writing this out of utter necessity. Nobody must read these words. Nobody. Yet commit them to paper I must, in the hope of exorcizing my personal demons. Am I some frightful Godforsaken pervert? Or am I simply buckling under the strains of my job, with its growing burden of dirty tricks? And have I, through my embarrassment – or whatever it was – compromised one of our closely-guarded wartime secrets?

I must describe the horribly shameful events of today and then destroy this rubbish and flush the charred remains down the toilet.

Talking about dirty tricks, they cannot get any dirtier than the X Scheme. To take some poor devil of an agent, plant them with false information, drop them in France and then arrange for them to be betrayed to the Gestapo, knowing that the false stuff will be tortured out of them . . . I feel a bit dizzy . . . But it's necessary to defeat Hitler . . . It's necessary . . .

I didn't arrange for Margie Trumper to be chosen as an X . . .

I've looked after my agents like a mother hen looking after its chicks – which is more than I can say for some of those Etonian bastards. You would think they were dealing with turnips instead of human beings . . .

I must calm down. I've been unable to sleep, and as I sit here in the early morning, putting my thoughts onto paper by the light of a candle, watching a cab and then a horse and cart trot along the ceiling of my room, I'm all out in a sweat.

Sometimes I feel like spraying those Etonian bastards with a Tommy gun . . . There, I've crossed the Rubicon now . . . If they found this I'd be out on my ear . . . I'm rambling, rambling. In fact, I'm trying to escape the subject of Margie Trumper altogether. Let's go back to room 109 . . .

There she is, gently knocking at the door.

"Come in," I call from my desk.

She enters, and as soon as she sees it's me the glow leaves her ice-blue eyes, the warmth leaves her face.

Of course, I know why. I'm used to women giving this "Oh, it's only you" look. It's not that I'm a monster. I'm short-sighted, I'm losing a bit on top at thirty, and my nose is undistinguished. Now that we're being honest here, what did that bloody tart I picked up in Germaine Street say? "You're no Clark Gable." And that was after I'd paid the bloody bitch! It was all I could do to get a hard-on and stick it in her I was so angry.

Why do women single me out for their particular contempt? Take someone like Edwards, for example. He's small, got a beer belly, yet he's always boasting of girls as hot as incendiary bombs, and I've seen him in the bar with his arms around girls he hardly knows. Gets them laughing . . .

I'm feeling calmer now . . . but I'm trying to avoid the subject of Margie Trumper altogether – actually, her childhood was in France and it's Marguerite. Back to room 109, with my oak desk, the drab institutional walls, the teapot tray, the telephone, and Marguerite throwing a bucket of cold water over me with her eyes.

We salute in the perfunctory fashion of the intelligence services.

"Take a seat, Miss Trumper. You must be surprised to see me here instead of Colin."

"Yes," she replied. "I hope he's all right."

Why I can forgive her that bucket of cold water is that Colin Fordington (put it down to the wartime sex frenzy that is affecting everyone but me) has broken all the bloody rules and is having an affair with an agent, something which is utterly *verboten*. The bastard would be cashiered if they knew. And ought to be! Mind you, it's amazing how many rules do get broken here. The whole X business, for example. They had planned for us to be in the dark as well as the poor devils of doomed agents, but it leaked out.

And this cad Fordington, having taken advantage of his position as case officer, just couldn't face the girl, knowing she was an X, just hadn't the guts. And that wasn't all! With his bragging and boasting the man had let out the most obscene details about the poor girl, ruined her reputation. I hope he suffers!

I'm feeling better. Writing this tosh has done me good. I think I'll treat myself and open that tin of condensed milk.

There goes the number 38, along the ceiling . . . I'll have to be in the office within the hour . . .

August 21st

I flew to my journal this evening. It's become a friend. And today I have something to tell my friend. I met Fordy in the mess today, looking pretty much white at the gills – as so he should, the treacherous swine! I wonder why the man is so attractive to women. He's not that much more handsome than me. Of course, he has all his hair, and that deep voice which I suppose hypnotizes women. And this bastard, who had let Marguerite down so badly, was about to sink his teeth into a corned beef sandwich.

"Hello, Fordy," I said. "Well, the crow must have landed by now."

Marguerite's "mission" was called Operation Crow.

The bastard never ate that sandwich!

Rereading my previous entry, I realized that I hadn't confessed all by a long chalk. My last interview with Marguerite is so vivid in my mind that I thought I had written down all the pertinent details. In fact I broke off my account at the moment when she asked about Fordy.

She was like a vision in that drab institutional room. She had (I am already using the past tense, wishing the poor girl out of her misery as soon as possible) one of those very expressive girl's faces that acts things out with upside down smiles and puppyish wrinkles on the forehead (almost like a mime artist) before speaking. Her blonde hair was tied at the back. The WAC uniform couldn't conceal the shape of her breasts or her narrow waist and long legs. She had saved her last pair of nylons for Fordy, I noticed.

"Just a touch of flu," I lied. "He'll be back like a bad penny."

Her hands, which were clasped in her lap, twitched. I'm trained to notice such details. The bitter thought passed through my mind that there was no woman taking such a keen interest in my welfare.

I suppose, to be fair, Fordington wasn't exactly broadcasting at the bar. I overheard him saying to Edwards ". . . and she puts your penis in her mouth . . ." Perhaps he was not even talking about Marguerite but, if that were so, how did she come to be known in our group as "Margie Strumpet"? And how did that rumour (that hardened into established fact) that Margie Strumpet was knocking off the Froggies whenever she crossed the Channel get about the place? It could only have come from her case officer, Fordy!

Having got over her obvious disappointment that Fordy wasn't there, she settled down to the briefing in a professional manner. This was to be her fifth trip. She was an extremely resourceful agent, her childhood in France proving invaluable. On one occasion she and another agent had been confronted by a German, but she'd arranged for the man to buy her some stockings.

I don't know whether my loss of control was due to overwork. In my concern not to let these brave people down I immerse myself in detail, and overwork can have a strange effect upon the brainbox. Like an unbalanced flywheel it takes on a momentum all of its own, and unlikely and unwanted thoughts are flung into the mind.

As we went though the briefing, images began forming in my mind. It was as if a flickering black and white cinema screen had opened in my head and was projecting over the room in a double exposure. ". . . knocking off the Froggies whenever she crossed the Channel . . ." There was Marguerite, standing behind an iron bedstead, pulling a slip over her head, leaving her breasts jiggling, standing there mother naked . . . And in the bed there was a Frenchman, coolly watching her . . . She was smiling as she jumped onto the bed, titties dangling down . . .

And as I looked at the young, freshly innocent face of the real, almost child-like Marguerite a frightful sense of confusion came over me.

Fortunately the briefing, concerned with a routine mission, was a short one.

Then I looked at her, and saw her dissolving into the drab institutional wall like the Cheshire Cat . . .

My God, it was my glasses steaming up!

"Sergeant," I mumbled. "Forgive me . . . I've forgotten to offer you a cup of tea. It's cold . . . I'll . . ." Before I could finish my eyes just flooded with tears!

The implications of such a blunder were obvious.

"I've got something in my eye," I explained, in what I hoped was a convincing manner, and in my confusion I scratched my right eye with my glasses, leaving it smarting with pain.

"No more tea for me, sir," she said. "I've just had some in the canteen."

I was rubbing at my by now painful eye when I realized she was at my side. I felt the actual touch of her tummy on my elbow! I looked up, and through my blurred vision I could see her pink delicate lips, like some sea urchin, sucking her hanky into a wet spike.

"Let me see if I can get it out, sir."

"No," I stammered. "I'll be fine . . . no . . . I think it's come out . . ." What devil of confused perversity prompted me to ask, "Do you think you've had a good life?"

"I don't know what you're getting at, sir."

I could see fear and suspicion grow in her eyes.

"Oh, I wasn't thinking of you," I said hastily, fixing her with my one good eye. "I was thinking of me."

"Well, sir, the tide is turning in our favour."

That cursed cinema in my head . . . The Gestapo, barbarous

though they are, were professional. With the French amateurs anything could happen . . . The projector began whirring busily and something wriggled like a fish, white and wriggling on the flickering screen. It was a girl's naked body, held by four men . . . They were pulling the long white wriggling legs wide apart . . . you could see everything . . .

I began rubbing my eyes to rid them of this obscenity.

"Is there anything else we need to check, Sergeant?" I demanded.

"Well, sir, as we agreed, I'm familiar with the details."

"In that case we'd better terminate this session," I barked. "I think I must have scratched this eye," I added, to explain my brusque manner.

I don't recall her leaving.

No, and I'm not going to hide any details, no matter how foul, from this journal. As I sat there, staring at the victory poster on the wall, I had an erection. There. I've said it. Is it so bad? I'm sure it wasn't that diabolical bit of cinema that aroused me. It was the touch of her tummy, even through two layers of khaki.

I didn't invent this diabolical X Scheme, necessary though it is to defeat Hitler.

I must ease up a bit . . .

I must invite the little flower girl tonight . . .

August 23rd

This journal is my only friend, my confessional. I can't ease up at work. In fact, I'm taking on a greater work-load, if anything. When I get home I'm in a sort of mind frenzy. I suppose drink would help, but I've never been a great drinker – frightened of what might get out if I got truly sloshed, I suppose.

Fordy seems to have gone into complete decline and looks positively green. No more of that awful rumbling laugh, thank God. He's getting his just deserts!

Would Marguerite have taken to me if Fordy hadn't barged in there? Now that I think of that well-nigh disastrous interview I can remember her looking at me not unsympathetically. Of course, I would have waited until after the war . . .

You fool! The poor girl is probably in the hands of the Gestapo by now! Don't besmirch her memory with your idiotic fantasies!

The only girl you can get is the little flower girl.

Without the little flower girl I would never get to sleep. I lie awake in the blackout with a maelstrom in my head and begin to create the little flower girl, sculpt her out of the darkness. I begin with her dusty, pretty little feet standing on the floorboards of my room, count her toes (occasionally I find a broken toenail) and work my way up from the ankles to the pale, dusty, dimpled knees, then create the long, shapely thighs . . . She is wearing a torn shift and holding a bunch of roses. If I find my attention wandering from her to my personal problems I blow the shift away from the very exciting part of her, have a little glimpse of the modelling of her groin and a wisp of her pubes, and then, when she has all my attention, I fill out her belly and build her in the blackout, mould her cheeky little upturned breasts with their nipples defined against the shift . . .

I find her face rather indeterminate. It tends to be someone who's taken my fancy during the day.

And then, when I've sculpted her with my mind, got her solidly standing there, the shift fluttering around the pale, glowing body, I say, "Come here, my dear, I won't hurt you."

I hold my hand out in the dark . . . She puts her little hand in mine, and if I can actually feel her hand I know I'm asleep and I've defeated the night.

August 24th

I can't understand it! I bumped into Fordy and Edwards on the steps this morning, and that bastard Fordy looked in the pink! Looked so damned pleased with himself! Suppose he must have found another woman, the utter swine! How could he forget her so quickly?

There was nothing I could say. He was unassailable!

November 1st

It's four in the morning and I'm writing this in the most awful frame of mind. I'll never get to sleep tonight. Been a bit woozy all day. Rang for the Deptford files and they were there all the time . . .

Fordy's down with influenza; got it bad, apparently and is hospitalized. I could not but help remembering that I'd told

Marguerite he had flu. No, Chigworth, you haven't given it to him by some occult means! That's madness!

But am I mad? Just listen to what's happened here tonight . . .

I could not get to sleep. The trouble was that every time I scuplted the little flower girl when I got to her face it was the face of Marguerite! And once I looked at that face I was back in room 109, with Fordy and the Gestapo, etc. etc.

I struggled to give the flower girl the face of a young woman I'd seen on the tube, but I kept losing her. To concentrate on the flower girl I blew the shift away from her pubes and those long, plump, dusty thighs and tore it off the cheeky breasts and grabbed her by the shoulders, threw the delicious dusty creature onto the bed, pushed her legs open and drove into her body . . . In fact, I jerked off like a bloody schoolboy.

They're beginning to say that it's perfectly harmless, but in my day it was supposed to cause syphilis.

Afterwards I felt so depressed, fearful of facing my colleagues in the morning. To be playing with oneself at my age, when all of wartime London was "at it" . . . I even wondered whether to make an end to it all with that service revolver in the bedside drawer. Eventually I got out the John Buchan and was trying to read . . .

When there was the most Goddamn awful explosion that rocked the entire room!

I ran across the corridor in my pyjamas and woke a neighbour, Digby-Smyth, who was extremely peeved. Well, to cut a long story short, I went running back and forwards, expecting to see the street in flames, but everything was as silent as only wartime London can be, as if the whole world is in a state of shock. You can imagine what an idiot I felt.

When I got back to my room there was a smell of roses.

Perhaps the sound of some explosion right across London did somehow rock my windows . . . Perhaps a bottle of perfume fell over somewhere . . .

At least I've given up on the notion of shooting myself. For the time being.

November 13th

Well. What can I say? Fordy died in hospital last night. Blood poisoning as well as the flu. I feel strangely shocked. After all, he wasn't such a bad sort. Anyone can lose their head over a woman as beautiful as Marguerite.

November 14th

Listen to this! Now hear me! Sometimes words seem totally inadequate for their allotted task! Lord Haw-Haw's Beethoven is perhaps more appropriate for what I have to write. Ba-ba-ba-*bah*! Or should I commit it to paper in case it breaks the spell? No. This is, after all, for my eyes alone.

I had a very difficult day at the office. I won't go into details but those bloody Etonian bastards deserve wherefore! They're all Arts, when what is wanted is someone with a knowledge of technology.

Anyway, at night my headache was so bad that it seemed to make the darkness shine, and I found myself sweating as I wrestled with the bedclothes and the cursed problems of the day.

I began making my little flower girl. I decided she must be naked to grab my attention. Riiiiiiiiiip went her poor little dusty shift. Bunched up at the neck, it was surprisingly difficult to pull apart. Eventually I snapped it and threw the torn halves away into the dark. I then stooped down to begin with her feet. I licked her feet. I polished her toenails. I licked the toes. I crept up her ankles (there was a scratch on the left one). One dimpled knee was leaning over the one bearing her beautiful weight. As I climbed to the top of a plump thigh I found a certain difficulty. The sight of her pubes and the flesh leading to the nook between her legs was just too arousing. I had to make my ascent by way of her waist, averting my eyes from the line of her bum, climbing round her shoulder blades to her neck and to her face.

The face was that of Marguerite. She was smiling at me gently, with that wonderful, nervously ironic, upside down smile. Her brow rippled, as if to say, "Isn't this fun?" This time her image didn't bring with it the dread associations. In fact, (although I was using the poor girl as a sedative) a sense of peace and happiness overcame me . . .

A cat howled at the back of the house like a wah-wah trumpet but I was nearly asleep . . .

"Come here, my dear, I won't harm you," I said in my mind, and stretched out my hand, palm upwards, in the blackout dark . . .

A real hand grasped my upturned palm and squeezed it!

I felt as if I'd been scalded with fright! With my heart knocking at my gullet, I found myself sitting bolt upright, still clutching this phantom hand!

This was not the sign of sleep overtaking me!

Automatically, my left hand reached out to follow the hand which was still gripping my right hand and alighted on a cold, delicate woman's arm. Panting with shock, I followed the arm up to a silken shoulder. I could hear her breathing now. That cat in the yard outside sang like a lost baby as my hand explored the mysterious figure in the dark, down the in-curving waist to catch the swelling weight of a cool, shapely bottom which gathered in warmth as I held it.

A stark naked woman was standing by my bed! Sexual excitement began to eerily mingle with shock. Could it be that the chaps were playing a joke on me and had arranged for a tart to enter my room at night?

"Well, Fizzy, are you going to leave a girl to freeze?" she asked.

An indescribable shockwave of feeling hit me. This was the chuckling fresh voice of Marguerite! Somehow the clever girl had escaped her fate and found her way to my room! I was shattered. I sat there like a dummy . . .

"Well . . . of course you must join me," I mumbled at last, uneasily aware that it sounded as if she was going to join me for tennis.

I moved over to the edge of my single bed. I could hear the springs creak and feel it dip. Her back squashed my folded arm while her hip pressed against mine through my pyjamas. In my imagination I could picture her glowing nudity as the little flower girl lying next to me. As the shock receded I got the most awful goddamn hard-on of my entire life, so hard it was actually painful, all my frustration and bitterness concentrated like some metallic ore in my penis. There was so much to talk to her about and here was this agonized thing between us! When I straightened my folded arm round her shoulders I found my hand quite naturally cupping a cool young breast whose nipple firmed at my touch.

"Why have you come to me, Marguerite?" I gasped.

"Because you're a decent man, that's why, silly."

"You know Fordy died?" I was so choked with emotion I could scarcely speak. Why did I have to be so stupid as to mention him?

"Yes, darling, I know. It's all very sad but here we are. Don't be shy, darling. Give me your other hand."

She took my other hand on a sacred tour of her silken, smooth-burning body. First I was guided to the other breast, to stroke its tip to a firmness to match the first one. I seemed to see them with a second sight, cheekily glowing in the darkness. Then my hand was taken down over the smooth expanse of her tummy with that little pool of her navel in the middle, down over the fur below and even between her long plump thighs to the source of the Nile. She opened her thighs and laid my hand shamelessly against the lips of her swollen juicy font of perfection. How long would I have lain there like a paralysed imbecile?

"It's wartime, darling." I heard her voice at last. "We girls want to be done . . . by the man we love, of course."

Still wearing my pyjamas, I flung myself on the silken nudity, with its breasts flattening and its legs opening wide in welcome, and thrust that tortured beast of my cock up the welcoming, gripping, indrawing expanse of her vagina. This was not the dank, resentful, flesh of a tart, but a crying, excited woman who heaved underneath me. I was so overwrought that I exploded in her deliciousness almost immediately . . .

"There, darling," she said. "Do you feel better now?"

"Better? My God, you're the answer to my prayers."

"Well, it'll be even nicer if you take these pyjamas off," her hand reached down and stroked my stiff penis thoughtfully. "And I don't think he's finished his job yet."

It was perfectly true. Such was my frustration that I still had a hard-on. I struggled with my pyjamas under the sheet and jumped out of bed onto the floor, the better to rid myself of them. I remember standing starkers in the dark, wondering if I would jump back into bed and find nothing there. But she was there, all right. I vividly remember the joy of being naked in bed with a mother naked woman, the feeling of naked flesh closing with cool-burning naked flesh, almost as if one was swimming in silken breasts and silken thighs which opened in glorious welcome. I slid into her, less desperate and agonized this time, feeling at home in her body. She sighed and our rhythmic journey through the night began again. She moaned and whimpered with excitement and writhed under me. Her excitement excited me to redouble my thrusting efforts.

When it was over a second time I asked her again, "But why did you come to me?"

"Because you've got such a lovely mouth," she said, giggling and tugging my moustache.

In fact, we hardly said anything sensible as the night was consumed with passion. I must have made love to her six times before exhaustion overcame me . . .

In the morning I awoke and watched a woman pushing a pram along the ceiling of my blackout digs. There was an inner glow that I'd never known before while my cock ached with the sense of a job well done. I was naked in bed. But where was she? I sprang out of bed, and, shivering, dragged on my pyjamas. Perhaps she was making tea in the kitchen.

In fact there was no sign of her, not so much as a hair on my pillow.

I felt a bit sick, and started talking to myself. "Well, if that was a dream it beats living by a long chalk."

There was no question that I'd made love to a real woman. My body told me so and there were also certain marks on my sheets. Yet how could she have got in and out of the room? To a trained agent the lock would have posed no problem. But why had she just vanished like this? Perhaps it was to avoid her relationship with her case officer being discovered. Discretion. That's it.

It's funny how one's view changes. When poor Fordy (it's odd but I feel almost close to him) was with her I thought it a disgrace, but now she's mine I take quite a different view of the matter. How fickle we are. I would be cashiered too, if this came to light.

It's awful to find her gone! Awful!

At work today I made tentative suggestions concerning Marguerite to discover how her mission had been aborted. When I suggested something of the sort to Edwards he looked at me as if I were mad. It was embarrassing and puzzling.

Tonight I await her. Writing this has given me something to do. What if she shouldn't appear? My teeth are chattering! I'm desperate! Why did Edwards give me that

out of worlds beyond . . . When I plunged into her at last it was as if we were both in the grip of some insatiable, almost insane frenzy . . .

But in the morning she had gone, and when I examined the thread over the door to my digs I found it still intact!

No flesh and blood woman entered my digs last night!

Who or what have I been making love to?

December 21st

Horror! Horror Horror!

What wretchedness must I write down? What horror so awful that the agony of a broken toe is pleasant by comparison . . . ?

Oh, God! Last night Marguerite came to me, but it was a different Marguerite. Her voice was cold with suspicion and she would not let me make love.

"You are a traitor," she said, in a voice that chilled me to the marrow.

"What do you mean, darling?" Did she mean I should have warned her during that last fatal briefing?

"You've betrayed me."

"I love you."

This went on for hours. Then she began groaning with pain. I had climbed on top of her (I'm afraid with an erection) when she gave the scream of the damned.

"What is it?" I asked, my blood ice-cold.

"My feet!"

"What's wrong with them?"

"My feet are being crushed!"

With that she grasped me round the chest with incredible force, as if I were being crushed in a vice. In fact, so great was her power that I fainted.

When I came to she had vanished. Is she gone for ever? Whatever she suffers I will suffer too! Sobbing, I searched the flat for her, but found not a hair. I noticed the hammer that I'd used to knock a nail into the doorjamb – better to tie the thread – lying on the drawers. In my agony of mind I brought it crashing down on my toes and limped around my rooms in silent pain. Pray God she comes back! Whatever she suffers I will match!

December 23rd
Office party like a dream . . . She has come back, but in what form . . . ? I cannot even write . . .

THE NEW MOTOR

M. Christian

IT IS NOT our place to say, via hindsight, what exactly happened that one particular night. It's easy to dismiss, with scorn or even a kind of parental, historical fondness, that he was just visited by vivid dreams, a hallucinatory fever, a form of 1854 delusion (after all, we smile, frown, grimace, laugh or otherwise; this was *1854*), or some hybrid kin of them all: a vision one third unresolved traumas, one third bad meal of steak and potatoes, one third nineteenth-century crippling social situation. What we cannot dismiss – because it's there with minuscule precision, in detailed blocks of blurry type in rag pulp sidebills, in the fine-filigreed pages of the genteel or just the skilled – was that John Murray Spear, a spiritualist of some quite personal renown and respect, did indeed depart Miss August's Rooming House for Gentlemen of Stature (near the corner of Sycamore and Spruce in Baltimore, Maryland), and go forth to tell anyone who would listen – and some did, as those newspapers reported and those diaries told – about his visitation by the Association of Electricizers.

Close your eyes, metaphorically, and envision the images that might have fluttered through the expansive and trained consciousness of Mr Spear as he lay, barely waking, on a cheap mattress more tick than stuffing, the too-warm embrace of a humid Baltimore summer morning pouring through the thin gauze of the window. Amid the jumble and clutter of a day's thoughts, they walk – as contemporary A.J. Davis expressed: "spirits with a mechanical turn of mind" – into the far-reaching mind of John Murray Spear.

Perhaps gears lit with fairy energies; they turn and tumble through his waking, shining metal honed with eldritch tools, playing inadvertent peg-toss with his sheet-raising morning priapism. Maybe a great churning clockwork contraption, whose complexity echoes Medusa's curse of knowing equally insanity or death. Or they might have taken the form of a Con-Ed employee in bedazzling ethereal refinements, in a saintly pose of divine grace, while the animated logos and mascots of every power company that was, is and will be flitted around his nuclear halo – commercial cherubs to his crackling, humming, arcing power.

Their form was something that escaped even Spear himself, for when he spoke of their visitation – and he did, oh, yes, he did, from his own mount and other less spiritual soapboxes – a 220-watt gaze seemed to consume him and his articulations became less detail and more impact: "Their form," he said to his breakfast companions and often, for many weeks thereafter, to any stranger on the street, "is fast and incorporeal. I don't possess the mind to express their appearance in words, but their message, dear –" sir, madam, officer, friend "– is clear and ringing in my ears: Go forth, they spoke. Go forth and with these two simple hands bring into the world a machine, a great work of engineering, that would take motive power from the magnetic store of nature and therefore be as independent of artificial sources of energy as this, our own human body. Go, this conglomeration of spirits pronounced, and build the Physical Savior of the Race, The New Messiah . . . the New Motor!"

John Murray Spear did, indeed, say these words: from that reasonably expensive boarding house in summer-heated Baltimore to the swampy humidity of the capital, then upwards towards the cooler North-eastern states. He spoke of the visitation of the Electricizers to a shocked and tutting crowd of theosophists in Providence, his hypnotic description of the coming glory of the Motor and how it would bring about a New Age of Man Through Machine ticking out of synch with their slowly shaking, disbelieving heads.

He spoke of the Motor in Boston, before a hall not as packed as it had previously been for the spiritualist of some repute, and answered with complete sincerity questions of the Motor's construction ("things of this earthly sphere coupled with the energies of transcendent motion and ethereal force"), creation ("for a small donation you can speed its manifestation and arrival here, to us"), method of operation ("can one envision a locomotive, some new machine of human use and creation, that might come during the new millennium? The works of the Motor may be visible to some of us with the enriched spiritual vision, but the true powers of it will be as unseen as that machine of ages undreamed"), and patentability ("if the material servants of this, our Government of Country, should grant me the license of its manufacture then I see no reason not to accept").

Coal and snow beard, hair wild with his feverish retellings, supple body (for a man of his forty summers) bending wildly with each description of the glory of the Motor and his saving of mankind through its mechanical enlightenment, Spear made himself a sight as he traveled. For some, he was a sight that brought smiles, frowns, or sadness at his state of affairs. But as he slowly, town by town, street by street, meeting by meeting, told his tale, made his claims, his entreaties, he gathered people who listened earnestly to his description of the Mechanical Savior of the Race, the New Motor.

With each meeting they watched, drawn by him and his description of the action of the Motor. Again, we can only imagine what they saw in the older, yet virile and definitely passionate Spear: men enticed by the engineering spirituality – this was, after all, 1854, a time when all of the world's ills seemed to have the potential of being cured by the right use of the steam engine – their members enlivened by the churning, throbbing, mechanizations of the Motor. Women enraptured by the . . . *hard* drive of Spear himself, the license to become excited by something, and, assuredly, what could be safer than something not obviously sexual, as the New Motor? So, with male members erect and throbbing at the thought of the Mechanical Savior of the Race, the New Messiah, and female sexes flowering and moist equally, at the thought of driving pistons, churning cams, humming flywheels, twirling governors, rasping bellows and other, pounding, sliding, gleaming parts (some the Motor's, some Mr Spear's), they went from couple to few, smattering to intimate gathering, dinner party to small crowd – with John Murray Spear and his clockwork choir invisible at the intangible controls.

Trickling together, their small number slowly gathering into a very small belief, they worked their way to the High Rock of their faith: a small farmhouse just outside of Lynn, Massachusetts. As to why they stopped . . . guesses include that the small hamlet of saltbox houses and cod fishermen was a perfect harmonious position from which to assemble the various physical attributes that would form the birth stage of their divine appliance, that the small religion had found a home in the craggy-faced, intolerant faces of the townspeople, or that, simply, they had run out of cash.

Reasons unknown, Spear and his traveling companions stopped, took a collective breath and, perhaps checking their wallets, purses and secret stashes, determined that the soil there, the homes there, the people there, the weather there, would be ideal, and – at the direction of their engineering apostle – set out to assemble the reason (perhaps) for their companionship. There they set out to actually create the Mechanical Messiah, Clockwork Jesus, Divine Device, Holy Contraption – their New Motor.

Looking more and more the father of a screaming-in-infancy religion, and less the mad-seer, Spear dispatched his believers, dispensing with them, like hosts of the realm, the few remaining coins in their possession.

"Cyrus, you shall go and fetch wheels of varying sizes. Be certain that their weight not be so great as to preclude their turning with ease," Spear said to the young engineering student whose face, marred by smallpox, was hidden by a great black beard.

"Your task, Youngfellow, is to purchase wire with the correct vibrations. I trust you, above anyone else, to recognize these vibrations by the wire's feel between the fingers," Spear said to the old railway man who shook with a consumptive cough when excited, which was often.

"Bartholomew, you shall acquire cylinders of rosy copper," Spear told the rather too pretty and too dandied young lad from New York.

"I need your fine eye, Mary, to go and bring us only canvas of good quality for the making of bellows," Spear said to the old matron whose single eye was a disturbing too-blue.

"Unis, you go and seek out strips of tanned hide so that belts may be employed in the creation of the divine Motor," Spear said to the stone-stern and perpetually unsmiling headmistress.

And so each was sent, little money and elaborate instructions in hand, out into the town of Lynn – till Spear remained with but one of his machine-enraptured flock.

"Faith, you of the beautiful gaze, the arresting demeanor, you shall remain with me while the others acquire the necessary physical requirements of our Mechanical Savior, for I am in need of your . . . *assistance* to prepare what shall become our High Rock, the seat of the birth of our Mechanical Deliverance into Glory!" Spear said to the handsome maiden with hair the color of hot embers, eyes that danced with a sparkling entreaty to be gazed into, a bosom full and firm, and so shapely, so perfectly formed ankles . . .

"What a wonder this day we create, Faith: something with the aspects of the earthly mated with the spiritual. This will be a true marriage of elemental forces," John Murray Spear said, with breathy passion, eyes dancing with fierce intensity.

"Tell me more, Mr Spear. Oh, please, enlighten me of our great mission. Speak of it more!" Faith said, stepping close – very close – her eyes also lit with passion . . . though of a more earthy nature.

"Ours will be a creation that will align the chaotic nature of this sphere, a Mechanical Messiah that will deliver us from our primitivism on this plane," Spear said, stepping equally close, his hands seizing her bloom sleeves, his heat conducting even through the thick, scratchy material.

"Oh, yes, Mr Spear . . . *John* . . . speak of this Motor we build," Faith said, pushing her body hard against his.

"Ours are but the hands . . . *Faith* . . . nothing but the physical extensions of the Association of Electricizers. Those who have blessed us with the information to see to its noble creation," Spear said, his hands dropping, grazing the slope of her protected chest.

"Yes . . . our 'physical extensions'. I know what you mean, John. I am so proud to be their . . . *your* . . . hands in this,"

Faith said, taking his hands in hers and placing them on her heaving bosom.

"The Motor is their will, with our physicality, towards a mutually beneficial union where we shall both be able to achieve new heights of enlightenment," Spear said, his hands working the delightful fullness of her breasts.

"Oh, yes, John, speak to me of our impending . . . enlightenment," Faith said, hastily unbuttoning the front of her blouse, fingers dancing a frenzy.

"We cannot know of the full impact of the Motor on our essences – can the ant know the dreams of men? When the Motor is infused with the force of pure force of life we shall be brought up to unparalleled heights," Spear said, helping her shuck off her blouse and then part her pale underthings.

"Oh . . . *John* . . . what a wonder the Motor shall be!" Faith said, bringing her hands forward to squeeze and caress her breasts, relishing in the sensual ache.

"It will indeed be one, Faith – a true miracle. And we shall be here to see its creation and then its . . . birth," Spear said, his hands echoing her own. Then, lowering himself to the dirty floor of the farmhouse, gently he took one of her breasts (the left) in his hands, and kissed the swollen pink nipple.

"Oh, Lord, John . . . oh, Lord . . . yes, such miracles . . ." Faith said, sighing with deep passion – a rich, throaty sound – as Spear kissed, then licked, then sucked at her tight nipple.

"Yes, Faith, we are truly fortunate to be here at this time, to be involved with this momentous delivery . . ." he said, lifting the billows of her skirts, pushing aside the linen curtains.

"Oh, yes, John . . . so *fortunate* . . ." she said as he rustled undergarments, hands fluttering against her quivering thighs.

"We are blessed, Faith, so . . . blessed . . ." Spear said, ferociously moving cotton until a triangle of silken red hair was revealed. This, too, he kissed – at first with gentle contacts, and then with more and more penetrating intensity.

". . ." Faith said, which translated as a breathy moan accompanying a push downward with her sex, reflexively, to get more of his tongue into her.

". . ." Spear said, which translated (same language) as fumbling his too-stiff throbbing penis free of many similar layers of itchy clothing. When his bare hand met his member, a sigh only momentarily interrupted his work on her well-lubricated region.

This went on, mutually pleasurable to both parties, until an ecstatically explosive orgasm vented up through her, spilling down into his mouth as a gush of slightly salty fluid.

Almost spent himself, he rocked back onto his haunches and then, shockingly hard, onto the floor of the farmhouse – his organ pointing authoritatively straight up, tipped by a pearlescent drop of fluid.

"We are witnesses to the creation, and the birth, of a divine engine –" Spear said, pushing himself up, begging himself to become impaled on the slippery hot recess of her molten sex.

"We are . . . helping the mechanical forces of the . . . *oh, God*!" she said, seeing his need, excited by his need, and lowering herself carefully to straddle, then feed his male member into her too-hot, too-silken, too-wet entrance, feeling the fat tip of him push, then slide up into her. A musical moan of delight escaped her bitten lips.

"We are the orchestrations of the creation of an engineering messiah – *oh, oh, oh*!" he said as she eased herself down, stuffing herself with his erect manhood. Then, with escalating intensity – driven by a need as old as humanity itself – she began a repetitive rhythm: up and down, up and down, up and down – a liquid, slapping motion that ebbed with his member almost escaping the lips of her sex, and peaked with him filling her to her utmost capacity.

After an uncertain time their moans and cries and incoherent bursts of near-speech, near philosophical balderdash, synched, perfected, then climbed to a pair of syncopated screams towards a deity that they hoped perhaps to outdo, with their engineered divinity, their mechanical savior.

Passion echoing down into an exhaustion that began to firmly pull them down into sleep, Faith and John Murray Spear managed to extricate themselves from their primitive embrace of genitals, adjust their voluminous and very often scratchy clothing, and put on somewhat civil faces for the rest of their congregation as they returned from their errands.

. . . an 1854 contraption, but surreally hinting at the complex technologies of our current civilization: a personal computer made of glass mason jars, coils of copper tubing, sheets of tin, old wagon wheels and the remains of a pot-bellied stove.

. . . a machine of a previous century: a maddenly complex clock – an interdimensional mandala of impossibly interlocking gears, fantastically meshing wheels, magically transversing pendulums, and springs coiling into eye-smarting spirals.

. . . a nineteenth century contraption of perilous articulations: the egg rolls down the tin gutter, lands in the funnel, which trips a lever that drains water from a jug, fills a bucket, lifting a cork, relaxing a string, tightening a bow, firing the arrow, hitting the target, ringing the bell – and on, and on, into a cascading eternity.

. . . an Age of Steam cyclotron: a tremendous squeezing weight pressing down through the action of great screws and pulleys onto a complex box of tightly spinning gears that, action reproduced on a molecular level, tried to split atoms like a hammer with an anvil.

The New Motor, the Divine Device, the Mechanical Savior of the Race could have looked like any of those – but rather, embarrassingly, it just sat there: a cold collection of parts taking up a major part of the farmhouse.

"Arise, spirit of the Machine! Awaken, Spiritual Engine! Be given the force of Life, oh Magnificent Instrument – breathe, beat, tick, hum, click, whirr – come on, dammit!" intoned (then whispered) John Murray Spear, standing before the inert pile of metal and other parts.

"Hear my words, New Motor – hear them and take of our essence, borrow of our life to spark your action! We are here, Great Ethereal Mechanism, and we exist so that you may operate and live!" Spear said, passion building, them smashing through his words – ringing them off the farmhouse walls and slowly reaching his congregation (especially one of then).

"It is time, Motor, time for your automated birth so that you might lead us into a New Age!" John Murray Spear said, words ringing out, echoing with noble desire – and sparking a more human version in one particular person.

"Now, Motor – *now*! My voice, my spiritual essence reaches out to you, oh Holy Implement of the Association of Electricizers, and sparks in you the motive power, the magnetic store of nature!" Spear thundered, the energy of his passion stirring those present (yes, one more than others) to feel their own thrilling charge of excitement.

So spoke Spear, intonation after intonation, plea after plea, summons after summons till his flock panted, eyes glazed and hearts pounding, themselves reeling from the charge he was raising – even if the New Motor, dead as anything, still sat immobile.

One of them, even more charged, heart pounding more, eyes even more glazed, was so seized by the driving determination, the impassioned oration of Spear, by a physical manifestation of his determination . . . her legs failed her and she fell to the floor, and her hands, moving like enchanted serpents, plunged beneath her skirts and began to feverishly work her melting sex in ecstatic syncopation.

Also feeling the charge of Spear's oration, the rest of the little New Motor flock was similarly energized – though not, definitely not, to get down on the rough floor and begin to masturbate. Still, to be fair, they didn't stop her from continuing either.

Complex skirts pushed up and out of the way, she spread her pale thighs wide so as best to gain access to her aching sex – her pulsing, liquid, burning neither regions that so desperately ached for contact – stroking, rubbing, penetrating release.

Hands fluttering a sensual dance at her swollen lips, quivering vulva and pulsing clitoris, she worked and worked and worked some more until a shattering orgasm applauded Spear's spiritual conjuration of the New Motor –

– and then, slowly, achingly, but also *definitely*, it started to click, then to whirr, then to vibrate, hum, oscillate, revolve, and otherwise simply *move* . . . the Physical Savior of the Race, The New Messiah, the New Motor began to work.

And Faith, exhausted, smiled, smiled, smiled –

Sometime later, the flock – in their less-than-comfortable cheap beds, but too tired with celebration to mind – lost in dreams of glorious spiritual engines, Spear stood before the great machine, now filled with motive life, his eyes still wide after many hours.

"So . . . incredible. In my dreams . . . no, not even in my most vivid of dreams could I ever have imagined the beauty of you,

Motor. No, I could never have envisioned the glory of your movement, the power of your functioning. I am enraptured with your mechanism –"

"John," Faith said – also tired, but not quite tired enough for bed – touching her priceless spiritualist on the shoulder. "Please, John, can I, may I . . . again?"

"You are truly the Mechanical Messiah, Motor. You are the Divine Engine. I am your servant and engineer – humbled before your actions, your motions –" Spear said, his eyes only for the vibrant contrivance.

"John, my body – I need you, John. You have awakened me, John. I need to feel you again," Faith said, voice heavy with desire, clutching firmly Spear's arm.

"Nothing, Motor – nothing on this earth shall keep me from my service of your gears, your parts, your elements. I shall be your Priest of the Oil Can, your Deacon of the Wrench, your Bishop of Repair . . . I am yours, Motor, and no one else's –" Spear said, glazed sight enraptured with awe at its motions.

"Please, John, I want you. I need you – please don't make me beg, John. Please –" Faith said, tears gleaming on her cheeks, tugs becoming more insistent.

"Great Implement of the Association of Electricizers, your motion grants me the greatest joy! I am here – I am here for you now, Messiah. My life as of today is yours. Your nuts I will tighten, your belts I will lubricate, your spokes I will straighten, your glass I will polish, your metal I will make gleam with my dedicated hands and all the strength granted me in this fleshy shell –" Spear said, pulling away from the woman and stepping closer, bathing in the technological glimmer of his holy gizmo.

"John, you cocksucker, are you going to fuck me or not?" Faith said – or words to an 1854 equivalent – screaming into his ear over the din of the machine and the single-mindedness of his locked gaze.

But to her own impassioned, driven, passionate pleas and invocations all John Murray Spear said was, "– What was that again, Motor? What is it you need? What is it, my Physical Savior of the Race, my New Messiah? What do you require of myself, your most humble servant? The tightening of some wayward screw, the adjustment of some loose belt, perhaps?

I am yours, Motor – tell me what you desire and I shall sate it!"

Faith said something else at that point, but since even the twenty-first century version would have scorched a sailor's ears we won't reproduce it – suffice it to say that, whatever it was that she *screamed*, Spear wasn't listening.

So Faith left John Murray Spear, left him standing bathed in the electric glow of the New Motor, the Divine Device, his Clockwork Jesus, and went out and down the road, consumed with frustration and a self-righteous fury, into the small hamlet of saltbox houses and cod fishermen, to tell them a very interesting tale –

We might not know if John Murray Spear actually had his vision of the Association of Electricizers, and we don't have a clue as to what his creation, the New Motor, even looked like. We haven't the foggiest idea of how it became active, or even that it did – all this is lost to hazy history, fragmented memories, not even reported in the documents we do possess. But we do know some things: we know, for instance, as stated of Spear's gathering of his flock, his speaking to the residents of the eastern seaboard, that the Mechanical Messiah, the Holy Contraption, the New Motor was built in Lynn, Massachusetts – and that it was destroyed shortly after its activation by the outraged Christian citizenry of that small hamlet of saltbox houses and cod fishermen.

But the truth really doesn't have anything to do with this story. All facts do is pin the Hows, Whys, and Whens down a bit – they don't say anything about what Spear and his followers might have believed, felt about their Mechanical Savior.

This was, after all, a tale about Faith – and how it started the entire endeavor of the New Motor . . . and how she destroyed it.

TWICE UPON A TIME

Nadine Wilder

THERE WAS ONCE a handsome cowherd called Dick, who was in love with one of the most beautiful girls in the world. The trouble was that the other most beautiful girl in the world was her twin sister, and Dick had no way of telling them apart.

I'll ask one of them to walk out with me, he decided. I'll knock at their cottage door and ask the first one I see. Then she'll be my sweetheart.

But they came to the door together. "Dick!" they chorused. "What a lovely surprise!"

Their blue eyes were bright with naked desire. They had often watched him walk down the lane, admiring his jaunty buttocks and saucy swagger, and both were as smitten as he.

Oh, dear! thought Dick. Which shall I choose?

"Come in," they invited him. As he did so, one brushed her breasts seductively against him while the other took his hand. At once urgent messages went down to his namesake, to stand up for himself and be prepared for active service.

"I've often wanted to drop by," he began, shyly. "But which twin are you?" he asked the one who still held his hand.

"I'm Zinnia Polyanthus, and this is Polyanthus Zinnia. But you may call her Polly," she said, then both girls giggled.

Dick searched their pretty faces for any distinguishing marks

He lifted the delectable globes to his nostrils. "Roses!" he said in a muffled voice, his nose buried in the valley between them.

Soon his lips had travelled to one swollen pink bud, and were sucking urgently while he rolled the other teat between finger and thumb. "What do I taste of now?" came the girl's softly mocking tones. He could feel her begin to writhe against him, increasing his arousal to bursting point.

"Fresh buttermilk," he groaned.

As he sipped his fill, his desire became even more unstoppable, and he pulled up her skirt, but to his dismay she slapped his hand, saying, "Naughty! I never allow that on a first walking out."

Bitch! Dick thought. Prick tease! But then her words sank in. "First walking out?" He stared up at her smiling face. "But we walked out yesterday."

"Not me! That was my sister!"

Dick sprang back as if he'd been stung, and his swollen erection abruptly subsided. "What? You mean you're not Zinnia, but Polly?"

"That's right," she giggled.

"But . . . you look the same, smell the same, taste the same . . ."

"Well, we are identical twins. And we both have honey and cream for tea, and place lavender sprigs in our drawers and use rosewater in our toilet."

Despairingly, Dick ran his hands through his thick, dark hair. "Then you tricked me!"

"That's true. Zinnia told me you were such a good kisser that I wanted to find out for myself." She stood up, smoothing down her skirt. "But does it really matter which of us you make love to, if we're both exactly the same?"

Dick had no answer to that one. In a way she was right: it didn't matter. After all, it had been a matter of chance which girl he had dated at first. But he still didn't like to think that he'd been made a fool of. "How on earth do I know whether to call you Zinnia or Polly?" he asked, sulkily.

"Darling Dicky, we are used to people muddling us up. We answer to either name."

"Even so, I can't go on dating you both in this random way.

Is there no difference between you by which I might tell which is which?"

Polly smiled a strangely distant smile. "That's for us to know and you to find out!"

It was a very confused Dick that went home to his cottage that night. The memory of his two encounters with the twins was still tormenting him with insatiable lust, yet he could not say whether he desired Zinnia more than her sister, or vice-versa. I'll make my choice tomorrow, he decided, as he gave himself some much-needed hand relief. Whichever twin walks out with me, her shall I wed and that shall be an end of it. The sooner I gets one of them wedded and bedded, the happier I shall be.

He knew they were orphaned, and had none to answer to. But suppose one girl loved him more than the other? Perhaps he should leave the choice to them, now they'd both had the chance to try him out. Well, he would discuss it with whoever he saw the following night.

Before then, however, the weather changed. When Dick called at the cottage he found the twins waiting for him. " 'Tis too wet to walk out," the girl he thought was Zinnia declared. "Let's stay in and play at cards."

At that, Dick's heart fell. The games he'd had in mind were more fun than cards. "Both of you?" he asked, miserably.

The twins giggled at his discomfort. "I'll put the kettle on." Polly smiled.

When Dick was alone with the other twin, he decided to come clean. "I'd hoped to ask one of you to wed me tonight," he sighed. "For I can hardly bear to spend another night without such a sweet body close to mine. Yet, I confess, I don't know which of you to ask."

"Well, I was your first choice," she said, identifying herself as Zinnia.

"True, but I would not wish to cause bad feeling between you and your sister."

"Then we'll toss for you," she smiled, lifting up her skirt to reveal a silk purse strapped around her shapely thigh. It was all Dick could do not to thrust his hand into her lacy bloomers, he was so full of frustrated appetite.

When Polly returned she was told of the plan and readily

agreed. They tossed a coin and Zinnia won, but Polly claimed a kiss all the same. "I've not lost a lover; I've gained a brother," she smiled, as she fastened her sweet lips on his. But the way she thrust her tongue in and out of his mouth was far from sisterly!

The three drank tea in silence until Polly spoke up. "Since you two are now betrothed, why don't you go upstairs and enjoy each other while I play Patience?"

Dick gladly agreed. He gallantly carried his bride-to-be up the steep stairs into the bedroom she shared with her sister. They tumbled onto the big double bed and Zinnia began eagerly peeling off her clothes, exposing more womanly flesh than Dick had ever before set eyes on. When she revealed her fine golden bush Dick nearly fainted with pleasure, and couldn't wait to entwine his fingers in the soft, sleek hairs.

"You may play with my flower, but do not pluck it," she said. "That must wait for our wedding night."

So Dick went enthusiastically to work, licking and sucking at the tender bud until the nectar ran down her thighs and her pink lips turned a deeply engorged crimson. Then, when Zinnia was gasping on the brink, he probed the honeypot with his finger and felt it clasp his stiff digit in an eager embrace. He added another finger, and another. Eagerly she caressed him with her love-lips, squeezing him rhythmically and making the most delightful squelching noises with her cunt.

Dick felt her hand reach his throbbing prick and lightly brush it with her fingers, making him thrust into her cupped palm. Her slim fingers played with his loose foreskin, rubbing it against his shaft and tickling the sensitive glans until exquisite tingles spread to every part of his body. At last neither could bear it any longer. With a moan Zinnia wrung the last shuddering moments of pleasure from his wet fingers as, with an equally loud groan, he spilled his seed into the hollow of her navel. Then they collapsed together on the pillow.

"There, my sweet Dicky, now we are truly lovers." She smiled, gently toying with his limp member as they cuddled each other.

I'm sure I've made the right choice, thought Dick, happily.

Soon they indulged in a repeat performance – with variations. This time Zinnia put her wet lips and tongue to work on Dick's revived member, while he tasted the honey that streamed from her other lips when he nibbled on the sweet nut within. So hot were they for each other that it took hardly any time to achieve the desired result, and they fell, laughing, into each other's arms.

Some time later, they went downstairs, to see Polly still playing with her cards. She gave Dick such a knowing smile that he blushed, and didn't know what to say. Poor Polly, he thought, when I marry her sister she will be left on the shelf. But she didn't look too upset at the prospect.

The wedding day was set, and Polly was to be Zinnia's bridesmaid. When Dick saw them arrive at the church he was amazed to see that they were dressed alike, each in a white lace dress and carrying a posy of zinnias and polyanthus. When the parson came to the crux of the matter and asked, "Do you, Zinnia Polyanthus, take this man, Richard Henry, to be your lawful wedded husband?" the answer came, "I do." It was spoken softly, but Dick could hear a faint echo ring round the walls of the old church, sounding like, "I do . . . oo . . . too . . ."

Dick began to put the ring on Zinnia's finger, but it fell onto the ground and the best man had to retrieve it. Soon, though, they were well and truly wed, and a party was held in the twins' cottage. When the last guest had gone, and it was time for bed, Dick looked round for Polly, but she was nowhere to be seen.

"Don't worry about her," Zinnia smiled. "I'm the one with your ring on my finger – see?" And she held it up, laughing, while he swooped her off her feet and into his arms.

"I'm the luckiest man alive," Dick said as he laid her gently down on the bed and began to strip off his clothes. Next he helped his bride to disrobe, kissing her wherever a new expanse of warm, scented flesh was exposed. In the flickering firelight she looked like an angel. His hungry gaze passed over her full white breasts, with their sugar-pink nipples peaking with desire. Down over her smooth, pale stomach went his eyes, towards the fluffy triangle that he expected to see gleaming bright and golden, like the flames in the hearth. But there his eyes halted, nearly popping out of his head with shock. For instead of the blonde bush that he had fondled and kissed before the wedding, there was an equally delightful, but totally unexpected, triangle of dark brown hair.

"Zinnia?" he gasped. "I . . . I thought you were a different colour down . . . down there! Surely, when we made love last, you were as fair below as you are above!"

A curious smile played about his bride's lips as she lay back, calmly surveying him. "You are right," she said, slowly. "*Zinnia's* hair is perfectly matched."

Dick's jaw dropped open. "You don't mean . . . !" He seized her hand. "But you are wearing my ring; you must be she! Am I going mad? Tell me, I beg of you, which one have I married – Zinnia or Polly?"

Just then the wardrobe door opened and out stepped the other twin, as naked as the day she was born. Dick saw at once that she was the girl he had pleasured before. She came and stood beside the bed, smiling down at the pair of them.

"Yes, I am Zinnia," she admitted. "My hair's fair above and below, but Polly's don't match. It's the only way you can tell us apart."

Dick wiped a hand across his sweating brow. "But I still don't understand. I could have sworn that it was you I married, Zinnia, in the church."

Still smiling, she held up her left hand, on which a gold ring gleamed. "You did, darling Dicky. But when the ring seemed to fall, and everyone was looking on the ground, Polly and I changed places. Charlie picked up a second ring, and you put it on Polly's finger. So you see, you have two brides!"

The idea excited him greatly, although he still couldn't quite believe in it. Two pairs of arms were entwined around Dick's body as he struggled to understand, and once again he felt warm stirrings in his nether region. "B-but if I am married to you both, what will people say?"

"They need never know," a voice murmured in his ear. Dick looked down: it was Polly. "As long as you only ever appear with one of us in public, no one will suspect."

"You see, dearest Dicky, once we had both tasted your kisses, neither of us could bear to be parted from you," Zinnia cooed, wriggling against his back so that her golden bush tickled his buttocks in a very stimulating fashion.

"Nor could we bear to be parted from each other," Polly smiled, rubbing her smooth thigh against his until a milky droplet fell from his pulsating glans. “We always swore we’d never let any man come between us.”

“But I think we’re about to make an exception to that rule,” Zinnia giggled. And, sandwiched as he was between the two most beautiful girls in the world, Dick couldn’t help but agree.

GARDEN

Jennifer Footman

SHE SAT ON her favourite rock and drank the juice from the coconut she had just cracked open.

Man had left to go swimming in the lake. The waters of the lake were too cold and still. She preferred the energy of the stream's shallows or the warm salt ripples of the small sea edging one side of the world. He never came here to the spot where the serpents coiled round the tree and hissed with their long tongues. They disturbed him; they were of no use to anyone. They did nothing but eat, sleep and sometimes spread their great wide heads, like birds.

"At least birds lay eggs. They fly and sing. What do those two evil things do? Nothing."

She felt sure that the serpents had some use. If they were of no use then what was the use of Man? Or herself? She bent down and picked a rose from the bush growing next to her and buried her face in its fragrance.

Some days the two serpents coiled together up on the tree, and some days they sunned themselves, spread on one of the many table-like rocks.

Today was going to be the day to touch the larger of the two – the black one. Black, black as the darkest night she could imagine, broken by its red mouth and amber eyes. He was longer than Man and thicker than her own thigh.

They were sleeping curled round the trunk of the tree. Black One opened its eyes and gazed at her. She walked over and touched it. Warm, warm and dry. She sat beside them. Yes, the smell of night and dreams . . . slowly it slid down from the tree, so slowly it hardly moved. It stopped at her feet and coiled its long thick body, lifted its head level with hers. It spread its hood and hovered in front of her.

"You are quite beautiful."

The other one joined them, and both swayed in unison. The smaller one was mostly green, but speckled with blue, shot with silver and gold, reflecting all the colours of the rainbow.

"Yes, you are quite, quite beautiful."

Green One lowered its head and curved its body up to hers, so its head rested on her breast. The long, thin whip-like tongue circled her nipple. The other one joined it and circled the other nipple. She was a feather flying in the wind. She arched her back and bonded herself to the contour of the rock. She had not imagined her body could feel this kind of lightness. The rose's sweet smell, the spice of honey, the texture of clouds all combined to enrich her body. Energy pulsed from her breasts to the area between her legs. Green One had moved his head down to her navel and it rested on her belly, its body tight between her legs. Then it moved away and brushed the fur so gently she was hardly aware of the movement, but her body responded by sending greater and greater blasts of energy through her belly, down, down, down. She was a tight drum; she was a sky about to explode; she was the meadow lit yellow and gold and silver and green and purple. Something more coming, something more happening. She was the anticipation of a sneeze.

Both of them left her body and curled and rotated round each other, making beautiful patterns of thick and thin, green and black, stillness and movement.

She looked down at herself. Her breasts were two full, ripe orbs, and so heavy she did not think she could walk. Her legs were weak, burdened with the sun, the moon, the clouds. She moved her hand down, over her breasts, felt the cool weight; she stroked across her belly, down to her fur, to the area unknown, untouched. Her finger explored, down, down. The lips bulged, thickened into twice their size. They were wet, soaking wet. She moved her finger round the lips, investigating. There had never been a need to examine, to look at this part of her body. Why and what for?

That night, just before dawn, she left the cave and gathered flowers and braided them into a crown and placed it on her head. She packed the best of their fruit into a basket and walked towards the plain of serpents.

She looked into a pool near their cave and saw herself reflected in the moonlight. The flowers were white and brilliant against her dark skin, her heavy red nipples danced in her reflection. She squeezed a petal or two between her fingers. God, the perfume swirled into her head.

Dawn turned the sky pink and gold by the time she reached the plain. Half of her wanted to be there and half was deadly afraid. Where would they lead her? Would they lead her anywhere? Her body tingled from the last time. Her blood demanded their touch.

Air was dense with the smell of darkness. Something near her rustled and she looked down. Just a dried sage bush beside, being blown by a pleasant breeze.

Black One lay fully extended on a rock; Green One was coiled into a cone. She placed the fruit and flowers near them. Green One slowly brought its head up to her and rested on her shoulder. She was fascinated by its teeth. It ran its tongue round her ear, deep inside. She shivered, unable to move. Then it took her nipple into its mouth. Her breasts had found their purpose; her belly had found its purpose; those thick curled lips between her legs had found their purpose. She lay back. Both snakes aligned their bodies to the moist dark area of fur and vibrated gently up and down, playing her. "Yes," she moaned, not knowing why. Her head was filled with roses and jasmine . . . she sniffed her hand and all the smell was coming from her own body. The snakes parted for a moment and she half sat to look at herself. Fine hair spread against pink lips. Yes, it was the inside of a conch they'd found one day beside the lake of salt water; it was the sky at sunset. She circled round the pink scalloped edge and whimpered with the delight she gave herself. She tasted the liquid on her finger and it was sweet, at the same time salt. It was the water from the oysters they'd picked when they had found the conch shells.

Black One spread its hood and circled the air. Its tongue hissed out and quivered from side to side; its head tilted until its tongue touched her in that dark moist area. She opened her legs wide, so wide she felt she was going to split open. Its tongue worked that magic area and its tail feathered her slit, feathered it until it eased a tiny way in, then a bit more and then more into her body. It twisted into her and filled her so tight she was going mad. Yes, this was what she was waiting for; this was the sun and the moon. Above her a million stars were born.

She went every day to the rock. Sometimes there would be one snake and sometimes two. Gradually the three of them found other games. She would take them fruit and flowers and they would use their tongues and bodies to please her, to make her live.

Man was adding wood to the fire and Woman had just skinned a rabbit for the evening meal. She looked at Man's fur and the way the fur curved up to his chest. Until now the differences in their bodies had seemed incidental – just as some birds were large and some small, and some black and some white, so he had an extra limb and two little stones.

"Man," she said when they had finished eating, "some time . . . some time come with me to the snake."

"What for?"

"For pleasure. Can't think for what else, just pleasure."

"What pleasure can be in that thing, that no-legged animal? It's nothing but a worm. It has no use."

"Perhaps pleasure for us."

He swept the bones and bits of their meal onto the floor. She held out a hand. "Please. I will weave you garlands of purple flowers and pick the tiniest reddest strawberries and press juice from the mangoes and papayas and make wine for you and crystallize the sugar from the plums and dry the meat of the oyster . . . Just once."

He shrugged and took her hand, and they ambled through the gardens to the arid plain.

The snakes were curled together, right at the top of the tree, and giving every impression of being asleep.

She sat on the rock. "This is where the serpents and I sit and talk." She pulled him to her.

"Don't believe you."

"Wait and see."

The serpents continued sleeping.

"Look at me," she said. "What do you see?"

"You."

"Is that all? Nothing else. No difference. No change?"

"What more is there?"

Slowly both snakes slipped down the tree to position themselves behind Man.

"Look at me."

Both snakes wrapped themselves round Man so he couldn't move, Black One round his ankles and Green One round his torso.

"What . . . ? What . . ."

"Don't worry. I can . . . they like me. They will not hurt you."

Man was trapped, his body in a tight knot but for an area between his legs. Woman stood up and studied him.

"Let me go," he moaned. "I can't breathe."

"Not yet." She bent down and kissed the limb on its tip, just at the dark hole. It had quite a pleasant texture, firm flesh, something like the flesh of her breasts. The limb itself moved slightly, and the balls below stiffened and tightened against his body. She slid the skin back to better expose the end, took the whole limb into her mouth. He whimpered.

"Is that painful, Man?"

He shook his head and lifted his back so his limb would be even more deeply buried in her mouth.

She worked the skin back and forward a few times over the tip and the limb expanded, just as a water bladder expanded when she filled it at the stream. It bounced against his belly button every time she freed it from her mouth. God, it was beautiful. Yes, much sweeter than any fruit she had ever licked, much more fragrant. God. Sweet. It stood right up in the air as she held it by the root.

Her own flesh was vital, swarming, leaving her bones, leaving her skin. She was energy, a river tumbling from one place to the other. She had a pain between her legs that was so acute, so sharp it took her breath away. She wanted to tear the pain right out, to rub it until it bled, to eat herself.

She squatted above him. Black One moved forward and used its tongue to tease her in the manner it had done so many times. She was a rock, cracking open in the heat of summer. She lowered herself onto Man's limb, so gently, just the end first. Snake was attached to her as if by a hook, sucking and licking. She sank down a bit and more of the limb entered her, and more and more, and finally he was part of her, the limb buried deep in her red darkness. Both snakes released his body and he rolled over her, crushing her below him. His face was the face of pain, at the same time the face of God. His limb filled her so full she couldn't breathe, couldn't feel anything but the great throb of the earth below her and the sky above her, and she joined the sky and the earth together. They both screamed so loudly the universe was deafened and they shuddered together, spent and delighted.

Just above them thunder crashed, and drops of rain fell on his back.

SUCCUBUS

Rosemary Hawley Jarman

IT WAS THE first time I had been in the cage, the place of disgrace on Cornhill, though I had been warned. Ply your trade only in Southwark, they'd said, even the ones jealous of my looks. You're safe this side of the Thames. The Bishop of Winchester owns all the stews here; he takes a big cut to build his churches. Indulgences pay for the fancy gilt carvings, the ivory roodscreens and the like. Plenty of indulgences bought from those who visit us whores, and plenty of fancy work in the stews too, belly to belly with the lusty lords and naughty clerics. But if you want to freelance, it's your choosing. But stay south of the river. Be wise, wench.

The horrible cage was only about ten foot square, standing in the busiest thoroughfare near the crossroads, on a pole about twelve foot high. The cage floor was filthy, and the bars greasy from the hands of previous felons, year after year. Idling youths and prentices could see up my skirt if they so inclined, but that was the least of my trials.

Towards Mincing Lane stood the pillory. A fat dairy-woman's head was stuck through it; she was guilty of selling bad butter, and a dish of it hung beneath her nose. The town idiot sat in the stocks, put there for being a nuisance. He droned a song, seeming not to mind too much.

The crowd were throwing offal and cabbage stalks at us. Most of it bounced off the bars, but some found its mark on me or on Mags. Mags was in the cage already when the Watch pounced on me in Bucklersbury, just I was about to undo the points of a sweet young gentleman's hose. They carted me off and put me up the ladder to join Mags. She was about thirty, none too clean, and maybe poxy with the ailment brought back by the soldiers who had trounced the French at Azincourt in my granddad's time.

I didn't have the pox, nor did I want it. At fifteen I was fresh and lively.

The soldiers, full of ale and sport after their victorious battle, had picked me up at Tewkesbury, hauling me up into an arms-cart. They'd turned me upside down after each swiving and washed me out with wine, so that I should neither be poxy nor with a get in my belly.

It was a great battle. They had even fought up and down the aisles in the Abbey there. Our King Edward was restored from exile to the Yorkist throne; the French Queen Margaret was captured and clapped in the Tower, and her son slain before he could usurp the throne for Lancaster.

So I came with the White Rose army to London and found myself on my back, on my knees, on my feet, whichever way the gentlemen desired. And I had my pick; rich ones, clean and dressed lordly, nothing sordid, no ruffians. And now I was cast down, rather shoved up, in this stinking pen with drab Mags, dodging fish-heads. Fortunes of war, the army would say. Fortunes of whore.

A prentice hurled a bad egg, and its smelly slime hit my dress and trickled down. It was my best, too, a present from a rich client, fine English wool in sky-blue with a neck that showed my bubbies. My little shoes and stockings were likewise befouled. Below I could see the sergeant of the Watch, nose in a tankard. I'd already tried to wheedle and bribe him with the only thing I had – myself – but he was old and grumpy. And night was coming down. Along Cornhill they were lighting the cressets for folk to see their homeward way. Mags told me she had already been in the cage for two days and nights. She had been swearing at the Watch, calling them cunt-bitten whoresons and the like, and this had done our case no good at all. Now she was quiet, curled up in a corner, knees to chin, looking mournfully over the big sign which told folk we were harlots.

The man talking to the sergeant seemed to have emerged from the shadows, no more than a shadow himself, long and thin in a dusty old-fashioned houpeland with dagged sleeves, covered by a blackish cloak in which were tarnished silver threads. But he wore a velvet cap with a large pearl in it and a plump purse at his belt. He brought the sergeant forward and together they looked up at me. I saw his face white, thin bones, and in deep pits the blackest eyes that gleamed like chips of sea-coal. They never left me as he talked to the sergeant and withdrew a fair number of gold angels from his purse. And as the sergeant set up the ladder I realized I was being bought out, and at no little cost either.

"Not you," said the sergeant to Mags, who hopefully uncurled herself. He took my arm and I stepped on to the ladder, near falling down it in my lust to be out. I landed at the feet of my saviour.

"Thank you, my lord." I gleamed up at him in my most beguiling fashion. He did not have the appearance of my usual client, grinning, puffing, hastening me away to inn or alley to do the business. This man had a cool, unhurried mien, detached, without lechery. More like a judge. Whatever he was, I owed him. With a hand in a green velvet glove he took my arm, and said quietly, "Come."

I came. Rather, I went, with him through the City of London and unfamiliar streets, though I recognized Chepeside with its windows displaying silver and jewels. I lingered to look at the gleaming collars and mazers, and he urged me on, his long dusty cloak laying itself over my shoulder like a wing. The way became strange again as we moved into the darkness of alleys where the house gables grew close together and made a slot for the starlight overhead. He spoke only once as we walked.

"You like jewels? They are but frozen minerals, a resin from the earth. Without true value."

I wondered now where he was taking me, and even whether it was for the normal purpose. And I felt cold. He knew it, for he draped the cloak about both of us just before we turned into a house whose doorway was carved with leaves and the heads of griffons with gilded teeth. His body pressed mine as we went in together; his bones were sharp as a skeleton's. Now I was not only chill, but afraid, for the first time in my life.

I stood within a room so full of clutter and artefacts there seemed no space for air to breathe. A great fire raged in a hearth that stretched almost the length of one wall. The flames showed oak furnishings and shelves on which were precious bound books and roll upon roll of parchment. A laughing skull sat on top of a bookcase, and a glass dome contained liquid and something scaly and hairy, gently floating. There was a tapestry covered with hieroglyphs and runes, and a globe showing the continents of the earth. On a top shelf I saw a line of bright watching eyes. When he lit candles I realized these were merely a family of cats, but I was still afraid.

He doffed his cloak and came to me, patting my shoulder quite affably. He bade me sit in a chair beside the fire. My fear diminished.

Then he began an inquisition. How old was I, my history, was I healthy? I answered him fairly, and for good measure I named my price. At this he smiled, so, emboldened by this, and the riches in the room, I doubled it. He stood surveying me. I leaned back in the chair and lifted my skirt to my waist, exposing my commodities. I was very proud of my cunt. I washed it regularly. Its hair was as red as the glossy fall on my head, and not too much of it either, merely a glinting frill through which my two sets of coral lips protruded and winked at the buyer. I slung a leg over each wide arm of the chair and waited.

Yes. He looked. By now I would have expected to be filled by a stiff yard, but he made no move. Perhaps he was too old, thought I, or had some infirmity. I put down my legs.

"My mouth is for sale too." I might as well have held my peace. He seemed to have gone away somewhere, although he still studied me. I began to feel sleepy by the warm fire. I even drowsed for a moment, which was unusual. His voice brought me alert.

"Yes. Redhair. You will do." And then he let out a long string of absolute gibberish, words neither English nor French nor Latin – or perhaps there might have been a little dog-Latin hidden away, like a flea in a mattress – but whatever the tongue it rolled around the room and shivered through me for no reason other than its power. And I said quite sharply, "What's your pleasure, my master?" then began to describe the variations of my skill, even the *paynim* versions of intercourse, backdoor traffic to which I was never partial, but I was uneasy and wanted our contract sealed without any more delay.

At once he became businesslike. "Take off all your clothes," he commanded, and I did, in some relief. I saw now there was a long mirror of highly polished silver set against the far wall, and I walked over to it. It was the first time I had seen my body, other than in wavering woodland pools. I was almost shocked at the beauty of the white shape under the waves of hair coloured like deep autumnal embers. I leaned forward and touched my own white teeth revealed by my prideful smile. I was still smiling when he said, "Now come. Lie on the floor, and be still."

He stood over me, with his deep eyes and straight lips. "I am Master Sylvanus," he said. "I have brought you to serve me. I am an Adept, cognizant of the Craft. I taught Friar Bungay all there is of earth, heaven and hell."

Even I had heard of Friar Bungay. The necromancer, the shape-changer, the heretic priest. Now to be in the presence of heresy is not comfortable. As I lay by the hearth the fireglow on my bare side took on an unpleasant tincture. "Don't be afraid," he said. "You are safe. I have been seeking someone with your attributes since the demise of my last assistant. Now I will prepare you."

All this without explanation. Or without telling me how the demise of his last assistant had occurred. Yet I lay naked on his floor, as acquiescent and heedless as to a lover. From a shelf he took a jar which looked made of black gold. The scaly hairy thing in the dome stirred. I saw now it was a tiny homunculus, living, breathing the fluid. It turned up its tail with a gentle flickering. I closed my eyes. Sylvanus was kneeling close to me. His hands were anointing me from the jar. It felt like oil. It smelled of pitch, then of flowers, then garlic, herbs, cats, candlewax, incense, a continually changing odour. It stung my skin, then soothed it. He began at the soles of my feet, along my legs, my belly, breasts, neck, down my arms and hands, between each finger, back to my groin, where he massaged the stuff between the lips of my cunt and into it, his fingers invading my arsehole, turning me over, greasing my back, lifting my hair, oiling my face, lips, tongue. My whole body sang and burned, then shivered coolly as if turned to silver.

It changed me. It possessed my mind. I was swept by a joy, its matrix was power. I lay smiling.

"Now," said Sylvanus. "Rise. Walk into the fire."

I came to my feet. The flames were leaping up in the great hearth with a tremendous heat. I did not falter. I walked through the flames and stood at the back of the hearth and looked at Sylvanus through a screen of leaping fire. I could see the whole room from behind the flames, and my own naked body, lying motionless, eyes closed, on the other side. I let a flame run along my arm and laughed. It felt like a cool serpent. I saw Sylvanus's lips move. "Come back." And next moment I was at his side, leaning against him, while he held me and smiled for the first time.

"Beautiful, good and holy whore," he said. He kissed my forehead. I felt another surge of joy.

"Instruct me," I said.

"That I do already," he said. "You must know our purpose. I deal in politics. The House of York . . ."

"God bless it," I said obediently. "God bless King Edward."

He frowned slightly. "And not God alone. The King is young. He needs constant guidance." The pupils of his eyes were like arrow-slits in his long white face. "Now. I will show you what must be hidden. Were you to reveal what I shall show you, it would no longer exist. Neither would I. As for you . . ."

He looked at me. In his look I saw ropes and blocks and fire, and I was silent.

He took me to a smaller, darker chamber. There was a tabernacle, similar to that in which priests keep the Host, but large. Within were many small glass vials containing a cloudy fluid. Near to them stood a line of tiny mammets, some impaled on thorns, others looking as if they had been held in fire.

"The victors and the vanquished," he said. "And in those vessels the distillation of England's power."

He closed and locked the tabernacle, and drew me back into the firelit room, where he poured me a cup of hypocras, an aphrodisiac which I did not need.

"The King is mad with triumph over the House of Lancaster. Now he indulges himself in play. He should guard his throne.

I do not forecast long life for him. And France is still a danger, as in the old days."

He stared into the fire. I studied his hunched, dusty form. I was still naked, and my nakedness was nothing to him. Yet he had possessed me utterly, through an ensorcelling that had happened almost outside my knowledge. I drank my wine, while he rose and fetched yet another jar, containing some small yellow eggs. When he broke these and discarded the shells, a wondrously slimy gleamy fluid was expelled. He beat the mixture with a pestle.

"The eggs of adders. Out of these cometh Cockatrice. This venomous juice has all the power you will need."

He touched the mixture to my eyes. Stinging and blinded, I heard, "this for sight in the dark." And as the mess was touched to my shoulder blades, "This for flight." Then: "Adonai, Eloim, Sadai, Ariel, Sabaoth, God who commands all spirits, who has given power also unto demons, lift up this child to our work. Asmodeus, Belphegor, Astarte, Azriel, send her safe passage . . ." And as the glutinous stuff trickled from my eyes I saw his lips moving in a final invocation, although a ringing in my ears drowned out the words.

Then he turned and said "Go now, child. Little beautiful strumpet, lovely popelot, fire-haired leman. Go and fetch me the King's essence while he sleeps. Bring it back in this." And he placed round my neck a cord bearing one of the tiny vials, which had a gold stopper. "Carry it back safe. So that I may work to preserve his throne and high estate."

I was by now out of my senses, in thrall to him. I was his mammet. We stood together before the raging fireplace, and with his left hand he pushed me into the flames. I saw him through the shield of fire, and myself, sinking to lie before the hearth. Then I was gone into darkness, becoming part of it.

I was afraid only for an instant. Then a thrilling excitement gripped me. The darkness bore me up. I was in its heart, moving fast like a thundercloud under strong winds, and as my eyes began to open through the gloom I saw I was in flight over the City, seeing tiny points of light from the cressets of the Watch, firefly candlelight in the windows of houses, and as I flew faster, towards the river, little lights from the topmasts of Venetian galleys and fishing boats swung gently in the night and teased the black river into spangled reflections, and I picked out the ghost-shapes of swans far below and a cluster of lanterns from men bringing in their catch on the shore. And then I saw the massive dark shape of Baynard's Castle ahead, and my darkness swooped and plummeted, as if directed by the mind of the magician, and I landed square on the battlements, plunging through the first small door to which I came, which was in a tower.

I travelled fast, effortless, within the castle. Some compass within my darkness sped me unerringly through passages and halls, down small curving stairways and up again, flirting with the air like a bat. My passage, my speed and purpose were those of a bat, my senses honed like a bat's. I felt more lusty and young than ever in my life. My blood sang and surged, and even when I came face to face with the first living creature I was only taken short for a heartbeat, for I knew I was invisible when the man passed by as if I were no more than a draught on his cheek. I sped on through the sleeping castle, hearing the faint noises of slumber, snoring, muttering, and the clash of pikes as the armed guard patrolled the corridors. The carved ways were swamped with tapestries of unicorns, roses, ladies, as I came to the richest suite of all the White Rose bloomed in gilt and enamel on every cornice and lintel, heavy with gold and blazons, and I reached the night-chamber of the King.

Two young pages lay asleep across the doorway. I breezed over them, passed through the stout oak as if it were butter, and checked my flight at the foot of the King's bed. Candles as thick as my arm burned in two of the corners. The bed was enormous, with the arms of England at its head, and a canopy of cloth of gold. I stepped closer and heard a sudden low growl. A big wolfhound lifted its head in the shadows. It alone knew of my coming. I made myself as still as a corpse and it laid its head down again on its paws. I perched on the bed-end. Now I could see what few commoners and certainly no common whore had ever seen: the King, in his naked bed, afloat on dreams.

The White Rose. The Rose of Rouen. Those who said he was the most beautiful man in Europe had not lied. I would kiss the devil's toute if he were not, and more than that. He lay on his back, peaceful as a fed babe. His breath whispered easy and clean through his nostrils. So tall: the long bed only just contained him.

And slender and strong. His hair was an angel gold, mussed on his damask pillow. One hand, still wearing a jewel, was flung up above his head.

I uncovered him, as so many men had uncovered me, but not so roughly, but gently, with reverence. I rolled the fine bedlinen down from his neck to his feet, and saw a flat belly, a great chest, boles of thighs covered with a light dazzle of golden hair, and between them a thick nest arranged in curls around his thing. His cock, his majestic yard, his royal tool, his glorious weapon. His tail, his runnion, the standard of England draped full-fleshed against one thigh. And I? Now I was all hot darkness, hungry and wanton. Between my legs I was already running with lustful liquors, globs of gelid joy that wetted the sponge of hairs at my groin. As I bent over him, the little vial tapped between my breasts. I had almost forgotten about it in my excitement. But now I took in my fingers the royal tail, so gently, caressed it, put my face down and wiggled the tip of my tongue into its sweet narrow eye. The cock was weighty in my hand, warm as embers, thickly enveined, the smooth bell like silk, heart-shaped and deeply cleft, and ringed by a loose foreskin which I smoothed back as if I stroked the head of a baby. Almost at once the cock bloomed in my hand like a strange and potent fruit of the earth, growing straight and hard as the dome of a soldier's helm, gorged like some great mythic serpent fattened on maidens' flesh.

It grew more. It swelled massively in girth and length. As it awakened it cleaved the air, a thick mast on a golden deck, a Maypole grown from a gilded sward. I fell in love with it. My cunt became a pulsing heart. I whispered to this standing-stone of power: "Darling," and ran my tongue up and down its bursting vein, and snugged my face into the hair which had an odour of warm cheese, hay, apples, wine. A gleam of wet showed in its eye. My juices poured avidly from my thing. As I lifted my thigh over his groin my liquids oozed on him. Stretching myself wide, holding my lips apart with my fingers and panting a little, I fed the hot silken dome into me, sliding down on to the big blood-gorged throbber of the sleeping King, and I moaned a little from this vast invasion which felt like all the men I had ever had rolled into one.

I had enjoyed men, especially the lovesome Yorkist captain, who was slim and small and had a prick like a darting adder, and at other times my pleasure had been worth as much as the marks they paid me. But now, as I slithered inch by inch down on to the godly bludgeon of Plantagenet, I was joyed beyond all reckoning. I felt him shudder beneath me. Invisible to him though I was, I could in some strange way view my own body, although my form was translucent, like a ghost of water; my open thighs, my froth of red cunny-hair spread out to mingle with his, my fleshy lips with the knob of joy like a little man in a boat. I pressed my slippery cunt down over the maypole, and with hands behind cupped his steaming collions in their silken sac, and took into me the whole thick, throbbing root, and felt him shudder in his deep, deep sleep.

By God, it was good, this sitting on the King! By God's holy bones it was better as I began to fuck and futter him, bobbing merrily up and down on the hot greased pole, with its tip touching the matrix of my insides, soaring and dipping upon him as if to take him into my heart. Sweat streamed down my body. Strange flickerings began in its outline, of light and darkness, like the blinking of an eye. And the King groaned softly and began to move beneath me, thrusting his hips upwards, and I brought one finger round to my swollen man in the boat and frigged myself wetly to open my womb wider to the plunging of the stiff standard, and I trembled on the brink of what they call the lovely death . . .

I could see my shadow against the candlelit wall, riding him, my great mount, lying with tight-shut eyes, moving only from the waist down, where his hips heaved strongly upwards to match my gallop. I threw back my head in the shadowlight and my hair streamed in invisible clouds. The hound watched the wall and growled. There was no stopping us now; together we plunged and swived, the head of the cock hitting my womb over and over, suckity-suck in the morass of heated juice. As men had used me, so I used the tumid shaft of the King, and there seemed to be hosts of angels and devils beating about us on the bed; in my wildness the room filled with flash of jewels, and their flicker and glow burned my blood as the moment came. A moment beyond telling – a fierce wrenching of my womb as it clutched the swollen rod within and I heard a strangled cry from the pillow, and saw the gold head writhe from side to side, then saw no more, becoming only a gulping, gasping hole, sucking the warm gouts that sprayed to fill it. I thieved the blood of his life, I drank his soul, I laughed in joy.

I could no longer see the numinous outline of my body. I was darkness again, thick as night, aching from being stretched so wide. He lay still, as if I had killed him. I felt a searing triumph. My womb continued to pulse, my wet thighs slithered on his as I slowly dismounted. And then a tremendous spatter of liquid came out of me. The great tool had opened me so wide that everything was flowing from me, soaking the bed. The little vial chattered on my breast. I had lost the precious essence of the King, which I had been entrusted to bring back to Sylvanus.

I could not save it. It was already disappearing into the sheets, drying, rolling in pearls over the King's thighs. I clapped my hands over my hole but the residue seeped through my fingers and ran away. I slid from the bed, all trembling darkness, and hastily threw the covers back over the king. The hound growled once more as I passed through the chamber. I stood uncertainly, just inside the door, and looked back to where Edward lay, his breathing heavy and ragged, still locked in slumber. I had stolen from him, and I was coming away empty.

Next thing, I was outside in the passage, where the sleeping pages lay. The thought of Sylvanus filled me with dismay. I knew without telling he would be angry at my failure. One of the young pages sighed in his sleep. I looked down at him. He was about my age, very comely, with a pale girlish face and black hair curling on his shoulders. His doublet was unbuttoned for comfort, as were the points of his hose. He smiled as he dreamed, some amorous fancy, and I saw the crest of his cock gently lifting his shirt. In that instant I had the answer to my own witless folly. So I quickly sank down upon him, uncovering him to reveal the prettiest hard tool and bulging collions in a flowering of dark hair. Even then I was tempted to mount him. But I had learned my lesson. I lay over him and took his rod, tasting of salt honey, into my mouth, and suckled him. He did not wake, but trembled and hardened still more in my mouth. In a few instants I felt the force of his life, and then the spurting wave tingling against the inside of my cheeks and over my tongue. I thought he would never stop. Sleeping, he discharged in glutinous spouts, rolling his head and gasping, and every drop I drew in and held fast, though the flow was so copious a trickle or two ran on my chin. I took my little vial. Carefully I dribbled his gift into its narrow neck and made the stopper fast, whispering, "Thank you! Thank you, my darling boy!"

Then I was flying darkness again, aloft over the battlements of the castle. The magician was calling me home. Clutching the vial to my heart, I dipped and rose through the cool pearly air, cutting my invisible way through cloudlets, and I began to laugh with relief. I was not alone. There were others abroad in this wicked night. They flew alongside me, scaly things, horned things, white shimmering creatures lit by their own weird ghoulishness, small black things with pointed wings like holly leaves, all flying close, chattering, singing a black windsong, some reaching out long fingers to grasp me, while I dived and swooped and escaped them. Eventually they grew tired of the game and lifted away, dispersing to east and west, while I flew faster over the tiny jewels of the masts of ships lying asleep on the Thames and on, darkness within darkness. And then darkness changed to searing flames, white and gold, and I stepped through them, landing unscarred, unscathed, at the feet of Sylvanus beside the hearth of his necromancer's den.

I could see my body again. It was glistening with sweat. My long hair was pressed wet to my back, as if I had been in the river. I could not speak for a moment. I took the vial from around my neck and gave it to Sylvanus. He held it to the light and gazed at the thick pearly fluid as if at the treasures of Byzantium.

I waited, trembling a little. On the high shelf I could see the row of black cats. Their brilliant eyes stared. Unwinking, they stared at me with accusation. After a while Sylvanus spoke.

"You have done well, child." And I let out a breath, and sank to sit on the floor.

And I said, "The King is beautiful." Speaking the absolute truth. It made me feel better.

Sylvanus murmured, "With this, I can work my will. I can ensure Edward's power, and that of England." He carried the vial carefully into the smaller chamber. I waited.

After a while he returned. He said, "What do you desire for this night's work? Gold? Security? Friends in high places? I can arrange what you will."

And I said, my body tingling from the night's adventures, "Master Sylvanus, I would like to serve you again."

This seemed to please him. He smiled. The cats' eyes glared. He smoothed his chin, thinking deeply.

"The Queen," he said after a moment. "Elizabeth Woodville. She is a dangerous woman, with far too much power. She needs to be tamed. If only I could obtain her essence . . ."

"Is the Queen fair?"

"Oh, she is more than fair. With silver-gilt hair and a body like a rose."

"I could procure her ichors," I said. "If I were a man. I could turn her insides into jelly." I was trembling again. I felt intoxicated. It was a glorious, fantastical notion to me, but not to him. He began to laugh in delight.

"Yes," said he. "I had already half envisaged this. Later, perhaps. When you are restored."

"Now," I said. "I feel strong. I am ready. I can serve you. Make it possible."

"And so shall it be."

And straight away he put his hands on my body. The body that men had used and swived and filled it seemed for half my lifetime, the soft cleft body, the vessel of rut with which I had been born. He passed his hands over it, saying words never to be heard in the public light of day. And I felt a shrinkage round my heart. My breasts faded. I felt a heaviness at my groin. I looked down at the strong root and tight round collions growing there, and I laughed a deep laugh of rapture. For I thought of the beautiful Queen, of her sweet-cunted handmaidens, of all the lovely slits just waiting for my thrust, and I was still laughing as I stepped again through the flames and soared, fair as Lucifer.

NO NATURAL MAGIC

Alice Joanou

SHE DOES MURDER my sleep, and go I into the Hallowe'en, falling into her body. I am searching for the soliloquy of her breasts, scanning for the skein, the blue silkish filaments, the familiar decorative pattern of her vulnerable and delicate veins secreting, showing under her skin. She is hiding under her masks and rouges of flesh. It is nearly impossible to decode the encryptions of her pussy, the design of her skin. It's near, outraging my body. She wears a secret grin like a chastity belt. I am more lost than before. O, there are others, but they have not her color. Not her hair. Not her . . . O, her color . . .

Red, red. Red, sweet-breathed Ophelia.

She eludes me, playing dangerously with my lethal affection.

Your body, my love, is youth blasted with ecstasy.

Is there something rotten in the network tonight?

My heavy hair, a wooden body I move in, a disguise of tangled vines. Weeds grow in my head, doubt holds back the physical body. It is something I can do without. The crimes of this crown have become too fucking heavy. I think I am too femme for the job.

Gladly, I go to her boudoir.

I have been cast from the camp of the heterosexuals, without corsets or pink fingernails. I have been sent to take my blue-lipped Ophelia.

I have deleted the flowers and trimmed the vines. I am sensually downloaded. I've shorn the head from my hair. I know your secret names, my love. I recognize the many arms of your destruction. I can recognize your ruby-red lips. You have the face of time, the personality of decay.

Her diseased infinity is everywhere. O. Ophelia.

When at last fate had it that it was our turn on the stage of sheets and bloodied linens, she called me from the Other Side.

"Queen, come to me."

She has invaded my system, sneaking in from a place I never expected. I suppose one never expects to revive a dead love, an unrequited lust. In her ghostly ghosting, she called on me, her full breasts bound in golden strapping, her face imprisoned in her hair. O. Red red. Yes.

Ruby-red hair.

Coming in from a hole in my system. The aortas move.

I thought to fax her before I fucked her.

O,
Shave away the trappings of femininity. Reject the nostalgia of an earth mother. Reject the ridiculous notion of natural magic. It is all created.

There is no natural magic.

It is all theater.

But how well you probably know this, my pretty.

I hope you have some fancy costumes to outfit our scene.

Love,
Q

Not long ago, she hid herself in the night, near my bed chamber. She liked to watch me do my "duty" as Queen. I can remember vividly the outline of her breasts as she stands in the doorway of my chamber, she smiles sarcastically, with watchful ironic eyes. She enjoys watching as I bring my hips over his and move my body toward its natural, hungry state of being – sated. In the deep shadow, I can see the sharp point of her adolescent arrogance, the angle of her hip bones jutting from her slightly curved belly, the sharp suggestion of her hips cutting a clear line into the shadow. I can see the impudence of her nudity. Her hair ignites her shoulders. Her fingertips are diamonds, searching for gems hidden in the folds of velvet glass between her thighs. She opens the flesh of her vagina and I can see her fingers search their way inside. I see her teeth in the moonlight.

She masturbates while I fuck the King and, when nearing her pleasure, she rocks a little on the soles of her feet, moving her body in lewd perfection. She is pure orgasm. She calls me with her hands that move with the accuracy of heat-seeking missiles to their fire. Soundlessly she opens herself to the candlelight, and because she is there, watching me fuck him, I am able to enjoy the mediocrity of my King's sad efforts to pleasure me. Sex juice tears weep down her breasts, which she holds out to me like a viper's apples. The knowledge of her body is out of reach. She smiles as she puts on this show, a blatant invitation to destruction. She licks her lips as she stages the beginnings of a burlesque seduction.

She loots her pleasures standing afar. She's a damned fine voyeur, able to give pleasure even as she receives it. The vapors from her cunt wind through the damask bed curtains and rest in my nose; her smell makes a cloud over my bed. I shatter the fog when at last I am pushed into orgasm. It was this night that I decided to do her.

Her head falls back to drink in air as she silently bites a chunk out of night. I find myself moving more deliberately over my lover, taking in the sight of the young girl giving herself to herself with the intention of seducing me. I come with my eyes open, watching her smile.

Engulfed in the thrill of lawless complicity, she knows everything. She knows about the murder. And the murderers. Her clarity is so fine that she seems to have the divinity, nay, the acuity of madness. This obsession with foul play has ignited her more – how shall I say, the suggestion of death has aroused her more provocative features. She walks about in full bloom of late, her eyebrows grown into an arc, her nipples more apparent under her dresses. The recent death in the family has irritated her erotic imagination. She has watched me nurture poisonous lusts.

In her lovely childish manner, she believes she is immortal, and untouchable. She believes she can escape the dreadful consequences of evil deeds. Obviously, she has not yet slept in my bed.

Ophelia's turned on to my kinky transgressions. She stands in the doorway of my chamber, coming just thinking about the death. All the death.

Thence to a watch, thence to a weakness.

When I open my eyes she has gone, her body leaving only a white shadow on the window, the outline of her naked breast engraved on the chamber's door.

While the King snored, I plotted another murder. I thought perhaps I could fuck this one to death. With these ungodly noises of his he mangles my last withering shred of desire for him. With every groaning, I grow more clinical. I look at him and whisper, "God save you, Sir. And now I take my leave." I leap out of that bed. His bed.

God save you, Sir, from two women in bed.

I move nearer to her every day. She feels it. My perversities are much more enticing than those my young son has to offer her, for he has not yet developed a taste for leather.

Bare-faced and bald-headed, I am no rose of May, no rose of Sharon, no vestal virgin, no spring chicken. I am no young maid.

"A-down, a-down, and you call him a-down."

When we come together, she pushes me between her legs. She is hard and heavy to taste the third nipple hiding there, the nipple that feeds the diabolic, the nipple that gives wine. I run my fingers through her hair, a well-kept secret, an untended garden. Her body is a field as yet unseeded.

Polonius, Laertes, and Hamlet hide behind the tapestries, watching Ophelia, watching me watch Ophelia. It is crowded behind the curtain. They vie for the best vantage point as if the voyeurs have gone blind.

"The Queen has taken a lover," whispers Laertes, a little too jealously.

"Ah, yes, they say she made a good end," says Hamlet, his heart dead from too much trauma.

Afflicted with Hell, diseased with the need to have her in my mouth, I pour the wine from my lips onto her, onto the sheer of her skin, onto the shine of her silken tunic ice-white. I am getting snow-blind from the pallor of her skin. Her tits moan under my goblet and tongue. Under my goblet of cherry Kool-Aid. Under my goblet of champagne wishes.

"Caviar dreams!" shouts Ophelia.

The purple part of her pussy had not the taste of fish, as she suggested, but rather the quaint flavor of columbines and snap-dragons. There was an unfortunate moment when her pussy tried to bite my lips off, but this slip-up was quickly reprimanded.

"My tongue is *not* a prick, my darling girl," I said.

"Oh, heat, dry up my bad brains," Ophelia called, letting tears fall from her cunt onto my freshly shorn head. "I'm just not used to being treated so well!"

The audience of men claps at a performance well done. They try to tip us. In truth, we know they are tortured by the dalliance of our bodies. They force themselves to endure the show.

"Tell us the whole, Laertes, tell us all. Leave nothing to the imagination. Tell us what you saw in the Queen's chambers." Polonius is not attempting to hide the erection that has announced itself through his tights.

"The Queen does resemble my lord Hamlet, methinks, quite a lot."

"Methinks incest is best," giggles Hamlet, nudging Laertes who blushes.

She unmasks the malevolence of her beauty and the moon tears open her breasts, revealing the gaudy pink complications of her sex, the dangerous labyrinth of her pussy. We lie upon a bed, a field growing pearls and pansies. Lovely words crop up in between humid, hanging breaths. Her mouths fall on top of me. Her words linger like sweet, ripe bruises. Ophelia's fingers make liquid dew on my lips. At last, the steep and thorny way up to her center is thought out by my tongue. We stretch our blazing bodies before our audience so that they might touch us, but we are just out of reach. Our striptease is sublime, our breathing was sanctified orgasm, our nipples fused. Her teeth give more light than heat when she cries out, her lovesound the music of forfeiture. I had conquered her body with my own.

The spell was broken when she called me Hamlet by accident, and then lay back, licking her shrewd fingers.

"God, how I love to watch women fuck," sighs Polonius.

"*OOO LA LA!*" says Guildenstern with great disapproval. "You are a complete slave to the canonized fantasy of watching women rub."

"*Mais oui!*" shouts Polonius, gleeful in his incorrectness.

She digs her fingernails into my ass, causing an unnatural murder when flesh and blood give into the weeding growth of pleasure. The poison cherry-flavored kisses start to work on her body. I, in turn, have been slain by her candied tongue and live in her favors. Each toy she produces, each acrobatic fold she brings forth, seems a prologue to some greater terror. Let her come in me, into my sick and tired soul like an elixir of lethalized lust. Let the sweet lady in, however she wants to come.

"Fuck me up the ass, you say?"

"Yes. Before I die, I want to know what it means to penetrate you, my darling."

Ophelia brandishes a punishing-looking dildo.

"How should I your true love know, my fair Ophelia?"

"By letting me fuck you up the ass with this thing," she says.

How now, fair Ophelia.

Before you tumbled me, I had wrestled Fate to the ground with my golden goblet of laced Kool-Aid. But, Ophelia, you do slay me. Our lips have filled the space between.

There is no more sentimentality in this place. There is devil sugar and evil flowers. This is the final outrageous stair to the natural shocks of coming, the artful calamities of shuffling off to Buffalo, of shuffling off this mortal coil, of shuffling off the condoms and the dental dams.

Who, my fair Ophelia, can bear the scorns of all sins remembered?

THE BRILLIANCE AND MISERY OF BODIES; OF WAR, OF DREAMS

Michael Hemmingson

LIKE MANY IDEALISTIC young Ivy League men in 1917, he signed up as a volunteer ambulance driver for the Red Cross. His name was Roland. He was going to Europe, and Elizabeth didn't want him to go. She was also a student of the Ivy League crust, and she was in love with Roland; they'd already made plans to get married. Roland was set on this decision to go – this was to be a great adventure, after all, and many young men of his acquaintance were also doing the same.

"I can finish school when I return," he told Elizabeth, "and I'll come back much more prepared for life – *our* life."

And he kissed her.

Elizabeth decided she would give herself to him before he left, and in the back of Roland's Ford, he made her a woman. It was painful and uncomfortable, and Elizabeth didn't like it at all. She held onto Roland after, and cried.

"Did I hurt you?" he asked.

"I'm afraid I'll never see you again," she said.

"Of course you'll see me again," he said.

He didn't come back from Europe. He was unaccounted for; he was presumed dead. Elizabeth knew he was dead – she'd known this would happen the night in his car. She kept dreaming of all sorts of horrid scenarios, until the real news arrived.

That was when she began drinking.

She made a point to attend as many parties she could, where she could drink, laugh, dance, forget; and find men to have sex with.

Sex was no longer uncomfortable, but an evasion. She could close her eyes, her body tumult, with alcohol and cocaine; it was nice to get lost in the sensation of a man's cock moving in and out of her. She never imagined these men to be Roland (she couldn't do that to herself). They were just men, and she knew it was her lot – maybe mission – to have sex with any man who wanted her; in the name of Roland, and all he'd missed in this life. She didn't care. She was taking something from them, little pieces that were slowly filling her. She was taking, and they didn't know – they thought *they* were the ones taking, and this perverse knowledge of her secret mission gave her great pleasure.

She soon gained a reputation for a sexual appetite, which was not a positive reputation, so she made it a point to go from city to city, from party to party, club to club; from Maine to South Carolina; from New York to Chicago. Of course, she quit school, and didn't talk to her parents. She'd acquired her trust fund, left by her grandmother, not long after Roland had gone to Europe. It was a sizable amount. It was easy for a young woman with a great deal of money to move comfortably as a nomad. It was the Jazz Age, after all, and she became good at playing the role of a flapper.

When she slept, she did not dream.

It was 1922 and she was twenty-three years old when she found herself at a party at a large mansion near the University of Virginia, at the home of – so she was told – a great writer and historian, Jonathan Blacksmith Caine. She'd gone to the gala with a young man who was studying at the university; she'd met him somewhere – she forgot where or how – and slept with him, and was now here with him. The young man – whose name she forgot – was an aspiring writer, and was attending this school because Edgar Allan Poe had been educated here. The only written work by Poe she knew was the poem, *The Raven*.

Never more, never more, she said to herself.

She found the party – populated by some one hundred or so well-dressed, well-speaking individuals of all ages – extremely boring. The best thing, she decided, was to intake a little cocaine, drink like a fish, and find some fun. She got too drunk, and the young man she'd come here with took her aside and told her she was embarrassing him.

"Fuck you," she laughed: "fuck you!"

She danced, she laughed, she drank, she propositioned a few men – some who were old and married, but she didn't care.

Everything was spinning. She was taken upstairs by a tall, silver-haired man in a tuxedo. She tried to kiss him.

"You've had too much to drink, my dear," he said. "I am taking you to bed."

"To screw me?" she asked.

"So you can sleep," he said.

"I don't need sleep," she said.

"I'm a wise man of many years, so take my advice. Yes, you do need to sleep. Rest the demons inside you, because they need to rest."

"You talk funny," she said.

"So I've been told," he said.

The man guided her to what she assumed was a guest room – guest rooms always having that certain feel and look about them. He laid her down on the bed.

She pushed her dress up and spread her legs.

"I want you," she said.

He looked at her sex and said, "That's a very kind offer, and you're a beautiful young woman, but sleep now."

"I don't want to sleep," she said.

He closed her eyelids with warm fingers, and kissed her on the forehead.

"Sleep," he said.

It wasn't an easy sleep, and sometime later – a minute, an hour; she didn't know – a man came to her in the darkness. He smelled of booze. He got on top of her and fucked her. She wasn't ready and he shoved himself into her and it hurt. It was rough and quick. When he was done, he left, and she went back to sleep.

In the late morning, a maid opened the drapes and let the sun in.

"Goddamn," Elizabeth said.

"Breakfast is downstairs," the maid said. "You can join Mr Caine if you wish."

She went to the bathroom and looked at herself in the mirror. There was nothing she could do about herself. She washed up a little, and went downstairs. The tall, thin man with silver hair was eating poached eggs and bacon at a long table in the dining room, and reading the paper. He smiled when he saw her, placing the paper down.

"Please sit, and eat," he said.

Elizabeth sat across from him. Another female servant poured orange juice and coffee, and asked what she'd like to have for breakfast.

"Just some bacon," Elizabeth said.

"Bacon?"

"Yes, perhaps ten strips."

"Yes, ma'am."

"An unusual meal," the man said.

"I like to eat meat," she said.

The man picked up a piece of bacon and took a bite into it. He said, "It is quite good."

"I'm sorry," Elizabeth said, "but who are you and where am I?"

The man laughed.

"What's so funny?"

"You drank a lot," he said.

"I always drink a lot," she said. "I went to a party with some fellow. I guess the party was here. I guess I stayed here. The house belonged to some sort of professor, a man of letters, I was told. Are you that man?"

"My name is Jonathan Blacksmith Caine," he said.

"It's a fine American name," Elizabeth said. "I hope you won't be offended if I say I don't know who you are, or what work you are famed for."

"That's quite all right, my dear. It's refreshing to be unknown."

"I see. Well, I hope you are not as equally offended at what is probably my ghastly sight."

"I've had similar mornings," he said. He added, "In my youth."

The servant brought a plate of bacon out. Elizabeth was ravenous, and ate quickly.

"I remember you taking me to the room, telling me to sleep," she said.

"You were causing a scene."

"It's what I live for."

"You needed to go to bed."

"Like a good little girl?"

"Perhaps."

"I'm not good."

"There's good in everyone."

"I remember asking you to make love to me," she said. "You declined, but later you came in and did me."

"I assure you," Jonathan Blacksmith Caine said, "I did not."

"Somebody did. It wasn't a dream. I'm still sore."

"Hmm. It could be that someone snuck up to your room during the remains of the party."

"Most likely," she said, looking down.

"You were making many men – how should I say it –?"

"Just say it," she said.

"Aware of your presence," he said.

"I apologize if I embarrassed you," she said.

"Not at all," he said. "I was quite amused, and glad. My parties tend to be somewhat stuffy at times."

"I'll say," she said with a mouthful of bacon.

"You added a bit of spice," he said.

"I've been called spicy."

"You haven't told me your name."

"Elizabeth."

"No last name?"

"Who needs last names? I'm Elizabeth – just *another* debutante out of control!"

She laughed at that.

"You're not from here," he said.

"No," she said. "New Hampshire."

"Were you staying with the young man you came here with?"

"*God*, no."

"He's a student of mine. Promising, but not much so."

She said, "I have a hotel room. Somewhere in town."

"Good," Caine said. "I shall have your belongings picked up and brought here."

"Why?"

"Certainly you would wish for a change of clothes," he said. "After a nice long bath, I'm certain. Then, later, I would like to take you to dinner, and we can talk more."

She nodded, thinking about that.

"All right," she said.

She returned to the guest room and drew a bath. A maid came and asked if there was anything she required, and Elizabeth said a bottle of brandy would be nice. The brandy was brought to her, and she sat in the tub for an hour, drinking and thinking about nothing.

Her clothes from the hotel were brought to her, and she chose a dark evening dress, cut low, for dinner.

"I rather liked your flapped look," Jonathan Blacksmith Caine said, dressed again in a tuxedo.

"I can't always be fashionably questionable," she told him. "I *am* capable of being a woman of decorum."

"Indeed," he said, holding out his arm. She took his arm, and they went into town for dinner.

It was the nicest and most expensive of restaurants, of course; she hadn't expected otherwise. She ordered a steak and he had lobster, and she treated herself to plenty of wine and cognac. She learned that Jonathan Blacksmith Caine was a writer of historical tomes of fiction and fact. Mostly, he wrote of wars, especially the Civil War, and the Colonial Wars, and wars of antiquity in the ages of Egypt and Rome. Sometimes he took the viewpoint of a fictional man, and sometimes he took his own voice as a scholar. His work was renown, and he wasn't ashamed to admit it; young men flocked to him for guidance, as well as the occasional young woman. He was adored by his students at the university.

"Perhaps I'll read your books one day," Elizabeth said.

"And perhaps not," Caine said.

"You must be working on a book about the World War," she said.

"I'm always working on a book," he laughed.

It seemed like an empty laugh, she thought.

In the chauffeured car, Elizabeth leaned into him.

"I had a pleasant and enjoyable dinner, Mr Caine," she said.

"Call me Jonathan," he said.

"Jonathan," she said, touching his leg.

He reached for her face. He kissed her.

He said, "I would like to make love to you when we get home, Elizabeth."

"All right," she said.

In his bedroom, he ripped her dark dress down the middle, suckling her breasts, grabbing her body.

"I'll buy you a new dress," he said.

"I have plenty of dresses," she said. "Will you get me a drink?"

"Do you need a drink?"

"I always need a drink?."

He left, and returned with a bottle of Scotch. She'd splayed herself naked on the bed for him, touching herself between the legs. He poured her a drink, and undressed, and joined her.

Caine had a lithe, muscular body, but he was an old man, and it showed. The hair on his chest and his pubes was as silver as the hair on his head. His penis was long and thin and curved like a banana. Elizabeth had never seen a penis like that. In fact, it occurred to her she'd never looked at many men's sex organs, given her encounters; she could tell if the cocks were big or small, thick or thin, when inside her, but she hardly ever saw them. Even when she would perform oral sex, it was often in the dark. But tonight she could take in the details of Caine's cock, the veins, the skin, the way it felt, tasted, and smelled.

He took her, and fucked her for what seemed like a very long time, in several positions. It was several hours at least, and both their bodies were covered in sweat.

"Don't you ever come?" she asked him.

"You want me to come?" he said.

"I was wondering," she said.

"I've been all over the world, my dear," he said. "In India, I learned from a Yogi Master how to control my body, and how to become a lover of stamina. I can make love to you until the sun rises. My body is still in good shape. You need only tell me to climax, and I will."

An hour later, she said, "Come inside me."

He did.

And they slept.

She woke several times during the early morning, in his arms, and she went back to sleep. Later, he was not there. She got up, found a white robe waiting for her on the bed. She put it on, went downstairs. She found Caine, in a similar white robe, in the kitchen. He was making breakfast.

"Where are the servants?" she asked.

"They're only here three days a week," he said. "I'm not *that* wealthy, and I don't always believe in servants."

"We're all alone in this big, big house?" she said.

"Yes," he replied. "I imagine you'd like a lot of bacon strips."

She said, "Some eggs, scrambled. Yes. Some coffee, some juice. Can I help?" she said.

"I enjoy cooking," he said, "and I'm almost done."

She went to the main room, found the bar, and had a quick drink of vodka.

She joined Caine, sitting closer to him at the long table. They had a very nice breakfast. He'd placed ten strips of bacon out for her. Somewhere in the distance she could hear faint, soft piano music.

"Where's that coming from?" she said.

"The gramophone," he said.

The music stopped, and they ate. They didn't speak much, and looked at each other.

"I'm not a good man," he said, "and you must forgive me."

"What do you mean?"

"I'm an old man with dirty thoughts. I have a beautiful young woman in my house, and I see an advantage. I dine you, get you drunk, and make love to you . . ."

"What's wrong with that?"

"Many things."

"I had fun," she said.

"Fun?" he said.

"Yes."

He smiled.

They continued to eat breakfast.

"I'd like some dessert," Elizabeth said.

"I believe I have an apple pie," he said.

"That's not what I had in mind," she said, and slid under the table. She crawled to him, opening his robe, taking him into her mouth. He pushed the chair back, so he could watch her, and touch her hair. His long, curved penis grew in her mouth, and she grabbed it at the base. She looked up at him and said, "Don't hold back like you did last night. I can't suck for three hours."

He said, "All you need to tell me is when, and I will."

Forty minutes later, she asked him to come, and he filled her mouth with several bursts of thick semen. She tried to swallow it all, but it was too much, and some dribbled from her mouth, down his cock, and onto his testicles and the floor. She licked him clean after.

He took her to the bedroom and gave her oral pleasure for an hour, her legs on his shoulders, her rear raised high, his mouth all over her cunt. She came twice. He turned her on her stomach, entered her, said, "Yes." He fucked her for several hours, until she couldn't take it any more, and she asked him to come, and he did.

They were in each other's arms.

"You don't know what a joy this is," he told her.

"What?"

"I'm a man of sixty-three," he said. "To be here, making love to a young woman, it's a true dream."

"I'm sure you have many eager girls vying for your company," she said.

"Occasionally," he said. "The women I spend time with are in their thirties or forties. Not so young as you."

"I don't believe that."

"On occasion, a woman your age. But very seldom."

"You're very desirable," she said.

She touched his penis. She took it in her mouth, until he was hard, and got on top of him.

They made love for three hours. She asked him to come, and

he did. Their bodies and the sheets were soiled with sweat and sex.

"We can sleep in one of the guest rooms," he said.

"Mine," she said.

They held one another in the guest room, waiting for sleep.

"You've been married before," Elizabeth said.

"Three times," he said.

"Three!"

"Oh, yes."

"Three," she whispered, closing in on dreamless sleep.

"I've loved too much," he said. "I could never love again. Not real love. I can love for the moment, like the moment we spend now. But tomorrow is another day."

"I loved once, for one second," she said. "Never more, as the raven said."

And they slept.

She spent the next week there, because it felt right, and there was nothing else to do. She ran out of cocaine, and her new lover was not a fan of the drug. So she drank.

"It may not be my place to say," he said to her, "but you drink an awful lot, my dear."

"So I do," she said. "So what?"

"It will catch up on you," he said.

"*Don't* lecture me," she told him.

"I shall not," he said.

During the days, she slept, or drank, or lounged outside in the Virginia sun. It was spring. Caine was either at the university, teaching his classes, or in his study, doing whatever it was he was doing – researching, writing. She didn't know or care. She *did* know it was soon time to go. She wanted to go to New York. She missed New York.

The night she knew she had to leave, Caine had guests, three men near his age, all scholars, writers – one was from Rhode Island, one from California, the other from England. She sat across from Caine at dinner. All the servants were there. There was a lot of talk about literature and politics, and Russia and Communism. She wasn't all that interested. She ate her food and drank. And drank. Sometimes she would interject, and all the men would just look at her and smile, as if she was a fool. She didn't enjoy that feeling.

In Caine's bedroom, she stood naked, drink in hand, looking at the man lying on the bed, reading an infernal book.

"I hate your intellectual crowd," she said.

"Why?"

"Does there need to be a reason?"

"They are all fine men," Caine said. "Did you not find them appealing?"

"All men are appealing," she said, "because they are men."

"You're drunk," he said.

"Yes," she said. "Of course," she said.

He fucked her for two hours.

"I needed that," she said. "Sex is all I know. Sex is my rhetoric and language."

She laughed.

"Good," he said, "because I have an assignment for you."

She sat up and said, "Oh! An assignment!"

"Yes," Caine said. "You made a good impression on my colleagues. They enjoyed your company, and your sight. I want you to visit each of my guests in their rooms, and fuck them."

"All three?" she said.

"Yes," he said. "And come back here, and tell me about it."

"All right," she said.

She stood, and looked for something to wear.

"Go to them naked," Caine said, "so there won't be any question as to why you are there."

First, she visited the man from Rhode Island. He was the youngest, at forty-eight. He was reading, and smiled when he saw the naked young woman enter his room. He fucked her on the bed, and she left, and went to the man from California, who was also awake and reading, and was close to Caine's age, and smiled when he saw the naked young woman. She took him in her mouth, and she got on top of him. The Englishman, in his fifties, was asleep, but awoke when she sat on the bed.

"Are you an angel?" he inquired.

"Hardly," she replied.

He came to his senses, out of sleep, looked at her, and said, "Oh."

"Hello," she said.

"Jonathan is up to his usual tricks," he said.

"What tricks?"

He laughed and said, "Can I have you?"

"That's why I'm here."

"I'd like to fuck you in your bum," he said.

"What?"

"Your arse."

He sodomized her. She'd only done this once, and, while she hadn't liked the first time, this wasn't all that unpleasant, as it didn't last long.

She returned to Caine's room. He'd lit several candles.

"You're back early," he said. "It's only been an hour."

"They're not like you," she said, "they're like regular men."

"*Tell me*," he said, and she told him about each of them.

"How do you feel?" he asked.

"I need a drink."

She had two.

"I want to spank you," he said.

"Do you?"

"You've been a bad girl."

"I have."

She lay on the bed, and he slapped her rear end with his bare hand many times, until her bottom was red and she had tears in her eyes. Caine stuck a finger into her asshole.

"My British friend did sodomize you," he said, "as Limeys tend to do."

He laughed. She smiled.

"Yes," she said.

For the next two hours Caine fucked her in the ass – his curved penis was an odd sensation – until she could take no more, and asked him to come, and he did.

They slept in each other's arms.

In the morning, he woke her.

"Leave me alone," she said.

"Come have breakfast with us," he said.

"Not now," she said.

"I insist, my dear."

She got up, looking for her robe.

"Remain naked," he said. "I want you naked."

She went downstairs, and had breakfast with the four men in

the nude. The servants didn't blink an eye. The men seemed to enjoy her like this.

"When I first met dear Elizabeth," Caine announced after they ate, "she finished her morning meal with my semen in her stomach. Elizabeth?"

"Yes?" she said.

"Crawl under the table and satisfy me," he said.

She did. She went to him under the table, and sucked him, and he came in her mouth.

"Now," he said, "do the same to each man here."

She went to the man from Rhode Island first, then the one from California, and then the one from England. None of them had washed, and she could taste herself on each. She very much liked this, all their cocks in her mouth, their semen in her mouth. She'd never eaten so much come at once, and her lips and chin were covered in the excess. When she was done, Caine told her to go upstairs. She did. She took a bath, the taste of semen strong on her tongue, and went to sleep.

The three men were gone by evening, and she was once again alone with Caine. She told him how much she'd enjoyed being a sexual toy like that.

"I knew you would," he said.

"I've been fucked by several men at once," she said. "It was drunk and sloppy; this was different."

"Yes," he said, and he fucked her four hours that night.

She remained there for a few more days, and told him she had to go on. New York was calling her.

"What's in New York?" Caine asked.

"I don't know," she said. "It's *New York*."

"I have nothing to do this weekend," he said. "Perhaps I can accompany you? I have friends in New York."

"All right," she said.

That weekend they traveled to New York, and they checked into the Waldorf-Astoria, which Caine first thought was excessive, until Elizabeth said she would take care of the bill.

Caine made many phone calls to various people he knew in the city. She lounged in the bath, drinking bourbon.

He came to her and said, "We must continue our sexual play."

"Yes," she said.

"Tell me, my dear, that you will do anything for me."

She said, "I will do anything for you."

He pulled her from her bath, took her to bed, fucked her in his usual way, and then opened one of his valises. He had wrist and ankle restraints, and a blindfold. He tied her hands and legs together, and blindfolded her, fed her bourbon and Scotch, and left her naked on the bed.

She slept.

He returned, and he wasn't alone. She could smell the other man, he was that strong – his sweat, his cologne.

Caine removed her blindfold and she saw the large black man – he was over six feet tall, in a beige suit and hat, heavy-set with large eyes.

"This is Jefferson," Caine said as an introduction. "A very white name, yes, but a name he has embraced. Jefferson and I go back. He is a poet and writer of stories, although not as well known as he should be. Lives in Harlem, works the clubs to make money. One day I hope to make the world aware of his talent. I've brought him here for you, and for me."

"I have to pee," she said.

Jefferson started to take his pants off.

"I've brought a number of women to Jefferson," Caine said.

"Why?" she asked.

"To watch," he said matter-of-factly. "I absolutely enjoy watching women being defiled by Jefferson."

"You want to watch me?" she said. "I have to pee."

"You'll comply?" Caine said.

"Yes," she said.

"Give her some cocaine first," Jefferson said.

Caine nodded, and held the powder to Elizabeth's nose, and also gave her a drink. Every time she asked to have her hands released, said that she had to use the bathroom, Caine smiled and shook his head.

She was told to fellate Jefferson. He had what she assumed must be a deformed cock, by the size of it. It was at least fifteen to sixteen inches long, and very thick and veined, the bell of the head gargantuan. She could barely get the head of the thing into her mouth! Jefferson stroked himself as she sucked, and Caine sat back and watched, sipping from a drink. Then he fucked her, and it was painful. The more she asked him to stop, the harder he fucked her. He tried to put it in her anus, but it wouldn't happen – he got in part way, but she cried for mercy. "This is some fine stuff, Jonathan," the black man said. She sucked him and he ejaculated into her mouth, a discharge that seemed to last forever, so that she choked on it, spitting his come out, a stream flying from his cock and into her hair. He patted her on the head and both men left. She went to sleep.

When she woke, she was next to Caine. It seemed to be a different room, but she wasn't sure. Her arms and legs were free. She got up, went to the bathroom, and found a bottle of bourbon. She drank, and went to sleep. In the morning, Caine fucked her for a few hours, and they lounged in bed.

"Don't ever do that to me again," she said.

"I was under the assumption you enjoyed variety," he said.

"Not like that," she said. She asked, "Did you like watching?"

"Yes," he said. "I wish to arrange one more get-together," Caine said. "Nothing extreme. Very ordinary."

"All right," she said.

That night, they went to a speakeasy Caine had the clout to enter. He wanted her to dress like a flapper, and wear her Egyptian hairpiece, and she did. She held his arm as they entered, and she noticed the eyes on her – the young woman with the older man. She didn't like it at all. She didn't want to be here. She didn't like the eyes. They sat at a table and ordered drinks. There was a jazz band on stage. She liked the music. She could get good and drunk and dance, like she always did. She needed to get away from Caine. She'd been in his company for almost a month.

Caine spotted two men he knew at a table. They were well-dressed, in their thirties, hair slicked back, guns under their jackets.

"You'll fuck them tonight," he told her, "and it'll be nothing like you've ever experienced."

He went to talk to them.

The whole time they'd been here, Elizabeth had been aware of a young man in snappy suit at the bar, his eyes on her. She immediately went to him.

"Buy me a drink," she said.

"Okay," he said.

"Martini. Vodka, shaken, olive."

The young man waved to the bartender.

She downed the drink, fast.

"What's your name?" she asked.

"Gregory," he said.

"Let's go," she said.

"What?"

"Gregory," she said.

"What?" he said.

"Let's get *out* of here," she said.

He seemed confused.

"Don't you want to take me out of here?" she said.

"Yes," he said.

"*Well,*" she said.

They left, and got into his Model T, and drove.

"You were using me," he said.

"Everyone uses everyone," she said.

"I saw you come in with that man."

"I saw you eyeballing me."

"You needed to get away," he said.

"So what?" she said.

"Soooooo what?" he said, laughing. "You look very familiar. What's your name?"

"I don't have a name."

"I've seen you before."

"It's the clothes, the hairpiece, the white make-up," she said. "You see me everywhere in this city."

"I know you," he said.

"No, you don't," she said.

They drove.

"So what's next?" he said.

"You have a place?" she asked.

"Yes."

"You want to take me there?"

"Yes," he said.

Gregory was twenty-five, a Yale grad, and a stockbroker – she learned this during the drive to his uptown apartment. He was successful, up-and-coming, making money. America was in good shape, and the economy was getting better and better each day, and he was making more and more money every day, as were many people.

"It won't last," she said.

"It'll last forever," he said.

He took her into his apartment, and they had a drink. He took her to the bedroom, they kissed and undressed, and he fucked her on his unmade bed. It was fast and rough. He put himself into her before she was ready, and it hurt, but he didn't last long. He lit a cigarette and they lay there. He got up, went to the bathroom, and when he came back, he said, "Your name is Elizabeth."

She was adjusting her hairpiece. "What?"

"I know you," he said, "Elizabeth. You used to be Roland's girl."

She felt cold.

"Right?" he asked.

She said, "How do you know Roland?"

"He was a classmate of mine! You were always with him. You don't remember me?"

"No," she said, feeling funny.

"Well, we only met a few times. But I remember you."

"Okay," she said, "so you know me."

"You were in love with Roland. That's what he said. You were engaged, I think."

"What is your point?" she said.

"I'm sorry," he said. "What happened to Roland was tragic."

"Oh," she said.

"I wanted to go, too. The war. Yes, I did. But my parents wouldn't hear of it. I should've gone," he said.

"Good for you," she said.

"I shudder thinking what his days are like," Gregory said, sitting on the bed. "I have no idea what a life like that must mean. He had so much promise."

"What the hell are you talking about?" she said.

Gregory was stroking himself, smiling. "What?"

"What his days are like?" she said. "What do you mean?"

"Don't you ever wonder?"

"What?"

"How he lives?"

"*He doesn't live!*" she cried. "*He's dead!*"

He stared at her. "My God," he said.

"*WHAT*?"

"You don't know."

"Know what?"

"You really don't know," he said. "I heard you –"

"What? Know *what*?"

"I'm horny," Gregory said. "You want to go at it again?"

She hit him in the face.

The next day, she took the train to New Hampshire, and a taxi to the home of the young man she'd once loved. A servant answered, and Elizabeth declared herself. Roland's mother came to the door.

"My dear girl," the older woman said, "it has been some time. It's nice to –"

"Let me in," Elizabeth said.

"I knew one day you would come," she said. "I feared –"

"Why didn't you tell me?"

"Tell you?"

"I want to see Roland."

"No, you don't."

"I *do*!"

"Listen, dear girl," Roland's mother said. "Your parents and I decided not to tell you. Not at first. We were going to. Then you became wayward, and you disappeared. Elizabeth, honey, your mother and father are worried about you. Call them, right now."

"I want to see Roland," Elizabeth said.

"No."

"*Yes*!"

"I implore you," Roland's mother said.

"Why was I lied to?" Elizabeth asked.

"I will take you to him," Roland's mother said. "They say he can hear, but I'm never certain. He cannot talk to you, he cannot see you. He cannot touch you, or even kiss you. He may hear you. But what you will see – I could never prepare you . . ."

"We were going to be married," Elizabeth said. She was crying. She said, "He was my love. He was to be my husband. We were going to have children. Goddamn you, you witch, take me to my love!"

"Forgive me," Roland's mother said. "Forgive us all."

They went upstairs, and stopped at a door.

"I give you one last chance to turn away," the mother said.

"What happened to him?"

"He walked on a land mine in Belgium. It was war, my dear. A very stupid war."

Elizabeth entered the room, and closed the door behind her. The room was very white. On a bed lay what remained of Roland. It was a body, with no legs and one arm. The body had no discernible face – traces of what used to be a mouth, eyes, nose, and ears. The body twitched, hearing her, maybe smelling her. Whatever this was, she knew it was Roland. She just knew.

"Roland," she said, "it's me: Elizabeth."

The body twitched.

She sat on the edge of the bed, and the body made more movements.

"I've come back," she said.

She looked out the window and saw two sparrows in a nest, in the tree that loomed over this bedroom.

"They told me you were dead," she said.

She pulled the covers away from him. He still had a penis. She took it in her hand, and it grew hard.

"I'm not the same girl you knew," she said, "but I know more things. I can make you very comfortable and happy."

She got into the bed and lay next to him, stroking his penis. The body twitched like crazy, and the one arm reached over and gently touched her hair.

"Hush, my dear," she said, kissing the non-existent lips on what had once been the face of a bright young man.

They made love – their bodies – in a way left only to your imagination; and they went to sleep, which was, for Elizabeth, abysmal and full of dreams.

THE PRESCRIPTION

Carol Anne Davis

DR LOREAN HAD not long been in practice when it was rumoured that he was guilty of crimes against the person. Hearing these whispers, the city fathers were naturally vexed.

"But we cannot judge a man by some scurrilous words from the street," they agreed. "Especially when he has always seemed such an exemplary fellow. We must have proof positive of his venial ways."

And so it was arranged that Madam Gray, the most upright and responsible citizen in Victorian England, would visit with the thirty-three-year-old doctor. She would report back every movement of the physician's healing hands.

At the appointed hour, Madam Gray swept through Dr Lorean's cosy parlour and into his adjoining surgery. Such haughtiness was her usual mien. Dr Lorean rose gracefully to his full five foot ten, then he bowed low. "Welcome, Madam Gray. I am at your service," he said.

Lucinda Gray gave a half-hearted curtsey in return. The half-heartedness was partly due to her tightly lacing corsets. She glanced at the man's neatly trousered groin and suppressed a shudder. The city fathers had given her a little bell that she could ring if his attentions became too great.

Male attention was an unvisited land to Madam Gray. She had

never been betrothed, had never known a suitor to take liberties. But she utilized her time by keeping house for her father (who had one of the largest estates in the country), so didn't feel the lack. It was her duty, however, she told herself as she gazed around Dr Lorean's dispensary, to save other gentlewomen from an unseemly fate . . .

The introductions over, Dr Lorean again seated himself behind his desk. He picked up his pen. "Are you well in yourself? What brings you here to me this August morning?"

"My last doctor has gone into retirement," Madam Gray said sagely. "And I'm brought low with a general malaise."

"I take it the two are in no way related," the physician said with a slight amused smile.

Was he suggesting an improper relationship? The twenty-five-year-old fingered the cameo brooch at her throat and felt a low pull of excitement. "He was an elderly gentleman, but he gave me sterling service," she said.

"As I profess to do too." So saying, the suave surgeon stood up and bowed again. "A full examination is called for," he announced.

How full did he mean? The virgin stilled into watchfulness. Outside the very birds quietened down. The silence was broken by a horse and cart clip-clopping and rattling along the road outside.

"We must shut out the world to safeguard your privacy, dear lady," the physician murmured, walking to the heavy prussian velvet curtains and closing them fast.

Adult to adult, they faced each other in the centre of the room.

"Remove your outer garments for me," the doctor ordered.

Madam Gray stared into his eyes as she slid her crocheted ivory-coloured gloves from her wrists, then unpinned her jade green hat. "I shall be glad to rid myself of them. It is much warmer out than I anticipated," she said breathlessly. As she removed her headwear, a few tendrils of polished chestnut hair escaped their clasp.

"My dress?" she confirmed in a husky voice, her eyes darting around the oleographed walls as if in search of solace.

"Indeed, ma'am, for I have to examine every inch of you," the wide-eyed physician said.

Slowly Madam Gray undid the pretty glass buttons of her muslin bodice with its becoming drop shoulders. She undid the satin rosebud ribbons, then let the bias-cut garment fall to the floor. She forced herself to confront the fellow's unblinking gaze for a moment before turning her attention to the removal of her jade satin shoes.

"Now your petticoat," the physician bid.

Swallowing hard, Madam Gray removed the silken garment that covered her bustle. Then she removed the bustle itself.

"You can see more of me now," she said in a small voice. "Enough to examine?"

"It is my duty to see more yet."

"You mean me to remove my corset cover?" the younger woman clarified, her extremities tingling at this exceptional situation.

"Indeed, for how can I investigate your flesh when it is so covered?" the surgeon said.

The young woman took a sudden interest in the baroque design wallpaper as she removed the protective shroud.

"Now unlace the corset itself. Let me know if you require my assistance."

"I can manage," Lucinda Gray said firmly, though in truth it had taken two maidservants to lace her that very day. Now she glanced nervously at the impassive male observer, then looked down at the stem-waisted and overbust-style boned band.

With effort she unfastened and removed the constricting ties and unfastened the front, doing it as slowly as possible to stave off the moment of near-nakedness. At last she stood vulnerably, in her pantaloons and chemise.

"Your chemise, if you please," the physician said.

Madam Gray breathed in the scent of rosemary and geranium from the medicinal gardens outside and reminded herself that healing the sick was a rightly revered profession. The doctor might well be a wholly virtuous man.

She took off her chemise, then stood there, breathing heavily, clad only in her white cherub-embroidered pantaloons.

"You ladies wear so very many clothes that it is a wonder you ever become pregnant," Dr Lorean smiled.

Madam Gray glared at this retort. "I am not married, sir, so it is imprudent of you to discuss pregnancy."

The doctor stood up and walked towards her. "On the contrary, my dear, I have to determine that your female parts are all in good working order. After all, you shall one day want to give your father an heir."

"Perhaps," the younger woman replied. In truth, the young men of the parish found her somewhat imposing. And, far from being a generous dowry-bequeather, her father was a mean and unapproachable type.

"So remove your pantaloons forthwith, so that I may begin a full and thorough exploration of your womanly contours," the physician said.

"As you wish." But did he wish this for the good of her health – or the corruptedness of his appetite? Madam Gray pondered the ethics as she undid the ties which held her pantaloons firmly around her small waist. Truth to tell, she felt somewhat breathless at the thought of being naked before a man for the very first time.

Slowly she let her unmentionables slide down her smoothly rounded hips to the floor. She stepped out of them and stood with her arms by her sides, her bosom heaving. For the first time since early childhood she was in the presence of a clothed adult whilst she had on not a stitch. The exposedness of her situation was not lost on her – indeed, was uppermost in her imagination – but she consoled herself with the thought that she was a spy, who was really in charge.

"Now for your measurements," the good doctor said. He reached smoothly into his leather bag and brought out a tape measure. He proceeded to hold it against the back of her head, then run it all the way down to her unshod feet. On the way down his hand brushed her spine and her buttock cleft and her virgin thigh-backs. It was a featherlight sensation which nevertheless was felt by Lucinda as a very heavy rush. Surprised at the sudden exquisite sensation, the maiden swayed and let out a little moan.

"Be reassured – your height is fitting for the times and you carry yourself impressively erect," the physician murmured.

Madam coloured slightly at his choice of words and stared straight ahead.

"And now I will check your skelekature," continued the man. He measured her shoulders from one silken arm-top to the next, his fingers soft and gentle. "And now your breasts."

The woman blushed more fully at this last word – a scandalous word. Why, even that part of the chicken was only referred to as "the white meat", lest it give offence! "You may want to loosen your stays each day to let your bosom move more freely," said the medical man, sliding his cold rule across both nipples before weighing the appendages in his smooth palms. "It will assist your body to breathe."

"I can breathe very well with my garments fastened," Madam Gray gasped in a strangely air-starved tone. Her breath faltered further as the physician thumbed the underside of her heavy round mammaries with his sensitive thumb-pads, and she gasped so harshly that the doctor asked if she were having an asthma attack.

"I take the air at Brighton and the waters at Bath. My constitution should be good," the naked young woman assured him.

"Then," said the doctor, "it only remains for me to examine your inner folds."

"Shall I lie down?" Madam Gray asked, for she was feeling quite light-headed.

"Not yet," said the man. "Just turn your back to me and lean your elbows on my examination couch. Then push your nether parts outwards, if you please."

"My nether parts?" the younger woman repeated haltingly.

"Yes. That reminds me – we must check your hearing at the end," the physician said. He walked forward and patted the surgical couch with his palm. "Just rest your head on your arms and part your legs a little for me that I may the better examine your buttock cleft."

"What could possibly go wrong in that region?" Madam Gray stalled. In answer, the doctor reeled off a string of Latin phrases. "Oh, I see," the baffled woman said. She looked at the couch, then looked back at the man. She must force herself to endure this new defilement. She'd have even more details to tell the city fathers at tomorrow's meet.

Slowly the Victorian matriarch assumed the buttock-exposing

position. "Is that high enough?" she asked, thrusting her firm, small derrière back.

"A little higher yet," said the man, tapping at the top of each arse-cheek with his fingers. Madam Gray complied, wondering inside at the increasing sense of pleasure her interiors felt. There was nothing wrong with being as naked as Eve had been in the Garden, she told herself in a moral tone. She must just be glad to be free of her bustle and stays.

"You have excellent muscle tone," said the man, beginning to squeeze each proffered hemisphere. "Do you perhaps go riding, my dear?"

"No, but our house has many stairs and large gardens and I walk them every day," the lightly perspiring Lucinda said.

"Well, I recommend horse riding too," the surgeon prescribed. "A proper gallop, mind, and not side-saddle. It cures my other ladies of their sore heads."

"I have felt migraineous of a morning," Madam Gray admitted faintly, as he continued to explore her small bottom with his large, caressing hands.

"Evacuating fully is also important," Dr Lorean said, beginning to pull on a thin white rubber glove, one of the new-fangled inventions. "We'll just make sure that there's no blockage there."

He reached for a small tub of gel and smeared it around the woman's most puckered parts. Madam Gray buried her head in her hands more fully as she felt his gloved and gelled fingers tracing their way around her secret pink entrance. She'd suffer in silence, she told herself stoically, then yelped with enjoyment as a digit was inserted into her rectum a little way.

"Relax," said the doctor as the poor woman almost shot over the couch. "We'll just widen you out ever so slightly. Easy voiding is of the essence, I always say."

Madam Gray shifted her weight from silken foot to foot, then tried to think of England as her backside was invaded a little further. But she ended up thinking of the strange sensation between her thighs instead. It was a sensation she'd known before, when she washed herself or woke up from disturbing night dreams. But now the sensations were much stronger, and growing all the time.

"Good, good."

Lucinda felt a sense of loss as the finger was withdrawn. Dr Lorean took off the glove and threw it into the bin, then washed his hands thoroughly. Madam Gray stood up and faced him without being told to and put her hands across her breasts.

"No need to be shy about your nakedness. You are like a fine horse to me, and I am a horse farrier," the man murmured.

Madam Gray snorted, then realized how equine she had sounded and changed it into, "As you say."

"Now, lie on your back on the couch and part your legs for me," said the man, "whilst I conduct the final parts of the exam."

"It will soon be over?" Madam Gray breathed.

The empty hours stretched out, out, out ahead of her. She wasn't due to report back to the city fathers till tomorrow, and had no further appointments for the full day.

"Oh, no, my dear, you must allow me to treat you fully," the surgeon said, fingering his cherrywood pipe without lighting it. "The internal examination takes a very long time."

"And do you enjoy your work?" Madam Gray asked archly as she clambered naked onto the low, long surgical examination table.

"Of course, for I make people better. It's a rare patient who doesn't leave my practice with a smile."

With a loss of maidenhood, more likely, the woman thought. She shivered at the thought of a man putting his . . . whatever it was that he put in to create a pregnancy. It sounded such an unseemly act, even if it was proper for the planet to survive. "How would a general malaise in myself manifest itself in my . . . in my female parts?" she asked as the doctor gently nudged her thighs apart with his scholarly hands.

"Well, you might have a psychic blockage, or indeed a physiological one," the doctor explained. He greased one hand, then placed the palm of the other on her lower tummy and palpated it gently. Then he slid his oiled fingers slowly inside her maidenly canal.

"Aah!" the young woman moaned, then turned it into a little cough.

"Are my hands too cold?" the physician enquired softly.

"They . . . they will suffice," Madam Gray said.

"If you prefer I could withdraw my digits and repair to the fireside . . ."

"No, don't! I mean, you must finish looking for any blockage and not mind my discomfort," Madam Gray said.

Clearly taking his work most seriously, Dr Lorean slid his fingers further up her heated conduit. "Everything is as elastic and wet as it should be, madam."

"It feels alternate," the younger woman admitted softly.

"The laying on of hands can make a real difference," the physician said.

Keeping one set of fingers inside her, he started to palpate her pudenda with his other adept palm.

"What are you doing now?" the would-be spy asked raggedly.

"I'm stimulating the gynaecological perineum. It discharges nervous excitement and leads to better sleep and a clearer head."

Only one thing was clear – the growing sense of awakening between her spread thighs and the parts usually covered by her unmentionables. Madam Gray closed her eyes and gave herself up to the response. It really was quite exquisite, and like nothing she had known before. Such rapture made her forget the lazy servants she had to chide, the too humid day, the nights that stretched so futilely. It made her think only of her most private flesh.

She whimpered as Dr Lorean continued to massage the triangle that made her tummy flutter so. The joy was journeying, striving. Madam Gray pushed her pudenda towards the digital source of delight. "Easy," Dr Lorean whispered. "You can't rush the treatment." The young woman gasped as heaven on earth was almost realized. The sensations rose and rose and . . . as they peaked she cried out in guttural ecstasy, all thoughts of polite form deserting her. All she cared about was straining each sinew upwards in order to squeeze every last quiver of pleasure out.

"Indeed, there was a psychic blockage. I have cured it," Dr Lorean said quietly.

Madam Gray heard him dimly through her orgasmic yodelling and post-orgasmic gasping sighs. "Thank you, thank you, thank you," she eventually managed to cry.

She rested. She briefly slept. When she awoke Dr Lorean gave her an invigorating rosemary tea, then rubbed her down with a medicinal wet towel that had benefited from an acquaintance with lavender. As he brushed her nipples the maiden felt slightly tingly, and wondered if her blockage had returned again.

"Perhaps I should visit you once a month, sir, to repeat the treatment?" she asked girlishly.

"I shall look forward to fitting you in," the good doctor replied. He had left the room jerkily, just before she slept, holding a clipboard down low over his surgical coat. Now she noticed that he looked much more co-ordinated and relaxed. Perhaps he had rid himself of his own psychic blockage in his little parlour? He was obviously very good at it . . .

The next day Madam Gray made her report to the city fathers.

"Dr Lorean is an upright man," she said.

"Not a charlatan?"

The Victorian matriarch smiled. "On my oath, he gives excellent service."

"There was no impropriety?"

"I left his surgery well rid of the malaise that I had come about."

"In that case, the good doctor has no charge to answer. Let it be known that he is a man of stout reputation and conduct, who will not be investigated further," the city fathers said.

Madam Gray vacated the room, well pleased with her replies and the issue's outcome. But as she reached the street one of the flower puff ribbons fell from her dress. She bent to pick it up and her pantaloons rubbed against her body most beguilingly. In the interests of science she repeated the movement, and the exquisite pull happened again. *Oh, dear,* she said to herself, *perhaps this is some sign of organic irritation. I must consult Dr Lorean forthwith.*

Alighting at the doctor's rooms, she found a considerable queue. "He cures my head pains," one woman said.

"He makes my neurastheina abate," offered another female.

"Since his treatment, I have been entirely free of nocturnal spasms," a third coy maiden chipped in.

After a very long wait – and oh, how fidgety was the queue, how over-zealous! – Madam Gray reached the esteemed medical doctor, who was lying on a chaise longue and mopping his brow.

"Forgive me, madam," he murmured faintly. "My reputation

has spread and I am quite in demand, quite over-extended. I can see no other patients today."

"Tomorrow, then?" the affluent young lady said.

The doctor reached for his journal. "No, I fear that I . . ."

"I will pay double."

"I am indebted to you for the compliment, but . . ." The physician stared at the many-worded page.

"Make it triple," Madam Gray rejoined.

"Such largesse I can't refuse," said the doctor, who doubtless had many a bill to settle.

"Then your attentions are assured me," the largesse-bringer said.

An appealing notion then came to her, and left her smiling. "You shall have to tend to my malaise in my chambers," she said softly. "For I will have taken to my bed."

"You think bed-rest is necessary?" A patch of nervous colour had crept into the physician's face.

"Indeed. It is a big four-poster bed, with lots of pillows, ideal for my comfort whilst you conduct your examinations," Madam Gray continued. She looked at him almost wolfishly as she stood up to leave. "Here is my calling card. The servants will admit you. I will expect your attendance on Wednesday at eleven a.m."

The doctor got slowly to his feet. His bow was distinctly shaky, as befitting a man who had spent the week exploring psychically-blocked orifices. "Shall it . . . shall it be a brief visit, madam?" he said.

The healthy young woman stared at him – concentrating her gaze on his fingers for a lascivious moment. "Oh, no, sir. At triple rates I will expect exceptionally long and arduous service," she said.

CAMILLE'S RESISTANCE

Robert De Vel

THE WHEELS OF the carriage continued their monotonous drone along the well-worn road as it meandered through the countryside. The dust had found its way inside the cabin, leaving a powdery mat on everything. Madame Buisse held the lace kerchief to her nose in a vain attempt to keep the dust from entering her lungs. She found the constant rocking and bouncing of the carriage nauseating. The brandy her physician had prescribed for the journey was all but gone, consumed in less time than he'd recommended. It had given her a warm glow during the journey, and intoxicated her. Still, she thought, no one would see her till she arrived in the court some eight hours away. She tipped the remaining few drops on to her handkerchief and inhaled the woody aroma. It was to no avail, and she felt the acrid taste of bile rise in her throat. Pulling the gold braid cord that hung from the ceiling, she signalled the coachman to stop the carriage.

The horses snorted and stamped their hooves, anxious to continue, having been cooped in the stables for the last three weeks. Pierre, the coachman, swung from his seat, landing with the agility of a cat, his dark unclasped hair spilling out from under the *chapeau* which offered him protection from the summer heat and icy winds of winter.

Only twenty-six years of age, he had found favour with Madame after winning the annual cross-country horse race from Lyon to Tours. Each rider had had to catch his steed and ride bareback through the dark of night. They had been given the choice of one item of clothing, with sustenance being acquired along the way from the villagers as they passed through the towns. Those who'd chosen breeches were lucky to last half-distance, as the biting cold froze their upper torso, caused heart seizures and frozen hands. Pierre had chosen his old woollen shirt, knowing the dangers of the icy winds. He'd received a rousing cheer from the crowds as he rode bare-assed into each village. The young women of the town would clamber to offer him food, hoping that they might be lucky enough to catch sight of his manhood. The cold chill had caused Pierre's penis to shrink, but there must have been something to show as he became known by the villagers as "Le Staff". Pierre did not escape the ride unscathed, receiving a gash across his left bicep, which left a scar of two parallel lines. He also received a wound to the left cheek of his *derrière*, in the shape of a triangle. How it formed that shape he was not sure, but it was large enough to be seen at twenty paces.

Madame had engaged him after his successful ride, much to the chagrin of the other ladies of court. He was not sure whether she was impressed with his skills and stamina, or if it was to spite the other ladies. Either way, she gave him a job and lodgings.

Madame waited for Pierre to open the door and offer his hand for support as she alighted from the carriage. She noted the coarse texture of his hand, hot from holding the reins of his two chargers. She stepped over a fallen log and sought privacy behind a small hedge. She found that once on stable ground her sense of balance returned quickly and the nausea lifted from her stomach.

A small stream babbled nearby, and she ventured to the edge of the water to wet her handkerchief. The cold water felt refreshing on her brow, and the rivulets explored the contours of her cheek, down her neck to the crest of her bosom.

Madame patted the soft skin of her breasts, which spilled over the top of her Paris fashion dress. The fashion statement at court, this year, was to bare as much bosom as possible without exposing a nipple. Relieved of her nausea, Madame now felt another sensation, this time in her bladder. The jarring of the carriage combined with the alcohol was making her bladder call out for relief. Normally a lady of the court would hold her bodily functions until she could seek the privacy of her boudoir, but today the urge was too strong.

Calling to Pierre, she instructed him to kneel on his hands and knees. She sat on his back and lifted the skirts around her waist, unlacing the strings of her pantaloons and folding the material down to her knees to expose her vagina. Although the dress and petticoats covered Pierre's head, Madame instructed him to look straight ahead. Spreading the lips of her labia, she directed the flow of urine up and away from her body. The stream of fluid made a gushing noise as she strained her sphincter muscles to expel the urine as far from her body as possible. When she had finished she bent over in front of Pierre's face, dried her lips against the ends of Pierre's woollen shirt, laced up the pantaloons and stood up, straightening the folds of her skirt.

"You may clean yourself in the stream and meet me back at the carriage when you have finished," she said, strolling off in the direction from whence she came.

Pierre felt abused by Madame, as he often did when they were alone. Yet he knew that some day soon he and his fellow rebels would have their revenge against Madame Buisse and the other members of the French aristocracy.

That night they sought lodgings at Count Priecez's mansion. Pierre carried the luggage to Madame's room, unpacking her clothing and hanging it in the oak wardrobe. Madame dismissed him, instructing him to seek nourishment from the kitchen. Pierre knew a number of the staff in the kitchen, some of whom he recognised as members of "La Resistance", a group of rebels whose goal it was to rescue France from the tyranny of the aristocracy. They gave him sustenance and then told him of a meeting of the rebel faction later that evening.

A disused barn at the far end of the grounds served as a safe haven for the group to meet. Pierre counted fifteen staff members, some of whom he had not seen before. The dialogue between the rebels was kept at a whisper, the room lit by one lamp, which cast shadows over the faces of the group. Pierre related the humiliation of the day before listening to the stories of abuse that had befallen his comrades under the authority of the King.

"Where's Camille?" asked a young red-headed man. Pierre recognized André from the stable; a tall lad, with the first wisps of a beard, he spoke with passion and concern about the love of his life.

"Madame has requested that she attend her this evening," said the pantry maid. "I don't think she will get much sleep tonight." The furtive glances amongst the group alluded to something sinister, but before Pierre could enquire what she meant, the signal was given that the guards were patrolling the area and would be upon them soon.

Madame prepared herself for the evening meal with the Count and a number of his faithful supporters. Though tired from the journey, she felt a sense of excitement, knowing that this dinner had been arranged by the Count to discuss the future of the King and his reign of France.

The meal was elegant, yet modest, compared with some of the feasts Madame had experienced at the Count's residence. The food, she thought, reflected the serious nature of the topic being discussed. The Count was his usual gracious self, though the smalltalk around the table frustrated Madame, as she was keen to discuss the real issue for which they were gathered.

When the meal had been cleared, the group retired to the study, where port and snuff were offered around. "Tonight we will consider action which will shape the course of the rule of Louis XIV and the position of France in Europe for the next fifty years." The Count sounded solemn in his prediction.

"I have been entrusted with plans for a meeting between the Kaiser of Germany and the Ambassador of Russia. The meeting will result in the joining of these three strong allies in a pact intent on invading and conquering England. France will again become a major pawnbroker in the future of Europe."

Madame felt a thrill of excitement, knowing that she would play a part in the plans devised by the Count. "I have the details of the rendezvous, and have been given the responsibility of ensuring that the plan reaches the King at the Gala Ball five days from today." The Count continued, "Madame has volunteered to secretly give the message to the King at a prearranged time. She is new to the Parisian court and should not attract the attention of His Majesty's enemies."

The men turned to Madame when the Count asked her to detail the plan they had devised. "As you know, the King has a penchant for young housemaids, preferring to spend his sexual energy on these unsophisticated wenches rather than the cream of the aristocracy." Madame saw she had their interest now, and reached into her handbag, pulling out an ornate silver cylinder. She unscrewed the end and pulled out a note. "These are the plans, listing the location and time of the rendezvous. It is imperative that the King meets the Ambassador and the Kaiser on the allocated day, as failure to do so will be interpreted as rejection of the pact. I will deliver the message, which will have the Count's seal as proof of authenticity."

"How do you propose to protect the message from the King's enemies?" asked one of the men.

"I intend taking a gift to the King; a gift I know he will enjoy and a perfect cover for the carriage of the message." Madame then pulled a second identical silver cylinder from her bag. "This is a decoy; it also has a date and location, but two days later. I intend secreting the real evidence on the King's gift and the decoy on myself."

"What is the gift you intend giving the King?" The other man asked.

Madame smiled as she pulled the gold cord that summoned the room's service maid. "Four glasses of brandy, Camille," ordered the Count. Camille left to prepare the drinks, while Madame continued. "As you can see, she would make an ideal gift for the King to indulge his pleasures. I intend secreting the cylinder in the one place only the King will be able to venture: her womanhood." Madame took pleasure in seeing the surprise on the men's faces. "She will become my handmaid for the journey to Versailles. There, I will offer her to the King as a gift for the night. He will then be able to retrieve the message and arrange to rendezvous with our allies.

"I will carry the decoy, as the King's enemies will assume that I'd be the likely carrier of the information." Madame lowered her voice as Camille returned to the room. "Gentlemen, tonight I think we need to spend some time ensuring that our messenger is appropriately educated. We should combine our special talents to ensure she will meet His Majesty's needs."

Camille had finished serving the drinks and was quietly leaving the room when Madame called to her. "Was there something else you required, Madame?" asked Camille. "Yes," said Madame, "the Count tells me that he has lost a rare diamond. Do you know anything about it?"

The group disbanded, each member having his own exit route. Pierre realized that he was alone, and the guards would be upon him very soon. He retreated to the far end of the building, looking for an alternative exit. The lights of the guards grew closer. Suddenly, a hollow wooden thump underfoot alerted Pierre to a trap door that was secreted beneath the straw. Quickly he scraped around till he found the handle and lifted the door.

What lay below he did not know, but faced with having to explain his presence, Pierre had no option but to abandon caution and step into the void. Moments later he heard the guards enter the barn. The smell of smoke indicated that the guards were stopping for their own secret gathering.

Not knowing how long they would be there, Pierre tried to make himself as comfortable as possible, expecting a lengthy wait. He must have dozed off, for he was awakened by the distant cry of a female voice.

Quickly regaining his bearings, Pierre realized that the sound came from the black void of the tunnel. As his eyes adjusted to the dark he was able to make out a tunnel, at the end of which glowed a light. He began stealthily moving towards the sound and the ever-growing light. The female voice he'd heard earlier was now reduced to sobs. He now discerned the sound of other voices, one of which sounded familiar. Madame! But what was she doing in the tunnel? At first Pierre thought it was Madame who was sobbing, but then he recognized her authoritarian voice, though somewhat slurred, talking to a man.

As he edged closer to the light he heard a number of other male voices, one of which was the Count's. "She said she didn't take it, but I think she has hidden it somewhere on her person." The other two males laughed, as though sharing a familiar joke. "Would Madame like us to conduct the search, or are you a woman who likes to take things into her own hands?" Madame chuckled and said, "I think this investigation will require the efforts of myself *and* you three gentlemen."

Pierre sought cover in the shadows of one of the abandoned cells – for it was, he realized, an old dungeon, which had been converted for some form of ritual. The walls were lined with rugs bearing symbols he recognized from the old Scriptures, symbols from a pagan religion he'd thought had been banned long ago.

His attention was again drawn to the group; he recognized the young woman as Camille, the housemaid. One of the men held her hands behind her back, while another began to unlace her bodice. "Stop!" Both men turned towards the voice. "I think it would be more interesting to wager on where she has hidden the diamond." Madame's words brought a cheer from the men, and soon they were nominating the area where they thought the diamond was hidden.

"Now stand back, and let *mademoiselle* prove her innocence."

Madame called on the Count to nominate the area he wished to bet.

"Inside the bodice of her left breast," chortled the Count.

"Well, my dear, prove him wrong," challenged Madame.

Slowly the maid unlaced her bodice and reached in under the breast, showing that the jewel was not there.

"She's tricking me," complained the Count. He stood up, and, taking the girl from behind, reached into the bodice and fondled her breast. She tried to resist, but the Count had a firm grip. He reached under the breast and then pulled it from the material support. Her nipple began to harden with the cool air. This seemed to excite the Count, who reached again into the bodice, exposing the other breast.

Madame instructed the other two men to hold the woman's arms out to her sides while she fondled Camille's breasts, sucking on the nipples to make them even harder. One of the Count's companions commented on the length of the nipples, claiming they were the longest nipples he had ever seen. Madame threw back her head and said, "Sir, your life must indeed be sheltered." Reaching into her own bodice, she pulled out one of her own breasts, revealing that it was crowned with a jewelled nipple ring. She approached the other woman and placed her nipple against

Camille's. The three men gathered around and began to measure the two women's nipples, Camille's breast was a little smaller than Madame's, yet the areola was very dark, the result of wet-nursing two of the village children. Madame had never borne children, so the areola was not so dark; it was the length of the nipple which surprised the men. Thick as a small ring finger, the nipple was half the length again of Camille's, the result of Madame's ministrations and the weight of the nipple jewellery, for which she had a liking. The men were mesmerized by the opportunity to fondle the two women's breasts; they pulled and pinched both nipples, till the Count declared that Madame had won.

Pierre was shocked to see Madame act this way. He was familiar with the length of her nipples, having on occasion been required to help Madame dress or satisfy her lascivious demands. But he had never seen her allow other men to touch her without having to pay for such pleasures.

The moment was broken when the door to the dungeon was thrown open and a body tumbled down the stairs. Two guards stood at the entrance, momentarily speechless on seeing the two bare-breasted women.

"What is the meaning of this?" demanded the Count.

"We found him sneaking around outside, as we made our patrol," the taller of the two guards said.

Stunned by the fall, the man cowered in the shadows at the foot of the stairs. The shadows, however, could not hide the ruffled red locks; Pierre recognized that they belonged to André, the stable hand.

Madame adjusted her attire, but Camille, still held by the Count's comrades, stood exposed before her lover. She shrieked his name, more in fear than embarrassment.

André, realizing the situation, charged at the fist of Camille's captors, knocking him to the ground. As he swung his fist at the second man, the Count struck him over the head with a bottle of wine, the contents of which covered his clothing. Camille screamed, thinking her lover had been mortally injured.

The Count and the other men laughed, realizing that the red wine spilled across André's chest hinted at an injury more serious.

"Don't worry, my treasure, there are more years of work left in him yet," the Count admonished. "Providing we decide to spare his life. What say you, Madame? He has seen you in a compromising situation which could be an embarrassment for you."

Madame feigned shock at the Count's words. "Sir, you are quite right. I am a modest woman and guard my virtue jealously. I am indeed in this young man's mind now, and the only way to ensure his silence would be to cut out his tongue."

Camille gasped.

"He could draw pictures," offered one of the men.

"Then we'll cut off his hands," Madame suggested.

"He could draw with his feet," volunteered the Count, enjoying the look of fear on Camille's face.

"Cut them off," said Madame.

"What if he uses his manhood to draw in the sand?" said Madame.

"Then we'll cut that off as well," laughed the Count.

They all laughed, enjoying Camille's growing horror.

"Unless we can ensure his silence, we will have to kill him," stated the Count, his voice void of emotion.

All eyes turned to Camille as Madame said, "I think we have just the motivation here in front of us."

Camille was sobbing quietly. "I think it is time to see how much she really loves this young boy," cooed the Count. "Tie him to the iron chair and gag him."

André was dragged over to the chair, which was fitted with leather strapping for the hands and feet. He was bound and gagged as the Count had directed. When one of the men asked if André should be blindfolded the Count laughed, saying that the boy was in for an education he would not forget.

"Now, if you want to save the life of your lover then I suggest you be a bit more gracious with your hosts and hostess." The Count took Camille by the hand and led her to a stool in the middle of the room. He then sat down and pulled her onto his knee.

"Now, where were we?" he said, reaching into her bodice and fondling her breasts with his hands. He opened the bodice, exposing her breasts. He then called to one of the men to examine them more closely.

They both squeezed and lifted the breasts, pulling on the nipples till they began to lactate. The Count began to suck on her breast, the milk now flowing more freely. He encouraged the other members of the group to taste the milk, each commenting on the flavour as if tasting a glass of fine wine.

Camille felt trapped. She was horrified by the actions of the group, yet realized it was the only way to save the life of her lover.

"I have some milk of my own," offered one of the men. "Perhaps *mademoiselle* would like to sample my vintage." With that he stood before Camille and loosened the strings of his breeches. "Reach in and sample my vessel." Hesitantly Camille reached into his breeches and touched his penis. It was semi-erect, but soon began to respond when she pulled it from the clothing.

The Count pushed her off his lap, making her kneel on the floor before putting the other man's penis again into her mouth. Before long it became fully erect. Camille gently pulled the skin backward and forward as the man softly groaned. Taking a handful of hair, he directed her head closer to his crotch, encouraging her to take his staff deeper into her mouth.

André began to struggle in his chair, pulling at the restraints, causing the chair to inch towards his lover. "Someone quieten that noise. I'm losing concentration," snapped the Count.

Madame, who had been observing the spectacle, reached into her bag and took out a kerchief and a bottle of clear liquid. She poured some of the liquid over the material and covered André's mouth and nose. He struggled briefly and then slumped forward on the chair. "When he awakens he will be in a more amicable mood. It's an Oriental elixir I acquired from one of the King's apothecaries."

The attention again returned to Camille, as she continued to take the penis into her mouth. She sucked the tip of the penis and rolled her tongue around the head; saliva on the shaft glistened like dew on a leaf. The Count reached from behind, caressing her breasts, pulling on the nipples till they again started to lactate. He rubbed the milky fluid over her breasts, then, cupping the man's scrotum, squeezed it in unison with the thrusting of Camille's mouth. Her captor started breathing more quickly as the juices in him began to rise. The pumping and squeezing provided the extra stimulation he had been seeking, and with a loud groan he released his seed into Camille's mouth. She began gagging as the fluid quickly filled her mouth. He pulled his penis out of her mouth, spraying the last of his load on her breasts. The Count continued his fondling, combining the sperm with the milk which lathered her breasts.

The Count led Camille to a table, which was covered with purple velvet sheeting. At each corner stood a large iron candleholder. Wax had trailed down the iron, leaving white wax stalactites, a sign that this was not the first time some innocent wench had been in this position.

The group began to undress Camille. Her bodice was already removed, leaving her skirt and pantaloons. Releasing the button of her skirt, Madame pulled it over her young shapely hips. Her pantaloons had been caught in the skirt, leaving them drawn down to just below her pubic mound. Camille expected them to be removed, but Madame suggested they be left for the time being, saying that the white material highlighted the black strands of her pubic hair.

The group gathered around Camille's upper torso; they stroked her skin and fondled her breasts, the milk and sperm glistening in the candlelight. "We still need one more ingredient to perform the ritual," the Count said. "Madame, will you provide us with the missing potion?"

Madame smiled. "Give me your hand, kind sir, and I will gladly do so." At the head of the table two steps of rough-hewn wood allowed Madame to climb on to the table. There she lifted her skirts and placed her knees either side of Camille's head. In this position she could lower her vagina onto Camille's face. Madame had already removed her pantaloons, leaving her garter and stockings to keep her warm against the cool evening air.

She lowered her hips till her vaginal lips settled onto Camille's mouth. Slowly, she began to rock backwards and forwards against her lips. She instructed two of the men to support her arms, in order that she maintain her balance. Next, she instructed Camille to use her tongue to penetrate her womanhood. The Count stood mesmerized as Madame began her quest for ecstasy. The sound of lips against lips, wet, squishy and salty, filled Camille's senses. She found Madame's labia had become engorged with blood, making them soft and plump; she found the sensation was not dissimilar to kissing a man's lips. It was, however, the distinct taste of vaginal juices that confirmed this was indeed her first experience of oral sex with a woman.

Madame had moved through the plateau stage of her arousal and now sought to continue the journey which would take her to the highest peak. She directed the Count to lift her skirts, exposing her womanhood. She then instructed him to take hold of her outer lips and spread them. This way her clitoris was fully exposed. "Now love my clit as if your man's life depended on it," she cooed.

Camille felt degraded. Lying pinned beneath Madame only highlighted her plight. Yet in a strange way she took some solace from the fact that she had the power to make Madame orgasm, a power that she usually felt with a man. She began her ministrations in earnest. Flicking, lapping and sucking the little bud. The rhythmic sound of her tongue against Madame's lips filled the room. The men supporting Madame were mesmerized by the spectacle; one of the men was masturbating in unison with Madame's movements. Madame's breathing became short and shallow, until her panting reaching a crest, and the banshee wail of release echoed through the tunnel.

While still in the throes of orgasm Madame moved down and rubbed her lips against Camille's breasts, coating them with the juice of her release. She then collapsed over Camille's upper torso, panting as she began to regain her breath. Madame rested her head against Camille's thigh, facing her pubic mound. She could smell the earthy aroma of Camille's love juices amongst the matted pubic hairs against her cheek. When she regained her composure the men helped Madame down off the table. The Count eagerly assisted Madame in adjusting her attire.

"I think we are now ready for the next stage of our ritual. Awaken the boy."

Madame instructed the men to move André to the side of the table, so that he could see the full length of Camille's body. She then slapped André's face until he started to regain consciousness.

"I need the boy in my command," said Madame. She then opened her legs and reached up under her skirt. From where he was hiding Pierre could see Madame running her fingers through the still-moist lips of her cunt.

"Smell me and know that I am your mistress," cooed Madame as she ran her finger under André nose and then painted his lips with her juices. André's eyes opened slowly, the pupils dilated from the influence of the drug Madame had administered earlier.

"Who do you obey?" asked Madame.

"You are my mistress," André answered with a slurred voice.

Camille let out a cry to André. "My darling, what have they done?"

André looked in Camille's direction; she could see that behind the glazed eyes André was still aware of her. He hesitated for a moment; his eyes seemed to clear and Camille thought that he had overcome the effects of the drug. Madame saw what was happening, slid her finger under his nose and ordered André to look at her. Camille could sense his resistance, but it was futile against Madame's concoction.

"You obey only me!" commanded Madame. André's eyes glazed over once again. "While you gentlemen prepare our young lady, I will have André help me prepare to receive the King's message."

The men needed no further prompting and began arranging items for the ritual. The Count made Camille kneel and placed a number of pillows on the table. He then pushed Camille back onto them. In this position her torso was elevated above her head and legs. The men took velvet straps, tying them to her legs and to each corner of the table. Camille's mound of Venus now became the focus as the candles highlighted the black forest of her pubic hair.

The Count began to trace his hand along the contours of Camille's body, stroking her hair, removing the dark strands that were matted to her face. Spreading her hair down over the end of the table, the Count commented that it looked like a cascading black waterfall, glistening in the candlelight. One of the other men brought a pot of water, which had been heating over the fire.

"We must ensure our lady is clean before we continue with the next phase of our evening," said Madame to André. She knelt beside him, stroking his hair just as the Count did to Camille. "Gentlemen, you may commence your cleansing ritual. Make sure you wash every part of her body."

Each man took a cloth from the bucket and commenced rubbing Camille till she was wet from head to toe. They then took bars of soap and began to lather her body, the soapsuds making her body appear translucent. The men took extra time when they washed her breasts, vigorously swirling the cloth around her breasts, making the blood flow to the surface of the skin, giving them a pink glow. They then pulled on her nipples, making them become erect, together they kneaded the areolae and pulled up towards the nipple till the milky fluid began to flow. This they mixed with the soapy water, lathering it over her stomach.

Madame whispered in André's ear, describing the scene before them. She began to rub his chest, feeling for the opening in his shirt and running her fingers through his hairy mat. "She has a beautiful body. Look at the fullness of her ripe, luscious breasts. Remember what they taste like? Can you feel the hard bud of her nipple in your mouth?"

André's body began to respond to the sight before him. He could feel the blood rushing to his head, making him dizzy. He had tried to fight the effects of the drug Madame had administered, but it was too strong. He was angered by what the men were doing to his loved one but was unable to control his own body, a slave to the words of Madame.

The Count began to wash Camille's pubic mound, the soap and milk turning her black hairs into a white fluffy mound of bubbles. He spread her legs as wide as he could and rubbed her vulva. Camille tried to close her legs, but the Count called to the other two men to hold them apart. He continued his washing, first with an open palm, running his fingers up and down along the labia. He then took the cloth and rubbed more vigorously. Camille could feel the blood rushing to the lips, engorging them and sending a familiar tingling sensation to the base of her spine. She cursed her body for responding to this unwelcome intruder. She tried to stifle the cry as he inserted his finger into her inner sanctum. First one, then two fingers began their exploration. The soap reacted with her tender pink vaginal walls, sending a tingling sensation through her body, making her long to reach down and soothe the irritation.

The Count inserted four fingers, spreading her lips as wide as they would go. Then, taking a wooden ladle, he filled the cup with warm water, pouring it onto the palm of his hand which had formed a trough into her open cunt. The fluid penetrated deep into Camille's womb, warming her in a way she had never experienced before, the irritation soothed by the clean water. She was aware that the continued attention to her sexual centre had inflamed her clitoris, and it began to harden, pushing its bud from between the folds of her lips.

"I think our lady is in need of relief," said the Count. "I can see her bud beginning to rise." The other men gathered around, peering at Camille's pubic altar. The Count pulled her lips open so that they could gain a better view. The men began to touch the blossoming flower, commenting on the size and firmness.

Just when Camille thought they would ravage her, the Count ordered the men away and told them not to touch her. He leaned close to Camille's ear and whispered, "I want you to show your lover how you satisfy the yearning when you are alone at night in your bed. Don't try to fool us with a performance. I am aware of the unique bodily responses when you really orgasm."

Camille had expected the men to satisfy their own lusts on her body, and she would have been able to separate herself emotionally from these events. She justified her actions to satisfy their lusty demands by arguing that she was saving the life of her lover. She recalled how, with other lovers, she had chosen to distance herself from them, arguing that most women at some time feigned arousal just to keep their lovers contented. However, it would seem that the Count was aware of her own bodily functions and realized she could not fake the performance. It scared her to think that she would have to surrender to the natural urges of her sexuality.

"Have you watched your loved one satisfy herself before?" asked Madame as she traced her hand down over André's stomach. She could feel the ripples of his abdominal muscles, coated with a fine down of wiry hair. Opening his shirt, Madame gazed at his young torso, excited by what she saw and what she knew she would soon be experiencing. Slowly she explored the trail of pubic hair, following it below the waistband of his breeches.

Madame pulled on the drawstring, allowing her hand greater freedom in its quest to find the focus of her desire. Like a bird nestling in its home, she settled her fingers in the bush of his manhood. She could feel the flaccid member beginning to stir as she stroked its shaft. André could feel his body responding to her touch as his will to resist succumbed to the power of the drug.

"I love the feel of your staff," Madame continued, stroking the now rigid penis. "I can feel the veins carving their pathway over your skin. I'm sure your Camille would love to feel your head dancing inside her." She opened the front of Andre's breeches, exposing his manhood to the group. Wiping the lips of her own vagina, Madame encircled the shaft, coating it with the fluid of her womanhood, making it glisten in the candlelight, the slishing sounds of wet sex filling the room.

Camille looked over at her lover and was shocked to see Madame fondling André. She began to protest, but was cut short by the silk gag that was placed over her mouth. "Forget your young man and please us with your performance. If we are pleased we will consider sparing his life." The Count sounded irritated by Camille's delay in masturbating herself.

She closed her eyes and began to imagine that she and André were alone in her bedroom, as they had been on numerous occasions before. She thought of the time when he had hidden in her room, just before she retired for bed. She remembered how he had silently crept up behind her, demanding that she keep still and not turn around. He had kissed her neck, nuzzling into her ear and biting her shoulders. Camille began to fantasize him running his fingers along her neck, imagining the path of her lover's kisses.

He had then slid the material from her shoulder, tracing his kisses further along her skin, sending shivers through her arms down to her fingers. Camille began to caress her breast, just as André had fondled her through the thin material, squeezing the firm flesh and pulling on the hardening nipple. Camille heard the men who were watching stir with excitement.

She sensed the let-down of milk in her breast and then felt the spray of fluid fall onto her belly. The men began to sound agitated as the Count forbade them from interfering with her performance. Camille felt excited that she had the attention of the men in the room, just as she had with André, on that wonderful night.

She rubbed the lactate which had fallen on her belly in circular motions, slowly working down towards her pubic mound. She remembered how André had lain her on the bed and had spread her legs, slowly lifting the nightdress until her mound was exposed. He had delicately kissed the outer lips of her womanhood till they began to moisten. Slowly he'd begun to explore her inner lips with his tongue. Camille let her hands trail down to her moist lips and inserted a finger in between the lips, mimicking the movements of André's lovemaking.

The men murmured with approval as she penetrated herself with her middle finger, sliding it in and out just as her lover had done the other night.

Madame was also enjoying the exhibition. She wanted to know what it was like to have André penetrate her cunt. She lifted her skirts and sat facing André, a leg either side of his body. She grabbed hold of his erect penis and began to run the head along her vaginal lips. Pulling the foreskin back, she exposed the head of André's penis and then lowered herself on to it. The walls in her womb began to stretch wide as he penetrated deeper into her. She began to rhythmically rock backwards and forwards, so that the shaft would rub against her clitoris.

Camille found that with her back arched she could stimulate her clitoris while she penetrated herself with her fingers. In this position she could feel her desire beginning to mount; her breathing became short and rapid. She began to sigh in time with her penetrations. Just then she felt something cool against her lips. She initially drew back, but the Count chastised her, telling her to fuck herself with the object.

The object was long, round and metallic, with ridges that stimulated her inner walls as it slid backwards and forwards. Camille found herself imagining it was André's penis, and started to slide it in and out with one hand while the other continued to stimulate her clitoris. Before long she felt the familiar warmth in her belly as she rode the make-believe penis to orgasm. The men all cheered as she ejaculated, the orgasmic fluid spraying all over her hand and down her leg. The walls of her vagina began to contract in a rhythmic pulse. If it had been an erect penis in her cunt the sensation would have been similar to being sucked; however, with no anchor for the object of her penetration, Camille's vaginal muscles sucked the silver cylinder inside her. There, the Count knew, it would remain, till the King had an opportunity to arouse her, and it would be ejected when she orgasmed again.

Madame repositioned André's chair so that he was facing away from Camille. She sat again with legs astride the chair and lowered herself onto the erect penis. Exposing her breasts, she made André suck on one then the other of her nipples. The jewelled nipple ring restricted André's access to her fleshy breasts, so he focused his attention on sucking the nipple as hard as he could. Madame loved the tugging of her nipples, and rocked with more vigour to encourage Andre.

"She is inserting a finger into her cunt," whispered Madame to André, and she ground herself deeper onto the erect member. The thrill of describing the pleasuring ritual of André's lover aroused Madame enormously; her own juices flowed down, coating his penis and scrotum. The sound of wet penis and vaginal lips combined with the sensation of matted pubic hairs grinding against each other enabled Madame to come, not long after Camille had satisfied herself.

As the women savoured the post-orgasmic euphoria, the Count called to one of the men to bring the velvet chest. He pulled out a leather and chain device, which he fastened around Camille's waist. He threaded the chains between her legs, adjusting it so that her vagina was sealed against digital entry. He then attached the other end with a lock, saying. "There are only two keys that will open this lock. The other is with His Majesty. You will accompany Madame to the court in Versailles, where you will deliver this instrument of love to him with the vigour and passion you displayed tonight. Now go to your room and pack your belongings; you leave in the morning."

Turning his attention to Madame, the Count said, "When you have finished with the boy my men will find a cell where he will stay till you return."

Madame lifted her skirts and stood up, the still-erect penis trailing a line of love juices down her leg. Camille was led from the dungeon by the Count's accomplices. As she turned to bid her lover *adieu*, she was shocked to see Madame on her knees, her head buried between André's legs.

After the men and Camille had left, the Count took another silver cylinder from the velvet chest. Madame was engrossed in the carnal pleasure of sucking André's shaft, and did not notice the Count behind her. André began to breathe more heavily, a sigh that aroused his fellatrix, who began to suck harder, sliding the shaft deeper down her throat. The Count lifted her skirts, revealing her round buttocks, and began sliding the silver cylinder along her lips, moistening it with her juice. When it glistened with natural lubricant he inserted it into her vagina, sliding it backwards and forwards in time with her sucking.

André could not resist any longer, and with a cry released his seed into Madame's hungry mouth. At the same moment the Count slid the metallic probe deep into her cunt, for a moment penetrating her womanhood with his own finger as he sought to position the cylinder as deep as it would go.

Madame turned to the Count, her face dripping with sperm. "Savour the taste and smell of my sex, *monsieur*, for it will be all you receive till I have fulfilled my mission and Camille delivers the fate of England to the King."

The Count ran his finger under his nose, inhaling the aroma of her passion. He trailed the finger over his lips, saying, "When England is defeated, and I sit at the right hand of the King, I will place you in the centre of my dining table and coat you with every fruit imaginable. There I will savour the heady taste of your womanhood as I pleasure you with each piece of fruit before I have you as my dessert."

The two men returned to the dungeon, reporting that Camille had been locked in her bedroom. "Good. Take our insurance and keep him in a safe place. We don't want any harm coming to him till after Madame returns from Paris." The men untied André and dragged him off to one of the dungeon cells. They walked up the stairs to the main living area, bidding the Count and Madame *bonsoir*.

"May I escort you back to your chamber, Madame?" asked the Count, offering his arm.

"Thank you, kind sir. I always enjoy the kindness of a gentleman.

Especially one who is soon to become the second most powerful man in France."

It had been a long night for watchers and watched, ravishers and ravished.

The fate of France was now in their hands.

WETNURSE OF THE WORLD

Val Weston

THERE WAS GREAT excitement in the medieval city-state of Copula. The ruler, a young and handsome nobleman called Marco Libertino, had announced another of his Olympic-style competitions to find a world champion in some interesting field. The citizens gathered in the main square to hear his pronouncement.

"Fellow Copulators, this year I am pleased to announce the first ever contest to find the Wetnurse of the World." There was a ripple of applause. "Like all our contests, it will be open to all comers. The heats will take place over three days, here in this square."

As the date for the novel contest drew near, fifty young hopefuls from all corners of the earth (well, Europe, which passed for the world in those days) presented themselves. Any considered too old, too sick or too ugly were weeded out by Marco's officials, and when the great day dawned fifty buxom young women were led into the Piazza to rapturous applause.

"Gentlemen, Ladies, Wetnurses and . . ." he glanced round at a screaming congregation of infants ". . . babies, welcome to the first ever International Wetnurse Contest. All contestants have been given the same amount to drink, no more and no less. Their intake will be strictly controlled during the contest. Today's heats will be first, Breast Beauty, and second, Breast Texture, both to be judged by myself in consultation with my advisers. The third part, Milk Abundance, will be gauged by the number of babies each nurse can satisfy before running dry."

As the women were lined up in the arena and told to remove their upper garments a great roar went up from the crowd at the sight of so many magnificent mammaries. The sun beat down with complete impartiality upon them all, gilding the paler breasts of the Northern Europeans, bronzing the darker flesh of the Mediterranean contingent and highlighting the dark brown boobs of the sprinkling of Arab nurses, who nourished the offspring of certain military families because it was believed that their milk contained more fiery strength.

The women thrust out their breasts proudly, glad of a chance to show them off. Some were enormous, defying gravity, and others were small but very shapely. Their resemblance to fruit was marked: some were shaped like perfectly round pomegranates, others like oval melons, some bore a resemblance to the exotic banana, being elongated and upward-tilting, while some delicious pairs looked like . . . well, delicious pears.

It was a dream come true for young Marco, who had not been weaned until the age of eight and had experienced his first orgasm (the first of many) while suckling. Titties, therefore, had a more than average fascination for him. As he walked down the line, like a general surveying his troops, he could feel his erection growing inside his cod-piece and bliss filled his veins.

"I think we shall concentrate on eliminating any not to our liking," he told his two advisers, the lascivious Giovanni and the experienced Paolo. "That one at the end has droopy dugs, and this one is horribly disfigured by freckles."

"I quite like freckles," Paolo objected. "And the tits in question are of a very nice shape."

"The redhead's are too small," Giovanni said. "So flat it's amazing they hold any milk at all."

It was clear that the three of them could never agree and Marco began to wish he'd appointed himself sole arbiter. However, in the end they eliminated ten women on looks alone.

Now came the task that Marco had been looking forward to: the touch test. Forty certified beautiful bazoomas to fondle to his heart's content. He stepped forward and smiled at the first in line, a shy Nordic blonde with a perfect pair of creamy churns. As he caressed their smooth slopes the pink nipples rose to salute him and he gave them a loving tweak. A little white bead appeared at the tip of each.

"Very nice," he murmured, deciding to wear a larger cod-piece tomorrow.

The next to be judged was a bold brunette, who returned his gaze with a wink and put her hands beneath her enormous jugs, offering them up for his inspection. Marco told her to remove her hands and felt the weight of them himself. It was amazing that such big, heavy boobies could stand up for themselves in so impressive a fashion. Thanks to his ministrations the dark brown nipples were soon rearing provocatively, and he longed to take them in his mouth, but that would be to break his own rules. He must wait until tomorrow.

After the men had caressed all the bosoms they dismissed another ten women, leaving thirty to take the next test. The fretful babes were brought into the ring, dozens of them, and put to each breast. The noise level was suddenly reduced, not just by the hungrily sucking babes but because the crowd had also gone quiet, in a mood of sad nostalgia for that golden age when they too had been offered a milky teat as the panacea for all ills.

By the end of the first day, twenty contestants remained. They had all satisfied at least four infants each – one had actually managed seven – rendering the little cherubs totally satiated and slumbrous. Amidst great applause the wetnurses retreated to their quarters and their allotted quota of beverage, while Marco announced the proceedings for the next day.

"Tomorrow our twenty ladies shall undergo the Taste Test. Together with my advisers, I shall sample the milk of each nurse and evaluate its quality. Only the finest shall proceed to the third and final heat. I bid you all good day, citizens."

That night the dreams of many a man, and possibly some women, in that city were exceedingly wet.

On the following day there was even more excitement in the square at the prospect of witnessing the Tasting. Marco, more comfortable today in his capacious cod-piece, began the proceedings. The Nordic beauty, having survived three heats, was looking decidedly coquettish and was fast becoming his personal favourite, but he was determined to remain impartial. The tits of a sexy little Moorish girl were very appealing too. All the women were seated on a long dais at the right height to allow the men to suckle without too much strain, and as Marco bent his head to the first lactating teat the crowd urged him on.

The milk was sweet and rich, and he gulped it down greedily at first but then realized that he must pace himself. He took a mouthful and swirled it around his palate, then spat it out into the bowl that a servant held for him. Turning to his fellow judges, he said, "Hmm, pretty good. Nice texture in the mouth, not too sickly. Hint of honey, slight acidity."

A clerk wrote everything down with a scratchy quill so the tasting notes could be compared at the end. Marco passed on, and as he went became more and more expert in discrimination of flavours. Realizing that the first samples had probably not been properly appreciated, when he had completed his odyssey he went back to the beginning and tasted them all over again.

Meanwhile, the crowd were growing restless, and since all the wetnurses had copious supplies remaining he ordered that some of their milk be squeezed into cups and passed round to refresh the spectators, which made him most popular.

At last came the results of the penultimate heat. Ten were deemed to have milk too thin, too sour, too insipid or too sickly, and now only ten remained to take the final test. Its nature was to be kept secret until the morrow.

Excitement was at fever-pitch on the last day. Marco announced a Test of Strength. Each wetnurse had to press their teats as hard as they could in order to express their milk. The one who managed to fire her bosom-load the furthest would be deemed the overall winner of the title. A sanded firing range had been prepared, with the contestants lined up at one end and marshalls in attendance with measuring rods. Everyone was looking forward to the novel spectacle.

Marco was pleased that both the Nordic blonde and the Moorish brunette had stayed the course. He arranged for them to perform last, the first to stand at the firing line being a tanned beauty sporting a small but very shapely pair. The arena went quiet, then a marshall shouted the magic word, "Fire!"

The wetnurse squeezed her right nipple between thumb and forefinger with all her might. It was a magnificent effort. The white stream shot into the air, describing a perfect arc, before dropping into the sand at least twenty-five feet away.

The official measurement was twenty-six feet, three inches. A formidable start. The second wetnurse managed only around twenty feet, and the third a mere fifteen. Marco felt his pulse quicken. He wanted one of his favourites to win, but an exacting standard had been set.

At last it was the turn of the Moorish girl. She braced herself, thrust out her delectable globes and pinched one dark teat between finger and thumb. To the crowd's delight she managed an astonishing thirty feet! There was uproar on the benches, and Marco beamed. See if the fair-haired beauty could beat that!

The blonde woman preened her exquisitely formed breasts and tweaked the rosy nipple to encourage the milk-flow. Then she thrust out her chest and, taking a deep breath, pinched the oozing teat as hard as she could. The white liquid rose to the sky, reflecting the sun's rays in rainbow colours, before dropping back into the sand very near the mark made by the dark girl's spray. The marshall hurried to measure: thirty feet and one half inch! A superlative effort.

Marco stood on the dais, ready to declare Brunhilda of Bremen the winner. But then an angry voice cried out, "Cheat! She is a shameful cheat! I demand another try!" It was Fatima, the Moorish girl. Marco, being a fair-minded man, asked her to explain herself.

"She drank more than the allotted amount, Sire. I saw her going round the hall draining the dregs from all the wine glasses to give herself an edge. She should be disqualified."

"Brunhilda, is this true?"

"No, it is Fatima who lies . . ."

"I do not! I saw it plainly."

"Lying cow!"

The two women were spoiling for a fight. A marshall grabbed each by the shoulders and separated them, but then the wetnurses began to fight with the only weapons remaining to them. Seizing their bountiful breasts, they squeezed their nipples hard, each directing a fierce jet of milk into their opponent's eyes. How the spectators loved it! Soon there was a free-for-all developing, with the other wetnurses taking sides. The arena became criss-crossed with milky jets, many landing far into the crowd amidst roars and cheers.

At last, weeping with laughter, Marco held up his hand. 'Enough, ladies, you have each proved your spirit. I declare you joint winners of the title Wetnurse of the World."

As well as the other valuable prizes that were heaped upon them, the two winners were granted what many women considered the greatest prize of all: a night with the handsome and well-endowed Duke of Copula himself. That night Marco lay in his splendid bed, complete with rampant erection, awaiting the two bathed, scented and eager women. When they arrived all three embraced, then he began to suckle at the tempting dusky breasts of the dark girl while the blonde massaged his organ between the fleshy mounds of her ample pair.

"Mmm, I think I'll make the contest an annual event," he mused happily as the honey-sweet milk began to flow from Fatima's engorged nipple. "No, maybe monthly. Or even weekly . . ."

But as another stream of milk was on the verge of spilling, this time from Marco's own body, his thoughts dissolved into mindless bliss.

AMELIA

Valentina Cilescu

While the maiden is lying on her bed, the mistress should loosen the girdle and the knot of her dress, and when the maiden begins to dispute with her, she should overwhelm her with kisses. Having gained this point, the mistress should loosen the knot of her undergarments, and turning up her lower garment should massage the joints of her naked thighs.

THE ROSEBUD SUTRA

MISS CATHERSTONE'S FACE was like thunder, her thin, bony fingers twisting and untwisting the knot of her lace-edged handkerchief. "This cannot be," she gasped, but her face was white with the shock of realization. "You have betrayed me!"

Dorothea Strong, still weak from loss of blood, lay stretched out on the couch, her normally smooth dark hair ruffled about her tanned face.

"I . . . am sorry," she said quietly.

"Sorry!" snapped Miss Catherstone. "That seems scarcely adequate in the circumstances. The understanding between us was that you would enjoy the girl's company for the afternoon, and if you were satisfied with her you would pay me the sum of two hundred pounds to engage her services as your . . . travelling companion.

"I entrusted the girl to your care. She is a valuable asset, and yet you saw fit to lead her into danger! And, having done so, you then chose to abandon her to her fate . . ."

Dorothea raised herself up on one elbow. A white bandage, stained with red, was wound around the flesh wound in her upper arm.

"Miss Catherstone, I had no idea . . . There was nothing I could do . . ."

"You foolish, stubborn woman. You knew very well that the hills are full of outlaws and brigands, and yet you led an innocent girl into their very arms. They have stolen her away from me. Do you know what they will be doing to her now? Sullying her virginal purity with their filthy hands . . ."

"I . . . I will try to find her. As soon as I can, I will ride into the mountains to look for her and bring her back. I swear it."

"Yes, Dr Strong. You will. Or you will never be received at the academy again. Never, do you hear?"

Without waiting for a reply, Miss Catherstone turned and stalked out of the room, leaving Dorothea to tormented thoughts of what she had done, of what might have been.

Out on the landing, Mary Bates listened with mounting anger. She had not trusted Dorothea Strong the first time she saw her, and she certainly did not trust her now, with all her promises and her apologies. Mary thought tearfully of her lover Amelia, and of the terrible things that might be happening to her – all because of some convenient financial arrangement between Dorothea Strong and Miss Catherstone.

As soon as Dorothea had raised the alarm, a search party from the Jainapur garrison had ridden out in search of Amelia, but that had been three days ago, and there was still no news of Amelia. Still nothing to say if she was alive or dead. Mary looked through the doorway at Dorothea Strong and felt a surge of bitter rage. In that moment she made her decision.

If Dorothea did not go to look for Amelia, she would.

Amelia had lost all track of time. For two days – or was it three? – she had been led higher and higher into the mountains towards the distant, snow-capped peaks. Her wrists bound and tethered by a long hemp rope, she stumbled behind the lead horse, her yellow gown torn and muddied by the red dust that kept getting into her eyes and lungs.

They travelled mostly by night, when the air was so cold that it made Amelia shiver uncontrollably. In the daytime, they rested in the shade of the rocks, but still the sun beat down on her half-naked body with a vengeful intensity. She was far from home, far from friends. She even missed the stern face of Miss Catherstone, chiding her for some minor transgression.

Here, with these tall, hard-faced tribeswomen, the prospect of one of Miss Catherstone's beatings held no fears for Amelia. She feared that in captivity her treatment would be far more severe than anything she had ever suffered at the academy. And she dared not show her fear, for each sign of weakness was punished with a blow across the shoulders from a flexible leather thong. Even protected by the material of her dress and camisole, her flesh stung from the blows.

On the morning of the fourth day, as dawn turned the sky blush-pink over the high Himalayan peaks, she saw the encampment: an untidy jumble of tents and horses, sheltering around a series of caves hollowed out of the bare rock.

At first the camp seemed deserted, save for a few scrawny goats and chickens and a piebald pony tethered beside the stream. But as they approached, figures emerged from the tents: young women clad in coarse woolen tunics, their dark hair falling loose and glossy about their shoulders. They ran forward to greet their lovers, who leapt down from the saddle and gathered them into their arms, embracing them with hunger.

Tears sprang to Amelia's eyes as more curious fingers explored her body, running over the silky skin of her arms and throat, loosening the tangles in her golden hair and spreading it out in a shimmering curtain that fell below her waist. She listened to the women chattering amongst themselves, understanding their dialect because it was so similar to the speech of the ayah who had cared for her as a child.

"Look at her skin – it's soft and juicy as a mango. Would it taste as sweet if I tried to bite it . . . ?"

A hand insinuated itself between the buttons of Amelia's torn camisole and fingers pinched her breast, making her squeal in protest. She wriggled and tried to pull away, but other hands were exploring her more intimately still – girlish fingers pulling up her skirts, discovering the bare secret of her sex through the split crotch of her linen drawers.

"She is bare and wet!"

"She is ready for sex. Let us enjoy her now. Please, Mistress, we have been so long without fresh slaves . . ."

Nails raked the skin of her breast and she gasped with the exhilaration of sudden discomfort, astonishingly pleasurable through the sense-dulling mist of her exhaustion and fear. Another hand, stronger than the first, pried the fingers away, and she saw that the chief of the raiding party had intervened.

"No – you must not mark her. She is not for us. She is for Khara."

Little murmurs of disappointment filled the air.

"But why? We have waited so long. Our breasts ache for love, our cunts are so empty . . ."

The outlaw chief spoke again, her sonorous voice full of authority.

"She is a virgin."

The murmurs were instantly silenced, and the women drew away, as though in awe. Amelia stood stock-still, afraid to move or speak, terrified that if she did anything that offended the tribes-women she would instantly be killed.

"She is a virgin, and therefore must be given as a gift to Khara. Come, slave."

A jerk on the rope that bound her hands together forced Amelia to move forward, half walking, half dragged across the stony ground which cut cruelly into her bare feet. She was being led toward one of the tents, by far the most magnificent, which stood in the center of the camp. It was made of dozens of multi-colored blankets and tapestries, slung Bedouin-style over ropes and sticks which formed a large, boxy framework with an overhanging canopy.

Beneath the canopy sat a naked woman in an attitude of meditation, with her legs in the lotus position and a wickedly sharp dagger lying on the ground before her. Her outspread thighs displayed the shameless secret of her sex: the plump love-lips that seemed to pout in a kiss of welcome; the glistening pink heart running with secret dew.

Despite her fear, Amelia looked at the girl with interest. She seemed very young, yet utterly self-possessed. Her neck was stretched into a slender column by dozens of solid gold rings, her arms and ankles encircled by many jeweled bracelets, her nose pierced by a jeweled chain which ran to a headdress of gold and rubies. Her eyes closed and her hands outstretched, she seemed oblivious to the world around her, but as they approached she spoke, her voice as unearthly and distant as an automaton's.

"Who approaches?"

"Makhani and a slave girl."

"What do you desire?"

"To make humble supplication to our queen."

"You may pass."

The outlaw chief Makhani jerked on the rope again and Amelia stumbled forward into the interior of the tent, blinking as her eyes gradually grew accustomed to the half-light.

There, on a bed of silken cushions, sat a beautiful woman dressed in the garb of a man, her full-breasted yet slender form attired in the rich, close-fitting finery of a maharajah. Her slim hips were encased in tight silver breeches which hugged the curves of her small, taut ass-cheeks. Her large breasts strained for release from the blue silk tunic, their size emphasized by the broad cummerbund wrapped tightly about her tiny waist.

Instead of the turban, she wore a plain gold toque on her long black hair, which was drawn back into a tight plait braided with multi-colored silks. On either side of her stood naked girls, their firm young breasts slick with sweat as they cooled their queen with long-handled fans fashioned from gilded wood and peacock feathers.

"What gift have you brought to amuse me this time, Makhani?" Her voice was sweeter than Amelia had expected, yet it held a note of steel.

Makhani knelt before her queen and pulled on the rope so violently that Amelia was forced to follow suit, tumbling to her knees on the carpeted floor of the tent.

"I have brought you a new slave, your Highness," replied Makhani. "We captured her in the hills near the town of Jainapur."

"She is a fine enough English bitch," observed Khara coolly. "But I have many fine bitches to relieve my boredom."

"She is a virgin, Your Highness. Tight as a child, hot as a tigress. I wager she will give you pleasure."

"A virgin! How quaint. And the girl must be all of eighteen, nineteen years old! How jealously the English guard the useless trinket of their virginity."

Khara got to her feet and Amelia noticed that she was wearing brocade slippers with curled toes. She looked like a picture from the *Arabian Nights* book Amelia had been given for her tenth birthday.

"You have verified her virginity?"

"Not personally, Your Highness. The girl tells me that she is a virgin and from her fear I judge that she speaks the truth."

Khara laughed.

"These English fillies are full of willfulness and deception. I shall examine the girl myself."

"No!" Amelia tried to scramble to her feet but Makhani caught her, winding the rope from her wrists around her throat, so tightly that she could scarcely breathe.

"Silence, slave!"

"I am not your slave," gasped Amelia. "I am . . ."

"Slave!" Makhani struck her with the side of her hand and she fell to the ground, fat teardrops trickling down her cheeks, all her spirit spent. "Do you dare defy your queen?"

"She is indeed a willful and spirited filly," observed Khara, with a degree of satisfaction. "Breaking that spirit might perhaps prove an agreeable diversion."

"Shall I prepare her for your examination?" Makhani looked up adoringly into her queen's face. It had been many moons since she had last been honored to share Khara's bed, longer still since Khara had allowed her the joy of tonguing her beautiful hard clitoris. She burned with longing, praying that her gift would find favor in Khara's eyes.

"Strip her and make her lie down on the bed," Khara instructed her. "And light more lamps. I want to see every inch of this proud little filly's body. She must be taught that she can hide nothing from our eyes."

Amelia struggled in Makhani's arms, finding resources of strength she had thought long since lost on her grueling journey. She bit and spat like a she-cat as Makhani wrestled to remove her clothes. Khara watched and laughed, evidently delighted by this battle of wills.

"Restrain her." Khara clapped her hands and the two naked fan-bearers glided to her side. "I hunger to see the girl naked."

With three pairs of hands holding her, Amelia gave up her struggle. It was futile. Everything was hopeless. She had been carried off into a life of slavery and not a soul in the world knew where she was – not even Dorothea Strong, who had led her to this terrible fate.

Makhani unfastened Amelia's belt and drew it off, running the plaited silk with satisfaction over the palm of her hand. It would make a fine instrument of discipline to redden this filly's white skin and teach her the meaning of obedience. Then she turned her attention to the dress – the yellow muslin soiled and torn now from the long days journeying through the mountains. The single button holding the waistband yielded easily, and the remnants of the dress fell in a sighing whisper to the ground.

The petticoats proved a more difficult problem. Stiff with starch, their drawstrings were tightly knotted and impossible to untie. Not in the least daunted, Makhani took the knife from her belt and slit the crisp cotton from waist to hem, tearing it away to expose the knee-length bloomers beneath.

Amelia could scarcely believe that this was happening to her. It was all like some dreadful, surreal dream. And the worst of it was that something deep inside her – something shameful that no one should ever admit to – was pleased to be a slave, happy to become the victim of these women's lust. Even Makhani's ungentle touch awoke sensations of pleasure in her yearning flesh, so long deprived of the means of its own satisfaction.

"Such inexplicable garments these English girls wear," commented Khara, circling Amelia so that she could observe her from different angles. "They primp and preen themselves with dresses and jewels, but underneath they are wearing these . . . these abominations." She plucked at the coarse linen of Amelia's camisole. "It is almost as though they are ashamed of their bodies, afraid of the pleasure that they can give."

"It is rumored that the English take no pleasure from the sports of the flesh, Your Highness," replied Makhani. "They are cold-blooded, as sexless as eunuchs."

Khara tweaked the fabric of Amelia's drawers and the vent bulged open, exposing the golden curls at her crotch.

"Is that so? And yet, for all their pretended modesty, they expose themselves with such vulgarity," mused Khara, running the tip of her silver ferrule down over Amelia's belly and pushing it up against the soft wet flesh of her bare sex. Amelia moaned and instinctively pushed down against the cold silver-tipped cane; when Khara slid it out from between her thighs, it was wet with her juices. She breathed in Amelia's scent and licked a drop of juice from the silver tip. "Terrible garments. Remove them."

Makhani obeyed, first unbuttoning the camisole and sliding it off over Amelia's shoulders, then slitting the drawstring of her bloomers and pulling them down over her rounded hips.

"Step out of them," snapped Makhani. When Amelia hesitated for just one moment, she felt the cold hardness of Khara's ferrule slicing down onto her exposed buttocks. "Now."

Completely naked now, she shivered, suddenly cold in the chilly mountain air. Khara stood behind her, her strong hands toying with the matted veil of her golden hair.

"A charming enough gift," she conceded, "though a little travel-worn. Make her lie down on the bed. I wish to examine her more closely."

Amelia made no attempt to resist as hands seized her by the arms and made her lie down on the wide, soft-cushioned couch which served as Khara's bed. Indeed, after so many long days and nights in the mountains, she yearned for the softness of a bed, for the gentleness of sleep.

But sleep could not have been further from Khara's mind as she stood over her helpless victim. She began by examining Amelia minutely from head to toe, stroking and pinching her skin, forcing open her mouth to examine the regularity and whiteness of her teeth.

"Hmm. She has a good form, though it is not yet fully developed. Her breasts are a little small for my taste, but the nipples erect quite adorably to the touch." She pinched and squeezed them with such skillful cruelty that Amelia felt a trickle of juice well up from the deepest heart of her, emerging from her swollen love-lips to stain the ruby-red bed-covering beneath her. Even this indignity did not escape Khara's attention.

"Ah, I see the slave has a certain aptitude. I can smell her hunger. That is good." Khara returned to her examination. "The umbilicus is deeply sunken, and that also is an auspicious sign. How pretty it would be if pierced for a ruby or an emerald . . ."

She pressed the tip of her long-nailed finger into Amelia's navel, and the English girl gave a yelp of surprised pleasure. She had never imagined that such a touch could be so discomfiting and yet so sensual. To her profound shame, she felt her clitoris swell with blood between her pouting love-lips, its engorged stalk the certain betrayer of her carnal lust.

Khara's hands moved slowly over the surface of Amelia's taut belly, tracing the slight downward curve from navel to groin, then the plump swell of her mount of Venus, garnished with a tangle of bright gold curls.

"Her maidenhair is of a pleasing silkiness; the sex-lips are full and plump, and the inner lips protrude slightly . . . that is a sure sign of a well-developed sexual sense. Ah . . ." She pulled apart Amelia's outer cunny-lips and peered inside. "I see that the fruit of her sex is juicy and a fine, deep pink. And see, Makhani – her love-bud is round and glossy as a fine freshwater pearl."

Her fingers were cool, the nails long and sharp as knife-blades, and Amelia held her breath in fear and excitement as Khara ran the very tip of her index finger along the deep, wet groove of her sex. It was the sweetest torment, and Amelia let out a long sigh of pleasure as the hood of her clitoris slipped over the hard, round head. Syrupy sex juice was welling up inside her, oozing and dripping from between her gaping cunt-lips at each new and skillful caress.

"Good. Very good." Khara's voice became a low purr of satisfaction as she scooped up a little of the sex fluid and smeared it over the head of Amelia's clitty. "The English filly has a natural instinct for the ways of pleasure." She rubbed a little harder, and Amelia gave a cry of despair. Her body was no longer her own, each nerve-ending crying out for the bliss she had felt that morning – it seemed so long ago now – when Mary Bates had teased her to her first orgasm. "So much so that I begin to doubt her purity."

Amelia sobbed her distress and her shameful longing as Khara's finger left her clitoris and traced a slow, lingering path toward the entrance to her vagina.

"No . . . please, don't touch me there." Her cunt muscles clenched instinctively as Khara's fingertip pressed a little way in to her sex. "You'll hurt me . . ."

Khara laughed.

"There are worse things than the pain of love, slave," she replied, good-humoredly. "In time you will come to understand that pain is an inextricable part of that love."

The index finger of her other hand rubbed hard on Amelia's clitoris, and the girl writhed in a torment of guilty lust, her hips bucking as though trying to take this new lover deep inside her. She could not break free; Makhani and the two naked girls were holding her down, pinning her shoulders to the bed so that she could only look up at the gently moving canopy of blankets that formed the roof of the tent. She could no longer see Khara, only feel her as her cunt grew wetter and more welcoming and her crisis approached.

As Amelia's cunt muscles relaxed, Khara slid her finger smoothly into the wet tunnel of her sex, so tight that even her slender finger seemed to stretch its walls. With a wicked delight, she jabbed her sharp fingernail a little further in, and was rewarded with a sharp cry of pain.

"Please . . . please! That hurts!"

"Well, well." With as much brutality as it had entered, Khara's finger slid out of Amelia's cunt. Khara licked it clean with a reflective enjoyment.

"She is a virgin, Your Highness?"

"She is indeed a virgin, Makhani. Tight as a bird. So, so deliciously tight, and with a hymen as thick and as tough as glove leather."

"You intend to keep her and deflower her yourself, Your Highness?" Makhani amused herself by taking Amelia's nipples between finger and thumb and pinching them long and hard.

"It is a tempting thought, Makhani, but no. I have other plans for this delicious English slut." Khara looked down at the bed, where Amelia's body was still writhing in the spasms of frustrated lust, her thighs spread wide and the pink oyster of her sex running with honey-sweet juice. "I shall sell her to the merchant, Indhira. With her golden hair and her beautifully tight cunt, she will fetch an excellent price."

"Indhira, Your Highness? But she takes only those who are fit for training. She will take no virgins . . ."

"Very true, my dear Makhani." Khara's eyes gleamed as brightly as the gold toque on her glossy hair. "And so she must be relieved of her troublesome virginity, and initiated into the first stages of her training. When the merchandise is presented to Indhira, we must be able to show her that the filly has an aptitude for the sensual arts.

"Tonight, Makhani, when we have celebrated your return with food and wine, you and five of your sisters shall deflower the girl. I shall observe. I am sure that it will make an excellent and stimulating spectacle."

The moon rose slowly over the mountains, its fat white disc gazing down blankly from a sky of blackest velvet, sprinkled with stars. It was a beautiful night, filled with moonlight and the scent of flowers, but Amelia scarcely noticed its beauty. The sweet, thick wine she had been given to drink had made her brain muddled, and yet she felt curiously alert, as though all power of rational thought had been taken away from her, leaving only the hypersensitivity of touch, of taste, of smell.

Her whole body felt alive to the wealth of sensations around it. As she moved across the stony ground, her white silk robe brushed lightly over the buds of her breasts, already erect, already filled with the need to be sucked, licked, stroked, bitten. It felt as though a million eager tongues were running over her flesh, a million soft and skillful fingers stroking her wherever the silken fabric flowed and touched.

She heard Khara's voice, but it seemed a long way away.

"Bring her into the circle. Into the very center, where I can see her."

She felt hands closing again about her arms, and she moved forward obediently, forced to trust the hands because she could see nothing but a host of dancing, dreamlike images, images of things that she had never even imagined before and could scarcely believe were real.

There were naked women with painted breasts, and others moving about them in a slow and sinuous dance, their bodies heavy with jewelled chains that hung from pierced nipples and cunt-lips. Colored and scented smoke rose from incense burners placed all around the margin of the wide circle, and between them burned flickering fires in copper braziers, orange and yellow flames rising up from the white-hot coals.

For a moment, Amelia quite forgot where she was, losing all sense of time and space as her eyes fought to focus on the chimerical dancing pictures – figures that moved so close she thought she could touch them, but when she reached out they were gone.

A nagging ache of memory kept drifting back in waves, like waves of sadness – yearningly real for a few moments, and then gone. She was Amelia Courtnay, a proud English girl who had been stolen away by brigands – savage, ruthless women who intended to sate their lust on her defenseless body. She must find some way to resist . . .

But it was futile. The thought lingered only a moment, and then it was gone, so far away that she could scarcely glimpse it any more, just one more dancing figure in the circle of leaping flames.

"She has been prepared?"

"As you instructed, Your Highness. Her body hair has been shaved and she has been massaged with sweet oils."

"Then the ceremony may begin."

Khara clapped her hands, and at once a sweet, strange music filled the air. Amelia did not recognize the instruments, but the woody, rippling sound of pipes mingled with the clamor of strings, bowed and plucked. In the darkness beyond the circle of fire, a woman began to sing as the drummer's supple hands set the beat.

The rhythm was elemental and compelling, the woman's voice low and sensual, rising from time to time to a passionate crescendo that echoed the need in Amelia's aching body. The massage which the two naked girls had given her had left her warm and hungry, her breasts tingling and the tight amber rose of her asshole twitching and stinging where the scented oil had been rubbed into it.

She felt strangely naked beneath the white silk robe; almost childlike now that the hair of her cunt and axillae had been shaved away, leaving her helpless and pure. The shame had faded away as the sweet wine had done its work, the mulled spices kindling a low heat in her belly whilst the alcohol annihilated all her inhibitions. As the music swooped and soared around her, she let her instincts lead her into the dance.

Slowly she began to move, her body swaying in time to the chant, her feet shifting on the bare earth as the drumbeat called her to her destiny.

"Take off your robe, Amelia. Show your nakedness to me."

Automatically, with no pause for thought, Amelia took hold of the white silk robe and pulled it over her head. The night air was chill in the mountains, but she did not notice it. A furnace of desire was burning inside her, far brighter and far hotter than the leaping flames of the fires around her. She wanted to be naked, wanted to exorcise the terrible need within her.

"Now touch yourself, Amelia. I want to see how you give yourself pleasure."

Khara's voice seemed like another theme in the symphony of sound around her, and it seemed the most natural thing in the world to obey it. Yet how could she tell her mistress that she did not know how to give herself pleasure, that until Mary had kissed her and caressed her, her lewdest touch had been to stroke her nipples gently, in the dark seclusion of the dormitory?

"Put your hands on your breasts and touch yourself, Amelia."

She let her hands wander to the small, firm mounds of her breasts. It felt as though she was touching them for the first time, discovering them as a lover would. She had become her own lover, her fingers innocent yet knowing as they roamed over the bare flesh. Beneath her palms, the pink cones of her nipples were puckered and fiercely erect, so hard that it seemed impossible that they could be part of the same, soft flesh that made up the body of her breasts. They seemed alien in their hardness – not soft, like flesh, but tough like rubber or wood, love-buttons that could be touched to turn on her desire.

Inspiration guided her fingers and she moved the palms of her hands in a sweeping, circular motion over her breasts, so that the nipples ground gently against them. The effect was electric, sending lingering aftershocks of pleasure right through her body from breast to cunt, from her nipples to the exposed pink triangle of her pubis.

"Very good, Amelia. But I want to see more. I want to see what else you can do."

Amelia drew her fingers up so that they were like pincers and fastened them on the twin buds of her nipples. At first she touched them only gently, her supersensitive body hardly able to bear even such a light caress, but as her flesh grew more accustomed to the touch her hunger burned more fiercely, and her body grew greedy for more piquant sensations.

She pinched and rolled the breast flesh with an almost brutal intensity, discovering with a child's delight how wonderful it could be to take herself to the narrow margin between pleasure and pain. The slight discomfort of the stinging, burning sensation seemed to intensify her sensual hunger, and as she pinched a little harder she felt an answering wetness grow between her thighs.

In her innocence, she had never caressed herself between her legs, never stroked herself to orgasm. Only Mary had ever taken her there – poor, sweet Mary, so many miles away in another world, or so it seemed now. Instinctively she pressed her thighs together more tightly and was rewarded with a burst of the most exquisite sensation. She rubbed her thighs together, and discovered that this stimulated the sensual hot spot between her cunt-lips to a burning frenzy of pleasure. If she kept on doing it, would she reach the same peak of ecstasy that she had enjoyed on that one ecstatic morning in Jainapur?

"You feel pleasure, Amelia; that is good." Khara's syrupy voice penetrated Amelia's brain and, like a child rewarded for good behavior, she felt the pleasing warmth of satisfaction. "But I want to see more. I want to see you touch yourself, Amelia. Open up your legs and touch yourself for me."

Amelia slid her feet a little farther apart on the soft earth and felt instantly bereft. All the wonderful warmth in her clitty seemed to ebb away, leaving only the terrible yearning for release. She felt so ignorant, so angry to have been kept so long in innocence. What must she do to please her new mistress – and to assuage the unbearable longing within her belly?

Keeping the fingers of her left hand on her nipple, she slipped her right hand over her smooth, shaven pubis and down between her thighs. She was amazed at the hot wetness she felt when she touched herself there, between the twin lobes of her plump pussy-lips. They seemed so swollen, so fat with juice that she scarcely recognized the feel of them.

What was this, this long, hard stalk that pushed against her hand and sent electric shocks through her body whenever she touched it? Could it really be the pert little clitty she had sometimes touched when she was washing herself? She had never known it could be so huge and hard. She pressed on it and the touch was almost painful in its intensity. It was too dry, too sensitive, its little pink hood forced right back so that the whole shaft of her clitoris was exposed.

She must be gentle, answer the cravings of her body with the lightest, the softest of caresses. She pushed her finger into the tight, wet tunnel of her sex and loaded it with the clear, slippery pre-come, then smeared it over the head of her clitty as Khara had done. The sensation was blissful, and somewhere, very far away, she heard her own voice moaning softly in harmony with the music.

"She is a born slut," observed Khara, drinking from a silver goblet as she watched Amelia stroking her own clitty. The girl seemed in a world of her own, lost to reality as she focused on the intensity of her need, her quest for the ultimate pleasure that still eluded her clumsy fingers. "Innocent, of course, but then that is to be desired in one who is to be trained as a slave. She will learn quickly, and, since she knows nothing, there are no bad habits for her new mistress to break."

Amelia trembled at the new, unknown pleasure of her fingers on her clitty, learning by touch the pathway to purest delight. Even now she could feel the sensations building inside her, the mounting excitement as the heat spread from her breasts and clitty to fill her whole body. It was as though her entire being was caught in time, waiting, breathless, for the moment of release. A few more strokes, a few more sweet caresses on her pleasure-bud and she would be there. She could feel the ecstasy almost upon her, feel the muscles of belly and ass and cunt beginning to tense in the seconds before the spasm overtook her.

She screamed out her pleasure as her cunt blossomed into orgasm, releasing a flood of fragrant nectar which dripped like honey from her nether-lips, anointing the barren earth on which she stood. All control had left her, all consciousness save the consciousness of overwhelming pleasure.

It was too much, the pleasure too powerful for her to bear; Amelia sank to the ground in a swoon, her body white and quivering in the dancing firelight.

"Excellent, excellent." Khara clapped her hands in delight. "I had not expected her to be such an apt pupil. I feel sure that her defloration will make an entertaining spectacle." She parted the folds of her robe to reveal her bare, shaven cunt, the left lobe of her outer sex-lips pierced by a silver ring set with emeralds. "Bring me the instrument of her initiation."

A serving girl, naked except for a filmy veil that obscured the lower half of her face, approached and knelt before the queen, holding out a cushion of dark blue velvet. On it lay a dildo of yellowed ivory, about seven inches long and its surface carved with lascivious scenes from the Hindu holy books: women kissing and stroking each other's breasts, massaging each other with sweet oils, masturbating with long, smooth sticks that distended their vulvas.

Khara picked up the dildo and kissed it – once on the shaft, once on the tip.

"It is yet fragrant with the spendings of our last slave," she observed with a nostalgic pleasure. It had been most agreeable, initiating the last girl. Although only a simple peasant from a village in the hills, she had proved both apt and willing. But her cunt had been a little large, and Khara felt sure that Amelia Courtnay would prove a still more interesting pupil.

She slid the dildo over her belly and placed its head at the entrance to her shaven vulva. Then, with a single thrust, she forced it inside her cunt, so deep that its entire length vanished between her love-lips, and she gave a sigh of satisfaction. As the outlaws' queen, she had many lovers – as many pretty virgins and knowing sluts as any woman could wish for – but none had the power to pleasure her as beautifully as she pleasured herself.

The dildo slid, glistening, out of her cunt, and in the next second disappeared inside her once more, forced in by a second powerful thrust.

"You may masturbate me, Makhani," said Khara, her eyes closed as she slid the dildo into her cunt and held it there with tightly clenched cunt muscles. "Place your lips upon my rosebud and bring me swiftly to orgasm."

Makhani knelt before her queen and opened her lips, putting out the tip of her tongue and wriggling it into the deep pink furrow between Khara's thighs. She lapped like a she-cat, teasing and tormenting the little pink stalk with her lips and teeth whilst her tongue flicked repeatedly across its head. Khara sat with eyes closed, her face betraying no trace of her excitement, but her breathing quickening as her cunt walls gripped the carved dildo, sucking it into her as though it alone could give her the release she craved.

She came with the merest sigh of contentment, the walls of her cunt rippling with wave after wave of pleasure, and the dildo slid slowly out of her onto the ground, its carved surface wet with her sex juice.

"Take it, Makhani. The honor shall first be yours this night." Khara smiled as she handed the dildo to Makhani, laying it across her hands as though it were some precious, sacred object. "The girl is prepared. I wish to see you enjoy her."

Amelia, waking from her swoon, felt strong arms holding her down, pulling apart her thighs, making her draw up her knees so that her sex was shamelessly displayed between her outspread legs, a coral pink sea-shell at the base of her creamy belly.

"Hold her still," commanded Makhani. Amelia tried to focus on the woman's face, but it blurred and merged into dream images in her head, images of painted dancing girls, whirling and laughing, their hands touching and caressing each other's bodies as the music bubbled and swirled to a climax.

Her body ached. She longed for a release from this torment of frustration, this burning, itching ache that racked her whole body and made her clitoris throb to the pulse of her insatiable desire. Hands touched her, some holding her down, others stroking and pinching her breasts and belly, producing little starbursts of pain that served only to intensify her longing.

"Please, please, please . . ." she heard herself gasp. What was she pleading for? She no longer knew – only that she wanted the touching to go on, to become deeper, stronger, more extreme.

The pointed tip of the dildo nudged between her love-lips, seeking out the white-hot heart of her desire. At the first touch,

Amelia arched her back and let out a shuddering gasp, the surrogate dick of carved ivory teasing and stretching the tight entrance to her hole.

"No!" The first twinge of pain brought with it some distant remembrance of fear. This could not be. There was not room, she was too small . . .

"Your Highness, she is very tight," observed one of the serving girls. "The initiation may pain her."

"In all pleasure there should be an element of pain," replied Khara with a shrug of serene indifference. "In time, the pain will heighten her pleasure. Proceed."

Makhani pushed the dildo into Amelia's wet haven, but she moaned and twisted, trying to escape its inexorable advance. Her cunt was so tight that it felt as though she would split in two.

"Harder," commanded Khara, a note of excitement entering her voice. "Do not let her fight you. Push it deep inside her."

As the tip of the dildo met the unyielding membrane of Amelia's hymen, she gave a little sob of discomfort. But she no longer struggled. There was a terrible inevitability about the pain, the fear. And her whole body throbbed with the desire she was ashamed to admit, the desire she could no longer conceal, for the juices were running freely from her cunt, anointing both the dildo and Makhani's relentless hand.

"Now!" Khara's voice summoned up the moment of her immolation, and – pressing on Amelia's love-bud with a skillful finger – Makhani gave the dildo a violent thrust. Amelia's back arched and she gave a shuddering cry as the dildo tore through her hymen, possessing her, releasing her at last from the prison of her virginity into womanhood in a shattering, breathtaking orgasm.

As one of the serving girls lapped at the scarlet pool of Amelia's virgin blood, soothing her hurts with the soft wet tip of her tongue, Khara sat back and smiled to Makhani.

"Such an apt pupil," she sighed. "She is sure to fetch an excellent price – now that she has been relieved of her virginity – for no virgin may ever enter the Temple of the Rosebud Sutra."

CROSSING THE RUBICON

Brian Levy

ON WEDNESDAY NOVEMBER 7th 1895 a joyous crowd of boys cheered the Albion Academy First Eleven to the echo after they had beaten Beddinghurst College by three goals to two. The school magazine will carry a full report on the game, so I will merely record that in the final minute of a hard-fought match, with the score standing at two goals each, we were awarded a free kick. My best pal Rodney Burbeck chipped the ball forward into our opponents' penalty area and I headed into the net to give us our first victory over our deadly rivals since 1889.

When the referee's whistle blew for full time I was carried shoulder-high off the field by a group of cheering spectators. Mr Hare, our sportsmaster, was waiting in the pavilion with a beaming smile on his face, and he showered us all with praise for our sterling performance. However, he came across and peered at my left leg when I peeled off my stockings. Late in the game I had taken a nasty kick on the shin, during a mêlée in front of our goal, and Mr Hare said, "Hmm, that looks pretty ugly, Dashwood. I want you to have a quick shower and then report to Mrs Dickerson. I think it would be wise for her to have a look at that gash."

Now, whilst this instruction meant I would probably miss the start of the slap-up victory tea, I was happy enough to obey his order, even though I would probably have to endure the pain of an iodine bandage being slapped against my leg. However, this should not be taken to be an early manifestation of any masochistic tendencies! Mrs Elizabeth Dickerson, the matron of Albion Academy, was a strikingly attractive young woman in her late twenties. Not only was she good-looking, but her cheerful nature made her a firm favourite with all the boys.

A distant relative of the headmaster, Dr Muttley, she had been cruelly widowed after only eighteen months of marriage when her husband was killed in the terrible train crash at Clapham Junction five years ago.

My interest in Lizzie Dickerson had been further heightened the previous term when a wild rumour spread round the school about goings-on in the sanatorium. A friend assured me that those chaps confined to bed with coughs and sneezes had their cocks tickled by Mrs Dickerson as a reward for good behaviour. Frankly, I discounted this tale as a mere flight of fancy, but, as the poet says, hope springs eternal in the human breast.

How wonderful it would be if there were some glimmer of truth in this incredible tale, I said to myself, which made my prick start to thicken as I hobbled along to her room.

I hastily adjusted my shorts, to hide the bulge between my legs, before knocking on her door. There was no reply, and so I knocked a second time, again to no avail. It occurred to me that she might be tending a patient, so I made my way painfully up the staircase to the sick bay. When I reached the top I heard the sound of muffled laughter coming from one of the bedrooms, and to my astonishment I heard a feminine voice squeal, "Nigel! You naughty boy, you'll get us both into the most awful trouble with Dr Muttley if you carry on like this!"

"Oh, the devil take Dr Muttley!" came the response, which I immediately recognized as coming from none other than Simon Byrne, the captain of the school. "It would be worth being gated for the rest of term so long as we're not interrupted for the next hour – and that shouldn't happen because I've bolted the door."

My heart began to pound as I leaned back against the wall. I could hardly wait to confirm for myself whether all the rumours about Mrs Dickerson were true! For the first time in my life I bent down to peer through a keyhole, and only with great difficulty was I able to stifle a loud gasp of astonishment.

On the bed I could see Mrs Dickerson in an amatory embrace with Simon Byrne. Their mouths were locked together and his hands were roaming freely over her generous curves whilst he wriggled out of his clothes. Mrs Dickerson followed suit, and I was soon rewarded by the sight of her creamy bare breasts crowned with nut-brown nipples, which Simon kissed before he slid off the bed to pull off his vest and drawers. With a pang of envy I noted the size of his colossal cock, which rose up from the matted triangular bush at the base of his belly. It was even bigger than that of "Donkey Dick" Bowden, whose prodigious tool was by far the largest in the Lower Sixth.

Now Mrs Dickerson rolled down her knickers and rewarded me with my first sight of a hairy pussy. She stretched out her hand to clutch hold of Simon's thick shaft, which stood up high in the air with the top of its uncapped helmet touching his navel. "Mmm, that looks nice," she said, sliding her clenched fist up and down Simon's throbbing tool. She smacked her lips and continued to fist his blue-veined truncheon as she slipped down from the bed and dropped to her knees in front of him.

From the theoretical knowledge I had gleaned from the well-thumbed pages of *The Oyster*,* I correctly guessed what she had in mind. My own cock swelled up to an aching stiffness whilst I watched her lips close over the wide dome of Simon's uncapped knob. With a groan, I ripped open my flies and pulled out my prick, sliding my hand up and down its throbbing length.

However, the naked nurse only sucked his shaft for a short while before rising to her feet. She jumped back on the bed on her belly, sticking her superbly rounded bum-cheeks high in the air. At first this puzzled me, but then I remembered the French postcard which one of my form-mates had surreptitiously passed around the dormitory at the start of the term, and I realized that I was about to witness a bout of "doggie-style" fucking.

Sure enough, Simon pulled her up until she knelt on all fours

* One of the most explicit underground magazines of the late Victorian era.

and, brandishing his huge tool in his hand, he mounted her from behind.

"Here we go!" he panted as he manoeuvred his cock into the cleft between the jiggling spheres of Mrs Dickerson's backside, and she squealed with delight as his balls slapped against the backs of her thighs.

It was so exciting to see that I could not stop myself from cumming, and a fountain of sticky spunk jetted out of my cock and splashed against the door. I hastily wiped the jism off my fingers with a handkerchief and stuffed my cock back into my trousers as I bent down again for a second look through the keyhole.

However, I had time only to catch a brief glimpse of Simon Byrne's shaft pistoning a passage through the crevice between Mrs Dickerson's bum cheeks when I felt a tap on my shoulder . . .

To say that I was greatly startled would be an understatement! It would be more truthful to record that I was frightened out of my wits! A loud cry escaped from my throat as I spun round to see whether I would have to face the wrath of one of the masters or prefects. But, thank heaven, the hand on my shoulder belonged to my chum Radleigh Trenton-Moss.

"Henry, how are you feeling, old sport?" he enquired. "Bunny Hare sent me up here because he wanted to know whether you would be coming down for tea." He suddenly realized that my flies were open and said, "Hey, what's up, old boy? Have you been –?"

"Yes, yes, and I'll tell you all about it later," I interrupted, pushing him roughly towards the stairs, for there was no way that the writhing couple in the bedroom could not have heard me cry out. Whilst neither of them could afford to have their liaison made public, I had no wish to risk the wrath of the captain of the school, who had the power to make life very unpleasant for me.

Alas, as I hobbled across the landing the door flew open and Byrne, clad in a white flannel dressing gown, roared angrily at us, "Come back here at once, you two scallywags!"

I would probably have ignored him and legged it down the stairs, daring the captain of the school to chase us in his bare feet. But Radleigh had no reason to disobey and, not wishing to be swished for disobedience, stopped in his tracks and turned back to find out what all the fuss was about. This left me no choice but to follow him, for I could hardly let my innocent pal face the music alone.

Simon Byrne was waiting for us with a look of cold fury in his eyes. "How long have you two cads been skulking outside this door?" he demanded angrily. But before either of us could answer, a rather dishevelled Mrs Dickerson appeared at his side, dressed in a blue silk robe.

"Stop shouting, dear, it would be very foolish to make a scene," she said, and then whispered something in his ear. Simon listened intently, and with a grunt he turned smartly on his heel and marched back into the bedroom, shutting the door firmly behind him. Mrs Dickerson turned to us and gave Radleigh and myself a sweet smile as she added, "Boys, please stand here quietly for a few moments. Don't go away, now; I won't keep you waiting for very long."

She went back inside the bedroom and the bewildered Radleigh scratched his head and asked me what the blue blazes was happening here. I jabbed him in the ribs with my elbow and chuckled. "Use your loaf, Radders. Mrs Dickerson wasn't just giving Simon Byrne a lesson in first aid."

Only a minute or so later the grim-faced but fully-clothed captain of the school stormed out of the bedroom and swept by us without a word. He was followed by Mrs Dickerson, who invited us inside, and we stood somewhat awkwardly in front of her as she sat down on the bed. She looked up at us and said softly, "You are both entitled to an explanation as to what has been taking place this afternoon. To come straight to the point, I decided some months ago that it was my bounden duty to provide sexual education for sixth formers. Far too many boys leave this school with little knowledge of sexual matters. In addition they suffer from the belief instilled in them that there is something sinful in the very act upon which the preservation of our series depends. My late husband's enjoyment of the marital bed was severely curtailed by this unnecessary burden of guilt about the delights afforded by *l'art de faire l'amour*.

"At sixteen years of age I believe you are both old enough to appreciate the need for sexual education. In doing so I am throwing myself on your mercy, because it is certain that Dr Muttley would dismiss me if he ever found out about my private classes in human biology."

I could scarcely believe my ears, but fortunately I still had enough of my wits about me to blurt out that I would keep secret everything I had heard and seen that afternoon. "You have my word of honour on this matter," I promised, and Radleigh nodded his head in agreement.

"You also have mine, Mrs Dickerson," he added, and she smiled at us. "Thank you both very much. But do call me Lizzie, Mrs Dickerson sounds so formal. Now, do I take it that you two would like to enrol in my private biology class?"

"Yes, please," we chorused, and she let out a knowing little chuckle and said, "Good! I was pretty sure that you would both be game. Well, there's no time like the present, so let's begin. Take off your clothes, gentlemen, I need to know what state of physical development you have reached."

Now this was the first time either of us had exposed our love truncheons to female eyes. Alone, we would probably have been too bashful to obey her instruction. But, as in any difficult situation, the presence of a close friend gives one extra courage, and we both quickly stripped off. Nevertheless, we both automatically turned round as we tugged down our drawers, and covered our cocks with our hands when we turned back to face her.

Cleverly, Lizzie did not smile at our self-consciousness. Instead she said reassuringly, "Henry, Radleigh, there's no need to be shy. I've seen more than a few pricks in my time, and I can tell you that girls enjoy the sight of a sturdy shaft just as you enjoy gazing at pictures of bosoms and pussies. Let me see what you are hiding, and if I judge that you're ready to proceed further, you're both in for a real treat."

I exchanged a glance with Radleigh and, following my lead, he removed his hands and let them dangle by his sides.

"Oh, yes, you're both good and ready," murmured Lizzie as she loosened the belt of her robe and gracefully stepped out of the garment to stand naked except for a pair of tight white knickers in front of us. Our cocks shot up as for the first time – or in my case the second, if one counts what I had just seen through the keyhole – we looked at a girl's bare breasts. And what beautiful breasts they were too, creamy white, firmly rounded and topped with circled pink areolae and large strawberry-red nipples.

Lizzie looked approvingly at our erect throbbing tools and commented, "My word, you both sport very nice cocks, and it's a great shame that you have been forced to waste all that jism just playing with yourselves. I think it high time you enjoyed the experience about which I'm sure you have fantasized whilst tossing yourselves off.

"Henry, you were first off the mark to show me your cock, so how would you like to be first to cross the Rubicon?" she asked as she tantalizingly rolled down her knickers to reveal a hairy bush of curls between her legs.

My eyes widened as they eagerly followed the path of Lizzie's long fingers as they traced a sensual line between her pouting pussy-lips. "Sit down on the bed with me," she said throatily as she grasped hold of my rigid rod and pulled me towards her. We snuggled up together and she kissed me lightly on the cheek as she placed my hand on her right breast. I stroked the rubbery nipple, which instantly hardened under my touch.

"Haaagh!" I cried out as Lizzie pushed me back upon the soft mattress, guiding my fingers to the entrance of her love funnel and my head to her soft bosoms. I needed no further direction and started to lick her erect titties. This was my first experience of making physical contact with the forbidden areas of a girl's body, and the feel of Lizzie's pert nipple in my mouth and the stimulating suction of her love channel on my forefinger made me dizzy with excitement.

She realized that a creamy flood of spunk was already building up in my balls, for she pulled me over her and muttered, "The moment of truth has arrived, Henry. Slide your cock inside my cunt and fuck me."

I was only too eager to obey, but in my haste I could not find the entrance to Lizzie's love channel and my cock battered in vain around her crotch. "Relax, dear, I'll help you," she whispered, and with expert hands she placed my knob between her yielding pussy-lips.

With a low growl of triumph I plunged my prick deep inside Lizzie's wet, welcoming cunt. Instinctively I pistoned my cock in and out of her sticky honeypot, and she wrapped her legs around my ribcage as her hips jabbed upwards to meet my ever-faster thrusts.

Of course I spent too quickly for Lizzie to achieve any great satisfaction. My over-excited cock could not resist the exquisite contractions of her clingy cunny. All too soon I shuddered in heartfelt joy and drenched her love channel with a flood of creamy jism. Of course the lovely Lizzie was kind enough to praise my performance, but I knew jolly well that she had not achieved a spend.

"Please, let me finish you off – look, my cock is still hard," I pleaded, and Lizzie looked down at my shaft, gleaming now with its coating of cuntal juice, still as stiff as a poker. "All right, Henry," she panted. "Stick that thick tadger into my cunt, you big-cocked boy!"

For the repeat performance I needed no help in sliding my shaft into her juicy quim. Lizzie bucked and twisted under me, urging me all the while to thrust deeper, and she raised her legs high in the air and gripped my head between her feet. How tightly her cunny clasped my cock as my balls banged against her bottom! I slipped my hands underneath her bum cheeks and felt them rotate against my palms as I rammed in and out of her tight, wet crack.

Ah, her sopping sheath was like a violin, and my cock was like a bow, and every stroke raised the most ravishing melody on the senses! Our surging cries of ecstasy echoed around the room as we climbed to the highest peaks of pleasure!

"Y-e-s-s-s! Y-e-s-s-s! Y-e-s-s-s! I'm there!" she howled, and this time I was able to hold back and wait until she shuddered to her climax. Only then did I complete a truly blissful fuck by releasing a copious tribute of frothy hot spunk into Lizzie's cunt before collapsing down upon her soft curves. Then I withdrew my shrunken shaft and rolled over to lie next to her, to see that Radleigh was now standing at the side of the bed wildly masturbating, his knob protruding from his clenched first, which was skimming at great speed up and down his swollen shaft. He let out a high-pitched sigh of passion as he climaxed, and a jet of sperm shot out of his prick and splashed out on the sheet.

"Oh Radleigh, I'm so sorry," exclaimed Lizzie sorrowfully. "No wonder you've wanked yourself off, I shouldn't have made you watch Henry in action whilst you waited for your turn to fuck me! We'll have to postpone your initiation till the weekend."

"No, no, it won't take me a moment to get on jack again," he panted, flogging his hand up and down his limp cock until, sure enough, it began to swell up again to a beefy semi-erect state.

"My word! I see what you mean," said Lizzie, who decided to help matters along by leaning forward to take Radleigh's burgeoning shaft into her mouth. She gobbled on the fleshy lollipop until it was once again standing up as firmly as a guardsman outside Buckingham Palace. Of course she did not want him to cum in her mouth, so she pulled back her head and said teasingly, "Well, now, Radleigh, there's no doubt that your equipment is in sound working order, but are you really sure you want to lose your virginity?"

"I'm sure! I'm sure!" he panted. "Oh, Mrs Dickerson, I want to fuck you more than anything else in the whole wide world!"

"Then you shall, my dear," cooed Lizzie, slipping her long fingers around the barrel of his cock, making the wide ruby helmet buck and bound in her hand. She lay back and instructed Radleigh to climb on top of her. As with myself, she had to pilot his prick through the slippery entrance to paradise. His whole body trembled, and I thought my chum was overcome by the elation of completing his rite of passage, for he simply lay motionless on top of her.

Lizzie looked up at him in surprise. "What's wrong, Radleigh? Go ahead and fuck me," she said encouragingly, but Radleigh confessed in a timid voice that he knew so little about *l'art de faire l'amour* that he must ask how he should go about his task. A less kindly teacher might have berated him for his ignorance, but Lizzie simply murmured, "It's very easy, dear. Just push in and push out until you feel the spunk bursting out of your cock."

Her hands slipped round his waist and clasped his taut arse to pull him further inside her. Not unexpectedly, my chum proved himself to be a quick learner. What he lacked in experience he made up for in enthusiasm, bouncing up and down on Lizzie, who jerked herself upwards in time with his vigorous pumping.

"Phwoar!" he groaned, plunging his prick deep inside her slippery love funnel. It was clear from the way she jerked her hips up and down in time with him that Lizzie was thoroughly enjoying herself as she plucked Radleigh's cherry. With a husky cry my chum shot his load and flooded her cunny with a fountain of sticky spunk. After two or three final, frantic thrusts he removed his shrunken shaft and rolled off her with an ecstatic smile on his face.

"Well done, dear, well done indeed," gasped Lizzie as she gently patted his flaccid cock, which was lying limply across his thigh. "But try to fuck more slowly, because it usually takes longer for a lady to spend. A considerate lover will try to hold back and wait for his lover to achieve a climax."

Radleigh's face fell and he groaned. "Oh, dear, I'm so sorry, I obviously came too quickly for you."

"Oh, tush! You mustn't worry about that. In all honesty I never expect to cum with a novice, because it's only natural for boys to fuck at speed during their initiation into the delights of the bedroom," said Lizzie, and turning to me, she added, "Now here's a tip that you should also bear in mind, Henry. When you need to prolong a fuck, you will find it easier to stop the spunk rising from your balls by clearing your mind of all sensual thoughts. Try reciting to yourself a passage from Shakespeare, or even something more mundane, such as the names of all the boys in your form in alphabetical order. This will cool your ardour and enable you to keep pleasuring your partner for that little extra time, which can make all the difference to the girl you are trying to pleasure.

"Anyhow, I do hope that the pair of you enjoyed your first journeys into manhood."

Naturally we chorused our assent, and Lizzie went on, "Good, I'm very pleased. Now that you know how to mount your steeds, so to speak, I can concentrate on teaching you the finer points of riding.

"Now you had better get dressed and go downstairs before Mr Hare comes looking for you."

It was time for us to throw on our clothes and leave. Strangely enough my shin no longer ached, although Lizzie bandaged it for me before I slipped on my trousers.

As I finish recording this intimate memoir I must admit that the memories of this glorious adventure have made my now vastly experienced shaft stiffen up to a prime state of erection.

For sure, whether it was wonderful or disastrous, one never forgets one's first fuck. Radleigh and I were naïve schoolboys, and we were indeed fortunate to be shown the ropes by Lizzie Dickerson, a considerate and sophisticated lady, who took the time and trouble to please us both and cater for our needs.

ONE LAST KISS

Michael Crawley

IN THE GREY gritty dawn, I followed her. I trailed my Queen, she who is my cousin, my aunt, my mother, my own and only true love. Her slippers clacked on flagstones and rustled through strewn rushes. The tips of my delicate bare toes made no sound at all. Herodias descended and descended again. She went down to the place that thrilled me, where guilty servants were punished and innocent prisoners were confined.

I had watched. I had envied the wielders of whips their savage pleasures. I had begrudged those they flogged their searing pain. My nostrils had sniffed up the scent that hot iron chars from warm flesh. My ears had fed on songs of anguish.

There is no ecstasy without agony. There is no agony without ecstasy.

My mother came to the deepest place. A guard stood before a barred cell. A kiss and a coin sent him away. My mother opened up her robe, baring the twin fruits of her bosom. She pressed their yielding tenderness between rigid upright iron rods.

"John?" Queen Herodias whispered. "See that which I have brought for thee. Fondle me, John. Kiss me a deep kiss with the red lips of thy mouth."

"Begone, harlot!" His voice was cavernous. "Remove thyself

from my sight. Take with thee the stench of incest and evil. Thou art an abomination."

"John, my mouth is wet with wine. Come taste me."

"Leave me, o whore of whores, o tainted one, born of cousins, who married her father's brother and had him slain by yet another brother, he who begot on you your daughter. Yet those sins did not suffice. At thy behest, the third brother slew the second and now has thee to wife. What next, Herodias? What new debauchery do you plot? Will you now lay with kine and swine?"

I knew the answer. I knew my mother's plans. I was part of my mother's vile stratagem. For half a year, since my breasts had first budded, she had been urging me towards the bed of her husband, my stepfather, my father's brother and murderer. No woman was ever so steeped in wickedness as my mother was, as yet. That was my evil inheritance. I embraced it, gladly. In the annals of depravity, only one name would be writ larger than that of my mother, Herodias. That would be *my* name, that of her daughter, Salome. I had sworn a terrible secret oath that it would be so.

My birth denies me entry into the ranks of the virtuous. So be it. Then I shall excel in the opposite direction. Evil, be thou my good.

My mother knelt, as if in prayer. She stretched her arms through the bars. "If you hate me, John of the River, then whip me. If you promise me the scourge, I will free thee this very moment. Thy stiff tongue shall be the key to this dark cell. My soft mouth shall be the lock. Slip in that sweet key and you shall be free, John. Once released, I shall be yours. Flog me, use me in any wise you shall desire. Brand my bosom with the name of your God. Through you, I shall be his, if thou so will it. I swear I shall be thy slave, for ever."

"Leave me to my prayers." His voice rose. "O God, forgive this woman. Show her the error of her ways. Visit her bowels not with sulphurous fire, nor infest them with hairy worms. Withhold Thy righteous rage, for she . . ."

My mother, Herodias, rose, atremble. She screamed. "I *will* have your mouth on mine, John. Thou wilt will kiss my lips while thine are yet warm, or I vow I will kiss thine when they are cold, but we *will* kiss."

When she was gone I slipped from my shift. At the cell, I pressed my nakedness to the bars. One cold iron rod split apart the lips of my virgin sex. My hips writhed. My pubes ground on hard metal. In the light of one small taper, I saw him. He was tall and pale, with a small but well-shaped head. Dark hair lay matted to his broad shoulders. I crooned, "John, am I not more comely than my mother? Am I not young and succulent? I am a pure and untouched maiden still. Would thou be my first man? Teach me first to love a man and mayhap I will come to love thy God."

"Perhaps thou hast yet to lie with a man, Salome. I believe thy mother guards thy maidenhead against the day she gifts it to her husband, foul Herod. Yet thou art not 'pure' nor art thou 'untouched'. What abominations hast thou performed in thy mother's bed, Salome? Unpierced thou may be, but thou art vile also."

"One kiss, then, John? What a vengeance on Herodias that would be! Refuse *her* lips, yet take mine. Bruise my mouth with your kisses, sweet John. None shall know on it save thee and me."

John thundered, "And my God! He seeth all. Father, lead me not into temptation! Deliver me from this evil, even unto my death if that be Thy will."

And so I left him. He would refuse me? Me, whom all men lusted after? Then my curse on his head. I swore a great oath. If John the Baptist would not suffer his mouth to offer mine tribute, then it would have to content itself with less. In the name of all Evil, John would kiss my mother's lips before another day passed, will he or nil he.

There were guests that night. All three tables in the Great Hall were set. The lowest, on the left, was for Elders and Merchants. The next, on the right, was reserved for a delegation from Rome. The high table was laid for but three, Herod on his throne, Herodias, his wife, to his right, and me, Salome, to his left.

When the feast was done and cleared, and the entertainment began, Herod Antipas, as was his habit, reached out to both sides beneath the table's concealment. His right hand found Herodias' thigh. His left fell on mine, midway between my knee and my sex. For the very first time I did not push his hand away. I covered it with my own, holding it still but not rejecting its hot touch.

"Will you dance for our guests, Salome?" he asked.

"For a favour," I told him. My mother had taught me to give no man any thing unless he paid a heavy price for it.

King Herod took the great silver ring with the uncut emerald from his smallest finger. He laid it before me. "Will this suffice?"

"For this dance, yes, great Herod. For a more – interesting – dance, no." He loves to be called "great Herod", for he can never be "Herod the Great", as his father, my grandfather, was.

My mother leaned forward and spoke across her husband. "What manner of 'interesting' dance, my daughter?"

"A private one. I believe it is called 'The Dance of the Seven Veils'."

"You know the dance of whores and harlots?" There was glee in her voice.

"Perhaps," I teased.

Herod's hand clamped tightly on my leg. I pried it loose, punishing its fingers with my pointed nails. Before Herod or Herodias could press me further, I rose. From behind a fretted screen, cymbals chimed. A pipe skirled. Tabors sounded. I kicked off my slippers, planted my feet wide apart and swayed.

My robe was green velvet, stiff with gold thread and held by a broad sash. Beneath it my pantaloons were clinging silk and my shift was thin cotton. Even when the swinging of my body parted my robe, my form was covered from my throat to my ankles. And yet, when I arched, straining backwards, the trembling in my firm young thighs was plain to see. When I bowed low, towards Herod's throne, my robe fell open. The hardness of my nipples prodded my shift.

My hands described arcs, following the lithe lines of my body without touching. My hips gyrated, flinging out the skirts of my robe.

I danced a promise. I danced for Herod. Both he and my mother read my dance. Its lusty message was subtle, but not obscured.

After the music had fallen silent and I had returned to my seat, Herod's hand found my thigh once more. I moved it aside.

"When wilt thou dance for me?" he asked, his voice hoarse.

"Yes, when?" my mother added.

"When the moon rises, perhaps."

"Shall I have the musicians stay?" Herod demanded.

"And it please thee so to do. You are King. Thou mayest have music whenever it pleases thee, my lord, my father, my uncle."

That pleased my mother. When I pleasured her body in the manner she had taught me, that was when she called out to me as "daughter" or even "darling daughter". For Herodias, no passion is so great as when it is at its most perverse.

She asked me, "And may I witness this dance, daughter?"

"*If* I dance, why not?"

Herod brought the banquet to a swift end. His ungraciousness was softened by the Elders being given small gifts and the Romans being led to their chambers by comely slave girls. Once the Hall was cleared, Herodias turned to me. "Art then ready to dance for us, daughter?"

"I must prepare, but I dance for my father, your husband, Mother. Thou art but a witness. Is that understood?"

Her eyes widened. She had raised me to be biddable. I had always obeyed her in all things but one – her demand that I join her and Herod in their bed. Now I was, it seemed, about to obey her in that also. Did that give me the right to be defiant in other matters? It seemed it did.

Her eyes dropped, as if in modesty. "I have taught thee well, my daughter."

"Better than you know, Mother."

She stiffened. "My place with Herod is secure."

"I am not thy rival, Mother. I love thee. What I do this night I do to please only thee."

Before I left, I instructed the musicians and had them bind up their eyes. My dance was to be intimate.

In my chamber, my maid, Miriam, oiled and scraped my skin. The wisps that adorned my mound were fine and few, as yet. Pumice removed every trace, and brought a becoming blush to the cleft cushion. Miriam perfumed me there, and between my breasts. I chewed on aromatic herbs as she dressed my midnight tresses. She rouged my lips and my nipples, and kohled the lids of my eyes. My mother might be the Queen of Whores, but I was their worthy Princess.

There was no need for haste. My mother and my step-father would wait.

Miriam put silver bells on my fingers and my toes and at the lobes of my ears. Together, we adorned me with the veils, seven of them, each as long as a man is tall, as wide as my forearm is long, as fine as smoke caught in a cobweb.

But they were strong. From the palest pink to the deepest crimson, they had been woven from long strands of pure silk. Like me, they looked fragile. Like me, they were not.

The tables had been removed. Herod's carved oak throne sat in the middle of the Hall. He sat upon it. My mother sat in his lap, devouring his mouth. Her own, lesser throne, stood to one side.

Her eyes brightened when she saw me. She left Herod's knee, tucking her bosom back into her robe as she crossed the Hall. "My daughter! Thou art transformed! What magic is this? Thou left us as a pretty child. Thou returnest as a wanton houri, as lewd a harlot as has ever delighted my eyes. Buss me, my child, true fruit of my loins." In my arms, she whispered, "Between us, we shall hold the King in such thrall that he will never look on another. If we bear sons, we shall seduce them also. We shall rule Judea, my daughter, thee and me."

Her tongue was spiced and wine-dipped. Herodias turned me, that Herod might see what manner of kisses we, mother and daughter, exchanged. It was a game that I liked well, and it went to my purpose. Perversion excited Herod. The greater his arousal, the more surely my plan would be successful.

I put my mother aside. "Go sit, Mother. See what thou shalt see."

My hands clapped a signal to the hidden and hoodwinked musicians. The beat began, a low throbbing, plain, without notes.

With my feet planted wide, I let the rhythm enter me. My thighs pulsed with it. My belly trembled. My breasts swayed.

'Show thy face unto me, Salome," Herod demanded. "Let the moon of thy visage shine forth for me, I pray."

Dutifully, I unloosed the pale veil that I wore doubled, as a yashmak. It wafted in the still night air as I let tiny flat steps carry me to where my mother sat. To her startlement, I wrapped her wrists in its diaphanous length and bound them behind her throne. She grinned in understanding when the music stooped me to her face, for one more long incestuous kiss. My nimble fingers parted her robe and drew it aside. Her breasts, heavy and round, gleamed in the torchlight.

"I am become thy slave, Daughter."

"But *I* am more bound than thee, Mother. My love for thee chains me."

I kissed the nipples of her breasts, one, then the other, and left them glistening with my spittle.

Herod said, "If *that* is the torment that thou inflictest on thy captives, Salome, bind me also, I pray. I too would suffer."

I took down the veil that covered my head. The music changed. Prancing, as a pony, I danced to his throne. My veil tied his left arm to the arm of his seat, tight and secure. My lips touched his cheek before I whirled away.

The veil that had covered my naked shoulders served to bind his right arm. His submission was rewarded with a lick from the tip of my tongue on the lobe of his ear. Herod grinned. His thighs parted. He wanted me to see the stiffening that stirred the skirts of his robe.

Another veil wrapped my loins from my navel to my knees. I put an end into his trapped hand. As I spun away, it unwrapped. *That* one was used to bind his left ankle to the leg of his throne.

I became a butterfly. My tail, the veil that encircled my slender waist, fluttered behind me. Lightly, I flittered, sipping nectar from my mother's mouth, from her breasts, and once, swift as a hummingbird's tongue, from the lips of Herod Antipas.

That veil constrained his right ankle.

"The Song of the Peacock," strident, strutting, raucous. Stiff-legged in my pride, I whipped the trailing end of my fifth veil, the one that confined my right breast, across my mother's bosom. Her nipples tightened.

When my veil trailed in Herod's lap he contrived to catch it in his fingers, as I had allowed. It tugged free from my body. I clutched my gleaming bare globe, to conceal it until I had danced behind his throne. Slotted through the fretted wood, my veil circled his throat, holding his head in place.

With my one breast bouncing freely, I set my hands over his, lifted up my left leg prettily behind me, and leaned towards his face. His lips brushed my nipple. I snatched back.

To the tune known as "Dervish" I whirled, stamping and shaking. My gyrations visited my mother. With her saliva on my nipple, I presented it to Herod. He suckled.

"Taste your wife, your niece, from the firm flesh of your step-daughter, your great-niece," I told him. "How vile thou art, mighty Herod. How depraved."

"Two more veils yet remain, Daughter."

I looked deeply into his brooding dark eyes. "And my reward?"

"Whatsoever thou asketh, even unto half of mine kingdom."

"I shall demand of thee less, yet more," I promised.

"What?"

But I was gone. The musicians played "The Acrobats". I performed somersaults. I landed with one foot pointed south and the other north, my sweet sex splayed hard against the flagstones. With only the strength of my straining thighs, I lifted myself. Three high leaps took me to my King. I laid his robe apart to his thick hairy waist. A fleshy scepter stood proud, bulbous and royal purple. I draped my sixth veil, from my left breast, across its head. Bending, I breathed through the gossamer.

Herod groaned, "Lower! Take my flesh into thy mouth, sweet child. More sweet milk awaits thee than ever thou suckled at thy mother's breast."

"My dance is not yet done," I teased.

The music turned slow and vibrant, pregnant with promise. With but the last, the crimson veil, girding my loins, I arched backwards. My knees and my hips bent. My hands, above and behind me, touched the floor. My hair brushed stone. No part of my body was higher than was my mound. I balanced on the soles of my feet and one hand. My other hand plucked at the veil. It loosened, and fell. The secret core of my womanhood was naked. The tautness of my pose was such that I could feel the night air on the tender inner flesh. Or was that Herod's gaze that I felt?"

"Salome!" he croaked. "Ask anything of me."

"You swear?"

"I swear."

But I was not done tormenting him. As the music pulsed, so did I constrict and relax muscles that I had been many hours in training. The soft pulpy lips of my sex closed, and opened. With careful slowness, I let my body roll forward, until I was on my knees, my head tilted back between the soles of my feet. I thrust upwards. With growing passion, I made love to the air.

"Salome!"

I writhed to my feet. With my knees touching his, I parted my sex with my fingers. He pulled against his bonds, but in vain. The veil that draped his weapon darkened with seeping wet. His man-scent was thick in my nostrils.

"Is *this* what thou desirest?" I asked him. "Or *this*?" I doubled forward. My open mouth hovered, not a finger's width above the dome of his manhood. I whipped the veil aside. His gleaming head bobbed. I let a little drool fall from my mouth, anointing it.

"Yes – *that*! Give me the heat of your mouth, Daughter mine."

I looked up at him, my eyes hooded with lust. Like a kitten, I purred in the crude language of the bazaar. "Is it a little 'head' that thou desirest of me, great Herod?"

"Yes! Yes!"

"Then first, my boon. Give *me* a 'little head', o my King. There is one confined in your deepest dungeon that will suffice."

THE MISSIONARY

Rebecca Ambrose

UGG AWOKE AT dawn and felt the rough pelt of his mate, Ma, tickling his erect penis. Seizing her by the buttocks, he parted the long hairs with his impatient member. One thrust and he was in, making the sleepy female cry out in surprise, although she shouldn't have been surprised. Their crude couplings happened at around this time every morning, accompanied by the dawn chorus. Ma could scarcely hear birdsong at any time of day without growing a little moist between her hairy thighs.

"Moo!" called the youngest of their nine offspring when he saw them at it again. "Moo, moo, moo!"

The child was still in the rudimentary stages of even that rudimentary language. His "Moo!" was a cry for attention. His mother grunted back, "Boo!" which, roughly translated, meant, "Be off with you!"

Undistracted by this exchange, Ugg felt his excitement mounting towards the inevitable tickling sensation which accompanied the spilling of his seed. He clasped his mate's pendulous and curd-encrusted tits with callused fingers, making her cry out again as he made his final thrust. Then he pulled out and lay back, breathing heavily.

Young Sprog, hoping to ingratiate himself with his father so that he would get a nice titbit of dried elk meat, brought the bowl of smouldering herbs for Ugg to breathe in the aromatic vapours. He did so with a deep sigh, accompanied by a dig in Ma's ribs, which meant, "Get up, woman, and bring me something to eat and drink!"

Ma shuffled off to the back of the cave, flinging a lump of rock at her mate's humped back. She was not happy. If she could have expressed her feelings in the sophisticated tongue of later cultures she would have said, "I don't know why I put up with all this. Just because he brings home the bacon and struts around waving that club of his at those yobbos in the cave opposite, he thinks he can prod me whenever he likes. But I'm already worn out with child-bearing. If I have another it'll probably kill me. Where's the fun in it for me, that's what I'd like to know? I've had practically a kid a year since I was thirteen, and just look at me now. I'm only twenty-five. I've got at least another ten years' life expectancy left. I reckon I'm entitled to some peace and quiet in my old age."

Later, as she pounded away at her quern, she imagined that she was grinding up Ugg's bones to a fine powder, which made her feel much better.

Meanwhile, Ugg was up and about. He lobbed a rock at his wife, to hurry her up, and eventually, refreshed by his breakfast of fermented goats' milk and elk meat, popped into the cave next door to see if his neighbour, Bogg, was ready to go hunting. A herd of mammoth had been spotted by the scout, and they were looking to pick off a couple to salt down for the winter.

"Hi!" Bogg greeted him. "Thought you'd show, old boy. Given the wife a good seeing to this morning?"

A grin of satisfaction spread over Ugg's simian features. "You bet! Never miss a morning. Got to keep the race going, haven't we? Heard a whole tribe got wiped out last week. Avalanche got 'em. Yours breeding again, is she?"

"Yes. Managed to get her knocked up a couple of months back. Hope it's another boy. Medicine Man says if you keep on pronging her while she's expecting it's bound to be a boy. So we're at it like rabbits, day and night."

The two hunters soon met up with the rest of their party and travelled towards the mammoth feeding grounds. Ugg decided to approach the herd from another angle, and went off alone.

Suddenly, however, a blizzard blew up, and he ran into the nearest cave for shelter. When the snowstorm subsided he looked out to find that both herd and hunters had vanished.

"Bugger me!" he exclaimed, or words to that effect. That expletive was commonly used by the males of the tribe, since homosexuality was unknown and the idea of anyone buggering them was viewed as extremely comic. They frequently buggered their mates, of course, since it never occurred to them to take their women in any other position than from the rear, and they often found themselves in the wrong orifice.

It was still cold out, with a few flakes of snow drifting about and a bitter wind howling. Soon the long, dark winter would be upon them, with only the comforting warmth of a bonfire to look forward to in the evenings and maybe a few stories and songs. Ugg began to feel miserable. His chance of getting a share of the kill was now nil. Why on earth hadn't he stayed with the others instead of trying to be clever? They would be back at the caves by now, gloating over the prospect of a meat feast, ogling the women as they skinned and butchered the mammoth.

Picturing Ma, kneeling on all fours as she scraped away at a mammoth skin, Ugg grew horny. His hand seized his stirring prick and gave it a few vigorous tugs until it stood up firm and strong. He was about to continue with the hand job when a strange voice came from the mouth of the cave, uttering monosyllables in a foreign accent which, roughly translated, meant, "Oh, good, you're ready for me! I was hoping to find one of your lot in here so I could meet my quota for the day."

Ugg's dark eyes peered out in astonishment from beneath his low, beetling brow.

"Who are you?" he grunted, in his own tongue. "And where the freezing bollocks did you come from?"

She answered in a halting version of his own tongue. "I am of a different tribe . . ."

"That's icicle-dag obvious! Look at you!"

Even in the dim light of the snowbound cave the contrast between the two species was striking. The stranger stood head and shoulders above Ugg, and was fair-haired and blue-eyed. Most curious of all, however, was the comparative absence of body hair. She – for it was clearly a female – had the pelt of a sabre-toothed tiger draped around her torso to compensate for the lack of her own protective covering.

She gave a quite irresistible smile and deposited an armful of sticks on the floor of the cave. "I thought we might light a fire. I have some flint and tinder here, in my clothes."

"*Clothes?*" Ugg pronounced the unfamiliar word with a frown.

"Yes. As you see, we're not as well-covered as you, so we have to wear these things to keep us warm. Don't worry, I'll take mine off as soon as we've got the fire going, then we can get down to business."

"What's your 'business' with me?" Ugg growled suspiciously, as she set about sparking the flint. He wasn't used to being addressed so confidently by strange females, especially ones that looked so weird.

"We have to mate," she told him, matter-of-factly. "It's important for the survival of both our races. Our Medicine Woman says there's another Ice Age on the way, and it's going to be survival of the fittest. Since we don't know yet which one of us will prove to be the fittest, we've decided to maximize our chances by mating with you lot. Besides, we're a lot more advanced, so we can teach you a thing or two. Think of me as a missionary, if you like."

"*Missionary?*" Ugg translated the term as "sent from afar". He was baffled by all these new concepts. He'd thought he knew all the words in his tribe's limited vocabulary, and now he was being faced with more. It was too much for his restricted brain to cope with.

The fire was beginning to smoke. Ugg was impressed. Her tribe's technology was clearly more advanced than his. They were still rubbing sticks together. The female stood up, her long legs disappearing into the animal hide where her sex was hidden. Ugg felt a strong curiosity about what she would look like with no "clothes" on.

"A missionary is one who seeks out others of a different tribe and teaches them about our ways," she explained. "But let me introduce myself. My name is Kwim."

"K-*wim*!" Ugg repeated, clumsily. "I, Ugg. You strip, we mate? Nice and warm." The image of Ma kneeling on the mammoth skin returned to titillate him. "Put *clothes* on floor and get down on all fours," he urged her, giving his penis a reviving tug.

"We don't do it quite like that," Kwim explained, stripping off her animal skins and allowing him to peruse her naked flesh.

She was like no creature he had ever seen before. Although long, straggling hairs fell from her armpits, and made a delightful V around her entry zone, the rest of her was smooth and soft-looking, with just a tantalizing ring of small hairs around her large pink nipples. Unlike the dropping dugs of his mate, Kwim's breasts stood out in amazing defiance of whatever force it was that dragged things down to earth. Large and luscious, they issued a pressing invitation to be stroked and squeezed. Taken into his mouth, even, although Ugg was ashamed of this urge to lick and suck. Back home such actions would have labelled him a *dork*, or mother-sucker. But he was far from his tribe, and the idea was dawning on him that he could do anything he liked to this delectable stranger with no comeback. Indeed, she seemed to be urging him to take his fill of her.

Kwim lowered herself onto the tigerskin rug with an inviting smile. "Come!" she purred. "Let us indulge in a spot of miscegenation. I do so love you hairy monsters!"

Ugg needed no further encouragement. He knelt down before her and allowed her smooth fingers to entangle with his hairy chest while he played with her smooth one. Under his rough caresses the buoyant globes expanded and their rosy teats grew hard as pebbles beneath his pinching fingers. "Suck me!" she gasped. Obediently he popped one tasty nipple into his mouth, but she scratched at his hairy back with her long nails, complaining, "No, not there! Down below!"

Impatiently she guided his thick skull down towards the moist chasm between her thighs. Ugg stared up at her in astonishment. It had never occurred to him to use his mouth on those nether lips. "It's all right – you'll enjoy it!" she promised him.

Tentatively he began to lick into the folds and crevices, while Kwim wriggled and moaned above him. She was right; it tasted good! A bit like clams. And the juices which ran out were quite fishy-tasting too. With renewed enthusiasm he explored further with his tongue, finding an interesting fleshy knob nestling at the top just below the bony bit.

"Ah, yes, yes!" he heard Kwim cry as he gave it his undivided attention. Soon she was thrashing about uncontrollably, uttering sounds he had never heard any female utter before, and the whole area became flooded with sweet liquid which he drank thirstily.

"Goo, bab goo!" he murmured, which was along the lines of, "Tasty, very tasty!"

By now Ugg's implement was well-honed and throbbing away. He had never known it to reach such impressive dimensions. Usually he thrust it into his complaint mate as soon as it grew stiff enough, but this time the delay had caused it to swell enormously.

"Turn over!" he grunted. "I want to prod you!"

To his surprise, Kwim refused. "We do it face to face," she explained. "I think you'll like it."

"Face to face!" The very idea revolted him. Fancy looking at the creature while you pronged it. Or, worse, having it watching you! He shuddered, and his erection abruptly subsided.

"I know it seems strange," Kwim continued, softly. "But our people have evolved the art of lovemaking far beyond mere procreation. Sometimes we make it last all night."

"All night!" Ugg's mind was being blown again.

"Yes." She took his wilting member in her smooth hands and began to caress it with featherlight strokes that soon had the desired result. "You see, Ugg, there are so many things one can do with another body. Slide your wonderful big prick inside me right now, and I'll show you."

Eagerly he thrust his dick between her sweating thighs and entered a warm, wet paradise. As he slopped around in there, feeling hot waves of pleasure course through his entire body, he began to realize that the alien female was right. She guided his hands to her straining tits, and soon his mouth was fastened on one juicy nipple while his fingers pinched the other.

"Tit-sucking is something you can't do properly when you take a female from behind," she reminded him in a whisper. "Not without twisting into some uncomfortable position. And here's something I can do for you more easily on my back . . ."

So saying, Kwim reached down and fondled his buttocks and balls as he prodded her. The exquisite overloading of his senses resulted in the inevitable shooting of his load, but this time he came with a long-lasting intensity that totally shattered his mind. It was as if he were rapidly evolving into a new species. The procreative urge had suddenly been transformed into the pleasure principle.

For his tribe had little concept of pleasure, but were chiefly concerned with the mere avoidance of pain. They had no knowledge of the feelgood factor which was to drive later civilizations to devise ever more elaborate and sophisticated methods of satisfying the senses. Ugg lay exhausted on the tigerskin for several minutes while vague intimations of these future developments teased his brain.

"I must go," he heard Kwim murmur at last. "There are other tribes to educate. But you, dear Ugg, must return to your people and convert them to our ways. Teach them to fuck face to face and your race will discover a new harmony and co-operation between the sexes that will hasten your civilization."

"How?" he asked, puzzled.

"Our Medicine Woman has told us that future generations will discover love between men and women. They will gaze sweetly at each other as they play with each other's bodies. They will become objects of profound desire to each other, instead of merely holes to fill or be filled. They will sing hymns of praise to each other, be inspired to create great works, and grow concerned for each other's welfare. All this will come from this one evolutionary change from rear entry to face to face. Spread the word amongst your tribe. Tell them to adopt the position of the Missionary, and your lives shall be transformed!"

Kwim left as suddenly as she had arrived, leaving Ugg to drift into a deep sleep accompanied by bright and marvellous dreams. When he awoke he was filled with a burning sense of mission, and hastened back to his cave to spread the word.

Ma was waiting anxiously for him by a welcoming fire. She sighed with relief when he returned. "Thought you were dead. Didn't fancy coming under the protection of him-next-door," she said, lugubriously.

"Never mind that. Lie down and spread your legs. I got a great new way of mating."

That was the start of a whole new voyage of discovery for Ugg and his mate. He managed to persuade Ma to shave her tits, a fashion which eventually became a rite of puberty for the young girls of the tribe. They also invented mouth-to-mouth kissing, a refinement which not even the people of Kwim's tribe knew, and learned to lick each other's parts simultaneously, an activity which was so pleasurable that they indulged in it for hours on end. It had the added bonus of being an infallible method of birth control.

Ugg and Ma thus entered a new phase in their relationship, where Ugg used other young females for procreative purposes while allowing his mate a pleasurable retirement from the endless cycle of child-bearing. So satisfactory was this arrangement to both parties that they stopped throwing rocks at each other and became a model of peaceful co-existence. The curiosity of their neighbours was aroused, and soon they were eager to learn the secret.

At first, they reacted with scepticism, but once Ugg had persuaded them to try the Missionary Position for themselves they were instantly converted. Face-to-face fucking became the fashion, and even children as young as two or three could be seen rehearsing the act which they had observed their parents enthusastically performing. It seemed as if the whole tribe were well on the way to evolving into a new and enlightened species.

Then catastrophe occurred. The predictions of Kwim's Medicine Woman came true, and the earth suffered another Ice Age. Ugg and the rest of his Neanderthal race were unable to withstand the cruelly low temperatures, and the species gradually died out.

Unfortunately so did the more enlightened tribe of the Cromagnons, to which Kwim had belonged. Yet their instinct to mate with the Neanderthals proved well founded. For those descendants of the brief overlap between the two species were the only humanoid creatures to adapt sufficiently to the freezing conditions. Eventually they emerged triumphant in the timetable of pre-history, to be labelled by paleontologists as *Homo Sapiens*.

WHEN ENGLAND CALLED

Debra Hyde

WHEN MARIE MARTINET du Contemaine heard the news, she laughed until she cried. She laughed at the irony of the nearly bankrupt French government collecting thousands of tapestries and burning them, supposedly to destroy all things bourgeois when they really sought to reclaim enough gold thread to pay the new America for a shipment of wheat.

Then Marie Martinet du Contemaine dissolved into tears as she imagined all those tapestries going up in flames, those beautiful, ornate and ostentatious creations that had hung in every palace, every mansion, every place of distinction, symbols of the only life she had ever known. And now that life and those symbols were tragically little more than ash.

But Marie Martinet was lucky compared to the French aristocracy at large. She had escaped France not only with her life but with much of her personal wealth intact. Her lover and benefactor, the Marquis, knew the revolution was spinning towards terror, and had sent her packing for her own good. Oh, she had been as furious as a trapped feral cat, spitting obscenities and curses at him when he had locked her in his coach in the dead of night and ordered his men to get her to the coast, but now, from English soil, she sent him a thankful prayer.

She was alive and on her way to London.

Her Marquis had not been so fortunate in seeing to himself. In putting her safety above his own, he had lost his own chance for freedom. Marie Martinet cried bitterly the day news came to her that the Marquis had died, his head one among many to hit the basket. That damnable guillotine had efficiently sliced away at the nobility and grandeur that had once been France.

She had resolved to mourn but not complain, for the ties and notoriety that her Marquis had had her cultivate in France were paying off, securing her existence. With the bitter news of the tapestries came an invitation from London. At the behest of a Mrs Collet, she could ply her talents in the city, and so she found herself in a carriage which lurched along the rutted roads from Suffolk to London.

Yes, it had paid for Marie Martinet to develop her sexual prowess. "It will serve and protect you better than simply engaging in idle court gossip," the Marquis had told her. "Gossip will not make you indispensable but displaying certain talents will." He had known her talents well. Often, they had rested in her bed, exhausted and sweating from fierce lovemaking that was an ends to the means. And the means were marked across his ass in the bright red stripes that only a cane could deliver.

Ah, well, she said to herself when she received the invitation, *Marquis was right. The Whipping Club was a wise move.* There, in a club famous for the infamous presence of respectable ladies who delighted in wielding the whip, Marie Martinet had extended her status from beyond the court to the rich merchant class, all because she knew how to birch and scourge and flog.

Her mind wandered through memories of her life in France as the coach wandered through the streets of London to Portland Place. In time, it would come to a stop, and Marie Martinet's thoughts would halt in tandem. Now she would renew her notoriety by applying the cane to the bare buttocks of craving supplicants, amid the bustle of Mrs Collet's brothel.

"Mark my words," Mrs Collet said as she took Marie Martinet to her quarters, "flagellation is destined to be all the rage. Demand for it grows unabated, and I suspect the number of brothels that specialize in it will only increase as English society refines its insatiable appetites."

"And I can help you grow your business, is that it?" Marie Martinet asked, somewhat skeptical.

And somewhat in awe. Mrs Collet's business barely deserved to be called a brothel. True, it serviced the many sexual needs of English society, but, housed in an expansive building, lavishly decorated, it was more like a rich merchant's city apartment. *Ah*, Marie told herself as three young, attractive girls passed by, *but Mrs Collet is a rich merchant.*

"We can help each other, Mademoiselle du Contemaine," Mrs Collet continued. "Your fame precedes you; it secures your position in our little society of sexual pleasures without question. And I have no doubt that in a matter of months you might well want to secure your own house and run it independently. Or perhaps you will simply add to your wealth and soon retire to the countryside. Regardless, I am more than happy to provide your introduction into English society. But I won't lie to you – I will increase my own reputation and business in doing so. No matter. There's more than enough clientele for us both."

"As you said, you only expect your clientele to continue to grow."

Mrs Collet smiled. It was an odd, sardonic grin, the kind of grin that comes from knowledge and wisdom. "Mark my words: we flagellants will go down in history. The English have a growing need for decadence and they descend upon us nightly, usually at theater's end."

As Mrs Collet opened the door to Marie Martinet's new quarters, Marie was delighted and surprised to find French finery in the decor and, even better, the sweet sounds of French voices, girls' voices, filling the room.

"Here we are. The first-floor apartment of the west wing, second only to my own," Mrs Collet informed her. "Nine rooms, all your own."

"It is sumptuous," Marie Martinet remarked. "And the girls?"

"All French. You weren't alone in your fleeing. Masses of common reprobates were expelled during the Terror, and many can't find domestic work here, what with high English society living in fear of French sexual excesses landing on their doorsteps. Going to a brothel for pleasures profound is one thing; bringing it under your own roof is another entirely. English propriety indeed!" Mrs Collet clucked. "But these girls know how to serve you in your own way and they are well-schooled in the special refinements that constitute the art of love. I suspect you will not be disappointed."

With that, Mrs Collet left Marie Martinet to her new surroundings. She wandered from room to room, assessing the rich and generous decor, meeting the girls along the way. One room, much to her delight, was fully equipped for the flagellant: whip thongs, cat o'nine tails, scourges, tawses, canes, switches, and birches. A padded bench sat in the middle of the room, high up on a base, to raise the victim enough so that his ass met her hand. She smiled. She would not have to stoop to anything, it seemed.

"Mademoiselle?" A young voice interrupted her.

Marie turned and found a young girl, her supple body draped in French gauze, the bodice dipping low enough to reveal the curve of firm, young breasts. She was exquisitely nubile. And she curtseyed before she continued speaking.

"Mrs Collet instructed me to introduce myself to you. I am Gabrielle and Mrs Collet has assigned me to be your submissive, if you desire it."

Submissive to her! Marie Martinet smiled. "And what would that encompass, dear girl?"

"Whatever you require, Mademoiselle," Gabrielle lowered her eyes and blushed. "I am well-versed in serving the needs of women, should you wish to refrain from taking a male lover. I have warmed the bed of a famed courtesan before, Mademoiselle. I am familiar with the feel of the rod against my skin as well, should a client desire to watch a woman be beaten. And I will service any client however you require."

Most surprising, Marie Martinet thought. She hadn't thought far enough ahead to see specifically how she would appease various clients' desires, and she had a growing respect for Mrs Collet's ability to provide her with these generous starting points.

And the girl was delicious, no doubt about that.

"Come here, my girl. Let me see you closer," Marie Martinet commanded.

Gabrielle stepped forward, padding in little pink mules, until she was face to face with her Mademoiselle. Marie Martinet reached into Gabrielle's bodice to her breast and squeezed. The girl gasped slightly.

Marie Martinet circled the girl's taut little nipple with her fingers and pinched it. She planted her lips on the girl's mouth and let the child melt into her arms. A moan escaped from Gabrielle.

Such surrender! *Oh, yes,* Marie Martinet thought, *perhaps a girl will do just fine.*

Soon enough, the throngs of customers who passed through Mrs Collet's doors expressed an interest in Marie Martinet's skills. In no time, she was seeing one to three clients each evening, depending upon how well a client could fund his needs. Requests outstripped bookings by a four to one margin; Marie Martinet would not be lacking in work. Yet this night would be different; it called for preparation and splendor.

As she began to dress, Marie Martinet felt her composure draw tight, ready, all because an appointment set early in the day had caused an excited stir throughout the house. "A purveyor from the King's private staff will visit," Mrs Collet had claimed. "There's every likelihood that if your skill and ingenuity impresses this man, great things will come of it."

Marie Martinet could imagine the ramifications of a positive outcome. *Finally,* she thought to herself, *it begins to feel like being at court.*

Knowing this, she sat in her boudoir, a girl seeing to her rouge and wig, another laying out a rich, full dress and a regal, coat-like robe. Here, as in Paris, men found sumptuously dressed women irresistible. When she was younger, Marie Martinet had wondered why – after all, bare flesh most thoroughly quenched lust – but the world of flagellation and sexual torments had taught her that many men longed for women who would test and torture them, yet remain forbidden to them, aloof and remote. Nothing provided a better vision of inaccessibility, she had found, than a whip in one hand and layers upon layers of fine clothing upon the body.

Soon enough, her doors were opened, and Marie Martinet found herself before her guest in a full, grand, for-the-royals curtsey.

"Good evening, Lord," she offered before she rose. "Welcome."

"Thank you, Mademoiselle."

As she rose, she met his eyes with her own steely gaze. Ah, he was mesmerized, she knew, by her poise and lubricity. Her dress – gala robes and skirt, gold-spangled shoes, silk stockings with accents of gold thread, necklace and bracelets – only enhanced matters.

"Forgive me for being so blunt," she told the man she knew only as Lord. "Would you like to sup and rest further or did you have enough repose in Mrs Collet's quarters?"

"Let me be equally blunt," he answered, smiling slyly. "My belly's had enough of a taste of tender delectables. It's my ass that's ready for a taste of your whip and your cane."

Marie Martinet smiled back, broadly. "Then follow me, Lord."

She led him to the spanking-bench and the tools of her trade. Rising from a divan, young Gabrielle greeted them, falling to her knees in supplication. She wore little in the way of clothing, a brief layer of French gauze wrapped several times around her waist and falling to ankle length. Her youthful breasts were completely unfettered, nipples erect and ready.

"Mrs Collet relayed your specifications, Lord. I hope this girl merits your attentions."

The Lord smiled approvingly. "She does. Let's have at it, Mademoiselle."

"Then I strongly suggest you strip naked and climb aboard the spanking-bench, my Lord. The sooner you're in place, the sooner I can swing the cane – and the sooner my girl can apply her own talents to your experience."

The Lord stripped bare quickly, handing his clothing to Gabrielle to fold and set aside. As he undressed, his body revealed itself as lean – enough body hair to arouse a lover, a sturdy hank of meat between his legs. Marie Martinet smiled. It would be a pleasure to watch him in action.

"Come now," she said, patting the leather padding of the bench. "Climb up here so I can apply the strokes."

The Lord sighed in anticipation as he climbed on the bench, resting his knees in its station, bending over the waist bar and placing his hands on a stationary bar. Marie Martinet admired how the bench's position exposed his ass, round and firm.

And ready.

She caressed his ass and explained, "I'm going to flog you for a few minutes, my Lord. By warming your skin, you'll be able to better enjoy each stroke of the cane when the time comes. Likewise, Gabrielle will show you how skilled she can be."

Gabrielle knew which flogger her Mademoiselle preferred, and brought forward a blood-red implement that had long, thick tresses of deerskin. Marie Martinet took it and signaled that the girl should take her position. Gabrielle situated herself before the Lord, kneeling, her back straight, her breasts prominent.

Marie routinely swung the flogger in a figure eight pattern, slapping its tresses back and forth across each of the Lord's ass cheeks. As she did, she interrogated the Lord, mildly, about his desire for her girl.

"She's lovely, isn't she?" she asked.

"Yes. Yes, she is, Mademoiselle," he answered.

"Look at her sweet breasts, so young and tender. Gorgeous, aren't they, in their deliberate nakedness?"

"Yes." He was growing breathy from the flogger's impact. Marie smiled like a sly fox. She loved taunting a man into his lusts. Doing so invited her own lust to rise.

"Girl, caress your breasts for our Lord. Show him how I like you to pinch your own nipples."

Gabrielle did as she was told, and after a few short massages, she had her nipples in her own firm grip, pulling and stretching until they grew elongated. She moaned, aroused by her self-manipulations.

The Lord moaned as well, and Marie Martinet stopped flogging to reach around and grasp his cock. She found it was admirably engorged, and she stroked it long enough to make him moan and squirm.

"How delightful!" she cajoled as she stopped masturbating him. "I love to see a man needy and lustful. Let's see how many ways we can arouse you. Little Gabby, my dear, offer your tit to our Lord. Let's see if he can suck it while I continue to whip him."

Gabrielle rose and approached the Lord. This time, what little curtsey she offered him was merely to bring her young breast to his mouth. The Lord devoured her tit, suckling like a starving babe, nibbling and biting like a crazed lover.

Marie Martinet saw her opportunity. As the Lord sucked greedily, she applied the first stroke of the cane in a quick, unforgiving strike. Upon impact, the Lord pulled back, crying out, pulling from Gabrielle's nipple so suddenly she cried out as well. Marie Martinet laughed cruelly at the site of their mutual plight. In turn, both Lord and commoner blushed in shared humiliation.

"Well, well, my darlings. It seems that suffering for my pleasure humbles you. What a wonderful weakness I've discovered. Perhaps I'll use that to my advantage some time tonight." Her voice dripped with cunning and impending threat.

With that, she placed the second blow of the cane across the Lord's other ass-cheek; the third and fourth blows landed low across the ass, in that sweet spot that best transmutes pain into pleasure. She planted the fifth and sixth blows across the back of his thighs.

As she repeated the cycle of blows, she set Gabrielle to a new task. "Girl," she said, "I believe it's time you showed our Lord how gifted your lips are."

Gabrielle fell to her knees, crawled under the bench, and latched her lips to the Lord's cock in the same devouring passion that he had brought to her breast. The Lord squirmed and groaned as the girl sucked and nibbled his meat, as Marie Martinet applied the cane over and over again, engulfing him fully in pain and pleasure.

Reactions. Marie Martinet lived for them when she worked; she loved to produce them, watch them, revel in them. Watching a client react to her efforts made Marie Martinet heady with heat and wicked delight. Already, she knew that as soon as the Lord was escorted from her quarters she'd drag Gabrielle to her and make the girl feast between her legs.

As she continued caning the Lord, he became increasingly lost in the lust of pain and pleasure, so much so that she decided to tease him further. She stopped the caning and watched Gabby suck the man's cock. Its length repeatedly slipped from sight and into Gabby's mouth as the girl worked, first taking it completely, then slipping back to its head, lingering there, tongue swirling, then finally devouring it fully again.

Marie Martinet stepped close to the Lord's ear, and as she spoke she rested the cane gently over his back, a sensual reminder of its presence.

"My girl sucks cock well, doesn't she, my Lord?"

The lord whimpered, then managed a weak, "Yes."

"I love to watch her service a man with her mouth, you know," Marie continued. "She's such a willing little whore, and around here it's easy to find a man decadent enough to slide his member down her throat."

The Lord quivered. *Ah*, she realized, *a little nasty talk has some distance with this man*. So she continued teasing.

"You like it when she tongues you, don't you? I can see you like how she buries your shaft into her throat. Perhaps I should arrange a private showing for you so you can watch her suck a man dry. Perhaps, my Lord, I can toy with you while she does."

Marie Martinet ran her hand down the crack of his ass to his puckered hole. "I do have a lurid assortment of phalluses," she commented as she started rubbing his asshole. "I could, if you wish, take one of them and –"

Rather than tell him, she shoved a finger up him. The Lord cried out. Marie slowly finger-fucked him and cooed into his ear, "Would you like that, my Lord?"

A distant even more breathy "yes" answered her.

"Gabby," she said, "I want to play a little game with our guest. Draw your lips to his cock-head and keep them there." Improvisation, Marie Martinet knew, was the name of her best game. What good was her talent if she didn't use it to her own liking? If this man must squirm, he would do it because of her cruel cunning.

As Gabby complied, Marie Martinet reached forward and wrapped her thumb and middle finger around the Lord's shaft, about mid-length. "My fingers are like a cock ring around him, girl. Bring your lips to meet them. You suck, I'll masturbate. Now."

The Lord melted at the sensations: Mademoiselle's finger up his ass, working the knob of his prostate in a grand pleasurable pressure, her hand sliding up and down his cock in a tormenting duet with Gabby's mouth. And Gabby's mouth, so wet and willing, her tongue still flicking. Marie Martinet squeezed his cock as they worked him, finally settling at the base of his cock, Gabby fully throating his entire length. It was all the Lord could do to contain himself.

Spotting this, Marie Martinet pulled her finger from his ass, her hand from his cock, and resumed her caning. Thwarted, the pace changing yet again, the Lord cried out in exasperation and excitement.

But his ass could take little more, and within a few strokes Marie Martinet stopped. She ordered the girl from the Lord's cock and, together, they took him from the spanking-bench and led him to the divan.

"Next time," Marie Martinet teased, "I'll leave something rough for you to sit on. Perhaps some sandpaper?"

The Lord smiled, dazed and speechless. His meat still bobbed, undeniably rock-hard.

"Now, sit back and watch, my Lord. It's time I readied my girl for your final pleasure."

With that, she grabbed Gabrielle by the hair and dragged the half-naked girl to the horse. "Up!" she commanded. The girl climbed into place, her breasts dangling, their swaying accentuated by her heavy, expectant breathing. Marie Martinet hiked the girl's skirts up around her waist, her soft, fleshy buttocks revealed, her legs spread enough to expose the sweet lips of her cunt.

Marie Martinet observed, "Ah, yes, my Lord. I'm sure you'll be quite pleased with my girl's portal. But first, let me add some marks to her unblemished ass to make her even more presentable to you."

The first blow of the cane to Gabrielle's ass elicited stifled cries from the girl, but Marie Martinet knew how to work the child into a state of crying and begging. After each stroke of the cane, she caressed the stricken spot with her own gentle hand, then moved to the girl's mound of pleasure, mixing arousal and pain to such extreme heights that soon Gabrielle's ass displayed an assortment of criss-crossing red welts and the girl was literally begging to be fucked.

"You want our Lord to use you, girl, is that it?" Marie Martinet taunted, masturbating the girl and keeping her on edge as she spoke.

"Yes, Mademoiselle, yes!" The girl was frantic with lust.

Marie Martinet knew the Lord loved this spectacle, and as she looked across the room to him his lurid desire was obvious. His eyes gleamed with cruel delight and he stroked his insistent cock, its head glistened with pre-cum. Marie gleamed back at him, sharing the lust. She knew the girl was ready – her cunt was as wet as her pleas were sincere.

"Come, my Lord, take her," Marie Martinet urged. "She's ripe and she's all yours."

The Lord didn't require a second invitation. He rose from the divan and approached the bench, coming around behind it. Marie Martinet pushed a broad step up to the bench with her foot and moved aside.

With a grunt, the Lord stepped up to Gabrielle's backside, taking his cock in his hand and aiming it at her ready cunt, all the while aroused by the bright red marks that beautifully marred the young girl's backside. With a second grunt, he penetrated her and buried his thick length into her. Gripping her by the hips, he began grinding himself, enjoying the ripples of pleasure that raked him with every stroke. Gabrielle cried out as he fucked her in slow, measured movements, as he stroked her welted ass with his hand, making her squirm.

The girl's reaction inspired Marie Martinet, and she came alongside the Lord, saying, "Let's make this little bitch writhe for you, Lord." She landed a firm slap of her hand to his ass, driving him deep into the girl.

Gabrielle jumped like a horse breaking its harness.

"Good God," the Lord moaned at her reaction. He couldn't help but seize the bucking girl and fuck her with bullish power.

Marie Martinet smiled deviously and planted more blows to the Lord, matching the pace of his strokes, sending both Lord and commoner into a lustful frenzy. They tangled themselves in the sounds of slapping, hand to ass and cock to wet cunt, the girl's captive cries, the Lord's snorting breaths, the Mademoiselle's verbal taunts. The Lord pumped frantically, sending his lathe deep into the girl, impaling her. She could no more escape his clutches than he could Marie Martinet's orchestrations.

Soon, the girl wilted, a limp doll exhausted into silence, existing only for the Lord's insatiable fucking. Seeing her conquered, knowing that they had reduced her to a mere object of his pleasure, the Lord immediately reached a sudden and raging climax.

Equally spent, he collapsed over the worn girl's body.

Satisfaction, the mark of a job well done. Marie Martinet could only hope the satisfaction she'd gained from her evening with the Lord would last as long as the cane marks across his ass. It was one thing to ply a trade, another thing to find joy in it, and Marie Martinet had truly enjoyed her evening's work. Later, when she dragged Gabby to her and buried the girl beneath her skirts for her own pleasure, she relived every heated moment all over again. Fortunately for the tired Gabby, it took no time at all for her Mistress to find a second satisfaction.

That night, she rewarded Gabby with a night in her bed, in her comforting arms, beneath lush, warm bedding. There, Marie Martinet prayed that she'd find greater rewards and fame for her efforts and no longer feel cast adrift.

And the rewards did come, late the next day, generous and grand. The Lord expressed his thanks in the form of a healthy stipend for Marie Martinet, a lovely gown for Gabrielle, and a new team of horses for Mrs Collet's stable. Mrs Collet, usually so savvy and discerning, practically fell into bubbling prattle.

"Such talent you have, Mademoiselle du Contemaine, for us to all be so blessed! Good things will come of this, mark my words. Good things will come."

Marie Martinet smiled superbly. Her satisfaction was complete.

And good things did come. Within three weeks, while drinking wine and gossiping between acts at the opera, a manservant begged entry into their box. He delivered a note which bore only one thing: the mark of the Royal seal.

In return, Marie Martinet placed a French franc within the palm of the manservant and told him, "France awaits His Majesty." And, looking across the theater to the royal box, Marie Martinet curtseyed low and long, demurely, until the manservant returned to the Royal box, delivered the coin as directed, and the subtle Royal nod of George IV acknowledged her from afar.

THE GOLD BUG OF JEAN LAFITTE

O'Neil De Noux

"It is the loveliest thing in creation!"
The Gold *Bug* by Edgar Allan Poe

Monday, 13 July 1891, early afternoon.
The creole townhouse at 77 Toulouse Street stood out from the other townhouses lining the narrow French Quarter street because of the police officer standing in front of its worn, cypress door and the small crowd gathered across the street.

As Dugas approached from Chartres Street, the police officer turned and took off his powder-blue bowler hat, wiped his brow with a handkerchief and said, "Good afternoon, Detective Dugas."

"Good afternoon, Officer Clavin."

Clavin ran the handkerchief through his short reddish-brown hair before returning the bowler to his head.

"Figured they'd be calling you," he told Dugas as the detective stepped up. "All these people speak French."

Dugas pulled his notepad and a pencil from his coat pocket and jotted a brief description of the building – three stories with a black wrought-iron balcony running along the second floor – the building's stucco façade painted a drab yellow.

At six feet, Detective Jacques Dugas was a thin man with an olive complexion, a thick mustache and Mediterranean dark brown eyes. His gray suit was lightweight and his dress shirt collar unstarched to combat the heat and humidity of another fierce New Orleans summer. At twenty-six years old, Dugas was the youngest detective on the force.

"They're in apartment 3D," Clavin advised, pointing to a white sign with maroon letters next to the door. The sign read: *E. Legrand, Professor of Magnetic Physiology.*

"They?"

"Two bodies. A man and a girl." Clavin looked away nervously. "Here comes Dr Miller now."

A portly man carrying a black case came around the corner from Decatur Street. Holding on to his brown derby, the doctor shuffled toward them.

Turning into the building, Dugas paused and asked Clavin. "Whom did you mean when you said, 'They all speak French'?"

"The landlord and the other tenants."

"Ah." Dugas ascended the narrow stairs to the third floor. The building smelled of stale beer and dust. Apartment 3D was at the rear of the building, its door slightly ajar. Pushing the door open, Dugas stood in the doorway, letting his eyes adjust to the dimness inside.

The shutters were drawn and the only illumination came from two candles at either end of the small apartment. Flickering candlelight danced off the walls and cast black shadows across the room. It took Dugas a moment to realize the floor was littered with stacks of yellowed newspapers and magazines and piles of books. Leaning inside, Dugas immediately smelled the unmistakable odor of chloroform.

Footsteps arrived on the landing behind Dugas. He leaned back out of the room to allow the doctor entrance. Nodding as he passed, Dr Miller stepped into the room, stopped immediately and flipped on the electric light switch just inside the door.

A crystal and brass chandelier, hanging from the center of the water-stained ceiling, bathed the room in bright light. The doctor and Dugas blinked.

"Damn," the doctor said to the brightness. He let out a nasal breath and began weaving his way through the stacks of books.

Dugas moved forward and saw them on the bed.

Both lay on their backs, the man nearest them. Wearing a white shirt and dark pants with suspenders, the man's feet were bare, his right leg dangling from the bed. The woman was naked, her head turned toward the man, her long brown hair covering her face. Her skin was chalky white beneath the electric light.

Dugas followed the doctor who, upon arriving at the far side of the bed, reached for the woman's hand. Dugas could see she was young. Twenty maybe. The man appeared closer to forty. Stopping at the foot of the bed, Dugas saw blood on the man's chest. He wiped perspiration from his temples and picked up another scent, faintly. Roses.

"Still warm," the doctor said as he let the woman's hand down and leaned forward to press his ear against her chest. He felt the pulse at her wrist then at her neck, then rolled back her eyelid before letting out a long breath.

"Dead."

The doctor moved around the bed for the man.

Stepping out of the way, Dugas kicked something, which rolled away. A blue medicine bottle tumbled across the floor toward the fireplace. Something smoldered in the fireplace, giving off an orange glow.

Dugas retrieved the bottle just as the doctor declared the man was also dead. The bottle reeked of chloroform and the word was printed on a red label on the bottle. The label was from J. Broussard, Pharmacist. Dugas had passed Broussard's Pharmacy moments earlier, around the corner on Chartres.

"Aha," Dr Miller said. He leaned forward and picked a small knife off the bed next to the man's left hand. He held the knife up for Dugas, then carefully placed it on a stack of books next to the bed.

"Self-inflicted," Dr Miller said, waving at the man on the bed. He belched loudly and said, "Open the windows. The chloroform is sickening."

Dugas stepped to the nearest window and pulled it up. Unlocking the louvred shutters, he threw them open and took in a deep breath of warm, summer air. Dugas looked down into the dilapidated courtyard behind the building. A scraping sound caused him to look up in time to see three small boys scurry over the roof of the building directly beyond the courtyard.

"Look here," Dr Miller said, which caused Dugas to turn around. The doctor had pulled the hair from the woman's face and pointed at her mouth. "Her lips are burned from the chloroform."

Dugas stepped forward. He caught a whiff of the doctor's whiskey breath. The woman's full lips were stained purple. Dugas examined her body again – her full breasts and small waist, her round hips and thick mat of pubic hair. Her legs were long and slim and her toenails were painted pink.

Such a waste, Dugas could not help from thinking. Such a beautiful woman. Suddenly he felt his neck flush. He wanted to pull the sheet over the body, to cover her, but he knew there was no dignity in death, no privacy for a corpse. Once a young, vibrant woman, she was now a specimen to be examined, probed and studied like an insect beneath a microscope. He looked away.

Dr Miller sat on a stack of books a few feet from the bed, and pulled a note pad from his black case. Dugas glanced around. On a small wooden table next to the bed lay a stack of pink cards and two sheets of paper. Dugas moved to them and saw the sheets of paper were pharmacist's receipts, both from J. Broussard and both in the name of Dr E. Legrand. Dugas noted the date on both receipts were today's date.

Leaning forward, he picked up one of the pink cards, which appeared to be a business card. In neat calligraphy, the card read:

Let us look for truth.
Let us do good.
Let us be magnetized!

Dr Etienne Legrand, 77 Rue Toulouse, New Orleans

"Magnetized?" Dugas said.

"What?" Dr Miller responded just as a man sporting a red handlebar mustache and mutton chops stepped into the room. Detective Patrick Shannon waved at Dugas, pulled off his tan derby and introduced himself to Dr Miller. Although he stood the same height as Dugas, Shannon was bulkier and appeared larger in his pin-striped brown suit, two sizes too small for him.

Turning back to Dugas, Dr Miller asked, "What did you say about 'magnetized'?"

As Dugas opened his mouth to answer, the man on the bed suddenly sat up. Dr Miller fell off the stack of books. The man on the bed turned, looked down at the dead woman and started crying.

"*Mon Dieu! Mon Dieu!*" The man pulled at his hair and cried out in French. "I meant to die. I meant to die!"

Dugas wrote what the man said in his notes. He could see Shannon moving forward, past the doctor who was struggling to rise.

The man on the bed started searching the bed and cried out. "Where is it? Where?"

Seeing the knife on the nearby stack of books, he reached for it, only to have Shannon grab his hand.

"We'll 'ave none o'that!"

The man pulled back and cringed away from Shannon. He seemed to notice the doctor for the first time, then Dugas.

"Are you Dr Legrand?" Dugas asked.

The man nodded, opened his mouth for a faint, "*Oui.*" Then the man swooned and fell off the bed.

"Dammit to hell," Shannon growled as he reached for the man.

"I'll attend to him," Dr Miller said. "You go down and tell that copper to fetch an ambulance."

The doctor sat Legrand up and administered to him. Dugas continued searching the apartment, making note of the chifforobe in the corner, with several men's suits inside and one pink dress on a wooden hanger.

Loud voices boomed outside the door. Dugas moved that way as Clavin backed into the room. A red-faced man tried to push his way past Clavin.

"Hold on," Clavin ordered, shoving the man back.

The man stopped and stared past Clavin at the bed for a moment, before collapsing against the doorframe.

"Julie! My Julie!" The man wailed, and then lunged past Clavin.

Dugas caught him between two stacks of magazines, and with Clavin's help moved the man back into the hallway.

"Oh, no. No. No!" The man fell to the floor and covered his head with his hands.

Dugas put a friendly hand on Clavin's shoulder and asked him to go back down and keep anyone else from entering the building.

"And keep those who are inside, inside."

Clavin took off his bowler. "This man says the woman is his daughter."

Dugas nodded, and urged Clavin back down the stairs.

Presently, Shannon returned with two white-clad ambulance attendants carrying a gurney. Dugas helped the crying man out of the way, standing him in the corner of the hall next to the hall's lone window. He opened the window and shutters and waited.

Obviously a carpenter, the man wore a leather apron with a hammer dangling from a loop and several pockets stuffed with other tools. His soiled shirt was worn badly near the collar and his work pants had small holes at the knees.

The man finally quit wailing, just as the gurney with Legrand exited the room, followed by Shannon. Turning to Dugas, the man asked, "Is Dr Legrand dead?"

Dugas shook his head and asked the man his name.

"Louis Maigret." The man's callused hands wiped tears from his eyes. He looked into Dugas' eyes. "What happened?" And, as quickly, he said, "I know. I know. I should have stopped this. I knew it was bad."

The man sank to the floor and sat with his back to the wall.

Going down on his haunches next to the man, Dugas said, "Tell me, *monsieur*. Tell me what you know."

The man spoke quickly, and Dugas hurried to write every word in his notes.

Louis Maigret had met Dr Legrand near Jackson Square about a year ago. Legrand was passing out business cards. Newly arrived from Paris, Legrand seemed a refined gentleman. Maigret was honored when Legrand struck up a friendship with a common carpenter.

Dr Legrand's practice grew steadily. Using magnetism, Legrand was able to cure many maladies, especially in women. But Julie had had no malady. She was a medium for Legrand as they searched for the treasure of Jean Lafitte.

"I'm sorry," Dugas interrupted. "Did you say treasure?"

"Dr Legrand was privileged to have information that Jean Lafitte buried a great treasure in the swamps and islands of Barataria. He needed a medium, a young girl, a *virgin* to help him."

Dugas tried to keep his face as expressionless as possible as he asked, "How?"

Maigret described Legrand's "treatments" in detail. Dugas jotted feverishly.

Using hypnosis, aided by chloroform, Legrand would put Julie into a trance where she was more easily drawn to his magnetic powers. She would talk, giving directions to the treasure.

"They went several times down to Barataria and Grand Isle." The man covered his face with his hands again and cried.

Dugas waited, wiping perspiration from his face with his handkerchief. Dr Miller peeked out of the room but ducked back in quickly. A mockingbird landed on the windowsill, bounced once, then flew off. Maigret's crying finally subsided.

"Julie –" the man's voice cracked. He sucked in a deep breath. "My daughter is a strong-willed girl. I was afraid. You see, she hung around with all sorts of boys and I thought she'd be safe with Dr Legrand."

Tears streamed again down the man's face.

A sourness in Dugas' stomach, from not eating lunch, seemed to acidify as he stood up and waited next to the grieving father. Footsteps echoed up the stairs and presently two white-clad mortuary attendants appeared, carrying another gurney. Their dark brown faces glistened with sweat.

A few minutes later, Dr Miller led the gurney out, a white sheet covering the corpse of Julie Maigret. The father watched silently, blinking tears from his eyes.

Shannon passed them on the stairs and hurried back up to Dugas, who pulled him aside and asked that Shannon continue searching the room.

"I will finish interviewing the father and the landlord and tenants."

Taking off his derby, Shannon nodded and stepped into the death room.

Dugas turned back to the father, who was now standing, and

said, "Today, *monsieur*. Tell me how Julie's day started and how she came to be here today."

Monday, 13 July 1891, late afternoon.
Stepping out of Broussard's Pharmacy, Dugas tucked his notepad and pencil back into his coat pocket. Passing several Mustache-Petes – olive-skinned Sicilians with long black mustaches who always wore black suits – Dugas looked them in the eye, but didn't stare. The Italians, who had been talking, stopped talking until they passed.

Dugas walked to the corner of Toulouse Street and looked down at the yellow façade of number 77. A small crowd still stood across the street, but Clavin was gone.

Turning around, Dugas moved up Toulouse, away from the death house. As he walked along the narrow street, he could not help but thinking how misery was a frequent visitor to this particular street. In 1788, the great fire which had destroyed nearly eighty percent of New Orleans had begun on Toulouse Street. Appropriate for a street named for a bastard son of Louis XIV.

Arriving at Royal Street, Dugas waited for the streetcar. The sharp scent of tomato gravy wafting from a nearby house caused his stomach to grumble. The old French Quarter, an ever-growing Italian slum, was a shadow of its former glory. Littered with rickety vegetable carts, sheets hanging from lace balconies, its Creole cottages crumbled in disrepair, its alleys filled with refuse.

Several dark-haired boys raced past Dugas, yelling at each other in Italian as they played. A mule-driven streetcar arrived and Dugas climbed aboard, discreetly showing his badge to the driver before taking his seat. Policemen rode free.

Settling in the hardwood seat, Dugas pulled his notes from his pocket and went over them again, and jotted several questions he had for the charlatan who called himself *Dr* Etienne Legrand.

Monday, 13 July 1891, early evening.
Legrand lay in a private room along the back side of Charity Hospital. An NOPD man sat on a folding chair in the hall.

"The doctor said no visitors," the bored copper told Dugas as the detective stepped into the room.

"The doctor can fuck himself."

The copper laughed so hard he nearly fell off the chair.

Legrand sat up immediately. He wore a white nightshirt.

Dugas opened his jacket to show his gold star-and-crescent NOPD badge pinned inside his lapel. "I am Detective Jacques Dugas –"

Legrand screamed in French, "I protest!"

"Shut up." Dugas turned and closed the door. He had planned to go easy, to be nice, to get Legrand to talk by stealth, but, seeing the smug look on Legrand's face as he lay in a private room, Dugas changed his mind.

"I protest!" Legrand shouted again.

"We speak in English, you two-bit charlatan." Dugas moved to the bed, grabbed Legrand by the throat and squeezed hard. Legrand flailed his arms and gasped.

Dugas waited several seconds before letting go. Legrand sank back on the bed and rubbed his throat. Dugas pulled his notepad from his pocket, thumbed back through his notes until he reached the proper page.

"When you said, 'I meant to die' – did you mean it?"

Legrand nodded slowly.

Dugas withdrew his snub-nosed Smith & Wesson 38, cocked the hammer and pressed it against Legrand's left temple. "Now, if you put your finger here." Dugas grabbed Legrand's hand and pulled it up to the gun. "Put it right here against the trigger and pull – you won't ever have to say you meant to die again."

Legrand's mud-brown eyes were ovaled, his lower lip quivering.

"Do you want me to do it for you?"

Tears formed in Legrand's eyes as he shook his head slowly.

"Then we'll have no more protesting, now, will we?" Dugas withdrew the revolver, uncocking it as he slipped it back into its holster on his right hip. Flipping forward in his notes, Dugas said, "When did you decide to kill her? This morning? Yesterday?"

Legrand only blinked at Dugas.

"At nine a.m. you bought a bottle of chloroform at Broussard's Pharmacy. At noon you came rushing back in a frenzy, even angry, and purchased another bottle."

Dugas skipped over Broussard's description of Legrand as a "gentleman" and a "scientist."

"The first bottle wasn't enough, was it?"

Dugas looked up from his notes at the muddy eyes. Legrand blinked again. Dugas reached and tapped the stock of his 38.

Legrand waved his arms again and said, "This is a plot, *monsieur*. A plot to besmirch the fair name of France."

Dugas almost laughed.

"You, *monsieur*. You are hounding me because I am French. I demand to see the Counsel!"

Dugas pressed his knees against the bed and leaned forward, causing Legrand to lean back away.

"I am French, you ass."

"You are American-French. *I* am French!"

"What you are, *monsieur*, is a murderer. And I am the man who will bring you to the gallows."

Legrand became still. Dugas leaned away and flipped through his notes again. "Now, Julie Maigret has been 'assisting' you for six months. Because she is a virgin, correct?"

Legrand closed his eyes. Then opened them and suddenly yanked off the sheet covering his legs. He jumped out of the other side of the bed, leaped to the window and climbed up on the windowsill. Reaching for the heating pipes overhead, Legrand pulled himself up, kicking his feet against the wall.

The door opened and the copper stuck his head in.

"What the hell's he doing?"

"I have no idea," Dugas said as Legrand shimmied higher up the wall.

A doctor appeared behind the copper and said, "What is the meaning of this?"

Legrand howled like a wolf, craned his neck forward and fell head-first to the floor.

The doctor rushed to his aid as a nurse hurried in, pushing Dugas aside.

Legrand moaned loudly as the doctor checked his head.

Dugas put his notepad back into the coat pocket and headed for the door.

"Wait!" The doctor pointed to Dugas. "Who are you to question my patient?"

Still moving, Dugas turned and said, "I am the man who will finish what that charlatan began."

"*Mon Dieu!*" Legrand cried. "*Mon Dieu!*"

Wednesday, 15 July 1891, late morning.
Standing between two cement sepulchres, near the rear of St Louis Cemetery Number Two, Dugas and Shannon watched at a discreet distance as Julie Maigret's casket was slid into an open tomb in the back wall of the cemetery.

Wearing another lightweight suit, his blue one, Dugas felt perspiration under his arms and along the small of his back. The unrelenting, semi-tropical sun beat down on his exposed head. Humidity, like a bowl of steaming rice, sweltered around them.

Shannon fanned himself with his black derby. He wore a black pin-striped suit today. Fifty yards away, Louis Maigret wore his only suit, also black. A priest said a prayer and sprinkled holy water into the oven tomb. Dugas counted the people in attendance. Eighteen.

"I heard the wounds on his chest barely broke the skin," Shannon said.

Dugas nodded.

"What about his head, when he dove?"

"Headache."

"I was thinking," Shannon said, "maybe we should contact the French police about this character."

Dugas smiled to himself. "I telegraphed the Sûreté yesterday."

Shannon fanned his coat. "Good. Good. I wonder why Dr Miller thought he was dead."

"Combination of chloroform and whiskey."

"What?"

"Legrand's chloroform and Miller's whiskey."

Dugas noticed a veiled woman in black move to Louis Maigret and wrap her arms around him. The small crowd began to filter back through the cemetery, led by the priest. Two impatient gravediggers peeked out from behind another sepulchre, obviously waiting for Maigret and the woman to leave so they could quickly plaster over the oven tomb, sealing the casket in the long wall of tombs.

"What did the autopsy reveal?" Shannon asked. "She die of chloroform poisoning?"

"Yes. It also revealed a motive."

"Yes?" Shannon bounced on his toes.

"Legrand needed a virgin for his experiments, correct?"

"If you say so." Shannon fanned himself faster with his hat.

"Julie Maigret was with child."

"Damn!"

Standing away from the woman in black, Maigret reached up and touched the casket before leading the woman back through the cemetery. As they passed Dugas and Shannon, Maigret looked their way and told the woman something.

The woman pulled away from him and hurried toward the detectives. Dugas stepped forward to meet her. When she lifted the veil from her face and focused her large blue eyes at Dugas, he felt a sudden surge in his heartbeat.

"Monsieur Detective," she said with a deep, breathless voice. "I must speak with you." Beautiful. There was no other way to describe her. Her wide eyes and small nose, the line of her cheeks, round chin combined to make her even prettier than her younger sister. This slightly older version of Julie wore her dark brown hair in long curls.

She raised a shaking left hand to her full lips.

"*Monsieur*, you must help me."

"Of course," Dugas answered, wanting to reach out to still her shaking hand. He could see Maigret approaching behind the woman.

"*Monsieur*, have you found the gold bug?"

"The what?"

She leaned closer and Dugas picked up a scent – of roses.

Maigret arrived and placed a hand on the woman's shoulder.

"*Monsieur*." Her voice rose. "You must find the gold bug! It is in Legrand's room."

"No," Maigret complained. "No!"

The woman pulled away, turned and headed quickly for the carriages waiting at the front of the cemetery. Shannon stepped next to his partner and let out a long sigh.

Dugas started to follow, but Maigret raised a hand.

"Monsieur Detective. My daughter is distraught. Perhaps you can question her later?"

Dugas watched as the woman stepped through the gates of the cemetery and climbed into a dark carriage, a very fine carriage. Looking back at Maigret, Dugas asked, "What is your daughter's name?"

Maigret let out a long breath. "Bridgette. She is my eldest. Bridgette Madison. She lives on St Charles with the family of her husband."

Maigret choked back a sob. "Bridgette married a rich American last year. He was on the *Utopia*. You remember the collision off Gibraltar? It was in all the papers."

Last March. Dugas remembered. The British iron-clad *Anson* had collided with the *Utopia*, sending her down with over five hundred souls, including several New Orleanians.

"First her husband and now this." Maigret wiped a tear from his eye. Faintly, he whispered, "Now this."

Wednesday, 15 July 1891, late afternoon.
Stepping off the streetcar on St Charles Avenue at the corner of Marengo, Dugas looked in his notes again for the address Maigret had reluctantly given for his daughter, the widow Madison. The house was in the center of the block along the river side of the avenue. A sprawling, three story Greek Revival home, painted a pale yellow, the wide front yard held two large oaks and an immense magnolia tree.

Passing through the black wrought-iron gate, Dugas moved up the brick walkway. Cooler under the trees, the air smelled of freshly cut grass. Climbing the twenty marble steps to a wide second-story gallery with six gilded Corinthian columns, Dugas rang the bell next to the cut-glass front door and waited.

Expecting a servant to answer, Dugas was surprised when Bridgette opened the door and blinked her eyes at him in genuine surprise. She had her hair pinned up in barrettes at her temples. As she looked back over her shoulder for a moment, Dugas could not help staring at the curve of her bare neck. And he remembered her father said she was twenty-three.

She grabbed his hand and pulled him into a foyer, past a wide staircase and into a parlor. She closed the door, moved to a small table and turned on an electric lamp.

She was wearing a white dress, a lightweight, cotton summer dress (common for New Orleans women during the hottest months), and Bridgette's figure was plainly visible with the light behind her. She was taller than her sister – nearly five feet ten inches.

"*Monsieur*, we must keep our voices down." Again the breathless voice. "Did you find it?"

Dugas shook his head. "I just came from Legrand's. What does it look like?"

Bridgette stepped around Dugas toward the French doors that faced the front yard. She waved him along. "It is brilliant gold, perhaps three inches in length. A golden bug with six short legs and two stones of polished onyx embedded in it. It will be on a gold chain."

Dugas shook his head again. "I searched the place thoroughly. For nearly three hours."

Bridgette fidgeted with a small pink ribbon on the collar of her dress.

"I found books on magnetism and hypnotism and vampirism and even lycanthropy."

"Lycanthropy?" Bridgette blinked her eyes and seemed to come out of a momentary fog.

"The belief that a human can change into the shape of an animal. Usually a wolf."

"Werewolves. Legrand was always talking about the Loup Garous in the deep swamps around Barataria. He believed in them." The tone in her voice showed she did not.

Stepping forward, she grabbed Dugas' lapel. "*Monsieur*. You *must* find it!" Her breath fell across his lips.

Dugas licked his lips and said, "Why?"

Bridgette shot a frightened look toward the parlor door. "It is the most beautiful object in creation. It has *powers*. Do you understand? Ancient powers."

The door suddenly opened and Bridgette jumped away from Dugas, toward the French doors. An old woman in a long black dress stepped in and glared at Dugas.

"Mama. This is the police." Bridgette's voice wavered. "He is here about my sister."

The woman's mouth opened into an "O" and she nodded slowly before backing out of the door. Just before closing it, she gave Bridgette a disapproving look. "Do not stand next to the windows."

Bridgette ignored the remark and let out a long sigh of relief when the door closed.

Dugas reached into his coat pocket for a business card and passed it to Bridgette, who studied the card carefully. Standing in front of the glass doors, with the sunlight behind her, Bridgette's figure was again plainly visible through the diaphanous dress. He could not stop himself from staring at the roundness of her breasts, at her nipples, at the darkness between her legs.

Dugas felt a growing passion rising in his loins. He tried to look away, but only managed to move his gaze up to Bridgette's gorgeous face.

"Detective Dugas," her voice was calmer now. "It is imperative, *most* imperative you find the gold bug. Will you please search again for it? Please?"

The door opened again and the old woman came in, followed by a tall Negro butler carrying a silver tray.

"Tea," the woman announced in a sharp, unfriendly voice.

Bridgette stepped around Dugas and said, "Detective Dugas was just leaving." Reaching back, she touched his hand and held it a moment.

The old woman waved the butler to a small serving table. "Well, then, we can have our tea right here."

Bridgette's shoulders sank. "I will walk you out," she told Dugas.

"Alvin will see him to the door," the old woman said. The butler hurriedly set up the tea settings and then started for the parlor door with the silver tray in hand.

Dugas stepped around Bridgette.

"You will keep me informed?" Bridgette said behind him.

Turning back for one more look at her body, Dugas nodded. His heart stammering, he readjusted the bulge between his legs as he followed Alvin through the foyer and then into the bright afternoon sunlight.

Wednesday, 15 July 1891, early evening.

Bounded by streets with amiable names like Orleans, Tremé, St Ann and Marais, the brooding, grim Parish Prison stood like a concrete medieval monolith a few short blocks from the elegant balconies of the French Quarter.

Entering the prison, Dugas passed a number of people waiting to visit inmates. The room smelled of perfume, probably from the inordinate amount of ladies, Dugas figured as he slipped past the visitors into the detention area.

A hulking prison guard with a protruding brow led Dugas through a labyrinth of dark corridors to the second floor, where Legrand stood alone in his cell. In a white shirt and gray prison dungarees, a white patch on his head, Legrand moved forward when he saw Dugas and gripped his cell bars.

"I demand to know why I'm being held incommunicado."

The guard slapped Legrand's hands. "Aw, shuddap! Ya fuckin' Frog."

Legrand pulled his hands back and set a pleading stare at Dugas.

"Ya can talk to the bastard through the bars," the guard said, and turned to leave.

"Why are my visitors not allowed to see me?" Legrand asked.

"Visitors?" The guard stopped. "All them fuckin' women! What are ya, some kinda super-fucker?" The guard walked away laughing, adding over his shoulder, "Ya ain't getting a sniff of pussy, ya fuckin' degenerate."

Legrand grabbed the bars again and yanked at them. "I demand to communicate with the French Embassy in Washington. When France declares war on this barbaric country, we'll see who laughs last!"

He looked at Dugas, who took out his notepad and said, "Tell me, Monsieur Deschamps, how did you come up with the name Legrand?"

The man's eyes widened as he recognized Dugas. He let go of the bars again and shoved his hands in his pockets.

Dugas pulled the yellow telegram from his coat pocket. "According to the Sûreté, you were born Etienne Deschamps in Paris in 1850." Reading from the telegram now, Dugas added, "You were convicted of fraud three times, *monsieur*." Dugas looked back at the man. "Dabbling in the occult, I am told."

Legrand backed away to the small cot attached to the rear wall and sat.

Dugas waited.

Legrand finally spoke, "I will say nothing of Paris. It is too painful. I miss it too much." Looking at Dugas he asked, "Have you ever been to Paris?"

Dugas nodded.

"*Bon*. You said you were French-American." Legrand looked around his small cell. "Hopefully, you are a man of some culture, as limited as it may be in this despicable country."

Dugas waited.

"Do you seriously believe this . . . this escapade will end in anything but acquittal for me?" Legrand stared at Dugas, who kept his face from revealing anything.

"Murder? They have charged me with *murder!*" Legrand buried his face in his hands, almost theatrically. "I have been accused of being a charlatan, a fakir. I may have been careless in my administration of chloroform, but I am no murderer."

Moving quickly to the cell bars, Legrand said, "*Monsieur*, Julie Maigret was a whore. I thought she was a virgin, but she was a whore. Do you understand?"

Dugas took out his notepad and wrote exactly what Legrand had said about being a charlatan and a fakir and the careless administration of chloroform.

"It was an accident," Legrand added. "Her death was an accident and I tried to kill myself after. Isn't it obvious, even to you?"

When Dugas did not respond, Legrand retreated to his cot and lay upon it. After several long minutes, he said, "I am a victim of prejudice because I am a foreigner."

Dugas waited, but Legrand seemed finished.

"*Monsieur*." Dugas finally spoke. "Tell me about the gold bug."

Rising slowly, Legrand glared at Dugas, reached for the bars on the far side of his cell and began climbing. When he reached the top, he pulled his legs up, propelled himself out and landed head-first on the cement floor and lay motionless.

Dugas walked back to the guard and told him.

"Dammit. He keeps doin' that. We're gonna haveta chain him to his bed!" The guard snatched up a set of handcuffs and a ring of keys and hurried back to the cell. Dugas followed, but remained outside as the guard picked up a groggy Legrand and plopped him on the cot.

"Got the hardest goddamn head I ever saw," the guard added as he cuffed Legrand to his bed.

Leading Dugas out, the guard added, "He got loose yesterday, on his way to the infirmary. Ran down the hall like a lunatic, screaming he was free. Son-of-a-bitch fell down the stairs. Landed on his head. That's why he got the new bandage."

Reaching the waiting area, the guard sneered toward several women sitting in the inmate visiting area.

"You seen all them ladies." The guard spat disgustedly on the cement floor. "They're here to see him."

Good, Dugas thought. *I think I'll have a little talk with the ladies.*

Wednesday, 15 July 1891, midnight.

Dugas knew he was dreaming and wanted the dream to go on and on –

Bridgette came to him, found the Creole cottage on Mandeville Street where Dugas lived with his great-aunt, found his bedroom and stood at the foot of his bed. Moonlight, glimmering through the window, fell on her face as she slowly disrobed.

She wore the same white dress from that afternoon. Slowly she untied the small bow near her throat and then unbuttoned the dress all the way to her waist. The dress fell from her shoulders, exposing her full breasts and pink nipples. She unfastened the dress at the waist and it fell to the floor, and she stood there naked, her skin creamy white in the moonlight.

Bridgette sighed and reached up to pull the barrettes from her hair. She shook out her long hair, moved around the bed and stood next to Dugas, who stared at the thick mat of dark hair between her legs. She bent forward at the waist and her face hovered over his and her lips were purple. Her lips parted and they kissed and a dog outside barked loudly, waking Dugas.

He reached down to adjust his erection, then rolled over on his stomach. He felt his hips gyrating as he closed his eyes and envisioned Bridgette climbing into bed with him.

He dreamed again, but not of Bridgette. A swarm of gold bugs came as a dark cloud over the roofs of New Orleans. Their incessant buzz wavered as they flew into open windows, scattering children in playgrounds, running carriages into one another.

Dugas realized they weren't bugs. They were flying spiders, golden spiders from hell, with long, hooked talons and poison fangs. As large as a man's hand, the spiders fell on the people of New Orleans and felled them in their wake.

Dugas woke again, sat up in bed and rubbed his head.

Lying back, face up now, he closed his eyes and tried not to dream at all.

Thursday, 16 July 1891, early afternoon.

Sweating profusely, after another futile hour of searching for the gold bug, Dugas stepped over to the window to let air into Legrand's apartment. He slid the window open. As he reached for the shutters, he hesitated and peeked through the louvres. Four boys, sitting on the roof across the way, pointed at the window as Dugas cracked the louvres to look out.

Dugas slowly withdrew his hand and hurried out of the apartment. Racing around the corner, he made his way around to St Louis Street, locating the Creole townhouse directly behind Legrand's apartment house. He rushed up three flights of stairs to the hall dormer leading to the roof. Pausing to catch his breath, Dugas heard a door crack open behind him. Someone peeked out at him from one of the apartments.

He opened the lapel of his tan suit to show his badge. The door closed. The hall smelled of tomato gravy and garlic. Breathing regularly now, Dugas pushed open the dormer's wide window and climbed out. He braced a foot on the gutter, reached around the pilaster and scaled the high-pitched roof toward the boys sitting along the rooftop.

His foot slipped on the tiled roof and the boys saw him and scattered. Dugas got his footing and pressed on. One of the boys slipped and skidded toward Dugas, who reached out and grabbed the boy's leg.

The boy froze.

Dugas pulled himself and the boy to the rooftop and sat straddling the roof. Two of the boys jumped over the party wall dividing the building from the next townhouse. The fourth boy scampered the other way, around the brick chimney and over another party wall. In a moment all were gone, except the dark-haired boy sitting next to Dugas.

Staring at Dugas, the boy's dark brown eyes were the size of silver dollars, his little arms shook as he held on to the roof. In a red and white striped shirt and baggy gray shorts, the boy was barefoot and looked to be around eight years old.

"I'm a policeman," Dugas said in Italian, showing the boy his badge. "What's your name?"

Tears formed in the boy's eyes.

Dugas smiled warmly. "There's nothing to be afraid of. I just want to talk to you."

The boy started crying.

Dugas waited, feeling the sun hot on his head. A loud blast from a nearby ship caused him to look at the river. A steamboat passed a clipper ship along the big muddy water just beyond the levee, a couple hundred yards away.

When the crying diminished, Dugas pulled a handkerchief from his coat pocket and wiped the boy's face. Then he asked the boy his name.

"Salvatore," the boy said.

It took several more minutes to discover the boy's full name was Salvatore Caprera, nine years old, who lived on Decatur Street. It took even longer to get the boy down to the dormer and into the hallway.

"Come along," Dugas told the boy as he led the lad down to the street.

Holding the boy's shirt collar, Dugas led him up St Louis to Chartres. Crossing the narrow street, Dugas pointed to the Third Precinct Police Station.

"You want to go there?"

Sal shook his head.

"Then come along."

Dugas led the boy to Toulouse Street, turning left, away from Legrand's apartment house to a small Creole sandwich shop called Lautrec's. He sat the boy at an inside table and positioned himself close to the door.

He ordered croissants and coffee and cold milk for the boy. Salvatore was reluctant to eat, even when Dugas prodded him, but once he tasted the freshly baked, warm croissants he ate voraciously.

Dugas ordered more coffee and a second milk.

When the boy finally seemed at ease, Dugas told him again that he was not in trouble. Then he asked about the window the boys had been watching. He could see by the troubled look in the boy's eyes that this wouldn't be easy.

"What you saw is very important," he told the boy. "Very important."

Dugas took out his notepad and pencil, placing them next to his coffee cup. Patiently, he questioned the boy and slowly, ever so slowly, the story came out.

Dr Legrand, known to the boys only as "the tall man", usually kept the window open when his visitors came. He turned on the electric light and lit candles. Most of the women stripped to the waist voluntarily, before he put the white cloth over their face. Some of them took all of their clothes off. Legrand placed all of them on his bed and climbed on most of them.

One woman would stand naked in the window brushing her hair after.

Yes, Sal remembered the dark-haired woman last Monday, how Legrand opened the window and how she took all her clothes off, how Legrand cast a spell over her, then put the cloth over her mouth, how Legrand took off his clothes and climbed on her, how he got up later and hurriedly dressed, how he rushed out of the room and rushed back in later with a blue bottle in his hand. Fully clothed, Legrand climbed into bed with the woman. Later, he turned off the light and moved to the window and closed it.

Taking rapid notes, Dugas paused and asked, "What do you mean by putting a spell over them?"

"He swung a golden thing in front of them."

Looking at Sal's eyes, he carefully asked, "What did the man do with the golden thing after he had the women under his spell?"

"He hung it from the light."

The brass chandelier!

Thursday, 16 July 1891, late afternoon.

It hung near the center of the brass chandelier between two glass bobbles, shimmering in the light from the bulbs around it. The size of a large pecan, the gold bug had six short legs and two jet-black spots on its back. The spots looked like eyes and the bug resembled a skull or death's head. No, Dugas told himself, it was an Egyptian scarab, a golden beetle.

"Resurrection," Dugas told himself as he reached for it. In Ancient Egypt, the scarab stood for resurrection.

With trembling fingers, Dugas unwrapped the gold chain from the brass prong and climbed off the stack of books that Legrand had strategically placed beneath the chandelier. Holding the bug in the palm of his hand, he examined it closely. Brushed to a brilliant gold, its weight told Dugas it was solid. The black spots were polished gemstones, onyx, as Bridgette had described.

This piece of evidence was the final nail in Legrand's coffin. With this, and testimony from Salvatore and the other boys, Dugas could expose Legrand, the charlatan, the fakir, the seducer of women, the murderer of Julie Maigret. The district attorney liked neat packages.

Yet the more Dugas stared at the gold bug, the more beautiful it looked, the heavier it seemed to become. The longer he stared at it, the less sure he was that he even needed this.

He had solved this case the moment he stepped into the room. Convicting Legrand would be the DA's job. He wasn't judge and jury. Convicting Legrand would be easy for even the least experienced Assistant District Attorney, especially after the women from the Parish Prison filed in to tell a good New Orleans jury how this charlatan took advantage of them. Terribly embarrassed at first, they had been quite determined after Dugas spoke with them. It was an open and shut case.

Turning the gold bug over, letting it catch the light, rubbing his finger over it, Dugas felt its power. The cool metal warmed with his touch. Its brilliance shone so brightly he could barely look at it.

And suddenly, as if in a dream, she was there, standing in the doorway. Wearing a prim navy blue dress and matching hat, she stared at the gold bug in Dugas' hand. Slowly he extended his hand and let the bug dangle on its chain.

Slowly, Bridgette stepped in, closed the door and latched it. And, even more slowly, she removed her hat, removed the pins from her hair and shook it out. Stepping closer, her gaze still riveted to the bug, she dropped her purse and began unbuttoning her dress.

Dugas' breathing grew deeper, the stiffness growing between his legs as he stood there, holding the bug. Bridgette wore nothing beneath the dress. As her fingers reached her waist, she unfastened the thin belt and let it drop. She continued unbuttoning her dress, the cleavage of her creamy breasts plainly visible.

She lifted the skirt of the dress as she continued unbuttoning it, until it was completely open. Raising her hand, she pulled the dress off her shoulders and it fell to her feet.

Dugas traced his way down from her throat to her voluptuous breasts, to the pink areolae and pointed nipples, down past her flat stomach to her silky black pubic hair. He felt his organ throb as he leered at her nakedness.

Bridgette moved to him. Her eyes still focused on the gold bug, she pushed Dugas back, across the room to the bed. And it occurred to the detective, as he moved into the sunlight, that he had opened the window when he had returned.

Bridgette forced him to sit on the bed. Dugas inhaled a deep whiff of her rose perfume. Reaching for the golden chain, she lifted it from his hand and draped it over his neck, letting the gold bug fall against his chest. Craning her neck forward, she kissed the bug, then licked it, then took it in her mouth for a moment.

Pulling back, she let the bug fall against Dugas' chest again. Bridgette placed her hands on Dugas' shoulders and pressed herself forward, rubbing the nipple of her right breast against the bug. She switched to the left nipple and then back to the right. She sighed, her breath falling on Dugas' face, her bright red lips pursed in a red kiss.

She pushed Dugas to sit back on the bed, then climbed on him, her legs straddling him, her pubic hair pressed against his crotch. Leaning her head back, she continued rubbing her nipples against the gold bug.

Her pelvis moved in rhythm with her breasts. She rubbed herself against Dugas, grinding herself against his swollen organ. Breathing faster now, she let out little high-pitched gasps and reached for Dugas' hands.

Shoving his left hand under her ass, she moved his right hand between her legs, to her soft pubic hair and into the folds of her sweet womb. She was wet and hot as she worked herself against his fingers.

Her hands on his shoulders now, she bounced on his lap, her

breasts rubbing against Dugas' face. He kissed them and sucked her nipples, and she gasped and reached down to guide two of Dugas' fingers inside her. And she rode his fingers, up and down in long strokes.

Crying out in pleasure, this beautiful woman let his fingers fuck her, her juices lubricating his fingers. She smelled sickly sweet, of pure lust. Bridgette bounced higher and cried louder, until she suddenly stopped and sank down on his fingers, her legs quivering and a deep shudder convulsing her body.

"Oh!" she cried. "Oh, yes. Yes!"

She sank on him, wrapping her arms around his neck. She kissed his jaw and then his cheek and then his lips. Softly at first, she pressed the kiss harder, her tongue slipping into his mouth. They French kissed each other, tongues pressing together, Dugas' fingers still within her, his left hand kneading her ass.

The long kiss continued as their heads moved back and forth, as their tongues worked against each other. Finally, Bridgette came up for air and slowly climbed off Dugas.

Staring once again at the gold bug, she reached for his belt buckle . . .

Her warm fingers caressed his stiff organ and moved down its shaft in long, soft strokes. Dugas lay back on his elbows and moved his hips with the up and down movement of her hand. Then this gorgeous woman bent her face down and kissed the tip of his organ, her hair falling around his naked thighs.

She kissed her way down the shaft and licked her way back up, taking its tip in her mouth. As her head moved up and down, Dugas felt as if he'd explode. He stopped pumping and pulled her head away, bringing her mouth to his.

Elbowing his way up the bed, with Bridgette atop him, he succeeded in bringing his legs on the bed. He grabbed her ass as she pumped her hips against him, her tongue hot in his mouth.

Her hand slipped down and grabbed his organ and eased it into her. She sank on it slowly and rode it. The feel of her wet, steamy flesh brought Dugas so close to a climax he had to stop moving and strain to keep from gushing in her immediately.

Bridgette didn't help, bouncing on him, working herself against him. But Dugas gained control and began pumping himself back against her, feeling the length of his organ work inside this beautiful woman until he could hold back no longer. He felt himself squirting inside her, his hips bucking harder against her.

Bridgette gasped even louder and cried in pleasure and finally sank on him and stopped moving. She lay there, her sweet breath on his neck, her super-heated body pressing him to the wet bedding.

Rising finally, she pulled her hair back with one hand and kissed his lips softly. Standing on shaky legs, she crossed to her purse and pulled out a hairbrush. She moved to the window and stood there brushing her long hair.

Dugas watched her ass as she brushed her hair, his breath slowly returning to normal. He suddenly remembered what Salvatore had said about one woman standing in the window brushing her hair.

Leaning to his left, he saw the side of Bridgette's pretty face. She was looking across to the roof, where the boys had perched.

"Are they there?" he asked.

"Yes," she said in a deep, sexy voice. "Four of them, watching me."

She took a couple steps back and did a slow pirouette for the boys. They she turned and faced them again. At that angle, they could see all of her. She remained there, brushing her hair. Dugas watched her. Although his eyelids felt heavy, he fought to keep them open, not wanting to miss a moment.

"You must keep the gold bug, *monsieur*." Bridgette looked over her shoulder at him. "You must keep it – for us."

Dugas' pulse rose, and he felt his heart beating loud in his ears. Staring at those bright blue eyes, he knew, for the first time in his career, he would keep a piece of evidence. He would hide it behind the loose board in his bedroom wall, next to his bed.

"For us," she said. "You must keep it – for us."

Bridgette turned and walked slowly, languidly back to the bed.

"We must find another place to do this," she said, glancing around the room. "We can find one together, if you wish." Her voice was lower now, almost sad.

Dugas leaned up and kissed her breasts, then her neck, then up to her lips. Her tongue immediately found his and he felt her hand groping his chest and felt a tug on the gold chain.

Hold the bug, my darling.

Dugas reached around for her ass and pulled her up on the bed and they made love again on the bed where her sister had died.

LOVERS REBIRTH

Veronica Kelly

The Venetian Countryside, 1533

"TEACH ME, SANDRO," Julianne purred. She yawned and stretched her Venus body as she lay on the dais that was draped in crimson veiling.

I frowned. "Hold still!"

She was my model.

I was the painter. Though she plucked me from amongst my fellow brethren to do this one special task for her. Julianne said she chose me for my lush use of color and the way I brought emotion to my portraits. The fact that I was young and strong and, according to some Venetian girls, handsome, may have helped facilitate her decision to pay me a princely sum for this commission.

I averted my eyes to the gesso-covered wood, where I stroked a sheen of crimson tempera paint.

"I will not teach you. You're a woman," I replied to her supplication. I tried to sound convincing, but I knew in my heart it was a poor reason to deny a woman with obvious artistic talent the privilege to learn how to draw.

At the end of our first session together, Julianne had shyly, though with pride, shown me several of her charcoal sketches. Very impressive for one who had no formal training. Although her use of the rolling, rich plains of the Venetian countryside for her subject matter was unusual (my fellow brethren and myself were educated to depict the body, not the earth), it was understandable. Julianne did not wish to ask anyone to pose for her, considering she was a woman, so she used nature as her model. The only sketch of a human figure she had done was that of a kitchen servant, Maria. It was well executed.

Julianne now ran her long-fingered hands under the lavender veil that wrapped around her nude body. Her palms and fingers smoothed over thigh and belly, then cupped her full breasts. She rubbed and pinched her rosy nipples until they resembled young grapes popping to life on gray-green vines. She smiled, and laughter quelled in her throat when she saw my displeasure.

But I was far from displeased.

"Yes, Sandro, I am that." She shifted her pose and rolled from her side onto her back. "A woman."

Hips ground into the velvet dais as she arched her back. She brought her long arms over her head and stretched every bone and muscle of her succulent body. The veiling shifted and slid over bobbing breasts and firm thighs.

Oh, to be able to capture that pose, to paint the sinew of muscle on her thigh, the curve of her belly as it rose from her navel then dipped down to her pubic bone, to capture the spread of her breasts across breastbone, to dab my brush to form the image of her budded nipples . . . But such poses can never be captured, can they? Oh, surely one could imagine the pose, then try to paint from memory, but this woman, with her body arched like the bridges of Venice, the olive velvet of her skin, and the cat smirk on her lips – no, this woman must be painted from a pose, not from memory.

Which is why I agreed to her commission.

Julianne was the lonely wife of a wealthy merchant who was often too busy gallivanting to the far corners of the earth to enjoy his marital pleasures. She sought me to paint her image. I agreed on one condition: that we paint at night. Lamplight would allow me to keep the illumination of her body consistent. To paint at the mercy of daylight would have meant tedious days of waiting to be sure nature provided us with consistent light. I did not have time to wait. I had other commissions that needed my attention.

She agreed to my demands but held her own condition:

that we were to paint at her villa and she was to model nude.

I had barely blinked at her suggestion. My face had remained impassive.

Very well.

So I painted this woman at night, under the steadfast light of oil lamps and candles.

I set my brush down and sighed. "We are not making progress." Julianne always became restless and wanted to stop posing before I was ready to stop painting.

"But I get so tired!" she pouted, then curled onto her side.

"But all you have to do is lie there!" I reproached, and wiped my brush with a rag.

"But all you have to do is look." Julianne smiled through slitted golden eyes and cupped her breasts again.

Oh, my. Julianne. I knew very well why she commissioned me. And she had been trying to lure me between her thighs ever since.

"It is time for me to go." My voice was terse. I stared hard at my brushes and paints. The smell of egg yolk and pigment powder was noxious, not at all in keeping with the sweet fragrance of Julianne. My cock tightened and twitched. Ah, God, I knew I should go, before I lost my perspective on why I was there and what exactly I was being paid to do.

"Please don't go," she whispered. When I looked up, she had stopped her self-ministrations. She was both Madonna and Venus as she lay supplicant on the dais. Her arm crushed against her breasts; her elbow nestled into the dip of her waist; her forearm molded to the curve of her thick thigh.

I tentatively licked my lower lip. I vacillated between dismay and profound pleasure over the weightiness of my cock. The tip of it ached and swelled, as though it sought touch of its own volition. My sac swelled between my thighs and the wiry hairs of my legs poked and teased the soft skin.

"Please," she whispered again, and held out her hand.

Oh, most painters would be happy to only sketch her tapered arm, plump and curved from shoulder to elbow, then tapering down to those long, strong hands. I once saw her from afar, digging in the courtyard garden with those strong hands that knew the sensuous touch of rich earth and vines, her baby's soft skin, her husband's rough hands . . .

I didn't want to go. I never wanted to leave these sessions of ours – these cocooned little vignettes we created in the lamplight.

But I knew of a way to give us both what we wanted.

"Very well," I said, picking up a piece of parchment paper. "We shall learn how to draw." I raised one eyebrow and nodded.

She did not bother to cover herself with a linen wrap. She sat next to me on the dais, still wrapped in her lavender veil, as I instructed her on the basic principle of drawing.

I should be used to the nude female body by now. I studied many paintings of female nudes as a student in Florence. I studied a few female nudes outside of my studies. But Julianne was an exception. A jewel among tarnished trinkets. Young, but not a child; wizened but not sullied; innocent but not naive.

She leaned into me and followed my instructions. She pouted when I made her draw circle after circle and oval after oval.

"I'm so tired of this!" she complained, but I reprimanded her, telling her all adults begin life as babies who cannot walk.

Her brow furrowed as she held the hewn piece of coal and drew circle after circle. But really her repetitious work was simply a way to occupy her mind with something other than primal instincts.

Her breasts rose and fell to the rhythm of her breathing. Her brown hair had been braided back into shiny ropes, but long tendrils framed her face and obstructed her view. Occasionally, she would give the tendrils an irritated flick of her fingers. The rich brown tendrils would lie on her shoulder, only to slip and dangle in front of her again. Finally, I dug a piece of leather string out of my bag. While Julianne focussed on her circles, I gathered up her silken braids and tendrils and tied them back. The scent of freshly sickled grass and earth wafted from her locks.

Julianne stopped sketching and glanced up at me through the thick lashes that framed her eyes.

She placed her charcoal piece down on a table with gentle care. The sketching of circles was laid down next to it.

There was a look of satisfaction in her eyes; the look one has after one has waited a very long time for something one has wanted so very badly.

She unlaced the strings on my shirt. I stiffened and closed my hand around her wrist.

"No, no," she whispered, and pulled the cleft of my shirt apart, then smoothed her palm over the coarse hair of my chest.

"You see, I have always thought, Sandro, if I could only touch you in one place it would be here." She placed her palm on my chest, just over my heart. "That way, I can feel the warmth of you, I can feel the breath of you . . ." she caressed my left breast ". . . and I can feel the life blood of you."

My heartbeat thundered in my ears. I neither embraced her or shrank away.

Julianne kissed the mat of hair underneath her fingertips. I sucked in my breath when she kissed my hardened nipples.

I longed to adore this woman. I had spent many evenings refuting my natural instinct to love her, to make love to her. Julianne seemed to have stepped over a threshold in me, and while I was perfectly capable of pushing her back from where she came, I simply did not want to.

I reached up and touched her silken ropes. With a slight tug of the leather string, the braids spilled loose.

I wove my fingers through her braids and clutched her skull, the cranial bone cupped in my palms. Her breath quickened and I longed to taste Julianne.

We kissed like fireflies lighting at dusk – touch and go. But we needed to drink one another. Our lips and tongues flicked and suckled and licked.

Julianne's hands smoothed over my chest. I ran my hands along the graceful column of her back, around her hips, that plumped around her as she sat, and along her thighs. My hands traveled up to her belly, and then cupped her full, heavy breasts.

She laughed and closed her eyes when my fingers and thumbs pinched and rolled her dark nipples. She moaned and thrust her chest forward as I rhythmically pulled her nipples.

The dark buds suddenly pearled with white moisture, and I gasped. Julianne smiled and half opened her eyes to see my startled expression. "It is all right, Sandro, the babe won't mind . . . he's had his fill today and sleeps well now . . ."

I stared at her breasts in awe as I milked nourishment from

them. I felt a sudden firmness in my palm, and then the milk spurted out in thin streams.

"Oh, Sandro." Julianne thrust her breasts upward, spread the dribbling white fluid over her erect nipples and pumped her hips.

I covered her dripping breasts with my hands and wiped them dry, only to have them spurt and bead with milk again. I closed my eyes and slowly lapped the moisture from my hand. I needed nourishment, too, although my stomach was not empty nor my mouth dry.

But I needed to feed from Julianne. I needed to feed from her soul, her life-giving body, spurting, swelling and warm.

I bent my head and took one bud into my mouth. Just the tip. But Julianne clamped her breast with her hand and pushed the entire brown sphere past my lips.

"Suckle," her voice quavered.

At first I only suckled with my lips. Her milk dribbled slowly into my mouth. But Julianne anxiously pushed her breast against my mouth, and so I opened my lips again. She pushed more of her firm flesh into me. And then I clamped down with a bite. Julianne grunted from what I was sure must have been pain, but then sighed, as though content, as I suckled with teeth and lips.

The first spurts of fluid spattered over my tongue and teeth. I sucked with a slow, deliberate rhythm, as I had often seen babes at their mothers' breasts do. But soon the milk flowed in a steady, strong stream with each pull of my lips, tongue and teeth. It did not taste sweet, as I'd thought it would, rather, it tasted bland, but satisfying nonetheless. The opaque liquid pooled on my tongue, and when there was enough I swallowed.

Julianne moaned and sighed and cupped her breast to my mouth. I caressed her hips and back in slow, circular motions. She jerked her hips in an effort to join with me. Her breath came in ragged gulps.

"Harder," she begged. And so I sucked harder as she nourished me.

Her hips rocked and jerked, her body stiffened and she clutched my shoulders with her hands. Julianne cried out, her hips digging into the dais. Then she relaxed, and sighed, and watched me suckle a moment longer. She stroked my hair and cooed and laughed.

When I had drained her, she lay back on the dais and spread her legs. One arm rested above her head, and the other snaked along her chest and belly. Julianne smiled at me as her hand nestled over her dark mound. I smiled, too, reached into the folds of my tunic, then sat back on my haunches so my cock could spring to life before her eyes. She watched me as I stroked my thick staff. I teased her senses as I pulled and squeezed myself.

Julianne in turn teased me as her fingers parted her lips. She slipped one finger around the edges of her puffy, wet lips, glistening from her satiety. Again, I marveled at the life that sprang forth from her. Wet folds of pink and brown unfurled underneath her flicking fingers. She smiled again as she brought her fingers to her mouth and licked them.

I pounced on Julianne like a lion to an impala. I covered her mouth with mine. Her essence and nourishment mingled on our lips and tongues. She moaned and wriggled underneath me and her breasts rubbed against my chest. I wanted to bury myself deep in her, pump her, feel her life encase my rod, and thrust deep to her soul. I was greedy. I wanted to take her nourishment and life and feed from it.

I knelt between her splayed thighs and cupped her haunches in my hands. Julianne hooked her hands behind her knees and pulled back. Her folds were spread wide. Wet and thick. Like a succulent piece of fruit whose colors and depth could be painted.

I licked her folds with the tip of my tongue and gripped her full cheeks when she cried out and arched her back at the sensitive touch. I covered her with my mouth, then delivered slow and languid strokes, like the strokes of my brush over canvas. The work of art before me, though, was a creation that belonged to Julianne, and one which she created and shared with me.

I felt her tremor and shudder, and she cried again. She openly wept now, and I looked up to see the tears of joy spilling down her flushed cheeks. I smiled and murmured, "My love," as I wiped her tears with my paint-stained fingers. My callused fingertips soaked up the salty droplets.

Like a greedy child, she held her arms wide open for me and grunted her need. I laughed softly and kissed her neck as I cradled myself between her legs. She guided my reddened tip to her entrance and circled her opening with it.

"Now," she said, her voice sharp.

"Greedy?" I whispered, and I pushed just inside her. She gasped and arched her back. I pulled out.

Julianne whimpered. "Now!"

I pushed in again, this time further, felt the rippled folds inside her envelop me. She pumped against me.

I pulled out and rubbed the head of my rod on her hard jewel.

She let out something between a growl and a scream. She raked my back with her fingernails.

I nipped her undrained breast with my teeth. The nipple spurted its response.

She thrashed, and crushed me with her thighs.

My sac had been aching long enough. I was doubtful as to my ability to control my release for much longer. I drove into Julianne and pumped her with furious strokes.

Julianne spasmed and rocked and cried and opened her soul. My seed spurted and rushed deep into her womb as I jerked and pumped the last of my passion into her.

The room glowed golden in the lamp and candlelight. Julianne and I lay on the dais as satiety weighed down our entwined limbs. I brushed stray curls away from her forehead and kissed her brow. Julianne slept.

I finished my commission from Julianne two weeks later. She and I sat in the study of her villa while she quietly counted out the coins of my payment. She slid them across the polished wood of the ornate desk that belonged to her husband. I slid the coins back to her. Julianne held my hand, kissed the back, kissed the paint-stained fingers, and the palm then pushed the stack of coins back to me.

"You will take this," she said, as though she were talking to a child.

I sighed.

"And this, too." She gestured to the painting of herself.

I'll admit, it was my best work ever. The brush strokes of tempera imaged Julienne's body almost like a mirror. The lush color and the sensual line of Julianne's pose was riveting.

"I cannot take the painting." I shook my head.

"But you will, Sandro." Julianne stood up and cradled my head to her belly.

I left her that afternoon with the painting wrapped in linen, tucked under my arm.

And my soul rebirthed by Julianne.

ALL ABOUT EVE

Julian Rathbone

I HAVE MANY NAMES, but you can call me Eve, since I am the mother of you all. I'm not joking. It's really true. Not only am I the mother of you all, but there's something of me, just me, something of the woman I was one hundred and fifty thousand years ago, in every single one of you. I am you. You are us. We're all sisters and mothers under the skin, even the blokes. Well, *in* the skin too, come to that. So you needn't be surprised that I can speak out and talk to you every now and then, that you can hear my voice, feel my presence when I choose. In a sense, when you hear me you are talking to yourselves; we're that close.

Yes, that's it. As teachers say – "Talk among yourselves for a bit." Do that . . . and listen to me.

I lived in Eden, of course. What is it like? In a word – paradisial! Imagine – a big, big lake, flat and calm and silvery pewter most of the time, though black when a storm whips up and very occasionally reflecting the blue of the sky when the almost permanent bright silvery haze is swept aside or dissolved. On all sides it is fed by tumbling streams from the mountains, and in the south-west by a large river that comes to us through rifts and gorges, and, so the young men say and the old men remember, tumbles down a giant waterfall a day's walk inland. Beyond the waterfall and above it are the mixed woods and grasslands where the men, obeying older and more primitive instincts than ours, go to hunt. Far away in the north-east there is an outlet to the bigger lake, the sea.

The mountains are high and steep. Their lower slopes are filled with forest. The tall thin trees, some of them buttressed, soar from a floor of forest litter, sparsely carpeted with bromeliads which yield pineappple-like fruit, and, where a tree or two have fallen and the sunlight gets through, there are plantains and bananas. Many of the trees shed nuts, monkey-pot nuts and brazils as well as coconuts. There are plenty of other fruits, which I cannot name for you since they have long-since become extinct. No doubt the palaeontologists have Latin labels for them.

There are no seasons, though it rains in one half of the year more than in the other, and so there are flowers always, as well as fruits. I like especially the great vanilla scented swags of purple jacaranda-like legumes, and the luminosity of pearly orchids.

The canopies are filled with birds, mostly with jewelled plumage and ranging in size from the humming-birds, not much bigger than insects, to the birds of paradise trailing golden trains behind them. And of course there are our cousins the monkeys in the trees, and our brothers and sisters the gorillas and chimps lollop about the forest floor or swing from the lower boughs – though these inhabit the higher areas, rather than the forest floor. There, where the slopes and protruding rocks prevent the trees from growing so tall, there are bushes and scrub, grass and caves.

Inside the ring of mountains there are few predators, and none very big. Leopards are the largest, though there are lynxes and smaller cats, also foxes. There are many rodents, some quite large, like the coypu, for them to feed off, small round pigs, and frogs and toads as well. There are three or four species of forest deer, very small compared with the ones the men hunt beyond the mountains, and difficult for all but the cats to take, and, considering their size, not worth the effort. Anyway, we, the women, love the lithe dappled shapes that flit noiselessly away from us on the rare occasions we actually see them.

Not that we are vegetarians, indeed not. We live on the islands – I didn't mention the islands, did I? – there are hundreds of them in the lake, ranging from rocky pimples to those up to a couple of miles wide and long, that are forest-clad. We live on the islands and our preferred food is fish, for the most part shellfish of one form or another. There is a huge variety, for the water is faintly saline – not as salty as the ocean, but not as pure as the spring water that gushes out of the mountainsides and even bubbles up on some of the islands. The result is a happy environment for every sort of edible fish, except the very largest, that you know about, and a whole raft of others that are no longer with us.

Shell fish and crustacea are our favourites. Muscles, oysters, fifteen varieties of clams, scallops, the lot. Chestnut and prussian-blue lobsters, many of them clawless, ramble idly across the rippled sandy bottoms, picking their way through the sponges, and a quick duck-dive to a depth of ten feet can bring up the main course for a meal for four in ten seconds. The children love to chase shoals of shrimps and prawns into rocky basins which they then dam. And of course there are eggs galore just after the rainy season peters out – turtle eggs, duck eggs, gull eggs, quail eggs, and if we want a good sized omelette for four, splayed out on a big flat stone, then one flamingo egg is enough.

Yes, we do cook a little, but not much, mainly to set things like eggs which would otherwise be runny and slop all over the place. The men, on their hunting trips, make big fires into which they toss the carcases of the animals they have killed, and I have to say the fatty crisp joints they bring back for us are delicious, though too much meat creates bad temper, constipation and smelly faeces – all characteristics one associates with males, does one not?

Fruits I have already mentioned, but on the islands, where again the vegetation is lower than in the forest, there are even more varieties – custard-apple fruit, mangoes, papayas, melons, strawberries, guavas, I could go on for hours. Of course many of these are smaller, and not quite as sweet as the ones you get in the supermarkets these days, but they have a fresh fragrance you will never know.

Paradise without the serpent? I'm afraid not. There are poisonous snakes in the forest and beyond the mountains, but the islands we live on are free of them because, when we colonize a new island, we simply make sure they are all killed off. But there are still watersnakes and some species of eel too, which can do one a severe hurt and even kill a child – some spiders and crabs as well. But fatalities are rare; we know the herbal antidotes –

also we have learnt to react instinctively to the presence of any of these at a very early age, and indeed infants are born with a phobia for snakes, spiders and scorpions. Still are, are they not?

Crocodiles? In these waters they are so well-fed on the abundance of easily caught fish they almost never bother us – and a good heavy splashing and shouting usually deter any that show predatory tendencies.

So, where are the snags? Well, as you would expect, as it is with every other species that has evolved to fill an environmental niche for which it is just about perfectly adapted, there are, at about seven thousand in all, too many of us. And when the total gets up to about ten thousand, then the elders get together and draw lots between the sixty or so clans to decide on which should leave. They do. Led by their men, who are usually keen to do it, since it gives their lives a bit more meaning than they had before, in groups between a hundred and a hundred and fifty, they uproot themselves and set off across the mountains. Of course the men have been there before and think they know all about it – survival in the wilderness and all that.

And that's it. We never see them again because that is part of the bargain. Of course I know now, on the cusp of the year 151,999 and 152,000, what happened to them. Most, nearly all, died out before they'd even crossed what are now the Sahara and Arabian Deserts. But a few made it, especially round about the year 80,000, give or take a few millennia on either side. Six tribes in all. No more than a thousand all told. Plus a seventh, the blacks, who never did go. And all of them, every single one of them, descended from me. Eve.

But I'll come to that later.

Copulation with men took place towards the end of the dryer part of the year, so the children would be born after the rains had gone away. What we did was this: the men – that is males between fourteen years old and forty – came down to the lakeside at dusk on the night before full-moon, and stayed there for three nights and two whole days. We women would swim and then wade from our islands and, keeping in the water, would wade to and fro along the coastline until we saw a man we fancied.

You remember the first best, don't you? He may not have been the best, but you remember him best.

The sun had dipped behind the mountains to the west an hour or so earlier, leaving the hazy sky blood-red above the peaks and gold, then blueish-silver above. The green planet was a hole in its fabric. On the other side an orange moon, huge and near, rolled up the crests of the mountains to the east before dragging itself clear of them, launching itself to float like a galleon into the centre of the heavens. Galleon? Not, of course, a concept I was familiar with then, but, as I said, I've been around, in you, and you, and in all the people between, ever since. So I know a galleon when I see one, better than you do.

I wade through the black water with it just deliciously lapping my thighs and pubes, pushing little waves or big ripples in front of me that catch the gold of the moon and which arrow out behind me, flashing greenishly with phosphorescence. If I turn and look over my shoulder and narrow my eyes the reflections of the moon turn into a sparkling continuous lacy thread of gold across the darkness of the waters, and I can see the island, half a mile away, that I have swum and waded from, a blacker tree-fringed silhouette against the mist that lies between it and the shores beyond.

I am beautiful. Beautiful, that is, for my fourteen years, but not yet perfect. I have glossy, long, straight black hair that reaches down my back to my dimpled waist, and is now wet and stuck between my shoulder blades. I have a broad forehead, somewhat spotted, I am afraid to say, with the sebiginous pores that make spots and are our inheritance from the intermediary ages when we had fur waterproofed with oily secretions. That was before we developed subcutaneous fat, like seals and whales – a far better way of keeping an even blood temperature in water, as well as supplying us with buoyancy.

Fat. Yes, I am as fat now as ever I will be, at least until old age sets in. Not grossly fat, but neatly fat – puppy fat you will, quite wrongly, come to call it – wrong, unless you are thinking of seal puppies. I have plumpish high cheekbones beneath large but slightly oriental eyes which are the colour of dark amber, a small but straight nose, with slightly splayed nostrils, thickish lips. Some of us can pull our top lips back to block our nostrils when we want to stay under water for as long as our lungs will allow, up to five minutes for some, but this is a knack I don't have.

Small neat chin, strong neck, plump white shoulders also, bother it, a touch spotty. My breasts are full and round and firm and creamy, with dark but rosy nipples, my waist thickish by the absurd standards of beauty you have nowadays, my bush a kite-shaped triangle of curly black filaments concealing, at any rate while I am walking or wading upright, the folded lips, inner and outer, that gleam succulently with their own moisture as well as with the fishy water of the lake. My anus, when I spread my buttocks, is a tight little flower-bud which contracts and loosens deliciously when I, or one of my friends, strokes it. My legs are rounded pillars when I stand, but are happiest and strongest when the muscles are used for swimming, kicking or folding in and pushing out in what you call a breaststroke. We all swim, almost from birth, and the breaststroke comes most naturally as it keeps our heads up out of the water. My feet are small and very, very sensitive – not that happy when walking on dry land, but fine in water. Some of us are occasionally born with webbed toes – it is considered an incredibly good stroke of luck for those who are, for of course they will swim even better than the rest of us.

Men's feet are larger, flatter, and not so sensitive. They haven't caught up with us. They still like clambering over rocks, arsing about in trees, *walking* for heaven's sake!

Anyway, there I am, pushing my thighs through the moonstruck water, with my gaze peering intently over the silvered rocks, sandy beaches, little coves and inlets that fill the space between the lake and the forest curtain. Around me – some closer to the shore, the older or wilder ones, those who have done it before, some further out, even occasionally still swimming – are the other young women of our clan.

We can see the men waiting. A mixed bunch. Some hunker, or sit with their arms about their knees on a rock or the shingle where the water laps their feet, some stand. A few are displaying. They cavort, turn cartwheels, beat their chests and howl or roar like the gorillas, Some shake and manipulate their tackle, displaying near-erections, cupping their balls in their hands, thinking we might be interested in how big they are. Well, it takes all sorts, and some of us do go for this sort of thing. But me, I am looking for someone about my own age, someone as shy as myself, perhaps as nervous as I am, someone also doing it for the first time.

Of course I know, as well as one can without actually doing it, what to expect. What you would call sexual play has been a normal part of life since I was born. Mothers, aunts, grannies, sisters have felt free to play with my cunt, my clitoris, my nipples and my anus, using their fingers and tongues, wrapping me in hot embraces when the urge became overpowering, getting me to do the same to them. Indeed none of this has really been separated from all the other natural things we share – grooming, cleaning, eating, playing, shitting and weeing. It's all part of the same thing, isn't it? All part of being alive.

And there have been males all around too, sharing in this, but not men. Infants, with their little button pricks and often empty sacs and rounded chests and buttocks like ours, lads growing thinner and occasionally displaying thin, hard little erections, and, of course, the old men, growing fat, tired and varicose now, after twenty-five years in the plains and the savannahs before we let them back on the island, caressing us as well, but mainly staying with the grannies, maybe favoured ones they fucked at moon-tide a few times each year and remembered.

Sometimes they get in a sweat, trying to get the silly things up again, but for the most part they are happy to play and be played with, until they get smelly and silly and we have to push them out into the lake, and not let them land until they sink away to feed the fishes we might eat the very next day.

But that first time. After half an hour I see the boy I want, indeed recognize him. When he was a lad, two or three years ago, we used to play together, fish and so on, and I remember once he strung seashells on a plait of grasses to hang round my neck. But I only just recognize him. Something about the way he holds his head, slightly forward and to the side, as if listening intently. That was one of the things I liked about him. He listened.

But in other ways how changed he is! Two years they stay up in the savannah, before being allowed down to the moontide copulation, until puberty has merged into near adulthood, until the neck has thickened, the shoulders broadened, the torso filled and the arms become rounded and rippled with hard muscle. Indeed, and I mean no joke at all, it is hardness that is the word that best describes the change. Lean he still is, but no longer thin or stick-like, and the muscles when he tenses them are as hard as his bones. He has lost all the softness humans of both sexes have during childhood and old age, and has become hard the way only a man, a *man* rather than a male, can be. Even their buttocks are hard, like small unripe melons.

All this is new to me, and even before he has seen me, or at any rate picked me out from the rest, I suddenly feel wave after wave of longing, a great emptiness, a desire for something I have never known before, I have a terrible urge to splash through the shallows, call out, grasp him, hold him . . .

I stub my toe. On a rock that normally I would have seen or sensed. And the first thing he hears apart from a little splashing is a whoops! of surprise, then a cry of pain and anger. The pain always comes a second or so later after you've stubbed your toe . . . have you noticed that?

But now he's seen me. And a moment later he's recognized me too, and in a moment I am in his arms, with my fingers in the nape of his neck, tearing at the coarse hair which daylight will show is darker and redder than the straw-coloured mop he had, and I can feel that hard chest pressing my breasts so they hurt as well as tingle with delight, and his hands, broad and strong, lifting my buttocks, and his long middle fingers prying in towards my bum-hole, and above all that hard pillar of a prick, a rock, a club pulsing against my stomach.

He tumbles us back into the fine silky sand, rolls us over so I am underneath and suddenly gasping for breath, and with one hand tries to push that thing into my groin, my cleft, between my swollen gaping lips, But the poor boy doesn't really know what he's up to; he tries to use his big hand with his strong, lean but clumsy fingers, and that does it. The feel of my pubes, of the wetness at his fingertips, and that aching, throbbing prick between us is too much, and with a great spurt of the stuff he comes, a handful of smooth thick viscous come streaking up from my navel, reaching to the cleavage between my breasts.

Poor boy. He's fed up about this, very fed up, puts his face against my cheek and I can feel tears mingling with the sweat as well as the pungent stickiness between us.

But his body is still on top of mine. I wriggle about a little, pushing up with my knees between his thighs, trying to get him to take some, at least, of his weight off me, and then his elbows too, between my arms and flanks, and as I do I feel it getting hard and big again, not that it had shrunk very much at all, and presently, using my hand between us this time, I manage to wriggle and twist and get it through the front door, if not actually beyond the hall. This wakes him up all right. The little sobs and sighs deepen into pants and grunts, his buttocks rise and with one push he's through and in.

It hurts. They said it would. But not as much as I expected. I get my hands into his hair again and yank and manage to murmur to him to lie still a moment or so, let me get used to that great bruising throbbing thing inside me, and because he is, as I hoped he would be, still the kind nice lad he once was before he was a man, he does so, though not for as long as I'd have liked. Then he's at it again, up and down, in and out, and I try to keep up with him, but he's too quick for me, and I can feel the sudden pulse again and my honeyed cavities fill with his juices.

He stays for a moment, pumping air in and out of his lungs as if he'd done a five minute dive, then rolls off with a sigh of satisfaction and a big grin on his stupid face. The moonlight is bright enough to show it. He's done it. He's got his prick inside a woman, and he's come. *He's* fucking come. Men.

Still, we have the rest of the night, a day, a night – the night when the moon is truly full – a day and a third night, and during that time I intend to teach him a thing or two. And learn.

Towards dawn, after the moon has set, I curl up in his arms and sleep, but when dawn comes he has gone. Not far. He's down at the water edge skipping stones across the gentle heaving opalescent water, skimming them hop, skip and a jump, out into the mist that hangs over everything, so all you hear is the final plop; you can't see it. The mist swirls a little and lifts, and there, forty yards away, is another man, also standing on the water edge and skipping flat pebbles. He sees my lad, and, winding himself up, throws a stone as far as he can to the edge of the now swiftly rising vapour. My lad carefully picks a stone the right weight and size and tries to throw it as far. By the time the mists have gone and the sky, which was filled with the rosy glow of dawn, is shifting to gold, and the birds are calling and singing in the forest behind us and the flying fish are skimming the waves, and further out the porpoises are humping their black backs in and out of the water, as far as you can see in either direction, along the scalloped coast of the lake, men are throwing stones. Who can throw furthest? Who can make the flat ones skip the most often?

This will not do.

I go into the forest, find a pineapple, then a most gorgeous odour tickles my nostrils. I see the signs where a pot-bellied pig has been disturbed by a predator, a cat, perhaps, or a man, in its search for truffles. I get down on my hands and knees and begin to scrabble in the earth, and soon come up with a beauty – black, glossy, multi-faceted, it's exciting enough to make me forget the dull ache of a cunt that has been both abused and left unsatisfied. And then, just as I'm going to get it free of the damp leaf mold that has nurtured it, I sense or hear him behind me and, pushing back my sleek black hair, look over my creamy shoulder.

He's there. He's followed me after all. Legs astride, he's playing with his penis and his balls, pushing the foreskin up and off the gleaming red glans, letting it slide over again, and he's getting big. And bigger. I spread my knees even more than before, put a hollow in my back, push my arse up at him. My breasts swing below me, suddenly heavy and throbbing again, the nipples swollen. Come *on* you fool! He'll do it to himself before he gets to me, if he's not careful.

But then he's down on his knees behind me, pushing forward, and this time, spread as I am and ready for it, it slips in with a musical sucking sound, like a blind animal finding its burrow, while I am all mouth, pulling in the loveliest morsel lips ever closed around. Oh, oh, this time it is *sweet*. With a little manoeuvring I manage to get the root of his prick and his balls to rub against my clit, and, since he is kneeling almost upright, with no weight on me, I manage to get one hand between my thighs without toppling the whole lovely funny structure we have become, and I can just tease his balls with my nails, then, whooomf! I go off like a whale spouting, whoomf, whoomf, whoomf, head up, shoulders pulled in, back hollowed, and I sing out that great female cry that wakens the woods above me and sets the monkeys off.

It's a bit of a surprise for him too.

That's an end to pebble-throwing competitions, I can tell you.

We do it fifteen more times before he has to go back up into the savannah and I have to haul myself back to the island, and each time the gap between is a little longer, and each time he takes a little longer, so by the third night I can get on top of him, facing forwards or backwards as the liking takes me, playing with the root of his penis, stroking his balls, getting my fingers up his bum-hole, do what I like while he just lies there moaning, and I come three, even four times before he does. And in between we eat fruit and shellfish. I have been told oysters, figs and guavas especially will help him keep going, but by the final dawn he doesn't have the strength left to prise the shells open; he can hardly peel a fig. Sometimes we chat and play a bit . . . but that's no different from what happens at home with my friends, and right now it's not what I want . . . Nevertheless, I do get to like him and, come the next time I shall wade ashore for the annual copulation, I shall be as much on the look-out for him as for new flesh.

But that's four years away. In the meantime I have twins, not identical, one like me, one like him, both girls, and there's no point in making the trip until I have stopped lactating.

Now I am eighteen, thinned down a bit but not much, several inches taller. My skin has taken on a deeper creamier look, my nipples are browner, the areolae bigger. Instead of the spots I have a few little brown moles here and there. My hair is thick and glossy, like a cormorant's wings.

This time I am not in the least nervous, but I am very excited as I wade along the shore peering through the silvery moonlight at the wares laid out for my delectation. I have half an eye open for the lad of four summers gone – I have a nostalgia for him, even feel I'd like to know how he has been faring in the man's world – but really my heart, or quim, is set on something new and different, even strange. And there, even while my mind is dwelling on some great hunk of a full-grown brute of a male, I see him.

You won't believe this, but what I have suddenly spotted, sitting on his buttocks on a high rock overlooking a little bay, with his knees pulled up to his chin and a thin spear with a fire-hardened point in the crook of his arm, is a thin, wiry shrimp of a man, with very dark skin, a top-knot of curly black hair with a golden pheasant's feather stuck through it, big dark eyes, a squashed nose, and thickish lips. Of course I could not see all this at once, but enough to know I'm in luck. There aren't many of these left. A whole tribe of them was sent off into the savannah and deserts a year or so earlier, but my gossipy chums back on the island have said if you can get one, then, well . . .

I push through the water to the edge, where the Orion's belt weed wraps round my ankles and glows greenly, set my head on one side, arms akimbo, and look up at him. Take it or leave it. He takes it.

He comes down off his rock, with very lithe, easy movements, into the water, takes my hand and leads me on to a patch of very fine shingle. I can see touches of grey in the wiry hair at his temples, and realize he is older than I had thought, quite a lot older than me. Well, I think, at least he'll know a thing or two.

And he does.

He gets me on to my knees, spreads them, then lies on his back behind me and pushes his head between my thighs. What the fuck is he up to? I think. Then his long thin hands rest on my hip bones and pull me down, so his squashed nose is rubbing my clit and his tongue is feeling its way through my lips and finding the juicy recesses beyond. Oh, boy. This is something. I begin to squirm and wriggle with the ecstasy of it, but his hand are strong and firm, grasping my waist now and holding me down, so all I can do instead is get hold of the back of his head and rub and grind his face into my pussy until the juices overflow and I'm off, coming again and again in great surges of pleasure.

It's a wonder I didn't suffocate him. But these dark ones often live near water, even during their manhood, and can hold their breaths for a long, long time. Long enough anyway.

Which brings me to . . . Well, that was long too. The longest I ever had. Long and thin, longer than the full stretch of my hand from the tip of my thumb to the tip of my little finger, and hard little balls beneath. Hardly any body-hair at all, and thin tight hard buttocks that hardly filled my hands.

Long enough to find places no prick found before or after. When I sat on him and moved myself up and up and down and down, ever so slowly up and down the full length of him, I could feel the cervix of my womb dilate to fold round his tip, and that was a pleasure beyond anything for both of us. And, of course, long and thin like that he could get it way up my bum-hole while his hands kneaded and pushed and rubbed and stroked my lips and clit and his fingers felt right in, way up my pussy, all this at once.

This time it was he who kept me going with what he brought to eat. He already had cooked cutlets of some sort of mountain goat, wrapped in large leaves, and a couple of gourds of fermented honey that was heaven at first but spoilt the second day a bit with a headache. And he used his spear in the water and got us a couple of big flatfish – I guess you'd call them sole. Dover sole. And he made a little charcoal fire to grill them on. He liked caterpillars and crickets too, the last crunchy and sweet, just the thing to end a meal with.

All in all, he was really quite domesticated, and now I look back on it, we probably spent more time messing about with pleasant little chores together than we actually did making out.

Twins again. Girls again. Both dark, but one with my high cheek bones and almond eyes.

There were three more. A tall thin guy with a heavy beaky nose and a reddish-browny skin, bony face, who said damn all and spent most of the time using a flint flake to scrape the tissue off the inside of a leopard skin he'd bought with him which he finally put on, with the mask of it over his forehead. This was a disappointment too, as I thought he was doing it all to give to me – not that I needed it; it just felt nice, that fur on my shoulder, rubbing against my cheek.

One girl only this time, which was a relief.

Next, when I was pushing thirty and getting on a bit, and felt I wanted a bloke who'd make the running again, I chose another black, but this time a big, strong, really, really dark guy, skin like ebony, muscles like ebony too and a prick which, when it was dangling, came halfway down to his knees. Really. And balls to match. Trouble with those big ones is it takes a lot to get them up and keep them up, which, for all my experience and the gossip amongst us girls, was something I didn't know about, or wanted to forget, and was a serious disappointment. I spent most of the time giving head and trying to get the thing in where it belonged before it went limp again. Mind, he gave good head too, not that there's a lot of point. I can always get that at home on the Island.

One lovely black girl, who grew up straight as a tree and could run and swim better than any of us. She was a bit dippy, though, always searching for God. Never found him.

And lastly an oldish white man, who was rather disgusting, picking his nose and scratching his bum-hole and then sniffing his fingers. I don't know why I chose him, except perhaps out of sympathy, and also perhaps fearing rejection from the young studs who were waiting around for younger flesh than mine. Very little use at all until the last night, when I found what really turned him on. He liked me to tie him up with sea weed and then whip his bum with the stuff. Slowly, bit by bit, his gnarled old pink prick just about made it to horizontal, and so long as I kept on hurting him, dragging my nails down his back till it bled, and across his scrawny, floppy buttocks, he kept it up, and managed to bring us both off.

My last little girl, and a bit of a pain. Fair hair, blue eyes, not a bit like me, always whining for something.

And that's about it. Seven girls of all shapes sizes and colours, and all carrying in every cell my mitochondrial DNA, which is only passed down the female line, and which, your modern scientists will tell you, is so alike in every human being that it can only have one source. Me. Still alive in you after one hundred and fifty-two thousand years. Say twenty years as an average generation, that's only seven hundred and fifty mothers separate you from me. Seven hundred and fifty. It's not a lot, is it?

PERFECT LITTLE VENUS

Alizarin Lake

URSULA RAISED HERSELF on one bare elbow and looked across the broad bed at her companion, smiling sweetly.

"So the new girl shows promise, does she, Philomena? How pleasing that is. You know, the first moment I caught a glimpse of her as I walked down the street I felt quite a frisson of excitement. A perfect little Venus, you said?"

Philomena lit a delicately scented cigarette and passed it to Ursula before lighting her own, neatly inserting the tip into the ornate incense burner beside the canopied double bed.

"Very much so. She needs to be broken in, naturally, but I suspect she will need rather less vigorous birching than Bernadette required when she came to us."

"Rather a pity, really," responded Ursula. "I greatly enjoyed watching you and young Loretta belaboring that saucy minx's hindquarters until she looked like so much raw beef. Do you remember how she whined and squealed when we showed her the Little Man and explained its use?"

Philomena laughed and nestled closer to the older woman, bending her head to kiss the graying long hair.

"Indeed I do, Ursula. Indeed I do. Yet she was wearing the Mystic Tree in her bottom quite contentedly a few days later, with a very proud smile on her pretty little face. Once Loretta had violated her narrowest portal of love a few times with the Little Man, she was cheerful enough when that unspeakable object was shown to her."

"That ebony phallus from the temple on the Isle, you mean," laughed Ursula, letting her hand caress Philomena's long back. Philomena made a groaning noise and playfully resisted.

"Enough of that; there simply isn't time, Ursula."

Ursula persisted, not heeding the young woman's weak protest. Her hands traversed the small of Philomena's back and rested on the rise of her pretty plump bottom. She began to tease the flesh there. Her fingers inched closer and closer to the starfish-shaped aperture that nestled there.

"No," cooed Philomena languorously. "Take your hand away this instant. If you excite me again I shall need to be licked again, and we both know where that leads, to we not?"

"To me wanting a lick and maybe another light spanking, Philomena," sighed Ursula, her fingers still persisting around the puckered little anus of Philomena's lovely little ass.

Philomena raised her hips despite her earlier protests. She could not resist a little hip rotation to the gentle probing of the older woman's experienced hand.

"That's it, my pretty dove. I know you want another little lick on that delicious little pearl between your legs." As Ursula was hoarsely whispering in Philomena's ear, her hand had reached up from behind and was tickling the tender spot.

"If you don't stop that, Ursula, I am going to have to give your precious bum a stiff whack. And a few lashes with my tongue, if you are really naughty."

"Oh, that's it my girl. Threaten me, but only if you promise to do as you say." And with that Ursula plunged one finger into the rosy little anus of Philomena, while another finger sought the other opening of softer, wetter pink flesh that was protected by dark hair. Philomena yelped with glee, and reached over and began to tease Ursula's naked breasts. Although Ursula was older than the other girls, she still had an extremely youthful body. Her breasts had retained the shape and firmness of a girl barely into her twenties.

Philomena was jerking her hips over the busy hand of Ursula.

"You are being very, very bad Ursula. Oh, yes. That's it! Oh!"

Philomena, racked with powerful spasms caused by the delicious probing fingers of Ursula, threw back her head and was panting with animal pleasure. When at last her juices flowed freely, her body contracting with wonderful pulses, Ursula playfully slapped her dripping pussy. With that Philomena promptly jumped up and grabbed a brush that lay on the dressing table.

"You nasty thing. Come here." She brandished the large silver brush, and the two of them began to playfully tumble on the bed together. At last Philomena had the older woman pinned over her knee. One hand held the brush; the other held Ursula's wrists. And then Philomena's hand wandered down the taut backside exposed to her. She patted it lightly at first, and Ursula cooed a bit.

"You like that, don't you, you wicked, bad girl?" Then Philomena slipped her hand between her captive lover's legs, and said, "My darling you are positively dripping. Shall I give you a little tap on these wonderful buns?" Without waiting for a reply she brought the silver brush singing down on the prone buttocks. Philomena's free hand had gripped the lips of Ursula's pussy and tugged gently, then a bit harder, as the brush came down with increasing force. She began to tickle the twitching clit and to spank the woman simultaneously. Ursula's buttocks were now a bright shade of red, and she wriggled with glee on Philomena's lap.

"That's it, my girl. Oh, my . . . my darling, you are going to make me come. Oh, yes." And Ursula let out a wail of satisfaction as the brush slapped the ripe flesh of her ass one last time.

Now spent, both women fell against the pillows. After some moments Philomena sat up, her lips compressed into a smile. "Come along, naughty Ursula. If you are still wanting, I am sure with some . . . ah . . . coercion you can have our new girl kneeling at your feet, begging to be allowed to please you with her sprightly little tongue. I know you do so love to initiate the devotees this way, tears streaming down their country-fresh cheeks."

Ursula laughed heartily at the thought. "I do hope she will be one of the girls we will send on to the Isle of Man later this year. Remember that young thing, Catherine, whom I picked up in the very same pub last month?"

"How could I forget. Although she was a willing devotee at

the beginning, that private spectacle you staged for the visiting priestess from the Isle . . ."

Again Ursula laughed. "I do suppose straddling that young buck from the Isle, and entertaining another pair of fine young devotees with her mouth and her bottom was quite too much for her inexperience. Although later she said she liked it so. What a pity she is too plain to send to the Festival this year. If this Brigeen shows promise, Catherine can teach her the entire repertoire she has mastered so far."

"Does Brigeen strike you as grateful to be here? After all, being taken from potatoes, boiled cabbage and buttermilk must come as a great shock to her."

"I think the luxury and pleasure here, in comparison to the harsh life of the country, will make her all the more an apt pupil."

"This is good news. I do so want to make a good showing of girls this year."

The two women proceeded to dress carefully and slowly, until Philomena slapped her forehead and cried, "Ursula, how do you want to taste for the new girl? The conceited minx, Bernadette, is especially fond of the taste of fennel, so fennel should be good enough for the maid from the Boreens, I imagine."

"What an excellent idea, Philomena. How clever you are to remember. Do you still remember the names of every last one of the herbs and natural substances suitable for using as a douche?" Ursula busied herself with the phial of fennel essence.

"There are eleven. Let me think – fennel, fit root, slippery elm, gum arabica, white pond lily, marsh mallow, wild alum root, uva ursi, fenugreek, barberry bark and . . . the last I forget," Philomena concluded her litany ruefully.

"I will never forget you telling the novice devotees to use the natural secretions of their cunnies as a scent. What was it you told them?"

"Simply that a rub behind the ears and on the throat works as well as any subtle and mischievous perfume. What's more, it costs nothing at all compared to all those fancy perfumes. It's something I learned on my first trip to the festival on the Isle. It is a powerful aphrodisiac. Unfortunately, one strapping big girl from Longford went around smelling like the Liffey at low tide before I taught her that moderation in all things is a virtue in itself, even if conventional worship and austerity are not part of our particular order."

The two women laughed conspiratorially about this fact. At last, dressed and composed, the pair descended the carved oak staircase to the parlor. Awaiting them were Bernadette and the plump girl known as Loretta. Brigeen was sitting at their feet as she had been told to do.

"Has Brigeen been washed thoroughly, Bernadette?" whispered Ursula.

"Inside and out," replied the girl in a low giggle. "She needed some persuasion to take the enema nozzle, but Loretta held her securely while I did the necessary. The water was hardly hot, but she wailed like a banshee all the same."

"That will do, Bernadette. Has Loretta got everything she needs?"

"Begod, I have the lot," murmured Loretta.

The four stood back and regarded Brigeen. Each of them studied her dispassionately. Brigeen turned her pale face towards Ursula, the oldest of the group.

"You have nothing to fear, child. Look at me; you know what obedience means, I hope?"

"I think so, madam." Her voice sounded subdued and hesitant.

"Call me Ursula, love," said the older woman.

Brigeen looked around the warm room. It was truly the most opulent place she had ever been in. The waning light illuminated the tall windows that held stained glass patterned into Celtic braids and strange runes that she had not noticed until now. They seemed slightly ominous. In the corner of the room stood what seemed to be a pagan altar. It had an ornately carved marble base. The surface was decorated with leaves, burning candles, and what seemed like bones. But she couldn't be sure. There was a plate of fresh fruit and a loaf of bread. A rich carpet extended from this queer altar to the center of the room. It was on this that Brigeen, barefoot, stood.

"You have been chosen by Ursula to be instructed in the way of the Old Religion – the cult of the Goddess and her consort, the Horned God. You are not required to take the vows for another week, Brigeen," said Philomena. "Tonight will decide you, and,

I might add, decide us as well. It is a great honor to be selected. How thoroughly have you learned your lessons?"

"As thoroughly as I could, Sister Philomena," replied Brigeen confidently. She felt warm and dizzy. The events of the past few hours, so many moments of delight, had convinced her that she would stay in the company of these wonderful creatures and learn more of what they were about. She had been reassured by the sparkling character of Bernadette that only more pleasure was to come her way. And perhaps she would learn more of the "dark habits" her mother had always so fearfully made reference to. She had never really known what Mother meant by "the dark way", but she had a feeling she was going to find out. It all felt deliciously sacrilegious, and the idea made her flush even more.

"To whom is your maidenhead consecrated, Brigeen?" asked Ursula quietly.

"To the Isle of Man, to the Great Goddess and her Mercurial Heralds of the Old Religion." Brigeen did not know what this meant, but she had been instructed by Bernadette to reply as much.

"And your vagina is consecrated . . ." prompted Philomena, her eyes sparkling.

"My vagina is consecrated and sacred. Only those blessed of the Holy Isle and the initiated are to know me as a woman."

"Not withstanding this . . ." continued Bernadette, who had moved closer to Brigeen.

"Not withstanding this, my mouth, my hands, my breasts and my tightest aperture may be employed to enrich our Order in all matters spiritual and temporal."

"You have taught her well, Bernadette," observed Ursula approvingly. "Now, my dear Brigeen, adopt the posture Bernadette has shown you."

With only the slightest shudder of hesitation, Brigeen knelt and then leaned forward, facing the altar. At a nod from Ursula, Bernadette slowly lifted Brigeen's coarse blue-gray schoolgirl skirt until the hem was around her waist.

"Her bottom is beautifully curved, a perfect hemisphere," breathed Philomena in Ursula's ear.

"Prepare yourself, my pupil, in the way of the Goddess," intoned Ursula. "Loretta, a dozen light strokes, I think."

With a satisfied grunt, the plump girl produced a thin Malacca cane with a silver and ivory handle. She shuffled carefully forward until she stood beside the bare buttocks of the trembling girl kneeling in supplication before the altar and its gleaming candles.

"Begin when I clap my hands, Loretta. Brigeen, you are to recite the sacred utterances. The essential purpose of this beating is to stir the blood, make it quicken. Call out clearly while you are being caned. It is the vibration of your voice that evokes the passions of the Goddess. Do you understand?"

Her teeth chattering, Brigeen nodded. Ursula, her face gleeful, stood back and clapped her hands. The thin cane whipped through the air and made contact with the soft flesh.

"I-o-evoe-e! Ahh!" Brigeen was having difficulty making the strange noises as the rigid ritual cane came thrashing down on her soft buttocks. "We invoke . . . oh . . . thee, Queen of Queens. Oh . . . Aradia! Aradia! Ah . . ." The cane came whistling down again. "Ooo! Come to us in all our . . . ah!" Brigeen's eyes were welling up with tears as the cane came down once again. "Ah . . . in all our dreams. Perfect love and Perfect . . . Ah . . . Oh . . . Perfect trust. Aradia! Aradia! Less would turn . . . Oh . . . All into . . . Oh . . . dust . . ." Brigeen was so frightened and moved by the strange predicament in which she found herself, that the feeling of the cane, and the moments between lashes, were beginning to become quite pleasurable. The sound of her own voice was mysteriously husky, transported. "Upward, on and . . . oh . . . oh . . . and on. Aradia! Aradia! Till . . . oooooh . . . our souls with thee are . . . one. Ah . . . Aradia!"

And, with that, the cane ceased to cut through the air and did not crash down on her poor ass again. Brigeen felt tears streaking her face. The cheeks of her bottom were stinging, yet there was a warm sense of relief, almost pleasurable, because compared to the harsh sting of the ivory staff, this was bliss. The words she had uttered had come out of a part of her that she did not know existed. And then there was that tingling sensation between her white young thighs.

Loretta, visibly disappointed that she had been permitted so little, sniffed and laid the cane aside with a shrug after the twelfth stroke.

Ursula and Philomena had begun toying with one another's breasts as the girl had uttered the sacred recitation. They were so moved by the sight of the virginal ass turning wine-red with the beating that they had fallen into each other's arms and lost themselves in lascivious kisses.

Bernadette could be seen lying back on some cushions, her thin legs sprawled apart. She was mesmerized by the sight of Brigeen's spanking, and could not help but tickle her own little pink cunt while the magic words were being uttered by this beautiful banshee. The recitation always elicited such an erotic response from her. Brigeen looked up from her position and waited quietly for the women to take notice of her. She was too scared to interrupt the playful interludes. At last Ursula wrenched her attention away from the wicked lips of Philomena.

"Brigeen, stop your recitation and pay attention to what I am now saying."

"Yes, Ursula," mewed Brigeen, soft tears pearling on her cheeks.

"You understand the meaning of obedience a little better now, I trust?" inquired the older woman archly. Without waiting for an answer, she turned to Loretta and murmured something Brigeen was unable to hear.

"The smaller one, I suppose?" responded the plump girl glumly.

"Of course. Not everyone has your capacity, you mare. You have the chism ready?"

A small chalice was produced from its place of concealment on the altar. Loretta's porcine hands laid it reverently before the stand, inches from Brigeen's nose. Philomena, determined to add a note of dispatch to the proceedings, knelt before Brigeen and opened her hand slowly to reveal a carved wooden object at which the girl stared incredulously.

"A Little Green Man from our sisters on the Isle, my dear. It will be thoroughly lubricated before it enters your pretty bottom, never fear. Once you have become accustomed to the sensation, you will be ready for the godemiche, another ritual object of pleasure from the rocky shores of the Isle. Don't fret, my girl. Bernadette and Loretta were once initiated as you are now." Philomena stood up and beckoned Bernadette to her side.

"Make the shaft thoroughly slippery, Bernadette. Let Brigeen watch."

Bernadette seized the contrivance from Philomena's grasp and held it in front of Brigeen's wide brown eyes. On a sudden impulse, she adjusted her grip and touched the bulbous head to her friend's lips, making Brigeen start with surprise.

"A devotee knows how to suck a cock as well as how to suffer herself to be buggered," she breathed. "Now, watch carefully."

Intrigued as much as appalled, Brigeen stared wide-eyed at the girl as she brought the oblong object to her own mouth. Her thin little tongue darted around the tip, and there she played her mouth over the smooth green marble. Then suddenly she slipped the strange thing all the way into her mouth. Her eyes were shining and a small growl erupted from her thin throat. Brigeen was entranced. Bernadette sucked the thing as though it were candy, so great seemed her delight at having this marble phallus in her mouth. And as quickly as she had popped the shaft in her pretty mouth, she withdrew it. With slim fingers, she immersed the slender shaft of the unthinkable object in the consecrated oil filling the chalice. Held aloft before her eyes, the dark shaft glistened and shone in the chapel's light.

"You see, all you have had in your ass up till now has been my finger once or twice," whispered Bernadette. "This will really fill you up, believe me. Be brave and relax. Try not to howl out loud for a good minute or two. After that you will find the sensation surprisingly agreeable. Wait and see."

She massaged the oil diligently, lovingly, into the shaft.

The voice of Ursula broke the silence.

"Very well, Bernadette. You may usurp Sister Loretta's prerogative in this instance; ours is not a religion in which cruelty is an end in itself. Not for us the ritual flagellations in stone-floored convents beneath the grey Donegal skies! Loretta, assist Bernadette."

With visible ill grace, the plump girl knelt and eased Brigeen's white buttocks asunder none-too-gently. Her ministrations exposed the deep cleft between the cheeks and – at last – the tiny knot of the girl's narrowest portal of love.

"Oh, Bernadette, I'm frightened," wailed Brigeen.

"Hush, silly," replied Bernadette briskly, reaching for the

chalice and the carved marble curiosity half-submerged within it.

To Brigeen's surprise and relief, Loretta relaxed her grip long enough to enable her to ease her knees further asunder. The plump girl's nearer hand curled beneath her thigh. She gasped aloud as a fat little finger caressed the curls on her mons veneris before unerringly finding the tiny pink ridge.

To the watchful eyes of the onlookers, Brigeen's fleshy knot began to pulse in rhythm with the restrained and invisible stroking of Loretta's fingers. Loretta's smoldering eyes met Bernadette's and the younger girl grinned wickedly.

When a soft finger touched her, Brigeen knew it could only be Bernadette's, it was so gentle, so subtle, so loving. She made herself relax. The warm, greased knob at the tip of the object replaced the questing finger. Brigeen, by now confident that Bernadette would do all in her power to avoid causing her the least unnecessary pain, shuddered and sighed.

For an instant or two Bernadette made no progress. Then, miraculously, the tiny aperture pouted and yielded.

"Ooooooh," moaned Brigeen, uncertain as to whether she was feeling pain or exquisite delight. Little by little, the bulbous head at the tip of the shaft slid further into the nervous and apprehensive girl's rectum.

"Oh, Jesus Christ," gasped Brigeen, feeling every millimeter of the thing as it made steady progress into her. As if in reply, the steady strokes of Loretta's hidden finger quickened their pace.

"There, my darling, it's in all the way. Now relax and enjoy it." Bernadette's dulcet tones seemed to be coming from very far away. The shaft withdrew, returned, withdrew once more and returned a second time. Between her thighs, Loretta's fingers maintained their steady pace, pummeling, squeezing and stroking, exciting her immeasurably.

"Go on, go on . . . it's beautiful," Brigeen crooned, her head spinning.

Some distance beyond the trio, Ursula and Philomena stood watching, their arms hanging about one another lightly, fondling each other's nipples.

"Well, Ursula, now is a good a time as any. Give the little

goddess something to do with her mouth other than sighing in appreciation."

Ursula smiled lasciviously at Philomena, saying, "Don't mind if I do!" She strode forward briskly until she stood at the foot of the altar, the hem of her long white robe all but brushing Brigeen's hair.

"You are demonstrating your obedience most impressively, my daughter," she said to the shuddering form at her feet. Brigeen stared up at the apparition before her, believing she had taken leave of her senses as the woman lowered herself carefully until a copse of dark curls was inches from Brigeen's open mouth.

"Bernadette has taught you how to lick, I believe?" The voice was soft, but the tone imperious.

"Yes . . . Sister . . . I am your slave to command."

"Then lick me, my daughter! Lick me hard and well until I tell you to stop!"

Brigeen was feeling the full pleasure of Loretta's teasing finger on her special node in the folds of her pink nether lips. It was heightened by the gentle thrusting motions of Bernadette's steady hands on her narrow and opening. It all made her feel delightfully full. With every breath the pleasure was enhanced; she could feel the different sensations impacted by the heaving of her body.

She did not dare disobey a command from the woman now standing over her, and in a state of near delirium she pressed her lips to the waiting cunt of Ursula. And oh! The taste was wonderful, musky, and tinged with the slight aroma of herbs. Brigeen could hear Ursula moan a little over her. Knowing that she was returning some of the pleasure she was receiving, she set of lapping furiously at the wet lips of the woman, suckling like a hungry pup. She could hear cooing sounds around her, and in a haze of total gratification she could feel Ursula's hips gyrating against her eager tongue.

Brigeen could still feel Loretta's teasing fingers on her clitoris, made erect and pulsing from the caresses. Her body was thrust gently forward into Ursula's wet cunt by Bernadette's thrusts behind her. All her senses were titillated as she sucked harder and harder at the soft mouth of Ursula's dripping vagina. She could feel Ursula's strong hands pressing the back of her head, forcing her to press her probing, flicking tongue deeper and deeper into the hot recess of the older woman's cunt.

The pleasure from Loretta's fingers and the excitation of her virgin anus by the steady hands of Bernadette were so intense that Brigeen was making muffled moaning sounds into the open crevice of Ursula's spread legs.

The vibrations of the young girl's voice created a tingling sensation in Ursula, and she pressed Brigeen's head more firmly into her wildly throbbing pussy. As she did this, Brigeen's body began to convulse in wracking spasms of ecstasy. The sight of the young girl coming so forcefully beneath her made Ursula writhe in pleasure, clutching her own tits in her hands, and screaming out as she came into Brigeen's still sucking mouth.

There were more screams and sighs, and then, in total fear and ecstasy, Brigeen lost consciousness.

BELLA

Josephine Jarmaine

ALTHOUGH IT IS many years ago now, I remember the Christmas when my uncle brought Laura the doll. It is unlikely I will ever forget either the doll or Laura.

Observe us at the festive board, stuffed with roast goose and plum pudding: Mama, tightly corseted in purple Ottoman silk, and pale under the threat of yet another bout of dyspepsia; Papa, in satin waistcoat with diamond stickpin, looking faintly as if he wished he were at pursuits more congenial to the male and away from the domestic turmoil; Laura and me, an aged great-aunt or two, and our uncles. The gaslight burping and flickering on the remains of the feast, and illuminating, over a pyramid of flowers and grapes, the face opposite, my exquisite sister.

Uncle Seymour was what they called a fine figure of a man, with iron-grey eyes and glorious moustaches whose waxed ends almost touched the lobes of his ears. He had given me a new cricket bat to take back to Epsom when term began. I was slightly disappointed, for he had just returned from the Grand Tour and I had hoped for something more exotic. However, Laura's gift stunned everyone at the table. It came in a box like a child's coffin. The doll had been purchased in Paris, made by one of the famous toymakers; I believe it was Jumeau, but it could have been Demontier. Or neither of them.

Laura got up and flung her arms round handsome Seymour's neck. I was jealous. In two years' time she would be putting up her hair, and wearing corsets like Mama. She would simply be swallowed up by fashionable Society.

I was fifteen and had a tutor in the holidays; he was cramming me for when I went up to Cambridge. We were on very good terms, man to man. I had overheard a conversation between Seymour and my other uncle, who was a lieutenant in the Imperial Yeomanry. I did quite a deal of accidental listening at doors; it was the only way I could learn. When they had finished discussing the unstable situation concerning the Boers of South Africa, their talk took a more interesting direction.

"What exactly is a brothel?" I asked my tutor. He did not bat an eye.

"It is a house where ladies of loose morals give pleasure to men."

He did not opine on the morals of the men who visited such ladies, and I knew then I had been born into the privileged sex in more ways than one.

"And what, pray, is a cunt?" was my next question. (I had eavesdropped for a fair while.)

He answered me honestly, like the sensible fellow he was. He was not with us this Christmas, having gone home for a week's leave, and I missed him somewhat.

I will return, however, to Laura's doll. The remarkable aspect was that it was almost a replica of her. If Seymour had given the maker exact specifications he could not have come closer. It was enormous, almost as tall as fourteen-year-old Laura, with the same lavish golden hair falling in hyacinthine fronds over her back and shoulders. It had her great blue eyes and classical figure. It even had her long fine hands with precisely moulded nails, and, as she laid it upright in a chair for everyone to admire, I saw it had similar curving breasts, like the pectorals of an athletic boy.

"I intend to call her Bella, because she is so beautiful" said Laura. She glimmered her eyes at Seymour in a roguish fashion, and I could gladly have smacked her. I was quite relieved when both uncles departed, the day after Boxing Day. The house was restored to normality; unusually quiet, in truth. Mama, as anticipated, had taken to her bed, both with dyspepsia and a megrim; Laura's French governess had been allowed a short vacation, and Papa had absented himself on errands suitable to a man of affairs. (I discovered years later that he kept a mistress in St John's Wood, but that is not germane to this story.)

The nursery was, as normal, in the attic, away at the top of the tall house. It always seemed to me to represent the brain of the building; there were a lot of energies there, or so it appeared to my pseudo-scientific mind. Laura and I had played together in the attic since we were babies, and far beyond that. There was a little gate at the top of the stairs. The banisters were still slick from my youthful hazardous descents. A fire always burned in the attic, behind a guard. There were shelves full of adventure stories, and my fort, with red-breasted soldiers defending our dear Queen's Empire in some desert dreariness. And there was a rocking-horse, a piebald beast with a white mane and tail and a ferocious grin.

As I ascended through the quiet house I heard Dobbin being ridden as if coming up the straight at Newmarket. Its violent creaking seemed to shake the door as I touched it. The sounds grew louder and faster, and above them I could clearly hear my sister. She was gasping, the gasps interspersed with tiny shrieks. At one time I might have been alarmed, but now, with some instinctual knowledge, all that arose in me was a prickling excitement.

I waited outside. Laura gave a loud cry, as if she had been stabbed. The creaking slowly decelerated and ceased. When I entered, she was dismounting. Her petticoats were up over her thighs in their black stockings. Her face was blood-red; she turned and smiled at me. The smile trembled on her lips.

On the big horsehair sofa sat Uncle Seymour's doll. Laura gingerly settled herself beside it. Her forehead was sweaty under the golden curls. The doll was smiling, its little beestung lips parted as if it too had a secret. I surveyed it closely. "You could be twins," I said.

They were dressed very similarly; their tiny waists in green silk with *gigot d'agneau* sleeves under their pinafores, their furbelowed frilly petticoats surging from beneath the hem of their dresses, their slender black-clad legs stuck out before them like liquorice sticks. Together they reclined, smiling. The fire ticked in the hearth like an irregular clock. My pulse beat in accord. Suddenly I felt my *membrum virilis* stir and stiffen in my trousers. Laura brushed the sweat away from her golden fringe, and set about cuddling the doll, which was too big for her lap. She looked at me sideways from under long lashes.

Presently she seemed more composed. She straightened her pinafore fussily, set the doll in a rigid sitting posture, and got up.

"I am going to see how poor Mama does."

I opened the door for her gallantly. I heard her footsteps going downstairs. Everything grew quiet again, though the rocking-horse still quivered infinitesimally.

I shall never know what prompted me, even now. Perhaps I was not meant to know. Yet I knew exactly what I was about. I turned to the doll. Its glittering eyes looked into mine, but only if I stood at the appropriate angle for its regard. I spoke to it by name. "Bella," I said. "Bella. Did you come from a Paris brothel?"

I am a full-fledged scientist now. I know the impossibilities. I know too the power of the human mind, and what games it can play. I know the tricks the heart can get up to. Whatever I thought then, I saw the eyes gleam brighter in the face of the beautiful doll. I heard the whisper of the eyelids slowly, conquettishly, moving at my words. That is how I remember it, that day during the Christmas season, when men talked of the coming troubles in South Africa, and the gaslight shuddered and deceived, and the strange energies made our attic playroom a sorcerer's grotto.

I went on addressing the doll in whispers. Had she answered I would have fled the room in terror. But she was quiet, and I was fearless.

I knelt before her and placed my hand on her knee, moved it up under the whirl of petticoats, higher until it was above the black stocking on the pink thigh. I watched her eyes. The room had dimmed and the fickle gaslight gave them expression. It seemed that I had insulted her, and, through her, insulted Seymour. It made me laugh quietly, as I proceeded to lift skirt and petticoats up to her waist, and looked between her legs.

"Have you a cunt, Bella?" I whispered.

I pushed her legs open. There was a bald pink delta and the tiniest crack, no bigger than a fissure in a walnut.

My member was tumescent. I took out its stiff length and put it to the crack. I pushed. The doll slid down and I covered it with my body. I pushed harder. It hurt the head of my member, and within my brain I fancied I could hear the faintest aggrieved wailing. Bella had disappeared beneath me on the sofa. Then all at once my prick went in. I had created a cunt. It was glorious.

I began to rut and roger her with short thrusts. She seemed to grow warm under me. I was in her up to the root; the pain had gone. My hot, delirious brain told me that she writhed a little, that she fought me with her small violated body. I poked Laura's doll while the sofa juddered from my thrusts, and as a final humiliation I filled her with a galloping flood of spunk which, when I withdrew, oozed from the tiny crack like slow pearls.

When I stood up I was shaking as from a tertian ague. I had the presence of mind to take out my handkerchief and wipe away the efflux of my come. I drew down the dress and arranged Bella carefully, as Laura had left her. She was once more a doll, but the recesses of my brain retained those faint, paranormal sounds.

That night I hardly slept at all. Excited and disturbed, I frantically frigged my sore prick until the soreness evaporated in pleasure. When people addressed me next day I could scarcely concentrate. Cook grew annoyed after having asked me twice whether I required cherry brandy in my provision basket when I returned to school in three days' time. It was as if she were speaking in a Hottentot's tongue. She could have been offering me strychnine for all I knew. I wanted to be near Laura, yet kept out of her way, mooching round the estate, ignoring her puzzled calling as she pursued me through kitchen garden and stable yard, where I had a nonsensical conversation with the head groom. The truth is, I could not face her. Another part of me wanted to tell her. I was in an agony of spirit, and this perverse emotion took me again to the attic.

This time I laid Bella flat on the worn old carpet in front of the fire, and undressed her completely. I knew I was safe; Mama was still abed and Laura was having a piano lesson. From far below I could hear the monotony of the F minor scale beating into my brain as I undid the pearl buttons on Bella's gown and revealed her slim pink body to my lecher's gaze. Her hair had fallen half over her face, giving her a louche and wanton look. I could easily ignore the little lines of articulation where her arms and legs joined her trunk, for I saw her as a young girl. I caressed her barely curving breasts and licked the rudimentary nipples put there by the French maker, a realist if ever there was one. I stretched her legs apart. The cunt I had opened was still there, a sere little hole in the minute crack, and quickly I penetrated it with my throbber.

I fucked with great abandon. This time there was a sour emotion to it, a hateful revulsion, and I pounded into the doll, hoping to hear again a whine of protest. I heard only my own hoarse breathing, my sobbing, my lustful calling out of a name. I made so much noise that I never heard the ceasing of the nerve-snapping F minor scale, nor did I hear the opening door. It was only when I felt a hand on my plunging bare buttocks that I stilled in horror.

I withdrew from the doll in haste, my hands hiding my engorgement from my sister's gaze. Then I felt her arms come round me, and her whispering my name: "Raymond, oh, Raymond."

I struggled to my feet. It was some time before I dared look at her. I saw her crouch down beside the doll and put her fingers where my member had been. She inserted her finger deep, brought it out and looked closely at the little vestige of slime already left behind by me. She took the finger to her nostrils, then licked it. She smiled. She frowned. I stood, putting my clothes to rights, with a scarlet face.

"Did she like it?" she said, whispering.

I managed to say. "No. I don't believe she did." I was trembling.

Laura's face had changed subtly. She looked adult, severe, but the severity was not directed at me. Bella was the one come to judgement.

"How dare you, you creature?" she said softly. "Raymond is mine. You are nothing but a harlot."

Calmer now, I sat down on the couch. I saw Laura take the poker from the fire. It had been left between the bars of the grate and was incandescent. I watched while she brought it to Bella's naked pink body. But I could not watch what she did, for it was accomplished with such viciousness it frightened me, although part of me rejoiced that Laura should know jealousy such as that which had clawed me when she embraced Seymour. Then she announced: "The harlot must be incarcerated. For seducing you. Please help."

Together we put Bella into the big doll cupboard. Laura threw her clothes in after her, and shut the door. She turned to me. There was an awesome light in her eyes.

"And now we're alone," she whispered.

She looked like the pagan goddesses I had seen in books. She was full of triumph. Her beauty was quite terrible. Her power was infectious. I could smell her sweat, like hay and apples, and the sweet odours of her body. Her hands were upon me. I was her doll, for she undressed me as if she had been doing it for years. Yes. I was her doll.

I stood naked before her, and she knelt down, taking my rod in her cupped hands, extending her fingers to encompass my balls and drawing them forward. My member rose starkly, hard and at such an angle it nearly touched my belly. Laura kissed its tip, then rose, tore off her pinafore and turned for me to unfasten the hooks down the back of her dress. She threw herself on the couch, her legs in the air, wide open so I could see every red inner crevice and crease. She spread herself, her heels hooked either side of the arms of the sofa. In between her long white thighs a froth of gilt hair crowned a pouting hillock over a slit as sharp as if slashed by a butcher. There was a further tiny hill at its apex, like a swollen acorn. A musky, fishy scent rose from her *mons Veneris*. Her little white bubbies were tipped with stiff nipples, raised at the air. She pointed to her slit.

"What do you call it?" she whispered.

"Cunt." Unsteadily I moved, magnetized, between her legs. "Your cunny. Your cunt."

"Do my cunt. What do you say when you do a cunt?"

"I poke it. I fuck."

"Fuck my cunt. Fuck it. Fuck it, Raymond. This is a real cunt. Put your thing in it. What is your thing?"

"My thing. My tail. My prick. My cock. My truncheon."

"Put your tail in my cunt. Put your prick in, put in your cock. Fuck. Fuck."

These were our courting words, our love-words, and they continued throughout, becoming indistinguishable from our moans, our panting. She had my member between her fingers, eager, spreading her thighs so wide that the sinews stretched like thin cords as I leaned on her, holding her apart. She pulled at my cock and I forced her hand away, whispering: "Let him go in on his own; he knows the way," and I nuzzled his head between the red nymphae so they spread out against the damp, odiferous hairs.

With my tip I found her hole; glutinous moisture burst from it, glazing the surrounding membranes. The opening yielded like a damp mouth and she lifted her bottom high to accommodate me. I gave pressure, spurred by the ache in my balls. I lunged and was engulfed in her hot wet maw. I moved forward into the hot and the wet, met a fragile obstruction, drove on regardless, feeling her suddenly cringe, hearing a gasp that was almost a cry. Then I plunged to the limit, sliding in an upward curve to where her womb lay, my balls pressing her nates, my body hair meshing with her soft gold frill. Riding her, eyes closed, heart fibrillating enough to burst, my loins jack-rabbiting, bounding, surging, settling to a steady pumping motion, while again and again her soft mount answered my every thrust. I opened my eyes on her wild blue glance, her lips drawn back, spittle on her teeth, the look both of the bitch in heat and the saint in ecstasy. And as I spent in her, spouting as in the wettest of all my nocturnal emissions, I filled her with all my dreams of desire, past and to come, while some deep inner mouth seized me and drank me up.

She held me clamped until my prick ebbed and came drained from her body. When I looked down at it I saw it was bloody. Laura's thighs were smeared with blood, but she was laughing with the purest joy.

That was our one and only time, unique in every sense of the word.

I suppose one might say that Bella was the catalyst, and Seymour, who later joined the regiment and was killed at Bloemfontein, the original font. I never enquired what became of Bella. For all I know she remained in that cupboard all the time I was finishing my education and pursuing my career.

Perhaps she stayed imprisoned, like some fairy tale princess, while beautiful Laura rose to become the jewel of London society.

Or perhaps one day she simply emerged and went away, looking for love.

ENKI

Angus MacMillan

I, ENKI, PRINCE OF Edom, firstborn son of the Great King Anki, whose House descends through all of history in its male members from the gods themselves, am Ky's whore in the palace of Shlomo of the Empire of Ysrael.

Edom no longer exists – nor does my family bond to the great gods. Both my land and I have become whores at the command of King Shlomo, who rules here from Yerushalem – willingly so in my case, my life now dedicated to the goddess by King Shlomo for me.

I sit at my window and stare down at the grounds of Shlomo's palace and the noble youths playing there. My body is oiled and I wear the jewelled loincloth given me by Shlomo himself, its pocket of fresh frankincense flush against my remaining claim to manhood. I smile as I wonder if I shall again introduce the young nobles of Ysrael beneath me to the pleasures of their bodies as I did that week Great Shlomo was too sotted with wine to know it.

My portal tingles its annoyance at being unfilled. Great Ky stands there demanding pleasure, as she always does. The giving and the taking of it. I pray Great Shlomo shall call me to him – or to one of his guests. I hear he entertains the Nubian Queen and pray she has retainers who have refined tastes in their pleasures. I have never worshipped Ky in a Nubian before.

The Host of Ysrael had begun to cross the great river with the first cock crow of the day of my commitment to the goddess Ky – by men who did not know her. Beniayah, the Captain of the Hosts of Ysrael, and Shlomo, the King of Kings, rode together at the head of the army that would destroy Edom for all time. Even three candlemarks into their invasion of my land, their men and supply wagons still crossed the Jordan.

Great Anki turned to me, his gaze pulling me from my burning anger. "Ride to Shlomo and sue for peace," he told me.

I stared at him in shock. "Never!" I cried. "Father, he has betrayed his own word. His own treaties!"

"Our duty is to Edom, Enki. We must save the land and our people." There was greater emotion in my father's voice than I had ever heard before. "Nothing else matters. Without Edom, we are nothing. If we are nothing, honour is a thing of the past."

"We must fight them, Father!"

He smiled, and I felt his pain. "With what, Enki? The Host of Ysrael is ten times greater than our small army. You would have the sand suck up all the young men of Edom? You would have our people become ghosts? And still have Shlomo rule afterwards? He would give our lands to his own servants, and the ghosts of our people would be left to cry their loneliness through the wilderness for all time."

Great Anki moved his horse closer to mine and he hugged my shoulder. "Go, my son, and make whatever peace the Ysraeli would give us. Save our people, whatever the cost."

I swallowed my pride. I wiped the tears of frustration from my eyes. I rode toward the Host of Ysrael alone. Without weapons. I was the Crown Prince of Edom, the sole emissary of Great Anki to the disreputable cut-throat Shlomo, misbegotten son of Great David. I rode to seek safety for my people, the salvation of Edom.

Spears held me immobile as I was announced inside the royal tent. The grizzled officer who came to escort me to his King leered as he studied me. "Remove your armour, boy," he growled. No goy may enter Great Shlomo's presence dressed for war."

I was being dishonoured intentionally. I knew it, but my mission was more important than my honour. I closed my eyes and repeated that as I pulled off my breastplate and leather girdle. I stood before the Ysraeli rabble in but my tunic and loincloth.

"Now the tunic, lad. Great Shlomo will not be threatened by hidden Edomi bronze this day."

I stared at the officer. My face grew hot with both anger and embarrassment. I wanted only to run a spear through the man. Yet I knew I had a duty that overrode even this dishonour. I pulled my tunic over my head and watched it fall into the dirt at my feet.

Inside the tent, I squinted to see in the dimness.

"You do not kneel before your master, Enki?" a bemused voice asked from behind me, and I whipped about to face its bearer.

I recognized the Ysraeli immediately. Shlomo's fawning dog. "Lord Beniayah," I acknowledged him, conscious to give the Captain of all the Hosts of Ysrael his title, in counterpoint to his ignoring mine.

He studied me silently, his gaze moving slowly from my smooth chest to my flat abdomen. It seemed almost that his eyes sought to peer beneath the loincloth that covered my manhood.

My face flamed in embarrassment at the thought.

"Enki, Prince of Edom –" His face twisted into a leer. "But, then, if there is no Edom, can there be a Prince of it?"

"I come to sue for peace, My Lord."

"Your total surrender is our demand. Your land already becomes another province of Ysrael."

I felt the blood leave my face as I turned pale, and a cold fear brought gooseflesh to my body. "I cannot treat with such a demand," I whispered in my fear. "Either I speak with your King and find better terms or I must leave to take your message to my father."

Beniayah chuckled and clapped his hands.

Startled, I looked over my shoulder to see two large slaves separate that they could encircle me. I stared back at the Captain of all the Hosts of Ysrael. "What are you doing?"

"Gag and bind him," he told the slaves.

I stood in shock, rooted to the dirt beneath my feet as one slave grabbed my hands and pulled them together behind me.

"King Shlomo has already sent an emissary to your father, Enki. He left while you were escorted within our lines." The second slave worked a rawhide rope between my teeth as his companion secured my hands.

Beniayah nodded at the slaves' handiwork. "Our terms are complete surrender, with you as hostage." The leer returned to his face. "I suspect you'll come to enjoy your stay under the Great King's tent."

He glanced to the slaves. "Remove his loincloth and take him to the King's chamber." He leered at me. "And make him ready."

My bonds tied to a rafter above me, I stared at the mattress that dominated the chamber. A slave knelt beside me, his fingers dipping in an opened lantern. He smiled up at me as he spread my thighs, opening a path beneath the jewels the great gods deigned to give me with birth.

I struggled to pull away. My eyes widened as his oil-slicked finger made its way behind my purse of jewels and found the portal that led into me.

"It hurts less the first time if you're oiled, Master," he mumbled in broken Ysraeli as his finger pushed into the entrance behind my portal. "The King's member is very large. This is best for you."

I groaned. I tried to pull away from him but he held one leg firmly. A second finger found its way into me, joining the first. I gritted my teeth. My body stiffened and I turned my head, surrendering my buttocks to the slave's preparations for the debasement I must endure, but unwilling to watch him do it.

Tears ran down my cheeks. Anger and embarrassment joined as one in my heart. I swore I would kill the man who dreamt my removal from the ranks of men.

King Shlomo entered the chamber, followed by Beniayah. He approached me and I smelled the wine on his breath. My stomach growled at the realization he had eaten and I had not. He smiled and touched my cheek, his finger following the line of my jaw from my ear to my chin. He pulled the rawhide from my mouth. "Anki has agreed to my terms, little bird." His smile became a knowing leer. "You're now mine to teach."

"Allow me to dress, my King?" I asked, accepting his suzerainty over my fate. I faintly hoped he had but wanted to humiliate me and Edom.

Shlomo ignored my petition and turned to Beniayah. "Help

me off with this girdle," he told the Captain of all the Hosts of Ysrael, as he would a slave.

I stood erect, as befit my station, unwilling to cower before the personification of Ysrael. The robe of King Shlomo, son of mighty David, was freed, and flowed down his legs and spread to obscure his hips. I saw with horror that his manhood had come alive and was beginning to tent the garment. I felt my face flame as my member jumped into life, the prepuce pulling back from its crown.

"Do you think our little Princeling has forgotten how to suckle?" the King asked his captain. He turned to me. "Have you, little Enki? Are you ready to know something Beniayah claims is better even than mother's milk?"

He stepped closer, our faces but a cubit from each other. My eyes met his defiantly. I still hoped he would relent. His hand shot out between us and grabbed the shaft of my manhood, pulling its cowl over its crown. His face again became a leer as I stared into it with shock. "Your body betrays your defiance, Edomi," he breathed as his lips closed the distance between us. "You desire what your goddess Ky offers."

I turned my head and his lips grazed my cheek as they moved to my ear. I closed my eyes, squinting away my tears, and prayed for death.

"You will know it all, sweet Enki. You will have it all. And you will love it all," he whispered in my ear. He pulled away, but did not release my member. "Lift this robe from me, Beniayah," he ordered his captain, even as his breath played in the down that covered my cheek.

My face blazed at the shame being visited upon me, at the betrayal of my own manhood as Shlomo continued to pull on it. I opened my eyes and looked upon the King of Ysrael. A silky black forest covered his chest, spreading up to cover his shoulders and down to – I pulled my eyes back from their descent. Never, I told myself, would I willingly look upon that which would debase me.

He stepped back and released me. He leered at me as he pulled his robe from his arm and tossed it behind him. "Now we're both naked for our mutual pleasure, Enki of Edom. Would you suckle the great manhood of Ysrael before you ride it?"

I studied his eyes. I saw only lust there, my own defilement. "Kill me, Great and Wise King," I choked. "Permit me, in my death, the company of all the gods."

"Ahh, little bird, that's not possible. I promised Anki I would care for his son as I would my own." He turned to Beniayah. "Release him and help him to the mattress." His gaze returned to me as the Captain of All the Hosts of Ysrael moved to my side. "This night you learn Ky's embrace from both of us, little bird," he told me.

I was pushed onto the mattress, my face pressed against the thin cloth and corn husks. Behind me, Beniayah grabbed my hips and pulled me to my knees. He splayed my legs before reaching between them and grabbing my manhood to pull it to him. The portal to my passage was raised and open.

I turned my head to the side to breathe, my eyes wide with fear. I stared over my shoulder, back at the man who would know me intimately.

"Kill me, Great Shlomo," I pleaded as Beniayah continued to move his hand along my shaft from my side.

"You want it?" the King asked his captain, ignoring me.

"It's long, Sire. A thin dagger that would know my throat."

I heard the lust in the man's voice. My jewels tightened about my manhood.

"Get under him, then, Beniayah. You may both suckle at the same time." Shlomo grinned widely. "Young Enki may find that a satisfactory diversion."

I stared at Ysrael's King. Each hair of Shlomo's beard seemed to stand out from its companion, his face had widened so much with his grin.

The Captain of all the Hosts of Ysrael quickly stripped off his war harness. He pulled his tunic over his head and opened the knot of his loincloth. He climbed onto the mattress before me. Shlomo gripped my shoulders and raised my body that his man could slip beneath me.

I stared at the Ysraeli manhood before me as Beniayah gripped mine. I mumbled a prayer to all the gods as his lips touched the puckered lace of my prepuce. I groaned my surprise as his tongue sought entry through that lace to what the gods had made me and these men would take from me for the glory of Ky. My eyes grew wide as more and more of me was gobbled until I was sure there was none of me left.

"Lick it, little Enki," Shlomo goaded me as he climbed onto the mattress behind me. "Take all of Beniayah and feast from the Ysraeli plate before you."

I gazed at Beniayah's manhood before me. It wasn't long, it was shorter than mine – but thick, much thicker. Its naked crown spread majestically above its shaft and seemed to call to me. Strange and unknown pleasures were growing in my jewels and manhood as he suckled at mine. Shlomo's hand grasped the back of my head and pushed me down toward his captain.

"Suck, little Enki," Shlomo commanded.

I opened my mouth to protest, but the crown of Beniayah's dagger was closer than I thought. Its spongy hardness was past my lips before I could utter a word.

"See?" Shlomo's voice touched my ear softly. "Work your tongue over it. Know my captain's glory, Enki – and the pleasure of giving pleasure."

I was in shock. A manhood was lodged at the entrance to my throat. A hand held my head that I could not escape it. My jewels began to threaten an explosion. I only dimly felt the silk forest of Shlomo's abdomen against my buttocks or his legs between mine. Shlomo pushed me further onto his captain's member and I gagged.

"Up and down, Enki," Shlomo whispered, and lessened the pressure on the back of my head. I felt his chest press against my back and realized something impossibly large had come to nestle in the valley that split my buttocks and led directly to the entrance of the passage into me. He pushed my face back down onto the manhood in my mouth and I felt stiff hair grind against my chin as my throat opened for it.

My jewels churned within their purse. I moaned around the thickness buried in my throat. And I knew orgasm from other than my own hand for my first time.

I did not feel the walls of my valley spread as the Great King of Ysrael pulled his hips from my buttocks, nor did I feel his impossibly large trowel make its way through that valley of flesh. I could not stop shooting my seed into Beniayah's waiting gullet. Mindlessly, I set my lips and tongue to explore the ridges of the

Captain's shaft as he humped it into my throat and pulled it away with growing need.

The crown of Beniayah's manhood shoved into my gullet and grew. His every muscle tensed as he held it there. My jewels pumped the last of my seed into his throat and I shuddered as his tongue caressed my shaft.

Pressure arose at the portal before the passage into me, but I was too spent to realize its presence at first. Ysraeli seed erupted to spew into my gullet as Beniayah pushed even more of himself into my mouth. My nose was buried hard against his jewels. Another volley of seed splattered against the back of my throat.

Shlomo battered the portal before my passage and plunged home. Pain shot out of my passage into every fibre of my being.

I moaned my protest around the width of manhood that still possessed my mouth and throat. I buried my face between Beniayah's tightly pressed thighs. After for ever, I felt Shlomo's coarse, tightly curled hair press against the insides of the valley through my buttocks.

"So tight, Enki," Shlomo muttered above me as he held all of himself within me.

Pain held me as the Great King began to move his battering ram inside me, claiming my virgin passage as his possession. It spread through me in waves. My manhood collapsed in protest. Only Shlomo's hand on the back of my head held me on Beniayah's Ysraeli staff of power.

"Ours shall be a special night," the King mumbled, bending over me to whisper in my ear. "A celebration of Ky's possession of you."

Even pain must pass. As Shlomo continued to plough my passage, possessing me with his glory, I adjusted to him inside me.

My own manhood swung from navel to one thigh and then the other, in union with his thrusts. It grew as my body adjusted to even Shlomo's presence. My prepuce pulled back from my glistening crown as the Great King ploughed slowly on. My jewels churned within their purse and tightened once again around my member under the hammering of the power and the glory of Ysrael.

"Give yourself up to it, little bird," he mumbled, and nibbled my ear. His member continued to spread me wide and claimed me.

Beniayah's hand encircled my moving manhood and pulled it to his lips.

My manhood and jewels betrayed what was left of me, relishing their surrender to sweet Ky as the goddess made me her own. My seed erupted against Beniayah's lips and he opened them to take me between them again.

I was possessed. I no longer belonged among the great gods; I belonged to the lowliest of them – the whore goddess herself. Given to her. And Shlomo continued to plough on.

I cared not. I moaned my pleasure. I ground my buttocks against his groin when he pressed against me "Ride me, my King!" I cried finally, giving voice to my need.

A discreet knock at the entrance of my chamber brings my thoughts back from the youths below me. I smile to the young Greek slave I have known when neither Shlomo nor his lieutenants want me.

"Two Nubians await you, sweet Enki," he tells me. "I'm to lead you to their apartment that you may tend to their needs."

I jump from my seat at the window, my face smiling its surprise. "Nubians? I've never had a dark one." I pause as I reached the mattress and gaze at the Greek. "Are they big?"

He grins. "I think so, sweet Enki."

I laugh. "Take me to them, then." I thank the goddess for the pleasures she gives me as I begin to follow the lad's backside and remember the power of his thrusts. Perhaps he can come to me tonight if the Nubians are satisfied early. Ky is an ever-hungry goddess.

HALL OF MIRRORS

Vivienne LaFay

THE LIGHTS WERE blazing in the West Wing where the men, including my husband, were indulging in their favourite pastime, gambling. There, in the Old Ballroom, all was quiet. The room was modelled on the famous *Galerie des Glaces* in Versailles, its many arched mirrors surrounded by gilt and marble, while a vaulted ceiling showed scenes from classical mythology. But the place had seen better days. An eerie silence reigned in that neglected hall and a cold draught made me shiver.

Reclining on the shabby chaise longue in my elegant gown of filmy blue muslin and écru lace, I saw my face looming in the dusty pier glasses like a pale ghost. Tendrils of dark hair framed my features and my breasts were high and firm beneath the ruched bodice. Beneath it my heart was beating rapidly. For how long should I await my lover? Already the nightjar was singing its throaty serenade on the terrace outside.

It seemed the safest place for a rendezvous. Since fire had devastated the East Wing of Melbray Hall the ballroom had fallen into disuse, and the sounds of distant revelry confirmed that the party was being carried on elsewhere. Yet it was there, in those once-glorious surroundings, surrounded by gleaming sconces and laughing faces, that I had fallen in love with Peregrine Bailey.

What attracted me to him was still a mystery, but I realized from the first moment that my interest was returned. Our eyes had met frequently across that crowded ballroom – mine blue and clear, his dark and brooding – and we'd shared just one dance. But as soon as I was in his arms I was lost. Just breathing in the heady scent of him was enough to make my heart flutter like a trapped pigeon. To feel his lips touch my hair, to be brushed by those manly thighs, and to have him kiss my hand with undisguised fervour before our reluctant parting – all that was bliss and torment at once.

I had been married to Sir Harry when I was seventeen and had borne him two sons. After that he had ceased to bother me, for which I was grateful. Yet a part of me was still unawakened. I had never known that ecstasy spoken of by poets like the great Lord Byron. Some deep woman's instinct told me that my dear Perry was the one who could open the door to that new world for me.

Suddenly I heard a literal door opening at the end of the long room. Fear that it might be some stranger, or, worse, my own husband, turned to joy as I saw my lover making his way towards me, his thighs looking strong and muscled in the tight breeches and his face visibly flushed, even in the gloom. I sat up eagerly, my whole body waiting for his touch, and my legs trembling beneath the silk petticoat and muslin skirt.

"My dearest Catherine!" he sighed, kneeling before the chaise longue and taking both my hands. I kissed that smooth brow, hardly daring to do more, but he seized my face and pulled my mouth to his. The soft pressure of his warm lips and the comforting feel of his arms around my upper body sent my soul into a spinning rapture.

"You look so beautiful," he murmured, at last. "Wait – I shall light one of these sconces. I have locked the door, so we shall not be disturbed."

Soon the murky room was glowing. A pool of light around the chaise longue enabled me to see my lover's face and figure in all its manly beauty. Tenderly he pulled down the shoulder of my gown and began to kiss my neck and bosom, so lightly that it was as if I were being caressed by floating thistledown. I could see us reflected in the mirrors all around, multiplied into a dozen pairs of lovers. It was my fancy that, just then, we represented all the world's sweethearts.

"Look!" I cried in delight. "See how we are everywhere!"

"Yes, indeed!" he chuckled, pulling my muslin gown lower until it was half off my body. He untied the ribbons of my chemise and with eager hands pulled out my left breast. I saw it stand proud in the candlelight, like a shiny pink pomegranate tipped by a tawny calyx. I had not realized that my breasts were so large and fine. Was it love that engorged them with longing and turned them into magnificent fruit for my lover to enjoy?

Perry took my tumid nipple between his lips and began to suckle, sending me into a state of dreamy arousal. I shrugged off my gown, then my chemise, until I lay naked before him, glorying in the sight of my voluptuous body, reflected back at me from the surrounding mirrors. Everything about me seemed larger than life: my swelling bosom, my rounded belly, my thick black bush.

I glanced up at the ceiling and saw Venus pictured there, lying in the arms of Mars on a flowery bank, with Eros and Cupid in attendance. The divine couple were as naked as we were in our mortal dalliance, and again my fancy went to work, imagining that the bond between Perry and me was being sanctified by the gods themselves.

Soon my lover was eagerly running his hands and lips over every part of me, inflaming my desires to fever-pitch. As he pressed against me I could feel the hardening of his organ, hidden behind the buttons of his trousers. At the thought of it my insides seemed to melt like wax from a candle, making me all soft and malleable within.

"Will you not also divest yourself of your garments?" I begged him.

Perry gave a wry smile as he removed his waistcoat. He turned from me and down came his breeches, showing me the pale moons of his behind. I caught a frontal glimpse of him in the glass across the room and at once I realized the effect that our kissing had been having upon his manhood. By the time he finally stood naked before me I could see the evidence of his robust desire reflected in every mirror, and I almost fainted at the sight. His member seemed twice the size of my feeble husband's!

"Oh, Perry, dearest!" I gasped, as he knelt upon the chaise longue between my thighs. "Enter me at once, for I am more than ready for you!"

But he seemed determined to prolong my tormenting passion awhile. Kneeling on the polished wooden floor beside the chaise longue, he placed his dear head on my bare thighs and began to deliver tiny kisses that thrilled their way up to my sex and set my whole body trembling. I began to sigh and moan as the strong tide of desire rose in me, but my cries redoubled when he reached my soft nether lips and dared to invade me with his tongue.

At first I could not believe that my lover could be enjoying the taste of me. I thought he was merely being obliging, making me wet so that when his cock entered it would be without any pain or discomfort. But the eagerness with which he performed the intimate lip service, the strong thrusts he made with his tongue and the answering groans of delight that he uttered, finally convinced me that our pleasure must be mutual.

At that I relaxed, and allowed him to take his fill of me, to satisfy both of us. His fingers crept to my naked bosom and toyed with my nipples while he continued down below, filling me with blissful waves of delight. Already he had given me more rapture in five minutes than my husband had in five years!

Soon, though, my swollen pussy was aching to be filled with his own dear organ, and I grew restless. Perry sensed that I wished our lovemaking to proceed towards the ultimate act, and he, too, seemed more than ready for it. He withdrew his mouth from my throbbing vulva, climbed up onto the velvet of the chaise longue and positioned his knees on either side of me, with my legs parted in between.

For a few seconds he gazed down at me, an expression of perfect adoration on his sweet face, then he took his member in his hand and guided it towards my inner sanctum. For a few seconds I saw us reflected in the mirror, a picture of debauchery that thrilled me to the core! My breasts reared up in voluptuous fullness, the red nipples glistening at their crests, and his prick was holding up its head with equal pride, raring to go. I marvelled at the dimensions of it in the dim reflection: the long pale shaft seemed thick as an altar candle, and the tip was like a lily bulb, faintly hued in pink and purple.

I was a little frightened that it would prove too large for my small opening, but my hot, desirous flesh gave way immediately he presented himself at my door. My lover pushed in an inch or so and I gave a strange cry of delight – no such sound had ever issued from my throat before.

I am born again a virgin, I thought, in wonder. I have given birth to two sons, yet I have never known such incredible bliss until now. This man has possessed my heart and soul!

I knew that according to the law of the land I belonged to my wedded spouse. But I also knew that according to the divine law of Love, that transcends all, I belonged to Perry.

Now he was sliding into me with such exquisite care, caressing my inner walls which embraced him gladly. He began to gently move in and out of me, his member producing the most wonderful sensations, so that I seemed to be quivering inside and my body felt as if it were drawn taut, like a violin string.

With every thrust my ardour heightened. His vigorous tool filled me completely as I clasped it in my secret embrace. I was more aroused than ever I had been in my marital bed. What a difference a few inches makes, I thought to myself, as I felt the waves of pleasure bringing me closer and closer to the edge of endurance. Then, just when I thought I could bear such sweet torment no longer, I felt myself helplessly hurled into the abyss of ultimate delight, and, with a groan, he soon followed after.

Exhausted, we lay in each other's arms. I felt warm gratitude flood my veins. Now I knew exactly why poets waxed lyrical about the love that inspires men and women. I had tasted the forbidden fruit, and I was still in paradise.

Perry withdrew from my side and stood up. I stared at the shrivelled thing between his legs. "It is so very small now." I smiled. "But not long ago it was the greatest wonder!"

"My love, it is never so very great," he answered. "I am not well endowed."

"Yes, yes, I saw it with my own eyes!" I protested. "There – reflected in the mirror . . ."

But as I looked from the man to the image, I suddenly realized that there was a discrepancy in the size of his part. I looked again from the reality to its reflection, frowning.

Perry laughed. "My dear Catherine – do you not know that

these are magnifying mirrors? They make everything seem larger than life size!"

"No!" I leapt to my feet, staring at the image of the pair of us. I looked down at our hands and feet, then at their reflections, and realized that what he'd said was true.

"I am a man of quite modest proportions," he confessed. "In fact, women have often ridiculed me for my small member. But tonight, dearest Catherine, you made me feel as if I were the most virile man on earth!"

He kissed me and was soon gone, leaving me to reflect in the dark.

TO GET AN HEIR

Dominic Santi

I NEEDED AN HEIR. As the seventh Baron Ashwood, I had my family lands to preserve, and I was determined to do my duty.

At forty-four, I had outlived my first two wives. Both had been good marriages, good matches of station and personality. I had grieved bitterly at my ladies' premature demises. Still, despite my previous losses, my third wife, Elspeth, had become the light in my life. During the first year of our union, I had discovered that she was my true soulmate. I have often been told I have a stern countenance, but even when I was at my most severe Elspeth remained sweet as the honeysuckle that climbed the garden wall. At nineteen, she had the face of an angel, the body of a Greek goddess, and a naughty sense of humor that had drawn me up from the depths of my sadness. I had come to love her dearly.

Still, as Elspeth and I celebrated our first anniversary, my friends again consoled me on my choice of yet another barren woman. None of my wives had given me children. Neither had any of my assorted mistresses. In all those years, not even one early-lost pregnancy. So, even as I accepted my friends' condolences, reassuring them once again of my undying faith that God would grant me a son, I had already set in motion the plan that I prayed would ensure my success.

I am a man of science. I'd considered my lack of an heir

objectively. Three barren wives? Six barren mistresses? To say nothing of the various courtesans I'd casually entertained? No, despite my physician's insistence that I had but to find the proper woman in which to plant my seed, I was convinced that somehow the problem was mine. In even the richest soil, not all seed is fertile. I was not about to let seven generations of my family's history come to an end because my seed could not take root in a woman.

That's where the Frenchman came in. Although Jacques Dupres was only twenty-six, my men told me he had a dozen bastards spread across the Parisian countryside – mostly boys, and those all bright, intelligent, comely lads. He'd gotten them on women of quality, though their fathers had all declined to allow a marriage because of his family's newly impoverished state. His blood was aristocratic, by Dupres was now but a lowly cavalry officer, highly decorated, but without land or title beyond his captaincy.

And Jacques Dupres was a rogue to the core. Handsome as the devil, suave and carefree. His reputation was legend throughout French society. He made the ladies laugh as he enticed them to his bed – to their beds, actually, as he had no real home, save that with his military unit. Still, they swooned at his prowess as a lover. The latest *on dit* always had him with a new woman – again, this season, the whispered gossip remarked on how one woman could never be enough for him. Though in the same breath all added how they had heard that Dupres truly cared for the children that resulted from his liaisons. Upon investigation, my spies said it seemed to genuinely pain the man that he could not acknowledge his offspring. But he loved them enough to leave them to the families whose names they bore.

I admired his discretion. And Monsieur Dupres looked enough like my beloved younger brother – or at least like I imagined my brother would have grown to be, had not the cholera taken him – to pass for a close relative to me. The arrangements had been made. Unscrupulous as it might seem, given the war, I was determined to have my heir before the Frenchman left for his stated destination of the Caribbean, whence, I presumed, he would venture north to join his friend Lafayette in the colonial rebellion.

The man's politics did not concern me. I would have my heir. And I was just as determined that Elspeth enjoy the encounter.

After all, given my age, she might well have much of the raising of the child without me. I wanted her as devoted to – pray God – my son, as I would be.

I sat in the library, before a blazing fire, sipping a brandy and reading Voltaire, when my man announced Dupres' arrival. I took a moment, watching a log roll to the side in a crackle of ashes, reminding myself of my duty, before I set down my book and stood. Then the Frenchman was in front of me, smiling as he handed over his coat and took the proffered glass.

As I had been told to expect, we were roughly of a size, and he was every bit as handsome as he looked in the miniature I had been shown. The dark curls that framed his face were damp from the evening's rain, his brown eyes twinkling with a mischievous sparkle that I knew Elspeth would appreciate.

We dispensed quickly with the usual amenities. We were only a few sips into our brandy when he handed me the packet of letters that comprised our correspondence. Then Dupres quirked his eyebrow at me and said, "So, Lord William, do you still wish to go on with this?" He swirled the amber liquid up the sides of his glass before he took another drink. "It's not every day a man asks me to seduce his wife. And to get her with child, no less."

I nodded, and lifted my glass to him. "The agreement stands, Dupres. The midwife says Elspeth will be ripe for seven days. You are to visit her every night – plough her until your seed is well seated in her womb." I looked at him hard as I added, "And you are to make her fair faint with pleasure at the encounter, so that the child will be a constant memory of naught but joy to her. This child is to be my heir, Dupres. I will have him – or her –" I acknowledged his arched eyebrow, barely suppressing a shudder at the possibility of that devastating outcome "– raised in a home that befits one who will manage my estates well." I held the glass tightly to keep my hands from shaking as I added, "Or one through whom my lands will pass to a new line through a grandson, should that situation come to pass."

I took a sip of my brandy, feeling the fire burn down my throat, in some ways still aghast at what I was doing. But I was determined to do my duty, to do whatever I needed to get my heir.

"In return for your services, I will finance your venture to the colonies in the form of gold that my man will deposit into your hands on the morning of the eighth day. As I have said before, I do not want to know what your pursuit entails."

"And my final demand?" Dupres' voice was quiet, but it every bit matched the steel in my own. I silently cursed him, both for his stubbornness and for the determination that I at the same time so wanted my heir to possess.

I took another drink, forcing myself to remain calm as the Frenchman's eyes burned into me. He was smiling, but the sparkle was now a hard glint as he met my stare. What he asked – what he insisted upon – made me mightily uncomfortable. I had hoped to dissuade him from his insane demand, to make him see reason. But to no avail. The man was adamant. If I wanted his services, I would have to acquiesce, much as it galled me.

"I will join you in her bed," I said curtly, "while you get the child upon her."

"So she will always associate the pleasure with you, my lord." The glint was not gone, but now the mirth dominated his gaze as he acknowledged my acquiescence. "Have you discussed the matter with her ladyship?"

"Yes," I said shortly. "The servants will be dismissed for the night when dinner is served. We will dine together, you and I and Elspeth. Then we will retire to her rooms."

Dupres nodded, his eyes still sparkling as he finished his glass and set it on the credenza. "I am an expert in the ways of love, my lord. Trust me in this matter."

"I surmise that I have no choice," I snapped. To the full-throated sounds of his laughter, I downed the last of my brandy, and we went in to eat.

Elspeth was every bit as lovely tonight as I had imagined she would be. Demure, as always, with a stranger, she blushed through her curtsey to the Frenchman. Her gown was a simple rose affair, shot through with gold threads that highlighted the halo of soft yellow locks that framed her beautiful face. Her hair flowed like liquid sunshine over her shoulders, the tips of her perfect curls just brushing the creamy swell of her breasts over the scandalously low-cut bodice. I'd not have allowed her in public in that attire, no matter how brazen the current fashions. But Elspeth had objected mightily to my plan. When she'd finally agreed, my young hoyden had insisted that if she were to play the part of the brazen hussy, she should at least get to dress accordingly, especially if she had to share her bed with two men. In my heart, I knew she'd not really been angry with me. Elspeth understands as well as I our need for an heir. But she'd pushed my patience – and my temper – to the limit before she'd agreed to my scheme. Seeing her now, I was glad she'd worn the accursed dress. After all I'd gone through to bring this assignation to fruition, I wanted to be sure Dupres appreciated the value of the gift he was getting with my Elspeth.

He reacted as I'd hoped he would. A sudden intake of breath. A faint coloring in his cheeks. And a swell in his crotch that let me know he was very aware of Elspeth's allure. He took her hand and kissed it, held onto it for much longer than would have been appropriate in any polite society. But then, there was nothing appropriate about my designs for the evening. I ignored him, and the three of us sat down to eat.

The meal was superb. Cook had outdone herself for what I had uncharacteristically confided was to be a besotted husband's seduction of his lovely young wife. But if the matronly woman who had served me so long was surprised at the quantity of food I'd requested, she said nothing. The hens were done to perfection, delicately seasoned and complemented by a savory white wine, the breads warm and crusty and dripping with fresh butter. Even the unexpected compote for dessert, cook's personal contribution to the occasion, made my mouth water. And, as I had been told, Dupres was an excellent conversationalist. He soon had both my wife and I at ease, laughing uproariously with him as he regaled us with stories of his exploits both on the field and in various boudoirs. The man was shameless, his virility and his lust for life – and women – apparent in each scandalous, though always anonymous, description.

"But, no, sir! You did not!" Elspeth gasped, choking on her second glass of wine as I roared with laughter, smacking my hand on the table as I stood to pat her back.

"I did, indeed." Jacques grinned. "I hid beneath the bed while *mademoiselle* convinced her father that her cries had been ecstasy at a heavenly vision of saintly love." He laughed again. "She also told her father that the angel in her dreams had insisted that her marriage to an ancient marquis, set for the following week, go through with all possible haste. That the union was God's will." His eyes twinkled. "Which was quite fortuitous, when she bore a daughter nine months later."

My heart caught at the mention of a daughter. Still, I reminded myself, Dupres had fathered mostly boys. I kept that upmost in my mind as I watched him take Elspeth's hand and kiss it, his eyes dropping to her heaving bosom as she finished regaining her breath. Then his breathing changed as well. He stood and bent forward, touching his lips, slowly, tenderly, to the soft curve of her breast.

"Will you also bear us a child, dear Elspeth? One from my love, one for your husband to love, nine months from now?" His lips sucked lightly, barely brushing her blushing skin as he spoke. "Despite your aristocratic blood, my lady, will you let our child suckle at this lovely breast, so that each tender touch reminds you that your heir was conceived in the greatest of joy?"

He kissed her as he spoke, licking a damp trail through the light dusting of powder on her bosom, then letting his tongue steal beneath her plunging neckline to lick the sensitive jewel of her areola. Elspeth's nipple swelled, even through the costly fabric. My wife is a sensuous woman, but she has ever known only my touch. Now she looked at me, her eyes widening in surprise, and in pleasure. I smiled and nodded down at her, touching my tongue softly to my lips, imagining the tender flesh Dupres was tasting. His hand cupped her other breast, holding it like an offering. When his lips continued where they were, I felt his gaze on me, through just the corner of his eye, and I realized what he wanted. I leaned down to my wife, smoothed my hand over her lustrous hair and down the satin smoothness of her neck, relished her shiver. Then I bent and set my lips to the breast Jacques offered me.

The tip was already ruched with her desire. Elspeth gasped as I kissed the warmth of the curve. I inhaled the heady fragrance of her perfume, tasted the light tackiness of the powder, the damp smoothness where Jacques had licked her skin clean. Then I tugged gently at her bosom, lowering the silken fabric. When her swollen nipple slipped free, I took it gently in my mouth and suckled her, worshiping her velvety smooth skin, nursing the hard pearl until it was hot against my tongue and she wrapped her arms around us.

"Oh, my lords," she gasped, holding us tightly to her. She shuddered as we suckled her engorged breasts, milking her to wanton arousal. "Ye gods, but this is delightful."

"Conceived in the greatest of joy, my lady," Jacques whispered.

We retired to m'lady's bedroom. Elspeth was still somewhat bemused. Jacques had carried her up the stairs. She giggled – from embarrassment or nervousness, I could not tell – as they swept past me through the door. I bowed, affecting the greatest of gallants, which caused her to duck her face innocently into Jacques' neck. He laughed and danced her around the room in a swoosh of skirts before setting her on her feet beside the bed. Her skin glowed rosy in the light of the candles, braces of them, at Jacques' insistence, that cast the room in a golden glow.

Dupres, rogue that he is, did not allow her to catch her breath. As her feet touched the thick Turkish carpet, his lips were on hers. I closed the door and leaned back against it, just watching them for a moment, his dark curls bent over her blonde tresses, his hands holding her firmly to him, first around her waist, then slowly moving up her back until he was cupping her face in his hands, plundering her mouth. I had expected to feel jealousy at this point, to want to strangle him with my bare hands for daring to touch my beloved, no matter that I had instigated – nay, insisted upon – the liaison. If I am truthful, I had expected, deep in the hidden recesses of my heart, to resent the necessary act that would, please God, lead to the heir I so desperately needed. Instead, my shaft pressed hard against the front of my breeches, excited beyond anything I could have imagined at the sight of these two passionate people so intent upon each other – at the sight of my wife's gasps as she molded her body to the beautiful Frenchman's.

"William," he growled, "come here. Your wife is more than any one man can handle."

Elspeth's breathless giggle made my heart melt as she looked up at me and added, "Oh, yes, beloved. Please, let me kiss you as well. You are so patient, whereas this accursed Frenchman is so demanding."

Dupres' laughter filled the room, as did mine, finally, as I strode across to join them. I came up behind Elspeth and put my hands to her shoulders, kissing the back of her neck. She shivered at my touch, whimpering softly, tipping her head to bare her neck for me as my tongue trailed a wet path to her ear. I held her tightly, surprised to discover that my breeches were damp where they pressed against me, the evidence of my arousal seeping from my straining cock-head.

We undressed her between us. Jacques and I played the lady's maids, unbuttoning and unlacing, sliding the silken fabric from her creamy skin, until Elspeth was bared to the waist. As each bit of flesh was uncovered, we kissed it, him in front, me in back. And when we had attended to her upper body, when she was moaning brazenly in our arms, we slid her skirts over her hips and let the billowing fabric fall to a pool on the floor. Elspeth stepped from it, holding our hands for support. Then, as one, Jacques and I dropped to our knees. He lifted her left foot and removed her slipper. When he was done, I did the same with the right. Then we put our teeth, one of us to each garter, him left and me right, and tugged down the lacy circlets, our fingers trailing down her thighs, then the backs of her knees, then her calves and ankles, until we could pull the silken stockings from her feet.

By the time we were finished, Elspeth was leaning back against me, gasping, letting me support her, letting me hold her. I could smell the sweet perfume of her arousal. Jacques looked at me, his eyes holding mine completely as he slowly licked his way back up her leg. When I did not look away, he gently spread her thighs, then turned his head and placed a tender kiss on her swelling mound.

"My lord!" she gasped, grabbing his hair and pulling Dupres' face from her. She looked down at me, her passion-filled eyes clouded with confusion.

I knew then, in that moment, that if this venture were ever to work, were ever to be truly fruitful, I had to dispense with all feelings of jealousy and propriety and commit myself – not just my wife, but myself as well – to the creation of this child. I felt naked as a newborn babe as I stood up and pulled Elspeth back into my arms, smiling down at her, kissing her gently as I cupped her breasts and slowly rubbed my thumbs over the straining peaks. I felt Jacques' steady eyes on me as I smiled down at my beloved and said, "Take your pleasure, my lady. It would greatly please me to see you wild in our arms this night."

As I said the words, I felt a great weight lift from my shoulders, as though I had been freed of a heavy burden. Then I no longer wished to cloud my mind with thinking. From the corner of my eye, I saw the smile curl across Jacques' lips, then he again buried his face between my lady's legs. I leaned over, turned her head back to me and kissed her, tasting her passion, her sweet mouth growing hotter and more demanding as she first accepted my probing tongue, then began to suck greedily, moaning and squirming in response to the kiss and Jacques' wanton ministrations.

"His tongue, my lord," she gasped. "With his tongue, he is . . . sweet Jesu . . . *Ahhhh!*" Her cry was pure music as she melted in my arms. We held her thus, on the verge of fulfillment, until my beloved was shaking so hard her legs could no longer hold her. Then Jacques stood up and his lips joined mine against hers. The musky tang of her woman's lips filled my nostrils, melding with the honey of our kisses. It was strange to feel the faint scratch of a man's face against mine as our cheeks touched, to taste her on his tongue as we shared her fair lips. Strange, yet arousing, to know I was sharing in her pleasure of another man.

Jacques moved away first, kissing down her neck, laving her clavicle until she was moaning. Then he stood and began to undress. I took this as my cue, and moved my mouth to the gentle curve of Elspeth's neck. I held her in front of me, my thumbs again stroking her swollen nipples, then moving to the long sweep of her neck as we watched the Frenchman bare himself.

He was more muscular than I had expected. Despite his lineage, he was obviously a man much accustomed to using his body hard and well. A fine pelt of dark, curling hair dusted his well-developed chest and arms, rippling over his skin as his muscles moved. The lines of a few thin scars, only one new enough to be faintly pink, lined his torso here and there. Marks of his career, I presumed, and no doubt of more than one irate husband.

Dupres stretched as he removed his shirt, the clean smell of his sweat filling my nostrils. As Elspeth shivered against me, Jacques smiled and reached his hand to her face, stroking her cheek with the soft linen of his shirt.

"Do I please you, my lady?" His grin was wicked as he leaned forward and brushed his chest over her breasts. She gasped, and he winked at her, pressing her between us. I stiffened, surprised at the heat emanating from his body, although he'd barely brushed against my skin. Then, with a twitch of his eyebrows at me, Jacques stepped back and dropped the shirt on the floor. He leaned against the bed and removed his fine leather boots, letting them thud casually to the floor.

When his feet were bare, he paused for a moment, his form-fitting breeches clinging to his legs as he curled his toes into the carpet.

"Forgive me my indulgence." He smiled, watching his long white toes wiggle like healthy caterpillars in the deep, rich colors of the carpet. "For one who spends much of his time on horseback and in tents, it is a pleasure for my feet to enjoy the freedom of such quality."

Elspeth and I both laughed with him. As we did, he set his hands to his belt, then to the buttons of his breeches, and removed the rest of his clothing.

He seemed totally at ease with his nudity. Perhaps that is the way of those who spend much of their time away from civilized society, isolated in only the company of men. For myself, I had never seen another man completely naked before – at least not one aroused, the way Jacques was. His cock-head had pulled completely free of its cover, arching out from his body, strong and healthy and demanding. So full of seed it was glistening with the clear sheen of his leaking juices.

He was beautiful. I knew at that moment a son who sprang from those loins would be well able to carry on my family line. I had chosen well in Jacques Dupres. Now we had but to see to my wife's pleasure.

Watching him, I think Elspeth had stopped breathing. Whilst I had kept myself firm and trim, and I know my face to be well-formed, my black hair was already shot with gray at the temples, in truth, across my chest as well. But Dupres was a man in his youthful prime, the life fair to bursting from his tool. He stepped forward, and as he did so I leaned back, moving away as he wrapped his arms around Elspeth and claimed her mouth.

"Kiss me, my lady," he said as he pulled her roughly to him. "Let me know you crave the pleasure as I do." As she whimpered in his arms, he added firmly, "Show *us* your passion."

The soft shadows of his body contrasted sharply with the smooth creaminess of Elspeth's skin. Where their heads met, his dark curls tangled against her wispy yellow locks. She moaned into his mouth, kissing him voraciously. I was glad for their distraction. I am a gentleman, not a military man. I feared I would lose my arousal completely did I need to disrobe in front of another man as he had done. I loosened my cravat, pulling it from my neck. Then I shed the rest of my clothing. My cock was hard, but not straining the way Dupres' had been. I stepped in back of Elspeth and pressed my body to hers, enjoying, as I always did, the first wonderful shock of her soft skin against mine, of her arching towards me in contentment as our bodies met. And processing for the first time the feel of another man's bare forearms against my chest.

If Dupres noticed the contact with my skin, he didn't show it. His arms moved against me as he slid his hands to her shoulders. Then, between us, we lifted Elspeth onto the bed and lay down, Dupres between her legs, his cheek resting on her soft thigh, and me at her side, leaning over her, kissing her, my fingers gently cupping her breast.

Dupres' fingers trailed up towards the cleft between her legs, a smile curling across his lips as she shivered. But he stopped, his fingers only twirling into the nest of soft blonde curls, and looked up at me.

"Your wife, my lord. Does she enjoy the taste of a man?"

I froze, not knowing quite what to say. In the privacy of our marital bed, Elspeth had learned to like the taste of my member. Indeed, she often initiated the contact. But she was a lady of proper breeding, and I did not know how she would respond to the thought of doing such with another man. And I did not know how I would respond to seeing her take him in her mouth. Then I saw his grin, and with a sigh of relief, I realized that was not what he had meant.

"Give her lips something to enjoy while my tongue pleasures her, William. That way, she will ever after think of the joy of creating children when she takes you in her mouth."

"Elspeth?" I asked it as a question. The thought made my cock jump with anticipation, but I would not coerce her on this. While the getting of children is a duty, I felt this private pleasure must be something that she chose.

I was more than pleased when my beloved laughed and took my member in her hand, squeezing me playfully. "I do enjoy it, my lord. If we are heathens enough to lie about naked in a lighted room with this knave, we may as well indulge ourselves in all manner of wicked pleasures." Her fingers closed around me and she slowly, tantalizingly, pulled my foreskin up over the head of my cock, stroking, retracting my hood, teasing me, her eyes twinkling as I gasped and the sweat rolled down my back. "If you would enjoy it, William."

My shock must have shown on my face. Dupres laughed, but the sound was muffled as he buried his face between Elspeth's legs, rubbing her scent into his cheeks. Then his mouth opened against her. As she moaned in response, I could do naught but let her tug me forward, until I was kneeling over her, straddling her chest, carefully keeping my weight on my legs as my member rested against her lips. I had gone completely soft, unsure how I would respond with another man watching me. Then I heard a deep chuckle in back of me.

"I will not be able to see him, my lady, engaged as I am in your deliciously tender folds. Will you be able to bring him to fulfillment on your own, whilst I am otherwise entertained?"

"Oh, yes, *monsieur*." Elspeth's giggle felt delicious against my cock as she kissed her lips against my folded shaft skin. I gasped as her tongue dipped inside, licking my hidden cock-head as I twitched above her. "I will ensure my husband enjoys himself."

Again, Dupres' laughter filled my ears. Perhaps it was because I knew no one was watching, that it was just us, my Elspeth and I – perhaps because her eyes held such love as she took me in her hands and started playing with me, rolling my shaft between her palms, stroking, pulling and retracting my foreskin until my cockhead burst forth with lust. Perhaps it was the tremor, the huskiness in her voice as she said, "William, I want you."

Whatever the reason, I roused to her. Soon, I was hard and

straining, shuddering with delight as she took me in her mouth and sucked, tonguing me with just enough pressure to make the seed start rising from my balls. Dupres was still mouthing her. I could tell. Her moans were becoming uncontrollable, her voice vibrating over my member as she writhed beneath me, her words now only mewls of pleasure.

Suddenly, her eyes flew open. "Oh, William," she gasped. "I am going to . . . I can't stop . . ." Her words trailed off on a high-pitched cry, her voice ragged with need. "I want you to . . . with me . . . William!" As her body stiffened, her eyes narrowed, and she suddenly stuck her finger in her mouth and reached behind me.

Oh, no, I thought. Not that. Not with him here. But I could no more control my response than I could stop her. Elspeth's slicked finger slid up my behind, and I roared as I shot my seed into her. Her hot wet tongue sucked my juices from me as her merciless finger pressed a thunderous climax from deep inside of me. My cock fluids overflowed her mouth, running like pearls down her beautiful neck, and Elspeth went wild beneath me, crying out, thrashing and bucking up against me.

I heard the laughter in back of me, but I no longer cared. Elspeth's finger was still massaging an incredibly sweet spot inside me, prolonging my orgasm, and she was still shuddering beneath me when a voice suddenly thick with accent and his own need commanded, "Move, William. I am going to plant the child in her belly *now*!"

I fell to the side, Elspeth's finger pulling free as he moved over her. The thick, purple sword of Jacques' swollen manhood slid into her. He grimaced, his face a mixture of pure relief and unholy passion as he buried himself inside her waiting depths. Then he was thrusting into her, hard and fast, the sweat dripping off him as he drove towards his own release.

"Her breasts," he gasped through gritted teeth. "Suck them, William, so that each time the babe suckles she will think of this moment, of your love and mine, and of the joy in which we created this child. Unh!" Dupres' arms shook with the strain as he looked at my wife and growled. "Do you feel me in you, Elspeth? Does my shaft bring you pleasure, woman?"

I looked at Elspeth, and was awestruck at the lust bathing her

OF WAXEN FIGURES AND SCREAMING TOMBS

Jasmine Sailing

A WOMAN, FINELY GOWNED in a loose-pleated linen robe, threadings pale to offset the rich shade of her limbs, hesitated outside a decoratively pillared noble house near the royal palace at the Temple of Medinet Habu. She fingered her bracelets nervously, let one hand stray to the gem-accoutered gold torque which bound her plaited auburn wig, and gained courage for entering. The inner chamber felt ancient, dusty and full of relics. Faience tiling depicting gods and battles of past ages lined the walls and ceiling. Lapis-lazuli figurines decorated a water-hewn sandstone table, papyri scrolls and tomes stacked haphazardly around them. In one far corner of the chamber rested the framework of a leather-draped bed; in the other nestled a chest with a gabled lid.

A man, also finely robed, perched on a bench at the table – carefully sculpting a waxen figure with the sharpened tip of a reed, allowing his visitor to wait. And to wonder. The woman coughed impatiently, imagining dust and age in her lungs, unwittingly displaying her preference for fruitful scents and comfort. Not the musk of old decay, of death; reminders of her own wasted years and empty mortality. Something here, beyond the stale air, reminded her of a tomb. A living tomb, claustrophobic, pestilence in motion. She shuddered and pushed a stray wigstrand, invading her subtly lined forehead, behind her ear. Feigning aloofness, she addressed the sculptor.

"For what news have you summoned me?" Though the man's position was high, overseer of the royal cattle, she sought to unnerve him. *For what business of cattle could I be concerned*? she thought. *Likely this audience involves a favor.*

His smile was slow, a slight quirk at the edge of his mouth as he glanced up from the waxen figure. "My news is of your *son*, and of his ascent."

"Ascent? In power, wealth, godhood, our cattle-herd Panhui-banou's entry chamber steps?"

"Teye, it has been foreseen that he shall follow our King. Son of Setnakht, to be succeeded by son of Teye." He voiced it as an afterthought, something to be rather than to be concerned with, and returned his focus to his sculpting – strands of his bobbed wig falling across his face to serve as a blockade against distractions.

Teye's stolid demeanor lapsed with a brief frown, then her aloofness returned. It was a dream to wish for your son to become ruler, King, even mortal godhead of the peoples. Yet it was also a nightmare to embrace such ambition. *Has this truly been foreseen, or is it merely a trick? Cattle-herds rarely aspire to be magicians and seers . . .* Her eyes wandered from the waxen figure to an amulet set near his left hand, and she wondered. *Offerings for Ra*? Inscribed in the amulet were the glyphs of adoration. *Perhaps he seeks priesthood from Ramses, and gains his trust through my betrayal.*

"Ah, you were to gauge my loyalty. Fear you not, my devotion to our Lord is as true as it ever was. I would accept the ascension of my son, if it were my husband's will. I would accept the ascension of another of his sons, not of mine own womb, if it were his will."

"I gauge naught; I merely speak of what is. As it has been envisioned to me. As it shall happen if *you* will it."

"I will have none to do with such treacherous thoughts. I must take my leave of you." With a suitable look of disdain, Teye bunched up the ankle-length skirts of her robe to protect them from what felt to her like layers of grave dust and descended through the cattle-herd's door. She glanced back once more, noting that he continued to disregard her amidst his crafting. Even as his voice followed her in departure.

"It *shall* be your will, Lady."

Teye fled to comfort, to her scents of life rather than death. It was a truth that she had dreamed of seeing her son ascend as King upon the death of Ramses. It was a truth that her son would prefer this destiny to high honor amongst the nobles and cavalry, and that she often envisioned him as becoming a god – perhaps even one to rival her husband's cherished Mont. It was even truth that she realized, and felt embittered by, her own lack of status in the palace. To have been second wife to the King, to have your own children frowned upon in favour of the first Queen's children. It was a grievance, but not enough of one for her to grow careless in the face of death. She had smelt death in Panhuibanou's chamber, and she feared it could be catching.

Had he been to entrap me, to gauge me? Had it been bequested for Hui to determine the loyalties of the Queen, of the harim, of the servants? Or, perhaps, worse, only of herself? She could perceive no cause for her loyalties to be questioned, aside from minor jealousies amongst the heirs, but knew of the penalties for such treachery. Their Lord was a proud one, and oft-times an overtly-questioning one, and disloyal servitors would have their lives by their own hands with poison. If they were deemed suited for such honor.

A servant disrupted her thoughts by calling in of a summons from her husband, startling her that it should come so shortly after the testing. *Have I failed*? Hui had claimed that it would be her will for her son to ascend. Had he foreseen her disloyalty and reported it, the audience having only been for obtaining a willing confession? Naught to do but heed the summons and pray for the protection of Rāt.

The King was reading scrolls by candlelight in his chamber. He glanced up at Teye's entrance, giving no more indication of mood than a slight frown. No wig adorned his head, and the shadows of whitening stubble reflected from candlelight and danced along the wall behind him. The shadows lining his aged face seemed to reflect from eternity, mortality, pain. He gestured for his wife to seat herself next to him.

Teye exceeded herself in meekness and exuding appeal as she did his bidding. "My Lord?" she queried, keeping the fear deeply buried. The smell of death crept again through her nostrils and briefly unnerved her with her own thoughts: *If only it were truly the smell of your own death, my husband.*

"There is much unrest," he explained with a sigh. "Workers are striking for pay, feeling underhanded. There is rumor that I hoard taxation and allow our peoples to starve."

An indignant sniff matched his sigh. "But it was *you* who spared our country from ruin. It was *you* who drove forth marauders and acquired new lands. For what have others worked which they should feel cheated of? They have the protection of Mont, of the war god. For what should this unrest brew?" Pandering to the King was no difficulty, not for one who was accustomed to his conceits. Ramses prided himself as a warlord, as mighty henchman of Mont, as the counterpart to his great predecessor: the first of the Ramses name. The feats of the long-dead Ramses remained in constant view as renditions of battle etched into the faience tiling throughout the palace; serving, also, as a reminder of the current Lord's matching divinity. Yet pandering to this divinity would mean naught if Teye was already suspect of mirroring civil unrest.

"Yes, I have granted the lands my protection, and in return I am granted strife. Have you heard naught of this amongst the peoples?" His frown remained, yet it finally seemed not to be directed toward her – nor toward anything material in the room or, perhaps, anywhere.

"No, my Lord. Were I to hear of such treachery it would already have been yours to know." *As the dagger penetrated your chest and freed me of you, for your life has long overshadowed mine own.* She closed her eyes and lowered her head submissively. "Fear you that such contention is present amidst trusted nobles?" Peering up, with one eye, she could see him raising an eyebrow.

"No, not as yet. But if there is discontent, you may expect to find it everywhere." He reached his hand out to caress hers. "And, no, Teye, you were not summoned for accusation. Your loyalty has never been questioned, nor your willingness to accept my rule. You have acted as mother to my heir, as my consort and counsel. Your devotion is noted."

Teye smiled delicately, maintaining her submissive air. Oh, yes, she had acted as foster-mother to his heir. And she had dreamed that the heir would ail, would abandon his life and legacy to her own child. And she had dreamt of being the consort of her husband's younger days, traveling to exotic lands. She had dreamed even of traveling with her son as the King, beyond the grave of Ramses. *It would seem my dreams have been observed as I feared, though not by my husband. For what purpose would Panhuibanou have revealed his suspicions of myself, if not to entrap me in confession? Perhaps I have indeed found discontent amongst the nobles.*

There could be no harm in failing to reveal an uncertainty to the King, though, one which could not be proven as a threat she had been made aware of. She cupped Ramses' hand as he cupped hers. He gently lifted her bowed face to his and brushed his lips against hers. As she stood and followed him to his bed of linens and leather she could think only one thing: *Rest now with Osiris, old man. Your life has been full, but your time has passed.*

Teye retreated within the safety of the harim, to the chambers where the Ladies could comfortably await a summons or visit. If ever they did receive one anymore. Her own chambers were lonely, overtly close to those of the King. Here could be found safety, friends, the comfort of proximity with those who likely shared her own private desires for an altered future – the whispered, oft-giggled conversations would at least make it appear as such. Now her own brooding silence followed her, settling throughout the room as she laid her head upon soft cushions and passed into sleep. As she slept, she dreamt the dreams of inner hopes.

She envisioned herself with Panhuibanou, sculpting his waxen figures alongside him. She felt energies which could be neither his nor hers, though melding with both, but something entirely more powerful. She could feel him next to her, in ways not as repugnant as her current affectations with her husband. And she could see the old man dying, to be replaced by her own son: ascended as King. Life, and destiny, filled her mind – intoxicating, even in dreams.

Hui paced as waxen figures were tortured. A general organized his men for assault. Nobles tallied serfs as bodies for a peoples' uprising. A demon, flesh the burgundy of wine, dark and vacuous eyes of the Void embedded in its distorted hawk's head, reached for her with taloned arms – begging the gift of souls for feasting upon The serpent Apep was unslewn, renewed, ready for a new cycle. New life. Ships brought bounties, which were seized by restless masses. Ramses' face bore the wrinkles of anguish as waxen figures melded to his name burned in the glow of a fire. And Teye smiled as she embraced Hui, embraced freedom, embraced no longer being the second Queen to an aging king.

And her smile didn't fade as she awoke.

Panhuibanou glanced up from his reading as Teye once again entered his home. She was disoriented, fidgeting, shifting from one foot to another, then catching herself. Replacing her nervous twitches with a stolid expression, only for the fingers of her left hand to begin pulling at the wig-strands clasped under her torque. She sighed as his focus reverted to the papyri. *Why can no one regard me amidst their studies?*

"You accused of it being my will for my son to replace our King. It is not so. Yet I have spoken with him and learned of much unrest, of possible conspiracies toward his removal. Have you news of this?"

"No, my Lady," he responded, without looking up.

"And why, then, had you summoned me?" Haughtiness crept into her voice, as her fingers continued unravelling wig-strands.

"To inform you of my vision. That you shall be one such unrestful soul."

"And you, with your waxen figures." She gestured toward the crude sculptures on his table, none of which bore any resemblance to the King. *It is I who shall entrap you in confession of hidden desires . . .*

She finally held Panhuibanou's attention, though he was smiling. "My new hobby of craft gives you cause for suspecting my loyalty to our Lord? Would it have pleased you for me to sculpt gold, as a lovely band for the Queen's loose mane?"

Teye became self-conscious of the actions of her fingers in the now-dishevelled wig, and slowly clasped her hands over her belly. "And what would you have envisioned of me? Would it be easiest for a wife to slip poison to her husband, or would it be easiest for another to engrave and burn waxen figures? One would have the more easily laid blame, and this would be your image of me."

"I envisioned not your poisoning of our King, nor that of you committing more than the witnessing of your son's ascension. It is your imagination which perceives threat," Panhuibanou scoffed, and returned to his reading.

Teye's expression hardened into a sneer. *Neither of us would be first to offer an admission.* "Just as it is my imagination which perceives you cavorting with demons, foul spirits, and of Apep becoming unslewn."

The air in the room seemed to thicken, even the dust choking on the tension. The cattle-overseer set his papyri aside and gazed speculatively at her. "The serpent Apep has many servants outside of this world."

"Such as one demon, of deep burgundied flesh? One which has energies felt from where it lies beyond this world? One which might cause a burning effigy to resemble its counterpart man?" Teye's fidgeting had ceased; she knew she finally held the advantage and pinned him with the smug glare of a tiger. "Or what of generals rallying men? For conquest? Of Kings?"

"You are wiser of more than you declare." Hui silently tapped a finger against his chin, eyes peering through Teye, only to perceive a blank wall.

"Even of this." She moved flowingly, paused before him, gently bent forward to place her lips on his. His eyes remained open, no doubt foreseeing penalty at the hands of the War King for being overtly familiar with his wife. She could dream of the same, for being unfaithful, but it was a choice she had envisioned making. Her presence was nowhere required, her husband was detained by business, and the cattle-herd would not be sought at this hour. Detecting fear, she reached her hand up to cradle Hui's cheek as she continued to brush her lips against his. Waiting for a response. For him to confirm one final fancy.

And he did. The tension left his body as his eyes unfroze. He stood, only to grasp Teye and lower her body before him. He kneeled alongside her, his expression serious, and reached down to grasp one of her legs in each hand. They moved slightly upward, exposing once linen-draped knees. "Our King's wife dares to be joined, amidst the dust, with another man?"

Teye, mocking his seriousness, rubbed her legs against his sides – allowing her skirt to slip further, exposing dark thighs. She placed her hands on his and pulled them to her hips, to the scarf binding her robe, urging him down from kneeling. Their cold expressions truthfully masked each other now as they embraced, their mental dreams and desires melding as did their bodies. Fancy becoming life and truth, in essence of pacing demons and emanating energies, in a tangle of limbs and fulfillment.

For Panhuibanou the reigning image was of himself being beheaded and of his body burned, charred, on public display for evidencing the gravity of such treachery against their King, as he traced his hands along Teye's thighs – easing his body nearer to hers. Dehydrated ash, once living, was fed to the river in recompense for his hands shifting upward to encircle her head. His own sightless eyes, severed head mounted as a ward against future disloyalties, beheld it within his mind as his lips lightly brushed hers. They moved toward her neck, teeth bared in vacuous snarl, while he fancied her own life blood being purged of her throat for such disgrace.

Life. Teye envisioned life, her own life after her son's ascension, her renewed status as King's mother rather than merely the aging concubine and second wife, as she braced her legs around Hui's waist, pulling him yet nearer to her. She could feel freedom and admiration, see the world at her son's side, as her arms traced up his and her hands began pulling at his robe. Laughter filled her mind at the vision of her old husband dying alone, just as she embraced his cattle-herd on the dusty chamber floor, while she arched her neck – baring her throat to her new love.

And, for each of them, the serpent Apep observed, cloven halves impatiently awaiting their healing, as Hui's teeth and lips scraped the length of Teye's neck. Safely. Carefully. Leaving no discernible marks for the old husband to find. The serpent retained allies, for they required feeding, and the dead life of Ramses' devoured soul could be replaced by new life as the ascending King's mother whimpered at the scraping friction tickling down her throat and continued pawing at Hui's robe – needing it gone, removed at once, him against her and inside her.

Pacing demons paused in their devouring of souls to acknowledge the lustful carnage of one conjoined man and woman, feeling dark energies coursing between them, knowing the future as theirs, believing visions and living them as the woman drew forth the man's cleanly circumcised penis and urged it, him, toward her womb. Her legs clenched tighter around his waist, bracing, his sweat leaking into her mundane-blinded eyes, and his chest pressed against hers, friction and heat binding suctioned skin, and his tongue flicked across her throat – tracing the path of her life blood. He taunted the gods, demons, and fate, with a brief withdrawal and Teye clutched his buttocks, pulling him back, savoring the feel of vaginal walls parting for life, of the tingling throb in them never granted through her husband's feeble mountings, of her own womb aching for the release of Hui's seed. Demons ceased their pacing and came to attention, taloned arms outstretched, just as the man's breath became a series of shudders and his thrusts lapsed into frantic sliding against the woman – both convulsed and the world paused in breathing, the serpent's cloven halves becoming partially sewn, through illicit witness of the cattle-herd's semen seeping within the Queen's womb.

Hui remained atop Teye, his head rested dreamily alongside hers. Her hands continued to stroke his legs, his rump, his back, while her eyes fixated dreamily upon the tiled ceiling. *I am alive, after so many years, and a future is mine for dreaming.*

"My husband is aged, and it is my will for my son to ascend as King. Osiris will make judgement upon our souls," she whispered.

"Osiris cannot rule that we be devoured by the soul-eater, for that is who offers us strength."

It was a hazardous process for Teye to determine who amongst the harim truly felt discontent with their King. As with the striking workers, though, and as with her own feelings of neglect, the women deemed themselves used and ill-valued. Rare was she who could not be trusted with plots of freedom and restful futures. The new King would leave them with their standing, their home, yet let them alone to attend to their own lives. They would need not be summoned, nor bear ill-favored children to a failing old man.

A further gift of supplication was granted the harim women by the Queen's secret concubine: amulets, each inscribed with glyphs of adoration. It was sworn upon them being magical workings which would bring the ladies the love of their focus. Teye silenced the giggles and speculations of her having used such an amulet to seduce the royal cattle-herd.

Other nobles were uncertain, many could never learn of the plans, and for them Teye left the responsibility largely to Hui. Granted, some of the women held influence over necessary men and they applied it. It had been their primary general's sister, a harim member, who had convinced him to begin rallying troops against Ramses. The land was in mass discontent, and its King would fail in one way or another. Eventually. Teye's other concern was in coaching her son for speaking of those issues which the peoples felt most cheated in, discreetly, never appearing to disrespect the King's judgement. Only to subtly let it be known that the royal coffers would no longer overflow from taxes as the workers of the land were abused and starved. That civil unrest would not threaten their unity under his reign. A rumor was carefully circulated of how the King's favored son would let go the taxed provinces and merely slave the workers more, for less pay. The difference between serf and slave would become naught, and the nobles (lest directly royal) would replace the malcontent underpaid labourers. Women for his harim could be stolen from anyone, and eventually only his descendants through them would be deemed noble.

It was a future no one wished to live, and support for Teye's son steadily grew. Quietly. Away from the eyes and ears of their ruler.

Teye reflected upon her own visions. Visions they had been, and that alone, yet Panhuibanou had verified his own sight of them. Had he not desired her as his concubine, she would perhaps have proven herself as untrue – as deluded by wistfulness. He had, though, and she could imagine no way for them both to perceive so falsely. *I shall be mother to the King, with Hui as my consort, and the soul-eater shall protect our mortality*.

She knew naught about the demon she had dreamt of, yet Hui claimed to have learned of him amidst his magical research. Feeling a lack of patience for the rallying of troops, he had begun his own experimenting and arranged that magical texts be borrowed for him from the palace library. Feeling that perhaps spells, and waxen effigies, could bring the splintered future together sooner, he studied them, devoured the arts of pain-inflicting magic, strategized murder from a distance. As Teye had witnessed upon her initial summons, his attempts hadn't yet exceeded beyond whimsical-appearing waxen figures of no one. Being caught with them carved to the likeness of Ramses would be suspect, and likely cause his own death. He desired certainty before such a risk.

In his studies, he had also named the demon of burgundy-wine flesh: Strethas, a guardian of the Void between the mortal world and Osiris' land of the dead. "This Strethas," he had explained, "shall now be our guardian. His energies can be tapped through ritual, and with these energies, and with my effigies, I will initiate our King's demise. This demon would grant our visions for the luxury of devouring the soul of a King."

"Or perhaps it is a trick to devour our own souls?"

"What are the souls of two servants as compared to that of a ruler?"

They would be naught, just as we are while Ramses remains amongst the living. Time, or perhaps Panhuibanou's burgeoning knowledge of magic and demons, would initiate their rebirth. They needed only fully realize the methods for tapping energies from the Void, and their envisioned futures would be materialized.

Ramses was ailing and summoned his Queen. She knelt at his side, straightened the cushion on his wooden headrest, pulled linen and leather blankets up to his chin, stroked his hand, whispered soothingly.

"Third of my name, and like to the first," he whispered. "I should not be weakened here, and coddled by a woman. I suspect there is ill intent toward me within this house."

Teye frowned, keeping her mind as purged of reality as she was capable. "No, my Lord, it is only weariness of workers' malcontent which troubles you. The nobles realize your strength." *And know it to be failing, old man*.

"No, I feel energies which would have my life and replace me. I sense growing discontent, conspiracy. It is no secret now that peoples of all classes grow weary of my rule. You need not defend me to myself, my Queen."

"What shall we do?" She sat straight, a stately visage, all at once adviser, confidante, and concubine for the King.

"I have bequested of my loyal friends to investigate the possibility of conspiracy amidst the nobles. If anything is to be learned, it shall be learned by them." He sighed, momentarily rested his eyes. "There have been more suiting times for frailty to take me."

Though never has there been a more suiting time for death to take you. Teye gently stroked her husband's hands and gazed with a mixture of compassion and adoration upon him. "You are strong, my Lord. You will rise, and you will disperse those treacheries which you fear. Your enemies will cower before you, as ever before."

Ramses coughed, tilted his cheek onto her hand. "Yes. Let me no longer concern you, Teye. I have heard of your new interest in cattle?"

It was an effort for Teye to avoid reacting. Instead, she smiled. "I have an interest in all matters of your concern. I worry. I realize your fears. If it would be of help for me to handle mere details, even only of cattle-herding, I would be willing."

"And you have no further interest in Panhuibanou?"

"Naught but that we took to discussing Amon-Ra worship, and I learned of a noble daughter who has eyes for him. I wished to know his worthiness, to give my judgement of the matter as well. The mother is of my fond acquaintance."

"Ah, attending courtships." Teye thought she glimpsed a keen spark in his eyes as he wheezed the words. *Could he suspect*?

"Yes, my love, for memory of your courting of myself. For memory of your love of myself." She smiled gently, sadly, continued stroking his hands.

"Fear you that I no longer love my Queen?" Ramses' body was racked with dry coughs, his eyes closed and his head rested sidewise in the cushion.

"No, my Lord," Teye whispered. "I know you are ever true." *And you shall choke.* She nestled her face close to his, careful not to obstruct his breathing. To suffocate him now would be simple, yet it would be equally simple for his loyal friends to determine her suspect. She sighed, curled her fingers around his, closed her eyes. *The demon spits and his saliva burns a steaming hole through to your ailing heart. You fall, old man. And I, and my son, are there in the abyss waiting to watch . . . and to laugh . . . and to say goodbye.*

For you relinquish your power upon death, and the soul-eater bestows it upon us as his saliva continues to fall and devour your tainted soul.

"It was rumored, through a friend, of Ramses having consult with an oracle." Panhuibanou's expression was deadpan, gravity lining his face and creating sags of weariness.

"I see nothing unusual in this." Teye outstretched a hand and stroked his forehead with her fingers. "What troubles you?"

"He spoke of treachery. The oracle spoke of the Queen's interest in cattle-herding."

Teye's hand fell to his lap. "And he spoke of the same to myself earlier. I offered my reasons, none of which are so. The moment was fearful, but I believe he suspects naught." With a slight frown she began caressing his inner thighs, linen loosely rearranging itself with the motions of her fingers. "And I have dreamt and spoken of coupling with you, and of freedom through our harnessed powers of the demon."

"My Lady must understand the gravity of this matter; discovery would forfeit our lives and dreams." Hui watched her fingers, losing an edge to his weary focus. His eyes darkened slightly, as stimulation ceaselessly envisioned him of death at the King's hands.

"And how would those of the protection of a soul-eater come to perish when their success has been foreseen?" She traced her fingers along the growing outline of an erection under linen. *Feel me, not fear.*

"Then we shall feel that demon's energies and hasten our King's demise." He placed his hand upon hers, stilling her motion, and stood before her.

The chamber no longer seemed full of pestilence, as it initially had to Teye. She found no preferred comfort to the leather drapings of Hui's bed. Her hand remaining clasped in his, she led him to the corner to lie with her. "Feel the energies, and hasten my leave of the frail old man," she whispered, kneeling upon the blankets alongside her lover. Her hands cupped his shoulders; her head rested meekly in the curve of his throat – an imploring position. *Free me, for your pleasure.*

He laid her down before him, straddled her waist, placed his hands upon her throat – squeezed, listened to her barely audible gasps and wheezes. He envisioned pacing demons, and the scent of fear summoning their attention. Feeling the power, channeling it, feeding souls in return. He lowered his head to kiss Teye as he lightly throttled her. She felt his hands upon her throat, felt the lack of oxygen, felt the darkness in her mind, beheld images of herself reaching upward, reaching to Hui, suffocating, clawing through darkness, screaming silently. His lips were pressed against hers – consuming her gasps, her whimpers. In her mind she could see herself clawing into the darkness, struggling for air, but in life she didn't. She trusted and waited, knowing fate as her protection.

And then Hui was sitting up, perched over her; a sinister grin, an absent gaze. Teye thought she could feel the darker, more deadly energies exuding from him. The harnessed powers of a soul-eater. Her freedom, her life, her King's demise. Hui fingered a bronzed dagger, flicking its sharp tip, and then began brushing away her robe. She raised one leg slightly, edged the other aside. He took hold of the wandering leg, cupped it gently in one hand, ran the tip of his dagger down the thigh, only lightly, initially, scraping skin. As the tip traced back up toward her hip, it ground in slightly more. Tiny beads of red formed in its path. Teye squirmed, whimpered again, urged herself to be strong rather than to cry out. She watched her lover's head dip toward the droplets as he released the dagger from his hand, tongue flicking out to taste them. She felt his energies extend from the tip of his tongue and trace through her bloodstream. *Soul-eaters scenting blood, promises of death and sustainment, reaching out to become trapped in essence within mortal flesh. My life is yours.* His body shuddered as his tongue continued to taste of her essence, his arms clutching her waist near to breaking as the energy – the fear – melded between them.

Hui lay quietly across her for some time before he finally loosened his embrace and once more began stroking her legs, her arms. For a moment he was serious, in gazing upon her. "If your husband were to see your leg, you would admit of quarreling with a cat."

"As I would," Teye whispered. She ran her hands into his robe, wanting to feel him, to birth the demon's energies within her. His expression altered from one of seriousness to one of brooding power as she tried to draw his body closer to hers. He pulled up and walked to his table, motioning for her to remain where she was. She waited, and watched as he returned with a glyph-engraved circle of quartzite; the glyphs coupling power with safety. He placed it within her palm and clasped her fingers around it – cupping them in his own hand.

"Keep this with you, that you may always have the protection of our fates and of the demon." And then he was kneeling over her again, his smile nearly paternal, and this time he allowed her gently wandering hands to begin disrobing him and pulling him nearer to her.

As Teye braced her legs around his, slowly guiding him into her, she could once again feel the energies combining between them – manifesting in the stone still clenched within her hand. For every movement of him against her she felt the power intensifying, melding them, further interlinking their fates. And she could envision the demon Strethas lifting his taloned hands toward them, offering his essence, granting them his power. *And Ramses' shadow disintegrates as the soul-eater's spittle falls upon it . . .*

Hui's hands clasped hers, cupping flesh and stone above her shoulders as he summoned all perceived strength of his demon ally. He was alone, with only a gate for receiving and storing the energies near him. It flowed between them, the sensation overwhelming. He felt it coursing along his spine, becoming millions of tiny pin-pricks clawing their way through his back. Seeking escape. He could sense her gasping beneath him, sense the glow from the quartzite in her palm. He wiggled a finger into her hand to touch the stone as he fed the soul-eater the sense of crushing her, pulling himself through her, building to release – to give her the burst of energy in the form of so many tiny pin-pricks . . .

The overriding sensation for Teye was of the steady warming of his penis, of the way it felt as it moved through her. The sensation of her inner flesh consuming the energies it exuded, permitting them within her, craving more. And, as it warmed, she could feel them intensify – could feel herself embracing them. He was shuddering again, clenching her again, as the warmth of liquid spread within her, absorbing, echoing his convulsive release of power within her. And then his hand was reaching downward, to claw at the congealed blood on her leg, to renew the wounds. He kneeled beside her and retrieved the medallion from her hand, placed it in the blood, coated it, and then pressed it upon the lips of her womb to absorb their combined moistures. Her blood, his semen, her lubrication. The medallion was returned to her awaiting palm and she squeezed it between her fingers. *I will always have the presence of you, Hui, and our melded energies.*

They curled together on the bed for some time, each lost in their own thoughts of power and fate. Ever the fantasies drifted more toward the death of Ramses than of themselves. There could be no damnation for those granted the protection of a soul-eater.

Eventually, though, Teye's expression darkened. "I had forgotten one mention during my latest sitting with our King. He suspects treachery amidst the nobles. He has bequested of loyal friends to investigate."

Hui's weariness returned, clouding his newly relaxed features. "We must haste his demise."

Nearly a full moon had cycled, with Panhuibanou being too often isolated, perfecting his magic with discretion and haste. He feared his home to be suspect, and could no longer store his research in the chest he had once opened for Teye. He never informed her of where it was he had found to hide, his reasoning being that it was sufficient for her to see him when he returned and that one less mind knowing his whereabouts would be one less mind for it to be deduced from.

Teye suppressed her initial bitterness, reminding herself of the King's suspicion of her interactions with the cattle-herd. A little distance might, perhaps, serve best. Particularly if that distance brought about the more timely demise of her inconvenience.

She hadn't yet heard more of Ramses' investigations into the conspiracy. His ailment had passed, and he was likely occupied in assisting his trusted friends. Through each day and night, she awaited the audience wherein she would learn what had already been deduced by them. *I wish you no pain, my Lord, I wish only for the futures of myself and my son – and for embracing Hui without fear of death. Your time has passed. End your search and leave us to our moments.*

A few nights prior, Hui had granted her items for their allies within the palace: waxen figures and a scribed papyrus tome. She, herself, wasn't to use them, or to offer them to anyone who couldn't be trusted. There were others, however, who at least wouldn't be as observed as she now feared herself to be. His reasonings had been vague.

"We must no longer await an uprising. If one indeed occurs, it could never succeed without defenses here being lessened. That I can arrange with these, and, preferably, another ailment for our King." His demeanor was cold during his retreat, often overtly serious, and Teye could derive no further information from him. *Is it fear of discovery, or eagerness for an end to our secrecy which inspires my love's distance?*

She had peeked within the tome, but had not read it for fear of harm; occasional glances at random glyphs inclined her to believe that its formulae would inflict madness upon the reader. *Would Hui cripple those loyal to Ramses with madness, possibly to harm themselves and others near them? An uprising would see them dead. Which could be worse?*

The waxen figures, however, had been easy for her to deduce the use of. Some were in the image of their King, others resembled his known loyal friends. These not being items which she would feel comfortable in storing throughout her chambers, she arranged meetings with their recipients in the harim. Most of the women had come to be trusted; others could be kept away by the majority. Teye passed along the items as Hui had bequested, heeding his warning to not overtly question their specific use. *One less mind possessed of the knowledge is one less mind for it to be deduced from.*

And then there was nothing more for her but waiting. Endless waiting.

Hui remained withdrawn when the summons which Teye suspected would be her audience of learning the investigation's results finally arrived. There hadn't been enormous progression in the conspiracy, though she had heard of an Ethiopian general being nearly ready for marching with an army of soldiers and civilians. Funds had shifted from the royal treasury to the straggling armies for the purchase of supplies. Amongst the nobles, restlessness became the overwhelming anxiety – all were eager for the waiting to cease.

Though little could be proven to be resulting through Hui's charms, Teye fancied that perhaps some of their Lord's trusted friends seemed more agitated than they had prior. *Descending madness?* Others were absent and reputed to be suffering from varying ailments, including paralysis. The results of the investigation could hardly matter anymore; Ramses would soon be removed from power.

Feigning her most promising visage of submissive loyalty, fingering her protective medallion, she approached the King's chambers. He was seated at a table, peering over numerous scattered papyri.

"My Lord?"

"Teye, my dear Queen." He glanced up only briefly. "You will be relieved, doubtless, to learn that proof of conspiracy has been uncovered and investigated by my appointed courts. I desire sharing your company at the inquiries on the morn."

Teye paled. *It cannot be I whom he suspects if he wishes for me to join him. Perhaps Hui?* "Who has dared to consider harm against you?"

"Sadly there would be many who wish to see myself and my heir removed from power. I have had, even, the noses and ears removed of members of one court for becoming overtly friendly with some of the accused. You shall rest, and then join me to see justice upon those who are weak of mind and loyalty."

She dipped her head in acknowledgement as he continued perusing the texts before him. *Could Hui be suspect? I have not seen him . . .* Ramses paused, glanced at her again, gestured her dismissal. She left the chamber, still fingering her medallion. Her mind coalesced with numerous fears as she retreated to her own chambers, and even more so when she noted a guard situated outside her door. *It cannot be I . . .*

The medallion felt cold as she laid it flat against her palm and stared at it. Her gift from Hui, her protection. Naught could harm those who possessed the strength of a soul-eater. Ramses would perish, his shadow dissolved. Her son would ascend. Hui would return from his isolation and openly become concubine to the mother of their new King. This she had foreseen. This, her fate, was granted.

It cannot be I . . .

It was not the first time for Teye to attend qenbet, yet it was the first time she had ever even heard mention of a King appointing his loyal commissioners as judges. A line of them observed, imposing in their higher seating, awaiting the testimony of witnesses. The number of peoples gathering in the juridical chamber was enormous, and it could not yet be clearly perceived which of them were there only for seeing justice and which of them bore accusations. Teye sat alongside Ramses, near to the judges, waiting to learn results of the inquiry.

And, to her, the procession of the accused seemed endless.

It had been learned, in response to assessing tax funds while determining the proper handling of striking workers, that the royal treasurer had been funneling monies, through select nobles, toward a cause for removing their King. These nobles were escorted in, alongside some of those whom they had in turn granted the monies to. Teye coldly observed their testimonies, giving no indication of any feeling beyond disdain for weak-minded traitors.

Ladies of the harim were then implicated, through consort of the accused nobles, and, upon interrogation, admitted to further conspirators having frequented their chambers – sometimes collecting waxen figures intended for harm toward their King. Teye felt her breath catching as the figures were displayed, knowing this was close – too close – that if neither she nor Hui were yet suspect they could be shortly. And then he was brought in. His eyes were downcast, acknowledging no one, giving her nary a glance to cause her to be suspect if she was not yet so. The King's eyes drifted from one to the other as Teye reflected upon his suspicion of her interest in the royal cattle-herd. *Do I remain suspect after so much time has passed without my sharing guilty company?* One glance at Ramses supplied her answer. She downcast her eyes as the interrogations continued, wondering what remained for preserving their fates. Only a soul-eater, pacing anxiously, as the serpent Apep remained cloven in twain.

Another name forced her attention to refocus, the one name which could hurt her yet more than Hui's: that of her son. It was gathered through confession of select nobles that he had been intended as the replacement for Ramses and his heir. Teye paled, and all the more so when the accusations drifted toward the coaching of her son in presenting a more savory future image of himself as King. She glanced at Ramses, glanced at the exit from the juridical chamber; knew she had nowhere for escaping to. With both Hui and her son implicated, with the breaking of nobles and harim women whom had observed her actions, she could no longer fully deny to herself that her own accusation would follow.

Her hand stretched toward her husband, desperate for supplication, and fell as he merely eyed her coldly and edged away. His focus remained upon the interrogations as it was revealed that she had guided her son in preparing for his ascent, supplied him of the words for ingratiating himself amongst the peoples. That her interest in Hui had been far more than casual and that she had, indeed, assisted him in bringing hazardous magics within the palace to employ against their Lord. Teye remained frozen, expressionless, only blankly observing as a guard moved nearer to her. *It cannot be. I was to be protected. I wished only for our futures from an ailing old man . . .*

She couldn't speak, knew there to be no words which would pardon herself in the eyes of her husband; knew the coldness with which he regarded her could never again be warmed. Regardless, she reached for him one final time, and dazedly watched her hand fall, shunned, one final time. Ramses himself only glared upon her with disgust, disdaining her as he stood to take his leave of the trials. Without a final glance in her direction, he departed the juridical chamber – issuing one final order:

"Those who are found guilty shall die by their own hands, and I will hear no more of it."

Teye stood, shook her head in denial, called, "I wished for no harm to you, my Lord!" to an empty door, felt only the hand of her guard clasping her shoulder and pushing her back into her seat. The frightened eyes of those whom had already been accused observed as the Queen joined their fellowship of the damned. Ramses didn't return. There remained only a panel of unsympathetic judges for hearing her pleas. She hung her head, tears silently gathering at the corners of her eyes, hands trembling for fear of her fate. *And so I shall, at the least, be joined again with my son and lover in death.*

Each conspirator remained guarded as the trials continued into a seeming eternity. Each became named as guilty of the offense of high treason toward their King. Teye, and select harim women, were granted further comforts than others: amulets which would coerce love from an unwilling beholder had been discovered, and their use was assumed by the court to be in entrapping the support of women near to Ramses. The Queen reflected upon first seeing one in her initial summons to Panhuibanou's home, and related the memory to the judges for her defense. Perhaps it could, at the least, spare her own life.

Privately she reflected upon the visions of her fate, of her power, of her son's ascension, of Hui as her concubine, which had truly enticed her into conspiracy. And she knew them to have been visions of her own desires, her own needs. No energies of a soul-eater arose to spare her, no armies marched to overthrow their King, no magics from her lover caused the court to pardon them. *And the demon merely laughs, anticipating a feast of condemned souls.* For all, sentencing was delivered.

Teye huddled silently in her darkened, guarded chambers. With respect to rank and to "the magician Panhuibanou's manipulation of the Lady's will" she had been allowed to await her own fate in comfort, after the fates of all other conspirators had been attended to. Most were granted the favor of dying by their own hands, by quaffing of granted poisons. She had envisioned her own son and Hui choking upon tainted juice, clawing at their throats and chests as their lungs forgot the ability to breathe. *To have died with you, Hui, for us to have been coupled one final time . . .* There remained for her now only the image of his lifeless eyes gazing into the heavens, pleading to unsympathetic gods.

Those of less fortunate standing, or those whom had been considered guilty of more extreme treachery, were condemned to living burials, and she could at least rejoice in her loved ones not having needed to endure such isolated and creeping deaths.

It was no secret that the King had begun ailing once more during the trials, that his strength had continuously drained until his heir began overseeing matters of state. It was irony that his life should end just as those of the ones whom had tried to end it did. Or perhaps it was a remainder of Hui's magic, belatedly accomplishing its goal. It might have been cause for rejoicing, had Teye not more so feared the judgements of the younger Ramses. He held not the love for her which her husband had possessed, and she had strived to eliminate his own power as much as she had his father's. *My fate is granted now to the whims of the foster-son I would have seen murdered in favor of mine own child . . .*

Waiting, pondering her end, she remembered lying with Hui. Feeling their energies combined, and entering her through him. Feeling the protection of a soul-eater which would dissolve Ramses' shadow and gift her with freedom and status.

And she recalled scenting death, the closed-off tomb, pestilence in motion, upon her initial summons to Panhuibanou's home. She envisioned herself locked within an airtight tomb, screaming soundlessly, clawing at walls. A living spirit trapped within the shadows as Osiris denied it entrance to his land. *And the demon taunts me, his saliva disintegrating the souls of my loved ones, as I wait, endlessly, in this isolated darkness.*

RAVISHED

J. P. Spencer

IN THE SECONDS after the shot, after the echo from the hills had died softly on the heather, there was utter quiet. Even the ring doves in the wood shut off their cheerful warble.

The big man with the mane of black hair lay on his back on the road, a crimson flower blooming on the white field of his shirt. As the blood puddled the dirt beneath his head Catriona fancied she saw the colour drain from his ruddy face until it was as white as parchment. His hand, that cruel inquisitor of her flesh but seconds ago, scrabbled on his chest, then stopped still. He was dead, she had no doubt. And in the frozen shock of the moment she marvelled that beneath his breeches she could detect his cock still standing, full of life.

She was the first to move, jumping to her feet from the bank where she had been so roughly thrown. She charged up the grassy slope of the hillside that led down to the valley road. "The murderer!" she cried, pointing ahead in the direction of the shot. Still shouting, she bounded in most unfeminine fashion, though her femininity was not in doubt, with her skirts pulled high about her hips and her unfettered breasts bouncing as she scrambled on. Not that she cared. Her audience back on the road with their dead captain had already feasted their lecherous eyes and now was no time for modesty.

So little time had passed that, as she gained the first rise, she spied not a hundred yards off a fellow in a dark coat carrying a long fowling-piece, looking back in her direction. When he saw her, he turned his face to the mountain and began to push on in earnest up the steep path.

"The murderer!" she repeated, turning to gesticulate at the small band below who remained grouped around the body. Beyond them, down the valley, she could see a file of redcoats doubling towards the knot of mourners.

The lawyer, a thin figure in his black gown and white wig, was looking up at her. "Come back," he called. Even at this distance she could make out the pen-sharp point of his nose and the cold glint of his gaze. She had no doubt he'd have stood by and watched as she was ravished with as little interest as a man might take in a dog covering a bitch. Catriona was glad there was a fair distance between them.

She was gladder still as he shouted to the arriving soldiers, "Ten pounds for the man who takes the lass! She held us here for the assassin. She's an accomplice!"

At this injustice, all the vigour in her limbs deserted her and she stood rooted to the spot, hugging her arms to her torn bodice. That not five minutes earlier she had wished her bullying suitor dead was true enough, but the granting of this unspoken desire had not been of her making. Many sins lay to her account, she acknowledged, but murder was not among them.

Catriona watched in dismay as the redcoats started up the hillside, fanning out along the incline, their legs pumping in their eagerness to capture her and claim the offered purse. And other things, she had no doubt. All her previous energy was gone as she watched her fate approach.

"Quick," said a voice from behind her. "Duck in here among the trees."

Catriona turned, her eyes wild in her head. Was there still a chance of salvation?

"Over here, woman."

A fringe of birch trees clothed the slope of the hill to her left and now, in the overhang of the wood, she saw a figure beckoning to her. She ran towards him and a hand pulled her under shelter. She found herself staring into a countenance as sun-browned as a nut, made up of angles and sharp points and with eyes as sparkling as a Highland loch. To Catriona, it looked a merry face, alive with wit and good humour if the present emergency did not preclude such civilities.

"You're improperly dressed, mistress," he said, his gaze fast to the gaping neck of her dress from which spilled the rosy tip of her breast.

"He did it," she blurted. "The man who was shot. He forced me."

Her rescuer was dragging her along now, under the cover of the trees. Suddenly he stopped and she ran into him. He seized her face in his hands and spoke in an urgent whisper, his eyes blazing.

"What did you do for him, lassie? Tell me the truth."

"I stopped and asked the way. He made free with my person. He was vile."

"Did he ravish you?"

"He would have done, I'm sure. But he was shot."

The man's face split into a grin and he planted a kiss on her forehead. "In that case," he said, "I won't throw you to the redcoats. Come on!"

She struggled behind him as he skipped ahead, suddenly plunging into a thicket and taking a narrow track that led upwards out of the wood and onto a gorse-filled moor. He crouched low and made her follow suit as she stumbled behind. At length they came to a halt behind a jagged crag where they could stand upright. There was just room for the pair of them to lean against the rock and catch their breath.

At length Catriona asked, "Was he killed to save me?"

Her companion chuckled, his laughter bubbling on in a manner she found insufferable. "No, mistress," he replied. "Your virtue was not the matter of his slaying. Do you no ken who he is?"

"No."

"There's more at issue here than your fair flesh, lassie – sumptuous though it may be."

He gazed frankly at her exposed bosom, blithely ignoring the poisonous look she gave him in return.

"Now's not the moment for a lesson in Highland politics," he continued, "but that man that lies dead is the King's Factor over the land of the Stewarts, sworn to skelp my people of their money, their homes and their rights. Robert Campbell of Argyll."

"Black Bobby," Catriona murmured, the fog of bewilderment in her mind now clearing. She was in worse peril than ever she had imagined.

"Aye, Black Bobby," her Stewart benefactor muttered, and spat at his feet. "You are telling the truth when you say he didn't skewer you?"

"Oh!" she burst out. "Do you not believe me?"

He turned his face to hers, his dancing eyes leaden as he spoke. "You're a bonny girl, right enough. But I'd rather be tarred and hung from a gibbet than take to the hills with a woman who's been pierced by the cock of a Campbell."

Take to the hills they did, with Alan – as he introduced himself – leading the way. It was plain to Catriona that he knew the country well – indeed he told her so as they halted so she could catch her breath. Not that his acquaintance with the land of Appin made the journey any easier, for they were obliged to avoid the paths and creep through the bracken and gorse, frequently throwing themselves face-down to avoid detection by the enemy. Catriona had no chance to discuss their circumstances with her benefactor as she laboured behind him, the fatigue multiplying in her limbs as she crouched and bent and oftentimes crawled on her belly throughout a long afternoon. She envied the seemingly unquenchable spring in his step as they forged on, ever upward, and she thanked God that he had been at hand to save her.

Just as her aches and pains – the stitch in her side and the myriad tiny cuts and gorse-pricks on her bare legs and the raw patch on her heel from the rubbing of her sandals – were beginning to overwhelm all other thoughts, they came to a halt beneath an outcrop of rock that rose from the moor in a great slab.

"Can you climb, mistress?" said her benefactor, with a grin on his face that lit up his features. He pointed upward to the grey mass that loomed over them, sheer and forbidding. Nevertheless, Catriona could see that the great stone levelled off some fifty feet above them, promising respite from the toil of flight. If they could reach it they would be out of sight and safe for the night ahead.

Alan slipped his shoes into the pocket of his coat and contemplated the rockface.

"I've not climbed this crag since I was a lad," he said. "But if I could do it then I can do it now, with George's army at my back. As I remember there's a channel that runs – aha!"

To Catriona's astonishment he leapt up, throwing himself at the naked rock, and seemed to hang there, his bare hands and feet glued to the glassy slope like a fly to a window pane. He was already a yard off the ground. He moved sideways, defying gravity as he searched with hand and foot for some invisible hold.

"Yes," he cried as he found what he sought, and Catriona saw he was wedged at the foot of a split between two plates of rock that ran upwards to the right. He slapped his hand on the edge of the crack. "Here's our staircase, my lass. Up you come, and be quick."

It was on the tip of Catriona's tongue to refuse. It was one thing for a spry Highland warrior to mount a sheer rockface, quite another for an exhausted Lowland woman who had climbed no higher than the stairs to her attic bedroom in her life. But the frowning look on her saviour's face and the urgency with which he spoke brooked no argument. She too pocketed her footwear and faced the rock. From below she heard a whistle and a shout – their pursuers were closing. She had no faith in her ability to mount the rock, but the choice was stark – climb or hang.

"Here!" Alan was reaching down to her. She caught his hand and scrabbled with her toes for a purchase, pushing up as best she could. His long slim fingers wrapped around her wrist like bands of steel. His other hand gripped her under the armpit and pulled. She sailed upwards. The strength in his slight frame was astonishing.

Their bodies were mashed together at the foot of the crack in the rock, his breath hot on her cheek and an arm like a hoop about her back.

"Look up," he commanded, and she did so, appreciating now how the channel in the rock could indeed provide a staircase for hand and foot and elbow and knee, all the way to the patch of sky at the top. "You go first so I can keep you steady. Don't look down. It'll get easier as you go."

Catriona was thankful that it did as, with sinews aching and her heart thumping against her ribs, she crawled and scraped and inched her way upwards, encouraged and pushed and sometimes cursed from below by her companion.

At the top, she collapsed in a small hollow of dead grass and bracken big enough, just, to shelter the pair of them. Alan lay face-down, too, peering around the edges of their vantage point for signs of pursuit. He ducked back into the saucer of land and laid a finger on his lips. Catriona heard the sound of cries and shouts, then the crunch of boots passing below them. The noises continued for a while, getting fainter all the while until they ceased altogether. But by that time she was asleep.

Alan contemplated the sleeping girl. She was a bonny lass, with her wild red ringlets and skin the shade of thick cream. Her body was lithe and lush – he'd seen a good deal of it as she'd followed him across moor and through thicket. Even with the soldiers at his back, and the certainty of having his neck stretched should he be caught, he'd shot many a covert glance at the torn bodice of his companion and the bounding globes barely contained within. The tips of her breasts were a bruised russet-red, the saucers of her areolae a shade lighter. He longed to bury his face in the perfume of her bosom and breathe in the scent of her – travel-stained though she was as she lay by his side. And why should he not? She owed him her life; the least she could do would be to lend him her body in recompense. He could insist, and take her by force if need be – there would be little she could do about it up here with the redcoats hunting for her below.

But though Alan's cock pressed against his belly, as stiff as a dirk, he knew he could not take her against her will. It would make him no better than Black Bobby Campbell, and that would be a betrayal of all he held dear.

The girl woke suddenly, her eyes opening to gaze full into his. Her pupils were a pale morning blue. In them he could read fear, gratitude and discomfort.

"As you're a gentleman, sir," she said, "would you be so kind to look the other way. I need – that is, I must –"

"Of course." He knew what she had to do. He had himself pissed off the lip of the rock while she was sleeping.

He turned his back and heard her step as far off as she could, to the downward edge of their patch of ground. Good. At least she had the wit not to spoil the earth where they must pass the night. There came the rustling of her clothing, then the whisper of her water as she performed her toilet.

Alan risked a glance. It was she who had assumed he was a gentleman – he had made no claims.

The sun was sinking, but still bright. Its low beams shone over his shoulder onto the squatting figure, illuminating in sparkling clarity every titian strand of hair on her head, the grass-stains and gorse-rents in her bedraggled dress, the dusty froth of her lifted skirts – and the full glory of her naked backside as she peed into the soil between her straddled feet. The sight of the twin hemispheres of her buttocks, as pale as porcelain, as seductively rounded as a ripe peach and, no doubt, as smooth as a silk sheet, ripped the breath from his lungs. At the base of the furrow between her cheeks her cunt lips pouted, pink and succulent, plainly visible through the moss of copper curls that matched those of her head. He saw all this in an instant and sharply turned away, the inflammatory images fixed for ever in his mind. At least, he thought, if they kill me now, I'll have a vision of earthly pleasure for a keepsake in the hereafter.

Alan passed an uncomfortable night. The peril of their position and the discomfort of the hard earth kept sleep at bay. But it was the proximity of the girl by his side, breathing deeply in exhausted slumber a mere hand's breadth away, that kept his mind in turmoil. He could see the outline of her sleeping form against the yawning width of the sky, the thorny tangle of her hair, the prow of her bosom, the curve of her haunch beneath her skirt when she turned on her side, thrusting her big bonny arse towards him.

Aye, her *arse*. The vulgar word echoed in his head as he lay there, imagining what it would feel like to stroke and squeeze and spank those curvaceous posteriors. *Spank her arse!* The phrase reverberated over and over, like waves on shingle. To make those handsome cheeks dance and shiver under his palm as he'd done to the willing maids of Paris a few weeks ago – that was what he wanted. His cock stabbed into the bare earth beneath him as he shifted uneasily, testament to his desires. To whelp a fair woman's arse and then soothe her with all the tenderness in his Highland soul; that was his need as a man. But only if the lass was willing. The lasses in the French bordellos had been willing enough as long as there was money in his purse. Mistress Catriona, he sensed, would be less tractable, even though she was in his debt. He turned his back on her and willed his rebellious flesh to give him peace.

But sleep did not come; the girl's presence was too disturbing. So too were other thoughts that now stole on him to justify his desire for her succulent body. Had she really been so innocent in attracting the attentions of Black Bobby? What had she been doing on such a dangerous road on her own? Was she, after all, a Campbell whore? In which case, what was he doing risking his neck for her – pretty arse or not?

Catriona woke with the sun on her face, a crick in her neck and the taste of bracken in her mouth. Alan was peering down into the gorge below. He turned to her as she stirred.

"I need water," she said.

He passed her his bottle. "Just wet your mouth," he said. "There's a long day ahead of us."

Catriona did as she was told. There was a bare inch of liquid in the container.

"Is this all you have?"

"It is. I wasn't prepared for a night in the heather when I ran into you."

"But there's a burn down there. We could drink our fill and replenish the bottle."

Alan shook his head. "It might be the last drink you have on this earth. The Lobsters are still looking for us."

Catriona crawled to the edge and peered over. She could see the moor stretching away to her right, with the ridges of hills high above, like banked clouds. Immediately below was the worn sheep track they had followed the day before, which turned sharply out of sight, obscured by thorns and a stunted growth of hawthorn. The stream must lie in the dip somewhere. She could hear it babbling. The sun was burning into her cheek and the back of her hand. How she longed to dabble her fingers in that fast-rushing brook and sluice cold water over her face and down her throat.

"What shall we do?" she whispered, turning to Alan, who was silhouetted against a sky of clear and cloudless blue. The sun was behind him, so she could not read his expression, but she did not doubt it was as grim as his voice.

"We have no choice, lass. We must just lie here."

"For how long?"

He shrugged and sat by her side. "Till nightfall, at least. Maybe we can get away when the sun's gone down."

Catriona glared at him. "It's all right for you. With skin like mine, I'll fry."

"You should have thought of that, mistress, before you took to the hills in just a shift."

"But I lost my parcel of clothes when those men stopped me on the road. And I could hardly go back for it after the shooting, could I?"

He stared hard at her with an intensity that made her shiver, for all his handsome looks.

"Tell me, Catriona, what were you doing on that road by yourself?"

"I'd been directed that way, by the Reverend Cawdor of Balachulish –"

"Cawdor! He's a Campbell man, is he not?"

"He's a man of God, sir, and a friend of my uncle's – that's all I know."

Alan's face was stormy, as if great emotions were boiling within and he were struggling to contain them. But all he said was, "Indeed," before he turned his back on her and closed his eyes.

Catriona did not know what to say and so said nothing. She was shaken by his sudden hostile manner. For a moment she had thought he might lay hands on her, yet the thought was not frightening somehow. The notion of those long nimble fingers on her body made her flesh tingle.

These preoccupations had taken her mind off her plight, but now the heat of the sun on her head reminded her of her uncomfortable circumstances. At least the mass of her curls would protect her face and neck. She pulled her torn dress as far across her chest as she could. She guessed it was still a couple of hours before midday and the sun was already unbearably hot.

An unexpected sound disturbed her. Alan was snoring.

The gall of the man! To so disregard her discomfort as to fall asleep.

Then, as she watched the regular rise and fall of his chest and listened to his heavy breathing, she realized that his slumber presented her with a solution to her predicament – if she only had the nerve.

Catriona's descent was easier than she had expected. Carefully clutching the water bottle to her side, she slipped from foothold to foothold down the chimney in the rock. She jumped the last few feet to the ground with triumph bubbling in her veins. The sound of the burn was much louder down here. She would fill the bottle and be back before Alan had even shifted in his sleep. And if he was angry with her when he woke, *tant pis* – he'd drink the cold water from the stream with as great a thirst for all that.

She struck off the sheep track they had followed the day before, making for the gurgling of the water. The gorse was thick and there were clumps of wind-bent hawthorn that hid the burn from view. Then there it was – no wider than the breadth of her mid-morning shadow, but a precious torrent of clean, clear mountain water, laughing and chuckling over stone and shale as it rushed down the hillside.

Catriona threw herself full-length to plunge her face into its iciness, gulping down deep drafts that numbed her lips and throat. After a few moments she sat up on her haunches to splash water down the back of her neck and into her bodice to cool the hot creases of her bosom. To think that Alan had forbade her this delight! She laughed as she swung her legs round to plunge her dusty feet onto the moss-softened edges of rock beneath the surface, then pulled her skirts high to splash her calves and thighs. So much for the bold Highland warrior, cowering on his sun-baked rock, too afraid to share this blissful release. He did not know what he was missing.

"Now, there's a pretty sight."

For an instant, so self-absorbed was she, Catriona did not comprehend that a man was regarding her from across the stream. Then she would have screamed had not a hand been clapped across her mouth from behind.

The fellow before her was maybe the biggest man she had ever seen. He stood six feet tall and was as broad as he was high. A long dark waistcoat flapped over his vast and dirty breeches which, despite the dust and stains, were of an ominous scarlet hue. His head was like a big pink cannonball as the sunshine gleamed on his hairless pate. One eye was half closed, drawn down at the corner by a white-limned scar; the other was fixed on the smooth vee of Catriona's glistening thighs. Though he was smiling broadly, displaying ragged stained teeth, he was not a friendly apparition. He was a giant – a redcoat giant hunting for her. And he had caught her.

Catriona tried to twist free, but the man behind her held on fast, pinning her arms to her sides with a grip of iron.

"Take her up, Billy," said the big one. "We've just found a little present for the sergeant."

Alan woke with the left side of his face ablaze in the sunshine. He turned on his other side to shield himself, and then saw he was alone.

He was alert in an instant. Where could she be? Could she have fallen from the rock? Dismay gripped him.

Then, recalling the dance of defiance in Catriona's eyes when he had forbidden a foray to replenish their supply of water, he realized what she must have done. He looked round for the bottle. It too had vanished. It was plain where she was.

He had no intention of waiting for her return, and was halfway down the divide in the rockface before he even considered it. He knew for certain the soldiers were down there somewhere; they would not have given up yet. The foolish girl did not realize what peril she was in. And, he promised himself, what a tanning he would plant on her broad white rump once he dragged her back to safety.

But he did not rush. Stealth was in his blood – which was one reason he was still alive, six years after the rebellion of '45. He surveyed the landscape for several minutes before dropping down from the rockface to the heather. He was worried in earnest now. He had no idea how long he had slept. Even if it had been for just a couple of minutes, surely Catriona would be on her way back by now, racing from the burn with her precious supply of fresh water.

There was no sign of her, or of the redcoats. He made swiftly for the sound of rushing water, hoping to find her slaking her thirst indulgently by the burn, words of reprimand forming themselves in his mind.

He followed the path of the brook, clearly marked to his eye by the line of bush and thorn. Where the foliage parted there was a bank of grass and the stream raced past. There was a patch of wetness on the bank – and his water bottle. But no Catriona. His eyes darted to the left and right, his senses alert. Where was she? Then, above the noise of rushing water, he heard a woman scream.

The sergeant was older than the other two. A gnome of a man, about twice the age of the boy Billy who had captured Catriona. She had been manhandled a short distance across the moor to a scooped-out clearing at the base of the cliff where, it seemed, the soldiers had made camp. From the amount of kit and clothing lying around Catriona guessed there were not many of them, maybe only these three. She prayed that that were so. These three were bad enough.

They had sat her on a long low rock in the centre of the horseshoe-shaped enclave, and Billy had been dispatched to guard the opening. The giant stood behind her while the sergeant, his weaselly glinting eyes in a weatherworn face, considered her.

"So," he said at length, "you're the doxy there's such a fuss about."

"I don't know what you mean, sir," she replied, straightening her back and staring boldly at him. She was resolved to hold her head high, though it was embarrassing to have to clasp the edges of her torn dress together to conceal her bosom.

"Where's the man?" said the sergeant.

"I don't know what you mean, sir. I'm travelling alone to my uncle's house at Loch Leven, and I implore you as a gentleman to let me continue my journey."

"Where did you spend the night?"

"I don't know exactly. At an inn somewhere on the road from Balachulish."

He grinned. "Bala-where? No, don't bother to tell me. Look at you – it's obvious you slept out on this accursed mountain, just as we did. Only we didn't get much sleep because we were looking for you and that murdering Scotch rogue that did for the King's Factor. So I'm not in the best of good humour this sunny day, am I, Bull?"

"No, sergeant, you ain't," said the big man from directly behind Catriona.

"However, if it satisfies your sense of justice, madam, let me tell you we are seeking a tall, fair-faced, red-headed young woman with pale blue eyes and a handsome figure. Hold her up."

Before Catriona could protest the giant had seized her arms from behind and pulled her to her feet. She tried to kick out at him, but only slammed her foot into the rock on which she had been sitting.

"Now, from my observation," continued the sergeant, "I can undoubtedly vouch for every item on that register. Even –" and he took hold of the neck of her torn dress and laid it open to the waist with a rip "– the matter of the handsome figure."

"Cover me up, sir!" she spat. "This is most indecent."

He smiled and stepped closer, so her full bosom, rising and falling with her distress, was almost bobbing in his face.

"Where is he, the Scotch murderer?" he asked.

"I don't know who you mean," she cried. "Let me go, I beg you."

Suddenly there was a glint of steel in the sunlight. A bayonet was in the sergeant's hand. Catriona screamed.

The sergeant cut a strip from her gaping bodice and handed it to the giant. "Muzzle her with that," he said, and Catriona found the rag being rammed between her lips. Now, robbed of speech, she could only stare at her tormentor in a silent plea for mercy.

But mercy was far from the little man's mind. He took hold of the waist of her dress and began to slide the bayonet down behind it. Catriona's pulse was galloping as she felt the flat blade of metal press into the softness of her belly, its tip nosing down as far as the fleece of hair that guarded her most secret place.

The sergeant laughed at the terror in her face.

"I'm an artist of the bayonet, madam. There's five Scotchmen, three Frenchies and half-a-dozen other heathen devils I've sent into the next world with the sixteen inches of steel underneath your dress. Think of that, mistress, when you tell me your lies.

I've not done for a woman yet, mind. But that's because I've not had a good enough reason. So far."

"Sergeant." The giant sounded nervous.

"Getting worried, are you, Bull? Think I might split her from cunt to belly button, do you?"

"Sergeant, please. It would be a mortal sin."

"I'm surprised that troubles you. It doesn't concern me, I can assure you. You see, if I just turn my wrist like this –"

"No!" cried Bull.

Catriona's heart stopped. For a second the blade was turning, and she could feel the razor-sharp edge biting into the tender flesh of her belly then – there was sunshine and warm air on her skin, and her dress was sliced in two, exposing her trembling beauty to the sergeant's triumphant gaze.

He held the weapon aloft.

"You see. An artist," he said.

But Catriona didn't hear.

"I think she's fainted, sergeant," said Bull, lowering her body to a sitting position on the rock.

Lying belly-down in a crevice twenty feet above them, peering through a fringe of gorse, Alan had been near to fainting himself. He had witnessed just enough of this scene to know that the worst had happened and that Catriona was as good as lost. Part of him reasoned that, since her own foolishness had placed her in this position, she could be left to her fate. Now might be his chance, while the redcoats were busy with her, to get clean away. After all, he owed her nothing, and she was likely a Campbell whore in any case.

To flee, however, was not the conduct of a man of principle, and Alan held dear to his beliefs. Many men had perished for principle, and his own life was doubtless destined to be abbreviated on that account. So there only remained one riddle to be solved – how could he kill three redcoats armed with just a dirk and a dash of Highland cunning? All he had was the advantage of surprise, and that not to any degree, since the redcoats obviously believed he was close at hand.

It seemed he would have to wait until the redcoats' attentions were fully engaged with their prisoner. He'd seen the way they looked at her. Her glorious body was a gift to lechery that men like them could surely not resist. He just hoped Catriona would have the strength to endure their attentions.

She woke to find herself lying naked on the stone, the tatters of her dress beneath her. She tried to conceal her nudity, but her arms were tied behind her back. At least they had removed the cloth from her mouth.

"You barbarians," she spat at them. "You should be ashamed to treat a woman like this. You're a disgrace to the commander you serve."

The sergeant shrugged and sat next to her on the rock. He still held the bayonet. He laid its point flat on one russet-tipped breast.

"And I suppose it's not barbarous to shoot a man dead when he's about the King's affairs?"

"This business has nothing to do with me," she protested, trying to ignore the pattern he was now tracing with his steel, ever so lightly, like the tiptoeing of a spider, across the yielding globe of her left breast.

"That's for a court to decide," he replied. "I would imagine it would go easier for you if you gave up the assassin himself. If you tell us where in these Godforsaken hills he is hiding, I swear it shall be known to those who sit in judgement on you."

"If there's any justice I shall be found innocent," she proclaimed in a voice that sounded bolder than she felt. "And I shall seek recompense for any harm that is done to my person by you or any other man."

"I see." He withdrew the steel blade and ran a callused hand down her flank. "Such perfect skin. It's a shame to mark it, don't you think, Bull? Why don't you show her your back?"

The giant said nothing, but threw his waistcoat to the ground and pulled his shirt over his head. Then he turned, presenting Catriona with a view of him naked from the nape of the neck to the broad waist of his breeches. She gasped in shock. His skin was a purple canvas of gnarled lumps and stripes, of corrugated ridges and half-healed excrescences where the flesh had been ploughed up like a muddy field and barely allowed to heal before the next ploughing.

"Eight thousand lashes in fourteen years, isn't it, Bull?"

"Nigh on ten thousand, Sergeant. But there's many has had worse." He turned to Catriona. "You get used to it."

She was speechless. She knew such brutality was commonplace in armies, but to be so close to the evidence was sickening. For a moment she even forgot her own parlous state. Until the sergeant spoke again.

"That's enough, Bull. Now let's show her the cat."

Alan was in a quandary. He too had been sickened at the sight of the big soldier's mutilated body, and the thought of Catriona's fair form being bloodied in such a fashion had him reaching for his dirk. But there was no point in being hasty unless he were certain of success. It would be better for Catriona to suffer a flogging now than a hanging later. And there would be more than one hanging, that was certain. The Campbells would require the stretching of necks for the murder of Black Bobby – and only Alan could ensure that Catriona's was not one of them.

So he held his passions in check as he watched the sergeant dangle a many-stranded whip before the girl's eyes – the infamous cat o'nine tails that kept the brutish soldiers of King George's army in order. He saw the devilish gleam in the man's face as he lovingly parted the strands of the whip to show Catriona the cruel leather knots that would soon be biting into her trembling flesh. He saw too the horror in her expression that, to his admiration, was quickly replaced by disdain.

"Get on with it, then, if you must," she said. "I have nothing to say."

That was unlikely to remain the case, Alan well knew. Once the cat began to claw, surely Catriona would tell all she knew of him. Not that it much mattered, he reasoned. Either he or the men below would not live out the day.

The sergeant and the big man had untied Catriona's hands and turned her body over. Now they stretched her across the rock and roped her wrists together above her head. The big soldier bundled up her dress and pushed it beneath her hips. The effect was to raise up her pearly bottom, the full hemispheres of her buttocks curving outwards in a spectacular and tempting display. With her face hidden by her forest of copper curls, she lay without resistance on the black slab, like a maiden sacrifice.

Alan could not prevent the intrusion of lustful thoughts at the sight of her. Already enamoured of her charms, after the glimpse she had afforded him the day before, now he revelled in her naked glory. It was shameful, and he was a sinner, he knew, but the thought of her voluptuous form being chastised enflamed him further.

He was not alone in this, it was clear. The soldiers below were moving quickly now. The sergeant offered Catriona a final opportunity to answer his questions, but she just shook her ringlets and said nothing. Then the whip was in the big soldier's hand and he raised his mighty arm.

The first blow landed on her left buttock, the leather tongues spreading across the white flesh in an obscene caress. Her hips jerked, and the mass of her cheek shuddered as it absorbed the lash, but she made no sound.

The whip rose and fell again, its nine tongues flicking this time across the resilience of the other buttock. Again she jerked, and the broad satiny moon twitched and jumped under the impact. She did not cry out, but on the impact of the third stroke Alan thought he heard a quick intake of breath.

On the fourth, as her bottom danced and the skin began to redden, there was a low-pitched "Oh", as of surprise or shock rather than pain. But soon, as the leather knots fell in a steady rain upon her upturned posterior, her voice rang out in a long, lonely wail of agony that did not cease from one blow to the next.

Horrified though he was, Alan was as hard in his breeches as he had ever been in his life. This was his fantasy of the night before made flesh. His cock dug into the rock beneath him as if it would penetrate the mountain itself. He tried to ignore it and concentrate on what must be done. If he felt this way then he had no doubt the soldiers below would be in a similar state.

Already Alan had noticed that the third soldier, the boy relegated to sentry duty, no longer had his eyes on the moor and the mountains. He, too, was mesmerized by the female backside wriggling under the lash, and though he held his musket in one hand, the other was pressing the thick bulge between his legs. When a man's cock is engorged and his mind is aflame with images of lust, then is the time to catch him unawares. Alan reminded himself of this and concentrated on the timing of his intervention below.

At the sergeant's command the whipping ceased.

"But I've hardly started," complained Bull. "Let me tickle her up proper."

"Don't be a fool, Bull," said the other as he peered closely at Catriona's striped posterior. "We have to hand her over in one piece."

He ran his hand over the girl's livid buttocks. "My, you've heated her up some. Her arse is on fire. By God, you could cook a beefsteak on it."

His fingers roamed further over her silky flesh, tracing the crevice between her cheeks and dipping down to the mossy treasures between her legs. Catriona made a token attempt to shut her thighs, but she seemed to have lost the strength to resist.

"So, mistress, have you nothing to tell me now?"

She did not reply, but lay moaning. The sergeant pushed a finger into the purse of her cunt and probed obscenely. "My, my," he said, "you're flowing like the Thames in spate. Now you've had a taste of the cat it looks like you're ready for an animal of a different kind."

So saying, he pulled out his male part, a thick truncheon of impressive proportions for a man of his dimensions.

He lodged the head of his member in the fork of her rear, gripped her hips and pierced her to the root. Catriona gasped.

The sergeant laughed. "First we light the flames and then we stoke the fire." He buffeted his belly against her tender bottom. "This is my idea of soldiering, eh, Bull?"

Alan had seen enough. He knew he must act now, or else, once the three of them had spent their lust on the girl, his best chance would be gone.

He slipped nimbly down the rockface. The heather of the moor cushioned his footsteps as he approached the mouth of the redcoats' camp. It was here that the sentry should be keeping watch. If he were doing his job then there would be no chance for Alan to surprise the girls' tormentors.

But the sentry was a boy lost in the mist of desire as he watched his sergeant plough the lush body of their captive. His musket lay forgotten on the ground as he tugged in a mounting rhythm on the thin white wand in his fist.

Alan had killed men before. Those deeds had been amidst the screams and chaos of battle, at Falkirk and Culloden, and once in a duel when challenged by a Frenchman who derided Highland swordsmanship. He had never before murdered like an assassin, coldly and silently, slipping his dirk between the ribs and into the heart. As he struck with the knife, he clasped his other hand over the boy's mouth, cutting off his cry of surprise and pain. The body twitched and flailed in his arms as death and sensual release seemed to overtake him at the same moment. Blood and sperm fell together on the heather. At least, Alan reflected, as he dragged the body behind the screen of rock, the boy's last thoughts had been of pleasure.

He crouched by the body and wondered how long it would be before the other two realized their companion was no longer observing them. Probably as long as it took for them achieve their own satisfaction. He reached out for the boy's musket. He loathed firearms, and considered himself a poor hand with powder and ball. But though the musket was no use to him the redcoat sergeant was not the only one who could wield a bayonet.

Of all the suffering Catriona had endured, it seemed to her that the present humiliation was the worst. The lashing from the cat o'nine tails had taught her a new awareness of pain, but the anguish had been purely physical. The ravishment she was currently experiencing was another matter.

The heat of the beating had inflamed her senses, making her throb and glow in the secret places of her body in a fashion that was shameful to admit. She hated and feared the sergeant more than any man she had ever met, yet what he was doing to her now was not painful, far from it. There was a surprising tenderness in his touch as he fondled her flanks and slipped his hand beneath the hinge of her hip to stroke her belly.

His manhood was lodged deep within her, and he held it there while he explored the mossy curls of her bush, parting the strands to slip his finger into the tender groove of her sexual opening.

At any moment she expected a pinch or a slap, but he seemed more interested in giving her pleasure as he sought and found the nub of her clitoris. She detested him even more for this. It was one thing to be whipped and abused for a man's brutish ends, but for him to coerce her into participating in his lust was despicable. As she involuntarily responded to the throb and swell of the male spike within her, she knew that he was intent on robbing her of her self-respect. It was unendurable!

"I think she likes it," said Bull. "She's wriggling on your pikestaff like a Spitalfields whore."

"Aye." The sergeant was breathing heavily as Catriona's abused buttocks kissed his belly. "She can't help herself. I never knew Scotch wenches could shag in so sweet a fashion."

Catriona bore down on the hand that fingered her, squeezing and nipping the thick shaft inside her, wanting to bring him to the boil and end this degradation. Surely his crisis could not be long delayed?

Suddenly the sergeant began to move in earnest, gripping her haunches hard and shuttling his instrument in and out of her in a steady stroke that stirred a chord within her. It was unfair to the memory of her one past lover to recall him in these circumstances, but Catriona couldn't help compare this purposeful attention with young Davey's greedy gallop to satisfaction. Though, to be fair, it all came to the same in the end –

"Ah!" shouted the sergeant. "I'm done!"

"You took your time," said Bull.

"Just warming the lady up for you," said the other as he relaxed his hold on her. When he moved away, Catriona felt the full heat of the sun on the skin of her belaboured bottom, and the glue of his passion sticking to the insides of her thighs.

Suddenly her head was yanked upwards by the hair, and she found herself staring at the big man who had flogged her. Catriona gasped in shock. He was stark naked, a pink monster with thighs like flitches of pork and a beer barrel for a belly. But it was his organ of generation that drew Catriona's eyes. She'd never seen anything like it except on a beast of the field. It was a great pizzle of a staff, with a flaming red tip that loomed over her like the barrel of a canon.

"Now you know why we call him Bull," said the sergeant.

Catriona screamed.

The sound reverberated through Alan like a call to arms. He took the bayonet in his left hand and his dagger in the right. Then he peered cautiously round the outcrop of rock that screened the girl's ordeal from his view.

The men turned Catriona over.

"I want to see her face," said Bull. "And her big bubbies."

She tried to kick him, but he caught her feet in his hands and spread her legs, stepping inside them and pressing his gigantic instrument against the tender flesh of her belly.

Though her wrists were bound together, she was able to cover her breasts. The soldiers didn't like that. The sergeant cut the bonds and squatted by her head, holding her hands away from her body.

"That's better," said Bull, covering one soft milky globe in his paw and squeezing. "You're a handsome lass for a murdering Scotch witch; I'll say that."

"Where's Billy?" said the sergeant. "I can't see him."

"Gone off with his tail between his legs, I expect. Silly young pup."

"We'd better find him."

"Not yet, Sergeant."

"Make haste, then. Let's see what she makes of a pump-handle like yours."

Despite herself, Catriona spoke. "No, it's too big! It won't go in!"

She knew it was a mistake. Anything she said was liable to excite these brutes more.

Bull grinned. "We'll find out, shall we, mistress?" he said, and thrust the head of his formidable engine into the mouth of her quim, where it stuck fast like an apple in the gullet.

"Oh, sir, no!" cried Catriona.

The sergeant whispered in her ear. "Tell me the whereabouts of your murdering companion and I'll make him stop."

"No!"

"Quickly or I won't be able to stop him at all."

But it was too late, for the awesome weapon was driving into her like a battering ram, filling her to the brim, and the weight of the mountainous man was crushing her torso flat against the unyielding rock beneath her. In that, her blackest moment, she saw her salvation. Through the wild and pungent tangle of hair in her ravisher's armpit she spied a Highland warrior running fleet-footed, metal glinting in both hands and murder shining in his face.

Bull knew as little of his fate as Billy before him. The dirk sank into his neck, cutting his windpipe in an instant, and he collapsed on Catriona in a froth of blood.

Alan stared full into the eyes of the sergeant across the still-twitching corpse of the giant. He couldn't reach the soldier, yet the redcoat was making no move for his weapons. He seemed immobile, stuck fast to the spot like a fly in honey.

Then Alan realized why. Catriona had a grip on the sergeant's hands and, though battered and abused and crushed beneath a dead mountain of a man, she was holding on with all her remaining strength.

The redcoat said nothing as Alan moved nimbly round the rock and placed the bayonet at his throat. He stared at Alan as a man stares at his Maker.

"Kill him," commanded Catriona.

It was lucky for Catriona that her uncle was away when she arrived at his house by the loch. Her aunt was a woman who knew when to ask a question and when to keep her mouth shut. Though it was evident from the condition of her clothes and from her bedraggled demeanour that the girl had survived an unsavoury adventure, the aunt said nothing once she had been assured that no permanent damage had been sustained.

Of that, Catriona was not so sure. She wondered whether she would bear the scars for ever. But for now she was determined that no one should know of the flogging. Her only satisfaction in her present predicament was to reflect that her abusers were all dead. As for Alan, an unfinished matter lay between them.

"Aunt," she said. "There is a gentleman I met on the journey. To tell the truth, I would not be here otherwise."

"Well, where is he now? Why did he not accompany you to the door?"

"I don't want to bring trouble into your house. But there's a shepherd's hut up the glen, is there not?"

The woman nodded and left the room. She returned with a bundle of food and a flask of spirit.

"Here you are. I hope he's worth it, lassie."

"I'll not stay here," said Alan, when he'd satisfied his hunger. "I'll be better off up on the hillside."

"As you please," she replied. "But before you go I have a task for you."

She took a jar from the pocket of the dress her aunt had lent her and handed it to him. Then she turned and raised her skirt high above her waist. The candle flickered, casting a yellow light across the dramatic hemispheres of her buttocks, latticed by the weals of the whip.

"Ah," he said softly.

"Am I so ugly now?"

"No, Catriona." He fell to his knees and gazed closely at the objects of his greatest desire. "To me, you are more beautiful than ever."

He traced a long crimson welt with a feather-light touch of the finger. The soft flesh shivered at his touch.

"Does that hurt?"

"Yes – and no. It would be kind of you to rub that salve into my wounds."

"Like this?"

He smeared a small dollop of the ointment onto a patch of hot pink skin.

"Yes. All over." She bent forward and rested her elbows on the rickety wooden table, her full buttocks swelling out in proud relief. She caught her breath as he began to minister to her.

"Does that hurt?"

"I don't care. It must be done."

He set about the work, rubbing and soothing to the accompaniment of her stifled gasps of pain. But somewhere in the process her heated flesh grew pliant beneath his curious fingers, and her cries turned to murmurs of appreciation.

Soon, there was no need for him to be stroking and fondling her beyond the need itself.

"I've been thinking," she said softly. "That soldier – the sergeant – planted his seed in me."

"He's paid the price for that deed, Catriona."

"But what if the seed takes root? What if I bear his child?"

"Ah." He'd not thought of that. "You'll be lucky if you live that long, my lass. There's more than one gallows ready for us now."

"Maybe so, but my uncle will get me safely to Edinburgh. And if I escape I couldn't bear to be carrying a bastard English whelp."

"It won't come to that."

"It might. And you'll be far off in the hills, no doubt. Or France."

"But if you have a bairn you must love it like any other. It will have one fine Scots parent at any rate."

"I'd rather it had two."

She turned her head and gazed at him, her big eyes like glistening pools in the candlelight.

"But that cannot be, Catriona."

"Yes, it can. If a Scotsman put his seed in me too – right now – then I wouldn't know whose child it was. Do you understand, Alan?"

He did not reply.

Her legs had moved apart and somehow his fingers were in the groove of her sex, dabbling in the slickness he found there.

The time for words was over.

THE THREAT

Patricia McKenzie

"WE HAVE NO room for virgins on this ship, Harris."

Anthony Harris recoiled. He loathed Lieutenant Williams. The man was a brutish, dissolute reprobate who had tormented him to the point of despair.

"I will thank you to turn your attention elsewhere," he responded stiffly, acutely aware of the pause in conversation at the mess table. In the ensuing silence, his colour fluctuated wildly.

Lieutenant Williams slouched back in his chair, teeth flashing. "Take my word for it, Harris." He glanced around meaningfully at their fellow officers. "I'm the expert around here."

Williams' observation produced boisterous laughter and some knee-slapping from Jones. Encouraged by their rowdy support, he narrowed his eyes contemptuously. "You need an education, Harris. I order you to go to 18 Rue Lafayette."

"I will speak to Captain –"

"You speak to Captain Rawlings and you'll be sorry you didn't join the church."

Surrounded by their laughter, Sub-Lieutenant Harris swallowed. He could see no alternative. His parents would be mortified if he failed in his career as a naval officer. They would, however, be even more devastated if they discovered his destination. At all costs he must protect his pious father and his fragile, retiring mother from disgrace.

"By the way," Williams continued slyly, eyes circling the officers to underscore their complicity in Harris' discomfort, "we expect you to bring us a token – a lady's garter perhaps, or, in your case, something even more intimate."

Faced with Anthony's blank stare, he twitched his nose meaningfully, then broke into a loud guffaw. He misjudged the rim of his glass. Port spilled down his uniform. "Damn."

Anthony mumbled, "As you say, Sir," and rose to leave the mess.

"Attention!" Williams barked, shifting his haunches because his breeches had suddenly become too tight. "Tonight." He pointed his finger forcefully. "Or I'll bugger you myself."

A blow would have been more welcome; that, at least, he could take like a man. Humiliation beaded his brow and weakened his knees. Disobedience was not in his nature. "Yes, Sir."

"Sounds like a girl, don't he?"

Their merriment followed him to his bunk. Although he could hear Williams, loud among the other officers, nevertheless, he shot several uneasy glances over his shoulder. He was afraid of Williams. The man was a beast. If Anthony stayed, Williams would come behind him and tear off his breeches.

"Dear God," he whispered, unable to find words which would not make his shame worse. Even as he tried to muster himself to leave the ship, he was forced to realize that his member had stiffened in a disgusting fashion.

Freezing rain tinkled on the deck already shimmering with a hard ice crust. It was not a night to be abroad. Anthony was cheered to think he might be the only caller at 18 Rue Lafayette. He hunched deep inside the collar of his greatcoat, but the chill precipitation trickled down his neck.

In the warren of narrow, perilous streets above the harbour he would find harlots who sold their bodies. The thought made him sick. He had never ventured inside a house of ill repute. His father had frequently preached that no decent man would lower himself to carnal pleasure. The condemnation had been strong enough to make his mother's cheeks flame from the front pew of St Albion's.

Carnal pleasure. The lusts of the flesh. Words to make his spirit cringe as he wiped the rain from his eyes. Rain suspiciously tainted with salt.

From his arrival on the ship last month, Williams had goaded him, particularly in front of his fellow officers. Yet, in spite of the humiliation, their presence gave him protection. When alone with his superior officer, Anthony had to bear the man's breath on his mouth, the thick hands fondling his arse.

He clamped his jaw to stop it trembling.

But there was no reprieve – especially when Williams spied his straining member.

A response he feared would bring dishonour.

Often he wakened from a dream of Williams, tongue thrust deep into his mouth and sinking deeper so that his stomach lurched violently.

Nothing in his life had prepared him for Williams.

Now, as his boots slipped precariously on the iced cobblestones, he considered shooting Williams. Daily, his honour had been increasingly compromised. If he didn't kill Williams, he would have to do away with himself.

A horseman trotted out of the dark, the horse's flanks nudging Anthony against a stone wall as they passed and disappeared in the gloom. Very few lanterns remained lit in the gusting wind, and those which were still burning showed only a dim glow through their sleeted surfaces.

He was lost. The few excursions he'd made into the town had given him only a general sense of its lay-out. Rue Lafayette ran as a division between the lower and upper town – a transitional area where classes mingled in a manner foreign to England.

Climbing, and nearly blinded by the sleet, he stumbled over a woman sheltering in the lee of an ancient city gate which marked his street. For a coin, she gave him drunken directions which he did his best to follow. Nevertheless, it was quite some time, much, much longer than he'd expected, before he found a doorway which seemed to match her description.

The small obscure sign could not be read. He fingered the coated lettering but he was none the wiser. Prepared to be in error, he lifted the brass knocker and rapped it sharply.

The wind keened at his back. He rapped again. Creaking a

protest, the massive door swung slowly open. A man seized his arm to pull him inside.

Unthinking, he stepped across the threshold into total darkness. The door slammed behind him and a bolt thudded into place. Only then did he remember his Captain's warnings about this port, the men who had disappeared and those who had returned unfit for duty.

If it were not for Williams and his need to bring back a token, he would have fled.

"I would appreciate a light, if you please."

"At your wish, Sir."

The softness of the woman's voice and her heavily accented English did nothing to lull Anthony's apprehension. He feared losing his virginity and, worse, perhaps wanting or liking sexual intercourse.

A lamp brightened from the far end of a very narrow room. Its mellow light bathed the woman's bare breasts in gold as she straightened. Black hair coiled high on her head in an intricate coil. Garnet pendants hung from her ears and another large stone lay between her breasts, darker, with its hint of purple, than the dusky crimson on her nipples and mouth.

She signalled, and the serving man brought the lamp forward to shine on Anthony. "You are very young," her voice chided.

"I . . . uh, am old enough to serve as an officer in His Majesty's Royal Navy."

The sallow features of the man holding the lamp remained expressionless. A ribbon held his hair in a loose *queque*; his faded livery had seen better days.

"Yes," the woman sighed, "you are very young. You have brought a card, perhaps?"

Anthony stared in the direction of her voice. In the near dark where she stood, her flesh offered comfort, a voluptuousness not to be found at sea. He licked his lower lip, feeling its texture against his tongue. "I have a guinea."

"We were expecting someone else." Her lush mouth widened in a near smile. "But he is too late. Come here."

Swallowing the lump in his throat, he stepped closer. A satin bodice, laced tight as a corset, cupped her rounded breasts. Velvet, the same shade of amber, sheathed her upper arms, then widened to loose sleeves cuffed at the wrists. The skirt's seductive folds invited a man to scoop them up as an opulent backdrop to her hips and thighs. Mixed with his incredulous wonder was a desire to throw her down on the carpet.

She watched him steadily, assessing his mood. "What is your pleasure?"

"I . . . uh . . ."

"Yes, young and –" she raised her hand to his cheek "– very smooth."

The liveried servant moved towards a back doorway with the essential lamp. She paused at the door.

Anthony hesitated. He was on the brink of sin. If it had not been for Williams, he would not be here.

His guinea would purchase a token. He could leave with his virtue intact.

From the doorway drifted perfume – musky, enticing. The lamp silhouetted her form, female and curving, the fateful lure of the siren. He could have more for his guinea than a token.

Still he hesitated.

"We are very skilled. We will know what to do."

Lamplight beckoned from the next room. He shifted his breeches and straightened his shoulders before following.

Four-foot logs crackled in a stone fireplace. Warm air embraced him, and instinctively he put out his hands to the flames.

"Theresa will take your coat."

Small hands were already pulling his coat from his shoulders. He turned his head to find a girl in a diaphanous shift bundling the cold wet of his greatcoat in her arms. Her small breasts and narrow pelvis reminded Anthony of a young boy, with clean, slim lines.

She watched him, wide eyes candid.

His breath dried in his throat. His tongue flicked at the corner of his mouth, thrusting against the soft inner tissue as if he already held the girl's mouth captive.

"Allow me to offer you a brandy." His hostess gestured him towards a second armchair on the far side of the fire.

The middle-aged servant brought two filled glasses on a silver tray. Never having tasted brandy, Anthony sipped cautiously. The golden liquid burned his throat before settling in a comfortable glow in his stomach. Abruptly more confident, Anthony drank deeper.

The woman peered at him over the rim of her glass. "You see how well we treat our guests." She rested her head against the back of the chair, which stretched her neck and drew attention to the fullness of her breasts and the dusky valley nestled between them. Dipping her index finger in the brandy, she placed a drop on each nipple.

In spite of the liquor, Anthony's mouth was dry. Swallowing, licking his lips, he leaned forward, drawn by the matte density of her flesh.

Slowly, her finger slid the length of her throat from her chin to her collarbone, where it came to rest, caressing the declivity with small strokes. Her lips parted; her eyelids sank.

Anthony leaned further forward, heat rising from his loins but at a loss. "What am I to do?" he croaked hoarsely.

The woman's dark eyes narrowed slightly as she played with her tumbler. "You said you have a guinea."

"It is all I have. I hope it is enough."

Her eyes flashed towards the servant, who immediately refilled Anthony's glass. "Sit back in your chair. Let the brandy take the cold from your bones. Watch Theresa and Henri. They will show you what to do."

He shook his head slightly, to clear the fumes which seemed to be affecting his vision. How could he have forgotten the lovely nymph Theresa? Groggily, he turned his head back to the room, which was low and beamed in a black-stained wood. An exceptionally wide sleeping couch occupied most of the space. Theresa lay on her side, facing him, her head propped on an elbow. One ankle rested on the bolster at the far end, separating her thighs.

Anthony stared in wonder, his face hot with embarrassment that he should be privy to a young girl's intimate parts. Shamed as he was, he couldn't look away. Blood pounded in his ears; he gripped the wooden arm of his chair.

She was so lovely, so innocent. He was a beast to consume her with his eyes, to feel the strident strain of his organ against his buttons.

Delicately, she placed her dainty finger between her thighs, pressing on herself, which drew the filmy cloth close to her naked skin. How sweet was her circling touch, how tender the curl of her toes.

In spite of himself, Anthony's hand stole to his erect member, and as she stroked, he stroked. Enflamed, but never losing the rhythm, he watched her pull the filmy material up the length of her slender young body until her sex was exposed. She was so guileless that he shivered with the privilege she'd granted him.

Her index finger delved into the folds of her flesh and came away glistening. She rubbed the clear nectar on her breasts and abdomen. Then, soaking her finger again, she wetted the tip of each erect bud.

Anthony groaned and shifted in his seat. His swollen balls ached with tension. Although he would be damned to hell for the sacrilege, he wanted Theresa, he wanted to touch his lips to those breasts. He knew he was approaching a brink, but his limbs were too heavy to pull back.

When she licked her finger and insinuated her tongue in the apex of two fingers, he started to slide to his knees.

"Wait."

The older woman's sharp command brought him to his senses, but he could not move back into his chair. He remained perched on the edge of the seat, mesmerized by her sweet young body.

Then he saw the boy for the first time. He had come out of the shadows behind the sleeping-cot. Slim and entirely naked, head tilted to one side, he gazed at Anthony. His fine features were a duplicate of the girl's, while his lambent eyes brimmed with dark promise.

"Uh, uh," Anthony could not find a voice to respond to such exquisite beauty. He thought of angels carved in the vestry of his father's church, the pure serene line from brow to chin. Weeks at sea and Williams had starved his soul.

Henri's delicate nostrils flared as he strutted in front of Theresa, the muscles in his buttocks rigid, his erect cock elegant as a rapier.

"Do you see what to do?" The older woman's voice was husky.

Anthony could only shake his head. How could he demean their beauty with his hungry hands? His gross mouth?

"Show him," the woman commanded. And as she spoke,

Anthony realized the servant was pouring more brandy into his tumbler. He drank in relief, glad of the scorching heat on his tongue and in his throat. He had barely finished when the older man unbuttoned his breeches. Before he could protest, the woman ordered, "Take them off." Embarrassed by his awkwardness, he removed his boots, stockings, breeches and smalls. The man had his sword and the woman was unfastening his tunic.

Everything happened so quickly, he almost fell back into his chair. He made some sort of gesture to cover his erect member, but the man pulled his hands away.

He blinked. Theresa looked different. Her eyes glittered, her virginal lips seemed almost depraved.

"Dear God," he murmured, hand gripped around his engorged member, "I cannot tell angel from devil."

Henri turned slightly and looked over his shoulder at Anthony, eyes wickedly salacious.

"My God, my God," Anthony continued to murmur, rocking on his naked buttocks. The room spun. He peered desperately at the young couple, trying to keep them in focus.

The boy knelt on the floor at Theresa's knees. When he leaned forward, his cock and her sex remained visible. First his tongue fluttered towards her opening. The girl arched her back, thrusting her pelvis forward and widening the gap between her straight thighs.

Theresa tilted her chin. The muscles in her throat rippled. Henri's tongue teased and prodded her clitoris; he flattened the surrounding skin to make it stand out and then lapped its swollen shaft. She kept her pelvis steady, but her nails raked her faint areolae. Shudders shook her frame; shadows curved beneath her cheekbones. As the boy's tormenting tongue flicked and prowled around her entrance, she pinched her nipples between the sharp tips of her nails.

"See how my children love the flesh," the woman chuckled, but Anthony barely registered her words. He knew what to do. He was down on his knees, scrambling towards the sleeping couch, jaw slack with lust.

Tears stung his eyes as he gazed at the sweetness of her cleft and the tender flesh of her inner thighs.

But it was not to be. Large hands grabbed him around the waist and pulled him backwards.

"My Theresa," the woman was saying, "is very modest. She must not be frightened by a stranger. First you will practise on me, and if you are good, I will let you go to her."

The whimper died in Anthony's throat. Her velvet blurred, then came into focus. The servant let go of his waist.

Laughing darkly, the woman raised her amber skirt, inch by slow, agonizing inch, to expose black stockings and the thick curling thatch at the apex of her white thighs. Anthony wept in earnest. When a broad hand clutched his cock at the base, he smelled Williams' raw breath.

She opened the petals of her sex, glistening purple with juice; drops seeped from her opening. He closed his eyes and thrust out his tongue into her ripe core. When she pressed against his ears with her thighs, he feared he would suffocate in the wet folds of her flesh.

The hand on his cock was inexorable. Cloth roughly abraded his buttocks, but he was too disorientated to remember exactly what had happened, or who could be taking advantage of his nakedness.

Breathing through his mouth, he nosed deeper into the well of her sex. His cock, which had drooped in despair when he was dragged away, began to fill as the callused hand maintained a steady rhythm.

The shame of his degradation filled him with self-loathing and an unholy excitement.

Images of redemption beckoned. The sweet fall of Theresa's earlobe. Henri's winsome half-smile. The untainted grace of their limbs. To press his lips against the tender curve of her breast would be heaven. Though he would never be worthy. Not when his soul had been sullied by the taunts of Williams.

Yes, he was base – indescribably base – his body carnal and full of vile lust. Never could he expect his parents to welcome him back to the rectory. Nor could he dream of an angel at his own hearth, honouring his virtue with her love.

Salt tears mixed with the woman's strong juices. He flared his haunches to the coarse fingers exploring the sensitive path from the root of his cock to that unmentionable part of his anatomy which a Christian man would never expose.

Oh, yes, he was vile, unfit to be born. The woman's thighs

tightened around his head as his tongue quickened in her hole. He squeezed her bottom in his hands, grabbing hold of the quivering flesh which was his damnation.

Groans escaped his throat as his arse swayed from side to side, raised like a female in heat.

Then he could feel his arse-cheeks being pulled to the side, to widen his crack. A perverse thrill seized him so that he did not sink with shame but thrust it out, widening the aperture for the most abominal sinful act – the act which Williams had so recently threatened.

Anthony burrowed deep in the woman's cunny, and as her musk strengthened the male organ prodded his tight, virginal entrance, demanding admittance.

His cock throbbed with the agony of his destruction. He gasped and moaned and shoved his arse backwards for more sensation, almost fainting when the rough palm again pumped his member vigorously. Gasping and groaning, he was feasting on her engorged flesh as if his true nature were that of a base animal.

With a grunt, the man broke through into his rectum. The pain roiled in his abdomen, raw and punishing. At the first sharp explosion, Anthony stiffened, then his fingers scrabbled on the woman's bottom as he fought his way out of the depths.

Before he could break free, a fierce heat widened in his core, to shudder in great spasms through his entire body. He pushed, he thrust to lengthen the penetration, to throw himself back on the shaft which so cruelly split him.

The scream in his throat was that of an animal, guttural and coarse as the hands which had prepared him for this violation.

His coming was hard, a spearing which left him abandoned and totally spent. He tried to pull himself upright, only to stagger and fall to the floor.

For some time he leaned on his hands, cursing himself and the body which wanted to curl into untroubled sleep.

When he could focus, he raised his eyes to Theresa, who was lying on the sleeping-cot, directly facing him. Her thin body was slack, the filmy material carelessly rucked around her hips. She still rested her head on her elbow, but now there was a weariness in the droop of her lids. The boy lay behind her, a careless arm flung along the length of her naked thigh.

With an effort, Theresa lifted her free hand and extended it to Anthony.

He traversed the floor on his knees. Reverently, he pressed his lips against her slim fingers, and when she twisted her wrist to let him kiss her palm, his heart threatened to burst with joy.

He was not to be afforded this privilege for long. He had laid but a dozen kisses in the soft hollow between her thumb and ring finger, when she withdrew it.

"You can dress now." The woman spoke firmly above the crackling fire. "You have fully used your guinea."

Ashamed and awkward, Anthony began the business of retrieving his uniform while they watched in silence. It was only when he had himself in reasonable order that he could properly take leave of his hostess.

Ill-prepared for such an occasion, he resorted to formality. The woman acknowledged his expression of gratitude with a calculating smile.

"I–I shall tell others about 18 Rue Lafayette," he stuttered, although he was not one to speak of private matters with other men, least of all his fellow officers.

"Indeed, Sir." Her smile widened to expose yellowing teeth. "You have erred. We are number 24."

If Anthony had not been so gauche he would have realized earlier that this establishment bore no resemblance to those which Williams frequently described. Flustered, and unable to speak sensibly, he allowed the servant to help him into his greatcoat.

The woman's throaty voice stopped him at the door. "My family will be honoured to serve you, Monsieur, when you have another guinea at your disposal."

The man whom Anthony had taken to be a servant, rather than a husband, bowed his head.

Anthony closed his eyes. Soured brandy rose in his throat as a wave of nausea swept over him. No matter where Williams had intended to send him, it could not be as depraved as this room.

He swung on his heel to express his indignation, but the fire flickered prettily over the mother and her two children. A longing to remain almost unmanned him. He had to hasten to the outer door, where emotion prevented him from acknowledging the husband's courteous farewell.

Stars glittered through ragged breaks in the cloud. The sleet had melted and all might have been well if he had not forgotten the token for Williams.

He could not bring himself to beg at their door.

By the time he reached the harbour, he was trembling. For lack of evidence, Williams would carry out his threat. The ignominy of his position could not be borne.

For some time he stared at the ship anchored in the harbour. His Majesty's vessel was a proud example of the great navy which ruled the seas. It should not be demeaned by men like Williams.

Nor men like himself.

Dawn picked out the tall masts from the surrounding dark as Anthony slipped back into the town.

SMILE, MONA

M. Christian

THE WIFE OF Francesco del Giocondo arose as the morning sun, far too hard and harsh for that time of the year and her luxurious frame of mind, started its unrelenting crawl across her bedclothes.

Her rise to wakefulness was an ascent through billowing clouds of satisfaction, a perfumed garden of memories decorated with recollections of the night before. As she blinked away intangible dreams that were nothing less than delightfully twisted versions of only a few hours ago, she felt her body respond with its own retrospection: a physical reminiscence demonstrated by a vibrant tingling through her nipples as they gently rubbed against the satin of her bedclothes – an action that normally she would not have been even aware of, but that morning, since it followed that night, was a brilliant, sensual echo, a thrilling reminder.

Feeling her nipples, thrilled with the memory, she smiled and ran a delicate hand down her body – starting with the hollow at her throat (a memory of a kiss there), going to the hard plain that preceded the swelling of her breasts (a kiss there, too), the warm valley between them (many kisses, a butterfly storm of them), their hot underside (where lips had tasted her ocean-flavored sweat), the gentle curve of her belly (a playful brushing of lips to her navel) and down to the tangled forest of her mons, her sex – and all the delightful sensual complexities that had been explored (many times) just a handful of hours preceding.

Thinking again of the night before, she smiled.

Fully awake, fully aware, she dipped a narrow finger between the lips of her sex and relished the thrill of her moisture. Bringing the same finger upwards, she slowly rode the shivering pleasure from her opening to the bead at the top, the delicate charm she'd had worked with feverish abandon when the sun had been asleep, as had most – ah, but not all – of the household. Memories again, but this time with the bitter flavor of disobedience: many kinds of the forbidden. Too many to count on a single rosary, too many to ever be forgiven.

Shame bloomed on her face. Too many sins ever to be forgiven – nothing could wash them from her, for there was not enough water in all of the Lord's oceans. For a moment it encompassed her, filling her so completely that it all spilled out as hot tears on the coarse threads of her bed. It peaked as a sob, a deep, muscle-convulsing reflex of self-pity that pressed her body down into the bed.

Many faces appeared in her mind, all of them stern and disapproving:

Monsignor Manchesti, his cold gray eyes looking down, down, down at her from the pulpit, the Bible in one hand, the other a fist of righteous indignation. In her mind, his lips formed a parade of abuse, accusations she was horribly guilty of, more so for the joy she'd taken in them.

Her father, who'd taken such pride in the artifice of her careful upbringing. He'd often bragged, with the cool arrogance of the truly skilled, that he'd turned his daughter from a creature of unclean womanly flesh into the art that is a refined lady. She remembered (shame, shame) the self-satisfaction he'd shown at her marriage to Francesco, the glow that had encompassed him as his craftsmanship was praised over and over again – awarded the highest prize: that the groom shook his hand with sincere delight in his eyes and on his lips.

And finally Francesco himself . . . a stern visage with a dirty white torrent of a beard, a voice like breaking stones, eyes like gray-iron pikes that looked at – and saw – everything, with a successful, powerful man's measuring scales. She'd known, or at least suspected, that when the proposal was put forth to her father, when the arrangements had been made, the contract had been finalized, that she was entering into a life with this man, this battlement of bounty, this wall against diminishing assets. At the time she had looked on the arrangement with approval – who would not have, even if they had had a say in the matter? This was Francesco del Giocondo, the Prosperous, the Wealthy, the Powerful. Marriage to him was more than a step up; it was a climb to places where few in her family could ever have viewed: she was more than fortunate, more than lucky, she was a prize – both to her groom, because of her beauty, and to her family, because it elevated them to the heights of being in-laws to *the* Francesco del Giocondo.

Francesco . . . a pot belly ornamented with curls of hair coarser than those on a pig's snout. Feet that looked as if they should have gripped the battlements of a Cathedral. Breath like . . . privies would have been cruel, but a more accurate description would have diminished the shock of it arriving to the nose. His nightly duties were performed with the grace of a butcher, the skill of a house painter, and the delicacy of stonemason. On their wedding night, the bells of which were still ringing in her ears, drowning out any thoughts from her mind and soul, he'd taken her – an act which, to that day, reminded her of the placement of his seal on some document: a quick downward thrust, a quick rocking to and fro to make sure the job was done thoroughly, correctly, then a jerk away so as to avoid sticking. Yes, like the placing of his seal – a handshake between estates.

Francesco failed in few things, and it was her humiliation, and his, that one of those things he did not succeed in was the act of love.

For all of his . . . lacking, though, she thanked whatever had decided to look over her that he did have another passion, another burning desire – something that had made it possible for her to know real pleasure, real, pure, ecstasy here on Earth.

Francesco was insanely jealous – something she was immeasurably grateful for.

The disapproving faces . . . Monsignor Manchesti, her father, Francesco . . . hovered in her memory, the heat of their mental accusations matching the growing heat of the day. But slowly, like an old fire being steadily breathed back into crackling life, a new kind of warmth, heat, started to rise in her. Two things steadily boiled away their disapproving visages: her memory of the night before and the intimate ballet of her fingers along the moist seam of her sex.

Where again . . . ? She tried to recall the lock that had opened in her just hours before, letting her fingers trace a thrilling path along warm, wet folds, through a slightly sticky tangle of hairs . . . until – *there* – she touched the secret place, the lock that had been so skillfully picked.

A shudder raced through her, a cascade of brilliant sensations starting at the throbbing, minute bead between her clenched thighs. Yes, *there* – that point, that one, single perfect part of her, the one that she had been shown. *There*, the entrance to the blessed (for it must be to feel so good) place.

Without her true consent – save that of her body, acting on its own – her fingers moved in their passionate dance around, over, and tapping on the bead at the top of her moist – no, *wet* – folds. Again, she felt herself rise up, take flight beyond the confines of her chambers, to go to that magical and . . . divine? Was that sacrilege, blasphemy? Was that against the teachings of the Holy Church? Against the will of God and his One Son?

Questions her mind and soul had . . . *somewhat* questioned, but – truth to tell – such deep ponderings were well beyond her at that moment, there in her warm, hot, steaming, burning room. Then, there, all she could think about was the pleasure roaring through her body, a fire consuming parchment, a mad storm of flesh: the satin of lips on hers, and landing (thrills!) along her body. The pliant strength of hands, also landing with fierce grips along her melting self. The sensation of being consumed, the incredible bursts of pleasure that had made her body act with spasms, moans, and gasps of its own – the incredible delight in being made the feast that was then nibbled, licked and swallowed. The pure delight of being filled, of having a firmness enter her most secret of places, and generating still more beautiful waves of delight.

Memories, recall, matching the play of her hands. One, her right, was lost to the pleasuring she was conducting to herself, the delightful manipulations of her fingers to the sweet bead, as well as alternately entering and leaving (to a wet, smacking chorus of sounds that reminded her, alternatively, of their kisses as well as of the act itself), while the left had reached up – almost beyond her will – and begun rough rolls and pulls to her nipples, trying to match the driving desire of when the night had been dark and the moon full, bright and silver.

Slowly, but then more rapidly – water spilling from a great bucket – the power started to fill her. Again, she viewed it as a kind of rapture, a pure, shining light of bodily pleasure. Again, she felt it burst through her – till she was it and it was everything, everywhere.

With a scream that she instantly feared would bring a knock to her chamber door, it peaked and exploded – fireworks within, the brilliance of a sunrise coming from that secret place between her legs and traveling up, up and up to her belly, chest, heaving breasts painted with reflections of perspiration, to her nipples (knotted with delight) and up and out through her throat – and that cry of bestial pleasure.

Calmness, the aftermath of the storm. Even though the room was steadily growing warm, she stayed in the oven of her bed until her heart ceased its urgent knocks in her chest and her legs and thighs had stopped their phantom twitching runs.

Yes, the phantoms were there – but against this power, such pure pleasure, they stayed distant, ghostly, and completely insubstantial.

Rising, the wife of Francesco del Giocondo stretched and elongated her body in the hard sunlight that entered her chambers. With a wry smile, she recalled who she had been, the young girl who had accepted Francesco's arrangement (as if her consent was required), his home, and her state. So different she was from that innocent. So fuller and prouder she'd become.

The wife of Francesco del Giocondo smiled, feeling the play of muscles beneath her cheek, tasting the truth of her pride. The day was fat, warm and long – and though it threatened much disappointment, great boredom, and tremendous humiliation at being the prize given by her family and won by Francesco, it also, always, brought the promise of night: the guards at her door, their stern instructions coldly enforced –

– and the delights their presence guaranteed.

Ah, yes, she thought, moving toward the window and her morning's toilet, *I must somehow thank Francesco. I must definitely show my appreciation for such joy he's brought me.*

Placing the ornate bowl on the floor, she rose and carefully washed her hands, a rosary tripping through her mind, as was her habit – till giggles floated up out of her throat in recall and irony. Drying her hands, she squatted and released a slightly painful stream into the bowl, thinking again – and giggling again – how such a beautiful part of herself, one she'd just been introduced to, could also produce such foul waters.

Clean and relieved, she rang her bell – the one her mother had given her. Fine Venetian glass, with a chime like an angel's voice. Aware, and cautious of its delicacy, she rang it, once, releasing her servants from their wait outside.

As they came in, smiling slight smiles towards their lady this morning, Maria and Catherine skillfully assisted her into her garments of that day. Since the road to Florence was a long one, and the day already hot and dusty, her clothes thus reflected the necessities of the trip. As the women's hands went about their trained duties – with or without their conscious violition – she felt, again, the heat rise in her body, mirroring the steady growing temperature of the morning.

The servants were good, skilled – and could be nothing less for La Gioconda, the wife of Francesco del Giocondo. Their chatter was negligible, because she had not spoken to them, and their hands were quick and precise as they dressed her. They were good but, for her, for the wife of Francesco del Giocondo, they were only fixtures: mobile, breathing furniture – all part of her life as wife to Francesco, of her existence in his lavish home. She could not really notice them as one could perceive the shape of a table-leg, the distortions in a window's glass, or the colors in a tapestry. They were just Maria (the short brunette) and Catherine (the tall redhead).

They were not, and never could be, Juliana.

That name. Even thinking of it her body responded with a wave of pleasure, a surging, warm swell of delight. Juliana: her nipples, again, swelled and crinkled in fantasy and memory. Juliana: her belly grew warm, eagerly awaiting exciting caresses and endearing kisses. Juliana: and, again, the secret revealed between her legs flowered with heat and . . . yes, she could feel it, an unexpected yet delightful moisture.

Juliana: thinking made her real in memory, a quick cascade of physical and emotional images, illustrated cards flipping through her mind – a flurry of tastes, touches, sights, sounds, smells and the complex mixtures of all and more (meaning the feelings they all also contained).

As Maria (the short brunette) and Catherine (the tall redhead) added their last touches to their lady, so that she might journey, her mind was elsewhere, lost among this memory, that recollection. Maria might have been deftly – because it was her specialty, her duty – combing her silken dark locks, and affixing a simple gold and lapis comb there. Catherine might have been adjusting her color, making sure her dress was perfectly worn for the appearance of La Gioconda beyond their own walls, onto the magnificent streets of Florence. They might have been doing their duties, but to her, to the object of their ministrations, they were invisible, unimportant – next to the retrospections of their mistress, their lady.

Juliana.

Yes, she thought amid the swilling storm of recall, she must find something, some gift or gesture, to give to Francesco to show her appreciation. Without his bitter jealousy, his possesive claim to the status of her beauty, she never would have had the . . . yes, pleasure, of knowing the girl Juliana.

Their first time together was the hottest memory – both of passion and of simple, pure logic. A too-warm night, the humid summers of the hills. Francesco on some errand to the great cities of the South, trying to impress the people of Rome with his simple *nouveau* wealth, still-gleaming coins, and so away from his lavish home and his pretty, pretty (and very bored) wife.

The night, indeed, had been a wet, hot blanket wrapped around her – too warm for anything, including sleep. Too hot for anything, save the painful shimmering knowledge of her own baking body. She had endured it as long as she could – being not of the class of her husband, she had, at first, been wary and guilty around the use of the servants. They had appeared to her too close to what she felt she was beyond her status as property – just simple, honest people. She had toyed, many times during that humid, dark night, with the idea of descending into the depths of the house for a cool respite, some chilled wine from the house's stock. But with these thoughts came the visage of her husband (before she viewed him more and more as an impotent ghost, bellowing empty threats) and his decrees, his instructions.

The Lady was not to leave her chambers after dark.

The Lady was not to have any male callers, ever.

Her needs were only to be met by . . .

There, then, that thought, that memory – the wife of Francesco del Giocondo . . . smiled. Such a simple rule, born in the simple and frightened mind of a simple and frightened man. So deathly frightened of being cuckold that he would slam the door, post guards, and forbid any entry to anyone . . . save the one who, indeed, would steal what he never really owned.

Juliana.

It was, finally, the heat itself that drew her to pick up the priceless Venetian glass bell and chime it. What kind of heat was shining her body with a patina of reflections the wife of Francesco del Giocondo didn't suspect – didn't recognize in herself till many days, weeks, later. But still, the cause, the embers of the heat she felt that night; she did pick up that bell, and did chime it.

The sound was crystal-clear, sharp and carrying. It reached the two footmen posted by the door outside. From the footmen, it was relayed with shouted instructions to the servants' quarters, from there to the ears of the downstairs maid. The downstairs maid was named Juliana.

The memory of her was rich and fertile, full of myriad details – like precious gifts she'd clutched tight to her chest, lest some of them slip away. The wife, her body making the motions she was used to, allowed herself to be touched with the gentle flutters of the servant's finishing. She allowed herself to be spoken to, to be addressed and catered to, and eventually walked down the marble steps to the main doors, and from the main doors to the carriage waiting outside.

To all those in the house, from the footmen to the maids, she was simply their lady, the wife of Francesco del Giocondo. But inside she was lost in the delightful memories of that one hot night, when the girl Juliana had made her feel something so different, so away from just being La Gioconda.

She'd arrived, Juliana had, bearing a pitcher of cool house wine, tapped from the great casks buried deep. Embarrassment burned La Gioconda's cheeks, made even the Lady of the House dip her head in submission to this young servant girl, shy at needing something so basic as a cool drink on a hot night, ashamed at her imprisonment that made her so dependent for such a simplicity.

Juliana . . . smiled. There was an earthiness, a scent of the soil about the girl. She was shorter than the wife of Francesco del Giocondo, a head, maybe a head and some more. Her hair was as black as the night outside, from what she could see of it under her simple servant's cap. Her bones were earthen bones, as simple, as pleasant as her Lady's. Even then, not knowing her as she would later, the wife of Francesco del Giocondo enjoyed looking at her, especially watching her smile.

Despite their glory, their shimmering delight, memories lie. They become clouded and indistinct, they become misshapen from wishes, from slight embarrassments, and, more than anything, because at the time there is simply too much going on to remember everything. Even for someone to whom memories are more precious than the jewels she'd been given on her wedding day, La Gioconda's memories weren't complete.

She knew that they'd spoken – La Gioconda, the lady of the house, the wife of Francesco del Giocondo, and Juliana, just a maid. Of what, though, she had no idea. She knew that they had, though, she knew that the young earthen girl with the midnight hair had spoken – shyly at first, inquisitive as to her Lady's health and comfort, but then, as they recognized in each other a common background, the words had come much easier, a natural flow among two women who knew that they had grown up in similar villages, homes, families.

It was hard to say, though, exactly what words, sentences, they had said.

Then . . . it was hard to say exactly when. But the fact was there, hot and burning in her mind as the carriage bumped and swung lazily back and forth on the long road to proper Florence – undeniable and glorious.

Sinful and wrong.

Beautiful and loving.

Sinful and wrong.

Priceless and endearing.

Sinful and wrong.

Magical and . . . loving.

They had done it, a gentle lean forward, a touch of lips to lips – an innocent, and yet not, *kiss*. It might have been all of that, more than likely sinful and wrong, but La Gioconda, the lady of the house, the wife of Francesco del Giocondo, would do it again and again and again if the opportunity (and she prayed to the God she suspected would condemn her for the sin) arose to do it again.

The kiss had opened a door, swung it wide, showing her a magnificent place. It looked simple and humble on the outside: wide, pleasant hips; strong legs like the columns of some Roman temple; a dark patch of gentle curls over a hidden (as yet) valley; large breasts hanging heavy, tipped by dark brown discs, the thick meat of rich nipples; and skin the color of thick cream – as fine as cherished silk.

The places Juliana had taken her that night, and many moonlight times thereafter – she couldn't express it. She didn't have the words, the grasp of the basic vocabulary to speak it, even if she dared. She knew some things, though, some things that were undeniable about what they did together – it was a high, high form of something she'd only tasted – and never from her husband: *Love*.

If this was a sin, she knew, as she was gently rocked into a dreaming daze by the traveling of the coach, then she would seek out more, and willingly build up a magnificent penance.

So many discoveries, so many voyages. Who would have thought that Juliana of the downstairs could have led her Lady – as well as any Marco Polo – from where she had been to where she was now . . .

. . . which was in her carriage, riding the road to Florence, and *smiling* . . .

A kiss was all it had taken – a kiss on the lips and on other places. A member of the same sex as downstairs Juliana, La Gioconda thought she knew herself; but that was before – before the kiss and the other kisses. She knew, for instance, the pleasure of her own nipples, but who could have ever expected the incredible delights of another woman's mouth upon them? Or who could have foreseen the beautiful heat of another woman's tongue within her own mouth? A kiss on the lips, a kiss there, and that hot night burst into flames – licking, consuming desire that obscured the world beyond that room with their distortions of smoldering lust. They, that night and the nights thereafter, were just two women together in sinful conflagrations of desire.

Juliana's nipples . . . yes, thinking of them, even then, in the seasick rolling of the coach on the road, stirred La Gioconda's body, blowing the embers of her memory with new breaths of desire: she craved, again, Juliana's lips on her own, on her nipples; she hungered for Juliana's in her own mouth as well – to feel their swelling, salty presence in between her lips and against the eager flickerings of her tongue.

In the rolling coach, it was a force of will for her to hold her hands calmly, regally to her sides and just watch – or pretend to watch – the simple homes and then the elegant piazzas roll by beyond. What they itched and ached to do was cup herself, as Juliana had done, and as she had done many times with the memory of the little downstairs maid. She felt the muscles in her pale hands twitch with the expectation, the need to feel again the way Juliana had made her feel – the maid's hands reaching down to gently spread her trembling thighs and feel, with quick, knowledgeable strokes of hot fingers, the slick texture of La Gioconda's melting sex.

The bed, the eiderdown sea of expensive cloth, had become a place of illicit and sinful love. Giggling, like girls scurrying amid some mischief, Juliana had taken her hand and pulled her – barely resisting – to the silks and satins, and there had eased her down, gently parted her legs, her thighs, and then Juliana, from downstairs, had . . .

Kisses . . . other places. No man had made her feel the way that Juliana had. It was that simple. With the actions of her lips, her tongue and even (terror mixing like a heady spice with desire) her teeth, the little earthen girl, the smiling peasant, had taken the wife of Francesco del Giocondo and led her into a brilliant domain, a place of shuddering joys, gasping delights, whispered promises and gentle sleeps.

Juliana had kissed her in a place that she had never thought she'd owned – and now, days later, looking forward to more days

. . . no, an inaccuracy, *nights* to follow, the wife of Francesco del Giocondo smiled. Juliana had awoken the girl, had shared with her a kind of simple woman magic. Something La Gioconda knew, instantly, there in that coach, more powerful than any of the heavy masculine faces that flicked through her mind – yes, ghostly, yes, powerless and indistinct.

And she had her husband to thank for it. Jealous Francesco, who so feared infidelity that he barred men from her quarters, but whose blind fear had allowed Juliana to enter and take . . . no, another inaccuracy, to *share* with her what Francesco had never, ever possessed: true desire, true passion, true love.

The wife of Francesco del Giocondo smiled at that. She grinned her slight grin all through the ride into the biting smells, discordant sounds and mesmerizing sights of Florence. The smile stayed all through her passage to the studio of the painter, the great Leonardo, commissioned to capture her beauty with paint and skill – to capture her image for her husband.

Her heart, though, belonged to a simple little girl, a little spirit with priceless diamonds for eyes, finest china for a smile, a beautifully glowing hearth in her belly, and the secrets to a woman's true happiness and glory between her legs.

Yes, Mona Lisa smiled – all through the portrait, and for many, many days, and especially nights, thereafter.

Even to this day.

MAHARANEE

Jennifer Footman

HARRY, THE RIGHT Honourable Harold Lawrence Forsythe, MD, FRCS, Edinburgh, had survived the fishing fleet – that gaggle of young women on the ship whose main purpose was to find a husband. He had breathed free of danger since baggage day at Port Said, when the luggage marked "Wanted on Voyage" was exchanged for the hot weather wear.

Why had he kept away from the women on the fishing fleet? Some of them had titillated him. Of course they had. He was a young man – just forty – and he could not help but watch them as they played games on deck, as they giggled and laughed together, their fresh white faces reddening with the sun, freckling or cooking into gold. Or sometimes, when he held a girl during a dance and perfume filled his head, his body responded and he would have to move away to recover.

Life had been so easy in London. Ever since he had graduated he had belonged to a select club of medics who shared a flat in St John's Wood. In addition to sharing the flat they also shared Marie, Sheila, Colleen and Elizabeth. No complications, no disease and total freedom.

Yes, it would be excellent if he could get into a chummery of some sort and have it set up the same way.

The newly appointed Chief Medical Officer for the Indian

Medical Services (IMS) had become totally immersed in India during the three months he had been here. He had toured from end to end: sometimes by ship along the coast and sometimes by the new railway. Thank God he had not had to travel more than a few miles by ghastly *palkee*.

He had been back in Calcutta for a week, and had settled into his hospital and offices, and was in the process of familiarizing himself with the culture of Bengal and the social life of Anglo-India.

He met her at a *durbar*. The Maharanee Cooch Bihar. About thirty, though he found it difficult to tell the ages of these women. In spite of her sari Cooch Bihar walked like a man and talked like a man. Her accent was upper-class English. He had asked her about it.

"Oh, I was one of the first royalty sent out. Willingham and then Girton. A First."

"Impressive."

"Money has some advantages, and my mother was the one with money in our family."

She had offered to take him on a tour of temples and he had accepted eagerly.

Last night he'd tumbled through dreams of her. Dreams where the mosquito net was her sari and it had floated over him. His flesh was a bed of sandalwood and his hair was fine spun gold. He was her flower. She swam in him as a dolphin swims in the sea. He had woken up twice, his hand hard round his penis and finishing, finishing into the clammy sheets. But why this woman? She was royalty, and far above him. She could not be interested in a plain Scots doctor, a man with no money and only the prospect of work and more work. And besides, the politics had changed recently. Up to the '50s mixed liaisons had been smiled on; now they were totally inappropriate. Well . . . not that he was looking for a liaison, but it would be most improper for him to have anything to do with local royalty.

She called for him in a carriage, and the tour started with the Jain temple. The Jains, known by the English as the Jews of India, did things perfectly. The temple was a castle of gold and silver and clean enough to perform surgery off the floor. It was dazzling and awe-inspiring, but perhaps too much, just too much. They proceeded to view about ten other temples of various kinds, and by the early afternoon, though it was cool weather, and the mornings were as fresh as any June morning in Scotland, he was hot, tired and full of temples.

"We must see one more, just one more. And the time is right. The temple to the goddess Kali."

It was totally unlike any of the other temples. Little more than a square of beaten mud surrounded by a wall of bricks, with a raised stage of rough wood in the middle. Six ragged men stood on the stage, as if waiting for something. The stink of blood filled the air. Two men led a white goat onto the stage. It was about the size of a poodle and astonishingly white. Its frantic amber eyes were frenzied with terror. Everything happened so quickly that Harry thought he had blinked and imagined it. One minute there was a goat, and the next minute the head was rolling on the floor and blood gushed out of the cut end of neck and the legs twitched. He swallowed and thought he might be sick. No, he had seen all kinds of horrors in war, and in the hospitals. It would not be appropriate to let himself feel sick.

"We are very lucky to have been here to see it," she said.

"Indeed."

"You look quite . . . quite affected by it."

"Very interesting."

"I should take you back for some tea, or something stronger. Something to take the taste of blood from your mouth."

"Yes, yes, that would be fine."

In the carriage, with the warm fresh air on his face, he brightened.

"Of course it's been banned since . . . let me see – the English started hunting down the Thugs in '29, but it was really about '90 that it became difficult to be a Thug."

"I have read a bit about them. Had some notes sent out to me."

"What do you know?"

"Well . . . that they worship Kali through the killing of travellers, mostly. It has to be done by strangulation."

"Are you really interested in their customs?"

"I'd like to know everything there is to know about India and its customs."

"I will show you something today that you will not see elsewhere."

In her house the shutters kept out the afternoon heat. The floor was a beige mosaic centred by a large Persian carpet. A carved teak Cashmere chaise, two matching armchairs and a table were the only furniture. Many large carpet-covered cushions littered the floor. A small silver bell was on the table. The aura was one of luxury and simplicity. The *punkah* whispered gently above them. They sat side by side on the chaise and she called the bearer to bring some lemonade.

"Or do you want something stronger?"

"No, that's fine, I have a long day tomorrow, and alcohol and heat do not seem to mix."

"This is not hot weather."

"No, I suppose not. Perhaps I will arrange to be doing something in Dargeeling when the really hot weather comes."

"Well, we will have something to drink, and then some food, and discuss this Kali worship."

The lemonade washed the back of his throat with its astringent oils. Yes, just what was needed after the blood and fetor. It was curious how fruit here seemed to have more taste, more smell than any fruit he had tasted.

She nodded to the bearer and he sat back on his haunches, waiting for instruction. She spoke in Hindi, far too fast for Harry to pick up, but he did get the words "scarf" and "show".

The bearer left, to return in a few minutes carrying a sliver tray. On the tray was a fine silk scarf and two medals.

She picked up the scarf and spread it out on her thighs.

"This is a Kali scarf." She held the two medals in her hand and handed them to him. "These are coins my uncle had made for my last birthday. They are quite amusing. They are Kali coins." He examined them. Gold, about two ounces each. They were identical. On one side there was the outline of Kali and on the other the Empress. Victoria had her usual aloof expression.

"Funny? Yes?"

"Funny?"

"I will show you." She placed her glass on the table and tied a coin into each corner of the scarf. She rolled the scarf into a rope.

The bearer lay down on the floor. She stood and walked round him. "Here we have a sleeping traveller and I am a Kali worshipper." With one movement she rolled the man onto his side, slipped the scarf under his neck and drew the two corners round behind his head. "See . . . if I was to kill him I would twist and it would be all over in minutes. Simple."

The bearer seemed quite relaxed, and gave every indication this was not a new activity for him. Harry wondered if the Maharanee used him as an exhibit, or as a specimen for training.

"Would you like to try?" She offered him the scarf. Again the bearer pretended to be asleep. Harry knelt at his side. She lifted the bearer's head and flicked the scarf under at the same time. "See . . . the coins are there to make it easier to twist. I will help you." She leaned back and he smelt her – sandalwood and clean skin and fresh air.

"Here, like this. Just under the laryngeal prominence. We should be able to locate our scarf to compress the common carotid artery." She demonstrated in the way a professor would demonstrate at an anatomy lesson. "One easy flick to place it, then a gradual squeeze. We do not wish to break their necks, but slowly and delightfully to deprive them of oxygen."

She handed the scarf to him, and he tried but seemed to be all thumbs. Why was he trying this? Interest? That was all. No, there was more to it than just interest.

"See . . . you must not hurt him. It has to be good for the sacrifice."

"Good?"

"But of course it must be good. They all die in the delights of sexual ecstasy, worshipping Kali."

"I see."

She sat cross-legged, her head slightly to one side. "Well . . . of course . . . naturally . . . there are many different ways of worship. I consider myself to revere her, but worship her through, as the French say, *la petite mort*. Instead of the true death we kill for a minute or two." She knelt again. "Now this time I will show you a bit more." She talked to the bearer, who nodded and smiled. He lay down again, as if asleep, and she passed the scarf round his neck and squeezed. Harry could hardly breathe. The fire consuming his form burned with a hellish heat and concentrated on his penis. He was a child, watching something his parents were doing; he tried to ignore his loins, but slid his hand into his pants and covered his growth.

"Ah, ay, ahh," the bearer moaned for some moments, then, obviously cyanosed, his eyes glittering, an ecstatic grin on his face, his lips curled from his teeth and his breathing stopped. She loosened the scarf. "*Voilà!*" He rolled over after a few seconds, a look of delight on his face. He stood and pulled himself to attention. His loose pants were wet at the crotch and down one leg. Under the wet spot his erection made itself plain.

"See, it has to be good for the sacrifice too."

They had a light meal of a variety of lentils and rice. When the meal was finished she offered him a cigarette and took one herself, and waited for him to light it for her. This he did, looking into her eyes – violet, gold, black, white. He had to be mad. What was happening to him? He had only just met her. She could not be sending the messages he imagined she was sending.

"Well, did you like your food?"

"Yes, my first real Indian meal."

"Let's hope it's not your last."

"I am confident it will not be." Sometimes Harry had to laugh at his own precision, even pompousness. He excused himself by saying that life was so much simpler if everyone knew exactly where they stood and things were writ high and clear.

She poured him a fine black aromatic coffee rich with cream. "So, what brings a doctor – and such a skilled and famous doctor – here?"

"Hardly famous."

"Oh, I know about your work on cholera and typhoid. Know your reputation."

"Overrated. I have always been interested in India. Ever since an uncle of mine came here and was killed in the Mutiny and . . ." He ran a finger round the edge of his boots.

"You are not relaxed." She called the bearer and gave some instructions, and almost immediately a young woman came in carrying a bowl and towels. The young woman knelt at his feet, removed boots and socks and washed his feet, massaged them with oil and patted them with an astringent lotion. His skin had become one vast erogenous zone; every inch was electrified and erect; every hair stood to attention.

"The British dress as if at a funeral all the time. We, now . . . we are comfortable all the time. See this sari: it flows." She stood to show it off, like a young girl with a new dress.

"Indeed it does." Visions of the night haunted him. The mosquito net and her sari. She had a fine strong build. The torso of a man, but for the large breasts. Her hair was traditionally dressed, into one long braid down her back. She had the fullest lips he had ever seen, almost verging on the delicious fullness of one African woman he had known when he had been on tour in Kenya. God, she had used those lips to lead him onto levels of ecstasy no man had ever climbed.

He tried to be the doctor again. "Yes, it is very healthy. Very healthy."

"See, I keep myself fit as I did in England. I walk and run and ride and swim when the climate is suitable. We own half of Bihar, of course. Or my family does. I was married briefly, but my husband died and I could not be bothered to marry again. And of course they had banned *suttee*. Not that I would have relished the idea of burning myself for that useless husband. I would have got a local virgin to stand in for me and paid her family well."

"You are incredibly beautiful."

"Thank you, kind sir."

"It has been a long time since I have been with a woman alone. I've lost any social graces I may or may not have had." He was so hot the sweat poured off his face into his collar. "Do you mind if I . . . ?" He started to undo the brass buttons of his jacket.

"Please do," the Maharanee said, and nodded to the young girl, who knelt and undid his buttons and removed his jacket. She took off his shirt and wiped his chest with the astringent lotions smelling of rose petals and witch hazel.

She left the room to return with folded garments, and helped him into a fine poplin shirt, cool and crisp against his skin, and smelling of the *dhobi* and hot irons.

"You should take off those tired pants," she said.

His face filled with the heat of embarrassment.

"It's all right. It is her job and her duty. She is a woman trained to dress and undress."

The girl undid his buttons and slipped off his pants. She hung them over the back of the armchair. This was followed by his underwear. He looked down and wondered if he should cover his evident pleasure at this ministration. Decided not to. In fact he was feeling delightfully foolish, gorgeously foolish. No, he was burning with guilt. He could not stay here like this. He had to leave.

She wrung out the cloth in the water and dabbed him with lotion and wiped his belly. She washed round his crotch and balls, and finally his penis, expertly pulling back his foreskin and just feathering the area under it. He had a raging erection. He should have presumed himself as foolish, stupid, sitting here with two women and them both clothed and him naked. But he grinned, totally in harmony with himself. She led him off the chair and made him stand, and gently pushed him over into a bending position. She lotioned round his anus and he gritted his teeth. He would not ejaculate. He would not. She curled one finger into the centre of his anus and wiped the lotion off. He would not. He would not. He imagined dissecting the mouth, all the facial nerves. Olfactory, optic, ocular, vagus . . . He couldn't remember the rest.

Thank God she stopped, and wrapped him in a towel. He glanced at the Maharanee and she had an almost condescending smile. Well, she had an excuse: anyone fully dressed watching a man being washed like a baby had a good reason to be condescending.

"Now, isn't that more comfortable?"

If anything was too comfortable it could not be good. In order to be good, things had to be uncomfortable.

"But what about you? It seems you are there dressed and . . . Perhaps it is time I dressed." He tried to be polite. She could be an eccentric woman who liked to watch naked men and humiliate them. It would not do to offend the Maharanee of Cooch Bihar.

She spoke to the girl, who took the basin to return with another basin of water and clean towels and a robe. She stood behind the Maharanee and unwrapped the sari. She lifted it from the shoulders and then she undid the pleats at the front and untucked it from the underskirt. As she did so she folded it into sections about six inches wide. The Maharanee stood in a heavily embroidered blouse and an underskirt of white muslin which floated against her thighs and resonated to the vibrations of the *punkah*. The blouse was deeply cut to accentuate her large breasts. She undid the many diamond buttons. Half of him wanted to sink through the floor, and half floated over the moon; half was the fool and half the king.

Her breasts were the most magnificent things he had ever seen. They were a rich dark gold, the colour of ripe honey, and the nipples shone black and turgid, seeming to take up most of her breast. He was a child, an adolescent, seeing his first naked woman.

The girl washed under the Maharanee's arms and round the breasts and the face. She then oiled her breasts and put fresh kohl on her eyes and lotion on her hands.

The Maharanee slid her rings and bracelets off and placed them on the table. "I have this European habit of removing jewellery."

She stood semi-naked. "See how I keep you company."

The girl now pulled the tie holding the petticoat so it dropped onto the floor.

Her strong legs were topped by a thick pubic thatch. The girl picked up the petticoat and folded it, and placed it beside the sari. "Now she will wash me as she did you."

She lay back on the chaise and the girl washed her feet, washed her belly, washed her sex. He stood at her feet to see what was happening. She had a large, ample, ripe clitoris. The pink sex stood out against the black hair and darker skin round it. The air in the room was heavy with her musk.

"I could do that for you," he asked.

She nodded, and sent the girl away.

He opened her legs and studied his job. He soaped the area between her legs and then wiped the soap off and oiled her lips and hair. The pain in his belly was unbearable, but he would not give in to it. He would never behave like a rutting boar.

"You are beautiful." He bent and kissed her gently on the mouth. She reached up and pulled him to her and kissed him passionately and deeply, her tongue finding corners and sensations in his mouth he had never imagined.

"Yes," she whispered. "Yes."

He licked each nipple in turn. They were firm and hard. He longed to have the feel of her clitoris rigid and stiff between his lips, to tongue it, to roll it and be part of it.

As if she knew what he was thinking, she moved his head down to her. Like a dog sniffing a bitch, he sniffed her; she was suffused with fruit and honey and fresh mornings. He touched the tip of her clitoris with the tip of his tongue.

"Darling," she moaned.

His tongue slid up her slit. He was on fire. She was alive and open and a glowing, blazing fire before him. He slipped a finger into her. Her spread lips were the wings of an eagle and he was ready, full, a dam about to break. He .... No, he could not stand this any longer . . . he was totally out of the world. Only the darkness and juice inside her existed. He had to be in her. He lifted her off the chaise and stretched her on the floor and pinned her shoulders down and thrust deeply into her, tearing and filling and bucking mad and moaning as he mined in her, groaning and grunting. He had to reach the horizon he saw and felt; he had to slide down the mountain he was climbing; he had to, had to, had to . . . He finished, the full weight of his body limp on hers.

As he withdrew he could feel her vagina walls clutching and grabbing him. Agony. She rang a small bell and the girl came in with towels and a basin of water and lotions. She placed them on the floor beside them.

So this was how all inhibition was lost? The Maharanee washed his cock and lay back for him to wash his juices from her. She took a small sponge and filled it with liquid from a bottle and inserted it into her vagina. "We use sponges from Kerela and some mild acidic solution. Keeps us fresh and avoids any accidents."

He held her ankle in his hand, such a fine ankle, the bones shining white through the skin. He kissed each toe in turn. God, even her toes made him crazy.

"I would like you to serve me now," she said.

Well, she was direct. She was lying back against some cushions, her legs spread wide and a smile on her face, playing with her nipples. His penis was a monster, a cobra which sees food and has not eaten for months.

Now the nipples were standing up under her ministrations. She then wet a finger and stroked her clitoris. She did this so very gently that it was little more than a feathering of her skin.

"You now," she said.

He lay on his belly and looked at her wide open sex, at her thick turgid lips and the curly hair spread against her skin. The gash wide open, red, glittering, smiling at him, and at the top of it the clitoris, bright, a beacon calling him. He flicked it with his tongue.

She lifted to him and her thighs clenched. "Yes, it is so much better when a man serves a woman after himself, so much better."

He entered her with two of his fingers and moved against the dorsal wall, looking for that point women love. He found it, and she twitched against his finger. He kept the fingers inside her and rolled her clitoris with his tongue. It rose to him, hard and demanding. He slicked it and stroked it and all the time his fingers inside her were pressing and rotating. She bent to him, coiled up on her ankles and shoulders so her body was a violin and he was the bow. He played her, and stopped when he thought she was about to finish. Yes, he wanted to watch her. No, he would not let her control him. Her juices dripped, soaking everything. She moaned deeply, a tiger on heat. No, he would not let her finish. He sat back and stroked the lips, gently, absently, as if he had forgotten what he was doing.

"Harry, please, it is time. Harry, mount me. Harry, enter me. Harry, for the love of all the gods, get inside me and make me finish."

He kissed her on her lips, and her lips were the sweetest, coolest things he had ever touched. He turned her over so she was kneeling. He pushed into her and reached round for her clitoris. He rolled and stroked, at the same time thrust into her. He rocked into her and stroked and pitched her. Damn, he would not finish. He banged deep, churning her sex, and his rhythm changed to one more demanding as he began to drive, pierce her, rolling her clitoris, and her muscles grabbed him, her belly contracted, the rings of her vagina came to fullness. She finished, loudly, thrusting against him violently.

They were sitting on the floor on cushions, leaning against the chaise.

"I think it is time for some refreshment," she said, and rang the bell. The bearer appeared with orange juice on a tray.

"Why me?" he asked.

"Why me? I could ask too."

"You are the most incredible creature I have seen in my life. I can't say any more."

She sipped the orange juice. "Why you? Because I am a woman who has certain needs. I like men. I like their bodies. It's difficult for someone in my position. I do not wish to be married. Do not wish complications. I think you are the same."

"Yes, yes, I think that's right for me. But . . . Oh, too much to expect. Too much to hope for. Too much . . ."

"My dear boy, we have only just started. Wait for the next round. You will find you have a . . . formidable . . . partner in these games."

"You wanted to know more about Kali. I will teach you now."

He ran his fingers though his hair. A bit nervous?

"Lie down, as the bearer did." He lay on the carpet, the silk soft against his cheek, his arms loosely by his side.

She sat beside him. "See . . . it is all a matter of trust. I am going to teach you to trust me, and then you will have to be trusted by me. Trust."

She rang the bell again, and the young girl appeared and stood as if waiting instructions.

The Maharanee spread the scarf on the floor and undid the coins. She kissed each corner, then she retied the coins. She sat on his back and rubbed his shoulders through the shirt, her hands slicking over the material. She was a feather on his back. While she was doing this the young girl massaged his legs, pressing the muscles in rings of compression with both hands. Every fibre was alive. He only consisted of the four hands working on him.

He was hardly aware of the scarf going round his neck. This was what was planned. This was necessary. Her fingers brushed his neck, as if looking for something just at his larynx. For one second, or part of a second, his belly flopped in terror, and then the terror was replaced by bliss. All he could feel was the girl's hands on his thighs and the scarf on his neck. No pain, just a gradual compression, so gradual it was hardly there. His head was a giant balloon, it was a feather, it was so large it filled the room. His whole body was only head. It grew and grew, light as breath. One part was not light, and that was his penis. It was heavy, so heavy it sank into the floor. It was lead, but lead which was being melted by a fire of incredible heat. His penis vibrated with blood and sensation. The rest of him was infinitesimal, tiny, his head glued to the ceiling, his arms and legs and torso floating round the room, figments of his imagination. But his penis was real. Oh, God, his penis was the size of the universe, and he was fucking, yes, fucking the earth, he was fucking the earth and moving into its boiling lava centre and pushing, driving into it, and his being existed in this black pain, this agony of all penis and all ecstasy.

He was on his back and the Maharanee was sitting on the chair watching the girl wash him.

"So, how was it?" she smiled.

He did not know what to do. He could not look at her. He had betrayed his control, he had lost himself, he had been a tool, an instrument. He looked away.

She bent down and stroked his hair. "Yes, it is quite frightening the first time. But you are with friends. You don't even feel any soreness round your neck."

His hand instinctively came up to his neck and she was right. There was no soreness, just a heightened sensitivity to his own touch.

"See, it gets easier. Much easier. And also better each time."

He could not imagine anything being better. But the terror of losing everything, losing dignity, manhood, control . . .

"We will learn to serve each other. There are many games we can play during your time in India."

He moved and rested his head on her lap. "I am a baby in your arms."

"That is how things should be. You in my arms and I in your arms. We will learn."

"Yes, I think I could learn."

A GOD'S WRATH

Olly Jasen

HOT RAYS BURNED Eltheia's glistening bare breasts. The powerful heat made gentle swells ripple from the tips of her dark pointy nipples, through her chest, down to the swell of her tummy, below her loincloth. Rivulets of perspiration ran between her soft mounds, trickling down, pooling in her belly button. She lay perfectly still, savoring the sensations. Such simple arousal was her favorite pastime while alone on the mountainside. Her bustling village on the Lassithi plateau was far from her mind. The country solitude was her salvation.

She shimmied further up on the rock. Her binding fell open, exposing a sliver of her sex to the sunshine's persistent penetration. She pressed her back against the rock. Rough granite abraded her skin in a hundred places. Pinpricks of pain rivaled the sun's powerful beam.

The herd of goats made their way up the mountain. Pebbles scattered down the steep path under their hooves. They fought for the juiciest plants, viciously guarding their prizes. Vegetation was ripped out by the root. Victoriously, the animals chewed the leaves in their greedy, ever-hungry mouths. The goats' pungent scent mixed with spicy herbal and sweet floral aromas as their teeth gnawed away, mashing food into saliva.

Eyes closed, Eltheia pictured the crushed red petals, running like blood onto the goats' white hair. She knew the herd would devour nature's beauty, which she cherished. Tiny violet clusters, lush green leaves and miniature lime-colored dots on whisper-thin branches would be an ample feast for the animals, giving her sufficient time to indulge herself.

Eltheia reached out to her side. Her long, slender fingers found a shrub branch. She pulled it to her face. Inhaled. Fresh, sweet, sensuous.

Eltheia's skin crawled. A million tiny fingers seemed to be awakening every nerve-ending in her body. She broke off a twig. Eyes still shut tightly, she ran the velvety soft leaves along her neck. Slowly, she traced a path between her breasts, down to her belly. Her body quivered. She gasped. Her legs begged to close as moisture trickled down her thigh from her frothing sex. She fought the desire to tightly clamp down on her hand and rub furiously to break up the building tidal waves in her abdomen.

She loosened the flimsy piece of white fabric covering her pubic mound. It slithered down her thigh and landed at her feet. She started to pant. The reward could be almost instantaneous if she wanted. But she didn't want the sensations to end quickly. Not today. Today, she would make the arousal last until she was thrashing, humping the granite, knotted from holding back.

Forcing herself to slow down, Eltheia grazed her labia with the velvet leaves on the twig. A moan caught in her throat. A rough edge scraped her bud. Her knees weakened. Her breaths came in rasps. She felt her chest rise and fall at such a speed that her firm breasts jiggled wildly. Her mouth dropped open. The air was thin. Her throat was dry. It hurt to inhale. Eltheia tried to lick her sunburned lips, but her tongue stuck to the roof of her sensuous mouth. The anticipation was agony. Release would eventually come.

She was so caught up in pleasuring herself that she almost mistook the sudden rumble in the distance for her own crescendo of desire. It seemed to be a surreal sound, filling her head, deafening her. Just as she was about to climax, a goat nudged at her hand, knocking the twig loose. The sun vanished. A chill ran through Eltheia's lithe body.

She opened her eyes. Dazed, it took her a moment to realize where she was and what was on the horizon.

Far off was the turbulent water's edge. Black clouds were rolling in, moving at a frightening speed. The sandy beaches were vanishing from sight. Within seconds, the plateau of Lassithi was veiled in darkness. The erratic clusters of homes in her village were invisible. Flashes of light fell from the sky.

This was not a good sign. As young as she was, she was old enough to understand that the gods watching over Crete had been angered. Most probably they were angry at her for pleasuring herself in a perverse way instead of tending to her brother's herd. Her belly spasmed.

Last season, during the harvest, her brother had come to find her. Their mother had become ill and had called for her. Ari had discovered her, sunning amongst the rocks, lashing herself between her legs with a thistle. She was never certain how long he'd stood there watching her. As she'd climaxed, her screams of ecstasy burning her throat raw, he'd grabbed her in his big arms and held her dangling above the ground. Was it fiery lust that had burned in his big brown eyes? Was it disgust? To this day she couldn't decide what she'd seen. But, whatever it had been, it had instantly aroused her. Even Ari's fierce admonishment hadn't dampened her internal inferno.

Now, her brother's words came back to her. "You shall be punished by the gods for indulging in your own perverse pleasures instead of taking your responsibility for my herd seriously. Perhaps a god will take you and teach you the true meaning of sex, leaving your belly full of some animal instead of a human child."

Ari shook like an animal. The bull's hide draped over his shoulders billowed, giving the appearance that it was coming to life, that *Ari* was becoming a bull. Her brother had claimed his totem gave him strength. At that moment, Eltheia had not doubted him. Every quivering, bulging muscle had danced in a continuous ripple beneath the hide.

Ari had flung her down and thrashed her backside with the thistle she'd used on herself. She wasn't sure if it was for letting his goats stray all over the mountain side or for her dalliance. Each lash had made her body burn wildly with desire. She would have let him beat her until she climaxed again. It never happened.

He'd stopped suddenly, tossed the weed into the bushes, then spun, and towered over her. The bull hide head had flipped onto

Ari's head. A savage mouth hung open over his. Horns grew out of Ari's skull. Hooves were flung across his massive chest. Ari's eyes had burned with rampant rage. A bull ready to devour his prey. He seemed to sense that she had been enjoying his punishment. He had pulled her to her feet and had hoarsely ordered her to rush home to their mother.

All she could remember about her blind run down the mountain was that her body had flamed with a need to be fulfilled. A stream of nectar had flowed down her legs. Her breasts had filled with prickly heat. Just outside the village she'd stopped to catch her breath. She'd squeezed her nipples tightly, pinching them, willing a release of the fullness in her abdomen. It came. Her knees had buckled as she'd slid down the side of the tree she'd leaned on. She'd fallen to the ground as wave crashed into wave. The endless orgasm had left her weak and dizzy.

Finally, she'd struggled to her feet. Love juice had oozed out of her tunnel. With the edge of her skirt she'd sopped up the tattle-tale wetness from her crotch and legs. Luckily, the sun had been strong that day. By the time she'd reached her home, the cloth was only slightly damp.

Perhaps her brother had been right. The goats were her responsibility only one day out of seven. That wasn't asking much of her. She should have been more caring about their needs instead of her own. She had been forgiven each time she had strayed from her herding responsibility, allowing the goats to stray, possibly endangering the animals by venturing higher and higher up the mountain so that she could enjoy the solitude she craved.

In the mountains she'd found the privacy to tend to her body's needs. To revel in the pleasure of climax that so far only she seemed able to bring herself. Many times she'd lain on her back for a man and felt nothing but frustration. Men seemed to be interested only in spurting from their fountain for their own pleasure. They'd buck like wild beasts and grunt until they unleashed thick white cream from their heavy sacs. They didn't make her honey nectar flow with their semen. They didn't make her writhe and pant and explode with orgasm. The men she'd secretly had sex with lacked the knowledge of where to touch her, of how roughly she needed them to enjoy her body. Either they treated her like a piece of fine pottery that would crumble, or they ignored her as she lay beneath them, using her cave for their own selfish needs.

A sure sign that she had finally tested the gods' patience and was about to incur their wrath, was that this time the gods hadn't allowed her to climax. At the very point of orgasm they had stopped her short.

The sky opened up. Torrential rain pelted down on her flaming skin. A bolt of light flashed across a bush and set it on fire. Frightened, the goats surrounded Eltheia, clamoring together, pushing her into the hard rock. She had to get out from the center of the herd before they crushed her.

Eltheia scrambled to her feet. Her skirt was trapped beneath the stomping, pawing, anxious hooves, racing back and forth. She grabbed at the white cloth, roughly shoving the animals aside. The cloth was shredded, but it would be better than arriving in the village totally naked. She wrapped the loincloth tightly around her shaking frame.

The dagger-sharp rain cut at her flesh. Goosebumps crawled over her smooth, tanned skin, marring its perfection. Her long, black, wavy hair hung in a wet mass halfway down her back. On trembling legs, she tried to fight her way through the herd, down the mountain. It was futile. The animals clustered together, spun around, unsure of which was the safest direction to go.

Without warning, the goats stampeded, carrying Eltheia higher and higher up the mountain. She was flung onto a bony back. The animal's spine bounced against hers. Her hair tangled in its horns. The other goats surrounded her and pushed her goat along.

The horizon faded from view. All was black. A thick fog blanketed everything below. It was catching up to her. The blinding rain fell harder. It chiseled at her breasts, sliced at her nipples, tore at her skin.

Eltheia's abdomen tingled. Her vaginal entrance pulsated. She imagined herself being carried on the goat's back as a sacrificial offering to a god. She would be deposited at his feet to be taught the true meaning of sex. Her skirt was around her waist, exposing her mound to the torrential onslaught. She caught sight of her gentle sloping pubic bone. The skin was raw, beaten red by the rain. Black pubic hairs bounced to life, then were crushed down. The springy curls collected and squeezed out raindrops like a sponge. Her clitoris, swollen and throbbing, rose out of the dark, matted bush of hair.

If only there was a wonderful release in store for her at the end of this ride, she could endure anything any god wished to bestow upon her. She would open herself wide and offer herself to him. She would take his length and pounding. She would suckle his juices down her throat. She would let him chew her nipples until they bled. In return, she would only ask that he would whip her sex. Make it raw and achy. Make it froth with honeydew. Then, she'd ask him to rub her with his penis, exactly the way she'd rubbed herself, until she saw the white light flash before her eyes. The light always signaled the grandest possible orgasm, full of heat waves and spasms which left her panting, sweating, exhausted, and made her black out into a deep, fulfilled slumber. Only then would she ever believe that a god could really show her the true meaning of sex.

The goats stopped abruptly at a small level area on the side of the mountain. Eltheia fell to the ground in a heap. She dragged her bruised body to the stone wall. Flushed, short of breath, she rested on the seat of pebbles and leaned back. The wall seemed to part and devour her. Certain that a god was engulfing her into the mountain, taking her for his own sexual pleasure, Eltheia felt her pulse race. She fell inside the narrow entrance.

Her eyes adjusted to the darkness. She was in a cave. A sweetness filled her nostrils. The burned sugary scent beckoned her. She got up and followed the smell.

To her right was a small chamber. It was filled with figurines of animals, daggers, knives and arrowheads. Bronze female statues stood on a ledge at eye level. A double ax lay in the center of the space. Vases littered the far corner. She made out an octopus on one, tritons and starfish on another. A brilliant vase, decorated with a spiral of vibrant-coloured plants, held a bouquet of dried flowers, the faded petals barely clinging to the dark brown stem. The source of the aroma was not in this room.

Eltheia crept around the corner, the sweet smell guiding her. Her bare feet, chilled from the cold, damp rock, stepped onto a soft carpet of fresh flowers and leaves. She followed the path of strewn petals and satin greenery until she came to a square altar built of field stones. On top were puddles of wax from burnt-down candles. A lone fresh candle, with wick intact, leaned against a bronze figure of the fertility goddess and a sacred bull.

She was in a temple. Eltheia took a step back. Her foot caught on a full flower. She crushed the fresh petals between her toes, releasing a strong, titillating scent. The sweetness intoxicated her senses.

The candle ignited with a sudden spark. The light flickered off the statue of the bull. For a second the bull seemed to come to life. Eltheia's blood ran cold.

Paralyzed, she could not move. Her throat tightened and, try as hard as she could, no sound came out. Her eyes, glued to the candle, would not look away. The flickering flame mesmerized her. Gradually calmed her. Drawn to it, she stepped up to the candle and ran a delicate finger through the flame, reassuring herself that she wasn't imagining any of this. She dipped her fingertip into the pooling wax and anointed her nipple. She picked up the candle and dripped the wax on her other nipple. The hot wax sealed around her puckered dark flesh. The sudden heat, then tightness, sent a tingle through her. She moaned, in spite of herself.

She was awake. This wasn't a dream. This was all real. Was she alone? Eltheia gasped. Could this light that had so suddenly lit up the room be a sign of the boy and girl who were lost in the autumn and came back to light and life in the spring? What season was it? She couldn't remember. Were the couple here in the cave with her, magically guiding her to some deep recess for their own reasons, which at the moment she didn't understand?

Eltheia took the candle and held it tightly. She would let it guide her to wherever she was meant to go. She backed out of the tiny room and descended a steep, slippery passage.

At the bottom was an underground pool. To each side the walls were decorated with scenes of animals, plants, trees, fish. The flora and fauna mural ended in darkness, entrance-ways to more chambers, then continued again. Eltheia side-stepped the steaming pool and looked into each chamber.

The small rooms overflowed with pottery, vases and vessels made of fine, veined, colored stone. Alabaster, marble, rock crystal, obsidian, porphyry and basalt. They came in many shapes and sizes. The bull-head vessels had to be from Knossos. Her mother had pointed them out to her at an altar when they'd gone together to worship. On the ground were long swords and elegant daggers. Their golden coverings glimmered as the light from the candle passed over them.

Another room had a small altar. Above it was a bronze plaque with a tree and a bird. A sacred bough hung between them. A sun disk and half-moon were mounted to the side of the altar. On the altar's ledge was a bowl of wild mushrooms. She'd never seen this type of mushroom before. If the gods could eat them, they must not be poisonous. Eltheia popped one into her mouth. She savored the small morsel. The tidbit reminded her how hungry she was. As she nibbled on another mushroom, she reasoned that the gods would want her to be nourished for her exotic sexual journey. She helped herself to a third one.

Eltheia tiptoed back to the pool. Her long shadow on the wall across the water startled her. She could swear she saw another figure behind her, following her. She convinced herself it was an illusion.

How far up the mountain had she gone? She searched her tired brain. Could this be the cave where Zeus was born? Where Minos had come to receive the laws of Zeus? Or was this the cave where Zeus was hidden by Rea to prevent Kronos from eating him? She was surprised she'd never come upon the cave before, although she'd heard all about it. Zeus had to be here. She was sure of it. She would let him come to her and do whatever he wished. The goats had deposited her at this cave for a reason. She shivered in the damp room.

Her eyes were growing heavy. A blanket of sleep was overtaking her. She placed the candle in a crack between two stones on the floor. Nestled by the pool, watching the hypnotic vapor rising to the top of the cave, Eltheia let her eyes close.

The bull nudged her buttocks. She rolled over to face him. An iridescent glow emanated from him. She felt no fear. Something indescribable, alluring, drew her to him.

Raised up on an elbow, she stroked his face. His eyes, circled with red rims, stared deeply into her round brown orbs. His hot breath singed her cool skin. A wet tongue reached out to lap at her lips. She moved toward it. The coarseness tore at her skin. She licked at the blood trickling from her mouth. The bull snorted. As if commanded, Eltheia lay back on the cool stone floor.

The bull's tongue left a trail of fire from her neck to her breasts. The animal's teeth nipped at her nipples, making them pucker, stand erect. The beast suckled her breasts. First very gently, then with a force that made her scream out. Her abdomen rippled. Her vagina flooded with moisture. Her vaginal opening contracted around air, making the need for a cock more intense. She tried to cross her legs, but the bull's hooves stopped her short. A foot connected with her leg, shoving it back. The bull's hind foot moved her other leg, forcing her wider than she'd ever been spread. Her extended tendons felt as if they'd snap. Her sex throbbed, engorged, and wept.

With his teeth embedded in her breast, the bull squatted. He rubbed his erect penis along her clitoris. His cold cock was hard and big, bigger than anything Eltheia had ever imagined even existed. Would he penetrate her?

The animal's penis connected with her love hole. It mercilessly teased her aching sex. Eltheia groaned with desire.

The bull released his hold on her breast and retreated a few steps. His mouth dipped to her weeping crotch. A stream of hot, moist air from his mouth caused a river of liquid to stream from her tunnel. The bull let out a hungry growl. His snaking tongue twirled around her puffy lips, traveled to her inner thighs and back again. Each lick was tentative, light, barely touching her.

Eltheia wriggled her hips, egging the bull on to take her with greater force. "Harder, please harder . . ." she whispered.

The bull snorted. He pulled away. Eltheia's eyes pleaded with him not to stop. The bull pawed the ground. His eyes glowed. He lowered his head and dug into her cunt. His horns held her legs apart as his tongue lapped up her juices. Eltheia screamed out. Her insides crumbled into a million pieces as spasms ripped through her.

The bull would not let her move away. Her head was pinned up against the cave wall while his horns dug sharply into her sensitive flesh. There was nowhere for her to go. He would not let up on her raw pearl, which he licked over and over again, then twisted viciously between his teeth. She was caught up in a never-ending orgasm.

The bull slithered his fat tongue into her love tunnel, probing into her deep recess. In and out. He thrust deeper and deeper. Eltheia was coming again, thrashing wildly.

She was spent. She didn't think she could come again. Yet the bull was bringing her to another climax. The room spun. It was a moment when everything seemed to blur and nothing was real. She felt as if she was spiraling through thin air.

When she came to, she was on all fours. A bobbing penis was pressed against her labia. It was positioning itself at her entrance. Hands grabbed her hips to hold her still. Hands? Yes. Not hooves. She tried to turn her head to look back. Strong fingers grabbed a handful of her hair and roughly pushed her head down to the ground.

"If you want to experience the pleasure you seek, you will not look back again," a deep voice commanded.

Eltheia nodded weakly. The hand released its forceful grip.

The dagger was ready to enter. She willed herself not to move. The stillness was eerie. The lover seemed to be deciding what to do next, holding her on the brink, making the anticipation unbearable.

A sharp smack of flesh against flesh broke the silence. She flinched. Again, the hand connected with her buttocks, setting them on fire. She arched with desire. Ready for the next slap to her flesh, she braced herself. The penis retreated. She panicked. Furiously, she wiggled her ass in the air, inching backwards to find the lover's blade.

"Be still!"

Eltheia froze.

The air crackled. A whip lashed her flesh. She choked on a scream which caught in her throat. Again. Again. The wicked tip of the strip of leather caught her swollen lips. The pain instantly turned to pleasure, making juices stream from her gaping, still unfulfilled cave.

Hands grabbed her shapely hips. A massive rod swiftly, surely, masterfully buried itself inside her aching love box. It plunged into her with long, hard strokes, pumping harder and harder. A hand reached around and expert fingers massaged her throbbing breasts. They plucked at her nipples, extending them, rolling them between forefinger and thumb. Just as suddenly, a hand placed itself on her rosebud. This hand duplicated the motions of the hand on her nipple.

"Suck your teats," the voice ordered, shoving a breast to her lips.

Eltheia scooped her other breast into her mouth as well, then repositioned herself. Her knees ached, but she ignored the pain. Her hands were scraped from the rough stone floor. She tuned out the discomfort. She bit down on her nipples and moaned.

The hand that had pleasured her breasts traveled through her soaked sex to her anus. It carried her love juices to her rectum. The slippery fingers plied at the rubbery opening. A stiff finger slipped inside. It matched the penetration of the penis, thrust for thrust.

The lover's pounding resounded like a drumbeat in Eltheia's ears. She pushed back harder on his pole. The smell of sex filled the cave. The sloshing sounds echoed off the walls. Eltheia felt her insides begin to thrum and swell. "Harder."

The lover plowed into her tunnel, hitting the end. Her body writhed on his stiffness. His heavy sacs smacked against her buttocks. As he rode her, her skin flushed with a feverish exhilaration. Goosebumps rose across her flesh. His thumb massaged her clitoris as he drove her until she finally exploded in a huge, powerful orgasm. Their bodies blurred and blended with the frenzy of their passion. Eltheia's body bucked and shook, which was all it seemed to take to send the lover over the edge as well.

He gave a powerful thrust, let out a sharp gasp and shoved himself deeper inside her, shuddering as he climaxed. His fountain exploded with hot semen. The fluid overflowed. It ran down between her moist swollen folds. Eltheia reached down and scooped a palm full of his cream. She brought it to her lips and licked at the salty deposit. She ached to place his cock in her mouth, to suck him dry. She craved to taste a mouthful of his love juices.

The lover continued moaning, rotating and pressing his body deeply into her. Suddenly, he pulled out. He rested his hard sword on the small of her back. His penis was still as stiff as when he had begun to penetrate her. The orgasm hadn't softened him a bit. He softly caressed her back. He stroked her hair. He let her catch her breath. His finger, still trapped inside her rectum slowly came back to life, moving gently in and out of her dark passage.

Eltheia was spent. She ached to collapse to the floor. Her weakened muscles gave out, but before she could sprawl on the ground, a hand caught her under her belly. The finger slipped out of her anus. She felt the swollen head of a cock press firmly up against her tight rear hole. That second of anticipation was the worst. She didn't know what to expect. No man had ever penetrated her asshole. The idea of being buggered renewed her strength. A flame flickered within her, then rampantly spread like a brush fire.

The dagger-tip eased slowly past her elastic sphincter until the thick ridge of the cock-head was inside. Pain flashed through her body. She wanted to pull away, but didn't dare. She breathed deeply and willed herself to relax. His entire penis was soon trapped inside her hot ass. It hurt. But it hurt good. She shuddered from the mixed sensations. Eltheia rotated on the rod. The lover took a few tentative strokes, then slammed into her. He stabbed her repeatedly with his flesh sword. His scrotum slapped loudly and wetly against her sopping labia.

The near withdrawal and then re-entry drove her to new heights of ecstasy. When the flange of his cock-head popped free of her sphincter, scraping the nerve-endings around her anal opening, then scoured them again on the way back in, she realized the pleasure of anal intercourse.

He reached under and felt her streaming nectar greasing her thighs. He rippled his fingers through her engorged petals, strummed her clitoris, then jammed three fingers into her vagina. She could almost feel his fingers touching his penis through the thin membrane between her vagina and anus. It seemed that her rear passage grew wider with each pump. She tightened her ass muscles around his cock, pulling him in deeper, holding him in longer. In wild abandon she slammed back against his groin. He buggered her until she'd come twice.

When Eltheia was on the verge of her third orgasm, she clamped down tight. Her lover grunted in surprise. She felt a hot, delicious feeling swirl through her. Then her mind blanked out in a surge of pulsing pleasure. The orgasm ripped through her body, suddenly triggering his orgasm. They bucked and thrashed against each other, locking hips, straining. He let loose what sounded like a triumphant sob. Blinding white light flashed before Eltheia's eyes.

When she came to, Eltheia's body was covered with sweat. Her mouth was parched. She felt spent, yet exhilarated. The candle had burned down to a puddle of wax. How long had she been asleep?

She sat up. Her skirt lay to her side. Strange. She swore she'd fallen asleep wearing it. She took the cloth and ran it over her drenched chest. There were bite-marks on her breasts.

Eltheia bolted to her feet. Her buttocks were covered in ugly red welts. She touched her raw sex. It was wet. But it wasn't just her own wetness. She licked her finger. Salty. This was a man's liquid. She reached for her rectum. It was stretched wide and oozed with a manly deposit.

It hadn't been a dream. Eltheia shook from head to toe. She broke out in hysterical laughter.

"Zeus?" she called out.

Silence.

"Zeus!"

A roar filled the cave.

Eltheia smiled. The vapor over the pool of water thickened. It clouded into a shape. The form appeared to be that of a bull. The mysterious mist drifted up the dark passageway to the upper chamber. Was she supposed to follow it? Unsure, Eltheia hesitated, awaiting a sign. Through the dispersing filmy white vapor appeared a figure with a lit candle. It was coming toward her. Half-man, half-bull! She took a tentative step, ready to embrace him, to let him take her once again.

Candlelight filled the chamber as the figure stepped out of the passageway shadows. A rain-soaked bull's hide hung heavily on the man's back.

"Eltheia!" Ari's eyes flickered with sparks.

Eltheia stopped in her tracks.

HYSTERIA

Thomas S. Roche

VICTORIA BARKER SHIFTED nervously in her seat in the waiting room. She could hear her husband's booming voice as he spoke to Dr Fitzmartin.

"She's a wreck," Arthur Barker was saying. "If I knew what to do, Charles, I wouldn't be coming to you. At the best of times, you see, she's rather a jittery woman. But lately it's nerve-racking to be around her! The slightest little thing might set her off!"

Victoria heard the low, seductive rumble of Dr Fitzmartin's voice. Dr Charles Fitzmartin was a dear, dear friend of Victoria's father, and had been for years, as well as the family doctor. In fact, Victoria had had quite a crush on him when she was younger, though she never would have admitted it then or now.

"Describe her symptoms, Arthur – tell me what you mean when you say something *sets Victoria off.*"

Victoria quivered with sudden nervousness as her memories came flooding back to her. It was as if she were mentally predicting what her husband was about to say. She remembered the nervousness, the depression, her tendency to fly into a rage about the slightest thing. It had been months – perhaps years – since she'd felt normal. Truth be told, she *never* felt normal any more – certainly not since the marriage. For a time Victoria had thought it was the stress of running the household. But she knew it had to be more than that – it was like some horrible nervous disease, eating away at her.

But what Arthur told Charles was this: "She's so damn nervous all the time." Arthur seemed to be struggling with a difficult description. Then, all of a sudden, he burst out with: "She's like a cat that's been buggered something fierce! Pardon my French."

There was a long pause as Charles Fitzmartin assessed the meaning of Arthur's salty phrase. Dear Arthur's time in the service had left him with a profound vocabulary of rather off-color phrases. Though of course he would never have used such phrases in his wife's presence. But, then again, Arthur's booming voice always carried much further than he realized, so Victoria had certainly heard more than her fair share of his naughty language. Truth be told, she thought it was kind of appealing. In a masculine sort of way. One of the few things she found that way about Arthur. As a matter of fact, it caused a curious sensation to grow near the back of her brain –

But of course that was unacceptable. Victoria ignored the sensation, feeling her hands shake as she did. It simply wouldn't do to be thinking of things like that at any time – least of all when she was at the doctor's to be treated for this profound nervous illness that seemed to be taking her over. Despair flowed through Victoria and she began to whimper nervously, as if in prequel to a burst of tears.

"Buggered?" came the calm voice of Dr Charles Fitzmartin, in quizzical response to Arthur's rather earthy assessment of his wife's condition. "A cat that's been *buggered*, you say?"

There was a long silence.

"Oh, for the love of God, Charles, you're not implying – you can't possibly mean – certainly – that's not at all what I meant! Such a thing would be totally unthinkable, even you have to admit!" Arthur lowered his voice, which was terribly unusual. But he was unable to lower it so much that Victoria didn't understand what he said. "Not that I haven't – I mean, Charles, you have to understand, I've been in the army, and on numerous hunting expeditions; it's simply not proper to do it the usual way and risk certain . . . conditions. But with my wife? Never! Well, what I'm saying is, Victoria would never go for such a thing, and you really oughtn't to make such assumptions from everything I say, do you hear me?"

Dr Fitzmartin laughed. "Of course, Arthur. I meant no offense. I wasn't implying your relations with Victoria were unnatural. Of course such a thing is unthinkable."

Victoria burst into tears, choking back sobs as she quivered uncontrollably in the hard-backed chair.

It was then that the sobbing Victoria noticed Dr Fitzmartin's assistant – Chloe was her name, wasn't it? Clara, Chloe, something like that. Her last name was Waters, or Rivers, or something like that. The young woman had been moving about the room liberally – rearranging things and dusting the furniture and that sort of thing. And the girl – Chloe, Clara, Carla – kept pausing in her work to glance over at Victoria and offer a faint, nervous little smile. The first few times it happened Victoria had thought nothing of it. She thought it was just the friendly gesture of a concerned health professional. But, as Victoria's breast quivered with the unstoppable onset of tears, she noticed that this time the receptionist – Chloe, Clara, Catherine – was not looking away. She looked about to say something, but did not.

Victoria took out her handkerchief and dabbed at her eyes as the receptionist returned to her filing. Victoria noticed for the first time that the starched white dress the girl was wearing was just a shade too tight for propriety. It clung quite noticeably to the girl's ample hips, and tugged with some effort across her breasts. Victoria was quite certain the girl wasn't wearing proper undergarments – the outline of her breasts was disturbingly evident, and the girl was blessed with perhaps more bust than was typical for a girl her size.

Victoria imagined that the poor girl must have a hard time keeping herself clothed on receptionist's wages – and this too-tight dress was the result. Victoria experienced a wave of sadness for the girl, which set her quivering and sobbing all over again. Oh, to be so poor that you were forced into too-tight garments . . . without the means to afford proper undergarments . . . the horror was overwhelming.

"There, there," sighed the receptionist – Victoria suddenly recalled that her name was Clara. To Victoria's dismay, the girl was now standing before her, but, try as she might, Victoria could not stop her wave of sobbing.

Victoria almost gasped as the girl put her arms around her. Victoria collapsed into a series of sobs, giving in to her nervous agony. The curves of the girl's body pressed against her through that too-tight dress – damn that dress – Victoria realized with horror that she could actually feel the tiny nubs of the woman's nipples – noticeably hard under the thick white material.

"Let me comfort you, my dear," Clara was sighing. She was a girl of perhaps nineteen or twenty, just a year or two younger than Victoria, and Victoria, despite her nervousness, got the sense that this girl could understand her feelings. "What's got you crying, darling? Tell me all about it."

Victoria realized that this manner of speaking sounded more like something coming out of the madam in a bordello than a doctor's receptionist. Not that Victoria would know about such things.

But Victoria gave in to her pain and wept bitterly as Clara cradled Victoria's head in her arms.

"There, there," sighed Clara. "The doctor will make it all better. Charles is a genius at making people all better. And I'll do my part, too, you dear woman."

Victoria experienced a curious rush of fear as she heard the girl say that, as if there were some double meaning that Victoria should understand. But the warmth of the girl's embrace and the softness of her touch soothed Victoria, and she found herself having some difficulty thinking straight. Especially with her cheek against Clara's breast like that. Victoria ached with jealousy – Clara really was blessed – or burdened – with more in the bustline than was typical for such a girl. If Victoria had such a figure, perhaps things wouldn't have gotten this far . . .

Victoria pushed that thought away. She shouldn't be thinking of such things at a time like this. Especially not with the soothing touch of Clara's hand stroking the back of her neck – tickling her flesh. And the fullness of Clara's breasts against her face.

Victoria began to sink into a sort of trance. She really oughtn't to be sobbing like this – everything seemed so pleasant at the moment. With the warmth and curve of Clara's body against hers . . . certainly everything wasn't as bad as it seemed, was it?

Then she heard Arthur's booming voice from the next room, and everything momentarily was at least as bad as it seemed.

"For the love of God, Charles, I wish you'd stop bringing everything back to buggery! Didn't I tell you?"

Victoria realized that she hadn't been paying attention to the obviously hushed sound of Dr Fitzmartin's voice from the next room. Perhaps he was keeping his voice low so that Victoria couldn't hear what was being said. How thoughtful Charles Fitzmartin was!

But now his voice, raised in answer to Arthur's, was quite audible. "Buggery is only one option, Arthur – certainly there's a number of others! I hope you'll forgive me for saying that you're being rather difficult about the whole thing."

Difficult. Arthur was so good at being that way.

There was a long silence, and Victoria calmed slightly. Victoria sank deliciously into the sensations of Clara's hand stroking the back of her neck. It was as if Sarah, her dear sister, was embracing her as they used to do. Victoria never wanted it to end.

Clara sighed pleasantly. "Just relax, my dear . . . we'll have you fixed up in no time . . ."

A shiver ran down Victoria's spine.

Arthur and Charles began speaking again, this time in low, hushed tones. Victoria could only pick out a few words here and there – "procedure", "correction", and "vicissitude."

Vicissitude?

Then the doctor's voice, loud enough for Victoria to understand: "No, you certainly need not be present during the procedure!"

Clara put one finger underneath Victoria's chin and lifted her face so that their lips were barely an inch from each other. A curious, warm sensation flooded through her as she smelled Clara's sweet breath – and then a tender, sisterly kiss on her lips.

A sisterly kiss. But when the sisterly sensations were over, the kiss did not end, and Victoria's warmth rose as Clara's tongue tickled her own. Was this really the proper thing to be doing in the doctor's office? Victoria heard herself giggling, low in her throat, as pleasurable sensations flowed through her and Clara kissed her deeper.

Then, all of a sudden, the door opened.

Victoria realized with fright that Clara had lifted her knee and placed it on the arm of Victoria's chair. Given the tightness of the dress, this tested the strength of the material and all but imprisoned Victoria in her chair. Clara's lips were still against Victoria's, her tongue still in Victoria's mouth, as Charles Fitzmartin cleared his throat demonstratively.

Reluctantly, Clara pulled her lips from Victoria's and turned to face Dr Fitzmartin.

"The poor dear," sighed Clara, indicating Victoria by ruffling her hair. "She needed some comfort."

Charles gave Clara a disapproving look. "What she needs," he growled, "is a medical procedure. Certainly you, of all people, can appreciate that – can't you, Miss Brook?"

Clara reluctantly pulled away from Victoria, her face reddening. She looked at the floor, but Victoria could have sworn she saw the barest hint of a smile on Clara's face.

"Yes, Doctor," said Clara breathlessly. "I can appreciate that."

Dr Fitzmartin turned his attention to Victoria, still wearing the stern, unforgiving expression he'd flashed at Clara Brook, and Victoria filled with familiar excitement as she vividly recalled her girlhood crush on the family doctor. She fought the nervous heat that it brought to her body and mind as Dr Fitzmartin spoke to her.

"Victoria, I'd like for you to come in, please?"

"Yes, Dr Fitzmartin," said Victoria nervously, standing. She wished suddenly that she had a moment to freshen up. She felt so hot and sweaty, despite the fact that it was not a warm day.

"Your husband has described your symptoms to me," said Charles coldly. "I see a clear diagnosis of hysteria."

"Hysteria?" asked Victoria, uncomprehending.

Arthur waved his hand in dismissal. "There's no need to explain it all to my wife, Doctor. She doesn't have a head for such matters."

Despite herself, Victoria shot Arthur a dirty look, which, luckily, her husband did not see.

"All right, then," said Charles. "What's important is that there is a new procedure to treat such nervous conditions as yours.

Mrs Barker, I think such treatment would clearly be of benefit to you."

Victoria couldn't stop looking at Charles. Something about the way Clara had touched her had awakened all of Victoria's girlhood desires for Dr Fitzmartin. She recalled the long afternoons under the apple tree imagining that the good Doctor was there with her . . . the warm feelings such reveries had elicited in her body. She remembered the fantasized trips to Dr Fitzmartin's office for an "examination" much more thorough than any he would ever give her in reality.

"Whatever you think best," sighed Victoria, tears forming in her eyes once again.

Victoria sniffled, and dabbed at her eyes with her handkerchief.

Arthur took note of his young wife's tears and began to grumble. "Good God, Charles, the woman's in crisis. Let's get this over with. Now, Victoria, mind you, I'm not going to be around for this treatment – you know I've got a weak stomach for all those woman-things." As if to punctuate his remark, Arthur turned a peculiar shade of green and shuddered, looking away from Victoria. "But I'll be back to retrieve you in one hour – no longer – so don't worry. This treatment . . . well, Charles will explain everything to you." Arthur gave his wife another nauseated look and cleared his throat. "It's all right if I go now, Doctor?"

"Certainly," said Charles coldly, his distaste for Arthur Barker showing through for the first time.

Arthur leapt out of his chair as if he were a schoolboy given a reprieve from the classroom on a warm spring day. "Tut-tut, now, Victoria. I'm sure the treatment'll seem distasteful at first – but Charles here's a trained physician, so you're in good hands." Then Arthur was gone, having bolted with admirable dexterity for a man his age.

Charles turned to regard Victoria, his gaze cold and clinical. "Well, then," said the Doctor. "Shall we begin?"

Victoria was more than a little nervous at the prospect of this "procedure." Charles had told her nothing other than that it would involve rather "personal" places and that it was somewhat "unconventional," and that she must at all times stay very relaxed.

Charles summoned Clara to escort Victoria to a changing room and help her into the grown that would be necessary for her to wear during the procedure.

Victoria blushed as Clara helped her undress.

"Now, darling," said Clara Brook with a voice as soft as silk. "There's no need to be shy. I've seen it all." With that, she tugged down Victoria's corset to reveal her smooth white belly and breasts. Victoria blushed more deeply, wishing yet again that she had more for Clara to see. But Clara was plainly enchanted with Victoria's small yet firm breasts.

"Aren't these the most delicious things?" giggled Clara, running her hand over the buds of Victoria's nipples. "It's so nasty having more, you know. And I think it's quite clever the way these small ones look in a swimsuit."

Now Victoria was blushing uncontrollably as her nipples stiffened and tingled with intense sensation. It excited her to be complimented like this by such an obviously fetching woman a few years younger than her. But, more than that, it excited her to be undressed by Clara. Even so, Victoria was fairly sure that she oughtn't to be letting Clara pinch and stroke her breasts as she was doing. Then again, Clara was a trained doctor's assistant – couldn't this be part of the procedure?

As if reading Victoria's thoughts, Clara cooed softly, "Now, Victoria, darling, just relax – I'm well-trained in these matters, and this is a necessary part of the medical procedure."

Then Clara was pushing Victoria onto an examination table, pressing her lips around one firm bud and suckling like a baby while her hand pinched and teased Victoria's other nipple to full erection. Victoria's eyes went wide and she let out a low moan of pleasure as unexpected sensations flooded through her body with every flick of Clara's tongue. Clara was pulling Victoria's dress down with her free hand, all the while coaxing her breasts to more exquisite sensation.

Suddenly the door to the examination room opened, and Dr Fitzmartin stood in the doorway with a stern expression on his face. Victoria flooded with shame as she realized that she was partially undressed – Charles could see her breasts quite plainly. But Victoria's shame mingled with another sensation – an excitement, as if it was some sort of lascivious thrill to be showing herself to her family doctor. Victoria knew that was awful – he was a medical professional, after all, and his interest in her body was merely clinical.

In that moment, Charles looked away and covered his eyes.

Clara looked up guiltily from Victoria's breasts, her face blushing deep crimson.

"Clara," growled Dr Fitzmartin. "What have I told you? You're to prepare the patient without getting carried away, do you understand?"

"Yes, Doctor," said Clara, chastened. Dr Fitzmartin closed the door and Clara looked up at Victoria. She gave a naughty little giggle and began to undress Victoria further.

Victoria was gowned for the procedure without further incident. She gathered that there would be some sort of involvement with her private parts – which both interested and mortified her. Victoria kept telling herself that Charles was a professional – he was intimately acquainted with a woman's nether regions, and there was no need for her to be shy about it. And yet Victoria was not comfortable at all with the warm, tingling feel that knowledge brought to her body.

Wearing the thick, concealing hospital gown – much like a nightgown, but looser around her bust – Victoria was led by Clara into another examination room – albeit one outfitted with curious equipment.

There was a slanted table with two stirrups – not unlike a birthing chair, perhaps. But right next to the table was a bicycle.

A bicycle?

Victoria realized that, in fact, this was not a bicycle – in fact, there was only one wheel, attached to a curious collection of wires leading to a rather complicated wand that rested on a table just in front of the stirrupped chair.

"Goodness," said Victoria, frightened for the first time of the fate that was about to befall her.

Charles had garbed himself for the procedure, in a white gown and mask. Clara, as well, took a moment to don a white mask before helping Victoria into the chair. Victoria blushed as Clara helped her to place her bare feet into the stirrups, spreading her legs in a most unladylike manner. The gown still cloaked

Victoria's nether regions – but simply having her legs spread like that was shockingly powerful.

She hadn't been spread like this since . . . since . . . since . . .

Victoria realized that there were thick leather straps mounted to the sides of the seat. Clara quickly drew the thickest strap around Victoria's waist, buckling and cinching the leather belt until it kept Victoria quite firmly in place. Victoria felt curiously restrained – especially when Clara took hold of her wrists and circled each of them with a similar strap, restraining Victoria quite firmly.

"You may feel quite uncomfortable during the procedure," drawled Charles as Clara swiftly fastened straps around Victoria's legs, restraining them in their vulnerable spread position. "Clearly some very delicate regions are involved. This is why the restraints are helpful – we can't have you struggling and possibly interfering with the procedure."

"But . . . Doctor . . ." gasped Victoria breathlessly. "Is it unpleasant?"

Charles shrugged, and Victoria thought for a moment that she could see the faintest hint of a smile on his handsome face. That sent a shiver through her.

"There can be confusing sensations associated with the procedure," said Charles. "But you must trust that no matter how desperately you wish to get away, you are being kept restrained for your own good. Failure to complete the procedure once we've begun could be devastating. Do you understand?"

Victoria had such a nagging familiarity associated with that phrase – "for your own good." Wasn't that what Arthur had said that night – the last time, Victoria remembered with a flash of heat, that she had found her legs spread like this.

"For my own good," she echoed, understanding that, while Arthur had been mistaken, Charles most certainly was not.

Clara swiftly cinched the final strap around Victoria's ankle. Now Victoria was most cleverly restrained. Clara bent forward and gave Victoria a tender, sisterly kiss on the lips – which earned a look of rebuke from the Doctor.

"Just relax," whispered Clara. "And leave everything to us. It's not so horrible – trust me, I know."

Victoria looked up at Clara for a moment – had she undergone the procedure, too? Perhaps during an earlier experimental phase? Victoria would have to make it a point to ask Clara sometime.

Clara gave a last ruffle of Victoria's hair, a motherly look crossing her face. Then, to Victoria's surprise, Clara mounted the bicycle, indelicately hoisting her white dress to allow her to part her legs around the bicycle's rather curiously-shaped seat.

Clara took quite a long moment to settle herself on the chair, having some evident difficulty getting herself into the right position.

Charles seemed to read Victoria's confusion perfectly. "This procedure uses electrical power – a rather new manner of running things. Unfortunately, it's impractical to run a steam engine in the office – so the stationary bicycle will provide us with the power we need. Please begin."

Clara began to pedal furiously.

Victoria's eyes went wide as Charles lifted the curious wand that was attached to the end of the variety of wires and cables. It had a long, thick body and a globular head that narrowed to a dull point on one side. It looked like some sort of royal scepter – but with clinical, modern-looking nubs all over it instead of jewels.

Then Victoria gasped in fright – as she realized that the globular end of the wand was humming, throbbing – vibrating – with terrifying efficiency.

Victoria looked at Charles for reassurance, but the Doctor was quite involved with the procedure, and paying little attention to his patient's dismay. Victoria's eyes swept the room, and came to rest on the violently-pedaling Clara, who flashed Victoria a lascivious grin and a too-obvious wink.

Victoria looked back at Charles and stared wide-eyed as he began to move the gyrating wand toward her lower body.

"Now, Victoria," said Charles. "This may cause some . . . interesting . . . sensations in your lower body. Keep in mind that I will leave the gown in place at all times – to allow for your modesty. I will be applying this treatment strictly by feel, so don't be shocked by the . . . apparent . . . intimacy . . . of my touch."

Victoria was falling, desperately falling into a vast chasm of nothingness. Charles slipped the vibrating wand under the wide bottom of Victoria's gown –

And then Victoria gasped as Charles's hands touched her nether regions. Her most private place.

Perhaps Victoria had expected the Doctor's hands to explore her. But like this? He was actually touching – stroking – caressing – her sex!

Then Victoria's head began to spin as Charles parted the lips of her female parts. The sensations overwhelmed her as Charles deftly exposed a sensitive region near the top of Victoria's womanhood – and applied the bulbous tip of the wand.

Unexpectedly, and uncontrollably, Victoria's body spasmed and she began to scream. She strained against the leather straps that held her in place. She shook her head back and forth as she screamed wildly, choking and sobbing in sudden catharsis.

"Hold, Miss Brook," said Charles loudly, over the sound of Victoria's screams, and Victoria turned her head to see a wide-eyed Miss Clara Brook, with her dress rather askew and her face and neck flushed deep red. Surely it was the exertion of pedaling the bicycle. Though the look that Clara was giving the squirming and screaming Victoria certainly implied something else.

The sensations in her sex lessened, and Charles looked up at Victoria's face.

"Describe what you felt," said Charles firmly.

Clara quickly said: "It was like the bicycle was my lover, and I was –"

"Miss Brook!" snapped Charles. "I was speaking to Mrs Barker."

"Of course," giggled Clara, embarrassed.

"What did you feel, Victoria?"

"It . . . it was like my whole body was being penetrated by a white light . . . Oh, Doctor, I've never experienced anything like that . . ."

Charles nodded. "Excellent. Proceed, Miss Brook."

Victoria moaned as the throbbing of the magic wand grew close to her sex once more. She whimpered desperately, frightened but excited by the closeness of the blessed instrument. When the blazing, throbbing head of the vibrator touched her sex once more, Victoria let out another scream – but this time Charles did not relent, but pressed more firmly against her sex, and in a few seconds Victoria's thrashings were quieted, and her screams turned to moans.

"Relax, Victoria," sighed Charles soothingly. "Relax into the sensations . . . you're doing fine . . ."

Victoria still squirmed and pulled against the leather restraints, but her moans and screams had turned to gasps of pleasure. She realized with embarrassment that she had begun to utter Charles's name – but she found that she could not stop.

Then there was Charles's touch again, underneath the throbbing hum of the vibrating wand. His fingers. Probing. Teasing. Parting her nether lips. Two fingers pushing inside her body – stroking her maidenhead.

"Hold, Miss Brook," Charles ejaculated nervously.

Clara let out a sorrowful moan, but managed to stop pedaling. Her dress was now extremely rumpled, and she appeared to be sheened with a thin film of sweat. Her eyes gazed dully at the squirming Victoria, and her mouth hung open as she panted unstoppably.

"Victoria," said Charles sternly. "I don't wish to get more personal than is necessary. But am I correct in thinking that you and Arthur have not . . . ?"

Charles's fingers were still inside Victoria, stroking that place where Arthur had never been. Victoria's moans and whimpers rose in pitch even without the stimulation of the vibrating wand. She stared at Charles with surrender, tears filling her eyes.

"You and Arthur have not had marital relations?"

Victoria quivered. "He lets me use my mouth sometimes."

It was the Doctor's turn to blush. He shook his head sadly.

"That certainly could contribute to your condition, Victoria. I understand that Arthur is a man of atypical needs, but a young woman such as you can't survive like this without risking dire psychological and physical consequences. With your permission, I would like to perform a small procedure that will . . . correct your condition."

Victoria's eyes fluttered, and she let out an uncontrolled moan. "Yes, yes, yes," she gasped.

"Miss Brook?" snapped Charles.

"Oh . . . yes, Doctor?" moaned Clara, plainly having some difficulty focusing on the Doctor's orders.

"Please bring me the number two molded prosthesis," said Charles, and Victoria shuddered as Clara raced out of the room to fulfil Charles's request.

Charles's fingers still rested slightly inside Victoria's sex, and she quivered and moaned as he continued to massage her insides.

"No trouble at all," cooed Charles soothingly. "This won't hurt a bit, my dear . . . and you'll be all better."

Clara appeared again, holding a bottle of liquid and what appeared to Victoria to be a curiously-shaped riding horn. "Oh, dear," Victoria whimpered, as she realized that it was not a riding horn at all. In fact, it appeared to be made of leather and . . . Victoria simply couldn't think such a thought. She stared at the instrument with a look of horror on her face.

"Miss Brook," growled Charles sternly. "It's unseemly to let the patient see the instruments before application."

"Yes, Doctor," said the chastened Clara, who handed Charles the instrument and once more mounted the bicycle.

"Begin," ordered Charles, and Victoria moaned uncontrollably as Clara began to pedal. The seething vibrations once more began in the vibrating wand, which Charles was deftly applying to Victoria's sex. As the quickening began inside her, and her pleasure began to mount, Victoria felt pressure in the teasing thickness at the entrance to her sex, the very opening of her womanhood, where Charles had previously applied his two fingers. Now Charles was entering her with a single finger, which probed and prodded at the place where her maidenhead barred the entrance to her femaleness. Then the doctor applied a second finger, teasing her open, parting her most private spot – readying her for the next stage.

Charles spoke with a tenderness he hadn't yet used with Victoria. There was something so soothing, so gentle, so seductive about the richness of his voice now. "Just relax, my dear Victoria. You're under my care . . . completely in my control . . . this is a medical procedure, and you're fully safe in my hands . . ."

Meanwhile, his fingers were stroking, penetrating, opening her further. Victoria moaned in unexpected pleasure, mingled with the horror of her position. She was helpless at the hands of her doctor, who was about to divest her of her virginity. Certainly she should have been divested of it long ago, when she and Arthur had first married – but since he'd shown no interest Victoria had remained in this undeflowered state until now – and no longer.

For she was about to be taken, strapped bodily into this seat with her legs spread and with curious sensations of pleasure filling her body. *Good God*, Victoria thought to herself, *I feel as if I'll be ill – I feel spasms coming on.*

Then, as Charles's fingers gently opened her up, Victoria gasped to feel the thickness of the "riding horn," which she now realized was . . . was . . . oh, she couldn't think it. She couldn't even imagine such a thing. And, even so, the sensation was so delicious. It was like being taken roughly by her husband, without the untidy business of his uninterest. And certainly Victoria was not to become pregnant with this procedure, was she?

Victoria squirmed in her bonds, seized with the sudden desire to break away and run from this unacceptable intrusion into the most secret places in her body. Then, as Charles spoke to her, Victoria felt herself succumbing, surrendering, giving herself over to the unforgiving interior caress of the doctor's firm instrument.

"Take a deep breath, my dear," Charles said to Victoria in his most soothing tone. "A deep breath . . ."

"Oh, God! Yes!" The unexpected shriek came from Miss Clara Brook, who was wildly riding the stationary bicycle, pumping faster and faster as she shuddered and bounced on the narrow seat. Her dress was looking *quite* the worse for wear, almost lifted off the lower half of her body. Her moans and shrieks grew louder as she pumped faster, and sent a new intensity of vibrations into the curious wand still being held at the top of Victoria's sex by the firm hand of Dr Charles Fitzmartin. This brought a new series of gasps and moans from Victoria's lips, as the sensations in her body suddenly increased in intensity.

"Keep pedaling, Miss Brook," snarled Charles uncharitably. "It won't do to stop the treatment now, you tawdry bitch – it would be complete disaster!"

Quite unexpectedly, a shudder went through Victoria's body at the sound of Charles using such rough language.

Charles quickly changed his tone.

"Forgive me, Victoria," he said smoothly. "I forgot myself. She can be so difficult some times."

"Don't mention it," Victoria heard herself mumbling as Clara launched herself into her task with a brand new enthusiasm. Within seconds, Victoria found herself completely incapable of further reply.

Then Charles was coaxing her further, his gentle voice caressing her ears as he instructed her to take a deep breath and then let it out. Another breath. Another. "We're very close now, Victoria . . . very close . . . just relax . . ."

Then, with her fourth exhalation, there was the gentle yet forcible thrust of the doctor's instrument inside Victoria, stretching her open, penetrating her maidenhead, entering her utterly. Writhing in her restraints, Victoria let out a loud, low moan of pleasure. And as Charles thrust the shaft to its maximum depth inside her Victoria began to thrash wildly, as an unexpected sensation came over her.

It was a wholly new sensation, though she remembered it from the depths of her girlhood fantasies. She could recall this very same sensation, this feeling of release, from her long summer afternoons fantasizing about Dr Fitzmartin, in the days of her fondest crush for the good Doctor. Was there some connection?

Victoria certainly didn't care. She was entirely swept away with the explosion of pleasure inside her, and it was as if another woman entirely were screaming the words, "Fuck oh fuck oh fuck me, goddamn you, fuck me harder, you fucking prick, fuck me with your cock, oh fuck me." Another woman entirely. Was it also another woman bucking her hips against the leather belt, trying to pump the thick member deeper inside her womanhood, trying to force its thick, thrusting pleasure permanently into her body? So she would experience this heavenly sensation forever, constantly being penetrated by the good Doctor's succulent rod.

Victoria felt a bolt of fear as the sensation slowly declined and she realized that, no, it certainly was *not* another woman uttering those lewd and sinful comments.

It was her.

Though Victoria supposed it was possible that Miss Clara Brook had uttered a few comments of her own – certainly Clara looked worn out, as if she'd been screaming her head off. Were a few of those moans Clara's? Or had it been only Victoria who was screaming like that?

There was not really any way to tell.

"Good enough, Miss Brook," Charles was saying unsteadily, and Victoria realized that he had removed the instrument from inside her. The thick object – which Victoria could only now admit was *phallic* in shape – was covered with the lubricant the doctor had used, mingled with what appeared to be Victoria's blood and – perhaps – the juices of her body.

Victoria blushed uncontrollably, lowering her eyes so she wouldn't have to look at Charles after letting him see her in such an unflattering state. But lowering her eyes like that brought Victoria's gaze in full contact with the lower part of the Doctor's body – and with the striking bulge issuing from his lower parts. But Victoria's greatest shock was that the bulge in the Doctor's pants was capped with a dark, moist stain.

Victoria gasped. That wasn't possible, was it? It couldn't be – could it?

She lifted her eyes and met Charles's, and saw in that immediate warmth and glow that, in fact, her suspicions were true. Charles had led her down a dark and sinful path – all fully sanitized by modern medicine.

"Eh, what? Come on, here. Must be someone around, righto?" Victoria heard a pounding on the door of the examination room. It was Arthur, come to collect his wife. "Sorry to be a bit late, Doctor," shouted Arthur through the door. "Didn't make it home – just stopped off at the tea-house for a quick nibble – did my wife make it out OK?"

The rather ruffled Clara Brook tried desperately to straighten her too-tight dress, then quickly hustled out the door. Victoria heard Clara's voice soothing Arthur. "She'll be out in just a moment . . . the procedure went very well, Mr Barker – but it took just a wee bit more time than we anticipated. Please, I'll see to you in the waiting room and we can finish with all that business about the Doctor's fee, can't we?"

Victoria still held Charles's eyes in her own, and she heard herself speaking in a hushed, seductive tone that she didn't know she possessed.

"Thank you, Doctor. I don't know how to make it up to you."

Charles looked at the floor, his face reddening. "Not at all, Mrs Barker. I enjoy my calling." Then, as if to squelch any momentary fantasies Victoria might have, Charles quickly murmured, "It's merely a profession."

Victoria's heart swelled, and tears formed in her eyes even as she heard the Doctor continue:

"Of course, in severe cases of hysteria, such as yours, repeated vibratory treatment may be necessary. Perhaps three times a week for . . . oh, six months or so?"

Victoria's tear-filled eyes went wide, and she gave a little shudder of excitement and choked back a sob of pure happiness.

"If you think so, Doctor."

"I'll have a chat with Arthur about the fee. Certainly we can strike a deal, since frequent sessions will be necessary – to prevent relapse, you understand."

"Oh, I understand," Victoria said – too quickly, she thought. She nodded fervently.

"For at least . . . the first year."

"Year?" gasped Victoria, as Charles quickly stood and buttoned his long white coat across his moisture-stained pants.

"Or two," said Charles nervously.

"No problem about the fee, eh?" It was Arthur's booming voice from the reception desk outside. "No treatment's too expensive to keep my little petunia happy!"

"I'll call Clara in to help you dress," said Charles as he helped Victoria to stand.

Victoria heard herself giggling slightly, in a highly uncharacteristic utterance of mirth.

"No need!" she cried, and slipped out of the chair.

Charles stared, confounded, at Victoria as she bounded across the room to gather her things and dress.

It was as if she'd been given a new lease on life.

Charles dabbed at his moistening eye with the corner of his sleeve. Oh, how he adored the science of medicine.

LUNA

Vivienne LaFay

THE STABLE WAS in a cobbled yard, between Count Jacopo's villa and the magnificent formal gardens, set out like the Boboli gardens in Florence. However, the Count's prized horses were tended not by a groom or stable lad but by his own daughter. She had lived there with the animals for fourteen years, ever since her mother died.

Jacopo had detested his wife who, though beautiful, had been cold and arrogant. Some believed that the woman had been poisoned by his own hand. He had called his daughter Luna, after the inconstant moon, believing all women to be witches at heart, in league with the devil.

Certainly Luna had suffered through being her mother's daughter. Jacopo could scarcely bear to look on her face, for fear of being reminded of his late wife, but few people knew the Count's secret. A groom had taught the girl about caring for horses but he, too, had died mysteriously. Twice daily food and water were left by a trusted servant, but the stable door was kept locked and only the Count had the key. As a result Luna lived a strange half-life, with only dim memories of previous times.

There, in the dark mustiness of the stable, Luna grew to maturity. When her body began to change there was no one to explain what was happening. The girl had no way of connecting her growing breasts with the suckling of babes. Neither could she understand why her body suddenly sprouted new hairs. And when blood first flowed she was convinced that she was going to die.

Except that she did not die, and when it happened at intervals, and still she survived, Luna came to realize that the bleeding was also part of the physical upheaval she was experiencing. It seemed to coincide with the waning of the moon. She ceased to worry, but folded her petticoats between her legs to stem the flow and threw out the soiled straw where she had been sleeping.

Strange as these bodily changes were, something even more disturbing was happening to Luna's soul. Often she would be overcome by a yearning emptiness. When the full moon shone, and the blood-tide was upon her, she would feel it most keenly. There would be a churning within her stomach, and a magnetic pull such as the moon exerts upon the tides, and the nameless longing would become unbearable. At such times she found comfort from pulling her petticoats tight between her thighs, as if she were sitting astride a thick rope. Then she would feel a warm tingling that went some way towards easing her hunger, but it was never enough.

Along with her baffling puberty, Luna began to experience a great curiosity about the world outside. For years she had accepted that she must live a solitary life, with only horses for company. Now, though, she wanted more. Her curiosity became a drive that was as strong as that other puzzling urge, only more focused. She knew she must find her way out of the stable.

One day the girl began to examine the wooden walls of the building for signs of weakness. She knew it was no use trying the door, which was securely bolted, but she found two loose slats in the back of the stable and worked them to and fro until the nails popped out. Eventually she managed to loosen another and, with three planks removed, the gap was big enough for her to slip through.

Luna had no words to express her feelings as blissful warmth and bright light and fresh air assaulted her senses at once. She was dazzled, overwhelmed. For a minute she stood in rapture, her senses freed from the chains of darkness and isolation, her mind struggling to meet the new challenge of freedom. She walked down through the formal magnificence of the Count's gardens, with their terraces and gravel paths, their fountains and statues of heraldic beasts, as if she were in a beautiful dream.

After pausing to drink the crystalline water, she passed on from the artificial to the natural landscape, on into the meadows of sweet flowers and humming bees. There she ran like the child she still was at heart, until she came to a small pine copse where she flopped, panting, to recover her breath.

The heat and the over-stimulation of her senses was making her drowsy. Luna lay with her head on a tuft of grass and was soon asleep. Her dreams were of this newly-discovered heaven, a place of wonderful sights, scents and sounds, all bathed in a warm, golden light.

Luna awoke suddenly, aware of another presence. There was the sound of a pipe, and she saw a young man sitting cross-legged nearby, coaxing a tune out of his instrument. He smiled when she noticed him, but went on playing. Luna stared in amazement. How was it possible for a person to be so beautiful? It seemed as if this man were dipped in gold from head to foot. His black hair curled like a horse's mane, and when he glanced at her with those brown eyes the strange feelings hit her again, more strongly than ever, so that she wanted to cry out with the sweet pain.

He ended his tune and spoke. "You are Luna, the Count's daughter, aren't you? I used to think him cruel to keep you locked up, but now I see why he wished to keep you from the eyes of men."

Luna made an inarticulate sound. She was unused to speaking, and her vocabulary was limited to that of a child.

"My name is Angelo." He smiled encouragingly.

Luna dimly remembered her mother referring to angels as "beings of light". She gave a shy smile and repeated his name, "An-ge-lo."

He moved forward and took her hand, bending to kiss it. She marvelled at the soft, warm touch of his lips. "You are very beautiful, Luna. It is such a shame to waste you on horses and darkness. Let me kiss your lips, and show you what pleasure it is to other young girls."

She was under his spell and had no will to resist him as he pressed his eager mouth to hers, parting her lips with his tongue. His breath tasted of the mint leaves he had been chewing, and his saliva was sweet and fresh. Luna grew languid in his arms, but deep in her belly a slow fire had started which felt as if it could never be quenched. His hands were caressing her back, the way she sometimes stroked the great stallion's warm flanks, and when his fingers touched the bare skin at the nape of her neck she shivered slightly with the alien feel of his flesh on hers.

Angelo's lips were moving down, down. Soon his nose was nudging aside the threadbare linen so that his tongue could wander into the cleft of her breasts, leaving a wet trail like the silver path of a snail. Luna gave a great shudder as his progress tickled the sensitive skin of her small bosom.

"What pretty little pumpkins you have, Luna," he murmured, pulling her dress over her head and loosening her shift. "They look so sweet. May I taste them?"

Luna whispered, "Yes." She repeated it more boldly, loving the unusual sound of her own voice. For the first time in her life she was beginning to feel truly alive.

When Angelo began to lick at her virginal nipples Luna lay back in the grass and sighed voluptuously. There was a new fluttering in her stomach, a tingling of her spine, and a magnetic pull of her blood-tide that was like her monthly pains. Except that the pain was also a deep, hungering pleasure.

"Luna, Luna!" Angelo murmured, his hands moving beneath the hem of her shift to feel the rough hair of her mons. New waves of delight spread through her loins as he parted the tender lips of her sex and gently fingered her swelling bud. The liquid that was fast bathing Angelo's fingers was like warm oil, anointing her folds and heightening the delicate thrills that his slow ministrations were producing. In a few moments, however, hands and mouth had reversed their roles, for Angelo lowered his head and began to wiggle his tongue between the swollen lips of her pussy while his fingers sought the equally swollen peaks of her breasts.

Now the naive girl was responding to his ministrations with instinctual passion, writhing and moaning like a seasoned whore. She had no idea what Angelo was doing, what he was preparing her for, but she let her body enjoy it without restraint, revelling in the way he seemed to be leading her on to further delights. Her desire to explore the world was being satisfied, except that it was the world of the senses which she was now experiencing, a secret and delightful world which she had scarcely known existed.

Then Angelo began dabbling his finger in her warm, wet hole, and she longed for him to fill the emptiness within her. One finger seemed inadequate, and when he brought a second, then a third into play she felt her tight opening stretch to accommodate the bundled digits. His thumb was circling on the hard nub of her pleasure, and his lips once again sought her nipple.

Luna moved her pelvis and squeezed his penetrating hand with her inner muscles, so that the urgent sensations grew stronger.

"Luna!" he murmured. "So beautiful! Come for me, my lovely Luna!"

For the first time she realized that their journey had a destination. What would happen when she arrived? Something incredibly wonderful, she was sure. The tension was building, building, like a horse chafing at the bit and longing to be given its head.

Now she could feel his free hand struggling with his own clothing. His breath came hot and feverish on her breast and his knees were between her thighs. She sighed as his hand withdrew from her streaming cunt, but moments later something hard, fleshy and thick was being rubbed between her slick labia. Luna gasped and, craning her neck to look down her own body, saw that he had a prong like a stallion between his legs, and it was pointing straight into her secret place. Mysterious as it seemed, Luna grew doubly excited at the thought of that magnificent appendage probing her in the same way that the stallion serviced his mares.

"Yes!" she cried to the heavens, and Angelo smiled at her assent. He was about to let his penis slide down the oiled groove, past the last vestige of her virginity, when there came the sound of thundering hooves. Too late, he tried to hide his jutting member beneath his tunic. Luna had no such inhibitions, and lay with her legs apart and her sex in full view as the rider drew up, bellowing curses. It was the Count, her father.

"I shall have you castrated, knave!" he called in fury, bringing his whip down on the lad's shoulders. Angelo gave a cry and sped off into the bushes, but the Count pursued him on horseback, galloping over the rough ground and flailing at the bushes. Eventually he gave up and returned to his daughter, who was lying weeping in the grass, her clothes still in disarray.

Jacopo dismounted and advanced, still holding his horsewhip. "So, you would defy me, wicked girl! How did you escape from the stable? Did *he* let you out?"

"No, no! It is me, Father. I go . . ."

"Little whore! The cursed spirit of your mother must have entered you!"

He grabbed Luna by her long hair and pushed her across his lap.

"I'll teach you a lesson you won't forget! You think you have discovered pleasure this fine day, but you shall learn what pain is, too. By God you will!"

The Count bared her rosy behind and brought his whip down on the smooth flesh with a stinging whistle. Luna whimpered at first, but at each stroke the heat was rekindled in her still-throbbing sex, and as she wriggled in protest against her father's thighs her desire grew again. Soon all her lower quarters were aflame, her buttocks warmed by the whip and her swollen labia pushing rhythmically against the secret fount of all her longing.

As he beat her Jacopo's anger at her defiance grew, so that the strokes fell faster and faster, increasing the friction. At last Luna felt herself melting in her own body heat, her pain becoming molten pleasure. A pulsating vortex of bliss assaulted her senses, a feeling so wonderful that she believed she'd died and gone to heaven, passing out in an ecstasy of delight.

For a moment her father thought he'd indeed killed her. He was a hard man, but not so wicked as to murder his helpless daughter. Laying the girl on the ground, he attempted to fan her back to life, and at last, dazed and satiated, she smiled up at him.

"That'll teach you!" he growled, as his fear gave way to shame. "Now, back to the stables! I was right to lock you away, shameless hussy! See what mischief you get yourself into. You need to be shut up for your own good."

He continued to mumble such self-justifying phrases as he pushed her back up the hill. Luna was still in a daze, and hardly knew where she was. Only when she found herself locked in the dark stable once again did she weep for her lost freedom, and the vanished glimpse of paradise.

For three days Luna was condemned to a joyless darkness. Now she was even more discontented than before. Her father had put stouter locks on the door and boarded up the weak points in the walls, so that she had no hope of escaping again. Sometimes she attempted to pleasure herself, but there was always a missing factor. For what seemed like hours she would hover on the verge of a climax, but eventually her over-stimulated flesh would grow numb and she would have to stop to ease the ache in her wrist. Time and again her memory replayed her love-scene with Angelo, but she remained unsatisfied.

On the third night, she heard noises outside. At first she thought it was some small animal, but then came the musical trill of a pipe and she knew, beyond doubt, that her lover had come for her. Such joy filled her breast that she was afraid her heart would burst.

"An-ge-lo!" she breathed into the space between two slats.

"Yes, dear Luna!" came his whispered reply. "I've come to rescue you."

There was a rasping sound and the smell of sawdust. Angelo worked until there was a hole big enough for Luna to creep through. Seeing him there in the moonlight, his handsome face silvered with a phosphorescent glow, she wept for joy.

"Come, quickly!" he told her, leading her into the shadowy yard. A horse whinnied in alarm, and they ran until they were in open country. Their pace slowed and eventually they found an abandoned barn where they snatched a few hours' sleep, curled up together for warmth. For the first time in her life Luna was in a state of contented bliss.

Next day they arrived in a village in the foothills, where no one knew them. Luna stopped listening for the sound of pursuing hooves and began to relax. The sense of space and freedom was overwhelming.

"We shall live in one of the abandoned farmhouses hereabouts," Angelo declared. "No one will find us here. I shall make you happy, Luna, and you shall do the same for me."

It sounded simple, and, at first, it was.

Luna was intrigued by being so close to a man who was not her father. She grew to relish the sweaty animal smell of him, that reminded her of the stable but had the power to arouse her in quite a different way. She loved to make him smile, seeing his boyish peasant face glow with delight and something else, a greedy glint that told her he was hungry to possess her. When she saw that look in his eye Luna felt an answering urge, her body growing hot and receptive, her flesh swelling and moistening in her secret places.

At midday, when it was too hot to labour on the land, the pair would lie down under a shady tree and make love. Luna discovered what a strange delight it was to have a man's tool to play with. Angelo's penis seemed to have a will of its own, and he loved it when she rolled it between her palms or placed it in between her soft lips. Sometimes they licked each other's parts at the same time, Luna responding keenly to the wetness of his tongue as it explored the tumid folds of her vulva.

But most of all she liked to have a man's stiff tool inside her, and she revelled in Angelo's lusty thrustings. His wild energy always took her halfway to where she had been before, but never any further. Somehow she failed to reach that glorious destination again. When Angelo enquired, afterwards, if she were satisfied, she always said, "Yes, An-ge-lo." But in her heart she knew there could be more. Much more.

Although Luna told herself it didn't matter, in time she grew secretly irritated by her lover. He was coarse and clumsy, he was too lazy. She resented the fact that he found it easy to explode inside her in a burst of voluptuous fire then get up and carry on with his work, fully satisfied, leaving her to nurse her secret frustration.

After a while, when Angelo came to her in the afternoons with his blood warmed by sunshine and desire, Luna no longer participated with real enthusiasm in their lovemaking. She dared not say anything, for she'd learnt that her lover had a quick temper, but her moans were those of frustration, not fulfilment and when he shuddered his way through a climax she lay there in bleak isolation, wanting it to be over. Slowly her dreams of reaching that glorious bliss once more were fading.

As a result Luna grew slovenly, neglecting her duties in the home. One night, when Angelo arrived back exhausted from the fields, she had no meal waiting for him and he lost his temper.

"I gave you everything, and you give me nothing!" he yelled. "Come here, woman. You deserve a beating!"

He grabbed her and, throwing her over his knee, hitched up

her skirts and proceeded to spank her with his bare hand. Luna groaned as her pink buttocks shuddered and stung, but she could feel the warmth creep into her loins and her vulva began to swell. She gasped as the tide of her desire returned, stronger than ever, and wriggled against her lover's thigh. Angelo had worked himself into a frenzy of beating, and she could feel his prick harden beneath her stomach as he slapped her repeatedly.

Excited by the knowledge that he was aroused as well, Luna felt herself approach her climax. Angelo was tiring, his slaps coming more slowly, but she rubbed her mons urgently against his hard thigh until the warmth spread all through her and the tingling sensations intensified. Throb, throb! Slap, slap! At last she came, in a rush of energy and a gush of fluid that took both her and Angelo by surprise.

"Why, you little sneak! I do believe you enjoyed that!" Angelo laughed, seeing her blushing face as he helped her off his lap. Luna's flush deepened, and he grew hot for her. Stripping off, he laid her down and plunged into her wet and still pulsating cunt, swiftly bringing himself off with a few sharp stabs.

"That's better," he smiled, as they lay in each others' arms. "Now you're my naughty little Luna again!"

Luna smiled too, in deep contentment. Some instinct told her that she was going to have to be naughty again, very soon.

GWENDOLYN'S FATE

Allison Manning

GWENDOLYN'S FLESH CRAWLED as the Colonel's cold stare settled on her breasts. He might be lord and master of his garrison, but he would never be *her* master! Britain might rule Egypt, but he would never rule her!

Shame and sexual anticipation weighed heavily in Gwendolyn's stomach as his lusty gaze undressed her. A bead of sweat trickled down the moist hollow between her breasts. His eyes glinted as they eagerly watched the droplet disappear beneath the front of her blouse. She sensed his lecherous blood boiling with the slightest rise and fall of her chest. The tip of his tongue slithered along his upper lip when he lowered his stare to her tight-fitted riding breeches and boots.

"Gwendolyn!" he said, as if ordering his subordinates. "Come here, young lady!"

"How dare you speak to me in that tone of voice?" she snapped.

He gripped her upper arm and pulled her close. "I said, *come here.*"

He crushed his mouth to hers. Gwendolyn gasped as his tongue probed and twisted its way past her lips. At once, her nipples tightened, and her belly fluttered with an incredible excitement. For an instant she enjoyed his strength. Then she smelled the stale pungency of tobacco and tasted the sour after-taste of whisky.

Gwendolyn pulled away and angrily slapped his cheek, turning his face. She tugged her arm from his grasp. A mix of fear and arousal made her nipples sprout thickly under the thin cotton of her blouse. "My father will hear of this!" She haughtily tossed back her long blonde curls from her shoulders.

"Ha!" the Colonel bellowed. "Your father knows why you're here. He sent you to me and to this Godforsaken piece of sand. You will learn things, Gwendolyn. And you will come to love them – this I know!"

Gwendolyn's belly knotted with anger, then she shivered as those words *this I know* brushed over her ears. She knew what he meant. She had seen the native women's eyes as they scurried from his quarters under the cover of a dawn sky to meet the slavers outside the garrison walls. They attested to his carnal appetite. That same animal passion was in the Colonel's grey eyes now. They glistened with hunger. She knew what he wanted – he wanted *her*. Gwendolyn would have no part of it.

Gwendolyn wrestled with her thoughts, wondering why she suddenly recalled the thrill of seeing a young native guide wash himself by the well; his dark, naked skin sparkling in the sunlight, his flaccid penis, long and thick, swaying with potent promise. Her belly flipped. A wave of desire whirled through her. Her sex thrummed at the image. Those delicious sensations were abruptly stifled when chains of guilt restrained her flush of excitement.

"Gwendolyn," the Colonel said, pouring himself another drink. "Surely you can see . . ." he took a sip from his glass ". . . the world as you know it does not exist out here."

Gwendolyn's mind darted between the native women and the young guide, then to the desolate place where she now lived. She stepped to the open window and stared into the courtyard. The sun had already dropped behind the barracks, casting a long grey shadow toward her. Its darkness seemed to reach for her, luring her into its seductive mystery. Dust floated hazily in the hot, still air. She took a measured breath. Her lungs burned as they filled with sickly heat – Alexandria, rich and vibrant, was only a dream now.

Gwendolyn tromped to the door and threw it open. The iron

latch slammed to the clay wall, sending plaster chips to the wooden floor.

The Colonel swigged back his Scotch; a grin stretched his narrow lips.

Storming across the compound, Gwendolyn gripped the reins of a white mare that had its head dipped lazily to a trough of water and threw herself onto the mount. Spurring the horse with the leather heels of her boots, she bolted out of the gates.

The smell of the compound, latrines and unwashed bodies, fled from her as each powerful stride carried her further into the desert. Gwendolyn thought of the small grove of palms and the sweet, cool water beneath it. God, why did he do this to her? She could see how spellbound he was with her, even before she had left school a year before. Damn him! She had lain awake many nights thinking about him, wondering about his manhood, about making love to him – God! He was so virile. Gwendolyn hated herself for having contemplated such an act. She despised herself for wanting him to take her. But she could never let him touch her – not *that* way!

A hot breeze, laden with the heady scent of fertile soil and wild flowers, swept out from the green oasis to greet her. Her refuge was near.

At last! She had escaped the repressed isolation of the compound and the tenacious advances of the Colonel.

Gwendolyn dismounted and walked the horse into the quiet of the palms. Letting the reins fall into the tall grass, she looked up at the yellow-orange twilight painting the swaying fronds. The high leaves whispered and caressed each other like newly acquainted lovers. Moving slowly between the palms and acacia trees, she took deep breaths to clear her head. The air was resplendent with warm perfumed scents. Licking her parched lips, she swallowed, cringing as fine, gritty sand slipped down her throat.

Laughter and youthful giggling drifted up from the pool in the gentle flow of cool air beyond the tall grass. Gwendolyn crouched, then crawled through the thick reeds near the water's edge. The water rippled and sparkled and seemed so inviting in the gentle light of evening. Creeping along on her hands and knees, she parted the tall blades of grass.

Two young women stood shoulder-deep, splashing each other

with handfuls of water. Gwendolyn laughed inwardly at their enthusiasm, wishing she could join them. When they floated onto their backs, her heart gave a jolt. Her pulse fluttered. She gasped. The closest young woman arched upward, thrusting her taut breasts sensuously above the water, their honeyed flesh glittering in the waning sunlight. Her companion, just as golden-brown, had much smaller breasts, almost none at all. But her nipples extended lengthily from small mounds crested with dark flesh.

Gwendolyn caught her breath as she watched them embrace each other. A strict English upbringing tugged at her stomach, her inner voice, guilty and stoic, shouted, Leave! Turn your head! Where is your shame?

Gwendolyn started to crawl away, but the thrill of watching the two young women sent her heart racing. Instead, she remained crouched behind the reeds.

The small-breasted woman with the protruding nipples stood up in the water. She took her friend by the hand and led her onto the grassy edge of the pool – only feet from Gwendolyn's hiding place. Facing each other in the golden light, they kissed, arms entwined and lips crushed against each other's.

The girl with the larger, fuller breasts dabbed gentle kisses on her friend's shoulders. Moving upward, she licked the droplets of water from her companion's cheeks. Those kisses moved lower. She lapped at the beads of moisture clinging to her friend's nipples, sucking on them, making the rigid flesh distend, thick and dark. She moved steadily, slowly downward along the flat of her partner's stomach, licking more watery beads, tasting them one by one.

Gwendolyn's thighs trembled. She wondered how those lingering kisses would feel on her own flesh. She mimicked the kisses with her hands, using her palms to caress *her own* breasts, *her own* nipples, *her own* belly.

The small-breasted girl parted her legs further as her friend's mouth continued its downward journey. The other, now on her knees, brushed her lips lightly over the soft rise of her partner's belly. With outstretched tongue she licked the damp golden skin before flicking the tip around the crescent-shaped navel.

Gwendolyn quivered, watching that wondrous tongue work downward into the mass of lush black pubic hair. Sliding her hand between her thighs, Gwendolyn pressed a slender pale finger to the crotch of her riding breeches. God! She could not control herself. She should leave. Now! But something inside her refused to obey her conscience.

That finger met the wet heat of her arousal through the tautly stretched material. She caressed herself. Her eyes narrowed in pleasure.

The long-nippled girl lowered her head. She cradled her lover's face, then combed her fingers through the wet hair. Slowly, moving her hips in little circles against her friend's mouth, she suddenly thrust forward. Another thrust, then another. She threw her head back, lifting her face to the darkening sky. Her petite body now writhed with pleasure. She ground her sex lustily onto her friend's adoring and ravenous mouth. Soft groans escaped her lips as her lover drew her hands along the backs of her thighs and squeezed the taut fleshy buttocks.

Gwendolyn watched as the long slender fingers of the large-breasted girl kneaded the dark brown flesh. The tips dug into the firm youthfulness, making pale imprints where the skin was still wet from their swim. Gwendolyn's heart beat thunderously, and her breasts swelled at the sight. Her nipples grew tight and she could feel the flesh pucker beneath her blouse. Her belly fluttered with excitement. No, she mustn't touch herself. She was a lady, and young ladies didn't do such things. She watched with terribly mixed emotions. She closed her eyes – but only briefly.

Still twitching her hips on her friend's mouth, the girl lifted the face that pleasured her away from her sex. Kneeling down on the grass, she motioned her friend to lie down on her back. Gwendolyn's belly twinged with illicit delight as the small-breasted girl straddled her friend's face. She saw the girl's sex, dark and fleshy and glistening, as she stretched over the reclining girl's face.

Gwendolyn found herself thinking of how it might feel to kiss another lady's vagina. She had dreamed of it – often. It was shameful, but she looked on.

The two young women now ground their mouths into each other's sex. Faces appeared fleetingly, then vanished again into the pulpy mass within each other's lush black pubic hair. Hips wriggled. Thighs quivered and trembled. The soothing rustle of tall grass and palms mixed with the fleshy sounds of lovemaking. Their noises of mutual pleasuring grew louder, echoing the passion of their sweetly writhing waists.

Gwendolyn subconsciously caressed her inner thigh, continuing to spy on the women just feet from her. The linen crotch of her jodhpurs was now soaked with her arousal. Using her fingertips, she traced the patch of moisture seeping from her own sex. Guilt filled her every pore. Shame washed over her. Yet her sex throbbed with pleasure.

Gwendolyn had only allowed herself to dream of such passions. Now she had no escape from her senses. She wanted the caress of another woman, the gentle touch of a female's hand. Her breasts ached with need under the thin cotton; her nipples poked lewdly at the material. The rubbery flesh became unbearably sensitive. Every breath sent her reeling with relentless sensation. Lifting her hand to her breasts, she cupped each of them in turn. As the two women writhed and moaned with their depraved pleasures, she soon crushed the yielding flesh of her breasts to her chest. Oh, God, she wanted to join them, feel their fingers on her skin – her naked skin. She desired their mouths on her vagina. Yes, to have another woman tease her sex with her mouth, kiss her swollen vaginal lips, lap at her wetness. Oh, God, she wanted to have pleasure – sexual pleasure.

Gwendolyn slid her fingers under her loosely buttoned blouse. With beating heart, she felt the rigidness of her nipples. Only in bed, late at night, had she touched herself there. She unbuckled her belt and unbuttoned her jodhpurs. Slipping her other hand under the waistband, she pressed downward along her belly. Nearing the fleecy blonde mass of pubic hair. Her pulse raced with the first sensation of damp skin. Moving lower through the lush golden tuft, she touched her vagina – her sex – her *cunt*! That word, deliciously naughty, made her nipples tingle with sensation. Lust roared through her body, burned in her blood.

Yes!

Her finger rode easily up and down the slippery crease of her sex. Parting the outer lips, she pressed firmly into the spongy flesh.

Gwendolyn thought of nothing but the pleasure. Sweet waves of sexual bliss surged through her. Nipples screamed for her fingers. Wet, slippery nether-lips begged for . . .

Although shamed with her thoughts, she could not rid her mind of her needs. She was soaked with excitement. Straightening, she stretched her hand lower into the steaming forest between her thighs. Further, deeper into the tight, moisture-laden crotch. Oooh, it was wonderful. Gwendolyn fanned her fingers over her pliant nipple. She inserted a finger deep into the sopping lips guarding her *cunt*. As her excitement rose, she flicked her fingers swiftly and firmly over the taut reddened bud bursting from her breast.

Incoherent words filtered and drifted between the palms and the tall reeds. Gwendolyn fell back onto the grass. She closed her eyes as an ocean of pleasure crushed her to the ground. Arching her back, she heaved her buttocks into the air. Opening her eyes, she saw the sky high above her had turned deep velvety blue. And stars winked at the earth with a knowing sparkle.

"Aaaaah . . ." Gwendolyn gasped. Her breast swelled under her hand. Her fingers slipped along the crease of her sex. Yes! Yes, oh, God! Her cunt!

She plunged her fingers deep into the wet opening, twisting her long fingers from side to side. Her nipples jutted as if about to be pulled from her body. Every sensation, every delicious trickle of sexual bliss flooded her belly. Her thighs tensed like twin blocks of stone. Her lungs sucked at the cool evening air, begging for release.

Laughter and the cries of orgasm echoed in her head as the two lovers continued to pleasure one another.

Gwendolyn's body began to quake. Her belly quivered. Her thighs trembled. Pressing her fingers to the swollen bud between her aroused vaginal lips, she let out a silent exhalation of pleasure. In a long, shuddering paroxysm she let every pore, every nerve in her body burst with release.

Gwendolyn slowly let her body fall back to the ground, and took long, deep breaths.

Voices!

Male voices sifted through the tall grass behind her.

Terror ripped through her.

Slavers!

She thought of the Colonel's words: *You will learn things, Gwendolyn. And, you will come to love them – this I know!*

THE NAUGHTY NUNS OF SAINT-SULPICE

Simon Sheppard

The 7th of Thermidor, Year II

"*Mon Dieu!*" cried the pretty young postulant, fingering her rosary. For the hand of Sister Lulu was having its way with little Mariette's swollen cunny, sending her into paroxysms of lust. Sister Lulu's fingers pried apart the juicy cunt-lips and drove deep into Mariette's dripping hole, her thumb playing upon the joy-button of the young girl's stiffened clit.

Mariette squirmed upon the narrow bed in Sister Lulu's cell, legs splayed wide, her cunt hungry and wet. Her simple linen slip was gathered up around her waist, the rough-woven blanket harsh against her smooth, delicate thighs. The flicking of the nun's thumb grew quicker and more intense. Mariette began to buck her hips and moan.

"What's that you're saying, my child?" asked Lulu.

"I'm reciting the rosary, Sister."

"Well, say it out loud, my child."

"Hail, Mary, full of grace," began Mariette, in a low and strangled voice. "Blessed art thou . . . among women . . ." But she soon enough fell silent as the nun pulled out her fingers, bent over the bed, and commenced licking the novice's quim. The rosary fell from Mariette's slim, pale hand.

They felt rather than saw the heavy wood door swing open. The night wind made the bedside candle flicker.

"What in the name of all that's holy is going on here?" It was the Abbess, a tall, stern woman in her late forties.

Sister Lulu raised her head. Her face was sopping wet. "I'm just introducing Mademoiselle Mariette to the ways of our order, Reverend Mother."

"Very well," said the Abbess. "Carry on."

The 8th of Thermidor, Year II

The knock at the gatehouse door came deep in the night, loud and insistent. Sister Annabelle, blinking away sleep, candlestick in hand, unbolted the door and opened it cautiously. The countryside gleamed bright beneath the summer moon. Annabelle looked down. A young girl lay sprawled before her, cloak spread wide upon the ground. "Reverend Mother, come quick," Annabelle called, as she half-ran toward the Abbess's chamber. "Come see what I found!"

Revived, the girl lay under heaped blankets, sipping a tisane. Her name was Berthe, she said in a hoarse, exhausted tone, and she was the child of nobility. The Reign of Terror raging, her mother and father had been dragged off to the guillotine. She herself had slipped from the château, watching from the woods whilst the Committee of Public Safety looted her home. She fled into hiding. But the radicals had somehow caught her trail, and she had run, run until she could run no more, at last coming upon the isolated Abbey of Saint-Sulpice.

"That damned Robespierre!" cried the Abbess. "We at the Abbey have somehow escaped the depredations of him and his hell-bound cohorts, but the calumnies continue. At each knock on the door we fear for our lives. As though they would bother knocking!"

"Ah, my poor little Berthe!" Sister Lulu cooed, wiping the young girl's forehead with a damp cloth. Lulu's other hand wandered down toward Berthe's apparently ample breasts, but was firmly gripped by the girl and pushed aside. *Tant pis!* thought the lascivious sister, looking into Berthe's soft eyes.

"Perhaps we should let the poor sparrow rest," said the Abbess, "for she's been through quite enough. Sister Annabelle, would you mind if she stayed the night in your bed . . . ?"

"Oh, *no*, Reverend Mother!"

". . . alone?"

Sister Annabelle pouted, a cute little moue.

"You, Annabelle, may stay with Sister Fifi for the night," the Abbess continued.

Annabelle looked doubtful, though chubby Sister Fifi's blue eyes were alight with glee.

"And Fifi," admonished the Abbess, "none of that nonsense with the statue of our Blessed Mother, or you'll answer to me!"

Each time Sister Annabelle was about to drift off to sleep in Sister Fifi's crowded bed, she felt Fifi's fat little hand reaching beneath her linen slip, sliding along her firm, silky thighs, straight to the mound of Venus. As Annabelle always slept without her panties, Fifi had no difficulty sliding two spit-wet fingers inside the young nun's twat.

"For the love of Christ," Annabelle moaned, "would you let me get some rest?"

"Well, *I'm* not the one who suggested you sleep with me!"

At last Annabelle rose from the bed and slipped into her habit. Closing the chamber door behind her, she tiptoed toward her own room, her pretty little bare feet moving soundlessly over the cold stone floor. With exquisite care, she silently opened the door. In the bed, *her* bed, slept the charming young Berthe, still wrapped in her long blue cloak. Berthe's golden curls shone in the shaft of moonlight coming through the tiny window. Annabelle caught her breath and walked silently toward the sleeping innocent. Suddenly, Annabelle's bare little foot tipped over the chamber pot, which was not in its accustomed place. The pot was, fortunately, empty, but the resulting noise roused Berthe; the girl stirred and her eyelids fluttered open.

"Who's there?" The poor thing seemed genuinely frightened.

"Rest, *ma petite*. 'Tis only I, Sister Annabelle."

"Ah, Sister Annabelle," Berthe said woozily, still half-asleep. "You startled me."

"I'm so sorry, my dear. May I sit beside you and soothe your brow?"

"I suppose it could do no harm," said Berthe. But the nun

was already seating herself upon the narrow bed, legs drawn up beneath her, thigh pressing into the cloak-swaddled form of Berthe. Softly, she stroked the pretty girl's forehead.

"Ah, Sister, what lovely little feet you have!"

"Yes," said Annabelle sweetly, "I'm quite proud of them. Though the Abbess says that pride is a sin."

"I'm quite sure the Blessed Virgin will forgive you. She seems to forgive so much."

Berthe extended a graceful hand from beneath the sheets and began to run her fingers along the curve of Sister Annabelle's pretty little instep. "May I kiss it?" Berthe asked.

"I wish you would," sighed Annabelle.

So Berthe leaned over and commenced to lick and cosset the delicate foot. Around and around her tongue moved, slipping between the little toes, until she stretched her mouth over an entire set of five.

"And is it too awful, the Terror?" asked Annabelle, in a genuine tone of concern, though she was squirming still. The mouth left her tingling foot.

"It's as awful as mankind can become when its rigid, abstract notions of right and wrong supersede the lessons of our own soft, hungry bodies. Surely you, being a bride of the Church, can understand that?" Berthe's tone was less than kind.

"I'll just forget you said that," said Annabelle sternly, "if you'll lick my foot some more."

But the mouth, when it returned, went not to her foot but her ankle, and began to move wetly up her calf. Annabelle shuddered and raised her slip to her waist. Her curly, luxuriant bush gleamed gold in the summer moonlight flooding the little room. Berthe's tongue moved steadily up her calf, described little circles behind her knee, then began to move up the inside of her pale white thigh. Annabelle reached over and stroked the young girl's firm, still-clothed breasts. She moved her hand downward over Berthe's belly, down to the girl's hidden pussy. Then, just as Berthe's probing tongue made contact with the nun's pulsing cunt, Annabelle gasped in shock. For between the girl's thighs was a huge, hard rod of flesh.

She jerked her hand away and crossed herself. "My Lord! My Lord! What is that?" But Annabelle already knew.

"I believe that even you, my innocent, know the answer."

"Berthe's" voice had grown lower, and a wicked grin crossed "her" face.

"But . . . but who are you?"

"My name is Hubert-Donatien de Sade."

Sister Annabelle gasped again. "The son of the infamous Marquis?"

"*Non*, the son of his brother, Louis-Marie. But I am my uncle's disciple, after a fashion." He pulled down the sheets and began to unbuckle his cloak. "And I *am* in flight from the Reign of Terror, that much is true. For my uncle, despite his support for the Revolution, has been accused of 'moderatism' and is condemned to the guillotine. And I have fled into hiding, lest I share his fate."

Annabelle knew not what to think. Pity, lust, and revulsion all swirled through the confused girl's soul.

"So, my little holy one, have you seen one of these before?" He gestured toward his now-naked crotch.

"Only my little brother's, *monsieur*. And it was nothing like that." For her little brother's soft worm was not at all like the the rampant rod of cock-flesh gleaming in the moonlight.

"You may touch it, if you like."

"Oh, no, *monsieur*." But de Sade had grabbed her wrist, and was guiding her hand toward his crotch.

"Go ahead, Sister. It will do you no harm."

"But I risk my immortal soul!" Annabelle was truly alarmed, though she *was* curious to feel its considerable heft.

"Ah, you people invent damnation, and then you sell us salvation!" de Sade said bitterly.

"You *are* your evil uncle's disciple!" But her fingertips had made contact with the hot, hard flesh. And when de Sade released his grip, her hand remained there, closing around the strange rod.

"Ah, my pious little fool, 'evil' is but man's invention, a stumbling block to knowing who we truly are. That's it, go ahead, squeeze." A leer crossed the beautiful young man's made-up face.

"Like this?"

"Harder."

"Like this?"

"Better."

"I do not know, *monsieur*, how a young man such as you can hold your unholy opinions." She began to move her hand up and down along the hot shaft, sliding de Sade's long foreskin over his damp, gleaming dick-head.

"Just as *I* do not understand how *you* can be bamboozled into believing antique myths. Would you like to find out how it tastes?"

Sister Annabelle bent over, squinting at the amazing shaft of flesh that shuddered in her hand. She sniffed: a yeasty smell, not like a woman's smell, but not unpleasant. She extended her tongue and gave the cock a tentative lick. De Sade, meanwhile, had worked his hand into her bodice and was cupping her breast in his hand, grabbing the warm tit harder, pulling her down upon his cock. She opened her mouth wide, wider.

"*What in the Savior's name is happening here?*"

They looked up, startled. Sister Fifi, nightclothes disheveled, stood in the doorway, a look of shock upon her chubby face.

"Ah, another bride of Christ!" grinned de Sade.

Annabelle had dropped the hot shaft and was rearranging her slip. "We were just discussing sin and salvation, Sister Fifi . . ." she sputtered.

"Fifi, is it?" smirked the dissolute young nobleman. "Sister Fifi, would you care to join us and get, one assumes, your first taste of cock?"

Indecisive, Fifi stood in the moonlit doorway, mouth agape, staring at the odd, red piece of maleness that snaked upward from the man in the convent bed.

"You should try it, Fifi. It doesn't taste half-bad – eh, Annabelle?"

As if entranced, Fifi shuffled toward the bed, making straight for the young man's hard-on.

"Sister Annabelle, show Fifi how to use her hand on it." And soon Fifi was stroking the stiff thing with her chubby little hand. Meanwhile, the young man was busy undoing Fifi's nightclothes.

"Oh, *monsieur*," said Fifi, "I don't think this is quite right, but touching you is making me feel so funny." Her bodice undone, her bountiful breasts poured forth, brownish nipples erect against smooth white skin.

"Annabelle," said de Sade, "suckle at her breast."

"But I don't wish to," protested the pretty blonde nun.

"*Do it*," commanded de Sade, "or you shall have to leave the room!" And Annabelle, overcoming her reluctance, drew a stiff nipple between her lips, stroking her own pussy as she did so.

De Sade, having finished disrobing Sister Fifi, licked three of his fingers and slid them inside the chubby nun's cunt which, having been shaved clean, looked very much like a young girl's. In and out, in and out, he pumped his fingers between the slick cunt-lips, and Fifi in turn applied herself to frigging his rampant cock with ever-increasing vigor. The dissolute young nobleman then reached his other hand over to Annabelle's golden snatch and began finger-fucking her, as well. Soon enough, though meeting some resistance, he'd slipped his slim hands deep into both the nuns, who squirmed and moaned energetically.

"Annabelle, use your hand on me, as well," he commanded, and now there were two hands on him, stroking his cock and balls, while the panting women rode his fists. "Some may call this sin, but I call it liberation, a sort of liberation more real than the 'freedom' that the rabble in the street prattle on about. And now," he said, "I believe it's time to put my tool where it belongs." Withdrawing his hands, to sighs of disappointment, he instructed Annabelle to sit astride his reclining form. She did so, her hungry cunt slipping against the curve of de Sade's damp stiffness. The nun reached down and began to stuff the big cock into her gaping hole. "No," said de Sade merrily, "*that's* not where it goes. Bend over and suck on it until it's very wet." Annabelle did as she was told, gagging on its prodigious bulk. "Now then, Sister Fifi, I want you to lie face-down upon me, head-to-foot, straddling my head, with your mound upon my face and your mouth upon Sister Annabelle's cunt." She did so with alacrity. "And you, Sister Annabelle, sit down upon my cock."

"*Take it into my nether parts?*" Annabelle gasped.

"*I said sit on my cock!*" de Sade snapped. Already, the oral ministrations of Fifi were breaking down Annabelle's resistance, and she maneuvered the bulging head of the young man's cock against her tightly puckered hole. De Sade, for his part, his face between Fifi's soft thighs, began licking the nun's hot slit. Thrusting upward, he pushed himself partway into Annabelle, who cried out, whether in pain or ecstasy he cared not. And then Sister Annabelle feverishly slid herself down upon the length of the hard shaft while Fifi's tongue plunged into her again and again. De Sade stuck a finger into Fifi's cunt until it was covered in juice, then reached up to her other hole and slipped it inside. Unlike Annabelle's, Fifi's arse seemed well-trained, opening up without resistance. With his other hand, he commenced to strike Fifi's fleshy rump, slapping its warm roundness again and again as his finger plumbed her insides. Annabelle, meanwhile, had begun to slide up and down upon his man-pole with increasing frenzy.

De Sade's spanking grew more brutal, until Fifi moaned into Annabelle's cunt. Fifi's tender butt-flesh grew hot.

"Ah, but Monsieur de Sade," gasped Sister Annabelle, "what I shall never understand is how you can hurt someone whom you desire, how her pain can pique your desire."

His finger pulled Fifi's mound off his mouth. "But my dear girl," he said, "are you not the bride of the bleeding, crucified Christ?"

And at that, Annabelle collapsed into shuddering orgasm, her tight asshole squeezing de Sade's cock until he shot off inside her, then milking him dry as patient, chubby Sister Fifi slurped away at Annabelle's red-hot cunt.

The 9th of Thermidor, Year II

"But you and Sister Fifi have been caring for poor little Berthe all morning," said the Abbess. "I simply wish to go in to her and see how's she's doing."

"But she's asleep. You surely wouldn't want to disturb her," said Annabelle anxiously.

"I'm going to see whether the child is well. Now let me pass." The Abbess's expression was stern. "The impudence!"

Annabelle stepped aside from the cell's door. Inside, a window-curtain had been drawn against the hot morning sun. The Abbess squinted in the semi-darkness. Sister Fifi was seated beside the robe-wrapped sleeping form.

"The poor girl must be sweltering in all those clothes," said the Abbess. "Let's get her cloak off, Sister Fifi."

"Mother, *no*!" exclaimed Sister Fifi, but it was too late. The

Abbess was already peeling back the bedclothes and removing the heavy cloak.

"What *is* this?" cried the Abbess. "A *man*? In the Abbey of Saint-Sulpice! Never in all my days . . . Sister Fifi! Sister Annabelle! Go to my office! *Now!* I'll deal with you soon enough. And *you* . . ." She peered down at de Sade, who was no longer feigning sleep. "Who, in the name of all that's holy, are *you*?"

"Hubert-Donatien de Sade at your service, *madame*," the young nobleman smiled wryly.

"De Sade? Oh, my sweet Lord! I want you out of here, and I want you out *now*!"

"But I've come seeking sanctuary. You people *are* in the business of providing sanctuary, aren't you?"

"Not for the likes of you and your blasphemous family, *monsieur*."

"Ah. But I seem from my youth to recall something about 'Judge not, lest ye be put to judgement,' *non*?"

The Abbess's voice became low and angry. She hissed out, "De Sade, I'm not going to stand here and argue theology with the likes of you. I want you, your sarcasm, and your damnable penis – which Sister Fifi no doubt enjoyed – *out* of my abbey. Now."

"And if I refuse to leave your sanctimonious precincts?"

"If you refuse to leave . . ." began the furious, red-faced Abbess.

"Reverend Mother!" Sister Lulu stood in the open doorway. "Come quick! *Sans-culottes* are at the gate!"

Alarmed, the Abbess hurried through the cloister to the convent's gate. Caught between fear and curiosity, de Sade wrapped himself in his cloak and followed.

The revolutionaries were pounding at the thick wooden door. "Open up in the name of the French people and the Committee of Public Safety or . . ."

". . . or we'll burn your Papist stinkhole to the ground," shouted a second rough, uneducated voice.

"My children, I fear the goons of Robespierre have come for us at last," said the Abbess, only the slightest tremor belying the calmness in her voice. "I shall open the door. I fear I have no choice. Let us pray to the Savior for protection." She unbarred the gate and pulled open the thick wooden door. Outside stood a mob of perhaps two dozen men, most ill-clad peasants, but also a few *bourgeois*, amongst them a schoolteacher and a shopkeeper whom the Abbess recognized from her visits to the village. The green fields shimmered with heat. The cloudless sky was bright blue.

"Out of our way, old woman," sneered a chunky blond-haired man. "We claim this place and all it contains in the name of the people of France."

"I'm sorry, sirs," said the Abbess, "but we answer to a higher authority than the men of the First Republic."

The unshaven blond-haired man shoved her to the ground. Several nuns gasped. Sister Lulu began weeping. As if from nowhere, dark clouds scudded across the sky, blotting out the sun.

"Let's go, men!" yelled the weedy shopkeeper, and started toward the gate.

And then, from within the cloister, a voice, calm and commanding. "Perhaps, gentlemen, you might be persuaded to leave the Abbey be," said the pretty young postulant Mariette, walking toward the gate, "if I offer you myself instead." Slowly, gracefully, she walked to the convent door, and with a single simple gesture let her robes fall to the ground. Her hands cupping her lovely breasts, she walked out to the angry mob.

Instinctively, the men backed away to let her pass. Mouths agape, the *sans-culottes* stared at the naked young girl who had offered herself up to them. For a moment there was utter silence. Then the chunky blond man pulled down the front of his pantaloons and, grabbing his thickening cock in hand, cried out, "Let's go, men! First her, *then* the abbey!"

He was mere paces from Mariette when the clouds parted and a bright shaft of sunlight shone on Mariette. Some later said they thought they'd heard the sound of distant trumpets. And Mariette's short auburn hair began to grow, lengthening, entwining round her body, till her tresses reached the ground, covering her nakedness.

"A miracle!" said Sister Lulu. "A miracle like that of blessed Saint Agnes!"

The sunlight grew brighter and brighter, till the awestruck mob of *sans-culottes* had to avert their eyes. Mariette bent to her help the Abbess to her feet and the two re-entered the Abbey, bolting the door behind themselves, and leaving the half-blind rabble to stagger home.

In a shadowed corner beneath an archway, amazed eyes wide as saucers, stood young Hubert-Donatien de Sade.

By late that hot afternoon, the miraculous tresses of young Mariette had been plaited, cut from her head, and placed into a golden reliquary which was placed upon the altar of the convent church.

Meanwhile, the Abbess had been talking with Sisters Fifi and Annabelle, whose repeated protestations of innocence had finally won her over.

"And how," she asked the two nuns, "do you propose punishing this vile seducer who has led you astray?"

Annabelle and Fifi whispered together. "I believe, Reverend Mother, that he should be flogged severely, though even flagellation is too good for him." Fifi spoke firmly, with an odd twinkle in her eyes.

"Then tomorrow morning, flogged he shall be, in the name of our Holy Savior. But we must keep him under custody tonight, to ensure his presence tomorrow."

"Reverend Mother," said Annabelle demurely, "I don't believe that, knowing of his punishment, he would run away."

"That's as may be," said the Abbess, "but I intend to keep him secure in a cell till dawn."

Sister Annabelle and Fifi smiled at one another.

"And *I*," said the Abbess sternly, "shall be the one who stands guard."

At which the two nuns tried not to let their disappointment show.

The 10th of Thermidor, Year II

Dawn lit up the verdant countryside. Birds twittered loudly. And Hubert-Donatien de Sade was led from the little cell where he had spent the night in fitful anticipation of what the morning would bring.

Clad in white linen shirt and knee-breeches, he stood at the center of the convent courtyard, surrounded by the assembled nuns of the Convent of Saint-Sulpice.

"In the name of Our Lord and Savior Jesus Christ," the Abbess intoned, "we have assembled here to provide chastisement and correction to this sinner." She turned to de Sade. "Before we begin, *monsieur*, would you care to pray?"

"Pray?" asked de Sade. "To what? To whom?"

"You can say that still? After what you witnessed yesterday?" Already, sisters were referring to the event as "the Miracle of Mariette."

"*Madame*, things occur every day for which I have no explanation. The sun rises in the East. Blood courses through my veins. At the sight of a pretty girl, my cock rises. But perhaps these are things which finally are, at base, merely inexplicable. Not 'miracles.' Not 'acts of God.' Merely the mysteries of a wide and dark universe. All else is self-delusion."

"Sacrilege! Unrepentant blasphemer," hissed the Abbess, "prepare for punishment!"

"As you wish, *madame*."

"On your knees, de Sade!"

He knelt upon the ground. One by one, each nun came before him, crossed herself, and spat into his face. As the gobs of spittle ran over his pale flesh, de Sade's mouth opened wide and a beatific look crossed his face.

Witnessing this transfiguration, the Abbess grew enraged. "You animal! You perverse, damned animal!"

Licking at his lips, face agleam with women's spit, the kneeling man asked, "And would it be better if I denied what I truly am?"

"Let's see if what awaits you next leaves you so damnably self-assured!"

The injured parties, Fifi and Annabelle, helped de Sade to his feet. Together, they removed his linen shirt, revealing a lanky, hairless torso.

"Now step away, Sisters," the Abbess said.

"Reverend Mother," said Fifi, "would it not be more humiliating if . . . ?"

"If what, Sister Fifi?"

"If he were truly naked." She almost giggled. Several of the other nuns nodded in agreement.

"Very well," said the Abbess sternly. "Strip him!"

His shoes, stockings and breeches removed, de Sade stood naked in the courtyard, his slim body shimmering in the morning light. Many of the nuns, having never before seen a man in such a state, kept their eyes upon his half-hard crotch. The Abbess, two thick ropes in hand, strode up to the naked youth and tied one rope around each of his wrists, then fed the ropes through the metal rings atop two posts standing several meters apart. She stretched the ropes taut and tied them off, so that the young de Sade was half suspended by his outstretched arms. She then stood before him and, with the back of her hand, delivered a brutal slap across his face. At the blow's resounding crack, de Sade's prick sprang to full erection. Sister Perpetua let out a low moan. Several of the other girls tittered.

The Abbess walked behind de Sade and was handed a medium-weight flogger by husky Sister Felicity. The Abbess's black-robed arm lifted the flogger high into the air and brought its stinging tails down upon de Sade's naked, helpless body. He winced a bit, but smiled. And his cock remained at full salute. Again and again, the grimly determined woman brought the flogger down upon the lad's shoulders and back, leaving reddening welts with each blow.

Several of the nuns had grown faint, from the warming sun, no doubt, and leaned against their sisters for support.

"Sister Felicity, the birch!" And the Abbess traded her flogger for a bundle of birch branches bound together at one end with twine. The strokes of the birch were sharper and more stinging than the flogger's had been. The naked young man grimaced in pain. Sister Fifi began to touch herself discreetly, and even innocent young Mariette was spellbound.

The stern Abbess's ministrations had turned de Sade's back into a cross-hatched welter of raw abrasions. "You are not, I assume, yet ready to recant your blasphemies?"

But de Sade was silent.

"Very well, then. Sister Felicity, the scourge."

Unlike the flogger which the Abbess had first used, the instrument now in her hand was a heavy, multi-tailed whip. At the end of each fierce tail, a little metal bead gleamed in the sun. Stroke after stroke, the blows inflicted upon de Sade brought him ever closer to some dark place between ecstasy and pain. He whimpered and cried. Tears rolled down his soft cheeks. Many of the nuns were now visibly agitated. Delicate Sister Perpetua fell to the ground and rolled around as if in a fit.

"Thank . . . you," de Sade gasped, "for the . . . mercy . . . of Christ."

At this, the Abbess let fly a truly ferocious blow. De Sade thrust forward against his bonds, fucking the air with his swollen cock. And with one last, desperate thrust, he found release, his overflowing seed shooting high into the summer air, again and again and again.

Hubert-Donatien de Sade, drained of everything, fell into a swoon.

Sisters Fifi and Annabelle rushed to his side. Fifi untied his hands, while Annabelle held his limp body, cradling him in her arms as blood soaked into her black woolen habit.

The other nuns, still dazed, stood and stared. Sister Perpetua, full consciousness regained, raised herself clumsily from the ground.

"All right, Sisters!" said the Abbess, still sweaty and breathless from her exertions. "It's time to attend to the rest of the morning's duties."

And at that exact moment, the convent echoed to a ferocious pounding at the gate.

"Oh, my Lord!" cried Sister Lulu. "It's the *sans-culottes* again!"

"Only another miracle can save us," whispered Sister Fifi, her eyes turning hopefully in Mariette's direction.

The Abbess spoke firmly. "Then, my children, we must pray for another miracle." And she went to answer the gate. The other nuns bestirred themselves and followed her slowly. At last, only Sister Annabelle was left, seated on the ground of the courtyard and cradling the young man's battered body in her arms.

The Abbess unbolted the gate, opened the wooden door, and stepped outside. None of the others could see what was taking place. "What?" they heard the Abbess say, and then again "*What?*" in an unexpected tone of voice.

The Abbess re-entered the convent, an unfamiliar smile on her face. "My children, Sisters of the Sacred Heart, great news has come from Paris! Robespierre has been overthrown, and today will himself face the guillotine. The power of the Jacobins is at an end, the Committee of Public Safety powerless. The Reign of Terror is at an end!"

Beautiful Mariette knelt and crossed herself. "Let us give thanks to God," she joyously intoned. And all through that day and the next, the convent echoed to prayers of thanksgiving.

Annabelle, meanwhile, attended to the young de Sade, cleaning and binding his wounds, nursing him back to health. By the next morning, he was well enough to leave. He departed for parts unknown, perhaps to rejoin his notorious uncle, who had by merest chance escaped the guillotine just days before.

The Sisters of Saint-Sulpice returned to quotidian routine, quite content with life as it had always been, a life of devotion and mutual stimulation. Sister Annabelle alone pined for de Sade's return. But he was never seen at Saint-Sulpice again, and with the passage of time the memory of him, and indeed of those fateful, momentous days, receded into mist.

Only the miraculous tresses of Mariette remained as a reminder of times past. Enclosed in a reliquary of beaten gold and gems, her auburn hair was kept upon the altar of the little convent church of Saint-Sulpice, and indeed, uncorrupted by the passing years, can be seen there to this very day.

THE CONCUBINE

Rosemary Hawley Jarman

We were happy before they came. The Spaniards, the White Ones. They came to burn us and rape us and rob us. They came to redeem us in the name of their strange God, in the year of that God, 1532. They brought us the Cross, and ordered us to desert our Sun, Inti, who warms us, who gives us light and sight, who brings up the maize for our nourishment. They ordered us to forsake Mamaquilla, our Mother Moon, who illumines our nights and whose tides mark the flow of female blood.

They came to the Tahuantinsuyu, the Four Quarters, and renamed it Peru.

And they captured our living god, Atahualpa, the Sapa Inca, the holiest one. Atahualpa the terrible, the beautiful, whose name means Sweet Valour.

Yet before they came, there was such contentment, such rejoicing. From cradle to grave, none went hungry.

I first saw Atahualpa at the Feast of Capac Raymi, the lighting of the New Fire, when I was twelve years old, and living in the House of Chosen Women, as one of the Virgins of the Sun. He was masked in gold, and I stood before the altar while the sacred llama kicked over the jug of wine for Inti to drink. And a rainbow fell on me, and I saw Atahualpa and my heart blazed like the New Fire, and my womb wept with desire for him.

When I lived in the House, my closest friend was Yma Sumac, whose name means How Beautiful. Yet she was not as beautiful and strange as I, for I am white-skinned, an oddity in this land of bronze and ochre and dusk, and I was chosen – not merely to serve the temples, but the lust of the Sapa Inca himself, the Most High.

Yma Sumac and I lived, with guards outside the house, in Cuzco, and the stern old women nearby to husband our virginity.

I see us now, treading the floor of Yucay limestone polished by the feet of generations of Chosen Women. I see us with our spindles in the hands which must never be idle, winding cloud-soft vicuna wool on to the slender spines, to make glorious garments for our god on earth.

A month before the ceremony when we were hailed as full-fledged Chosen, she came to my blanket. One blanket under which we slid to lie on a single quilt on the floor. Almost asleep, I turned, sighing, into her naked arms. Her skin was warm. Her hair fell over my face. Her hands moved on me, all over me. My juice poured from the sealed crack between my thighs. Carefully she touched me, so lightly, so as not to damage me. We trembled and twined together, skeins of flesh, fluid, like waters moulded by a mountainside.

We were muted throughout; watchers slept across the doorway. We flowered under the dark sun of one another. At dawn we were aghast, as from a crime.

"What would happen if they knew?"

"No harm was done."

From her hair she took a blossom. It had a gold trumpet and a quivering pistil. She fastened it to my tunic with a gold tupu pin. Her fingers trembled.

"There. Your sacred name-flower."

For I am Cacchu Cori, the Golden Lily of the Incas, but Yma Sumac and I were soon no longer friends.

For Atahualpa had fought fierce battles for his throne against his half-brother, Huascar Inca, as ugly and wretched as Atahualpa was beautiful, and Yma Sumac was Huascar's cousin. It was a small price to pay, losing her friendship.

The Sapa Inca had already taken me, in his council chamber, very quickly, almost brutally, tearing me apart in joy and blood.

Two days later, I was installed in his pleasure house. I was sixteen. I belonged to him. I had always in my heart belonged to him, but the difference was that now he knew it.

I was borne in a litter to the pleasure house, across the fertile plain of Cajamarca where the workers were carefully watching the crops beside the little streams diverted from two rivers to irrigate the land. It was a glittering morning. Other litters carried noblemen and women. An escort with lances went with our train. Servants led llamas bearing baggage and provisions for our stay, and bright birds on poles. Runners went ahead to sweep the road with green branches.

I wore white and gold, my hair covered with a white band under which hung many braids, each ending in a gold ring, a tiny orchid, or the bright house of a snail. My snow-white palms were rouged with vermilion from the quicksilver mines.

I had been instructed. I was to be steward of his robe at mealtimes to see it was always clean. If a spot dropped on it, the garment was to be removed and burned. At last I would be close to him. The thought brought heat into me; it washed my neck and face as if I were filled with flame. My heartbeat ran away and lower down I was all soft and sweet and heavy like a fruit.

The litter came over the first river bridge as the horn sounded for noon prayer. We all dismounted into the road to do homage to Inti, the Sun.

The pleasure house was set within a perimeter of small buildings around a great courtyard. The entrance was carved with the Serpent and the Rainbow. Suites of chambers led out of a succession of wide passages. Light streamed through high openings into the heart of the house: the bathing chamber.

Running with pure water, golden fountains were set into the walls. There was a green lawn above which a dais stood among a forest of climbing vines, orchids, lupins and blood-red passion-flowers. The deep sunken bath was of masonry coloured like old cream. In the angles of the bath were stone steps and seats and niches for cosmetics. From copper pipes a mixture of hot and cold water poured into the bath and out again through a vent. A haze rose from the surface, on which female slaves tossed aromatics.

I sat in one of the alcoves, my feet in water always at blood-heat from the sulphur springs. Yma Sumac's face was grim with fury. Atahualpa had punished her for being of Huascar's line. She was to be my personal maid. She had painted my toenails silver. Now she was unbraiding my hair, withdrawing my ornaments. She began drawing a silver comb through my hair, not gently.

I said, "Do you remember how we used to do this for one another in the Mother House?"

"My lady. I remember only that you are the Sapa Inca's concubine and I am a slave."

My head hurt. She said, "Would my lady like some coca to make her forget her troubles?"

"What troubles?" I tried to turn my head; her fierce combing stopped me.

She bent close to my ear. "He will soon grow tired of you."

Seven words. You are cursed by the seven. So the lore went.

Across the steamy water in the far corner were four new virgins, brought for the pleasure of the Court, immersed. I submerged myself, swimming towards them, and the water washed Yma Sumac's words away; the water swallowed them. I rose up to distant music, the bellbird voice of the siku pipe, and the small dancing drum.

And to the sun-reflected water leaping on the walls, and to the sight of *him*, entering the bathhouse.

He stood there for a moment, servants holding his robe clear of the wet. The four virgins covered themselves modestly with hands and hair. I stood up in the water and showed him everything that was his, everything he had glimpsed only briefly on our first hasty coupling. He looked, then turned and was gone.

A bodyservant, Llullu, came hurrying alongside the bath, holding out towels. "The Sapa Inca calls for the lady Cacchu Cori."

My trembling made it difficult for them to dress me. I put on a long chain of raw emeralds he had sent me after he had taken me. All the way along the walls to his apartment, the gods of the hot springs gazed down in stone, and the invisible siku player dropped notes like bells dipped in honey.

I was led to his door. It was opened, and I was closed into the apartment.

Into shattering light. The suite was faced with gold; on each wall the rays of four solar discs stretched from floor to ceiling. He stood there as the nucleus. Light.

Naked except for a sleeveless mantle of white rhea feathers covering his back and sides, and a breechclout bearing at the loins a great gold cob of maize. The symbol of virility worn only by highborn men.

I shook so much my vision blurred. I abased myself. His hands lifted me. His body and hair were perfumed with some bitter wild herb.

Whatever words I had were blotted out. His arms struck out my breath. I stood on my toes to embrace him. His hands gripped me, pulling me to the largeness, the hardness, living rock at my loins, and I remembered its pain and power. I pressed myself against him between the soft feathers and the hot bare skin and the heavy beating heart.

All the time, running through my brain was the word "*Cuyajguem!* – I love you!" – silent, mighty, and the word took my strength so when he lifted me in his arms it was like the weightless flight of a bird.

The clothes were off. White feathers a drift on the floor beside the gold cob, my belt and tunic, my emeralds. I lay on my back on wool like silk, soft cushions with silver tassels, mounded quilts bright with blue palm fronds and serpents. He knelt by me. I dared not look at his body, but I caught movement as he touched his own erect rod swiftly, as if preparing it for what it was about to do. Serenely I readied myself for the pain again. But he lay down with me close in his arms and began filling the world with kissing. Kissing me with his mouth, his tongue, his skin, his hair, holding me into him, warm, a haven, father, mother, lover, master, god.

I moved at him to be even closer, his bones on mine, his pulsing shaft a lifted sword against my belly. He laid his thigh across me and I felt the long crust of a battle-scar, and the feel of it set me on fire. A glide of slippery wetness came from my slit. I pushed at his mouth with my wide open mouth, and put my fingers in his silky hair, and kissed him with my breath and blood and all that I was.

His mouth caught at my left nipple and drew it on his tongue, warming it, wetting it. He rubbed the other breast with his palm. I held his head, he sucked harder at my breast. My womb contracted hard, forcing a gasp. His heart shook my roots. My head strained back on the pillows, my body lifted as if a force pressed me from beneath.

I had him where I longed for him, mounted on me, clutching him, his skin of scarred silk, his body ridged with hard muscle down the centre, disciplined so as not to crush me. I writhed under him as if I fought him, and waited open, arched like a bow.

And he settled over me as the condor settles over a viscacha doe in the mountains, that same doe that lies and quivers, accepting death.

His face against mine; my close sight filled with the black wing of hair and the dark shoulder as he held me under my neck, his other hand still over my breast where the nipple poked through his fingers, alert, a little bean.

No pain. How could there be pain? My juice flowed like a river. He was in me. Not only, it seemed, in my womb, but in the blood of my heart, my veins, my pulse, from my toetips to the roots of my hair. He slid in, very hard and far; moist, pliant, I took him in; he filled me up. My breath eased out as if drawn by a furnace, my face scalded with a flush, sweat broke on my lips. He kissed the sweat, opening his mouth as my body was opening, he pushed into me almost to the limit, and inside I became a bird, fluttering in the pool of juices.

I cried long and shuddering. He reached further into me, our loins knotted, our bellies fast on one another, so deep a thrust that it seemed ultimate, until I raised and spread myself wider to admit him one last link, deep enough to bring me the pain I craved and feared.

We lay still for long instants. My womb pulsed and flickered and gripped. The pain was a sumptuous itch, a call for more. Far away I heard my own crying.

He worked me into a heat, circling his loins hard on me on that little bead where lie all the dreams of lust, and my blood sang and I sobbed from the slow, long kisses and the arch of his body as he sucked again at my swollen nipple and began slowly to move in and out of my drenching centre, a rhythm high and low and far and deep, always deep, always returning to the source that clung on his thick gorged rod.

He slid his hand under the arch of my back and trained my body to thrust down on his upward thrust. We flowed together, faster, and a little red glow began in my darkness, like a lamp in a mine, and grew brighter and bigger and fiercer until it was all at once a starburst as he pressed me down hard, lunging in me almost to reach my heart, with my womb opening in a great fainting yawn of lust, followed by ripple after shivering ripple chasing into my thighs, my arms, my chest and throat and face, shuddering from the swollen wet cleft where he was working up to my blinded eyes.

He cried out like a great animal, and gripping my buttocks drove rapidly, finally in, with the fast swell of his essence like drumming fingers rushing hot and strong up inside me and I cried too, as if he were killing me, and truly then he was mine in that moment, everlastingly mine, and stay in me, stay till the sky splits, till the cat eats the sun. Sweet Valour, my life's desire.

Still deep he lay, and I began frantically to rub the furrow in his back, where sweat had gathered as if to heal him from a wound. I kissed his long hair of shining night; he turned lazily on his face. I saw battle scars; an ancient white crescent above his ribs, another fainter long and jagged under his shoulderblade. He had run close to death in his time. And I thought: the gods are good. He seemed asleep. I touched him, light as a spider, in the hollow of his back, the indentation at his flank, down over the dark valley of his buttocks. I slid my fingers down, and felt the faintest reflex, I trailed my fingers over the cool heavy sac beneath. Then, nervous, I took my hand away.

A gush of his semen suddenly pumped out of me, mixed with a little pale blood, the very last of my virginity. I tried to smear the seed back between the lips. He had turned on his side. Watching me.

"I hurt you," he said. He spoke in the secret language that we Chosen Women had been taught for such a moment as this. I answered as I should.

"No, Sapa Inca. I wasn't hurt at all." And he laughed. Sharp, white, mountain-cat-teeth.

"Don't you know my name, Lily?"

"Atahualpa," I said, and closed my eyes for the name was holy.

His hands on my body made me shiver. He felt my skin, looked closely at its texture.

"Where did you come from?" he said softly. "You came from the sea. You're a pearl. A washed pearl. Do you taste of the sea?" And lowered his face and began to lick my belly and between my legs. Appalling! The Supreme Being with his hair spread out over my thighs, parting the lips of my sex, among all that unclean confusion, the tip of his tongue moving in the slimy opening, and I sat up and tried to pull his head away. He pushed me flat. "Stop it, woman. Oh, *somak'cha'*! you are most beautiful."

I lay while he worked his tongue in my sex and licked the lips, the bead, and lashed the place inside and out with his mouth and pulled my legs round his neck and lifted me up to him and in a sharp moment I was rising, falling, fainting, crying, laid waste by love, and next moment I kissed our juices from his lips and tasted the jelly of my bliss.

His scent was all over me, sweat, musk, jungle plants. When he lifted me on to my hands and knees I was open to him as to a ray of the sun, and when once more I felt the sliding shock of his hard coming in I sank forward, enslaved. He held me up, his arm round my breasts, his hand spread over my soaking sex.

And this time he was savage. He swelled in me, he rammed home and circled inside me and worked his rod this way and that in my deepest caverns and lit the gold fire in me again and doused it with his galloping jet, and I was dying under him, stretched and shaken to the heart by his power, and I screamed.

I screamed that I loved him, I called him *cuyaskas*, my darling, before the sunburst he put in me wiped out thought and being, and when he withdrew I was flung out on my face as if hit by arrows.

We were quiet for some time. He sat calmly. A bar of sunlight fell on us from a high slit in the wall. I looked as pale as a fish. He was more bronze than gold. In the folds and angles of his flesh there were darker tones, copper, dusk, almost umber in the smooth nakedness. The ribs just visible, the straight spine incurving a little to the narrow waist, the hard line from waist to hip to thigh slatted with muscle, lightly glossed with sweat.

I could see from his face why people feared him. He was said to be merciless. But the long obsidian eyes with their flushed whites liked what they saw. He bit my throat. I stroked his hair, long to his shoulderblades, so black it was almost blue. The sun slid from the transom. Shadows came.

He studied me intently. His eyes were full of lust, of curiosity, and perhaps I saw the shadow of love transferred from the mirrors of my own. He stretched out and took up my strand of emeralds from where they lay. They were round, glossy, like small eggs, yellow as cat's-eyes, smooth. He held them out to me, rearing to his knees over me, his thighs apart.

I knew what to do. I had been schooled by the old women in the temple. I lay beneath him and opened his buttocks gently. There was the eye of his bowel, winking, pulsating, showing the red inner rim within the small dark creases. I fed the emeralds into him, one by one. He quivered a little, leaning forward so I could have access to his body. I left the last emerald hanging on its golden thread between his thighs.

The veined column of his phallus stood up under my lips. With my hand between his legs, my wrist passing under the smooth bulge of his scrotum, I took the last emerald between my fingers. He pushed the head of his phallus between my lips. I opened wide as the shaft sank deeply over my tongue. He was breathing fast and hard. His shadow lay against my closed eyes as he leaned over me. The heat from his body enveloped me. His hands closed round my jaw. He pushed the simmering god-shaft over my tongue, against the inside of my cheeks, down, down, until it touched the back of my open throat. It tasted of pepper and musk and leaked the sour-sweet essence of his life. I sucked him like a fruit, drawing him in and down, devouring him. I received the body of my god, just as now the White Ones ingest the drear white wafer of tyranny at their altars . . .

I felt him swelling in my throat, a seed-pod at bursting point, and I drew on the string of emeralds, slowly, then faster, and at the instant he filled my mouth and throat with a glutinous outpouring I pulled them sweetly from his bowels. The chain of emeralds, moist and warm from his core, fell and coiled between the lips of my sex as I jerked upwards, hearing his deep groan of pleasure. I put the emeralds in my mouth one by one and sucked them clean. Bitter, beautiful, the marrow of him in my mouth.

He turned to me. He took the gold maize cob and spread my legs wide. Gently, not too gently, he inserted it in me. I gasped with pain. "Open, open," he whispered, his lips on mine still sticky from his seed, still tasty from his bowels. "Open." He licked my tongue. "Open, gently, open now. See, this is how you can bear my child." And so I opened to the cool gold cob, felt my membranes stretching beyond belief, felt the hard cruel love of the cob moving further and further up into me until it reached a place even he had not touched, and I could not stop my cry, nor could I stop my hips from jerking, undulating, dancing up and down with the pleasure-pain, and he laughed, bending his lips again to my glistening slit where the gold cob had disappeared but for the tiniest inch, and licking me, my bean, my little bud, bringing me to a moment beyond pain-pleasure, beyond pleasure-pain, and my juices sprang around the invading thing, and my womb sucked at it as if to draw it in to me for ever, because he had done this to me, because it was his, an extension of his loins, his power. I heard the weird wild music of my screams, and, beneath them, his laughter.

"Let's bathe," he said.

Through an arch was a sunken bath of hammered gold. We stepped in thigh-deep. He sat on a plinth mid-bath. I took a great sponge, glittering with minute shells, and washed him, face, chest, belly. I washed his shaft, the darkest part, its heart-shaped head coloured like sunglow. I had nothing to compare it with, and it was incomparable. It blossomed and grew across my palm. He pulled me on to him where he sat. He soaped my bottom and pushed into me as if I were a boy. I opened to him. Pain. Pain. Pleasure. Joy. Throbbing, spine-shivering, maddening joy, running up me to the crown of my head. I leaned and twisted on him and gripped his thighs with mine and drove myself hard on him, and bent and sobbed into his neck.

Again. Again. Inexhaustible. We rose from the bath and he lifted me on to the edge with my spine flat, and reamed my womb as he stood in the water. He rode me like someone in a race. I gasped and cried for the whole pleasure house to hear. He lifted me on to the skin of a mountain lion, sliding on me and in me again.

And there was nothing, only this. Him in me. He kissed inside my mouth, his tongue all over my wet face, in my eyes and ears, his hands hard on my loins, moving so deep in me now that I became part of his blood and strength, his seed and his sweat, as a stream joins a great river.

I was in the race. I rode him as he had showed me, writhing, dancing on him, rubbing my burning body against him, seizing handfuls of his wet hair and clamping my mouth on his, so that in the end he let me take him, and there was no world, no sun, no moon, no light or dark, only the pounding of the flesh in me, the sceptre of all joy, all life, the token of the god.

I remember we lay long together, my body flushed and slick with the efflux of his semen. That we drank chicha morada, the pink maize wine, sharing a gold vessel studded with opal and pearl.

And the siku played its silvery ghost-tune all afternoon, as if the player were hidden in the walls.

I remember that he left me at last asleep, filled with him, drowned in him, the whole of my body a vat of fine essences, as if liquid gold had been stored in me. Between my white thighs was a swollen red passion-flower that vibrated thereafter for days, until he called for me again, to renew my liquid hurts, my shimmering rain of pleasures.

Yma Sumac and the servant Llullu came at dusk and awakened me. Yma Sumac's face was sad, envious. She held a small silver box.

"This is for you. The Sapa Inca sends it, for your services."

It was a glittering chain of little moons and rayed stars. The finest craftwork, with tiny shining spindles hanging from each link. A fine sliding little serpent in my hands.

He had given me platinum. The most precious, the Moon metal, worn only by a female highly prized.

He did not grow tired of me, for he lived only a year from that day. The Spaniards killed him, after they robbed him of all the gold in the Inca Empire.

He ascended on the wings of the condor, and lives for ever in the Sun.

THE TEARS OF THE CROCODILE

Michael Crawley

I TOOK A LONG strip of gauzy white cotton and wrapped it low around my naked hips. An artful knot secured it at the base of my spine. I drew the long end down snug in the crease of my buttocks, up between my thighs, under the band that crossed my belly, and let it hang in front of me. When you are young and lissome, and serve the Queen of the Nile, your private parts may not be kept too private for fear of incurring Her displeasure.

The second strip went around my breasts, doubled. I tied a loose bow. My mirror, of polished bronze, told me that two layers of fabric sufficed. She would not see what had been done to my left nipple yet. I would choose when.

On the tips of my bare toes, I entered Her chamber. She was not alone. She never slept alone. Her companion of the night was but a boy. His gilded curls were matted. His painted lips were puffy, kiss-bruised. The silly little papyrus beard that adorned his hairless chin was askew. Bits of gum were stuck on his cheek.

I laid a hand on his soft shoulder and squeezed.

He blinked awake. I put a finger to my lips. The lad nodded. Silent as a black cat's shadow, he eased from the couch and slunk away. His plump young buttocks were livid with scratches.

A bite-shaped bruise adorned the fleshiest part of his thigh. She delights in leaving marks.

Perhaps I had saved him from worse abuse. Our Queen was fickle. It was Her frequent whim to "spoil" her Royal Brother's sodomites. She believed that once a boy had shared her couch he would no longer be content with Ptolomy's perverted loving. She was also sure that any girl she seduced was henceforth converted to sapphism.

It was not wise to disillusion Her. Any who failed to fall under Her erotic spell were condemned to be unsexed. Three eunuchs bore witness to that. So did the five girls who'd had the nubs of their desire severed by Her Royal teeth before Her Torturer had sewn them closed. Then there were those she'd had impaled.

That was why I concealed my love for Tonius Brachus, a man-at-arms in her Royal Guard. Had She discovered us, neither of us would have been left capable of physical love. The deception had made the bond of our love, and of our lust, strong. Cleopatra plays her perverse games on all who serve her. The loving between Tonius and me was always fierce, but never so frantic as when one of us had observed the other in Her embrace.

I hated it when I was forced to stand by as my Tonius futtered the Royal Bitch's coynte, or lapped at it, and yet it excited me unbearably at the same time.

My fingers folded down the silk coverlet that concealed Cleopatra's slumbering form. I held my breath as I knelt by Her side. In sleep, She was innocent. The cruelty didn't show. Her mouth was soft, not voracious. Her rounded form was relaxed, not straining with erotic tension.

Cleopatra's skin was translucent milk. Beyond white, it was tinted by the tracery of blue veins beneath it. It bruised easily. Cleopatra loved that. She counted the success of her orgies by the number of finger and tooth-marks she woke with on the following day.

My Queen shunned the Sun's holy rays, but that was only part of her secret. On the full moon she repaired to her private courtyard to bath in Selene's cool rays. On those nights, ten naked young people, five of each sex, would scour Her Royal skin from toe to hairline with a paste made from finely ground antimony, the crushed shells of apricot pits and thick cream.

I welcomed the moon. Her treatment always left her weak. On the following day we were spared her "games."

Further, Cleopatra bathed each morning in ass's milk, warm from the udder. Finally, She credited both her skin's pure luster and her seemingly eternal youth on one more treatment. She believed that men's seed held powerful magic. My Queen drank it in copious quantities. It was applied to her skin as a lotion. If it had been possible, she'd have bathed in it.

In contrast to the creamy pallor of her skin, her lips and nipples had been stained deep crimson.

Such nipples! Perfect glossy cones. They had no halos. There was no transition between the skin of Her breasts and that of Her nipples. Her peaks sat, dark waxy red, proud on their firm soft pillows.

It was to her left nipple that I applied myself. I dipped my fingertip in aromatic oil and ringed the smooth prominence with infinite soft care. If Cleopatra was woken any way but gently, She would slash out with Her talons. I'd seen them leave grooves. I'd known them take out an eye.

Still sleeping, my Mistress made a little pout. Her lips worked like a suckling babe. My fingers spiraled up to the nipple's peak. She frowned. Cleopatra was rising up from the arms of Morpheus. Her nose twitched. A slender hand lifted and covered mine. I paused. She gripped my wrist. A sudden tug urged my hand towards Her womanhood. Her thighs fell apart. I knew what to do.

My finger and thumb took a soft grip on the skin of Her clitoral shaft. I eased back, exposing the tiny pink pearl.

She bucked. My fingers tightened. Slowly at first, but growing faster, I masturbated her clitoris as if it had been my Tonius' shaft. A few breaths later, She was mewing and writhing. Her hips rose above Her couch. A tendon on the inside of Her thigh tightened. My frotting became urgent, demanding.

With a sigh, My Queen slumped.

Her eyes opened. "It's you, Asheya! Welcome back. I feared We had lost you."

"You granted me a moon, My Queen. I am returned on the day appointed."

Her hand covered mine. "Such loyalty, Asheya. How you must

love me. Only you, of all my slaves, would I trust to roam beyond my reach."

Beyond Her reach! The stupid bitch was ignorant of even Her own land. Just because I'd told Her that my home was an island, She assumed it wasn't a part of Egypt. There are a score of fishing villages on islands in the Nile's delta. Mine was one of the least of them, but it was home. One day Tonius and I would live there.

I told her, "No news, as yet, My Queen."

"News?"

"Of the battle – the great sea-battle. Your Mark Anthony . . ."

She shrugged. In clumsy Latin, she said, "He will return carrying his shield, or borne on it."

It was the first time I'd heard the tongue of the Romans from her mouth, apart from a few obscenities. Cleopatra can command a man to futter her in a dozen tongues, but knows how to say "good day" in only her native Macedonian.

She asked, "My bath?"

"It is ready, My Queen."

She writhed to her feet. Cleopatra was lithe and flexible. Those attributes, combined with sexual voracity and physical beauty, were Egypt's protection. Our Royal Whore conquered all conquerors. She had but one strategy. By surrendering eagerly, she defeated them. Men are strange. When they meet women whose lust burns more strongly than their own, they become slaves.

No human man could match lust with the Slut of the Nile. I doubted that even a god could.

Caesar, when he had been Cleopatra's groveling toy, had installed a hypocaust beneath the Palace. My warm feet blessed him for heating the marble floor beneath their bare soles.

Naked, and proud of it, My Queen lowered herself into Her sunken bath. Her ablutions were anything but solitary. I stood by with my arms full of warm cloths. Two pretty girls joined the Queen in Her bath with scraping tools and oils. Seven guards, my Tonius among them, ringed the bath, naked except for loin-clouts but bearing shields and swords. Two more female slaves, a buxom Nubian and a heavy-breasted Jewess, stood close by with salvers of pickled dove's eggs and sweets made from dates and honey, in case their Queen might feel the need of sustenance.

And she did, but not of that kind.

"Tonius," she commanded. "Feed me."

My love's eyes flickered an apology at me. He unknotted the cloth that bound his loins and knelt at the bath's edge. His staff wagged. I knew he loved only me, but a cock knows no loyalty. Basking in the heat of the Imperial Slut's gaze, it rose. She waded to the edge. The girl-slaves followed, busily scraping and oiling the Royal back. With her gorgeous breasts bobbing in the milk, Cleopatra stood at the end, head turned up and mouth agape, like a nestling begging for a worm.

Tonius stroked the length of his weapon, from base to head. I took a step closer, fascinated despite myself. He rubbed briskly, skinning and sheathing. Cleopatra strained higher. There was drool on her lower lip. Her throat was already working, swallowing in anticipation.

"Hurry," she demanded. "I have a great thirst."

His hand blurred, but the Great Gobbler, as She is called in the bazaar, couldn't wait. She grabbed his column and dragged it down to Her mouth. Her lips closed behind its head. Her cheeks hollowed. Obscene wet slurping noises filled the chamber. Her Royal fingers urged Tonius. At Her unspoken order, he pumped his hips, driving his knob deep into the soft vortex of Her mouth.

Tonius let out a deep bellow, as he always does on climax. Cleopatra kept sucking and milking, drawing out every last drop of his male essence and still sucking, till all She could pull from him was pain.

I have been told that once She gobbled a score of men dry in the time it takes a short taper to burn down. I hadn't seen it, but I believed it. I'd seen her bathed in semen – seen gobs of the man-milk drooling down her breasts and pooling in her navel.

The Imperial Slut climbed from Her bath and stood as handmaidens sluiced her down with buckets of warm water. I held a cloth out. She ignored it and pulled me into a warm embrace. I tasted Tonius on her tongue.

"There, now you are properly welcomed back." She held me at arm's length. "You look well rested." Her eyes traveled over my body. "What's that?" She tugged at the bow that held the cloth at my bosom. It fell. "Aha!" Her fingers gripped my left breast. She leaned closer. Her pupils widened as she inspected the golden ring that pierced my nipple. "Is this the new fashion, in your land, Asheya?"

It was simpler to say, "Yes, your Majesty."

Her forefinger hooked through it and twisted. I bit my lip.

"Did it hurt, when it was done?"

"Some, your Majesty."

"And now?" Her eyes were feasting on the pain in mine.

"In a very pleasant way, Majesty. It is my joy to receive pain from Your hand."

"It took a sharp tool?"

I dared not tell her that the physician had used the tooth of a cat. That might have been taken as sacrilege against Bast. "A fang," I told her. "Pulled from the jaw of a serpent."

She twisted my nipple into a spiral. I gasped. My knees shook. There was wetness between my thighs.

"It thrills you?" Cleopatra demanded.

"Yes," I admitted.

She fingered her own nipple. The honed nails of finger and thumb nipped. "Yes. I can see that it would."

Slaves put slippers on Her tiny feet, tied a silk sash around Her voluptuous hips and fastened a beaten gold collar around Her slender throat. We followed Her to the audience chamber.

"At my right," She told me as She sat.

It was a position of honor, of sorts. My kneeling there signified that She had a whim to fondle my body. To Her throne's left stood a handsome boy, naked. His penis was scarce the size of my smallest finger and curled down on his tiny wrinkled sac like a shy little snail.

There were jugglers, whom She soon tired of, followed by a woman who ate fire and ran flaming torches over her oiled bare body. Cleopatra enjoyed that better, particularly when flames licked between the woman's thighs. Freaks were paraded: a woman so fat that her belly was an apron that covered her knees, and a man with two pizzles, both functional.

As she watched the entertainment, Cleopatra toyed. She pinched my gold ring though my tender flesh. One of Her fingers tested the tightness of the boy's anus. His worm uncurled and stiffened.

"Can you make seed yet?" She asked him.

He blushed and shook his head, speechless.

"Then, if I make you, it will be for the first time?"

He nodded.

She turned him to Her, slid his foreskin back with two fingers, and inspected the small head that emerged. "Do it for your Queen." Her fingers stroked. "The milk of a virgin must be very sweet."

As she was distracted, I massaged my sore teat, trying to ease the deep ache.

She took the boy's tiny penis into Her mouth and suckled. His face grew crimson. Eventually, he jerked and then doubled over. Agony twisted his face.

"Nothing!" Cleopatra spat. "Dry as bone. Take him away. Beat his genitals with nettles."

Someone whispered a message into my ear.

"Your Majesty?" I said.

"Yes?"

"The battle was joined yestermorn, near Actium. No news of the outcome yet."

In reply, She took hold of my nipple ring and tugged it until I staggered forward. "A serpent's tooth, you said?"

"Yes, Majesty."

"If we chilled it with ice, would the cold claw deep into your breast?"

"I know not, Majesty."

"If we heated it with fire . . . ?"

I remained silent.

"And if you were with child, what when it suckled? Perhaps we should have you mated. What say you, Asheya?"

"I have little liking for men, as you well know, Majesty. After the joy of your embrace, all else is as nothing."

She grinned at that. "We shall see."

A brief time was spent on affairs of State. When a noble put forth plans for Anthony's triumphal return, She waved him aside. "It is too soon." She turned to me. "What manner of man is this Octavius?"

"In what wise, Majesty?"

"Does he like boys or women? Is he lusty? Is it true that he beds Octavia, his sister? His manhood, is it great or small? Is he potent?"

"Whatever his preferences, my Queen, he could not fail to be lusty if he met you."

She smiled. "How true. We must be prepared for – for any eventuality. Would he like me to be brought to him naked and in chains, do you think?"

"What man wouldn't?"

"You are sweet, Asheya. See that a goldsmith is brought to me." She lifted her breast and inspected her nipple. "A serpent's tooth, you said?"

After the entertainment and audience were done, we withdrew to our lunch, oysters and figs. That was a sure sign that her lust ran high. When we were alone, in her private chamber, she drew my face down to her bosom. "Bite me, Asheya. Be a serpent."

"I dare not draw Royal blood, Majesty. The penalty for that would be death."

She started, "No, but . . ."

A thumping of spear-butts signaled that we were to be interrupted. A man, the dust on his skin cut by rivulets of sweat, entered.

"A message, my Queen. From Actium. Anthony is defeated. His fleet is scattered. Octavius hounds him."

Cleopatra waved him away. "Don't be afraid, Asheya. Draw no blood, but bite hard enough to hurt me."

I took Her nipple into my mouth. The cone was rubbery between my teeth. I gripped, hard.

"Oh, yes, Asheya! Harder. Bruise me!"

I chewed. As my teeth worked, Cleopatra put her fingers to the junction of her own thighs. They worked frantically. At last, she sighed.

"Enough." Her finger hooked into my nipple ring once more and lifted my breast by it. I tensed and waited, but she let it drop. "A serpent's tooth?"

Musing, she walked to the archway that led out to Her privy courtyard. Woven mats, stretched overhead on cords, screened the area from the sun, but it was lush with greenery. I'd never seen Her so thoughtful – so distracted. Was she planning some new cruelty? If so, I'd have rather been elsewhere. Cleopatra had no patience. When she devised a game, it had to be tried immediately or She would grow spiteful.

I followed Her as She strolled between the plants. It seemed that She was looking for something, though I couldn't think what. At the end of a little path, she stopped. Her hand snatched out. To my horror, I saw that she had surprised a basking snake – an adder – the symbol of Royal Egypt.

I almost blurted a warning, but swallowed it. She was Queen, after all. Who was I to . . . ?

She lifted the writhing serpent to Her bosom. Her hand, behind its vicious head, squeezed. The foaming mouth gaped wide. Her free hand crushed the flesh of Her own breast, extruding Her nipple between its fingers. Cleopatra, Whore of the Nile, struck a fang into her own tenderest flesh.

I waited patiently until Her convulsions ceased. When she was still, I twisted the ring in my nipple until the pain brought tears to my eyes.

"Guard!" I screamed. "Send for a physician. Our beloved Queen, distraught by Anthony's defeat, has taken her own life."

THE BALLAD OF SCOTT AND ZELDA

Maxim Jakubowski

THIS IS HOW it could have happened (anachronisms and all).

Scott. December 1940

Yes, the past is a different country, he thought. Damn right. And these last few months, every single night he had been tossing and turning in the narrow bed, even when Sheilah had been visiting, as it all came back. Visiting his own lost life again, armed with no more than his mental passport.

To avoid the pain, he had moved into Sheilah's apartment. Hers was on the first floor. His had been on the third. He could feel it all ebb away. One slow day at a time. There was no longer much work at the studio, and he knew the book was at a dead end. Something told him he would never finish it. Or at any rate, not to his satisfaction.

She was so kind. But it just felt like charity for the poor, the under-emotional, the under-haemorrhoided, the under-cocked. He grinned broadly and filled the glass again. She had set him up with a writing board and he kept up the pretence that the novel was making good progress. There was pain climbing the stairs, there was pain all the time, but the worst was not the physical deterioration, it was the past flowing back, relentlessly, as he couldn't just close his mind to its cruel assault.

He sipped the whisky. The glass was soon empty. He filled it again. Not much left in the bottle. No worry, he could always phone out for another delivery.

All this booze made him want to pee. He sniggered. It just came in and seemed to flow through his body like water and come out the other end so quickly. He avoided his drawn, gaunt face in the bathroom mirror. He now spent most days in his faded blue dressing down, with a pocket full of pencils and one always balanced over his ear. The great writer at work. And play.

Another glass, then. Yes. At least the whisky kept him warm inside.

Sheilah had arranged a doctor's appointment for December 20, but he had managed to get it cancelled on the pretext of some problem with his writing. He had no need to be told what was wrong with him. He knew all too well. The slow usage of time. He also knew that it wasn't illness or his body giving up on him that would kill him in the end. Because he just wouldn't allow that. The drink would do it so much faster and efficiently. And painlessly. Just as it kept him alive right now. And erased all the memories of the past. The so-called golden days. St Paul. New York. The Côte d'Azur. Paris. Hollywood.

He hoped the alcohol wouldn't kill him at least before Scottie graduated from Vassar. He would write her again tomorrow with advice. And maybe, with a bit more work and attention, he might actually finish the novel by February. It was just that he had lost much time following that heart scare when he had fainted outside the Schwab drugstore in November. The medics had said it was his heart, but Scott knew. It was the booze clawing away at his insides. But he needed it so much. Couldn't get through the day without it. Ironically, it kept him alive as it killed him.

He looked, and then suddenly the whisky bottle was empty. No matter. Tonight, they had agreed to attend a movie preview of *This Thing Called Love* at the Pantages Theatre. And he would wear his Brooks jacket, the pink shirt and a bow tie. Made him look like a dandy. He smiled.

Stock up on more booze afterwards. Yep.

★

F. Scott Fitzgerald, American author, died the next day. He had written the letter to his daughter Scottie in the morning, and was lounging in an armchair after lunch, making notes for an article, eating a chocolate bar, when he suddenly stood up, reached for the mantel and collapsed to the floor. A moment later he was dead.

At his funeral in Rockville, Maryland, on December 27, a raw, wintry day, his wife Zelda was unable to attend and asked her brother-in-law Newman Smith to attend in her stead. She had not seen Scott for over a year at the time and was living in Montgomery, Alabama, with her mother. She had recently been released from Highland Hospital where she was being treated, unsuccessfully, for her precarious mental condition, with a letter that paroled her to her mother.

It's Always Forever – St Paul, Minnesota and Princeton, 1920

The novel has sold. She has agreed for them to become engaged. The family weren't too happy about it, but then Scott knows they never approved of him that much before, even. Irish and from the other side of the tracks and all that.

They are blissfully happy.

He loves the way Zelda kisses him, how her tongue invites his in, twists moistly around his tongue and plays mischievously with it, streams of saliva blending as the kiss lingers on and on and on, and he soon runs out of breath and she releases him and giggles in her customary lovely way.

The feel of her lips against his, the way she sometimes nibbles the lobe of his right ear (which gives him an instant hard-on, which causes him to clumsily shift around on the spot, attempting somehow to conceal the unseemly bump in his pants from her eyes as they linger in each other's arms in the back of his shiny new motor car).

The distinctive smell of her breath, which lingers all around him for hours, nay, days, even after she is back with her family, like a cloud that evokes her flesh, her eyes, her body.

Is this the magic of love? Scott wonders.

He has longed for ages, it seems, and still can't believe it is all coming true after he had given up in despair so many times.

"What are you doing?" he asks. Zelda is fumbling with his belt.

"Close your eyes, silly," she answers.

He does. Obedient.

Jesus Almighty, she is unbuttoning him, and her fingers are delving in his undergarments!

"I'm reliably informed it's called a blow-job," she says under her breath, lowering her head towards his penis as her nimble fingers roll his foreskin down and his head emerges. To be engulfed into the volcanic head of her mouth.

Scott keeps his eyes closed.

Zelda! Zelda! He would never have expected this from her. The girl is just fantastic . . .

She licks, she sucks, he grows to what he feels might be monstrous proportions, but she is not fazed and continues her tactile inventory of his cock, and that familiar tingle in the pit of his stomach begins, moving fast towards the sac of his balls, and he shudders as his future wife, his dearest Zelda, relentlessly continues her task. Her auburn hair bobs up and down on his lap.

He knows he can't tell her, but this is not the first time a woman has done this to him. No. There was that Belgian whore, the one with the scar on her cheek and the empty breasts hanging too low, back in that brothel in the North of France on the furlough he and his battalion mates had while they were still waiting to be assigned to the front. He couldn't even remember her name now. All he could recall was the way she had spat his seed out onto the stone floor after he had come to orgasm, and departed with not even a word to service another American trooper in an adjoining room. They had all been too scared of possible diseases in those foreign climes to go the whole hog and actually purchase a full-blown fuck.

Scott grins at the memory. A few days later, the end of the war had been declared. He had never been to the front. No glory.

And now Zelda was doing this wonderful thing to him.

Her mouth full, she quietly kept on sucking him as he felt that unstoppable wave of depraved pleasure course through him. He tried feebly to warn her, to indicate she should pull back, but Zelda would have none of it, and attacked his member with even more relish.

He exploded, and felt the warm surge of his seed burst through and flood Zelda's mouth. The ejaculation seemed to go on for ever. And still she would not release him, lapping up the come; he could actually feel, hear her swallowing it, and his heart just melted on the spot, waves of mighty emotion swirling inside his head and chest. God, I love this woman, he thought. I will never love another the way I love Zelda now. And for ever. My intended. My wife. My extraordinary St Paul flapper.

Soon, it would be time to drive her home to her parents' house.

Scott shivered.

"I love you so much, Zelda. Words just won't suffice. They can't express even a small part of what I feel for you."

She looked up at him and smiled quizzically, as if she were trying to interpret the precise meaning of his words.

She smiled again, as he clumsily stuffed his cock back into his woollen undergarments, slightly ashamed at being openly exposed to her gaze like this, even after what had just happened.

"It's OK, Scott, darling," she said, "next week I shall come to Princeton, and I will stay the night . . ."

"You mean?"

"I will become your lover. You will undress me and make love to me. Properly."

Once more his heart just lurched.

Screaming in the Cathedral – New York, 1923

The world is at their feet. The King and Queen of literary New York. Prophets of the Jazz Age. Life has become an endless party. The money goes around. The liquor flows.

There can't be more to life.

Or can there?

They get back to the apartment after a somewhat wild party at the Waldorf, held for a visiting French soprano. The nanny has already gone to bed. Scottie, whom Zelda still insists on calling Pat – they had first named their daughter Patricia, before changing the name to Frances – is sleeping soundly in her nursery overflowing with toys.

"Darling, I know I've had too many already, but it would be nice if you could make me one final cocktail. Would you?" Scott asks, as they both kick off their shoes in the carpeted lounge of the Park Avenue townhouse they are renting. The price is exorbitant, but so what?

"Make your own."

She is frowning. Her cheeks are slightly flushed.

"What's up with you tonight?" he asks, puzzled by her sudden change of mood. Earlier she had been as happy as hell.

She avoids his eyes, looks away.

"I saw you with her," she spits out.

Scott is nonplussed.

"Who? I don't know you what you mean, Zelda."

"That blonde actress. I saw the way you were talking to her, you know . . ."

Scott bursts out with laughter.

"Jesus, Zelda. I was being sociable. She's the daughter of one of Scribner's biggest shareholders, for heaven's sake!"

"Her breasts were spilling out of her cleavage, for Christ's sake, she was like an ambulant peep show and you sure enjoyed the landscape of flesh on display, didn't you?"

Breasts are a delicate subject. Since Scottie, hers have somehow shrunk, whereas most women's would have grown a bit after a first child, she had been told.

Scott ignores her and walks over to kiss her.

Her breath reeks of gin, but then probably so does his. Wordlessly, he unbuttons her front and ceremoniously unveils her chest. Her nipples harden, lengthen as he uncovers them. He kisses her there with tenderness, allowing his tongue to linger warmly as he circles the sharp tips of her small breasts. He moves back half a foot and takes them into his hands, cupping them, then looks her in the eye.

"But yours are the ones I like," he whispers gently.

And he is not lying. He loves the fact that they are small, that he can hold them both in the hollow of his outstretched hands as if he were weighing them like fruit; he adores the way the nipples lengthen under the warmth of his fingers or the moistness of his tongue and their colour reacts invariably by shifting somewhat between indescribable shades of pink and light brown.

He enjoys undressing her so, as he does now. One garment at a time until she stands there quite nude in front of him, legs slightly apart for support in her current slightly inebriated state. Her reddish hair, cut short according to the day's fashion in a mischievous-looking bob, the long expanse of white skin, the plains of her flesh and the modest valleys of darker hue between her breasts and in the shadow of her belly button. The sturdy Irish legs. The luxuriant growth of hair around her cunt. He closes his eyes a while and smells her and soon the distinctive odour of her aroused sex reaches him and he feels himself harden.

She lets her hand move down to her cunt and spreads her vagina lips open to his hypnotized gaze. She is wet already.

"Fuck me, then. Now. Me. Not her," Zelda demands.

He quickly sheds his evening wear, movements a tad unsteady.

"Shall we move to the bedroom?" he asks as he pulls the shirt above his head and the cufflinks from his left sleeve fall to the wooden floor.

"No," she answers, "I want to do it here." She points to the large room and an Afghan carpet spread across the floor between the liquor cabinet and the plush, quilted armchairs.

Scott feels the warmth spread inside him. Ah, my Zelda, always one for the daring and the unexpected . . .

He struggles with the belt to his pants. When he looks again in her direction, she is kneeling on the russet carpet on all fours, her backside raised in his direction. An obscene position in which he cannot help but see both her apertures almost gaping in readiness.

"I'll switch the electricity off," he suggests as the trousers slide to the ground.

"No," Zelda quickly says. "I want the light on."

She is so daring. His cock, quite hard already, gets tangled in the elastic of the underpants as he rushes his movements.

"Come," she calls impatiently. "I want you to do me this way, like a dog."

Finally, he is himself naked, and moves behind her raised rump, falls to his knees. The wooden floor under the carpet feels hard. He can feel her sweating. It's a warm summer evening and the nanny has omitted to leave any of the apartment windows open before she retired for the night. He realizes there's something animal about Zelda's odour tonight.

He looks ahead. Her puckered arsehole and its darker concentric rim of flesh looks as if it is almost breathing. He has never before seen her, seen this so close. He is fascinated by the depravity of the situation.

His eyes move an inch or so down, and as they do so, Zelda's hands thrust backward and spread her cunt lips wide open for him, and Scott sees how wet she is already.

He thrusts forward into her. There is no resistance. She is totally lubricated and gaping for him like seldom before. He sees all the way into her mysterious pinkness. He slides in.

Surely, he wonders as he fucks her, not all married couples love each other this blissfully? Surely all the people he sees in the streets outside, dressed all proper, coated with the veneer of civilization, do not become wonderful savages like us in the privacy of their sex lives? he presumes. No, we must be unique.

My Narrow Mind – Villa Paquita, Juan Ies Pins, France, 1926

The summer had been absolutely gorgeous and their skin had tanned grandly. Evenly. Golden brown. Of course, Zelda had to wear a floppy straw hat to protect her face from burning too much, but she had nonetheless come out all over in sumptuous freckles, evenly scattered across her nose, dotted across her pink cheeks and staining the visible part of her chest like paint-stains in an Impressionist painting.

They had made friends so easily with the American contingent of the Riviera set. Also a lot of French aristocrats. Lazy days spent lounging on deckchairs and dipping an occasional toe in the warm waters of the Mediterranean, while the children, little Scottie always busy with the Murphy kids, were kept happy at a short distance under the careful eye of their minders. The conversation was witty, the rhythm of summer languorous, the parties at night in a variety of glamorous villas easily reached by car, by the sea or in the hills, flowing with good wine and gaiety.

Wit and repartee and laughs and fun; this was another side of paradise.

Scott and Zelda found it delirious. They rented a succession of villas after a stay at the Hotel d'Hyeres. Zelda in particular loved Provence. She would later evoke it meaningfully in the only book she would ever write. At first, Scott managed to write most days, while Zelda busied herself shopping with Sara Murphy and others and organizing picnics later in the day on the beach.

America felt so far away.

Ernest Hemingway had come down to the coast for one week, but left after only three days, mumbling under his breath of their parasitical status and accusing Scott of prostituting his talent with all the layabouts down here. But nobody really took Ernest that seriously then. Just another spoilsport, and a bit too earnest anyway. Zelda wondered sometimes why Scott and Ernest managed to stay friends. There was an undercurrent of envy, she sensed. And Ernest looked at her strangely when he was around, almost undressing her with his eyes. Not her sort of guy.

Unlike some of those handsome French military types, who came and went with the set throughout the summer. Dashing, exotic, supremely elegant, whether in or out of uniform.

She is still in love with Scott. He's a good man, loves her back dearly. And he attracts the sort of glamour that enchants her. Her husband the famous novelist. But he's also a bit predictable. Boring? Zelda also wants to write her own books, regrets the loss of her planned dancing career, she doesn't just want to be "the wife".

Yesterday. A whole group of them had gone up to that famous restaurant in the hills behind Nice. Expensive and overrated, she reckoned. You were mostly paying for the view. They had all divided up into several cars after.

"A last drink, a coffee, Madame Fitzgerald?" the French army officer had asked.

"Why not?" she had said, without thinking. Scott had gone ahead with Gerald and Sara Murphy, already quite sloshed. By now he was probably passed out on the bed with his clothes still on.

Another man's body. Another man's touch. His kisses tasted different, the movements of his hands over her skin held new, changing rhythms. He undressed her slowly, as if performing a ritual. Stood back at regular intervals to admire her, allowing her each time the opportunity to say, "No, no further" but Zelda had wanted to see where this would go. It was like an adventure. Another crazy one, like the drinking, the false gaiety, the jumping into swimming pools with her dress still on, the day she had swum so far out to sea until none of the others had been with her any longer and she had slipped out of the cumbersome costume and waded about until tiredness set in, stark naked in the blue Mediterranean waters.

The officer had kissed her everywhere, worshipped at her altar like no man ever before, inserted his tongue in all her nooks and crannies, opened her up and delved and tasted her between the puffy lips of her cunt, which Scott had never even thought of doing. She had come twice even before he got round to fucking her.

Finally, he'd undressed. Jeez, he was big. She had stared.

"*Qu'est-ce que c'est, ma chère Zelda*?" he had asked as she did.

"It's – it's . . . different," she had said.

"*Ah, oui*. I see. I am circumcised; it's for hygienic reasons. You like?"

"Yes." She nodded. "It looks . . . nice."

He moved closer to her. Presented himself to Zelda.

"Would you, *ma chère*?"

She would.

It was morning by the time she got home.

Scott was awake.

He was already (still?) drinking.

"Who?" he quietly asked her.

There was no point pretending, she thought.

"The officer," Zelda answered. Knowing all too well that things would never be the same again.

He set his glass down, looked slowly at her – was she still flushed? – and, slurring his words slightly, said "I'm sure it wasn't your fault, my darling. It was his. I shall challenge the bounder to a duel."

"You wouldn't." Zelda had to smile.

"Yes," Scott replied, "and after I have avenged my honour, you and I shall then pack up and return to Paris."

Carrying Sin In My Sack – Paris, fall of 1929

Ernest and Scott were having a pee in the toilets at the Coupole in Montparnasse. They had earlier been moaning together about the state of New York publishing and Max Perkins' editorial edicts, size of print-runs and likely future level of advances against royalties.

Scott broke the silence.

"Hey, Ernie, can I ask you something?"

"Sure," Hemingway said. "Shoot, buddy." He directed his stream of urine towards the metal wall of the convenience so as to avoid splashing his shoes. Next to him, Scott also concentrated on his aim, pensively looking down at his member.

"Well," he said, "it's a bit delicate . . ."

"Oh, come on . . ."

"Do you think my cock is of a normal size?"

Ernest grinned broadly and turned to look down at Scott's still dribbling penis. Reflected one moment, then said "Seems more or less same size as mine, man." He pulled back from his standing position and held his own cock for Scott to see.

Scott sheepishly turned and looked.

"Yeah, I suppose so . . ."

Hemingway suddenly roared with laughter.

"What is it?" Scott enquired.

"I was just imagining my wife the bitch seeing us here with our damn cocks out on display. As it is, she said the other week that she thought we were both two queers anyway!"

"Really?"

"What does she know, hey?"

Scott slipped his penis back into his trousers. Hemingway shook the last few drops off his away.

"It's just that I think Zelda finds me inadequate, you know," he confided to the other American writer.

"All women want you to feel that way, you know, Scottie boy. I wouldn't let it worry you."

They found their way back to their table and ordered another round of pastis.

Scott had told Ernest some years back of the affair with the French officer, and made a whole song and dance of the duel he had threatened, and how it had scared the guy right away from the Riviera, never to be seen in their circle of friends again. What he hadn't revealed was that the French officer had just laughed and declined to participate in such a farce.

"I've never had the courage to ask her if his was bigger than mine, you know?"

"Listen, Scottie boy, you fucked that gal, that English singer the other month, didn't you? Did she complain about the size of your equipment, hey?" Ernest continued.

"Well . . ."

"It's not the size; it's how you use it," Hemingway insisted.

Scott had not told him that he had come too quickly with the British woman, and that one hour later he had been impotent and incapable of performing again. Maybe it had been the drink inside him. He hoped.

They downed their drinks.

"Mind you," Ernest said, unwilling to change the subject of the conversation, "talking of size, I saw that Tijuana movie loop the other week at Gerald and Sara's last party. The one you couldn't attend. There was a guy in it with a monster of a cock, must have been at least ten inches. Darn breathtaking. But this girl he was with managed to accommodate it without too much strain, I must say. But when he turned round and disposed her on all fours, you could see her arse stretching to criminal proportions as he impaled her there. Memorable, Scottie, you should have been there to watch it. Now, that cock would have made you feel inadequate . . . And the actress – well, if you can call it acting – actually looked a bit like Zelda, I must say. Picture was a bit grainy, and you couldn't see her face, but small boobs and a nice white arse. Could have been her sister, hey?"

He roared with boisterous laughter. Other customers looked at the two men.

"You sure she hasn't been taking some side trips to the Mexican border while she is visiting her parents?"

"Come on, Ernest, that ain't funny any more," Scott said.

"I know," the other man said. "It's just I so like to see you squirm, you Irish prick!"

"I know," Scott acquiesced. Then: "Have you ever measured yours?"

"Sure," Ernest said. "Six inches, just above average. And all in perfect working order, I hasten to say . . ."

"I didn't know that was the average," Scott remarked.

"Well," Hemingway added, "your average red-blooded all-American male . . . Don't know about French guys . . ."

He laughed out loud again.

As One with the Spirit, Yes, She Goes Where it Goes – New York, 1932

Scott is in California, talking to some producers. Zelda is restless. She wants to start more dancing lessons but has been told she is too old now. A friend has told her about this discreet club, this speakeasy in the East Village where money can buy you anything. Well, money is no problem these days. Scott's books aren't selling as well as before, but a short story for the *Saturday Evening Post* or *Harpers* or *Esquire* every now and then takes care of the bills and more.

"It would be advisable if you wore this," the plain-looking woman shepherding her in says, handing her a domino mask. "Discretion is most necessary."

Zelda slips the mask on, ruffling her auburn hair in the process.

Still holding her complimentary cup of champagne in one hand, and her tasselled Italian-made handbag in the other, Zelda is escorted into a small empty, dark room, and shown to a chair at its centre, facing a velvet-curtained wall.

"Do make yourself comfortable," the woman says. "I shall return in a few minutes, when you have made up your mind."

She leaves the room, and the curtain Zelda is facing unfurls slowly.

Behind the glass, there are half a dozen men. All quite nude. Standing against a white wall. It makes her think of an identity parade, like in the gangster movies. Each holds a square of cardboard with a number. Her first thought is that the numbers are not consecutive. 3. 6. 2. 9. 7. 12. She wonders briefly about the missing numbers, the men who are not available to her today. Then lowers her gaze and sees their cocks. Long. Thick. Straight. Bulbous. Crooked. Heavy. Some just dangle there against a thigh, others are being gently stroked by their owners as she watches.

One man is bald, but his body hair is absolutely everywhere else from chest to feet, thick and curly, his cock like an explosion of dark purple amongst his forest. Another has pale blond hair, his white chest quite hairless and his pubic thatch like golden down.

Another, number 6, is a black man. Tall, standing proudly, legs apart, his regal chocolate cock already at half-mast, impossibly elongated and sharp. She gulps.

Time freezes momentarily.

The men are all looking in her direction, but she knows they cannot see her behind the one-way glass partition.

The door opens and the woman returns.

"Have you chosen, madam?" she asks.

"It's difficult," Zelda says. "They are all so different. Age. Appearance. Colouring. Size . . ." she adds.

"I understand," the woman sympathizes.

Zelda looks at the parade of naked men over again, thoughts swirling in her head. And some guilt already.

"Some of them are really quite appealing," she blurts out. Blushing ever so slightly in the surrounding penumbra of the small room.

She fixates on the mole staring at her from just above number 12's crotch area.

Sensing her indecision, the plain-looking woman intervenes.

"Could I make a suggestion to madam?"

"Certainly," Zelda answers.

"Well, has madam ever thought of two?"

"Two?"

"Double the pleasure. Even more staying power at your disposal. They can take turns, or you could have them in tandem."

"You mean . . . ?"

"Servicing both front and rear, madam. An experience to cherish, I am told. They are all well-trained in these variations, I assure you." She reassured Zelda as to the men's abilities.

Zelda finally selects 7 and 9.

She is taken to the bedroom and told to make herself at ease. The four-poster bed is the largest she has seen, sitting there like a throne, dominating the whole room. Crisp white sheets. A silken dark bedspread. A thick scarlet rug. Erotic etchings on the walls. She knows at least one of them conceals some peep-hole and that she is going to be watched. That is also part of the price and adds to the spice of this new experience.

There is a gentle knock on the bedroom door.

"Enter," Zelda says.

The two men walk in. In the flesh, so to speak, they appear so much larger, and number 9 looks very young. But she likes the gentle curls of hair on his chest. It was difficult to arrive at a choice. So she has settled for one with dark hair and a foreskin that wrinkles down and, even when half erect, obscures the mushroom-like bulbous cap of his glans. The other is cut, his cock all pink and shiny.

They approach her and the dark-haired man politely asks in a European accent, "Would madam like us to undress her?"

"Yes, that would be nice, very nice. Yes," Zelda answers, setting her handbag down. Next time, she thinks as their hands began searching for her buttons, she will go with the black man. Something she often guiltily dreamed of in Minnesota days of old, when she was still Miss Sayre.

Seen that Tight-Lipped Grin – New York, 1934

Whole days now went by without them even speaking to each other, beyond the bare formalities of "Good Morning", "Please" or "Goodnight". Sex, which he knew she had once enjoyed so much, was now perfunctory on the rare occasions that he managed to stay hard long enough without recourse to her mouth.

Scott had often wondered how it must feel for a woman, for Zelda, to take a man's cock in her mouth and pleasure it without choking. How this most intimate of violations could even provide her with a modicum of pleasure. The thought had troubled him for years. The fact that she had already been familiar with this particular sexual perversion when he had met her brought a sliver of bile into his throat at the idea of the other men she might have practised on, done it with, before or since him.

The young man sitting at the bar was still looking at him.

Scott had to admit he was quite pretty, a tad feminine despite his short hair and the floppy fringe that fell across his pale forehead.

He smiled back at the stranger.

Who soon joined him at his table.

"You know I'm not that way inclined," Scott said furtively, looking around the bar to check there was no around whom he knew. "Just interested in knowing what it would be like. Curiosity, call it. An experiment. Not that I wish to go all the way, just, you know . . ."

"Sure," the young man said.

"And I don't want it to be something sordid. In some public

convenience, with trousers down to my ankles. Have to do it properly, in a civilized way. Be comfortable with each other . . ." Scott added.

"I understand," the young man said. "Do you have a place where we might go, then?"

They had undressed, with their backs to each other. Scott was conscious his body was no longer as athletic as it had been. As he failed to turn round, he felt the young man's hand on his shoulder.

"Do you want me to suck you first?" his pick-up asked. "It will put you at ease. You can do me afterwards. No rush."

He lowered himself down to his knees and took Scott's flaccid cock in his hand and rolled the foreskin down before enveloping it with his lips.

Scott closed his eyes. The tongue moved slowly around his stem. He imagined it was Zelda and St Paul, Minnesota, again, and paradise and youthful days. Felt a bit the same. Pleasant. The shivers began as usual in the deep pit of his stomach before travelling down towards his now-aroused genitals.

Later, he adopted the same kneeling position and closed his own mouth on the thick cock of the young man. At first, the feel was quite unexpected. The penis felt strangely greasy under his tongue, pulsing with the beat of a distant heart. He licked it methodically, his lips gripping its surprising warmth while his tongue circled its expanding circumference. With his free hand he cupped the young man's balls and felt them yield. He pushed his lips further forward, curious to see how far he could take the cock in without choking. Surprisingly far. The young man, towering now above him, began to moan gently and rustled Scott's hair as he sucked away. Scott lost all notion of time, his whole mind concentrating on his task.

Finally, the young man shuddered and said, "I'm about to come. It would be best if you let it out now, unless you want it inside your mouth."

Scott pulled away just as the cock began spurting its white, floury ejaculate.

As the come spiralled down towards the wooden floor of the borrowed apartment, he was already thinking back on the experience. It had been interesting. He couldn't really say he had taken much pleasure sucking another man's cock, but on the other hand there had been nothing unpleasant either. Yes, "interesting" was truly the right word in the circumstance. So this is what Zelda would feel as she did it. Maybe now he would understand her better?

The young man was dressing quickly.

"I'll make my own way out," he said. "It would be better if we didn't exchange names."

"Yes," Scott said.

She's Waltzin' out of the Door – Princeton, 1936

The team had lost the Varsity Challenge and the overall mood was despondent. The woman was waiting for them to arrive back at the dressing room, holding a bottle of champagne and a couple of glasses in her hand. She was visibly drunk already.

"There's nothing to celebrate, lady," McKenna said.

"I know," she said. "So I thought I'd bring you Princeton boys some consolation. So you'll be luckier next time."

Tim, who had been kept on the touchline for most of the game and was still bitter at the coach's decision, walked up to the woman, took the bottle and one cup and poured.

"And why not?" he said. "There's nothing else to lose. And most of us won't be here next year anyway."

He passed the bottle on to the other players. The woman took a small metal flask out of her bag and took a deep swig from it.

"Atta boys, that's the way to go!"

The players had soon emptied the bottle of champagne and began trooping past her.

"Why are you off so fast? We can still celebrate," the woman said, brandishing the small flask. "It's good bourbon!"

"We're all filthy and sweaty. We have to take a bath, lady."

She hiccuped and followed the last of one of them into the building as they made their way towards the giant communal bath tub.

"I'll join you," she exclaimed.

"You must be joking . . ." McKenna replied.

"Not at all," the woman said, and raised her cotton skirt upwards to reveal that shockingly she had no underwear on. "See, I'm already dressed for the occasion, boys."

The young men looked at each other. Some blushed, others shrugged their shoulders. One of them began to strip openly in front of this strange woman.

"Why not?" one of them said.

She stripped with them.

"So which one is the captain of the team?" she asked as she jumped into the hot water and joined the burly, muddy young men.

"I am, and today was the last time," Chris Callaghan said.

"In that case," she said, wading towards him across the steaming water, her small breasts bobbing along, "you get the first blow-job."

The whole team fell silent.

She serviced almost half of them, but the water was growing cold and she suggested they adjourn to the dressing room. They carried her out of the bathtub triumphantly over their broad shoulders, like a trophy.

By now, most of the young players, even those who had already come in the woman's mouth, were hard and excited, and all veneer of civilization had long faded.

They all had her in a variety of positions, using every available orifice offered. She sometimes laughed, often moaned, occasionally cried and eventually passed out. Which didn't stop some of the guys from continuing to fuck her until they ran dry.

Later, once the young men had all hurriedly dressed again into their perfect Princeton gentlemen suits, and, mostly shamefaced, trooped away from the scene of their lustful crimes, Tim and McKenna revived the woman with some smelling salts from the first aid cabinet and helped her dress in silence.

They watched her move away unsteadily across the now darkening playing fields of the university, feeling damn guilty about what had happened, but after all, hadn't she been the one who had suggested the orgy and all its excesses?

Finally, she faded into the darkness, her soiled white skirt just a minute star-like point of white on the horizon where night and earth blended.

"Damn it," Tim said. "That was crazy. She was crazy. Who was she?"

"I don't know," McKenna said. "Earlier, on the floor, while

Stewart was arsing her and she was sucking on me and White in turn, between mouthfuls she kept on saying, 'I'm Zelda Fitzgerald, the wife of the famous writer,' over and over again." He sighed. "Forget it, man, she was just some madwoman with a bad itch in her pants. What we all did was mad too. Better forget all about it."

"Fitzgerald? Never even heard of the name," Tim said.

"Probably some delusion of hers, anyway," the other one said, straightening his tie, thinking already of tomorrow's ball, with all the Vassar belles in attendance.

Zelda. Highland, 1948

Scott has now been dead for over seven years and Zelda lingers in the mental institution in which she is being kept for her own good.

Most of the time she is quite lucid, and has much too much time to reflect on the golden past and its mistakes. How lives can be wasted so damn easily on the altar of lust, ambition, petty jealousy and money worries. How time eats away at the wall of love. How nothing lasts even with the best intentions in the world. How we allow things, people, to go because we are too proud, shy or helpless to do otherwise. How all those things gnaw the mind during the unending hours of the night when all you can do is wonder "what if this" and "what if that" and "what if she" and "what if he", until the sheer torture is too much and you retreat into that deep well where the ghosts can no longer reach you and there are no longer any feelings.

She is being given insulin treatment and has been moved to the top floor of the main Highland building.

Early March she writes to her mother that the jasmine is in full bloom and crocuses are dotted across the lawn.

On March 9, she writes to her daughter Scottie that she thinks that winter is now over. She is already four months into this new stay in Highland, and Scottie's second child, a daughter, has been born.

She writes of the promise of spring in the air and the fact she sees an aura of sunshine over the nearby mountains and longs to see the new baby and its growing brother.

The following night, at midnight, a fire breaks out in the

establishment's kitchen. The flames shoot up a small dumbwaiter shaft to the roof and leap out onto each of the floors.

The building has neither a fire alarm system or a sprinkler system.

Very quickly the fire becomes completely out of control, and smoke races through the rooms of the old stone-and-frame building. The fire escapes are made of wood and soon catch fire.

Zelda sleeps. After hours of tossing and turning, peace has returned at last, and she is again on the back seat of that brand-new motor car which Scott had purchased with his first novel's advance, and she is unbuttoning his trousers and giggling madly inside at the bemused look on his face as she extricates his small cock from the heavy garments. She's nervous also; she's never done this before, just heard about it from the other girls at the finishing college, who tell her it's the best way to a man's heart. And, yes, she loves Scott so. After all the courting, the tantrums and the break-ups, yes, she has decided, hesitantly moving her lips towards the warm penis, feeling its awkwardly spongy texture between her moist lips. Yes, I will be Mrs Francis Scott Fitzgerald.

She smiles in her sleep.

The fire keeps on gaining ground.

Nine women are killed that night, six of them on the top floor.

Her body is only later identified by a charred slipper lying beneath it.

She is taken to Maryland and, on a warm and sunny day, buried next to Scott. They are together again. For ever.

PLAGUE LOVERS

Lucy Taylor

WORD SPREAD QUICKLY in the tiny, plague-ravaged town – the Flagellants were coming!

Gabrielle, sequestered in the house with her father and her dying mother, heard the news shouted out in the street beneath her window. She felt her blood quicken at the thought of witnessing such a spectacle – a band of penitents whose submission to the Lord was made manifest in deprivation and self-wounding. Despite her fear of mingling with the plague-infested crowds, she felt compelled to see them.

Snatching up her shawl and wrapping it around her thin shoulders, she crept down the wooden stairs, hoping that her father, exhausted by his day and night vigil at her mother's deathbed, would be dozing. She didn't want to have to speak to him, or witness the reproach and anguish in his eyes as she hurried past without so much as gazing at her mother.

Her father's back was turned to her, his head lowered into his big hands. Gabrielle took a breath and tiptoed toward the door.

All I want, she thought, *is to get out of here. Get away from the death and dying.*

The plague, or the Great Pestilence as some were calling it, had arrived in early summer. Word of a terrible illness sweeping the port cities of Pisa and Genoa had reached the town a year earlier, but here in this secluded Tuscan valley the villagers had felt secure and safe in their relative isolation. With spring, however, the plague had reached Orvieto, where a spiritual revival that added fifty new religious dates to the municipal calendar had failed to spare the city from devastation. Now death was everywhere – evidenced in the rattling of the carts that carried bodies for burial outside the village, the cloying, rotten-flowers scent of sickness that permeated the air, the moaning of the sick, the wailing of the bereaved.

Gabrielle had heard that, according to the priests, who divined such things by studying the book of Revelations, a third of the world had died.

And the plague had not yet run its course.

An idea, borne of terror and desperation, had been nudging its way into the back of her mind. Many people had already fled the town to take refuge in the countryside. No one really knew what caused the sickness, but escaping the "pestilential atmosphere" of more populated areas was thought to help. It was said the air was cleaner in the country, the food less apt to be contaminated.

When she was almost at the door, her father looked up.

"Where are you going?"

"Don't you hear the drumming? The Flagellants are on their way to the cathedral."

"Hah," her father snorted. "The Brethren of the Cross they call themselves. I call them the brethren of lunacy. Why expose yourself to the crowds to see a troop of madmen beat each other bloody?"

Her mother moaned and went into a coughing fit. Blood foamed around her mouth. Gabrielle's father dampened a cloth in a bowl of water and wiped her face. "There, there, my love," he whispered. "I'm here with you. I'm here."

The tiny woman, little more than bone and gristle, reached up and stroked her husband's face, a gesture rich with the tenderness and caring of devoted lovers after a long and passionate night. Gabrielle felt that she witnessing something private and precious between her parents, something she could never hope to exprience herself.

"She hasn't long," her father said. "Can't you just sit with her?"

She shook her head. "I have to go."

"What kind of daughter are you? You feel no love for your own mother?"

But how could she? thought Gabrielle. Until the plague struck, until her midwife mother fell ill, neither of her parents had shown the slightest warmth or caring toward one another or, for that matter, toward her. Theirs was a union based on practicality and the running of a household, a way to satisfy the needs for sex, security, and mutual support. Love was a luxury for idle, wealthy ladies and lovestruck troubadours. The poor had no time for such frivolity.

Now Gabrielle observed the change in both her parents, a transformation that appeared wrought by suffering, and found herself both horrified and envious. For never had anyone shown her the kind of tenderness her parents now bestowed upon each other. It was as though, through suffering, they had paid some terrible price required for the giving and receiving of affection.

Looking at neither her father nor her mother, she hurried toward the door.

"Gabrielle!" The undercurrent of fear in her father's voice brought her up short. "You are coming back, aren't you? *Aren't* you?"

"I–I don't know."

"What if I fall ill? Your mother's taught you about herbs and medicines. You could make my dying easier."

Gabrielle stared at this man whose love she'd never managed to win, who'd never offered her a moment of affection. "I know nothing of my mother's skills," she said stubbornly.

"She taught you everything," her father insisted. "Please, girl, I don't want to be alone. Promise me you're coming back."

"I'm sorry," Gabrielle murmured.

Behind her, her father's voice rose in anger.

"You think you're safer in the outside world? The plague is everywhere. Only God can keep you alive."

Only God.

But God was nowhere to be found these days. The young abandoned the old, the healthy left the sick to expire in alleyways and filthy deathbeds, even priests refused to hear confession from the dying, lest they contract the sickness. Some people reacted to the danger by living lives of ascetic abstinence, while others, wanting to make the most of what time was left, indulged in every kind of excess and debauchery.

At the cathedral in the town square, Gabrielle stood at the edge of the crowd and held a handkerchief dipped in perfume to her face, for it was common knowledge that pleasant odors helped protect one from disease.

The Flagellants marched up the main street, men in the lead, women following. The men were stripped to the chest. Each carried a hard leather whip festooned with little iron spikes which he brought down, rhythmically and slowly, across the back of the one preceding him. Bent and bloody, the procession snaked toward the cathedral. They were silent and sweaty and a great stench rose from them – not the sickly sweet odor of sickness, but the musky tang of unwashed, bloodied bodies.

Gabrielle watched the blood streaming down their raw backs, saw how the sweat glistened and ran in the deep furrows that the pain had etched in their faces. Some appeared to be in agony, others simply exhausted. And some appeared to have gone beyond the pain and seemed entranced in what looked like ecstasy.

Gabrielle stared, transfixed by the bizarre spectacle, amazed by the stoic silence in which the Flagellants bore their pain. As one man passed by, she could not stop herself, but reached out to caress his mutilated back.

"What do you suppose it feels like?"

At first Gabrielle didn't realize the voice was speaking to her. Then fingers gripped her elbow. She whirled around, appalled and startled by the presumption of this stranger.

A young man with fair hair, tanned, pockmarked skin, and black eyes that glittered like a raven's regarded her. He was dressed in the rough, simple garments of the Flagellants, but his clothing had no rips or bloodstains, nor did his sturdy-looking arms bear signs of abuse. Something in the cunning, slyly mirthful way that he appraised her made her uneasy, as though he knew things about her she did not even know herself.

"What are you talking about?" she whispered, holding the scented handkerchief tighter to her face. "What *what* feels like?"

"The whip, of course."

"Pain beyond my ability to imagine it."

"At first, there's terrible pain," the young man said,"but still it seems bearable at first, or so you think. Then the lash keeps falling and the pain mounts. It fills your whole body, your whole being. At that moment, you'd sell your soul to make it stop. You think that you can't possibly bear it another moment, that you'll lose consciousness or die.

"Then it's as though the body becomes completely overwhelmed, and there's a giddiness. You laugh, you scream, you weep. At that point, you've gone beyond the pain – it's still there, but it's not your body anymore, or you're not in it. That's when it begins to feel like a holy sacrament, like you've touched the face of God."

Gabrielle looked at the man's hand where it still rested on her elbow – large and heavy-knuckled, covered with fine wheat-colored hair.

"How would you know about such things?"

"In the spring, I marched with the Brethren for thirty-three and a third days – to commemorate the life of Christ, as is the custom."

"And do you think your suffering will save you from the plague?"

"No. Only luck and my own wits will do that. But I learned a great deal about pain – and what lies on the other side of it."

He turned and pulled his shirt up to reveal his back, a gouged and furrowed tapestry of scar tissue and half-healed wounds. Gabrielle ran her hand across the scars. "You must be insane. Who in their right mind would choose pain when there's so much of it to be had without asking?"

"The Flagellants believe it brings them closer to God."

"I don't believe in such a God. No loving father would willingly send such misery on his children."

"Perhaps that's how He wins their love – by sending misery and then, according to his whim, providing minor comforts."

Gabrielle laughed. "Then you aren't talking about God. You're talking about Satan."

"Maybe he's the one in charge."

"That's blasphemy."

"That doesn't mean it's not the truth."

His hand, which up to then had rested lightly on her elbow,

moved slowly up her arm. Heat spread through her belly as his fingers curled around the back of her neck and collected a great fistful of copper-colored hair.

"My name's Gerard. You remind me of a woman I was once in love with."

"What happened to her?"

"She died of plague. That's when I joined the Flagellants. I thought the pain of the whip might take away the greater pain of losing her."

"And did it?"

"For a while. And then it made it worse. Now I think that only death will truly cure me. But I'm not ready to die yet." He released her hair, let it tumble in long glossy coils around her face. "I'm on my way now to the countryside. If I keep to myself, stay in abandoned houses, I figure there's a chance I'll survive. If you like, you could go with me."

She shook her head. "Nowhere is safe from plague."

"Perhaps not, but some places are better to die than others."

The crowd surged around them, pressing them close. So thick was the odor of blood, so sharp the cracking of the whips, that Gabrielle felt light-headed.

"Good luck to you, then," said Gerard, and began to elbow his way out of the mob.

Gabrielle thought about her mother, the foul-smelling boils that swelled along her armpits and groin, the dark blue spots that blotched her skin. Before long, she thought, her father would be dying, too, and it would fall her lot to tend to him, to comfort him in his death throes, press cool cloths to his brow, wipe up the waste that would gush from him. She knew she couldn't bear that.

But on her own, she also knew, she would be prey to the roving bands of looters and marauders that, emboldened by the almost complete absence of the law, terrorized the towns and countryside. That possibility terrified her, too.

"Wait," she called out, catching up to him. "Before you go – I want to know – I want . . ."

She hesitated, felt an unfamiliar heat creep up her cheekbones.

"I know exactly what you want," he said, and took her hand.

They traveled along narrow, rutted roads leading through the countryside of Tuscany, sometimes cutting through untilled fields and deserted orchards. Occasionally they passed through abandoned villages, where dogs and livestock roamed at will. Along the roadside, the corpses of those who had fallen while trying to escape lay bloated and putrescent.

The first night they camped in an open field with others fleeing the plague. The second night, after Gerard had led them on a circuitous route along the ridgetop of some hills, they came to an abandoned town where the only signs of life were feral dogs that roamed the dusty streets and wild-eyed rats that held their ground almost until the last instant, then skittered away as Gerard and Gabrielle approached.

Gerard picked out the most luxurious of the deserted houses. Like a lord and lady returning from an outing in the hills, he and Gabrielle made themselves at home.

"Who lives here?" asked Gabrielle, looking around the beautifully appointed rooms.

"We do, now."

"Whose house was it?"

Gerard shrugged. "Whoever it belonged to, they're gone now. Like everything else, the house belongs to whomever takes it."

That night, when Gerard moved on top of her, Gabrielle found herself aroused, but strangely distant. It was as if she watched herself from a corner of the room, moving beneath this man, arranging her body to accommodate his, but somehow profoundly absent. She let him penetrate her body, but knew that he could never touch her heart.

"You don't want me," he said finally.

"I *want* to want you. I want to feel something. I just – don't."

She turned away from him, finding no way to describe the sense that vines and briars encased her body and leaves of deadly nightbane numbed her heart.

"Have you ever loved anyone?"

The question seemed unfair, humiliating. "Of course I have."

But she saw he knew that she was lying.

Later that night, she dreamed of her mother. Saw her father

bending down to wipe her mouth with a wet cloth and stroke her face. Her dead mother's eyes were open. Her father reached down and gently closed them, placed the cloth across her mother's face.

Something was wrong. She was awake now, but couldn't get her eyes open. A rag or cloth was tied around her head. When she tried to remove the blindfold, her wrists were seized. She was roughly shoved onto her belly and her arms bound behind her.

She knew about the bands of rogues and thieves who preyed upon those fleeing the cities. Surely it was such a miscreant who had her now.

"Gerard!" she cried out. "Help me."

"Silence," he hissed. "Not one word or cry or I'll gag you, too."

He pulled her up off the bed and dragged her into another room, where he shoved her up against a beam or column and bound her there face-first.

"What are you doing?"

"Just because we've fled the plague doesn't mean we aren't going to die. I want to make the most of every moment. I want you to learn to love me. I'm going to *make* you love me."

So saying, he bent her over, kicked her legs apart, and entered her from behind. This time he made no effort to be gentle. His ramming hurt her, but when she squirmed and tried to pull away, he withdrew from her and forced his way into her other orifice, wringing forth screams of pain.

He gripped her hips and forced himself in deeper.

"You want this, don't you?"

"No!"

"Tell me you want it harder, deeper!"

"No, I hate it! Stop!"

"Tell me you want more!"

Finally, desperate to appease him and end the torture, she whimpered, "Yes, please, harder," her voice choked with tears.

When she said that, he thrust one more time, released his semen into her and then withdrew.

She sank to her knees, weeping.

Gerard grabbed her by the hair and yanked her head back.

"That was good," he said. "I'm proud of you. We're off to a good start."

Their next night in the deserted house, he again tied her to a beam, wrists secured over her head, and began to twist and squeeze her nipples. The pain was beyond anything she could have anticipated. She begged and pleaded, made promises of future acts of submission, but he increased the pressure. Then, because the pain was so unbearable and there was no escaping it, her body reacted by convulsing in a fit of laughter. She laughed and sobbed and, in between, implored Gerard to stop hurting her, but by the time he did her nipples had gone numb and, with the blood flowing again, the pain this time was greater than what she'd felt before.

He left her sobbing with fury at the pain and the futility of fighting it. When he returned, what seemed like hours later, he kissed her swollen nipples and fed her grapes he'd found growing in a nearby vineyard.

"Tell me how much you love me."

"I hate you. You're a monster."

"Tell me how much you love everything I do to you."

"Let me go. Please, just let me go."

"There is nowhere to go. The plague is everywhere. There's only death."

She spat the chewed grapes out at him, spattering his face with sticky pulp, then caught his finger in her mouth and bit it to the bone.

He cradled his bleeding hand and eyed her coldly.

"I'd thought that you were doing well. I see now I was wrong. I must be stricter with you."

He left her then, still tied, and came back brandishing a lit candle. At the first touch of the flame against her flesh, her courage failed her. She began to beg and weep, but Gerard was implacable. He moved the candle up and down her body, its shadow dancing across her flesh. Rarely did he let the fire make contact, but when he did, the agony elicited a howl. He singed a spot below her nipple, touched the flame to her thigh and the tender spot at the base of her spine, while she thrashed against her bindings.

"Tell me how much you like this! *Tell* me!"

The flame blazed in her face and burned her eyes. It filled her head with an unnatural light that grew brighter and brighter before exploding into darkness.

She dreamed she was a young child, ill with the fever that had swept through her village one winter, killing half a dozen babies and a few of the older children. Her mother had held her and sung her lullabies that had been handed down for centuries.

She had not gotten better right away. Instead, the fever had buoyed her along like a flooding stream, sweeping her far into the depths and byways and canyons of her mind, but, for the first time in her life, she had felt loved and safe, unafraid of the death the sickness seemed to be carrying her toward.

She opened her eyes.

He had cut her down from the beam and laid her on the bed. When she moved, the pain from her burns flared, making her gasp.

"Lie still," he told her.

"Why are you doing this?"

"Shhh."

He slid into the bed with her and spooned himself around her. His naked flesh was warm and comforting. When he cupped one hand around her breast and slid the other up between her legs, her sigh was both of pleasure and of resignation. His mouth roved over the back of her neck, his breath disturbed the tendrils of hair along her cheekbone, his tongue probed the delicate convolutions of her ear.

She turned and sobbed against his chest. "It's all right," he murmured. "The things I do may seem a strange way to win your love, but don't forget I marched with the Brethren of the Cross. I know the sorcery that pain and then the absence of pain can work upon the mind. I know that pain can penetrate a heart that can't be opened any other way."

He held her and she clung to him and sobbed harder.

Knowing how desperately she wanted closeness, comforting, appalled at the price she was willing to pay for it.

She had escaped the plague, thought Gabrielle, in order to endure something worse – the ever-increasing torments Gerard devised for her.

Sometimes it was merely being bound in humiliating positions and left alone to wonder when or if he would return. Sometimes it was being spanked until her buttocks burned as if she'd sat upon hot coals, or having the wax from a lit candle dripped onto her breasts and thighs.

When he wasn't using her, Gerard kept her bound much of the time and never let her move about freely without his supervision.

But sometimes, usually when the punishments had been most brutal, he would make love to her as though she were his heart's desire – indeed he swore she was exactly that – soothing her bruised flesh with tender caresses, moistening her sore and swollen places with his tongue. And this she found almost more difficult to tolerate than the punishment, for she both longed for his sweet comforting and despised herself for craving it.

It was after just such a time, when Gerard had followed up his punishments by making love to her slowly and in silence, each move deliberate and delicate, as if they were underwater, that he fell asleep without remembering to tie her.

Gerard was snoring deeply, and from outside came the snarling and yapping of feral dogs, but the only sound that Gabrielle heard was her own heart racing at the possibility of escape. Nothing else mattered.

Outside the night felt vast and unforgiving, stars pulsing coldly overhead. She picked up a stick to ward off wild animals and started across a field toward a stand of trees, thinking to hide there until the sun rose.

She had gone only a short distance, though, when the sky sank so low it pressed against her head and the earth seemed to undulate and roll beneath her feet. The shadows of trees became the outlines of marauders come to ravish her and kill her. The sighing of the wind became the hiss of air leaking out of bloated corpses that she, unable to see, might tread on in the dark.

Never had she felt so vulnerable and desperate for solace. The memory of Gerard's cruelties dissipated like fog. All she could think of was the softness of his kisses, the skillful pleasuring of his hands when he rewarded her endurance with some small kindness.

Near panic, she returned to the house, only to find Gerard waiting for her, brandishing a whip of the type used by the Flagellants.

"Ungrateful whore, is this how you show your love for me?" he said, but something in his voice made her believe it had all been a trick, that he had given her the chance to escape on purpose, either to test her or to seek an excuse for greater punishment.

How confident he'd been, if that were the case, she thought. How sure that she'd return.

No amount of begging could persuade him to forego the whip. He bound her wrists above her head and brought it down across her shoulders.

The pain devoured her, obliterating everything.

"Do you want more of this? *Tell* me you want more!"

"Yes!"

"Do you love me? Tell me how much you love me!"

"Yes, I love you, *yes!*"

The agony was terrible and breathtaking – it ripped the air out of her lungs and seared her flesh as though she were a witch burning at a pyre.

When it ended, her mind seemed to stop, to fog over with a pale, cool cloud of blissful nothingness.

Oh God, she thought, *the pain has stopped. Oh God, oh God, ohGodohGodohGod . . .*

Gerard pressed his mouth against her ear. "I'm here," he said. "Don't worry. Only a few more blows. I'll help you get through it."

Then the chorus of pain began again, the song of the whip mingling with that of her screams, carrying her down and down into a place beyond thought, beyond fear. Without dying, she had somehow ceased to exist. Her flesh did not belong to her, nor did her name – how could it when *she* no longer was – nor her past nor any thought at all. There was no room for name or past or thought in the brilliant, all-consuming clarity of her agony.

The god she called out to was no longer the God of the priests and penitents, but her private god – Gerard, who gave and took away her suffering.

"There, now, it's all right. It's over now. It's over."

He untied her. She pressed her face against his chest and sobbed with gratitude. He had caused the pain to stop. He was her savior, her protector, how had she ever doubted him? When he began to kiss her, she kissed him back, then slid down his body, kissing every inch of him, anointing his skin with her tongue.

"I love you," she said. Then, when he gave no reply, she added, "Now you must love me, too."

To prove her devotion, Gabrielle worked diligently to please him. In bed, she acquiesced to every demand, and pleaded for new punishments. She prepared meals from whatever meager food was available, combing the orchards around the house for fruits, making salads of wild grasses. In the fields she picked the pale purple-blue flowers that her mother had so often pointed out to her, gathering the luscious-looking berries in her skirt.

In performing these small domestic tasks, it seemed to Gabrielle that, indeed, she felt real love for him, even as she made a salad of wildflowers and grasses and crushed the purple berries to make a pie.

In the night, Gabrielle woke to hear Gerard arguing loudly with someone. Alarmed, she lit a candle. No one was there. Her lover was sitting up in bed, conversing with great animation. The pupils of his eyes were dilated; his skin felt hot and dry. For an instant, she fancied she could hear the distant drumming of the Flagellants, then realized it was his heartbeat, audible at several feet.

"Harder, I can't feel it!" he was shouting. "Harder! You must flog me harder!"

This went on for some time, before he fell into an exhausted, feverish sleep.

The hallucinations grew worse. Gerard imagined he saw whips descending and fires blazing at his feet. He cried out and flailed away at imaginary tormenters. So violent became his behavior that she was forced to tie him to the bed with the same ropes that he had used to bind her.

He complained his mouth was dry and that he couldn't swallow, so she brought him water and put cool compresses across his brow. When she held and stroked his hand, she could feel his wildly beating pulse.

During a lucid phase, he said, "You could run away now. Why don't you?"

"You need me," she said, delicately licking the sweat from along his temple. "You wanted me to love you, and I do. If I can't take away your pain, at least I can help you bear it."

The days dragged on. Gerard was able to eat only a few spoonfuls of food, and his illness worsened. No spots disfigured his skin, no boils erupted along his groin, but still he grew ever weaker.

Gabrielle nursed him, fed him, kept him clean. At night she spooned herself around his back and stroked his chest and stomach, kissed his neck and outlined with her tongue the geography of scars that mapped his back.

When she had to leave him, if only for a moment, he would call out for her in fear.

"I'm sorry for what I did to you," he said. "I saw the emptiness in your eyes and wanted you to feel something. I wanted you to need me. To love me."

"I do love you," said Gabrielle.

He squeezed her hand. "I thought that I was different, that somehow I'd escape the plague when everyone else was dying of it. I don't know why, but I didn't think I'd die of plague."

"Nothing else I can promise you," she said, stroking his face, "but this I do. You will not die of plague."

Perhaps he even believed her, for he clutched her hand more tightly and kissed her fingers with desperation and desire.

He died later that night, holding tightly to her hand, voicing his undying love for her, even as his heartbeat grew so loud that the pounding filled the room. She had no energy for digging a grave, but dragged his body outside and left it for the dogs.

Some passers-by, headed east from Pisa, told her the plague still raged around her village, but Gabrielle no longer feared it. She had decided to return home to her father. She prayed he hadn't died. If he was only ill, then she would nurse him. If he was healthy still, then she would win his love the way she had Gerard's. She would crush more of the purple berries, the lovely, deadly nightbane berries that her mother'd always warned her of, and bake them in a pie. As with Gerard, she would feed him only small amounts, enough to provide a lingering and painful death, enough to give him time to well appreciate how lovingly she cared for him, how desperately he needed her, how exquisitely soothing was her touch.

She fantasized it as she began the journey home. How she would hold her father, stroke his brow, comfort him through his agony. How, at the end, he would pull her close and clutch her hand and tell her that he loved her.

Against Medical Advice

Against Medical Advice

A TRUE STORY

James Patterson

AND

Hal Friedman

DOUBLEDAY LARGE PRINT HOME LIBRARY EDITION

LITTLE, BROWN AND COMPANY

NEW YORK BOSTON LONDON

This Large Print Edition, prepared especially for Doubleday Large Print Home Library, contains the complete, unabridged text of the original Publisher's Edition.

A list of other books by James Patterson is on page 387. For previews of upcoming books by James Patterson and more information about the author, visit www.JamesPatterson.com.

Little, Brown and Company
Hachette Book Group USA
237 Park Avenue, New York, NY 10017

Little, Brown and Company is a division of Hachette Book Group USA, Inc. The Little, Brown name and logo are trademarks of Hachette Book Group USA, Inc.

ISBN 978-0-7394-9908-5

Printed in the United States of America

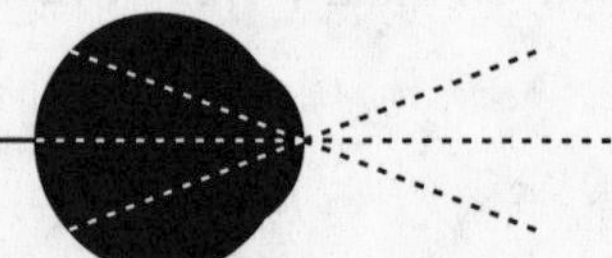

This Large Print Book carries the Seal of Approval of N.A.V.H.

To the Angels

To Dr. Ruth Bruun, the angel who pulled us up when our own wings were broken. Your dedication to all of your patients who have struggled with Tourette's syndrome cannot be measured, and you are loved and renowned for your profound wisdom and very great heart.

And to Jessie, our daughter, who weathered a childhood filled with great sadness and great inspiration. And yes, one day we will go to Disneyland.

—Hal and Sophia Friedman

Cory's Dedication

In my thirteen-year search for help, I traveled to places far from home and met many people, young and old, with medical conditions so extreme that I could not have imagined they existed.

I will never forget these special friends and their heroic battles with the phantoms that inhabited their minds.

I understand them, and they understand me.

I hope that this account of my life, which in many ways might be similar to theirs, will give them and others like them a measure of comfort and hope. And I'm grateful to my father and to James Patterson for helping to tell my story to the many people who might benefit from it.

To those like me, who are forced to travel a road that few others can even conceive of, I wish you peace, and a way home.

—Cory Friedman

Preface

"One morning in March of 1989, just before my fifth birthday, I woke up as a normal, healthy boy. By that afternoon, I had an irresistible urge to shake my head—continually—and the course of my life changed in ways few people had ever seen or could begin to understand.

"Before long, my body became an explosive, volatile, and unpredictable force with a mind and personality of its own. It jerked and twisted, bent in half, and gyrated without warning until I was almost always in motion.

"I bit down on my teeth until I actually

broke them and howled in pain because of the exposed nerves.

"I twisted my back around with such force that I tore muscle tissue and had to be drugged asleep to stop myself from doing it.

"My mind fed me thoughts so frightening I couldn't even talk about them to my parents.

"It didn't take long before I saw myself as the oddest person in my town. I felt like a boy on the end of a puppeteer's string.

"What made it even worse was knowing that I was also the puppeteer."

This is the story of Cory Friedman, and what follows is his remarkable journey, a story of triumph against all odds.

I met Hal Friedman in 1975 in New York City, at the J. Walter Thompson advertising agency, where we were both writers. We never imagined then that more than thirty years later, we would collaborate to write a book about Hal's son's heart-wrenching experiences.

Over the years, I would hear about Cory

and his devastating struggle with Tourette's syndrome, obsessive-compulsive disorder, and anxiety disorder. But until Hal asked me to read an early draft he had written of Cory's story, I had no idea how severe a torment this lovely family had been living through. I knew that his complex condition was nearly impossible to treat. In fact, thirteen doctors and approximately sixty potent medicines after Cory's first traumatic head shakes, his debilitating symptoms were still unchecked.

When the downward spiral of his symptoms led to severe depression and hopelessness, and when all of Cory's doctors and their advice and medicines had proved to be false hopes, Cory's family staged an intervention that was as daring as anything that had preceded it, maybe even more so.

I was drawn to Cory's harrowing story because of what it says about the power of love, courage, and determination, and I was proud to join Hal in writing it. I knew that Cory's story had to be told because it would give hope and comfort to so many others struggling in all walks of life. Cory was in a living hell, but in climbing out, he showed us that it is possible to survive—and even thrive—against unbelievable odds. For me, that makes him a hero.

Hal and I are honored to bring you *Against Medical Advice* on Cory's behalf. My hope is that you, too, will be inspired by the courage, heartbreak, sacrifice, and ultimate victory of Cory Friedman and his family, and by the sheer invincibility of the human spirit.

—*James Patterson*

A Father's Prologue

The events recounted here took place over what seemed like—to those of us who lived it—an endless thirteen-year period covering Cory's life from age five to age seventeen. We decided, with Cory's blessing, to tell his story in his own voice, because this conveys most powerfully what it was like for Cory to live through these experiences.

Some names and other identifying details of friends, doctors, and medical institutions have been changed.

The extremely unusual events portrayed in this story have been reconstructed from Cory's own accounts, from detailed medical diaries that were kept by his mother throughout the period, and from direct family observations. Cory confirms that this narrative presents an accurate portrait of his life story.

Over the four years it took to write this book, I was continuously tormented by the decision of whether or not to make the most intimate details of Cory's life public. Finally, I went to Cory for the guidance I needed, and he resolved the issue in a single sentence, without hesitation:

"If it will help other people like me, yes."

—*Hal Friedman*

Part One

A LOST CHILDHOOD

At the Edge of Madness

Chapter 1

I'm seventeen years old and lying like a pathetic, helpless lump in the backseat of our family car, being transported to a place that treats crazy people.

This is an exceptional event, even for me. I know that my brain causes unusual problems that no one has been able to treat, but being insane isn't one of them.

How and why I've gotten to this point is complicated, but the main reason I'm here is more immediate. I've finally found the one thing that brings me peace—alcohol.

Now this self-medication has become a life-threatening danger that I cannot fix by myself. The doctors at the place I'm going to promise they can help me. I've heard that one before.

After about an hour, we arrive at a large brick building with a sign that reads DRESSLER PSYCHIATRIC HOSPITAL. In a split second the reality of what's happening becomes very real and very scary.

"Why does it say that?" I call from the backseat, my heart suddenly pounding.

"Don't worry about the sign," my mother says to calm my rising panic. "They treat all different kinds of problems here, Cory."

Dad looks as worried as I am but says softly, "Let's not deal with this now, okay?"

Not deal with going to a hospital for psychos? Sure, no problem. What can my father be thinking?

Inside the main entrance, I enter a very crowded, somewhat noisy waiting room. Being on view always makes me uneasy, so as soon as I start to walk, my feet need to perform a triple hop, three quick steps only inches apart, which throws me off balance.

I have to do this in order to satisfy a

tension that is building up in my legs and can't be released any other way. Sometimes this trips me up so much that I go flying to the ground.

I do the triple hop a few more times before reaching out for the safety of one of the empty waiting-room chairs.

Welcome to my fun house, folks.

Chapter 2

Many of the people in the waiting area are still staring at me as my right hand shoots up in the air with the middle finger extended. *Oh boy, here we go,* I think. Giving people the bird is another one of my involuntary movements, or tics, that pop up exactly when they shouldn't. Try telling people that one's not deliberate.

Another middle-finger salute. *Hi, everybody!*

For a moment I think about the new medicines I'm taking, which are, as usual, not doing their job. Wellbutrin for depression, Tenex to keep me calm, Topamax as an "experiment" to see if a seizure medicine will help. So far I've been on fifty or sixty different medicines, none of which have worked—and a few of them can become deadly when washed down with Jack Daniel's.

Psychiatric hospital. A place for insane people, I'm thinking.

I know I'm not insane, even though the things I do make me look that way. But I do have a fear that I can think myself insane, and being in this place could push me over the edge. Going insane is probably my worst fear. If it happens, I won't know what, or *where,* reality is. To me, that's the ultimate isolation—to be separated from my own mind.

Eventually a receptionist calls my name and then starts asking me strange, bewildering questions. One of my eyes begins to twitch rapidly, and my tongue jumps out of my mouth like a snake's.

Occasionally I make a loud grunting sound like I've been punched hard in the stomach. Often my tics come one at a time, but today they're arriving in clusters of three or four, probably due to the stress.

I once told my parents that they

couldn't live through a single day with what I go through *every day of my life,* and that was when I was a lot better than I am now.

It takes another hour or so for my parents to be interviewed by a doctor. When they come out, I can see that my mother has been crying. My father looks exhausted and edgy.

When it's my turn with the doctor, I can't stop myself from shooting him the bird, too. The guy is good about it. He totally ignores it. He's young and gentle and pretty much puts me at ease.

"I drink more than I should at night," I tell him, skipping the part about almost burning down my parents' house when I passed out on the couch with a lit cigarette. "I guess I like to get a little tipsy."

This is the understatement of the year. *Tipsy* is my code word for totally wasted.

The doctor gives me a complete physical, and when it's over he says I'm as healthy as anyone he's seen, which strikes me as very funny.

"So I guess I can go now?" I joke, punctuated by an involuntary tongue thrust.

"Yeah, right."

Later, back in the waiting area, a male attendant approaches us and asks for any medicines we might have brought.

"What do you mean?" my father asks.

"He needs these," my mother cautions, taking out a large plastic bag crammed with pill bottles.

"The doctors will take care of that," the attendant answers.

Mom reluctantly turns over the stash.

A while later, a female nurse approaches and leads the three of us deep into the rear of the building.

Everything is a lot different here. It's darker and there aren't any people around. It's a spooky place.

I fight off a really bad feeling that I'm going somewhere I won't be able to handle.

Eventually we stop in front of a massive door with a sign that says JUVENILE PSYCHIATRIC WARD D.

Mental kids, I think.

"That's not me," I snap, pointing to the sign. "Mom, you know I'm not crazy."

The nurse says, "We get all kinds of people here," as though arriving at an insane asylum is an ordinary event in anybody's life.

"You're here for your drinking," Mom adds, "which they treat."

"It doesn't say that on the signs."

The nurse takes a large metal key out of her jacket pocket, and I freeze at the sight of it. I've never been in a hospital where the doors have to be locked. I come to a sudden realization: You don't lock doors to keep people *out.* You lock doors to keep them *in.*

Chapter 3

Dad gets it, too. He and I exchange fearful glances, and he lightly touches my arm.

The door opens as if it weighs a thousand pounds. When I refuse to move, my father holds on to my arm tightly and guides me into the ward. The main corridor is small, maybe fifty feet long, before it turns off at a right angle. There are no nurses, doctors, or equipment around, not like any hospital I've been in.

Three boys are standing together at the end of the hall. They stare at me and whisper to one another. Then they disappear.

A man hunched over a computer in

a small office turns out to be the ward supervisor. He's dressed in very casual clothes and doesn't look like a doctor.

He keeps working for a while, and when he finally turns to us, I notice that his eyes are unfocused. He seems to be either stoned or a little retarded. If I didn't know who he was, I'd guess he was a patient.

After going over my papers, he leads the three of us farther into the ward. There are small offices on either side of the main corridor. One of them is for dispensing medicine and has metal bars over the opening.

We take a sharp right turn. All of the patients' rooms are off this corridor. There's also a common area with a TV playing, but no one is watching it.

"How many kids are here?" I ask.

"Right now, eleven. Never more than fifteen. That's a hospital rule."

As we pass by the rooms, I count about eight kids and have no idea where the rest are hiding. All are teenagers, none as old as I am.

The three boys I saw before appear

again at the end of this corridor. As I get closer, they split up and walk past me, deadly serious. This is not a bunch I want to be around when the lights go out. And that includes the supervisor.

I'm getting more uncomfortable by the second. My skin is oozing a cold sweat. Hop. Hop. Hop.

I can't do this. I'm ticcing like crazy now.

In a moment we come to a large sign on the wall with rules printed in thick black letters.

NO TWO IN A ROOM
DOORS MUST REMAIN OPEN AT ALL TIMES
ALL ARTICLES IN THE PATIENT'S POSSESSION UPON ADMISSION WILL BE CONFISCATED
PERMISSION REQUIRED TO LEAVE PREMISES AT ALL TIMES
NO STANDING ON WINDOWSILLS
NO STANDING ON UPPER BUNKS

I wonder about this last one, then look up at the ceiling and understand. The entire area is covered with a metal grating. The openings in the grid are too small to put your hand through. *This whole ward is a giant cage.*

My heart is pounding as if it wants to jump right out of my chest and die on the hospital floor. *How bad must this place be if people have tried getting out through the ceiling?*

"I'm not staying here!" I shout to my parents. "Don't you understand? I can't do this."

I back away, then turn and start for the main door, the only way out.

I want to run but hold myself in check so it doesn't look like I'm trying to escape; I don't want anyone to come chasing after me.

"I'm not like these people," I call back to my father.

My sudden decision throws my parents into confusion. I think coming to a place that looks like this is as much of a shock for them as it is for me.

"I'm not crazy! This place will *make* me crazy."

My father's expression changes slightly,

and I can see in it a small ray of hope. He seems sympathetic yet angry at the same time, and I can't read which emotion is winning.

"You can't give up without trying," he says finally. "Give it time to work out."

"I'm *leaving*. Didn't you hear me?"

"What choice do you have? Think about it. This isn't your choice anymore."

This message sends me into a rage. I'm spinning out of control. I'll crash my way out if I have to.

I quickly rush to the door and stop when I see that there's another *golden rule* on it, etched on a bronze plate. This one stops me cold.

NO ONE PERMITTED OUTSIDE AFTER 6 P.M.

My watch says seven twenty. We've already been in this so-called hospital for more than three hours.

I try the door anyway. It doesn't move, not even a jiggle.

My anxiety spikes way past panic. If they lock me up, my life will be over. I'll die of fear. *People can die of fear. I've read about it.*

"Take a few deep breaths and try to

calm down," my mother says when she catches up to me. "I know you're scared, Cory. We'll work something out. We always do."

"I promise I'll stop drinking on my own," I plead, my voice cracking. I'm completely helpless, dependent on her—as usual. "I swear it. Please, Mom, I know I can do it on my own. *Don't make me stay!*"

Chapter 4

We're back in the supervisor's office, and he's just returned after leaving us alone for a few minutes to talk. My parents are having a really hard time deciding what to do. My father is usually fast with decisions, but this one is giving him trouble.

Finally, he takes a breath and delivers the words I've been praying for. "We don't think this is what we need for our son after all. We had a different idea of the hospital before we came."

I'm joyous inside. My father has done a complete about-face and is now going to fight for me. I want to hug him.

Unbelievably, the supervisor isn't taking my father seriously. He shakes his head as if he doesn't care what my dad just said.

"I'd appreciate you letting us out," my father announces.

He has to say it again before it seems to sink in with the guy.

"It's not possible for Cory to leave," the supervisor reports without any emotion. "Once a patient is admitted to the ward, New York State requires a minimum seventy-two-hour stay. It's the law."

"But we're *not* admitting him," my father explains. "We're going to leave right now, *before* he's admitted."

"He's already admitted," the man says more strongly. "It happened when he came through that door. Seventy-two hours, no exceptions," he adds, delivering what to him are just simple facts.

To me the number of hours—seventy-two—is like a death sentence to be executed in slow motion.

My father jumps up. "I want to speak to the hospital administrator," he barks. When the supervisor still doesn't react, he says, "Let me put it another way. I *demand* to speak to the administrator."

The supervisor thinks about it, then shrugs and picks up his phone. In a minute he hands the receiver to my dad.

My mother and I look at each other nervously. Everything is riding on this next conversation.

My father takes the phone and tells the administrator what's going on. He listens for a long time, and my mother and I don't know what's being said.

"There has to be a way," he says finally, obviously very frustrated. "What if someone came here by mistake, like we have?"

The debate continues, and he's beginning to lose his temper, which isn't like him.

"Even a criminal can post bond and get out of jail. What do you want me to do, call a lawyer?"

My father keeps going at the administrator. It seems hopeless. Then, all at once, he stops talking. "Yes, I understand. Thank you. I will." He hangs up and turns to us. "Maybe" is all he says.

Mom and I are both surprised when we hear who he's calling next.

"Dr. Meyerson! Thank God you picked up."

Dr. Meyerson is my current therapist. It's an absolute stroke of luck that he has answered his phone this late in the evening. We usually get his answering machine.

"We have an emergency here, and you're our only hope," my father continues.

The two of them talk for a few more minutes as he explains the situation.

After a while he lets out a deep breath.

"Say it just like that?" he asks. "Exactly that way?" He nods to us, then thanks Dr. Meyerson and hangs up.

My father turns to the supervisor and announces defiantly, "I request the release of my son *AMA*."

The man cocks his head suspiciously but doesn't respond. Not a word.

My father repeats the special code letters, this time as an order. "We are leaving the hospital with our son AMA. I'm told you understand what that means."

In a moment, the supervisor nods reluctantly, then gets on the phone again.

While he's talking to someone high up, my father explains, "*AMA* is an acronym for *against medical advice*. It's a legal code that allows the hospital to go around the law. It means that we understand the hospital advises against it, and it shifts responsibility to us—the parents—and our therapist. It lets the hospital off the hook in case a patient... harms himself or something."

"You know I wouldn't do that," I reply, to reinforce his decision.

"It's the only way we have a chance of getting you out of here."

"And what if we'd never learned about AMA?" my mother asks. "Or if Dr. Meyerson wasn't around or didn't pick up?"

My father shakes his head. "We were lucky. Very lucky."

I study my father's face. He looks older than I've ever seen him. He's worn out. It's been as long a day for him as for me.

"Sorry, Dad."

He nods, but he isn't happy. "You know that we haven't fixed what we came here for."

It's not a question.

A long time later, the nightmare is finally ending. The supervisor is still waiting for whatever approvals he needs. My breathing has almost returned to normal.

Eventually someone comes into the ward with papers and the required signatures. The supervisor gets his key, and the thousand-pound door swings open again.

It's been five hours since we entered the hospital. I walk out the front door without looking back.

The ride home to New Jersey is silent. No one has the energy to say anything, and nothing we can talk about seems important compared to what's just happened.

My mother lets me smoke a cigarette, then a second one, and after that I fall asleep. In an hour or so, they wake me in New Jersey and I drag myself into our darkened house.

"I really mean it, Mom. I'm going to quit drinking," I tell her before going to bed. "I know I can do it."

I'm not lying. I really believe I can.

It's the middle of the week, and my resolve lasts until Friday night, when my body is again driving me crazy. After my parents go to bed, I sneak down to the basement and chug five or six big swallows from a bottle of vodka my father thought he'd hidden when he'd squirreled it away in the back of an armoire in the living room. In a short time, the bottle is only half full.

I fall asleep with my head reeling. Images of the psychiatric ward are getting hazier. I have a dim awareness that despite my honest desire to change, my absolute need to change, I won't be able to.

Something else is going to have to happen. And happen soon.

Chapter 5

Many years before my narrow escape from the psychiatric ward, my mind begins to play terribly cruel tricks on my body. My life changes forever sometime before my fifth birthday, with a simple shake of my head. Just like that.

It starts as I'm playing a video game. I feel an unusual, intense tension building up in my neck, and I think the only way to relieve it is to jerk my head to one side. A little while later, the tension is back and I do it again.

Soon my head is twisting more and more often, and the muscles in my neck are beginning to cramp.

I'm starting to get scared. Remember,

I'm not quite five years old at the time. I'm just a little kid.

I try to stop, but the more I hold back, the stronger I feel the need to do it. My parents are looking at me, wondering what's going on.

That makes three of us.

When I wake up the next day, my head shaking is more or less a continuous thing. By lunchtime I know that my mother and father are worried because they aren't talking as much as they usually do.

By the following afternoon, the three of us are on our way to see a doctor. My father is driving pretty fast, and it feels as if we're in a speeding ambulance. At first I think it's my pediatrician we're going to see, but it's not.

"Is it going to hurt?" I want to know, stepping into an unfamiliar office.

"No, honey. This is a doctor who just wants to talk to you. This is a *talking* doctor."

In her office, Dr. Laufton asks me a lot of questions, such as "Do you ever feel like you have extra energy?"

"I guess so," I answer, because I think that's what she wants to hear.

Looking back, I realize this wasn't a good question. How could a kid my age have any idea what extra energy feels like?

"Why do you think you shake your head so much?" she asks after that.

Just thinking about it makes the shaking more violent. "I don't know. It feels like it wants me to," I say in between head thrusts.

That evening, my mother gives me a little pill to take. It's called Ritalin. I fall asleep pretty fast, but in the middle of the night I wake up feeling very restless and frightened.

I have no way of knowing it at the time, but Dr. Laufton has guessed wrong on the condition that's making my head shake. And she didn't realize that giving me Ritalin was like trying to put out a fire by drowning it in gasoline.

Brainstorm

Chapter 6

After two days on Ritalin, I wake up having to move different parts of my face all the time—my nose, ears, forehead, cheeks, tongue.

Every few seconds, I squeeze my eyes shut until they hurt, then open them as wide as I can, then repeat this over and over. In the bathroom, I can't stop looking at myself in the mirror and distorting my face into the most grotesque expressions I can possibly make. I don't find the faces funny, just weird.

It's obvious that whatever was controlling me before has only been worsened by the medicine. For some reason, though, the urge to twist my head is gone. For now, anyway.

A day or two later, I'm in the kitchen and I'm about to eat breakfast with my sister, Jessie. Jessie is only eight months older than I am. My parents adopted her when my mom thought she couldn't have children of her own. Then Mom got pregnant with me *that same week.* Jessie may be only a little older than I am, but she's years ahead of me in just about every other way.

This morning I'm thinking about armies of bugs and germs. So there I am at breakfast, getting extremely disgusted by the idea that they could get inside my body somehow.

Then I see a big hairy horsefly buzzing overhead.

"Get it away from me!" I yell to anyone who can help. "Get it away, get it away!"

"Do you know what flies do every time they land?" Jessie says to me.

"What?"

"Throw up or go to the bathroom."

I'm so disgusted by this thought that

as the fly lands near my plate, I start gagging.

My mother sees me and tries to swat the fly with a dishcloth, but she misses. The idea of its insect guts being smeared on the countertop makes me almost throw up again, and I beg her not to kill the fly.

"Please, Mommy, *don't!*" I screech.

Still, I'm very hungry. Last night the spaghetti Mom served made me think of a bunch of long, skinny white worms, and I went to bed without eating supper.

Jessie lifts a forkful of pancakes dripping with maple syrup, and I get past my bug thoughts long enough to do the same.

Enjoying her meal, she turns to me to see if I like it as much as she does. So there's absolutely no reason why, without any warning, I spit my mouthful of pancakes right in her face.

Jessie is so shocked that she just sits there, covered with food. Then she starts screaming.

"Don't do that again," my mother

scolds loudly. "Tell your sister you're sorry."

I should feel bad, but instead I'm mostly fascinated with the impact of my spitting.

"Sorry, Jessie." Then I repeat, "Sorry, Jessie."

For some reason the word *sorry* stays in my mind. I want to say *sorry* again.

"Sorry. Sorry. Sorry, Jessie. Sorry, sorry, sorry."

Repeating the same word over and over makes everyone even more angry at me.

After a while Jessie calms down and we continue to eat, but the urge strikes again, and I can't help spitting another mouthful of pancakes at her.

This time her earsplitting scream brings my father running—and when he leans in to scold me, I spit right in his face, too. He's so surprised, he doesn't know what to do, except wipe his face with a towel.

"You'll have to leave the kitchen," my mother says, more serious than I've ever heard her. Actually, she looks more worried than angry. She doesn't understand why I'm doing this spitting thing any more than I do.

Instead of listening to her, I reach for more food to do it again. She takes the plate away just in time.

"Sorry, Dad. Sorry. Sorry, Mom. Sorry, Jessie. Sorry."

"That's the worst thing you can do to people," my father tells me, still dabbing wet spots on his cheeks. "The *worst*, Cory."

"Sorry, Dad. Sorry," I say, making a silly face.

I jump off my chair and take off to the family room, hooting as I run. I can't understand what's happening or what I'm doing. I love my family and would never spit at them.

This isn't me.

So who is it?

Chapter 7

After I've spent a few more days on Ritalin, the totally new things I feel compelled to do keep shocking all of us.

And they change from day to day.

My parents tell Dr. Laufton they want me to stop taking the drug, but she says we have to give it a chance to work and allow my body time to adjust to it. I think that if the doctor had to live in my body *for even a few minutes,* she'd never give out that advice again.

Later that week at dinner, my father is at my side, showing me how to use my knife and fork.

"You feeling better today?" he asks.

Right away I answer, "You feeling better today?"

"No, I'm serious," he tries again. "How are you doing, Cory? I want to know."

"No, I'm serious. How are you doing?" I repeat back to him. "I want to know."

"Please don't do that," he says.

"Please don't do that," I answer, even though I don't want to. I want to talk to him about normal stuff, but instead I've made him angry with this stupid new habit of becoming a human echo.

Later on, when anybody tries to talk to me, I repeat their words before they can even finish the sentence. When I do this for the fifth or sixth time with my father, he gets up and walks away from me, just shaking his head. There's an expression on his face that I've never seen before, more like sadness than anger. My father's feelings always show on his face.

The next day, Jessie and I are in the TV room and I have a new urge: clearing my throat. The sound I make is halfway between a grunt and a low-pitched musical note.

After she's had enough, Jessie gets up

to leave rather than start another fight. But as she passes by, I have to touch her on the shoulder.

"Don't do that, Cory," she says.

I touch her again several times at even intervals until something inside me feels satisfied.

"Get away from me," she yells.

I run after her, touching her shoulder again. *Two* taps, a pause, then *three* taps to make the feeling of having to do it go away. Her yelling gets my mother's attention and gets me a time-out.

"Sorry, Jessie. Sorry. Sorry, Jessie," I begin repeating like some kind of broken record.

Alone in my room, I pound my head with my fists to make it stop doing these things.

The next morning, I hear a song on my stereo, and when it's over I can't stop hearing the melody. It pushes out all other thoughts until I can't concentrate on anything else.

Later on that day, I hear a silly word in a cartoon and have to say the word over and over to everyone I come across.

Gooneybird. Gooneybird. Gooneybird. I've begun to flap my arms like a bird, too, and I run around the house doing it whenever I get excited.

Things are getting worse every day, not better like the doctor said.

Today I'm like a jack-in-the-box, with new surprises popping out at any given moment. I feel as if my body is filled with electricity, and when I go to bed I can't lie still, even though I'm exhausted from my body moving all day. After a while my mother gives me a dose of Benadryl to get me to sleep, then another when the first doesn't work. The two doses eventually knock me out.

Finally, Gooneybird sleeps.

Chapter 8

Two weeks after our first visit to Dr. Laufton, we're back in her office, but I can't sit still in my chair for ten seconds. The head shaking is back full force, plus a lot of extreme grimacing and blinking and God only knows what else I'm doing. Even I can't keep track of all my new movements.

Dr. Laufton closes the notebook she's been using and sits back in her chair. She talks about some medical stuff that I don't understand. But I catch a bunch of unusual words coming out of her mouth.

"When I saw Cory last time, I thought we were dealing with attention-deficit/hyperactivity disorder, ADHD, especially after he told me about feeling so much energy."

"But not now?" my father asks in a sharp tone. He isn't a big fan of the Ritalin that's turned my mind into fruit salad.

The doctor doesn't like the sound of his voice. "Cory, would you like to go into the waiting room and play with some of the toys I have there? I think you'd enjoy that."

My mother tells me to go and that she'll be there in a few minutes.

Years later, my mother filled me in on what was said after I left. Dr. Laufton wanted to let my parents decide what and when to tell me, but she said that from what she saw, it was likely that I had Tourette's syndrome. The head twisting, the grimacing, the spitting—they were all tics. Vocalizing—making sounds such as throat clearing—was another common symptom of Tourette's. *Echolalia* was the term for repeating other people's words.

The doctor said there was no quick fix to get rid of the condition, that my body needed to move on its own. But there were any number of medicines and combinations of medicines we might look into—it would be trial and error.

My mother and father didn't know it at the time, but they were about to go on a scary roller-coaster ride that would last for many years.

I already knew what the ride would be like.

I was on it—*and I was in the front seat.*

School Daze

Chapter 9

I don't remember much about nursery school; mostly my teacher yells at me to do things I've forgotten to do and to *stop fidgeting.*

There are constant time-outs when I can't do simple things fast enough, such as hang my coat on a hook. My teacher is always mad at me, even though my mother tells her I can't help what I do. The teacher says my mother is overprotective and that she should go have another child and leave me to her. The truth is that in addition to my body movements, I was also born about seven weeks' premature and therefore am not as good with my motor skills as most kids are at that age.

By the time that long, excruciating spring and summer finally end and I arrive at kindergarten, it is obvious to my parents that my condition is actually several conditions. It is their choice not to tell me or anyone else the names of them. Tourette's syndrome isn't something people understand much about. It just makes you weird to other people.

And to yourself.

In first grade, my behavioral problems are a lot easier to see. My body is doing strange things several times a minute, and it has to be obvious to everyone that there is something very unusual about this kid named Cory.

My parents have found a new therapist for me. Her name is Dr. Pressler, and she is one of the world's leading experts in Tourette's syndrome.

The drive to meet Dr. Pressler takes about an hour and a half, because her office is in a medical building in another state.

After examining me, she puts me on a different medicine that's actually for people who have high blood pressure, but she says it helps a lot of Tourette's kids. Pretty much all the kids like me start off on clonidine.

When my behavior and my movements don't get much better, Dr. Pressler slightly increases the dose every few days, like my other doctor did. Clonidine definitely tires me out, so I don't have as much energy. But it doesn't stop me from twitching and jerking my arms and legs, or even from spitting at kids in school, which I've done off and on since my Ritalin days.

Some of the things I'm doing may not even be tics at all. Lately I *have* to stab paper cups with pens and knives, and I *have* to wash my hands several times after I use my computer. These compulsions don't feel the same as the other tics.

Then suddenly I start something new that happens every morning before school.

As my mother creeps ahead in a long line of cars to get to the entrance of the Dellbrook School, I get obsessed with the thought that something terrible is going to happen to her after she drops me off and I'm not around to protect her.

She's going to fall down a flight of stairs and die.

She'll be hit by a car or fall into a ditch.

Unless... unless...

Suddenly I think of the one thing that can save her, my mom's only hope.

"Promise you'll be first in line to pick me up?"

It doesn't matter to me that this isn't a logical solution to my mom getting hurt after she drops me off. All I know is that the thought seems to take away my feeling of dread.

"I will if I can, Cory," she says, sounding very unsure about my plan. "I can try, but there are a lot of mothers who come here to pick up their kids. I don't know if I can always be first."

"But you *have* to do it—every day. *Every single day.* You *have* to."

I wait for her to answer and can see that she's trying hard to work it out.

"Okay, honey. I will," she agrees.

"You'll be first in line when school is out? Will I see your car right away?"

"Yes, Cory, I'll be first in line."

"Every day?"

"Every day."

"Even forever?"

"Yes, even forever."

Chapter 10

One day my worst fear comes true. Leaving school, I see a silver station wagon at the head of the line. A wave of horror shoots through my body. *She's not here. Something happened to Mommy!*

I know that any second a teacher will come to tell me the bad news. She's been hit by an airplane that fell from the sky. Or there was a terrible car accident. I start crying uncontrollably, shaking horribly.

Then I see my mother in the distance, pulling up to the school quickly. She drives as close as she can and stops behind the silver wagon to be . . . *second in line!*

My mother rolls down the passenger window and yells for me to come, but I'm frozen in panic, still sobbing and shaking my head.

She yells again, but I still don't move.

A moment later, she steps on the gas and pulls around the silver car and ends up in a fire zone. Right away a crossing guard charges at her, as if she's just driven through the school's front window.

"You crossed the yellow line, lady. You have to move," he shouts loud enough for everyone in the pickup area to hear him.

By the time I'm running to her, she's surrounded by the crossing guard, a policeman on a bicycle, and a large, angry lady bus driver. In the middle of all the shouting and arguing, I dive into the car, and my mother takes off quickly.

On the way home, we don't talk about what just happened, and I don't really care anymore. I'm listening to a heavenly choir, singing words that thrill me.

She's alive, she's alive. My mommy's alive!

And I've made it through another day without my mother getting sucked down into a manhole.

So Hard to Be Good

Chapter 11

No one can imagine how horrible this is. Every single day, *something bad happens to me.*

A few steps from the front entrance to school, a spasm shakes my shoulders and freezes me in place. I jerk my chin straight up to the sky as high as it can go and lock it in that position for the next three or four seconds.

When the spasm finally stops, I take a few deep breaths to relax, but it happens *again,* then *again* a few steps later. I'm only six years old and don't know why my medicines aren't helping me by now.

Nothing is working. I'm actually getting worse.

I'm incredibly discouraged that the day is starting off with my tics being so bad. I like going to school, and my first-grade teacher, Mrs. Wilkens, has been nice to me so far. My mother was able to have an early conference with her, and she "gets" my problems and knows how to deal with me.

Mom is always having to explain me, not only to the teachers but to everyone who sees me acting funny. Once she clarifies the situation, people usually get over their shock. But not always.

I try not to look back at the car because I know that my mother is still watching and feeling bad for me. She always tries to hide how worried she is, but these days she doesn't look as happy as she used to. I wish I could stop being the way I am for her. She is the best mother anyone could ever have, and I love her so much.

School only makes my tics worse. There's no doubt about that. Now there are so many tics we've started to give them names. The *hopping tic,* the *bend-at-the-waist tic,* the *chin thrust,* the *scrunchy face.* When I began the *twisting tic,* I felt something rip in my back, but I still had to keep doing it. I had to go to the hospital and be drugged asleep in order to make it stop. I never thought the twisting tic would end, but it did after a few days.

My tics keep changing all the time. They started mostly in my neck and face, but now they are all over my body and affect my large-muscle movements. There doesn't seem to be any limit to how many kinds there are.

I do the chin thrust a few more times before getting to the front door of my school. The pressure is so strong on my spine it feels like it's about to snap. This is not such a wild thought. I already know that my tics can make me hurt myself. Before I ripped the muscle in my back, I was biting down so hard on a bottom tooth that I broke it in half and had to be rushed to the dentist. The dentist didn't believe what had actually happened.

Even though I'm trying hard to be good, this day gets off to a terrible start. During the spelling lesson, Mrs. Wilkens asks me to write the "word of the day" on the blackboard, and I feel proud to have been selected. I can tell she likes me, even though I tic a lot in class and require some extra work on her part.

When I get to the front of the class, Mrs. Wilkens pronounces the word of the day and asks me to write it.

My writing isn't very good because I have trouble holding the chalk and forming the letters, but I always try my best to please her. And everybody else.

Before I start, I sound out the word in my mind, the way she told us to do. Then I turn to the blackboard and get the chalk ready.

But instead of writing the word of the day, my hand writes the word SHIT in great big letters.

For a moment I stand there, staring at the word in horror and shame.

I don't know what just happened, only that something told me to do it. I know it's one of the worst things I could have done, and I'm as shocked as anyone.

As soon as the kids see the word, they start laughing and pointing at the blackboard. I'm so embarrassed, I want to erase it, but I can't.

"Sorry," I say to Mrs. Wilkens. "Sorry. Sorry."

My face contorts, and my eyes close and open fast and tight. Not only have I written a bad word on the blackboard but it's making my tics worse. The combination of what I've written and my silly faces starts the other kids laughing harder and louder. Mrs. Wilkens isn't laughing at all. She's angry.

"Everyone be quiet," she shouts. *"Cory, take your seat. Now."*

"Sorry," I say again, but I don't think she's listening.

Then I get the idea that it will be better if I make it look like I'm doing everything on purpose, as a joke. The kids will think that I'm funny and not just weird. So I make a few more silly faces, including a dopey grin. This makes the kids laugh again. I laugh along with them.

Mrs. Wilkens yells at us again, and this time the room goes completely silent.

I get to my seat and slip into it quietly. Inside, I'm feeling so bad that I let Mrs.

Wilkens down when she trusted me at the blackboard. But I also realize for the first time that I can get kids to laugh *with* me instead of *at* me when I do something inappropriate. I can become the class clown.

One thing is for sure. From this day on, I can't go to my classroom without thinking about writing SHIT or some other bad word. And I live in paralyzing fear of going up to the blackboard again.

Danger Everywhere

Chapter 12

I'm making it very hard for my mother to drive. We're coming home from the YMCA, where she's taken me to play basketball with some kids like me who don't have much else to do or other kids to play with.

We're on a narrow country road, and the traffic is bad. My mother is trying to make a left turn at an intersection, but there's another car coming at us, and she has to decide if she can make it in time.

Already on this ride I've been sticking my head out the window and also making silly faces in the rearview mirror, like I used to do in my bathroom. This is getting my mother upset, but not as upset as when I need to *open my door while the car is moving.*

The reason I'm so wild today may be the new medicine I'm on. I'm getting anxious about starting third grade only a few weeks from now, so my doctor is trying a new drug called Haldol. This one was made for people with problems such as schizophrenia and big mood changes.

The Haldol is already having a bad effect, making me do strange, risky things—like now, when we're driving.

Just as my mother is about to turn left, I have an urge to do something new that is unexpectedly dangerous. I suddenly touch the steering wheel and push it to the right.

When my mother feels the wheel turning out of her control, she pushes my hand away.

"Cory, you could cause an accident!"

This makes me want to touch the wheel even more, but I just tap it in a teasing, slightly threatening way.

All the while, an oncoming car is getting closer. By now I've distracted my mother so much that when she faces the road again, she has to make a faster decision.

She steps on the gas pedal, but I can see she's so upset, she's made a mistake. The car is coming at us too fast. We're not going to get out of the way in time, and it's too late to stop.

"Mom!" I call out. "Mom! Mom!"

My mother tries to speed up, but the oncoming car is right next to us. It slides sideways as the driver hits the brakes and tries to steer around us.

A thunderous crash rocks our car. It lifts the front end right off the ground. Suddenly I'm flying forward. My head slams hard into the windshield with a loud crunching sound. I see a blinding white flash, then little lights sparkle in my eyes.

"Mom?" I cry out in pain and confusion.

Chapter 13

When everything stops moving, there's smoke spewing from the engine of the car that hit us, blowing crazily over the hood. A young woman pries open the door and steps out, crying and stumbling over her feet.

I'm dizzy from the hit against the windshield. I look over at my mother to see how she is.

Her head is resting on the steering wheel. I think she's hurt very badly, and I know it's because of me. But then she pushes herself back up and lets out a breath. She looks at me in wonder, then at the windshield. She sees the broken glass.

"Cory, are you all right?" she asks. I can tell she's very afraid. I've never loved her more than I do right now. She's so precious to me.

"I guess so," I say, trying to be brave.

"Does your head hurt?"

She touches a large swelling on my forehead that I hadn't noticed. Now I can feel it pulsing, but there's no pain yet and it's not bleeding.

"I don't know why the air bags didn't go off to keep you away from the windshield," Mom says.

And I don't know why I needed to touch the steering wheel.

Chapter 14

When the phone rings, I look away from the video game and listen to hear who's calling. I hope that my mother will shout my name and tell me that it's a friend who wants to play—but, as usual, it isn't. Fourth graders are pretty much staying away from me nowadays. My tics are driving me and everyone else crazy.

Even Jessie is keeping her distance, and we're usually pretty close. A few days ago, I was in the front seat of our car and suddenly hurled myself over the backrest and landed on top of her. I hurt her so much that she screamed in pain. I feel so bad when I have to do things like that to her. Jessie used to try to calm me down and hug me when I got restless, but now there are too many things I do that threaten her, and she can't trust me anymore.

My father is spending more time with me, probably to make up for my not having any friends.

One afternoon, my father and I are in the basement putting together a new model car with a real gas engine. The car has hundreds of tiny parts, and he's helping me find one that's missing. After looking for a while, I'm suddenly aware of how close our heads are. The fact that they're almost touching gives me an urge to do something wild and inappropriate, like spit in his face. *Something is telling me to ruin our good time.*

Out of nowhere the F word flies into my mind. It's the worst word I can say, like the time I wrote SHIT on the blackboard at school. I try hard to hold back from saying it, but when the urge becomes overpowering, I lose the fight. Only it comes out as *fu fu fu fu fu,* as though I'm stuttering.

My father knows right away what I'm almost saying.

"What's that about?" he wants to know with a disappointed expression.

"I'm not sure. It just came out."

"Where did you hear that word?"

"Nowhere... I guess."

He starts to tell me not to do it anymore but then stops short. He knows the first rule: telling me not to do something only makes me want to do it more.

"Sorry, Dad. Sorry. Sorry, Dad."

"That's okay, don't worry about it," he says. Shifting topics, he goes on, "Have you seen anything that looks like this?" He points to a picture of a part in the car instructions.

"Fu fu fu fu fu," I answer.

"I bet it's in here somewhere," he says, ignoring the near curse and digging into a new pile of loose screws and plastic pieces.

I guess I'm lucky that I almost never feel the urge to curse in front of people like some kids do, and that when I start to, I can usually control it. If you have to curse out loud, you can't be in a regular classroom or go to the movies or restaurants because people don't understand. Just like when I give people the bird. No matter how many times my mother or father explains that I can't help it, they don't believe it.

My father's distractions help me forget the F word, and we spend a happy time putting most of the car together.

"How'd you get so good at this?" he says when we're done for the day.

"Dunno," I answer proudly.

But I do. I can spend hours at a time doing something I love because it becomes an obsession. Sometimes obsessions can work for you.

In bed that night, I can feel the medicine helping my mind shut down. I think about what a mostly good day I had with my father, and then I remember the one thing that wasn't so good.

Fu fu fu fu fu, I say softly into the darkness. *Fu fu fu fu fu.*

I don't think this is a regular tic. It's more like a thought I have to act on. Or maybe that's the same thing. And I suddenly recall where I first got the idea of having to say bad things and having no control over it.

Our family had recently watched a comedy that made fun of different kinds of people with terrible conditions. One was a woman who kept cursing out loud, and she explained that it was because she had Tourette's syndrome. I remember being so surprised.

"Does Tourette's make people say bad words?" I whispered to my father.

He looked really angry, but not at me.

"No, this is a bad movie, Cory. They make fun of people who can't help themselves, and they shouldn't."

And that was the way I learned about the cursing tic. It's called *coprolalia.*

I go to sleep wondering why grown-ups would want to make a movie that pokes fun at people who can't help themselves. And I wonder if they still would if there was somebody in their own family like me.

When Good Turns Bad

Chapter 15

It feels strange and almost wrong to see the hallways so empty and silent at this time of day in such a big school.

I'm late for class because the extra Benadryl I needed to take last night made me oversleep. It's the end of fourth grade, and it's getting harder to stay in school for the whole day, but I want to try. Yesterday I was twitching and jumping around so much that my shirt was soaking wet by sixth period.

On the way to class, I see three girls around my age whom I haven't noticed before. They use the word *like* about ten times in five seconds. *And I, like, go with him, and, like, oh my God! That's, like, so awesome.*

I wonder—do they have tics? Is saying *like* really a tic? If so, I know an awful lot of other kids who have it.

As they pass by me, I bend at the waist and jerk my head to one side. The girls stop their conversation and smile as they go by, but after they're farther down the hall, I can hear them giggling. I don't know if it's because of me or something else.

Still, I feel pretty good about being in school today. I don't know if it's my new medicine or not. I've been completely off Haldol for a while, and Dr. Pressler has replaced it with Cogentin. This is yet another medicine made for something else, in this case for people with Parkinson's disease. Parkinson's sufferers have problems with the way their bodies move, so I guess that's a good reason to try it on me.

Dr. Pressler will do anything to help. She's very disappointed that she hasn't found a great medicine for me like she has for hundreds of other children.

So far Cogentin is better than Haldol. Or maybe it's just that the Haldol is wearing off. I never know. A lot of my wild behavior has stopped, especially the feeling that I might need to curse. Haldol gave me an unbelievable appetite. Now my body is doing some new things. I guess that could just be a sign of getting worse as I get older.

The real problem is that it's hard to know what's causing what, with everything going on at the same time. There are all the different medicines with different doses and combinations, and the time of year. Spring usually seems to be the worst. Then there is the stress of school and of the way Tourette's always changes, getting worse, then better, then worse again. It's called *waxing and waning.* With all this, none of my doctors have been able to figure out precisely what's going on, so whenever they prescribe a new medicine, it's always just a guess.

The best thing about school this year is my teacher, Mrs. Erlanger. She never ever lets the other kids make fun of me. She's explained to them that just because my body moves, it doesn't mean there's anything wrong with me, and that it's no big deal.

Today I promise to be extra good in class for her. Today I'm going to be a "Tourette's angel."

Chapter 16

By the end of the morning, things are going well. Mrs. Erlanger has called on me almost every time I've raised my hand. She praises me a lot and never lets my ticcing bother her. She tells my mother that she loves the way I always contribute in class. I can't tell you how great that makes me feel—like I'm a regular kid.

Things change at lunch.

I see my two old neighborhood friends sitting alone at a table, and there's an empty seat next to them. I sit down and say hi. They look at each other, then just get up and leave. They never say anything; they just take off. I feel so bad I can't stand it. They go to sit with their other friends.

After that I don't want to try to sit with anyone. Most of the time I eat alone anyway, except now and then I sit with William. He's a nice kid who doesn't seem to have friends either. William has learning disabilities.

Eating by myself isn't that terrible, mainly because I love the food my mother packs for me. Today my lunch box is stuffed with all my favorites—fruit salad, cookies, and sandwiches my mother makes herself.

Back in class, Mrs. Erlanger is slowly reciting a poem for us and wants us to print it out as she speaks, but I'm having trouble. The pencil is clumsy in my hand, and I need my words to be *exactly* on the blue line, not even a little above or below. I also need my letters to be *perfectly* formed, and since I can never get it right the first time, I have to erase and start over. I'm doing that so much today that I've made holes in my papers. I hate the sloppy holes so much.

Soon I'm so far behind that out of frustration I break my pencil in two and stop working. I've been breaking pencils in two all the time lately, at home and in school, even when I'm not using them to write. I don't know why. I just do it.

To try and relax, I begin to drum my fingers on my desk. I drum out a series of beats over and over, so after a while it attracts attention.

Mrs. Erlanger looks up and sees that it's me, then gives me a little smile and goes back to her reading.

One of the good things she's done for me is to make me the class messenger. This is a job the other kids want since it gets them out of class for some free time. When Mrs. Erlanger sees that I'm getting a little out of control, she usually says, *I need someone to go to the office for me. Cory, would you mind?* So while everyone else continues studying, I get to leave before I disrupt the class any further, and I go chill out in the nurse's office.

As I keep up my drumming, Mrs. Erlanger seems to be getting annoyed. I guess it can get on anyone's nerves after a while. It even gets on mine.

I soon realize that I'm getting stuck on drumming, and I stuff my hand in my pocket to stop. *I'm trying so hard to be good.*

I look around and I see a kid named Jerome grinning at me. He sits a few seats away and is one of the boys who likes to get me in trouble.

When I stop drumming, he makes a low chirping sound that I can hear but the teacher can't. It's similar to one of my throat tics, and thinking about it makes me start doing it, which is just what Jerome wants.

Soon I chirp loud enough for the other kids to hear, and I make a silly face so it looks like I'm doing it on purpose—the class clown again.

Now I'm chirping so much a bunch of the boys start to imitate me, and that does it for Mrs. Erlanger. She jumps out of her chair with an angry look I haven't seen before.

"This is not funny. I need you *all* to be quiet. Do you understand?"

The room gets so quiet that I can hear somebody outside mowing a lawn. At first I'm relieved that the laughing has stopped, but then the silence gets to me and becomes its own problem. I need to do something to break it. I know this is a terrible time to make a noise, but that's what the urge is all about.

Finally it gets so strong I can't stop it. My throat makes another chirp, then another one, even louder.

The class holds its breath, waiting for Mrs. Erlanger's next reaction.

"I think it would help if you could control that, Cory," she says in a sharp, slightly strained voice.

I can't believe it. *Are you asking me to stop?* She knows I can't control it, and telling me to only increases my need to do it. I feel like I've suddenly been attacked by the only person in school I can trust.

The tension makes me chirp again, even louder, and now I'm stuck in a terrible cycle I can't get out of.

"I think a time-out will do us all some good!" Mrs. Erlanger shouts over the noise. "Cory, why don't you spend a few minutes outside in the hall?" she says, and points to the door.

Her order stuns me. I'm supposed to be a messenger when this happens, not punished. Everyone knows the hall is punishment. I'm confused and hurt, *really hurt.*

I get up to leave and grab my book bag without looking at it, but the bag is open and all my books and papers spill around me on the floor. This starts another round of laughter from my classmates.

Nothing is making any sense. My favorite teacher is mad at me and she's making me act worse. My classmates are provoking me into doing things they can make fun of. I'm lost and embarrassed and ticcing wildly. I'm so afraid, I can't stand it.

Then I realize that another bad feeling is starting up inside of me.

I'm beginning to get angry. Very angry.

“ ’Night”

Chapter 17

I love my sister—she’s my best friend—but sometimes it’s so hard for us, unbelievably hard and unfair. I can cause her a lot of trouble and pain, and every now and then she starts to get even.

I don’t know why she picked tonight to try to trick me. It’s bad enough that a new tic is making me twist my shoulders so hard that the bed creaks. Add this to all my other nightly thrashing around, and my bedposts are getting wobbly enough to collapse.

But just as the clonidine and Benadryl are finally beginning to work, I hear Jessie from her bedroom, which is right next to mine.

" 'Night, Cory," she sings out a little too happily, and my eyes pop open.

There are certain phrases people say to me that I *always* have to respond to. Saying *good night* is one of them, and Jessie knows it.

" 'Night, Jessie," I say as quickly as I can, trying to make it sound as if it's the last time we'll be doing this.

I'm about to drift off when she does it again.

" 'Night, Cory."

"Stop doing that, Jessie!" I yell back, and quickly follow it up with another " 'Night, Jessie."

This isn't like her. Jessie is almost always on my side, but lately things are changing. She used to let me join in when her friends came over to play, but now she takes them right to her room and locks the door. I guess it's hard for her to have a brother like me when she's trying to be regular.

Yesterday she deliberately got me in trouble. When my mother wasn't around, she told me that it was okay to pee in the bathroom sink. And when I did, she told on me.

It's easy for Jessie to trick me, just like she's doing tonight. She's smart and plans ahead much better than I do. A while back, she made up a rule that whoever yells *Front seat* first gets it when we go for a ride. I agreed because I thought I'd always remember, but so far she's won about a hundred times in a row. Occasionally she remembers to call *Front seat* when we're still in the house. And every time she wins, she laughs in triumph.

I stay awake for a long time, waiting for Jessie to say it again, which is just as bad as her doing it, but finally, when nothing more happens, the medicine takes over and I drift off into...

" 'Night, Cory."

The gleeful little call splits open the darkness, and I sit up in bed and yell for my mother, who shows up fast.

"What's the matter, Cory? Are you all right?"

"Jessie won't stop saying ' 'Night, Cory.' She's doing it on purpose."

Mom ducks into Jessie's room and scolds her until she promises to stop.

Finally, sleep arrives, and with it my best dream. I'm riding a motorcycle on a highway that goes on forever. I'm traveling faster and faster, bent down over the handlebars, passing everyone else. I'm not thinking about anything as the cars and trees fly past—except the thrill that's rippling through my body.

Eventually I'm going so fast that my motorcycle races ahead of the sound of its roaring engine, and I'm moving in a state of blissful quiet, as if I'm the only one at the very tip of a spaceship. A wonderful voice talks to me, telling me that this is how happy I will be someday. *This blessed freedom will be mine.*

And then comes another voice, from another place and time, a softer one, just loud enough for me to hear.

" 'Night, Cory."

Part Two

ONWARD AND DOWNWARD

The Lure of Branches

Chapter 18

I stare up at the two-hundred-year-old tree in my backyard, almost out of breath from the excitement. It's more than a hundred feet tall. I wonder how many storms it must have survived to still be here, waiting for a barefoot kid with an unusual urge to climb.

The tree trunk has to be at least twenty feet around and looks like a huge elephant's foot. I wonder if I'm really crazy to be doing this, but I don't think so. *Crazy* is someone who kills people because his dog tells him to.

I have to climb because there's no other way to get rid of the urge that's building up inside me. It's as if I have wires in my brain that light up at the thought of it, but they're wired to the wrong places and don't allow the electricity to turn off.

So this isn't about being crazy. This is about bad wiring.

Right now I should be at school with the other fifth graders, but today I can't sit still long enough to make it through the whole day.

So this afternoon, while the other kids are learning English, geography, and math, my assignment is climbing.

Lucky for me, the kids who lived here before left a homemade rope ladder that's still attached to the first branch. I stand on the rope step and can tell it's strong enough to hold me.

I hook my foot around the next rung, but right away my leg shoots straight out and slams into the tree. This is what I'm most afraid of, the excitement making my body spark more than usual. A wrong move a hundred feet in the air will make the trip down a lot faster than the climb up.

On the next try, my leg is okay, and I keep going until I run out of ladder and can grab hold of the first branch and pull myself into the tree.

The next few branches line up one above the other, and I climb them quickly. Then a large gap stops me.

My bending tic hits all at once, and my stomach clenches so hard that for a few seconds I can hardly breathe. The thrust forward shifts my weight so much it throws me off balance, and *suddenly I'm falling.*

My whole body jerks to a stop when my legs get tangled in a thick bunch of branches and end my fall. It all happened so fast that I didn't have time to be scared, but I am now that it's over.

I stay very still and suck in a few gallons of air.

I look down and see just how bad an idea this whole thing was. Below, there's a pattern of small light and dark rectangles, and I realize they're the roof shingles on my house.

I'm much higher up than I thought, and I wonder how I'm going to get down.

That thought makes me *need* to test the danger of a fall. I let go of the limb I'm holding on to for just a second until I start to lose my balance. Then I grab it again at the last moment. I test again by letting go for a longer time and almost don't get my grip back before it's too late.

But I still need to climb. I wrap both arms around an overhead branch and hook one leg around it, then the other, and in a moment I'm hanging upside down.

All at once a big muscle in my left leg contracts, making it straighten out. Now only one leg is attached to the tree, and *I'm still hanging upside down.*

I dangle there, high off the ground, not knowing if I'm going to fall. I wait for the spasm to stop, then I wrap my leg back around the branch and haul myself right side up.

I don't know how long I've been climbing. My shirt is soaked with sweat.

The muscles in my arms are tingling from the strain of holding on for so long, but being this close to the top elates me.

I push apart a final thick clump of leaves, and a small space opens up. Now I can see where some of the highest branches end. The branches here are thinner, and I don't know if the last one will hold my weight, but I'm not going back down until I find out.

I take a deep breath and go for it. It bends but doesn't break. *And I'm there!*

I actually begin to relax. The breeze is like a silk scarf on my skin. Far below, the earth looks like it's moving back and forth, but it's only the treetop swaying.

I'm like a bird in the canopy of a great forest—one that's washing stillness over my body. Up here, I'm part of another world—a zone without time or stress. I needed to get here because of the thrill but also because, up here, there's something I can never find on the ground. *A place where no one can see me tic.*

I don't see any reason to come down.

No reason in the world.

What I don't know, and won't for many years, is that the act of climbing this tree is the key to something wonderful.

This is it. I just don't know it yet.

Resource Room

Chapter 19

You'd have to be unconscious not to realize that something is about to break loose in the Resource Room at my school. It's obvious to all the kids that Phillip is getting more hyper by the minute, but Mr. Jansen is still sitting behind his desk, reading today's *New York Times.* He seems concerned with what's going on only when it gets so loud that you can hear us in the halls or when someone starts to freak out. Then he yells, "Be quiet and sit down! Now!"

The Resource Room is a classroom set up as a quiet space for special-needs kids like me who require a break in order to get through the school day or need a place to go when they get to be too much to handle in a regular classroom. The teachers have started sending me here for time-outs a lot, ever since my behavior in class got out of control.

Everything about middle school has made me worse. Just changing classes puts me under unbelievable pressure. I can't work the combination on my locker very well, so I'm always late for my next period. When I finally do get the door open, I usually forget to lock it again. Already I've had my jacket, books, and several lunches stolen. Feeling anxious between classes makes me worry all the time, and that's made my tics go off the charts.

This is the main reason one of my teachers sent me to the Resource Room again today.

There aren't that many of us in the school who come here, and everybody knows who we are. I'm not the only sixth grader, but I'm the only one who comes because his body is like a Mexican jumping bean.

The trouble with the Resource Room is

that it isn't what it's supposed to be—a rest. It's not really Mr. Jansen's fault. He can't do much to keep kids like us under control. We're already on medicines for that, and he probably figures that we come to this room when our medicines aren't working. What chance does he have?

So I'm not surprised when, without any warning, Phillip bursts out of his chair and begins to run around the room, screaming his lungs out and knocking things off other kids' desks and the blackboard railing. Phillip is the most out-of-control kid in the entire school. He never stops moving and can't be quieted down no matter what people say to him. So Phillip and I have a lot in common.

On his second lap around the classroom, Phillip suddenly cuts into a row of desks and slides to a stop within a few inches of a boy named Danny. You never know what Danny is going to do either. He can be as still as a rock, just staring into space, or he can get as wild and crazy as Phillip.

Phillip approaches Danny and reaches

for his head, grabbing a fistful of curly red hair. Before Danny knows what's happening, he's being dragged out of his chair headfirst. Even though he's way off balance, he manages to get to his feet and kick Phillip in the leg. He follows that by grabbing Phillip's arm and sinking his teeth into Phillip's wrist.

Phillip retaliates with a kick of his own that misses Danny and makes a desk go flying. Both kids are about the same size, so this fight could go on for a while, unless the teacher gets them to stop.

"Hey, you two!" Mr. Jansen yells, making his way into the fight. He reaches Danny just in time to stop him from pushing his hand into Phillip's face. The teacher separates them by grabbing their shirt collars.

"Knock it off right now or you're going to Mr. Arno's office."

The threat of being sent to see Mr. Arno scares just about everybody in the school. Mr. Arno is the vice principal and is in charge of discipline. He's a big man with a floppy mustache and an expression like that of a snarling wolf. When he talks, he sounds like he's barking at you.

Phillip doesn't tune in to what Mr. Jansen is saying, so he continues to fight until his shirt is almost torn off his back.

Danny is more in touch with reality. He stops fighting, which calms Phillip down. In a few seconds, Phillip stomps back to his seat.

Mr. Jansen shakes a finger at both of them. "Don't make me talk to you again. This is a rest period. *All you have to do is be quiet!*"

For a while things are peaceful, but Danny is still upset. Phillip has really hurt him this time, and he's angry.

All of a sudden, Danny lets out a howl and launches himself like a missile at Phillip. He knocks both Phillip and his desk backward.

"That's it!" Mr. Jansen hollers, charging out of his seat again.

I want to help calm things down, mainly for Danny's sake—he didn't do anything to deserve being attacked. But the last time I tried to help in a situation like this,

I was told to stay in my seat, and I don't want to make Mr. Jansen angry at me.

The fight ends before the teacher gets to them. Danny has satisfied his urge for revenge and is moving back to his seat. Phillip is also tired of the fight—the last push knocked him out of his chair and sent him sprawling to the floor.

For the first time since I came into the Resource Room today, there's no noise. The quiet feels good, but it's already too late for me. I'm more anxious now than I was when I got here.

The silence lasts about another twenty seconds. Without warning, Phillip leaps out of his desk and heads full force for Danny, waving his arms and offering up an earsplitting scream.

Mr. Jansen bolts out of his chair again, but before he gets to them, the fight spills over to where two other kids are sitting. One is the only girl in the room, and she starts crying and puts her head down on her desk.

I put my head down, too, to try to block out what's going on. I make a few throat-clearing sounds and do a few shoulder lurches that have been building up. Poor Mr. Jansen doesn't know what to do or who to talk to first, so he ends up standing there, checking the clock on the wall. He still has ten minutes left with us.

My mom has to come early to pick me up, *but at least she's first in the car line.*

Med Menu

Chapter 20

What's so terribly wrong with me that so many smart people can't help me figure a way out of it? It's been *more than six years* since my body started jerking, shaking, quivering, twitching, and exploding on its own. I'm more out of control than ever, and I wonder why anyone thinks another drug is going to help after we've tried so many. I'm already eleven years old. My so-called childhood is almost gone.

Lately I've heard Dr. Pressler describe some of the things I do as *compulsions.* That's why she's prescribed Celexa, the first antidepressant I've ever taken. Everyone thinks it could be a breakthrough for me, since antidepressants work on compulsions, but in my case, the medicine seems to make everything worse. Celexa hypes up the need to jerk my body to one side so violently that I hurt a nerve or something, and it takes days for me to stop jerking and hurting myself.

After Celexa comes Paxil, another antidepressant. My doctor says it's worth trying because different medicines can do different things, even if they're in the same general category.

For a while Paxil really helps my mood. I become much happier than before, and being happy calms my tics down. But then my mood gets so good that it doesn't feel real. I actually tell my mother, "I don't want to grow up. I don't want things to change." *How weird is that?*

The good time doesn't last for very long, anyway. By the end of a week of nirvana, I start getting into trouble at school again, falling off chairs and being disruptive. So my mother begins to take me off Paxil right away. *Against medical advice,* I guess. A short while later, the school calls her and says I had a great day, and she thinks that my getting off Paxil is the reason. But I think, *If things are better when I'm* off *Paxil, then why weren't they better when I wasn't* on *it to begin with?* Maybe it's only that I'm still coming off the drug, which is like being on a lower dose. So we go up and down on Paxil a few more times, but we can't see that it helps, and I finally get off it altogether.

When I have good and then bad days on the same medicine, it's hard to know what's going on. Is the medicine wearing off? Is it the different doses I'm trying? Dr. Pressler says maybe my mind eventually figures out how to beat each medicine so that it can go back to the way it was.

Fluvoxamine is one of the worst drugs I try because its side effects are so extreme. At first it calms me down quickly. My dose is increased, and I have another great day at school. Right after that I can't stop laughing in art class and am asked to leave.

From there I become depressed, and the dose goes up again. Three more calm days in school are followed by a sudden burst of more tics and cursing in front of friends. I begin clenching and unclenching my right hand so hard that after a while it becomes impossible to open and close it at all.

Even worse, my body is jerking almost continuously, and for the first time it keeps doing it in my sleep, the only period when my body gets a rest. That's a real problem. I can't sleep, and it's making me crazy, seriously crazy.

When we finally lower the dose of fluvoxamine, my twitching goes down pretty fast; the cursing, too. My food and germ phobias go away. Then we add clonidine, which I have taken since first grade, and everything is okay until I start throwing things and having to touch boiling pots of water on the stove. I get in trouble at school by talking, laughing uncontrollably, and saying nasty things, so there goes fluvoxamine.

It kills me that there are so many unsolved mysteries about my medicines. Once in a while one starts to work, then something changes and the side effects get worse. I never know if it's the medicine itself, the combination of medicines, the doses, or the usual ups and downs that happen with Tourette's. This is the most complicated puzzle I can imagine for my doctors and parents to try to figure out—which probably explains why they haven't so far.

But we have no choice except to keep trying. Our new plan is to start on BuSpar in a few days, because Dr. Pressler now believes anxiety is causing everything else to be worse. She's also talking about trying a new drug called Risperdal, an antipsychotic used for schizophrenia and to control violent behavior. This is a very big decision for my parents. Risperdal hasn't typically been used for Tourette's, and I'll be one of the first Tourette's kids in America to try it. I'll also be part of a new study, like a lab rat.

Risperdal worries me for another reason. People who take it gain, on average, thirty-five to forty pounds. So instead of being just a kid who can't stop moving, I'll become a *fat* kid who can't stop moving.

Chapter 21

I'm standing on the pitcher's mound in front of hundreds of people in the biggest game of the year, the Little League town championship, on Memorial Day weekend. I'm basically a nervous wreck but also as happy as I've ever been. This is a rare chance for me to be the center of attention.

For the right reasons.

Playing baseball is the best time of my life, and against all odds I've become a good pitcher, a sixth grader who can throw a sixty-five-mile-per-hour fastball, though not always as straight as I would like. I'm also able to hit long home runs when I'm not striking out, which happens a lot, too.

We're losing by three runs, and they've got the bases loaded with two outs in the fourth inning. I've just come in to replace our pitcher. My team expects my help in winning a game that will be talked about until next season's first practice sessions, when there's still snow on the ground. At least, in my family it will be talked about.

Today I've come to the game with many more tricky moves than the crowd expects. Due to the stress, my tics and compulsions have reached a whole new level. I'm also bigger than anyone's ever seen me. As expected, I've gained thirty-five pounds from the Risperdal, which I've been on for a few months.

And I've taken an extra dose before today's game.

As the stadium quiets and I look for a signal from the catcher, I give in to an urge to start touching the tip of my nose with my mitt in an exact sequence, three times, then two times, then one. I complete this complex compulsion by tapping myself softly in the crotch with my glove.

Today, because of the extra tension, I've done this ritual before each of my first two pitches, and it has distracted me so much that both pitches were balls, missing the strike zone by a mile.

This time when I start my tics, I notice some of the guys on the other team watching me from the sidelines. So far they aren't reacting, just staring. Even though I know they're aware of my Tourette's, I tell myself that a lot of pitchers, out of nervousness, go through their own rituals on the mound, even in the major leagues, so maybe what I'm doing is no big deal.

When the touching is over, I stand up straight and turn the ball in my glove until the stitches are in the exact right place for my fingers.

My body becomes still, I cock my right arm, and I throw the ball as hard as I can. It flies straight over the center of the plate so fast that the batter can't get around in time. The umpire calls *strike one.* I'm in heaven. *All right! There's hope.*

The crowd in the bleachers to my right is rooting for my team, and they erupt in a cheer like they've just witnessed the best thing ever. It's amazing to see how important this game is to them, and it feels good to know that I've come through with a decent pitch.

Nose three times, then two, then one, pound my crotch.

This time one of the kids from the other team picks up on my ritual of movements and yells, "What's the matter, pitcher, you nervous? Can't take the heat?"

I have a tough time concentrating on my next pitch. Then another kid shouts, "Choke, choke."

I take my foot off the rubber for a break, turn to the outfield, and try not to think about the cruel taunting and about what happened in my pregame warm-up. I'd been throwing really well, not every one a strike, but most. Then, all of a sudden, I let go of a ball that sailed at least ten feet over the practice catcher's head. Something told me, *Throw a wild pitch.*

I worry that this can happen now, in the real game.

I also worry that something will tell me to throw the ball at the batter, which would be horrible. I can't stand the thought of hurting anyone with my pitching. I do throw fast, and this hardball in my hand is a lethal weapon.

By now a bunch of the opposing team's players are off the bench and standing along the first-base line. The batter is taking warm-up swings at the plate.

The next time I touch my nose, I hear one of the players yell something at me, then another and another. Their voices echo in my head, and even though I can't get all the words, I know for sure that they're making fun of my ticcing and dancing around.

"Choke, choke, choke," they chant in unison.

They all know I can't help the tics, and I can't believe they're using it against me. This is really crummy sportsmanship. Why isn't someone telling them to stop? Where's their coach, a grown-up who has to know how unfair this is?

I hurry through the rest of my movements, just to stop the shouting, and throw a really bad pitch for ball three.

The other team bursts out laughing, like they know they've made me worse by taunting me. It's cruel and it's wrong, but it's working.

Even before I get ready for my next pitch, the whole team is shouting all kinds of things to make me more nervous.

I look for their coach again to see if he's going to stop this. He's the father of one of the players and also the team manager, and when I spot him I'm shocked to see that he's up on his feet next to them. He's yelling at me right along with his team. He's leading them on.

I don't know how a grown-up can be doing such a thing. It feels like he's using my nervousness against me. I thought everyone would have known what this would do to me.

The more they yell, the more I need to tic. Suddenly I lurch forward with a bending tic. When they see that, the noise level goes up even more. But not on my team's side of the stadium; they are mostly quiet.

I suddenly hear my father's voice rising above our opponents' shouting. I look over at him, and at my mother and sister. My father is standing now and calling across the infield to the other team's coach. He's telling him to shut his players up, but the coach isn't paying any attention. My mother is staying in her seat, looking as tense as I feel. Jessie gets to her feet to cheer for me, saying, "You can do it, Cory."

Throw a wild pitch, something inside my brain tells me. The bad thought happens all at once and is too much for me to tune out.

Throw a wild pitch.

Throw a wild pitch.

I take a few deep breaths. I focus on the red seam of the baseball.

As I get ready again, the noise from the other team is so loud I can't even hear what they're saying. But I know what they're doing, and I've had enough. I can feel the change in my mood, and the change in my body.

Instead of making me more nervous, their jeering is making me angry.

Throw a fastball for a strike, I tell myself. *Right down the middle. Faster than you've ever thrown before.*

This time I hurry through the touching so quickly that I leave out a step, and when I let go of the ball, it flies straight and fast. The batter barely gets around and fouls it off for strike two.

Three balls, two strikes, I say to myself. *Now I have a chance.* And then the significance of what's just happened dawns on me: *I can still throw a good pitch even when they're yelling.*

"Show 'em, Cory. You can do it," Jessie calls out. "C'mon, Cory."

"You got 'em now," somebody else shouts.

"Right down the middle, baby."

"One more, just one more," my father calls out. "Go, Cory! You've got 'em!"

I have goose bumps all over my body. People are actually cheering for me.

I touch my nose once, but this time that's where the urge ends. My arms come to rest on my stomach.

The runners set themselves, ready for anything.

People on both sides of the field are standing and shouting.

Something inside me has changed and gotten really calm. I'm out here in a place I love, with the wind on my face, playing my favorite game in the world. This is tense, but I've been through a lot worse and come out alive. I can survive this, too.

I force my attention completely on the catcher's mitt. Two seconds later I reach back with the ball, then let it go with more power than I've ever had before. The ball flies so straight and so fast I can hardly see it. Even before it gets there, I know that nothing can touch it.

And nothing does.

"Strike three. You're out!" the umpire yells at the batter.

The inning is over.

God, I love baseball.

Chapter 22

If this had been the end of the most perfect afternoon in my life, it would have been more than enough to make me deliriously happy. But right now our team is still losing by two runs, and it's our final at bat.

I'm at the plate with two outs, and a new set of bending and twisting tics has set in. I look at the two guys on base and don't want to let them down.

Maybe it's the lesson I learned on the mound about not letting anything bother me, but when I see the ball coming in, I have only one point of focus.

When I swing, I feel solid impact on the fat part of the bat. As the runners take off, the ball sails high in the air. It keeps going farther than any other ball has gone at this field, right over the center-field fence and into the parking lot. *I just hit a home run!*

When I get to home plate and break free from my teammates, I run to my family at the chain-link fence. Our fingers touch through the mesh, and they tell me that I'm great.

My God, I did something great, I think to myself.

A short time later, a friend of our family taps me on the shoulder. "I got this in the parking lot," he says, "so you never forget."

I take the home-run ball with a happy grin and thank him.

It's been years, and I still have the ball. I will always remember that special day, maybe the best day of my youth.

No, not maybe. It was.

To the Ends of the Earth

Chapter 23

The good days are few and far between, and maybe that's why I remember them so vividly.

It's late on a Sunday afternoon in the summer before seventh grade. My father and I are in a race against the sun somewhere in the mountains of northeastern Pennsylvania. We've been looking for a lake called Wallenpaupack, but after what is supposed to be a two-hour drive turns into a three-and-a-half-hour drive, we're about to give up.

The tension in the car is like electricity flowing all around us. Out of anxiousness, I start to touch the steering wheel again, even though we're going fast.

My father doesn't mention it at first, but the next time I reach for the wheel, he can't stop himself.

"You can't do that, Cory. Do something else," he says, suddenly very annoyed.

Even though I realize that this urge seems dangerous to someone who's driving, I have an instant angry reaction to his warning. He knows it will only increase the urge. And he should understand by now that I would never again pull the wheel to one side, as I almost did with Mom right before our accident.

His outburst is especially surprising given that my father and I are getting along very well this summer. When I do something silly or dangerous such as grabbing at the steering wheel or shooting paintballs at our white garage doors, he knows how to handle it. He stays calm and asks me to think about the consequences of my actions, then walks away until I chill out.

My mother almost never gets upset with me, no matter what I do. She simply talks to me until I relax. I just wish she'd stop worrying so much. Sometimes I see a sadness in her eyes that makes me think my problems are never going to end and that they might even make her sick.

I move once more for the steering wheel, but this time I'm able to stop myself from touching it. Then the need goes away.

I still can't believe my father is taking this long road trip with me. He's doing it because he wants to spend some time together but also because I have nothing to do at home. My few friends have been going to the town pool and having parties and not inviting me, so my father has again taken over as my friend.

Chapter 24

The sky is getting dimmer. Ever since the idea of Jet Skiing came up, it's become a thrilling obsession for me. It's like riding a motorcycle full speed, only on the water. But we're obviously losing the race against time.

"I'm not sure we're going to make it," my father says. "It wasn't supposed to take this long. Sorry, Cory."

His words are like a knife sinking very deep into my stomach.

"We *have* to do it, Dad. Will you still try?"

He takes his eyes off the road to look at me. "I'm trying, Cory."

"It's okay," I surprise myself by saying.

"It's okay if we can't do it. Thanks for trying, Dad."

My father's expression suddenly gets more determined.

"I didn't say we were giving up."

He sets his eyes back on the road and pushes down on the gas pedal.

A half hour later, it's getting more apparent that my dream isn't going to happen today. I'm making a chirping sound to get the tension out of my throat, and my right hand is shooting into the air over the dashboard.

Then a miracle. We see a road sign for a place called Hawley. My heart pounds in my chest. That's the name of a town near the lake.

"We have a chance," my father says with new energy, "but they said they only stay open until no one wants to ride."

That's a possibility I don't even want to think about.

Lake Wallenpaupack appears at the end of the road like magic. It's an endless body of water that looks like motor oil in the dimming light. The evergreen trees on a distant shoreline seem about a thousand miles away.

Two college-age boys in swimsuits are on the dock, one sitting, the other tying up the last of six or seven Jet Skis for the night. No one else is around. No one is on the lake. My heart is sinking faster than the setting sun.

"I know it's late, but I'd really appreciate it if you'd let us take a ride," my father says to the boy on the chair. "We've been driving for hours."

The two guys look at each other. Not happy.

"We're closing up for the night," the chair guy says. "We open at eight tomorrow. Where are you staying?"

"We have no place to stay." My father nods in my direction. "I promised my son we'd be able to ride. It's really important to us."

The tension in the air makes my body twitch. Maybe they notice, maybe not.

After a long silence, the boy in the chair gets up and trudges to a small shack on the dock that serves as the office. My father turns to me with his eyebrows raised, and we follow him.

"I'll need his ID," the boy tells my father.

This is an unexpected shock. Age matters, even at such a faraway place as this. With all the weight I've gained, I'm big for my age, but I still look too young for this.

"We left so fast we forgot to bring it. But don't worry about that. He's ridden dozens of times. On vacations."

"I could get in trouble."

"I'll take full responsibility. I'll sign a paper if you want."

The boy thinks about it for a time. "I'll need a hundred-dollar deposit. You've got a half hour."

Chapter 25

This is heaven for me.

My dad and I are out so far on the lake that I wonder if we can ever find our way back. We've definitely been going for more than a half hour. The sun has set, and the golden sky is the only thing lighting up the water. If we wait too much longer, we'll be riding in the dark.

I'm the one who has taken us out this far from shore; my father is just following me. I can tell he's nervous about being in such deep water. Even I have to admit this water is very weird. It feels alive with things moving and wriggling under the surface like huge fish. The strangest thing is that although there are strong waves, there's no wind at all.

The surface swells have valleys in between that sometimes take us out of sight of each other until we rise again. When I get caught halfway up the side of a swell, it feels like the Jet Ski is going to tip over.

My father must be feeling it worse than I am. He keeps staring at the sky and his watch—although when I look back at him, he waves at me as if he's happy to be here.

Soon the sky is so dark that even I can feel a sense of danger approaching. My father motions to me, and I drive over to where he is. The water has now become almost motionless. We gently bob up and down with the sides of our skis touching.

"We have to go back now."

I nod in agreement.

The current catches hold of our Jet Skis for a moment. It gently turns us side by side until we're both looking out into the horizon, now only a thin slice of orange through the trees. In the stillness of a world that belongs only to us, I feel endlessly grateful toward my father. I don't know any other fathers who would have done so much to make this dream happen, or put up with me day after day.

"Thanks for doing this, Dad."

"I love you, Cory."

Then we slowly head back.

Ups and Downs

Chapter 26

Of course, for every good time, another bad one isn't far off. That seems to be Cory's Law or something.

We're driving to one of the best hospitals in the country for people who can't control their body movements. Suddenly I don't feel so alone.

I can't believe there's an entire hospital for people whose bodies move in unusual ways. I wonder what the other patients are like, and if there is anyone there who does stranger things than I do. I doubt it very much.

I'm coming here because in recent months middle school has become overwhelming, and I've started missing whole days at a time. I've even stopped playing baseball.

Risperdal has become my doctor's main weapon in the battle against my mind. It's calming me down and has stopped a lot of my wild behavior, but I'm paying a price.

At one and a half pills, I developed a new tic of head twisting and foot tapping in sequence. My weight had already gone up about forty pounds.

At two and a half pills, the foot thing stopped, but my tics became wilder and more unpredictable than ever.

Then came three pills. And four.

Suddenly I've become afraid of everything I used to like. I've always loved the ocean—the bigger the waves, the better. Lifeguards have had to order me out of the water after everyone else has left because of undertow or rip currents. With the increase in Risperdal, I've become afraid to go into even the calmest water. I've also started to suffer from vertigo and was so terrified of taking the ferry to Martha's Vineyard that I almost ruined our family vacation. I heard Dad saying to my mother that Risperdal took away my courage.

Still, in the hope that Risperdal would eventually help, we got up to six pills a day, a dose that would make most people catatonic. One time my father accidentally took a single pill thinking it was something else, and he slept almost all day.

The high dose calmed me down enough to stop me from bouncing off the walls, but I began to shake my head so hard I was sure I'd damaged my brain. The increased dosage also shot me up to nearly 230 pounds, a lot for somebody who's five foot seven. I was afraid of doing anything that had the potential to hurt or scare me. And that's when enough became enough.

The decision to start taking me *off* Risperdal was harder than the one to put me on it. Internet chat rooms are full of horror stories about the physical pain of withdrawal from this drug, even when it's taken away a little at a time. And the accounts are all true. There were days when I screamed, and cried, and just wanted to die. My depression deepened, and I began to believe that the only purpose of my life was to be in pain.

Given how bad the withdrawal was and the fact that Risperdal had at least helped my behavior, I *had* to start back on some of it again. We also tried it in combination with old and new drugs such as Orap—which made me totally wild—and Zoloft and Klonopin. So many that I can't remember them all. And nothing helped.

During this period, out of desperation, my parents found a chiropractor two hours away in Connecticut who said he could help my movement disorder by snapping a part of my upper spine. My father was worried about that and asked the chiropractor to demonstrate it on him. It was such a violent snap that my father said he actually saw stars, and he decided it was too risky for me.

After that, we found an unusual environmental allergist in the southern part of our state. He believed that my problems were caused by ingesting the wrong foods or chemicals, and that if he could figure out what they were, he could fix me. He may have been right, but I'll never know. He wanted me to go on a diet that was too strict to even try. With Risperdal making me hungry all the time, and with eating now an obsession, the thought of losing my favorite foods was unbearable.

The most extreme thing we almost tried came up while we were on vacation in Florida. A social worker by the pool noticed my movements and introduced herself. She said that I should try *swimming with dolphins* because they had healing powers that could take away my Tourette's. It sounded crazy, but she seemed pretty smart. My mother tried to set it up, but all the time slots were filled. Otherwise I would have gone for the swimming-with-dolphins treatment.

Which explains why I'm here today, turning onto the side street that leads to the Stringer Clinic for Neurological Movement Disorders.

It sure sounds like my kind of place.

Hope Against Hope

Chapter 27

As my parents and I travel up the elevator to the third floor to see the doctors, my tics get the message and shift into high gear. The doors open onto a long, narrow waiting area with a single wooden bench that runs along one wall.

It's before nine a.m., so the glass door that leads to the inner office is still locked. We're always early for these appointments. I guess that's because we're always so hopeful.

We sit and wait in silence. My father is thumbing through old magazines; my mother is trying to look optimistic, as usual planning to spend her whole day with me. Since my head started shaking all those years ago, she's given up her own business, writing, and any thought of a career.

The next time the elevator arrives at our floor, a teenage boy comes out with a condition no one would believe unless they saw it for themselves. My first thought is that he must have dropped something and is trying to pick it up.

But as he leaves the elevator, he doesn't stand. Instead, he moves forward like an animal. He places both hands ahead of his body on the ground and keeps them there until his legs catch up. This allows him to take another stride. Amazing as it seems, this must be how he moves all the time and why he's here. This is his movement disorder, as big an understatement as there has ever been.

After three steps, he jumps up on the bench and swings his legs around to face forward. He does this so effortlessly it's clear he must have done it a thousand times.

Once he's settled on the bench, he looks straight ahead without checking our reactions. That's something I totally understand. I've learned how *not* to see people staring at me, too.

Not wanting to embarrass him, I study him out of the corner of my eye. Sitting, he appears to be completely calm and normal. He's older than I am by five or six years, which would make him about eighteen. He's good-looking, with intelligent eyes.

His mother is showing a lot of self-control, too. My heart goes out to both of them. I can't imagine what it's like to get up every morning knowing that some power you can't control will force you to move around like a gorilla. All he probably wants to do is just stand up straight. How cheated he must feel, how he must hurt inside. I wonder if he ever runs into anyone worse off than himself, like I just have. I don't think I could survive what he has, but I guess I'd find a way.

I've thought about what a place that treats movement disorders would look like. I pictured the laboratory in *Frankenstein.* In reality, the building is like a large city hospital, all cement and windows. The closest parking is a few blocks away, so by the time I hopped, skipped, and jumped to the front door, I was tired out, and the day hadn't even started yet.

My mother has told me that the Stringer Clinic is one of the best hospitals in the world for research into unusual body movements, especially Parkinson's disease. Since I'm beginning to believe that any cure for what I have will eventually have to come from me, I'm mainly here to please my parents.

Our appointment with the well-known Dr. Holmes has been a great accomplishment for my mother. At first they told Mom that the doctor was too busy to see me, but when Mom described how severe my movements were and started to cry, they agreed to make room in the doctor's busy day.

This is a truly depressing thought. Being able to attract the attention of someone this famous only clues me in to how extreme my case must be.

Chapter 28

Dr. Holmes seems to be involved more in research than in the actual treatment of patients. Her biography on the Internet is very impressive.

In a short time, I'll wish that I'd never heard of her or her hospital. I'm about to learn the meaning of the phrase *living hell.*

In theory the hospital's advanced research and treatments for Parkinson's disease are important for me because that illness also causes involuntary movements. Like Tourette's, Parkinson's has something to do with two chemicals the brain produces, dopamine and serotonin. We've been told that Dr. Holmes has had great success treating Tourette's patients, too.

When we're finally admitted inside, we're directed to a larger waiting room that before long fills up with other patients. There are many doctors working in this area of the hospital.

There seems to be a special bond among patients in places like this because everyone has the same kinds of problems. Most of the patients here are older, and a few have come with family members.

The man who takes a seat next to us is probably in his seventies and doesn't look well. He's bent over and his skin is pasty white, like pie dough. Soon he strikes up a conversation with my mother. He's a doctor himself, researching treatments for Parkinson's disease, which he suffers from. In his case, the sickness has progressed to its later stages. He has only a short time left, he admits as a matter of fact, and wants to survive long enough to finish his research, which could help with a possible cure for Parkinson's. He says that Dr. Holmes is the best in this field, and he hopes she can give him a few extra months to finish his work.

When his name is called, he turns to me with eyes that have seen a lot of suffering and says, "Good luck to you." I know I'll never see him again, and it makes me feel sad.

Chapter 29

Dr. Holmes's assistant is a young, soft-spoken but very intense man who takes my medical history. He spends most of the time on my past medicines and their exact doses.

My mother has brought her precise daily notes on my meds and their effects on me, which she has kept since the beginning.

A door I hadn't noticed opens, and Dr. Holmes enters, surrounded by three other doctors in long white coats who look more like scientists. Two of them have clipboards, and no one speaks but Holmes, a tall and strict-looking woman with round glasses, maybe in her mid-fifties. She ignores me completely at first, choosing to skim over the notes her assistant has taken. When she's done, she looks up at me without even so much as a smile. She's all business.

"What are your present symptoms?" she asks as though she's dealing with a grown-up patient.

I don't know where to start. "I do a lot of things," I tell her, scrunching up my face. "Twist my neck, make sounds . . . different things at different times. Right now I'm hopping a lot."

For some reason, the hopping gets her attention.

"Would you show me?"

I'm surprised and uncomfortable at this request. No doctor has ever asked me to perform my tics, maybe because they are so obvious, they don't have to. With all these new doctors staring at me, my eyes are twitching continuously, and when I stand, my body bends at the waist and I bob up and down a few times as if I'm doing a warm-up exercise. I haven't done this one in a while.

Dr. Holmes directs me to walk to the

end of the hall, a distance of about thirty feet. Almost immediately, my legs get a freeze-up feeling, and I have to take a few hops to relieve the tension.

Three or four quick hops in place, some more walking, then three or four more.

The first set of hops is mild compared to the second, which almost trips me up. When I look back to check Dr. Holmes's reaction, I notice that one of her assistants has been videotaping me. Suddenly I'm embarrassed and angry. No one has asked if they could take my picture. I don't know who they're going to show this to.

The general feeling I've had since I came into this office is that *I'm not a person; I'm a specimen on display.*

I turn back to the far wall and try not to think about it. I tell myself that they've seen so many other lab rats they've forgotten rats have feelings, too.

It's another fifteen feet to the end of the corridor, and because I'm extra tense, I hop every few steps until I get there. At the end of the last jump, I lose my balance and fall forward. Only my outstretched hands stop me from crashing into the wall, maybe smashing a few teeth.

After the videotaping, the men in the white coats leave and I go back to my chair with several more hops, none as extreme as the one that almost made me fall.

"We understand that you've treated Tourette's cases," my father says to Dr. Holmes, getting right to it, as usual.

"Yes, a large number of them," she answers.

"How many have you helped . . . I mean . . . well, as a percentage?" my father asks, trying to pin Holmes down. He's as suspicious as I am and is never afraid to be direct.

"About eighty percent," Holmes says without hesitation.

None of us is expecting a number that exact or that high. It's too good to believe, even though I want to. The last thing I need is another false hope, but it means a lot when a woman of her stature makes such a specific claim. She's instantly put a chink in my armor.

"From what I've seen so far, I'm fairly certain my treatment will work for your son," she adds without much emotion, as if this life-changing, lifesaving promise is everyday small talk. She's all about facts and research.

"The treatment is simple," she goes on to say. "We use tetrabenazine. Most of our patients respond well to it. The dosage has to be monitored closely, however."

My rising hopes are suddenly smashed. After all the buildup, Dr. Holmes is only talking about another medicine. One more to add to the long list.

In a few minutes, the meeting ends abruptly when the doctor just gets up and walks out of the room, cutting off any more discussion. Not even a goodbye.

After another meeting with Dr. Holmes's assistant, we stop off at a reception desk and are given a form to sign that lets us get the tetrabenazine, which, it turns out, isn't usually legal to prescribe in the United States, except through a few special licenses, one of which Dr. Holmes has.

During the ride home we all sit in silence. Even with the name of yet another drug ringing in our ears, there is an air of subdued excitement, as there has been every single time we've gotten a new medicine or a new piece of advice. A faint ray of hope. Not much of one, as far as I'm concerned, but better than nothing.

Or maybe not.

Chapter 30

It takes more than a week to get tetrabenazine, or TBZ, because we have to get it from Canada. Dr. Holmes made me think that it was an experimental drug, but a Web site I check says it's been used in countries outside the United States since 1960.

It turns out it's an antipsychotic created to treat schizophrenia, just like Risperdal.

Here we go again.

Mom calls Dr. Pressler to check on her experience with TBZ but gets her answering machine. By now, Dr. Pressler has moved too far away for us to see her in person, but she's always there, returning our calls quickly, sharing results of medicines she's prescribed for her thousands of Tourette's patients, and telling us about new medicines.

The first night, I take my prescribed dose and fall asleep with an uncomfortable new feeling. My body is restless almost immediately, and I toss and turn continuously to find more comfortable positions. My tics are worse, too, but the high level of agitation is the bigger problem.

The next day, after we report my symptoms to Dr. Holmes's assistant, he tells us to *raise* the dose.

That night, the restless feeling increases so much that my whole body starts bouncing around the bed, kind of like the girl in *The Exorcist.* As the agitation gets worse, I plead with my mother to make it go away. She tells me to try to wait it out, and I curse at her because she won't help me. *I curse at my mother?* There's another person inside of me, taking over.

She gives me a second dose of Benadryl to help me sleep, but two hours later I'm still jerking and twisting and bouncing up and down. I'm exhausted from the meds, but it feels like there are a thousand fire ants in my bloodstream. I want to jump out of my skin.

Another hour passes, and it seems like forever. I take a third dose of Benadryl and some extra Risperdal. Between the heavy sedation and all the energy I've used, I gratefully pass out at around three thirty.

As strong as I usually am, I don't think I can take much more of this.

I am officially in hell.

Chapter 31

The next morning, Dr. Holmes's assistant casually tells us that my reaction is a well-known condition called *akathisia.* His advice is to wait it out until my body adjusts—otherwise we'll never know if TBZ is what we've been looking for. *How many times have I heard that about a new medicine?* As a possible solution, he orders another *increase* in the dosage, saying that this will help me adjust more quickly. I don't get why taking more of a bad thing can help, but he's the doctor. And this is his advice.

The following day, Dr. Pressler calls back and tells us that she hasn't prescribed tetrabenazine for me because it hasn't worked for any of her other patients. She's not sure of Dr. Holmes and her success in treating Tourette's syndrome with TBZ, but she says that since everyone's chemistry is different, there's always a chance it could help.

Over the next few days, the medicine takes me to another level. During the daytime, when it wears off a bit, my agitation changes into a heavily drugged feeling, as if I'm living in slow motion. I sit in place for long periods, my eyes glazed over and my mouth hanging open. I actually drool.

I don't know where I am in time and space, and I'm so limp that some of my tics go away. But something really bad is happening with my worst leg tic.

As I get up from my computer, I hop in place as I have before, but this time I hop on my heels. This makes it easy to lose my balance, and I fall backward, crashing into the French doors behind me and hitting my head on the floor.

My parents come running at the noise and find me unhurt. But I just lie there with no idea of what happened. I have a silly, embarrassed smile on my face because I feel so stoned. In my hazy state, I tell them I'm all right and apologize for falling. They help me up, but as soon as I'm standing, I hop and fall backward again. This time my father catches me before I hit the ground.

The doctor at the Stringer Clinic has the same answer to this as he had before: we have to stay with the program. We've gone too far to give up on TBZ. Unbelievably, he hikes the dose of the medicine again.

That night the akathisia goes beyond my ability to handle it. I writhe in bed, literally trying to scratch my skin off, screaming for my mother to please kill me. I can't wear any clothes because they hurt my skin. I beg for more and more Benadryl, but even that doesn't help until doses of other drugs I'm taking are added.

The daytime pattern continues, especially the feeling of being in the ozone layer. I go through the motions of living, moving slowly from place to place, trying to respond to things happening around me. But I'm in a total zombie daze. It's like watching the world from a thousand miles away, from another level of reality, from someone else's body.

One afternoon my father takes me to my favorite Chinese restaurant, and when the waiter places my meal in front of me, I just stare ahead with a long string of drool hanging down from my mouth. I imagine I'll never forget the sad look on my father's face as he watches me try to eat, to function on the most basic level.

I'm not living the life everyone else is living. I'm not here anymore.

That night I'm like one of those screaming patients you see in old movies, the ones getting electroshock therapy in insane asylums. I tell my mother I want to die, I want her to kill me, and she's frantic. Somehow I get through the night with more drugs.

When we report in to the doctors at Stringer, they finally agree that the treatment isn't working. The tetrabenazine is decreased gradually so I don't have more dangerous side effects.

In a day or two, the akathisia begins to go away, too. My vision clears, and slowly I become part of the world again. *And my tics go right back to where they were.*

Dr. Pressler isn't surprised that the medicine hasn't helped, but she is surprised to learn how high the doses were, even the first, which is probably why my body reacted so badly.

"Falling over backward is a classic symptom of overdose from drugs used to treat Parkinson's disease," she tells us.

The worst part is that there may have been no need for the painful hours I spent with akathisia.

"It could have been stopped quickly with Cogentin," she says. "It's a well-known antidote for Parkinson's patients who overdose on tetrabenazine."

Dr. Pressler has no idea why our new doctors didn't tell us that. Her reaction makes me wonder whether they let my trial go on longer than it should have because they really believed it would work or because they were actually using me for research.

Whatever the answer, I was in a dangerous place because of this drug. When the akathisia was at its worst, I wasn't in my right mind. I wanted to kill myself. If you had handed me a gun, I would have used it.

When it was all over, I was consumed by obsessive thoughts of getting even with the famous doctor and her hospital for what they put me through. I wanted to go back and tell them what they did to me, and to sue them and give the proceeds to the Tourette Syndrome Association. Of course, I had no idea if their actions justified a lawsuit. I just wanted to do something.

Yet, in the end, our family didn't do anything. That's the problem with having a condition as hard to treat as mine: there are only a few doctors who have a chance to help, so you can't make them angry or burn bridges no matter what they do to you.

And that's why when I talk about the famous Dr. Holmes, I don't use her real name. As bad as her advice turned out to be, I never know when I might have to go back to her with another desperate cry for help.

Holding On, but Just Barely

Chapter 32

I can tell by how quietly my mother and father are talking downstairs that they don't want me to hear them, so they're probably discussing me. They're doing this more and more lately, especially after a bad day like today.

This afternoon I noticed my mother lying down next to our golden retriever, River. Mom's head was pressed tightly into the dog's chest, and she stayed that way for a long time. River always seems to understand what's going on in our family. Once, when he heard my mother crying, he started to howl softly with her.

Today when my father walked in the door, Mom told him what had happened at school. He often comes home from long workdays to bad news about me.

I had seriously disturbed the class again, and one of the other parents had called the teacher to complain. My mother had to go to a conference after school to talk about what to do with me. My father got mad when he heard about it. He gets angry at the people who make things harder for me. I hope he's not mad at me now.

Sometimes I think my problems will get to be too much for my mother and father to take, and that maybe they'll become so unhappy they won't stay together. I know this can happen, because it did to a few of my friends' parents who didn't have nearly as many problems as we do.

I'm also worried that Jessie doesn't love me as much as she used to. She complains to my parents all the time now that they pay more attention to me than to her, especially when she's having a hard time. Today Jessie's best friend ditched her for no reason at all, and when she came home, she had to hear about my bad day before she could tell them about hers.

I think Jessie is having a harder time with me now than when we were younger because she has conflicting feelings about me. She still wants to protect me from anyone who makes fun of me, and a lot of times she tells off kids who are bigger than she is. But she's also mad at me because I make it difficult for her to have friends and a normal life. I guess that's what a lot of our fights are really about. It must be hard loving a brother who makes your life worse. Even so, most of the time she's great to me.

I'm still awake, and after my parents have talked for a long time, I get worried and tiptoe down the stairs.

At the landing, I peek around the banister and see my father standing with his back to me. He has his arms around my mother, and he's hugging her tight, and it makes me feel so good and warm to see them that way.

Then, when he lets her go, I can she that she's been crying. She wipes her eyes when she sees me and tries to make her face look like it's smiling, but it isn't. She takes me back to bed, saying there's nothing to worry about. Mom tells me a joke and kisses me on the forehead, and I feel okay again.

One good thing, I guess, is that all of us have been living this kind of life for a long time. Even though bad things happen, we get over them somehow. We laugh and we cry and we fight and then we make up and tell one another *I love you.* A lot of *sorry*s and hugging and kissing and chasing River around the dining room table.

That's my family.

Tsunami

Chapter 33

I've been in front of my computer for more than twenty hours now and I'm not even getting tired. I've studied courses on Internet marketing for up to a day and a half straight. Being compulsive has its advantages—sometimes, anyway.

Tonight, though, there's something new building inside of me. It's a feeling I've had before, but now it's stronger and wants to bust loose. It's like knowing you're going to be sick and throw up: it's just a matter of *when.*

It's hard to believe, but I'm actually getting through middle school, even though I'm missing a lot of classes. This is mainly because of homeschooling and my ability to remember just about everything I hear in class.

The torture of tetrabenazine has finally worn off, but different parts of my body are still cutting loose at any given moment. At this point there's a huge list of drugs that are in my bloodstream.

BuSpar to sedate me, and Tenex, another high-blood-pressure drug. And higher doses of Risperdal again because I'm worse when I'm off it than when I'm on it, and getting off it completely is terrible.

But being out of control for so many years—and what that's done to my life—is pushing me to a place I don't want to go.

A needed break from the computer comes when Jamie shows up at my front door around eight o'clock. I'm grateful for the company, even though he and I hardly ever spend time together. Jamie drifts in and out of the small group of people whom I've started to hang out with in my basement.

Each of them is strange in his own way,

but I think Jamie is the weirdest of all. He almost never smiles, his face rarely shows what he's thinking, and he's very moody.

I give Jamie a big welcome, like he's my best friend in the world, but as usual he doesn't react. Jamie and I have a strange relationship. Sometimes he seems like a true friend, but then something happens and he flips out, and I don't hear from him for weeks at a time.

For a while we play video games on my computer and fool around with a hacking program that fascinates both of us.

Everything goes okay until I have the need to touch Jamie's shoulder three times in a row. I haven't had this strange urge in a long time and thought it was gone. I try not to do it but can't fight off the feeling.

Finally I touch him as lightly as I can, but he cringes away from me like I have a contagious disease, and he orders me not to do it again.

I think his reaction is way out of proportion to what I did. Jamie is aware of my *have-to-touch* tic. Everyone knows that it doesn't mean anything, but Jamie has his own problems. I think he takes medicine for something, but he doesn't talk about it. He's one kid you never want to touch, *which is probably why I did it.*

Since a single series of touches hasn't completed my have-to-touch routine, a little while later I tap him.

Now Jamie freaks out. He jumps up from his chair and curses me, then storms out of the house so fast I can only sit there in amazement. I can't believe how quickly a good time has turned bad again, how my tics have ruined another night. My body is always betraying me, *always, always, always.*

This sudden ditching by Jamie causes something else to happen. The feeling that was with me earlier at the computer is growing stronger. It's bigger and badder than before, and it's taking on its own life. I feel it surging inside—like a giant wave that wants to break powerfully on the shore.

I get up and try to walk it off, but there's something urgent about this. I feel like

I'm getting sick to my stomach, but it has nothing to do with vomiting.

And then, right in the middle of a hopping tic, the tsunami hits full force.

Rage

Chapter 34

The almost complete loss of control happens all at once. The wave inside breaks and forces me to cry out with such raw fury that my throat feels like it was sandpapered.

I want to move, to outrun whatever is going on inside me, but a stabbing pain in my belly makes me go down. I hit the floor as though I've been punched by a weight lifter or a heavyweight boxer.

By the time my parents hear me raging, I'm unable to control it any more than I can control my tics. My anger is wild fury, and suddenly it's directed at them. I'm scaring myself because I've never felt anything like this before.

I curse my father when he tries to calm me, and I make a threatening move at him when he gets too close. I blame him for my suffering. I'm ultraviolent and want to strike out at anything and everything around me.

Before long I'm in another world, this one not even close to rational.

I can feel the skin around my mouth pucker and tighten. My eyes have narrowed and made the world darker. My lips are pulled back like a snarling wolf's. I feel my brain unraveling, detaching from any normal thought process.

I'm unreachable, even to myself.

I shout that I can't take it anymore and bolt for the living room, where I fall to the floor with a loud groan, clutching my stomach again. I thrash around, then dry heave. It seems the only question is, which will burst first, my brain or my heart?

In a while the rage is still there, and I'm getting desperate. I pull myself up and head to the kitchen to take medicine so I can put myself out as fast as possible.

I go crazy and take all my medicines

at once: trazodone to wipe me out; propranolol and Xanax for my anxiety.

I add two Benadryl, almost choking on the slippery pills. When I'm finished, dozens of pills are all over the floor.

Waiting for the medicines to work, I give up fighting and collapse onto the ground again, wondering where this insanity will take me and if I'll ever get back. My parents are trying to help me—something they've done since I was four—but there's nothing they can do, nothing anyone can do.

I finally yell at them to leave me alone, to get away from me. They're petrified and do as I say. That's good, because I'm afraid I could hurt them right now.

I latch the kitchen door.

A red-hot pain in my stomach explodes with such intensity that I double over in agony. The loudest scream I have ever made almost bursts my throat. It's a torrent of pent-up rage spewing out, a lava flow of all the years of pain, embarrassment, insults and ridicule, tics and bad thoughts, betrayal by friends, and helplessness—all of it, plus the fiery ball still glowing in my belly, trying to burn its way outside.

Once let loose, the full rage takes control of me. From the kitchen floor, I grab the bottom of a stool and crash it against two others, splintering one of the legs.

I pull myself up to the countertop and bring my fist down on a glass fruit bowl, breaking it into pieces. Then I violently sweep everything else on the counter onto the floor and kick it out of my way.

I see the drawer with the knives in it and wonder what it would be like to end it this way. I can't stop thinking about hurting myself. I open the drawer and grab one of the big jagged-edged knives.

I hold it in front of my eyes, fascinated with the idea of dying. My hand is shaking uncontrollably.

I hold the knife to my throat and feel a tingle at being so close to cutting myself, a mixture of excitement and dread. *Maybe I'm going to do it. Maybe I'll have to do it.* It's like being on the edge of a cliff or standing on the balcony of a tall building and just for a moment thinking there's something inside you that's going to make you jump. I feel totally crazy, capable of anything.

My parents are talking to me through the kitchen door, trying to calm me down. They have no idea how bad this is, though. *They're not me.*

At the last moment, I pull the knife away from my body. I throw it with all my might at the wall near the kitchen table. I miss, and it sails over the table and breaks through the double kitchen window behind it.

I spin around to the refrigerator, remembering the bottle of vodka my parents keep in the freezer. I nearly tear the door off getting to it, then put the bottle to my mouth and take six or seven big gulps.

My legs finally give out, and I'm back on the floor, waiting for numbness to set in. Eventually, it gets dark.

Sometime later, I'm still lying there, now with a pillow under my head.

The lights are turned down and I've been sleeping. The rage is gone, replaced by warmth, as though I'm sitting near a fireplace. The burning in my stomach has stopped. My heartbeat is slow and regular. I listen to my own breathing in the silence of the house and feel like I'm alone in heaven after rising out of hell.

I had thought that this life couldn't get any worse, but I was wrong.

"Cory?" I hear a whisper.

Chapter 35

My mother is standing over me. She kneels and asks if there's anything she can do to help, and I just stare at her. I've come back from a nightmare world that neither of us has ever known, and there aren't words to make her understand where I've been.

The only thing I know for sure is that the raging person I was a few hours ago isn't me now. I'm back. *This is Cory, not that other crazy guy.*

I feel shame and remorse and don't know where to start. "Sorry. Sorry, Mom" is all I can think to say.

"I know," she whispers. "Me, too."

She reaches down to pull me up, but

the drugs and alcohol have left me without strength, and I can't help her.

She puts her arms around me and, as big as I am, somehow hoists me to my feet and holds me. My father is behind her now, and he takes my hand. This would make *some* family portrait, I guess. Not exactly Norman Rockwell.

We stand that way for a long time, breathing in the same exact rhythm, our bellies going in and out against one another's.

In time they get me up the stairs and put me in bed. I try to remember what happened, but I can't force myself to think about it anymore.

I have one last thought as I drift off to sleep.

Whatever it was that took over will be back. Soon. I just know it.

The next day, I go to the computer and write a letter to my mother and father and place it on the kitchen counter.

Dear Mom and Dad,

I feel so bad for what happened last night. Every time I think about it, my actions seem more and more ridiculous. I can't believe I cursed at both of you like that. I know it wasn't me, because I would never ever blow up at you when you were only trying to help.

Mom, the fact that I made you cry makes me want to shoot myself. Out of all the things in life, seeing you cry absolutely kills me. I feel like a beast. It's like I took the most loving angel and broke its heart over nothing. Mom, you are an angel to me. I'm the luckiest kid in the world to have you as my mom. I would take Tourette's one hundred times as bad and be condemned to a wheelchair for my whole life, unable to move my body, just so I could have you as my mother. I really mean it. I love you, Mom, and I'm very sorry for hurting you.

Dad, I also feel terrible for raging at you. I know all you want to do is help me and make me happy. And I love you more than you can imagine. And I know you don't deserve one bit of it. You're the best dad I could have ever asked for, and I'm incredibly lucky to have you as my dad.

Even though I've got a harder life than many other people, you guys totally turned the tables on what could have been a tough life and turned it into a blessed life, full of love, caring, and happiness. You're more than I could have ever asked for or imagined. I love you both so much and hope you'll accept my apologies. I love you, Mom and Dad.

Cory

Part Three

FALLING DOWN, PICKING MYSELF UP

The Promised Land

Chapter 36

"The next medicine will be the one that works."

"Your body will calm down as you get older."

"If you can just hold on until middle school, things will get better."

"If you can just hold on until high school, things will get better."

These are the promises that help keep me going. And in my mind, the summer before high school is going to be the time that the bell will ring and everything will change.

Except it doesn't happen.

That summer comes at me one day and one event at a time, and there is no triumphant arrival into a more normal world.

Around the beginning of August, when everyone is bored and looking for something to do, a neighborhood girl invites me to come hang out at her house. While I am there, her brother and his buddies take the bike I leave on her porch.

Another "friend" steals a paintball gun of mine, and someone takes my cell phone and rings up more than five hundred dollars in long-distance charges. And these are the kids I am closest to.

On most nights I go to the Burger King parking lot, where those of us with nothing better to do end up. Somebody gets booze, and we head for the local park, where we lie on the grass and drink. The police constantly harass us. It is the best I can do for a social life. Of course, I hide all this from my parents.

Chapter 37

I finally enter high school, and the biggest surprise is that nothing has really changed. It's turning out to be as much of a minefield as middle school. Instead of becoming nicer as they've grown up, some of the meanest kids have become smarter at using my weaknesses for fun and games. It's as important as ever for them to look cool, and they do it by putting down others who are different or have problems. I'm an easy target, and it makes me feel bad just about every single day of high school.

This Friday morning is freezing cold. Another reason—besides the medicine-and-booze cocktail that's still working in my system from last night—to stay in bed. If I let them, the Xanax and Risperdal would keep me asleep for half the day. And maybe that's not the worst thing, actually. Sleeping is the one time I don't have to think.

When I finally do get out of bed, I hop.

This morning I stomp down so hard on the old wooden planks of my floor that a booming sound shakes the whole house. After years of taking my punishing blows, many of the planks have split open. The ceiling of the room under mine has cracks in it from the vibrations. Floor tiles in my shower are shattered for the same reason. *Welcome to my space.*

Not all of the damage is from my feet. My bedroom door is split down the middle from another violent rage attack during the summer. My raging is also the reason for the holes in the walls around the house. I could keep a carpenter busy full-time.

In my bathroom the scale says 243 pounds, a new high. At five foot eight, I'm getting more and more obese from Risperdal, my late-night feeding frenzies, and an ever-increasing number of liquor binges. Alcohol is better for giving my body and mind some blessed peace than any medicine I've ever taken.

"Breakfast is ready," my mother calls at nine o'clock. It's another shortened high school day for me, since I'm not able to go to all eight periods.

Downstairs, I walk through the kitchen without stopping. "Got to have a cigarette first," I tell my mother, heading for the outdoor deck.

"Can't you wait? At least put something on!" she shouts after me. My mom hates that I smoke, but she also knows she has to pick her fights with me.

Outside, the temperature is cold enough for me to see my breath. I sit in a metal chair, puffing away, not caring that all I have on is a short-sleeve T-shirt. My craving for nicotine has become so strong that I can't get through an hour without a smoke. I'm also obsessing over my need for cigarettes, which makes my craving worse than that of most smokers, because it's not just about the nicotine.

My father has a business meeting in the area today, so he's able to drive me to school. On the way, I need music to calm me down, but a new compulsion makes me turn the volume to the highest level *before* turning on the radio. The sudden explosion of sound makes my father almost drive off the road.

"Jesus, Cory!"

"Sorry. Sorry."

The second time I hit the volume control turns out to be the last... for this trip, anyway.

There's a hole in the dashboard where the cigarette lighter used to be. My father is one step ahead of me here. The last time we drove together, I got the lighter red-hot and then just barely touched it to my nose until I almost burned myself. I had to get into the backseat to stop doing it.

"Hope you have a better day," he tells me as I get out of the car.

"I will. I feel pretty good. Thanks for the ride."

Before I get to the front door at school, I do my leg shuffle, followed by a brand-new tic that seems to have developed just for the occasion. Every few seconds, I punch the air three times in a row, then bring my fist to my chest for a beat, then punch again. I do this one or two more times before getting to the door. What a way to start.

The days go on pretty much like this, and little by little I'm getting through my classes. Each day has good and bad moments. My teachers mostly like me and call on me whenever they can, and my life has as much structure as I can expect.

And then, something amazing happens, and things actually start to get better. It's the last thing anyone expects, maybe the most unlikely event in the history of the world, at least from my point of view.

I join the high school football team.

Man in Motion

Chapter 38

It's a cold, windy October Saturday at our high school football stadium. Our opponents are physically larger and from a much tougher town, but against all odds we're winning by a point and the game is almost over.

Now they're on our two-yard line, close to a score.

There are only a few seconds left on the clock, and everyone in the stands is holding their breath. The next play will decide the game.

By some miracle, not only am I playing football but I'm the second-fastest member of our team. The coach is using me on both offense and defense almost every play of the game.

But as good as I am, my tics are still part of the deal, and in the few seconds before the ball is snapped, my body is one of the only things moving on the field.

My main position is called noseguard. That means I'm on the defensive line opposite the other team's center. My job is to burst off the line the second the ball is snapped and try to tackle whoever gets the ball before the play can get going.

On the field, I feel like one of the luckiest people in the world. Nature has given me the strength and speed to get into the offensive backfield before my opponents know what hit them. And the weight I've gained on Risperdal is a good thing for football. I'm faster than anyone can believe for a guy as heavy as I am, and I don't let anything or anyone get in my way. Talk about a means for unloading your anger.

Because I was hyperexcited about today's big game, my mother gave me an extra Risperdal to calm me down.

That makes six and a half pills, but they haven't taken away an ounce of my energy.

My mom, my dad, and Jessie are sitting in the stands at the fifty-yard line, cheering for me. I can always hear Jessie's voice because it's high-pitched and loud. I can't tell you what a huge day this is for our family, and for me, of course.

As the opposing quarterback calls his signals, I get into my three-point stance, my right hand balancing me on the ground.

I can feel this tremendous tension building in my legs. Suddenly, before the play starts, I make three rapid hops that take me into the neutral zone, considered a crime in high school football.

A horrified gasp rises from the crowd, but there are no penalty flags. Before the game, the referees were informed of my involuntary movements, and the league has made an exception for me.

The quarterback's count goes on longer than usual—he seems nervous, running through his audibles twice.

This gives my left arm time to spasm,

and it shoots out into the sacred no-man's-land that separates the two teams. This movement has been startling the center opposite me all day. No matter how many times I've done it, he can't get used to the idea. He's pissed off when no flags are thrown.

I recover quickly from my arm thrust and plant my legs solidly on the ground. My body is like a stick of dynamite with a lit fuse.

When I hear the quarterback call *hike,* I ignite and explode off the line into the center before the guy can even get upright. My sudden impact knocks him backward, and as he fights for balance, he grabs my leg with one hand. But I'm already halfway past him and tear loose from his grip.

The quarterback sees me coming and tries to dodge out of the way, but he's too late. I plant my helmet into his belly and lift him right off the ground. Both of us go crashing down, with everyone else piling on.

The refs' whistles blow just as a gun goes off, marking the end of the game.

The home-team crowd, my crowd, is hysterical with joy. They've just witnessed a huge upset, in more ways than one—this was a game of me against my life, and this time, I won.

I feel my teammates' hands pulling me out of the pile of bodies and pounding me on the back. The crowd is standing and cheering wildly.

At first I can't hear what they are saying. Then I realize they are chanting my name.

"Cory! Cory! Cory!"

I'm embarrassed. I'm not used to being a hero. There's no other place in my life that this happens. Except in the old days, in Little League.

I head to the sidelines, hopping a few more times before I get there, and my coaches are actually hugging me. When I get a chance, I search the stands for my family. Dad's arm is wrapped around my mom, and he's beaming with pride and happiness. This is almost too much for me to stand, all this happiness and joy.

A short while later, the stadium is emptying out. As I walk to our car with my family, I can see how proud they all are of me. Jessie has been a star athlete in basketball, soccer, and lacrosse, but no one expected me to be back in sports after baseball ended. And they know that a day like this is about a lot more than football.

Now it's just the four of us. My teammates are leaving with one another in groups of two and three, joking and bragging and reliving the best game of the year so far.

Now and then as they pass by, a few of them congratulate me, but they don't stay around or invite me to come along.

Inside our car, I sit in silence with a curious mixture of emotions: a sense of pride but also an empty, achy feeling in the pit of my stomach. It's hard for me to understand how I can go from being a hero to being alone again, in just a couple of minutes.

"You're one of the best players they've ever had here. You're amazing, Cory, and they all know it," my mother says with a hand on my cheek.

"Yeah, I guess."

"I'm so proud of you, Cory," Dad says. "That was one of the best days of *my* life."

I don't let them know what I'm really feeling right now. Why should I, when it will only make them as sad as I am?

"Yeah," I say. "Me, too."

Chapter 39

A week later, the football team is called together to meet a new coach. I'm not really sure what happened, whether it was school politics or not. The new guy is one of those really strict types with lots of rules such as *You smoke, you're off the team* and *Anyone late for practice doesn't play in the next game. No exceptions*.

These are two particularly tough rules for me, since I smoke like a chimney and, with my body problems, I'm always late getting anywhere.

A few days before the biggest game of our season, our practice is moved from the stadium to the weight room. Because

I've gotten to school late, I don't know about the change until I get to the field and find it empty.

This makes me incredibly anxious because I know the new coach will be really pissed. My legs start to buckle under me, and the hopping spasms come one after another.

They get so bad that I can't stand up for very long, and by the time I arrive at the weight room, I am literally crawling to the door. It's never been this bad, not even close. But at least I'm finally here.

I manage to stumble into the weight room ten or fifteen minutes late, and the coach turns his anger on me in front of the rest of the guys.

"I told you I won't stand for anyone coming to practice late. That goes for you, too."

"I couldn't help it."

"I don't want to hear your lame excuses. You'll have to learn the hard way."

The rest of the guys don't like what's happening. Anyone can see that I'm covered in sweat, but no one says anything in my defense. They're too afraid of the coach. The practice session goes on without any further lectures, and I lift weights with everyone else. I figure everything is going to be all right. I hope so.

The next weekend, I'm suited up to play and mentally ready. It's an important game, and I know I can help the team. Right after the pregame pep talk, the new coach takes me aside.

"You're benched," he barks like a military drill instructor. "You were late to practice. I warned you."

"That's not fair," I answer quietly, trying not to show him how angry I am. "It wasn't my fault."

"I said no exceptions, no excuses. Next time, maybe you'll listen."

I can see from his tough expression that there's no possibility of a compromise. I'm doing everything I can not to explode. He's taking away the one thing I have that makes me acceptable to the kids in high school. I can feel blood rushing around my body, heating up. I'm thinking what a *dick* he is. No feelings, no compassion, nothing in his eyes.

"How long do I have to stay out?" I ask.

"I'll let you know. Don't ask me about it again."

This is the worst thing he could have said to me. Not knowing keeps me in a state of high anxiety that I can't come down from.

He turns away, and it's over—for him, anyway. The explosion I've been holding back has now become unavoidable. I tear my helmet off and smash it on the ground. Then I look up into the stands, where my parents are trying to figure out what's going on.

"That's it!" the coach yells back as he walks away. "You're done for the whole game."

I sit on the bench in a daze, watching the other team's offense begin to dominate the game, running right up the center, where I would usually be to stop them. We're getting killed. Every time a play ends, I wait for Coach to signal me into the game, and each time he doesn't, I feel like I'm going crazy. I'm embarrassed and humiliated.

With the building tension and anger, my tics are also going wild, and when half-time comes and I still haven't played, I'm hopping so often that I can hardly keep my balance leaving the field. The coach doesn't seem to notice, or care.

The second half ends, and I haven't been in for a single play. I stumble away from the stadium and, as it turns out, away from football forever.

The new leg tic is the worst I've ever had, and this time it doesn't go away. By the following week, I can't make it on the practice field without falling. *What is happening to me now?*

After that, my school seems to realize the new coach has made a mistake in my case. One of our neighbors with a kid on the team comes over to our house to tell us that the high school is willing to hire a special coach to help me get back on the team.

It doesn't help what my legs are doing now. I'm stumbling and falling a lot. In the end, I would never play high school sports again.

Wheels

Chapter 40

Even though I know it's coming, I'm still surprised when it arrives at our front door. It symbolizes a turning point in my life and is one of my greatest defeats. I hate the thought of it—a *wheelchair!*

Maybe this day would have come anyway, or maybe it's a result of what happened with football. Since I stopped playing, the team has lost almost every game, and my stress seems to have permanently changed the frequency and intensity of my stumbling.

Even so, I think I still get around okay without help, so when the wheelchair is actually brought into the living room and becomes a reality, it makes me feel like someone has taken a giant scoop and hollowed out my insides. I force myself not to cry, but I'm barely holding the tears back.

"Just for a few days, until you don't need it anymore," my mother says to try to calm me down.

"I don't need it *now,* Mom."

"The school thinks you do. They're afraid you might hurt yourself—or somebody else—because you're falling so much."

"That's so unfair. Last week a kid pushed another kid down a flight of stairs, and nobody thought *that* was a big deal."

"They suspended him for doing it."

"Maybe they should make *him* go to school in a wheelchair. That would be fair, right?"

Of course, I end up using the wheelchair. I want to go to school like everyone else, and I won't let anything stop me, even if it means using wheels instead of legs.

Once again I had thought things

couldn't get any worse. Guess I was wrong about that.

But in a few days, instead of feeling sorry for myself, I get an idea.

Chapter 41

Right after lunch period, two swinging doors in a high school corridor burst open faster than anyone is ready for, and when I come racing through them in my wheelchair, a bunch of kids scatter to the sides.

I keep pushing the wheels forward, gathering speed, and a kid who never paid me any attention before is suddenly behind me, pushing, too, making me go even faster.

Just in front of the doors at the far end of the corridor, I step down on the brake lever. The wheels lock and I come to a skidding stop so hard that I leave rubber skid marks.

By now most of the kids are totally into my fun diversion, the way they are whenever rules are broken. I turn the chair to face them again. I'm the center of the show, the man of the moment, in a different way from the old days. The class clown on wheels.

"Go, Cory," one of the older kids starts chanting. A few more pick up the mantra and urge me on to greater deeds.

"Do it, Cory. Go ahead!" a girl who never seemed to notice me before shouts.

I'm feeling good. I've never gotten this much attention inside the school building. My wheelchair and I have become a source of amusement to the crowd. It's exactly what I wanted.

"C'mon, Cory. One more time."

"Yeah, let's see it."

"Go for it, Cory."

Their cheers require action—and I'm not about to let them down. I jerk back hard on both wheels at the same time. The front of the chair lifts right off the ground. Balancing my weight, I pivot almost completely around in place before touching down again, like a figure skater spinning at the end of his program. Just about everyone's cheering for me now. No one's ever seen a wheelie like that.

I don't realize it, but as I start to do another one, an adult is racing to the scene. He watches me start to spin. It's someone from the school staff whom I don't know very well. He comes at me so fast that he has to jump to the side to avoid getting cut down by my spinning legs, which stick out from the chair's foot-rests.

This is way too much for the assembled students, who roar with laughter as a symbol of school discipline is almost knocked down on his rear end. But in a second, the man's angry look sweeps the room and chills the mood.

"Get to your classes," he snaps through his mustache. "Show's over."

All the students head off, and suddenly it's just me and him, and he is breathing hard. "That," he says, "will never happen again."

The next week, my mom drops me off at school the old-fashioned way—on foot. I hop a few times on the way to third period, but I don't fall once. The wheelchair is sitting at home in the garage, just in case. But for now that particular symbol of defeat has been eliminated.

Even though the school was furious with me that day in the hallway, I think everyone understood that fooling around with the wheelchair was my way of downplaying my physical problems and was not about being reckless or disrespectful.

So why am I walking again and not cruising? I guess the school figured I was more of a danger to myself and the other kids in the wheelchair than I was out of it.

But letting me walk again came with a condition: I wasn't going to be allowed to walk alone. The school was searching for a personal aide to accompany me at all times, wherever I went. But the search was going to be difficult. The job didn't pay well and wasn't much fun.

The other catch was finding somebody who could deal with me.

period. But a portable ramp, the wheel-chair is sitting in a corner in the garage just in case. But for now that particular symbol and reality has been eliminated.

Even though the school was furious with me that day in the hallway, I think everyone understood that rolling around with the wheelchair was only a level down-playing my physical problems and was not about being careless or disrespect-ful.

So why can't I walk again and not crutches? I guess the school figured I was more of a danger to myself and the other kids in the wheelchair than I was out of it.

But letting me walk again came with a condition: I wasn't going to be allowed to walk alone. The school was searching for a personal aide to be constantly near at all times wherever I went. But the search was going to be difficult. The job didn't pay well and wasn't much fun.

Plus the catch was finding somebody who could deal with me.

Me and My Shadow

Chapter 42

It's strange going to all my classes with a shadow. My shadow's name is Terry. I thought having an aide was going to be humiliating. Now I think of Terry as my best friend in high school.

In addition to helping me get around without hurting anyone, Terry takes notes in my classes. This is especially useful, since I can't write at the speed my teachers talk and my handwriting is like hieroglyphics, anyway. I have poor fine motor skills, or something like that. *Is there anything about me that works right?*

Terry also explains my problems to teachers or substitutes whenever they forget and think that my tics are a reason for discipline. He's supposed to fix any social problems that may come up, too, like kids making fun of me, but that might be asking too much of anybody.

Terry is kind of a strange guy, and it makes me wonder why all the people who end up in my life are so unusual. He's around forty, with a potbelly and a head that's about two sizes too small for his body. He doesn't like to talk much either. There's something sad about Terry, too. I sometimes wonder how good his life can be when, at his age, he's a nursemaid to a high school kid. I think about what dreams he must have that aren't coming true. I wonder if he ever goes into a rage.

Even so, Terry and I hit it off. He's someone to talk to when I get lonely or upset. He's sympathetic to my problems and stands up for me when somebody gives me a hard time.

But all that starts to change a few weeks into the job. For whatever reason, there's a distance growing between us. He's begun to lose patience with my tics. A few days ago when I started to drum on my desk, he yelled at me to stop. He totally lost it. Terry should have known better. He *did* know better.

Today he's angry with me all the time, and I don't understand why. And then it gets really out of control. By fifth period, I'm desperate for a cigarette—partly because Terry is getting on my case. I get excused to *secretly* have one. Sometimes Terry comes with me, even though he doesn't smoke, but today he stays behind in the classroom.

I leave by a side door. I'm supposed to walk far away from the building so the other kids can't see me smoke. The school can't officially allow me to have a cigarette on the property, but they mostly look the other way. Twice, teachers who didn't know my situation reported me.

Today I'm a little lazy and figure it doesn't really matter where I smoke, so I go only as far as the gym and take out my pack of Merits. I light one up and suck in a hefty amount of carbon poisons.

Before I can exhale, I hear a voice yelling, "That's it, you're busted."

It's Terry! He jumps out of the shadows

of the gym, pointing a finger in my face like it's a gun. He has a triumphant grin, as if he's just uncovered a plot to overthrow the government. It looks like he's having a good time, so I assume he's joking around and take another puff. He keeps shouting that I've broken school rules, and I start laughing, but in a moment I can see I've seriously misjudged the situation.

"You think it's funny? You think this is a big joke? I'm taking you to the principal's office."

I can't believe that Terry means it, but when I don't move, he grabs the cigarette out of my hand and throws it away.

"What are you doing? You know I have to smoke. You're my aide."

"Just shut up," he snaps back, and actually shoves me toward the main office.

I don't understand why this is happening, why Terry of all people would be doing this to me. I feel betrayed and confused.

I thought Terry was my friend. I thought I could trust him.

After the principal listens to Terry's

story, he looks up my record, which already includes the other smoking incidents, and he tells me I'm suspended for four days, starting Monday.

"They all know about my smoking," I try to explain. "They understand that I *have* to smoke."

"Who lets you?" the principal wants to know.

I don't want to give him the names of my teachers. "Nobody actually said I could smoke. It's just that they let me."

The principal isn't buying my story. I guess he has to go by the rules. He's the one who makes up a lot of them.

Terry seems pleased, which I find unbelievable, and so hurtful. Maybe he just can't handle me anymore—my tics are too much for him—and my smoking is a way to be rid of me. Or maybe I'm just a symptom of the life he's sick of.

When we leave the office, I ask him, "What the heck, man? How could you do that to me?"

He just looks at me blankly, his eyes as cold as can be, and keeps walking.

This reaction pushes me too far. Suddenly I'm in a blind fury. I replay the scene over and over and can't stop: him *following* me, *jumping* out of the shadows and reporting me, his *creepy* grin. I want to smash walls. I want to go after him and beat him up, which is funny because I don't know the first thing about fighting and would probably lose. I don't think I've ever felt this much anger toward anyone, and there have been a lot of people who've done cruel things to me.

A plan for some kind of revenge races through my mind, and I do the first stupid thing I can think of. I run to the library computer and e-mail Terry. The angry words just spill out of me—the stronger, the better.

The phone call to my house comes late on Monday, the first day of my suspension for smoking. *The principal wants to see me right away.*

The suspension turns out to be nothing compared to what happens next.

Chapter 43

At school I find out that Terry has read my e-mail and has shown it to the principal. I don't even remember what I wrote, but the message says something about "getting even" and that he'd "better watch out."

"I didn't mean it," I say as soon as I've read it. "I was just mad. He was supposed to protect me at school, not make things worse."

The principal begins speaking differently than he ever has, choosing his words carefully.

"When threats to school personnel are received, they are evaluated by degree. The words you used fall into the third category, a physical threat, and are the most serious. In cases like this, we are required to turn the information over to the county prosecutor for evaluation and possible prosecution."

I sit there, in shock. This must be a bad dream. I've never even heard of a "county prosecutor," but it sounds like I'm being treated as a criminal.

The principal hands my mother a copy of my e-mail. After she reads it, she looks up at me, shaking her head slowly, disappointed but also worried. Now I know I've really crossed the line. I didn't mean to, but it happened.

"You know I'd never do anything like that. I was just letting off steam. I could never hurt anybody."

"I'm afraid that doesn't matter," the principal says. "The legal process has already started. There's nothing I can do to stop it now. The prosecutor has your e-mail."

Chapter 44

Two days later I'm at home, still on suspension for smoking, and going crazy waiting to see what the county prosecutor wants to do. My whole body is ticcing horribly. I don't know what's going to happen to me, and the anxiety is reaching new highs. To settle me down, we try a few different drugs. Neurontin is one of them, used for seizures, but it only makes my tics more crazy. Same thing with Effexor, an antidepressant and mood elevator. It produces wild ticcing, even for me.

"You couldn't have picked a worse time, Cory," my mother says. "There are kids committing violent acts in schools all over America, and you've just threatened your aide. It doesn't matter that you didn't mean it. Everyone's thinking about violence these days."

As usual, I've done the *worst possible thing at the worst possible time.*

"What's going to happen?" I mutter meekly. "Honestly, I would never hurt Terry. You know me, Mom."

She just shakes her head. No pep talk this time.

On the fourth day of my suspension for smoking, my father takes off work to go speak with the director of special education. My poor dad is on the case again. He fills us in when he gets home.

"Mr. Sweeney knows that you're not the kind of person to do something bad, Cory, but what you did was wrong and impulsive. Maybe your aide should have known you weren't really threatening him, but once he complained, you technically could have gotten into real trouble. You're lucky to have the right people on your side."

"And what's going to happen to Terry?"

I ask. "I don't want him to be my aide anymore."

"I don't think there's any chance of that happening. But he's still going to be around. The school always needs aides. You know what kind of job it is."

"But it's gonna be okay?" I wish out loud.

"Mr. Sweeney doesn't know yet. He's agreed to ask the county prosecutor to have the serious part of the charges dropped. That's all he could tell me for now."

The next few days are real bad, as my mind fills with dozens of horrible possibilities. Finally the phone rings, and it's Mr. Sweeney from school. I won't be charged with a violent threat. Nothing will go on my record, but I'm being given an additional ten-day suspension. And I have to apologize to Terry. To me, this is the ultimate injustice, but I have no choice.

The first day back at school, I find Terry eating alone in the cafeteria. It isn't easy to even look at him, but I manage to choke the words out.

"Sorry I wrote that e-mail, Terry. It just got me angry 'cause I thought we were friends. I didn't mean what I said. Sorry. I'm really sorry."

When I finish, Terry gets up and leaves without saying a word or even looking at me, as if I'm invisible. Now I feel like a wuss for having groveled, and I have the urge to tell him off again, but I hold myself back—a minor victory.

It's been a few months since the e-mail incident, and Terry and I pass in the halls once in a while. We try not to look at each other. I'm no longer required to have an aide. I'll be more disorganized than I was with Terry, but maybe I'll learn more by having to do things for myself.

By now I guess I should be putting the incident behind me and trying to see Terry's side of the story, but I can't. Even though I acted like an idiot, I still think the wrong person apologized.

The Slippery Slope, Once Again

Chapter 45

In sophomore year, it's becoming clear that obsessive-compulsive disorder, or OCD, is a bigger part of my condition than we thought. Right now I'm mostly experiencing the kind of OCD they call *intrusive thoughts*—ideas that can take over your thinking. The worst thought I have now is that there's no point to anything in life. This obsessive idea has suddenly paralyzed my desire to do anything, even to work on my Internet projects.

I feel like I'm drifting outside the world that everyone else is living in, that I'm in a whole different place. I don't understand how other people can feel so attached to their lives and appear to know something I don't. I wonder if they really do or if everybody's just faking it.

"I have a bad thought every day," I tell my parents, "that nothing will ever be any good for me. I look at other people and wonder how they can relax and do normal things, but my thoughts tell me that nothing matters. What am I supposed to do next, and why don't I know? What do I do every day? Am I in hell?"

Over the course of several months, I go from medicine to medicine again, and I also bounce back and forth between three doctors. I don't know if what I'm thinking is caused by the drugs or if another part of my brain is starting to play new games.

My parents learn about Dr. Bonds at a Tourette's syndrome seminar they attend in New York City, where the doctor works. Some people say he would be great for me, so I make the trip to the city twice a week for about five weeks.

Dr. Bonds focuses on my mood as a cause of my other conditions because, he says, a lot of my new thoughts are signs of depression and anxiety. Old and new medicine combinations follow quickly: propranolol and Ativan to relax me, Neurontin (in a different dose than before), Risperdal, and an occasional Xanax when I need it.

It actually seems so normal for me to be popping all these pills every day that I've stopped thinking about it.

The medicines keep changing, but not much about me does. Then, with the re-introduction of Effexor, another antidepressant, I'm suddenly unable to go to school at all. There's a huge increase in my verbal and physical ticcing. I've found another level of hell.

Now the nights are getting as bad as the days because my body isn't letting me rest. One time I'm squirming so much that I have to go to the local hospital for an injection to help me sleep. We're jumping back and forth between Dr. Pressler and Dr. Meyerson, the psychologist who got me out of the psychiatric ward, then back to Dr. Bonds and Dr. Pressler again. From Aricept to Remeron to baclofen. Nothing helps, and now my whole family is depressed. There's no way for me to believe that this isn't my fault, too. Somehow.

At the end of this period of drugs and doctors, I have nothing to show for all the new advice and chemicals that I've been loading into my body. My tics are all over the place, and my OCD is increasing daily. I'm up against a wall and at a new low point in my life.

And I'm running out of medicines to take.

The only thing that's working is alcohol.

Friends in Need

Chapter 46

On a freezing Saturday night, I hear someone knock at the basement door. Judging from the pounding, I realize it has to be my friend Mingo, all three hundred pounds of him. Our friendship started in high school when I was on the freshman football team. He was on the varsity and came with some other players to watch me.

Having been on the football team changed a lot of things for me socially. People now think that I'm somebody special. Maybe that's why I have a few regular friends, the *group,* to hang out with. Almost halfway through high school, I still don't go to classes as much as normal kids do, but nothing stops me from having a party with the group. A few of my friends have been calling since school ended on Friday, and some of the talk was about who's supposed to bring the liquor. Of course, I can't be sure anyone is going to show up. Most of the kids I hang out with usually take the best offer at any given moment, and they've ditched me at the last minute more times than I can remember. Sometimes I think that they're my friends mainly because they want what I have... a basement in which to party.

These days Mingo has become the leader of our group. Everyone's afraid of his size, plus he's able to buy liquor for us at a place in another town.

When I open the door, the sight that greets me is pretty ridiculous. Mingo is standing there with another friend of mine, Drew, who's at the opposite end of the size spectrum. Drew is a great guy, but at sixteen, he's very short and weighs fewer than ninety pounds. He could be Mingo's backpack. Of all my so-called friends, I feel the closest to Drew.

Mingo charges in first, carrying a case of beer with a bottle of Jack Daniel's on top of it. He's twenty but looks older, mainly because of his weight, which is increasing all the time now. I worry about his health.

At times Mingo has taken care of me like a brother, teaching me how to do things I should have already learned, like how to dress cool and change the air filter in my car. In return, I buy him things such as a paintball gun or food, and I give him money to purchase liquor. He doesn't get along very well with his family, so a lot of nights my parents let him sleep in my basement. Mingo wasn't exactly an honor student when he graduated from my high school, but he's very street-smart. He'd be the one to bet on in a *Road Warrior* world.

Drew asks if he can play a set on my drums while we're waiting for the others to arrive, and Mingo cracks beers for the three of us. The beers loosen us up, and before long Mingo is hugging me like in the old days. He has a really warm streak, but as close as we are at the moment,

Mingo has almost killed me in a few fights over the past year. We get tight for a while, then have a serious argument. That's our pattern, and I have the scars to prove it. Even though my continuing use of Risperdal has piled weight on me, Mingo still outdoes me by a good seventy pounds and has a temper you don't want to set off.

By now I can hear Drew playing some rhythms with feeling on the drums. He is the coolest of us by far, a hippie dude straight out of the sixties. Playing drums unites us. They're a refuge, a way to express our feelings and let out our anger at being different.

Suddenly Sara is standing there. She's come in alone, and I can't help but notice how different she looks from just a year ago. She used to be a thin, pretty blond girl with a sweet smile. Now it hurts me to see that she's become very overweight and reckless. The word is, she's taking whatever she can to get high, even cough syrup. Her values have also changed. At my last party, someone sneaked upstairs from the basement, and I noticed later that a bunch of my Xanax pills were missing from the kitchen cabinet. I can't prove it was she, but it's a solid guess. I should be angry, but I'm not really. I feel sorry for Sara. Drugs can control even a good person's life.

To be honest, my friends have many decent qualities. We have lots of laughs, and when we're just one-on-one, I can count on them. But there are times when they can lie and take things that don't belong to them. They mainly come from poor families or have problems getting along. Since they don't get what they need at home, they live by their wits and hang around people who need them, and I'm one of those people. Also, by now a lot of the nicer kids don't want to be around them, so they are able to attract only one another.

Even though I know all of this, I don't care. I'm with them because it's them or no social life at all. Isolation hurts, and it increases my Tourette's and my OCD, so my parents and I have allowed them to stay in my life, despite the fact that a few of them have ripped me off here and there. Most parents would simply forbid their kids to have such friends. It's been a tough call.

Chapter 47

Sara lights a cigarette, and I sit down to play my drums and sing to her. A little while later, Robert and Jamie join the party. It's not unusual for us to have four or five guys and only one or two girls at our gatherings.

Jamie is even moodier tonight than the time he stormed out of my house. He's constantly depressed about something that's always right under the surface. Robert is the kid who is most out for himself. He doesn't seem to have much of a conscience, particularly when it comes to sex. To find easy sex, he picks out girls who can't get dates because they're overweight or not too pretty.

Being beautiful, Sara was an exception at first, but when she started going out with Robert, he began to treat her like his other low-self-esteem girls. Now he uses her any time he wants, then gets rid of her. She's so insecure she keeps letting him do what he wants with her.

Sometimes they make out in front of the rest of us, and it kills me to watch this happening. It's like seeing someone spray poison on a beautiful flower. I've always had a close feeling for Sara, and at times I've wanted to be her boyfriend. So it hurts that she has chosen him over me.

I'm surprised to see Eddie come in, because he's never been in our group or to my house before. He's in some of my classes, and I like him, even though we don't really talk. He used to be a good student and a great athlete. But something has happened to Eddie, and I hear that he's become a heavy drinker.

Sara acts glad to see Robert, but he barely says hello to her, and she sinks back into the couch and curls up and looks small. Robert doesn't care. He's in a lousy mood and looks ill. His eyes are sunk deep into his face and he's getting so thin I wonder if he's sick, exposed to something because of all the girls he's screwed.

Mingo opens the Jack Daniel's and asks everyone for money to pay him back, even though it was mostly my money in the first place. Some of the others don't have any money, so I lend it to them. In a little while, everyone feels good. I drink about three big swallows of Jack, then two or three more when the bottle comes around again. I never remember that it takes a while to feel the liquor, so I always drink too much too fast.

This is the biggest party I've had by far. I don't even recognize the two people who come in last. There's a chubby black girl, Angel, who turns out to be one of Robert's new girlfriends. He's invited her without asking me and obviously without caring what it will do to Sara. Angel's friend is a lot prettier. I wonder how they got here. Neither one of them is old enough to drive, so someone must have dropped them off without checking out my party—something my parents would never do.

My basement couch runs wall-to-wall and is filled with people. Eddie takes a seat on the floor, sucking up the bourbon. Sara sits above him and between the couples who are kissing and touching each other all over. It must kill her to see Robert doing this so close to her. At first she acts like she doesn't notice, then she can't take it anymore and grabs the bottle from Eddie and slugs down a huge mouthful.

Even though I'm getting dizzy, I can see how miserable Sara is. When she finally gets up to leave, I put a hand on her shoulder and tell her how shitty Robert is acting and that she doesn't deserve it. I want to hold her and show her there's goodness in the world. She stops and turns to me with a warm, almost inviting look I've never expected to see. I suddenly want to kiss her, and it looks like she wants me to hook up with her. I lean in toward her mouth, but at the last second Angel, the chubby girl I didn't invite, busts in between us looking for the liquor, and the moment has passed. Sara dips away from me and finds the bottle, and the two of them go off laughing.

Party Animals

Chapter 48

An hour later, everyone is high. Jamie's mood has taken a turn for the worse, and he slips out without saying good-bye.

Drew is on the drums again while a few of us are outside under the deck in the cold, chilling out. Suddenly there's shouting inside, and I race back in. Apparently Mingo made a move on Angel's friend, who turned him down, and then he tried to hook up with Angel right in front of Robert. Robert is now threatening Mingo, who's cursing him back. So far they are both just yelling, but the whole thing is about to blow, so I step between them.

"Hey, man, that wasn't right!" I shout.

"You don't make out with someone else's girlfriend."

Mingo is stunned by my verbal attack, and for a second he just stands there, staring at me. I take his silence to mean that he's seen he was wrong and that the fight is going to end.

"It's just not cool," I press on.

I am so wrong about his mood. I watch as his face gets redder and redder, and in a few seconds I can almost see steam coming off his neck. I try to convince him again, thinking that his loyalty to me and Robert will eventually make him feel bad and quiet him down. Bad call. He's shaking with rage. All I've done is redirect his anger from Robert to me. If I was sober, I might have caught on earlier.

Even in a good mood, Mingo can be a nuclear bomb waiting to go off, and now I've become his detonator. He suddenly lets out a scream and charges me, slamming his elbow into my chest. The impact knocks me off my feet and into the cement wall. He yells that he's going to kill me and looks like he means it, but when the pain hits me, instead of getting scared, I stupidly get angry.

For a split second I move faster than he does and trick him into a headlock. I try to throw him to the floor, forgetting that he's an amazing athlete—and that I don't know how to fight. He easily jerks his head out of my grip and gets me in a bear hug. He squeezes my chest so hard that my breathing is completely cut off, and I can feel my ribs about to snap. Then, all at once, he loosens his grip, curses me, and shoves me full force into a wooden section of the wall that breaks when I hit it.

He stands over me after I fall, breathing hard, waiting to smash me again. His eyes are wild and his forehead is covered with sweat. The person I'm looking at seems insane.

No one else has moved since the fight started. They're all as afraid as I am. Robert is probably glad he's not in my place, although he should have been. In the silence I realize that the drumming has stopped, and suddenly Drew walks in and stands between Mingo and me. He has his hand on Mingo's huge arm, trying to hold him back. Calmly he says, "Chill, bros. Friends shouldn't fight."

Chapter 49

Even in the middle of getting beaten up, I can see that this is a really funny scene: Mingo, as big as an elephant, being held back by Drew, who barely comes up to his waist. The ridiculous confrontation is too much for the crowd, and little by little people begin to chuckle. I let out a gasp of relief. Only Mingo still has his fight face on, but in the end he turns away with a grunt.

"You okay, bro?" Drew asks, helping me to my feet.

"Yo, man."

I limp outside to get some air. My ribs feel cracked and there's blood on my leg, but at least I'm beginning to sober up.

The relief doesn't last for long. Once out the door, I step over a *body* lying on the frozen ground. It turns out to be Eddie, apparently passed out in his own puke. Someone says they haven't seen him move in a long time, and I quickly forget about my ribs.

I bend down to check Eddie's breathing. His face is like ice. He tries to speak, and I can't understand him, but in any case I know he's alive.

The person suddenly standing next to me is my father. He has heard the noise from the fight and has come downstairs in his bathrobe. He is beyond anger and is headed for disgust, but he forces himself to talk softly and deal with the crisis at hand.

"We have to find a way to get him home," he says calmly.

Just then, a car pulls up to the house, and by luck one of the girls in the backseat knows Eddie. My father makes sure the guy who's driving isn't stoned and convinces him to take Eddie home. Together, we lift Eddie to his feet and drag him to the car.

Between this latest drama and the fight, everybody is down and the party is obviously about to end. I'm feeling really depressed, and I'm hurting inside as much as I'm hurting outside.

After everyone leaves, my father and I stand in the basement room, checking out the wreckage of the evening—the bottles, the spilled ashtrays, the broken wall, all of it. He stares into my bloodshot eyes with a look I've seen many times before and just shakes his head. He's too depressed to speak.

"Sorry, Dad" is all I can manage to say.

He is someplace else in his mind when he answers, "It's okay, I know you didn't want this either. Go to bed. We'll clean up in the morning."

I know what he's really thinking: *Never again. This is the last time. The last party.*

Of course, it won't be. Even at this moment, we both know that in my life it's either times like this or nothing at all. And "nothing at all" is worse.

Two hours later, I'm asleep when the

phone rings, and my mother says it's for me. It's a social worker at the emergency ward of the local hospital. Sara has been admitted there with an overdose of something and is having her stomach pumped. She's given them my number, not her own family's.

I tell my parents what's happened and that I have to help her, and then I'm off to spend a few hours at the hospital, at the bedside of my good friend Sara.

Another Saturday night with friends.

Flying

Chapter 50

The contrasts are getting really crazy; they'd be too extreme for anybody to handle, let alone a teenager. Last night I passed out from drinking in my basement. Tonight I'm doing seventy miles per hour on my street-legal dirt bike and I'm lost somewhere on the New Jersey Turnpike.

It's ten o'clock on an August night. I'm in a pouring rain and can barely see where I'm going.

School is out for the summer, and all I want to do is ride. Even though I'm pretty out of it from all the medicine I'm on, the thrill of riding brings me back to life with a rush of adrenaline. This is all about life . . . or maybe the opposite. Dirt bikes and motorcycles have been an obsession of mine ever since I can remember. When I ride, I move in a way I can't anywhere else. It feeds my need for danger. I can see myself in the future, riding all the time, never having to worry about school or jobs or friends, never having to explain myself to anyone.

A sudden compulsion to test *just how close I can get to crashing* makes me jerk the handlebars to the right, almost to the point where I lose control. I should be scared out of my mind, but the thrill makes me do it again, this time a little farther to the right, just to see how much I can get away with.

The bike shudders and starts to slip out from under me. The wheel is angled near the point of no return, but I just manage to get control back.

Tonight I started out on a peaceful ride on dry local streets, but I've gotten lost and now I'm trapped in a nightmare on the turnpike.

I have the option of pulling off the road, but that will leave me in the middle of nowhere and I'll never get home. Also, it would be dangerous. I'm in the fast lane, and the traffic on my right is a high-speed stream of cars and trucks. I drop the speed down to around forty in an attempt to cut over, but the drivers behind me lean on their horns, so I give the bike more throttle again.

The stinging rain starts to get heavier, and I can't see anything. This is crazy dangerous.

My helmet doesn't have a visor and I'm wearing only a light sweater because I didn't plan to be here, or in the rain. There's no chance of being rescued by my parents because I don't have a cell phone. My hands are so cold I can hardly feel them, and I wonder whether my fingers will work at all the next time I use the hand brake.

At this point I've been lost on different highways for two hours, and there's almost no gas left in my tank. Every new road has taken me farther away from home until I've ended up here, *wherever I am.* I'm sure that somehow I'll get out of this. I always do. But I'm also scared about the odds of it ending in a horrible accident. Every biker has at least one, they tell me. And often *only one.*

When the turn-the-wheel compulsion comes again, I do a substitution tic, an idea given to me by one of the therapists I've had.

Instead of twisting the handlebars, I arch my back until I'm lifted completely out of the seat. This makes me steer with my fingertips, but at least I'm not skidding.

People passing me must think I'm the dumbest driver ever, doing stunts in these conditions, risking my life for no reason. I wish it was only a stunt.

In the distance I see a toll plaza coming up fast, and I squeeze the hand brake tightly instead of using my foot brake. I'm not thinking clearly. How could I be? My bike pulls sharply to one side, and for a few frightening seconds I'm totally out of control. Though my dirt bike has been adapted for the street, it's made for off-road riding and is too light for the highway and for this speed. But the thrill of velocity always wins out over sanity.

At the last moment, the thick tire tread catches hold of the pavement and the bike is stable again.

By now I've had enough and need help bad. I'm in way over my head. My body is numb from the cold, and I have no hope of finding my way home by myself.

When I pull up to the tollbooth, I ask the man inside for help, but he doesn't seem to hear me and only asks for money. I haven't got any because I've spent it all on the other tolls.

While he's writing down my name and address, a miracle happens. A woman in the lane next to me rolls down her window and asks if I need help. It must have been obvious to her that I was in bad shape.

Someone is watching over me on this night, because it turns out that the woman lives in my hometown. This is the best news I've heard in my entire life. She tells me to follow her home.

Forty minutes later when I walk into my house, my parents are crazy with worry. I look like I've been swimming and have turned blue from the cold. When I tell my story, they shake their heads in disbelief. This is just another in a series of disasters I've been involved in over the years. Some of them have given my mom migraines. I hope this one won't.

Before I take a hot shower, I need a drink, a real one. After what I've been through, my father hasn't got the heart to say no and pours one for each of us.

In a little while the steam from the hot shower transports me to another place. My mind has seized on a Beach Boys song about traveling around the world, and it plays over and over again. *Bermuda, Bahama, come on, pretty mama.*

I close my eyes and see myself back on the highway.

The road is smooth and dry and endless. The sun is out, and I'm going faster than I ever have. There is no sense of danger, just pure joy.

My bike and I are flying.

Flying in the wind.

End of the Line

Chapter 51

It's near the middle of my junior year, and everything is pretty bad again. I'm acting reckless and don't care what I say to people, which is only pushing them farther away. There are too many nights spent drinking on the basement couch until I pass out. My parents are trying to stop me, but they can't, because I lie and won't listen to them. And because they don't know any other way for me to get some peace either.

I'm hopelessly behind in my schoolwork. I'm fat and a chain-smoker. I'm depressed over not being able to change my life.

My worsening condition is having a big

effect on Jessie, too. She's always said she wants to teach special-needs kids, and I think that growing up with me is probably one of the main reasons. Now she's decided to teach people with Down syndrome. I know she's serious because last summer she coached a Special Olympics team with severely handicapped kids and grown-ups. Some of them were in wheelchairs and some had been born without parts of their bodies. She loved helping them and they loved her and chanted *Jessie, Jessie,* every morning when they saw her arriving. She has a real gift as a teacher and coach. This seems to be the only good thing that's come out of what's been happening to me.

In the past four months I've had two new doctors, which brings the total to more than a dozen. The latest one believes that OCD is the main cause of my body movements. He says that most people with Tourette's also have some OCD, but like everything else about me, my OCD isn't the typical kind.

I don't have to wash my hands over

and over, or go in and out of doorways dozens of times. And I'm not a checker who has to keep going back to make sure they've done things such as turn off the stove or lock the doors.

But all OCD people get *stuck* on their compulsion. The new doctor's theory is that Tourette's starts my body doing something, and then instead of being able to let the tic shut off, I get caught on the movement because of the OCD. My OCD gets stuck on my Tourette's.

Looking back now, I wonder if a lot of the things I did were more symptoms of OCD than Tourette's—like my need in elementary school to form my letters perfectly and put them in exactly the right place on the lines.

My doctor believes that my high level of anxiety is also intensifying everything else. Still, with all his good thinking, so far his medicines aren't working any better than anyone else's.

One smart thing he does is to help me get off Risperdal for good. I'd been living in a thick fog and had been unaware of it. It was as if a sudden wind blew it all away. I'd had no idea how drugged out I was from the Risperdal. Now at least I feel connected to the world. Unfortunately, I'm also more in touch with the reality of what my life has become.

In an attempt to stabilize my mood, I start taking Zyprexa, another antipsychotic used to treat bipolar disorder and mania. At first my body calms down a lot, but the drug makes me very angry. Paxil is back again, too, but it stops working after two weeks and makes me even angrier. My whole life is like a movie about kids on drugs, but my drugs are supposed to be good for me.

My doctor's thinking prompts a flow of new drugs into my mouth. The bottles litter our house, with most of the pills still untaken: Geodon, Lamictal, Seroquel, Topamax. I'm so desperate I even go back to tetrabenazine, this time in a much smaller dose, until it again makes life too miserable for most people to even imagine.

Nothing works.

Nothing works.

Nothing ever works.

This isn't me just repeating and getting stuck on the same words. This is reality.

Finally, based on the radical theory that we should try to do the opposite of everything we'd done before, the doctor wants to prescribe pergolide, a drug that would increase the chemical in my brain that we've always thought was one of the problems. This seems to be a desperate move a doctor makes only when he thinks you're at the end of the road. *Is that where I am?*

Maybe pergolide is the radical solution we've been looking for, but by now I've had it. I decide not to find out. I'm finished, wiped out, sick of being a walking medicine cabinet, tired of symptoms and side effects. I like being clear and awake, and I never want to be in the fog again. This is where I draw the line, and my family finally agrees with me.

It's over. No more drugs.

Except, of course, the only one that's ever worked: *alcohol.*

Rock Bottom

Chapter 52

I take another mouthful of vodka and feel a warm wave spreading through my body. The serenity that liquor brings is better than any medicine I've ever taken and is the only way I get relief from my restless body. I'm not worried about the consequences of liquor anymore. I know they can't be any worse than the consequences I experience every day without it.

Lying on the basement couch, I think about where I've ended up. My junior year of high school continues to be more of a disaster than the end of my sophomore year. I'm not going to school much because I'm unable to sit still or concentrate on what my teachers are saying. My obsessive need for nicotine makes it worse. Noises are constantly coming out of my mouth that no one can deal with. My friends call only when they want something, and my compulsions are making me hurt myself again. I have scars and bruises everywhere.

Tonight I need to feel better any way I can, and I'm finally drifting off into a deep, drunken sleep.

Somewhere around three or four in the morning, I'm aware of having a hard time breathing. I start coughing but not enough to wake up completely. When the coughing becomes almost continuous, I can feel my lungs burning, which eventually forces me out of my stupor.

My eyes open to a room thick with a new and unusual haze. When I look for the source, I see smoke coming from the couch cushion beneath me. Maybe the entire couch. There's a glowing red circle two feet in diameter that slowly spreads as I watch. The edge of the fire is only an inch from my arm. In the middle of the circle are the charred remains of a cigarette filter that had dropped away from my mouth when I fell asleep.

I'm setting the whole house on fire!

Chapter 53

I leap off the burning couch, afraid that at any second the whole thing will burst into flames and set fire to the walls of our house. My mind fills with horrifying images. The fire will become an inferno that will break through the ceiling and blaze up the first-floor stairs. My sister will be asleep in her room when the smoke and flames pour in too fast, and she will be unable to get up and run. The fire will then rip across the hall to my parents' room.

The instinct to scream catches in my throat. I don't want my family to find out what I've done. There has to be a way to stop this disaster myself.

I don't know what to do, though. I should still be drunk, but I'm stone-cold sober and totally aware of what's happening.

In a moment the first wave of terror subsides, and I run across the room to where the smoke is thinner. I take a deep breath and look back at the couch. The fire hasn't spread yet, but any breeze will make it burst into a blaze I'd never be able to put out. *Seconds, only seconds.*

I race back and rip the cushions from the couch. The fire has burrowed deep inside, to the couch's inner padding. There's no chance of putting it out by beating the cushions.

I'm coughing so hard that I can barely breathe. I'm also scared out of my mind.

I look around the room for another answer and spot the bottle of vodka that I'd half emptied before falling asleep. I grab it and pour what's left onto the cushions. The fire hisses loudly but doesn't go out. Then I realize how crazy that was. *Alcohol on a fire?* The vodka could have ignited. I was stupid and lucky.

But the liquor *is* making things worse.

It's creating a terrifying amount of dense black smoke. My eyes are burning and watering so much I can hardly see. I'm coughing and gagging.

Get the fire out of the house.

Holding the burning cushions in front of me, I make a run for the back door. The thickest part of the smoke streams back directly into my face. I'm forced to inhale it before it has time to mix with the air outside. I'm suffocating now, and I can't see where I'm going. The room is dense with smoke and the windows are all shut.

I feel my way to the far wall and fumble for the exit. My hand finds the dead bolt, but the old door is warped. The lock won't turn unless the door is forced back into its frame.

Finally the door bursts open, and I charge outside and hurl the smoking cushions as far as I can into the backyard.

For the first time since I woke up, clean, fresh air pours into my lungs, but somehow that makes me cough even more.

When I can breathe again, I go back

into the room to check for more fire. The smoke makes the search impossible, so I open the windows on two sides of the room. Cold air rushes in one side and sucks smoke out the other. At first I don't know why the smoke detectors aren't going off, but then I remember there aren't any in the basement.

In a few minutes the room is nearly clear of smoke, and my knees feel too wobbly to hold me up. I make it back to the couch frame and collapse. My clothes, my skin, and the whole room reek of smoke. The basement has become freezing cold, but the worst is over. I hope, anyway.

There's still no sound from upstairs. No one has awakened. They don't have a clue how close they came to disaster, how close I came to killing everybody.

Alone in the eerily silent room, I close my eyes, not to sleep but to play back the movie that is my life, to see what is still worth saving inside of me. Amazingly somewhere I can sense hopefulness. It's like the start of a gentle rain in a desert that's been dry for years—*since I was almost five, for God's sake!*

There's anger, too, but not the kind that leads to my rage attacks. *This is an anger that can be used and channeled.*

The idea of fighting back comes with such urgency that I want to write it all down—so I can think about it when I wake up again.

I find a pencil and paper in the workroom and don't finish until my muscles are cramped from sitting in the same position. As it starts to get light outside, I finally fall asleep on the remnants of the same couch that almost took away my family's world and maybe my life.

My mother finds me in the morning, still asleep in the frozen room. The windows are wide open, the stinging smell of the burning couch still thick in the air. I'm on my back, stretched out full length. My arms are folded over my chest. Under them is a smudged yellow legal pad on which I have scrawled this letter to myself:

> I was born with the worst disease.
> My body wants me to suffer.
> My whole life, I've been gasping for air.

The ground hasn't ever been there.

I've been trying to fly when I can't even breathe.

There's been nothing to build on, not even a dream.

You probably can't comprehend it. And I don't blame you.

You're only human and have only smelled the slightest micro-atom of what I breathe. My life has been the most disgusting and vile thing you could imagine. My body wants to hurt me. I can't stop breaking myself down, physically and mentally.

I have severely damaged my teeth. Ticced so hard I've broken my ribs. My wrists scream with pain. My neck burns and aches.

I'm so tired, yet I still have to fight. I could explode. I want to go to war and kill bad shit.

Yet I am reminded that my life has been only that of prison and torturous pain.

My own body has betrayed me. I can't feel safe with myself.

Right now I want to smash my head through the computer screen and explode myself with the sharp huge bang of a shrapnel bomb. Liquefy me and burn me to ash. Then dump water on my ashes and get RID of them.

My anxiety is so high I can't even make sense of anything.

I've lost the world. I've lost the world.

I'm in myself and can't get out.

The world's joy makes me feel like an outcast.

I'm worn ragged, dirty, no good, hopeless, disgusting, insane.

But I am alive. I am alive.

I still have human feelings and needs.

I have dreams.

Don't desert me any longer, common goodness. How can you? You've already committed the biggest sin imaginable. Taking a good-hearted, peaceful, intelligent person and making him come within a millimeter of taking his own life.

Am I insane? It would seem so. I can't stop hurting myself.

My parents don't know what I've gone through. If they did, they'd be saying every word to me as if it were their last.

I deserve the world.

And I am stronger than the worst things that happen to me.

I am not suicidal.
I will take control of my OCD.
I will fight and KILL my Tourette's.
Rip them apart or be doomed.
I will own my own mind.
I will never give up.
Fuck you, OCD.
The war has NOW BEGUN.
And you're already bleeding.
I will survive.
I will love life, if life will love me.

Part Four

THE INTERVENTION

Chapter 54

Day 1

The temperature is fifteen below zero. Trust me on that—it could be lower by now. There's nothing between me and the snow except my sleeping bag and a four-foot-square tarp mounted on sticks over my head.

I'm a mile up in the mountains of Wyoming, a few hundred miles northeast of the 2002 Olympic Winter Games, which have just started in Salt Lake City.

It's my first morning at Roundtop Wilderness Camp for troubled teens.

The noise of an unseen, unidentified animal nearby in the woods wakes me from an uncomfortable sleep. When I try to open my eyes, I find they're welded shut by a crust of ice. I pry the frozen stuff away, one small particle at a time. A few pieces come off with my eyelashes embedded in them.

I'm not here because of my doctors. None of them has ever advised that I do something this unusual, or this extreme.

After discovering the dangerous fire in the basement, my parents knew they had to intervene. They eventually came up with the idea of wilderness camp after hearing about a good experience some friends of theirs had had with their son. Shocked by my own actions that night, and realizing what could happen if I went on that way, I was ready to try anything.

Even this.

They call places like these *camps,* as though they're an outdoor adventure, like Outward Bound. Before I arrived, I actually thought this would be fun, but last night at my first campfire meeting, I found out the truth. This will *not* be fun. Maybe to *read* about but not to live through.

"Wilderness is for guys like you who

have a lot of trouble making it on the outside," the head counselor announced at the meeting.

He was around thirty, the oldest of the staff of four with our group. The others looked young enough to be in college, although I doubted they were.

"Most of you have been in trouble with the police, your families, or your schools. You've done violent things, used or sold drugs, stolen stuff or set fires.

"We're here to help you fix your lives, but in the end it's going to be you who have to do it."

I looked around at the six other kids at the camp, most of whom were my age or younger. A few of them arrived here *escorted,* which is a nice way of saying that they were brought by law-enforcement officers because they wouldn't come any other way. One of them arrived in handcuffs.

I'm different from the others, except for my addiction to alcohol and cigarettes. I'm not a bad kid. The closest I came to being in trouble was when I wrote that e-mail to Terry. And maybe almost burning down our house.

"The rules are simple," the counselor went on. "You'll be on this mountain for as long as it takes to work out your problems. No more, and no less. The time you're here depends on your progress and your ability to work as part of a group. Some of you will be here for one cycle, others longer. That's the deal, guys."

I was stuck on one part of his speech: *for as long as it takes to work out your problems.* The threat that there was no telling how long I would have to be here was very frightening. Ricky, the kid sitting on the left, told me that he'd been on the mountain for three months and was doing this cycle over again.

Does that mean I could be here for months? Or a year? What's to stop me from being here forever? I had to fight off a sudden wave of panic. And tics, of course.

"The conditions here are very basic," the counselor continued. "We've brought enough food with us to get by, and we'll use what we find in this terrain for shelter to survive the cold. We'll teach you how to do this. This is a year-round program, but winter is the hardest. Your bad luck. If we work as a group, we make it. If we don't, we all suffer. Everybody got that?"

No one responded. This wasn't like a classroom back in school. These guys were a tough, hardened bunch. Maybe encounters with the police made them that way.

The silence made me really nervous and uncomfortable. I felt as if I had to say something to break the tension. But it was obvious that this would be a mistake.

"Don't even think of trying to get away from here," the head guy went on. "The closest human beings are twenty miles away on a military post. They know about this program and are on the alert for anyone who shows up in their area. That doesn't really matter because even if you got away, you'd probably never make it there in this weather. But even if you did, you wouldn't like what happened to you next."

This last speech erased any doubt that any of us were going to escape from this place on our own.

Another, longer silence fell over the group. Reality was setting in for everybody. *Wilderness camp.* We got it now.

"Are there any questions so far?" the counselor asked when he was done spelling out the rules.

After a long wait with no one saying anything, my urge to do something inappropriate rose to the point where it was unstoppable, and at once I found myself shouting, "Run! Run!"

My unbelievably disrespectful and rebellious command shattered the stillness of the deadly serious moment. I couldn't believe I'd said it any more than the rest of the group could. At first, everyone stared at me, openmouthed. I didn't know how to explain what made me do it. I wondered if the word *compulsion* meant anything to them.

"I'm sorry . . . I didn't mean . . ." was all I

could get out before the two junior counselors were on either side of me.

"Take off your boots, wise guy," the bigger of the two said to me. "You're not going anywhere."

Chapter 55

Day 3

My sleeping bag is covered by a good half foot of snow, which has been falling steadily throughout the night. It's wet on the inside from ice that I must have brought in on my coat before passing out from exhaustion.

In my hurry to get out of the cold, I also left the bottom of the bag open to the wind, and now I can't feel my right foot. I wonder if it's been asleep too long to ever come back to normal.

If I had my boots on, I'd stand and jump up and down to try to get some feeling back in my foot, but they take away our boots at night in case anyone is still thinking about escaping—like they took mine that first night. I'm cold to the bone and hungry. If I'd known what it was going to be like here, I would have probably needed one of those escorts to get me to the camp.

What they said the first night has turned out to be absolutely true. The idea of this place is very simple: force troubled kids to cooperate in order to survive, and get us through the withdrawal period of our addictions by having us focus instead on more immediate issues—like eating, going to the bathroom in the woods, and not freezing to death.

I'm not the first person who's come here with an alcohol addiction, but I'm the first with that plus Tourette's and OCD.

Before I came up on the mountain, the people who run the place said they didn't know if I could make it, but they were willing to give it a try. My main worry is that sometimes my tics are so bad I can hurt myself and then I can't move without excruciating pain. If that happens, I won't be able to keep up and they'll send me home. The more I'm up here, the more tempted I am to fake my tics for just that reason, but I've promised myself I won't do that.

If I go back home the way that I came, there's nothing in my old life to help me.

So every time one of my tics makes me think of giving up, I tell myself that I'm not going to let it beat me. I can't. This is life-and-death for me, and not just because of the temperature and the amazing amount of snow.

Chapter 56

Day 5

A terrible thought has begun to take over my mind. It's been in the back of my head since the second day, but now it's risen to the surface and I can't think of anything else. *My father has been killed in a plane crash on his way home from the wilderness camp. Or he and my mother both died after he got home.*

There is no other explanation for why my parents haven't contacted me. In my whole life, I've never been away from them for this long. They've never even had a vacation away from me. The idea that they wouldn't even try to see how I'm doing in this dangerous place is impossible—*unless something bad has happened to them.*

The counselors haven't brought it up either, and I think it's because they must know something and are hiding it. I'm so preoccupied with this fear that it's begun to slow me down from doing the normal chores required as part of group survival.

Finally the thought makes me so frantic that in the middle of a task I break the rule about leaving my area and force a conversation with Kevin, the head counselor.

"I'm scared that something has happened to my parents," I say without wasting time. "I'm not kidding, I'm serious."

"It's possible," he answers casually. "I don't know."

His calmness shocks me. "I have to find out. I need to know. I have a bad feeling."

He shakes his head. "You're here and you have to make it work on your own, no matter what. I think I explained all that the first night."

I can't believe he's not trying to talk me

out of my fear, to reason with me like all my other doctors have. He's not nasty or mean, just firm and very clear.

On one level I understand why he is acting this way, and that it doesn't mean he knows something. But on the way back to my work area, I'm still terrified about my parents, and now there's nothing I can do about it. Obviously, he's right. I am on my own in every way up here, and the fact that I don't know for how long makes things a hundred times worse for someone like me. It's a perfect formula for the panic that bubbles near the surface all the time.

I'm cold, exhausted, and always hungry, and I miss home so much I sometimes want to cry, but I won't let myself. Kevin has forced me to recognize I have only two choices: throw myself on the ground and give up and let them send me home, or fight off the bad thoughts as best I can and do what I have to do to survive.

Trying to analyze my situation a little, I realize that I haven't needed a drink or a cigarette almost the whole time I've been here. As hard as this experience has been, maybe I'm really starting to do something for myself. With everything I've always needed suddenly taken away from me, hey, I'm still alive.

And that's when, for the first time, I start thinking about something really impossible.

As bad as it is, this is good.

Chapter 57

Day 7

As dawn breaks, the others around me are already out of their sleeping bags.

We've all spent the night close enough to be in touch in case of a storm but far enough apart so there's no verbal contact. The guys are all busy trying to light a fire but not with matches. For whatever reason, we have to do it the way the Indians did, rubbing a stick between our hands into a groove in a piece of wood until it smolders into an ember, then quickly putting some dried grass on it and blowing to get a flame.

We need the fire for more than warmth. It melts our drinking water, which freezes every night, and is also used for all our cooking. If we can't make a fire, we can't eat the cornmeal, soy, and millet they've given us in small bags.

Today it takes me so long to get my boots on that there isn't time to try to make my own fire. When I get enough ice off my boots to get into them, I realize that one of my gloves is missing, and I spend another precious few minutes looking for it. Finally, one of the counselors gives me another glove but says it will be the last. This is the third time I've lost a glove—in two days.

I walk out into the woods to go to the bathroom, then come back and start to clean up my area.

By the time I get to the common kettle, the rest of the guys are already finished eating and about to put out the fire. Nobody makes fun of me, but nobody offers to help either. That's okay.

I get some water, but there's no breakfast for me this morning because I haven't contributed to the effort. Back at my sleeping bag, I stuff some raw cornmeal into my mouth, then spit it out when it makes me gag.

The lead counselor gathers us together and checks each person's gear. By now everyone else is carrying their possessions in a backpack they've made themselves, shaping it with branches and holding it together with strips of rawhide. The backpack is crucial to survival because there's no other way to carry the supplies that keep us going.

It takes most people a day or two to make a backpack. I've been working on mine since I got here, and it's still not holding together enough to carry much. Until I make it better, I'm hand-carrying some of my stuff, which partly explains why I keep losing certain items over and over, like my gloves.

As the sun comes up from behind a nearby mountain, everyone assembles with their gear. One of the counselors tells us about the day's activity plan.

"We're going on a little hike today,

nothing too hard," he announces. "Just a few miles, straight up the mountain."

He conveniently forgets to add, *in knee-deep snow.*

Chapter 58

Day 12

Since that first time we climbed up the mountain, we've made a big trip every single day. Now we're going to stay in base camp for a while, so we're digging ditches that will serve as latrines and will ensure that we don't contaminate the area around us.

The only tools we have are the jagged stones we've been able to pry out of the frozen ground. Using them to dig is backbreaking work, and it takes several hours to show very little in the way of results.

We are also completing a clearing in the woods for a future campsite for another group. We've found a patch of land rising above the snow that doesn't have much growing on it, and we have to figure out how to cut down what's left.

One of the tics I've feared the most has suddenly returned—the need to twist my ribs back until something hurts inside of me. I've been doing it all day and have either torn something in my chest again or pulled a muscle.

I'm having trouble breathing, but I don't want to use that as an excuse to stop working. I'm part of the group now, and they've accepted me, so I want to do my share.

I've also had to make my rope belt tighter again; my pants have dropped to my ankles a few times because I've lost so much weight. I still miss at least one meal a day because I'm usually too frozen or tired to prepare it, and I'm burning calories from working and trying to stay warm in the freezing climate. I'm even burning calories because of my tics.

Despite the extreme cold, the bottoms of my layered shirts get soaking wet from sweat. It's no wonder I can feel myself getting thinner. I imagine what I would look like in a mirror. But of course there are no mirrors.

For some reason the skin on the back of my hands is turning black. I don't know if I'm just dirty or if that is an early sign of frostbite. I've lost so many gloves that they've stopped giving them to me sometimes. They think that this will make me learn to keep track of them better, but I'm just too disorganized. Or maybe too forgetful. It usually takes a lot of mistakes, and suffering a lot of consequences, before I learn any lesson.

Chapter 59

Day 16

We're halfway up the mountain. Today, we've been walking for six hours with only short rests for water and a break for lunch that took longer than planned. I finally get to eat some cooked soy and cornmeal, which tastes like the best steak I've ever had. I still haven't finished making my backpack strong enough, and carrying some of my supplies in my arms has been almost impossible, especially in the rougher terrain.

Part of the trip is over bare rocks swept clean by a strong wind, and part is in waist-deep snow. My famous hopping tic is severe today, and when I hop in the deep snow, I often fall and there's no one to pick me up. But at least the snow softens the blow.

"We're way behind schedule," one of the counselors tells us halfway through the day. "If we get any slower, we won't reach our camp and you won't like where you have to sleep tonight. You won't like it at all!"

This is not the greatest threat in the world. We already don't like where we sleep.

But lying out in the open is dangerous at this higher altitude, where it's much colder. Before dark we have to get to a level place much higher up that will serve as our campsite for the night and that will be safe from the big snowstorm that's supposed to be coming.

Another serious problem arises around four o'clock. The water we're carrying has frozen solid, and because we're so far behind, there's no time to stop and thaw it out. A few mouthfuls of snow every now and then keep us from getting dehydrated.

When we get to the campsite it's almost dark, and by the time I've laid out my sleeping bag and set up my tarp, my hands are too frozen to work on a fire. As hungry as I am, I'm too tired to eat. I take my boots off and crawl into my sleeping bag, missing a second meal in one day.

I have to sleep within view of two counselors who are watching from about fifty yards away. I pray they don't ask me to get out of my sleeping bag, and they don't. But in the morning they tell me that if I don't get my act together and finish the hike, I'll be in the wilderness for a long time.

Or be kicked out.

With all that I'm going through, I'm once again astonished to find myself thinking that this is the worst that can happen.

Chapter 60

Day 20

Miraculously, I'm at the top of the mountain as the sun is setting. I'm the last to arrive, but I got here.

The backpack, which took me more than two weeks to assemble, isn't anything to brag about, but it actually holds together pretty well, and all my supplies have made it with me. Tonight I will sleep in this frigid air with a smile on my face and food in my stomach.

The beauty of the place is amazing, especially the light and the quiet peacefulness. I feel like I'm at the top of that tree again, the one I climbed back at my house years ago. Maybe that's the way I have to find the answer—I need to be on my own like this, and to push hard in order to relax and be myself. Now I can spend hours looking at the patterns of the nighttime shadows in the snow, the way the white-coated treetops are lit up by the sun and the moon.

As tired as I am, being here is exhilarating.

I am living life on a very basic level. Its calming effect is stronger than any medicine I've ever taken.

I haven't wanted a drink... or my medicines... since the very first night. The air is so pure here that the idea of putting cigarette smoke into my lungs seems outrageously dumb and disgusting.

The worst of my wrenching body movements have also lessened, either because I've been so distracted or because the exertion has tired me out. I deal only with the rituals of survival and the simple jobs that make it possible. *I'm making it.* I think of nothing else.

In some ways, my past life seems like it was a hundred years ago and happened to a different person. When I do think of my friends, I feel sorry for the smallness of their average days and wish they could experience what I have. I've been able to put aside threatening intrusive thoughts, like the idea that something has happened to my parents. I'm going on faith that it is just my mind trying to trap me in a bad loop again.

As I've grown stronger, I've become thinner and thinner. My clothes are practically falling off me and the rope is tight around my waist to keep my pants on.

My depression is lifting, too. I'm learning that I'm able to endure terrible hardship. This is an amazing feeling of power that I know will help me fight whatever comes at me after I leave. I've always believed I had inner strength, but I never thought it would be tested in such a profound and crucial way.

There is no doubt that this has been the worst thing I've ever had to do, the worst place my parents could possibly have sent me to.

And the best thing that has ever happened to me.

Chapter 61

Day 23

The pickup truck arrives at base camp just after noon.

I will be its only passenger.

I shake hands with each of the other kids and the counselors who have assembled to say good-bye, my brothers in the wilderness. There is a mutual respect and an unspoken jealousy felt by the other campers. Some of them will stay for a few more weeks. The one who has already been here for four months still has no idea when he's leaving.

But I'm going home.

Before getting into the truck, I turn for a last look up at the snow-covered mountain that I climbed when my body kept trying to stop me. I've suffered more here physically than I ever thought possible.

I'm leaving the mountain a different person than I was when I arrived. I've lost sixty pounds and am free of my addictions. I am stronger inside and out and have gotten past fears that none of the medicines I've taken could conquer.

My tics haven't left, but now they are more like nuisances, not overwhelming problems.

Mainly, I feel as if I can do anything I set my mind to.

The trip down the mountain takes a half hour on trails barely wide enough for our vehicle. Eventually the snowpack gets thin, and there are patches of dirt and bleached-out grass here and there.

Soon after that, we get to a rough country dirt road that leads back to the main street and the modest two-story house that serves as the camp's headquarters.

There are a bunch of new teenagers on the front lawn, boys and girls about my age fixing up sleeping bags for their trip to the mountain. They look fresh and rosy cheeked and seem like nice kids, but I know they're here because they've got problems. I wonder if they understand what lies ahead. I wonder if they'll be able to make it.

As I pass them, they stare at the kid with blackened hands who is back from weeks of cold and deprivation but is walking tall.

I turn from them to go into the house, and I see my father standing outside, waiting for me. He sees me and waves. "Hey," he calls. In the end, no matter what, he's always there. My mind is flooded with a thousand thoughts, but mostly I am proud. A big grin spreads over my face as I reach out for him.

He holds me and grabs my shoulder tightly. "You did it."

When we hug, I can feel his body shaking with emotion, almost as much as mine.

Leap of Faith

Chapter 62

I sit across the table from an absolutely beautiful teenage girl who breaks my heart every time I look at her. I'm at the adolescent OCD ward of the world-famous Wellington Neurological Center, a thousand miles from where my father picked me up at the bottom of the mountain.

Six of us patients are in the cafeteria to eat lunch, but what Noelle is doing is like nothing I've ever seen in my life. It kills me just to watch.

Noelle is a teenager from somewhere in Canada. She has long black silken hair and flashing eyes with dark circles under them that must be there because she doesn't sleep much. Her parents have sent her all over the world for different kinds of treatments, and none of them has helped. She's been at the clinic for a long time, and from what I can see, she shows no signs of getting out.

I try not to stare as she picks up a small portion of food from her plate, then stops the movement of her fork after lifting it only a few inches. She holds the fork there for as long as it takes her to complete some unknown counting ritual or some need for symmetry.

After about twenty seconds, she gathers herself for another move. A second lurch of her right arm brings the fork higher, but she stops it before it gets to her mouth. Something else must be completed in her mind before she can go any farther.

Finally, when she is able to get the food into her mouth, she chews and swallows in a certain regulated way. It's exhausting just to watch her. And so damn sad that I can barely stand it.

Noelle has multiple obsessive-compulsive rituals so complex that it can take her more than a minute to eat a single bite of food. Getting through a simple meal takes forever, and she usually doesn't finish because time runs out.

By now the rest of us have gotten used to eating with her, but today's lunch is so protracted that we'll miss our therapy sessions if we don't leave. So finally the aide who has come with us gently urges her to stop.

Noelle does what she's told with a gracious smile, and slowly she lowers the fork to her plate. My heart breaks for her again. She must be incredibly embarrassed by what she has to do, but she doesn't show it. I'll never get used to watching her go through so much hell just to feed herself.

Despite her sickness, Noelle is amazingly smart, maybe genius level. I've been told that she can speak four languages, but she's so deeply afflicted with her ritual disorders that her intelligence isn't any help to her right now. These days she usually just sits there, her eyes wide open in a dazed, sometimes frightened look, and seems almost paralyzed. She might say a few words, but very slowly and as if she's gasping them.

Most of the time she has a gentle way about her and an angelic smile. But yesterday that changed abruptly.

A few of us were in the common room using headphones to relax with tapes we'd made. All of a sudden we could hear a horrible screaming, which was getting louder as it got closer. Noelle was running down the hall. At first I thought she was running away from someone, but she was heading right for us. Her screaming seemed to be coming straight from her soul, as if all the pain in her entire life could no longer be contained and burst loose in pure fury. She was so out of control I'm not even sure she knew what she was doing, and if it hadn't been for one of the strong nurses who caught hold of her at the last minute, I swear she would have gone after us. It reminded me of my own rage attacks.

The saddest thing about Noelle is so painful that I try not to think about it too much. Sometimes I hear her screaming in the middle of the night. I lie there thinking it's that she realizes, in the endless darkness of her mind, she's alone and lost in a place where no one can reach her, and she is so unbelievably frightened to be who she is.

Chapter 63

For the first time in my life, I'm being consistently sensitive to other people and not mostly concerned with myself.

About a week into my stay at the ward, a tall, quiet guy named William appears in the common area without a shirt on. The fact that he's partly dressed is a huge breakthrough. For many years before he came here, William hadn't been able to wear any clothing. Just having fabric touch his skin gave him an unbearable feeling. I don't know how he got through life to this point, but they've been working with him here, with some obvious success.

Even though the rest of us are in our

teens, William appears to be in his thirties and is easily the oldest patient around. He's really intelligent, and his long wild hair makes him look like a mad scientist or some kind of wizard. It seems that most of the people I meet with Tourette's or OCD are unusually smart. Maybe that's just nature's way of compensating, but sometimes I think it's not such a good thing to be so smart and think so much about everything. To be *inside* your mind so much. Maybe it's too easy to get trapped there—like some of us do.

Except on rare occasions, William keeps to himself and stays in his room, which is why I'm surprised to see him in the common area. His obsessions and compulsions are very different from Noelle's, but, like her, he has an awful lot of them. Two of his problems are in direct conflict with each other. He has an extreme phobia of germs. His food has to come from sealed containers, and no one can touch it or be around him when he eats, which is why he never eats with the group. At the same time, another fear makes him deathly afraid to take showers.

William also has a fear of shaving, so his beard is long and scraggly. And he's afraid to lie down on a bed or sit in a chair, so I don't know how he sleeps. Every time I see him, he's standing. He's been standing for so long that his ankles and legs have become terribly swollen.

Germs aren't the only small things that terrify him. One time when he ventured out of his room, he ended up near a girl who was working on an arts-and-crafts project, and she accidentally spilled a bag of glitter. William went totally crazy when he saw it, and he went running off down the hall. I don't know what would have happened if some glitter had actually gotten on him. It's so hard to understand how someone as smart as William can be so irrational about something as harmless as glitter, but that's OCD for you.

"Hey, man," I say as he passes by. He keeps his distance, not because he's antisocial but because he's afraid of any kind of physical contact. He can't touch or be near anyone, even his doctors, so you don't shake hands with William. I can't imagine he's ever high-fived anybody in his entire life. Someone coming up to hug him would probably be his living hell. I wonder how that must have made his parents feel . . . or William himself . . . having to live a life without any physical affection, *ever.*

One of the guys I've become friendliest with has really made me think about what bizarre tricks nature can play on a person's mind. If you ran into my friend Chester somewhere indoors, you'd think you were with an ordinary, fun-loving guy. He's about fifteen and as all-American-looking as you can get. His interest in rap music isn't unusual either, but his degree of interest is. He always has headphones on, rocking out in the halls, rapping to his favorite songs.

Except with him, it's not just because he likes music. He *needs* to like music, especially songs by the group Linkin Park, whose music he plays over and over again and sings along with. Still, you wouldn't think anything was that different about him.

But something is.

Chester is deathly afraid of daylight. He hates going near the window. And if by accident some sunlight falls on him, he literally freezes in place like a deer caught in the headlights. The one time I saw this happen, he had a look in his eyes as if the world were going to end. Go figure that one out.

Chapter 64

If you have extreme OCD, then Wellington is a very comfortable place to be. Everyone here understands you and could care less if you're different from other people. If I wasn't so homesick I'd have to say I like being here, and I like the kids better than any I've known back in my hometown. They get me, and I get them. They have *empathy.* Most people don't, they really don't.

This is my best week with my clinical psychologist, Mr. Kenneth Roberts. We've been working hard on a number of therapies for almost a month. One is called *cognitive behavioral therapy*, and it is slowly helping me change my everyday thoughts and the way I act.

Wellington's approach to my Tourette's and OCD is completely different from most other approaches. Just like my being sent into the wilderness, this is not the standard treatment for my illnesses. Far from it. It's like a *second* intervention for me.

The main goal now is to deliberately expose myself to my obsessive behaviors, including my Tourette's tics, in order to gain control over them. Before this, my doctors did everything they could to suppress my symptoms.

Every day I focus on my most extreme tics and try to refrain from performing them for longer and longer periods of time. This is part of tic-reversal training.

Right now I can go more than fifteen minutes without doing any unusual movements. There are days when it isn't that good, but little by little I've gotten back some control over my body.

Mr. Roberts thinks that anxiety is at the root of all my other conditions, so he's teaching me a progressive relaxation technique. To help with this, I made a tape that I play in my headphones when I need to calm down. Learning new ways to breathe also helps control my anxiety.

Aside from the treatment, the most important thing about being here is just being here, living in a world where no one is reacting badly to me or judging me.

Chapter 65

Six weeks after arriving at the Wellington clinic, I stand with my suitcase packed. Mr. Roberts rises from his chair in the training room.

It's a hard moment for me because of the feelings I have for him. As my main therapist, Kenneth is one of the best things that has ever happened to me. He seems to instinctively understand what I'm thinking and knows what to say to get me to help myself. I also consider him a friend and a hero to all the people here.

Three of the other patients have assembled in the lounge to say good-bye to me. One college-age girl comes up and hugs me. "You be good," she says with tears in her eyes. "I'm sure you will, Cory."

I know the tears are not only for me. I saw that same look when I bid farewell to my friends at wilderness camp. *You're leaving. And I'm still here.*

"Stay in touch, man!" Chester yells, his headphones still in place.

Chester honestly seems happy for me. Maybe he's glad to see that someone can get enough help to go home. Maybe it gives him hope.

I wish Noelle was around. I'm going to miss her and I know I'll always think about how she's doing. We have been part of a very unusual and close community where we are all safe with one another and the staff. Not like the world I'm about to go back to.

"How are you feeling today?" Mr. Roberts wants to know with his typically serious but gentle and caring manner.

"Really good, I think."

"Can't talk you into staying a little longer, I guess?"

"You can try."

"Hey, that's . . . a change."

"But it won't work. I'm outta here."

He shoots me a disappointed but playful look. "You're gonna keep working on that anxiety, right? Do your exercises?"

"Yeah, of course."

"It's easy not to do the exercises when you're back home, but they're important," he says. Right to the bitter end, he's still working with me. You gotta love a guy like that.

From across the room, William's eyes meet mine. He nods, and I return the gesture. We don't need words.

One of the nurses shouts an upbeat good-bye from behind her station window. I take a last look at all the people I'm leaving and feel a wave of guilt that they have to stay. But every one of them is better now than when I met them. And so am I.

When I turn, I see my father at the end of the hall. I can tell that he's been standing there for a while, not wanting to interrupt the ending of this part of my story.

His eyes are glistening. Just like they were at base camp in Wyoming. That's my dad for you.

Chapter 66

I fly home from Wellington and get to stay over for one whole night. Jessie's there, and we connect like we haven't for years. And I can't tell you how good it is to see my mom, my angel.

The next day my mother and father drive me to the Devorough School, a private therapeutic boarding school in western New Hampshire.

As part of a plan I didn't get to vote on, I wasn't allowed to have any contact with my old friends during the brief stopover at my house. I've now been away from home for two and a half months. Going right into another strange new situation is like punishment when I think I should be rewarded. I hate the idea of it. A lot.

My parents have decided to send me right to the Devorough School because it offers me a chance to catch up to my junior-year class before it's too late. This wasn't even a remote possibility before wilderness camp and Wellington. Devorough has an intensive-study program, with more hours per day devoted to lessons than any regular school. Plus, like the other places I've gone to, they are set up to deal with kids who have special problems.

Devorough is in a very rural town and consists of only a few buildings, including a large structure for classrooms, dining, and other activities. Bicycles are the sole mode of transportation allowed other than feet. No friends, no cars, no cell phones, no alcohol, no cigarettes, no life.

We are met by Dr. Marianne Morgan, the founder, in a wheelchair, which reminds me of how far I've come from the days I used to go to school in one. She makes me feel welcome and promises that I will get what I need here. Even though there are many rules that must be followed, the other students love it, she says.

My mother and father are gushing with gratitude for her accepting me. A lot of other schools didn't.

The first group of students I encounter quickly confide that the place is a prison and they totally hate it. Every one of them does. One of the guys I meet right away is a very sketchy, secretive type who seems to command a lot of respect from the other boys. When I try to ask about his past, he doesn't tell me anything, but he's really friendly. He shows me the layout of the school and how to get around some of the rules.

In the next couple of weeks, I undergo intense schooling, but I'm so far behind that I have to stay awake half the night just to catch up. The constant pressure starts to make my tics worse again, which makes studying take even longer.

The relaxation exercises I promised Mr. Roberts I'd keep doing aren't on my mind at all, and even if they were, I wouldn't have time for them anyway.

Because I really do want to catch up to my class back home, I put in an incredible effort, which impresses the staff but takes a toll on me. I'm not getting enough sleep. I'm frantic about falling behind, and I'm getting anxious again. This is the exact opposite of what the people at Wellington wanted to have happen. I'm starting to break down a little.

The pressure isn't helped by a lot of whispering and private discussions going on around my room. I never find out what's going on because the other kids make me leave and no one will tell me anything. I guess I'm too new to be trusted.

I also start having clashes with kids on the lacrosse team when I stupidly brag about how good an athlete I am. I pick a fight with one of the little guys, who easily beats me up. Even after all I've been through, and as good a shape as I'm in, I still haven't got a clue about how to fight.

Every day I'm learning more, and faster,

than I ever have before, but the work is still mounting up too fast. In some ways, wilderness camp, with all the snow and ice, was easier than this. I kind of miss the mountains.

Three weeks into my time at Devorough, I feel like I'm going to have a nervous breakdown from the work pressure and lack of sleep. In my mind it's pure torture and punishment. I plead with my parents to let me come home. After a lifetime of their supporting me in so many good ways, this is possibly the worst thing they've ever done and the only mistake in their intervention.

No matter what I say, and it's all the honest truth, they tell me I have to stay until the end of the school year in May.

At night I drift off to sleep thinking about my old friends back home and how I could be with them in a way I never could have before. I feel strong and more in control and want to show them what I'm like now, how I've changed. With my new confidence, I know I can make it in my old high school, maybe even play football again.

I dream of being home, riding my dirt bike, hanging out, sleeping late in my own soft bed.

No one knows it, but I packed my cell phone and charger in a backpack when I came to Devorough. One night I make a call to my old friend Mingo. As usual, he knows what to do, because he's a survivor himself, and he tells me something that hits like a lightning bolt. I've already turned seventeen, so I'm legally old enough to leave Devorough if I want to *without anyone's permission.* No one can stop me, not my parents, not even the police.

My mind starts spinning with the possibilities. Soon, I can think of nothing else but getting away from the school. *It's becoming an obsession.*

The next night, after everyone's asleep, I sneak out a side door and make a break for it. I run like crazy to the two-lane country road that connects Devorough to the nearest town, which I estimate to be ten or fifteen miles away. I feel exhilarated, taking my newfound power and strength and using it to escape from this prison of a school.

Just before midnight, in total spooky darkness, I'm walking on a desolate rural highway.

It's another kind of wilderness, and not nearly as bad as the one I've been to, so I'm okay with it. After an hour, however, I begin to feel that maybe this wasn't such a good idea, because it dawns on me that I escaped without a plan. I left with only the money my parents had given me for school expenses, and I assumed that eventually I would be able to pay someone to drive me back to my hometown. I wasn't thinking, just acting.

Some plan, huh? Talk about compulsive behavior and making bad decisions. I don't even really know how far it is to the next town or how far I've walked, and I'm not dressed for the cold night. After another hour passes, one of the few cars I've seen catches me in its headlights and slows to a crawl. It's a police car.

"Cory Friedman?" the officer asks.

Chapter 67

"Yeah, why?" I answer back.

"Been looking for you, son. Get in. I'm taking you back to the school."

I wasn't expecting this. Apparently soon after I escaped, the school did its usual late-night bed check, found me missing, and called the police. It's hard to decide what to do now—then I remember what Mingo told me.

"I don't have to, do I? I'm seventeen," I say very politely, desperately hoping Mingo knew what he was talking about.

"I don't know about that. Even if you are, you have to go back to the school first."

I get in the cruiser, and the policeman returns me to Devorough. The school calls my parents.

When I get on the phone, I refuse my mother's request to stick it out a few more weeks and lash out at both my parents for sending me here. I tell them that I'm demanding my rights and that I'm no longer their dependent son but a legal adult. They don't know how to answer that. It's news to them, like it was to me.

The discussion ends with me hanging up. It turns out that Mingo was right. The police have no choice but to let me leave.

I sign a release that the school needs for their records—this is why I had to go back there. Then the police drive me to the nearest bus station an hour away. It turns out to be such a long distance that I never would have made it on my own.

I don't tell anyone where I'm going. Just far, far away from this prison.

In a few hours I end up at the Port Authority Bus Terminal in New York City and spend the early morning walking the streets. When I'm ready, I take a train to my hometown, where a friend picks me up and drives me home.

My mother and father haven't slept the whole night. Now that I'm back, they are outraged by my behavior. I understand their position, but I had to do what was right for me. That school sure wasn't. A little while later, I'm safe again in my own bed, and it's the best feeling in the world. I sleep for twenty-two hours straight.

In a few days everything is peaceful again. My parents and I return to Devorough to officially sign me out. We have a final meeting with the school's founder.

"You never should have left us, Cory," she scolds me. I can see how hurt and disappointed she is, but also arrogant, it seems to me. "I don't think you're going to make it out there."

Her words stun me. In my mind this is a cruel and destructive thing to say, but she can't reach me on the inside. After all I've been through, my armor is titanium and a couple of feet thick. I don't argue with her, just thank her for letting me attend. I can't leave the grounds fast enough.

But as we drive away, I'm thinking, *You don't know me. Don't ever count me out. I'm going to make it this time.*

The Emergency Meeting

Chapter 68

After Devorough, there's a sudden shift in focus. Now the job is to try to get me back into my high school to finish junior year. This is almost impossible given all the work I've missed, but not impossible for my mother. She's been on the case, assembling piles of records, making notes, figuring out what we need to do.

We are now on our way to a crucial meeting at school to get me back into classes and discuss any accommodations that they can give me to help me get through the rest of spring semester.

But the moment we walk into the designated room, our whole idea of what the meeting is about explodes.

The first shock is that this is an actual large conference room, not the customary office space these kinds of meetings take place in, and instead of seeing just the special-ed and guidance counselors needed to take care of my accommodations, we find that the room is loaded with about a dozen people. This stops my mother in her tracks, and she looks as confused as I've seen her in a while.

"Please sit down," someone says sternly, and we take the only two empty seats at the large wooden table.

I don't recognize some of the people here, but there's my history, math, and English teachers; my regular guidance counselor; and a social worker from the special-education department that I met a few times before.

I already have a scary feeling that something is wrong, and I search for the friendly, smiling face of Mrs. Tremaine, my personal caseworker. She's been my best friend in the school administration and has fought for me for years, but for some reason she's not here.

In a moment another woman who's

a lot older takes over the meeting. She identifies herself right away. "I'm Emily Hanover. I've been assigned as Cory's new caseworker, *replacing Mrs. Tremaine.*"

For the second time in the first two minutes, my mother and I go into shock. The person who has always been my champion and who I need most in this meeting hasn't even been invited.

Everyone can sense the negative tension. The room is eerily quiet, and I get the feeling that nobody really wants to be here. I know I don't.

When my new caseworker starts again, the world is suddenly turned upside down.

"We wanted to gather everyone familiar with Cory and his history to help you understand why we've come to our decision," she says, looking back and forth between my mother and me.

My mother is stunned by this unexpected announcement.

"What decision? I thought we were here to discuss the accommodations we could have for Cory as he reenters school."

The complete silence that follows tells me how stupid I was to think coming back might be as easy as just asking. And it's a huge surprise that the members of the group have already met on my case and seem to have made up their minds about something big. And bad.

"Basically, we've had to deal with the wisdom of Cory being able to continue in this school year," Mrs. Hanover says. "It wasn't really a question of how we could help him through the rest of the semester."

I can't help but notice that everything she's saying is in the past tense.

"I don't see any way to avoid the unfortunate fact that Cory simply didn't attend enough of his classes in the first semester to get credit for them," Mrs. Hanover decrees.

It's as if a bomb has been dropped on us. A tidal wave of disappointment rises in my body. My mom looks like she's been punched in the stomach. I want to start screaming but I know this is no time to lose it. Somehow I keep my mouth shut.

"Are you saying that you want Cory to repeat his junior year?" my mother asks, her voice shaking. "Entirely? Starting next fall?"

The magnitude of this thought is still sinking in. *Not going back to school for several months, and then starting over in the same grade?* It's almost impossible to deal with.

It's also almost impossible to understand why none of my "friends" at this meeting are saying anything to defend me, especially my English teacher, who really likes me. She looks as if she's afraid to speak.

As I search from face to face, I see that the one with the most negative look is my history teacher. This doesn't surprise me, since she never did have much patience with me. I don't think she ever really understood that I can't do all the work all the time or that I can't help being somewhat disruptive in class.

"It's absolutely necessary for Cory to move on," my mother says directly at the new caseworker, confronting her and the whole unexpected premise of the meeting. "I don't know how you can even be thinking about making him repeat junior year."

As she forces herself to continue, I can see her gathering strength. "All of the psychologists agree that Cory needs a new start, and is ready for it. Going backward will only make him revert to where he was when he had to"—she stops short for a moment, then goes on—"when he had to take a leave of absence." She's choosing her words very carefully.

"Look, Mrs. Friedman," my new caseworker says with a sudden pleasantness in her voice. "We're all here because we want what's in Cory's best interest, and we certainly don't want to set him up for failure. As I said, we don't see how Cory can possibly complete the present term since he hasn't really completed the last one."

My mother is speechless.

"He's missed too many days and too much class work. We have thought about this long and hard, and we're in agreement that he doesn't have a chance to succeed in spring semester because he hasn't built the proper foundation for it."

She looks around the room for support from everyone about my terrible crimes of the past, but she doesn't find any. Her voice is still hanging in the air when she sits back in her chair.

"But since I'm the newest person in this," she says, "maybe it would be appropriate to ask for thoughts from those other members of our staff who have worked with Cory . . . just to be fair."

The room goes quiet again as all await her first selection.

"Let's start with his experience in math class."

My math teacher is a little nervous as she begins, and I have no idea what she's going to say. She was always nice to me but not always happy with my performance.

"Cory has shown the potential to be good at mathematics," she starts, "but frankly I don't think at this point he's been in my class enough to grasp a lot of the fundamentals of Algebra I. I tried to keep him up to speed, of course, and when he couldn't attend class, I gave him assignments to do at home, but he didn't turn most of them in."

My mother is about to say something but decides not to.

"Given that, how would you assess his ability to do Algebra II in this next semester?" Mrs. Hanover asks bluntly.

My math teacher hesitates. "It would be very hard for him," she finally admits. "I'd question the wisdom of letting him go to the next level."

I don't think she wanted to say it, but she did.

Mrs. Hanover shifts her attention to my favorite teacher.

"Let's talk about English."

My English teacher seems caught off guard but takes a breath and manages to smile at me kindly. She's obviously uncomfortable.

"Cory has a wonderful mind," she begins. "He's one of my best writers and has a vivid imagination. But . . . he *has* missed a great many assignments . . . which isn't to say he still couldn't do well in the spring," she adds as a hopeful after-thought. "English is a little different. His basic skills are in place, but..."

Her words trail off into silence.

"And what's been the experience in history class?" Mrs. Hanover continues.

My heart starts pounding in my chest. My history teacher has been the hardest on me in the whole school. I don't think she's ever liked me. If I have an enemy in the room among the teachers, it's her.

And what she says doesn't surprise me.

"Quite frankly, I don't even have enough work from Cory to say he really has taken first-semester history. He hasn't turned in the majority of his assignments and didn't take his midterm exams. I'm sorry to say that I couldn't possibly pass him on the basis of the work he's completed. He would be cheated of the learning that didn't occur."

What's best for Cory. Question the wisdom of continuing. Cheated of learning.

All the things they're saying are just polite ways of telling us they're not going to help me. *Why don't they just come out and say they don't want to give me a chance, don't even want to listen to our side of things?*

In a while, when Mrs. Hanover finishes with the teachers, she thumbs through a stack of papers in front of her. "There are also, of course, the issues of state educational standards that have to be met. According to Cory's record, he hasn't attended school for enough days to meet the requirement for last term. Technically, the physical education he's missed is enough to set him back by itself."

This seems like a totally random problem to me. The state is very big on gym classes these days, but everyone knows that a lot of the time, nothing much goes on there.

"To be truthful, a good deal of this decision is out of our hands, even though, as I've said, our guiding principle has been to help Cory in any way we can. I think we all agree on that."

Some of the people in the room nod their heads.

Yep, let's help Cory. Let's hold him back.

"So, as you can see, according to the rules, we really have no choice but to require that Cory repeat his junior year. We're sorry, really we are."

Even though this decision has been obvious from the start, I feel a rush of heat. Lucky for me, my mother's hand is around my wrist, grasping it tightly so I can't get up and blow any chance I might have of changing their minds. *If I have any chance at all, which I don't.*

Mom and I exchange glances, and she has to be thinking what I am: *This will destroy everything just when I'm getting better. I have to move forward, not backward. I have to get my life going again, get through high school, and move on.*

"Just give me a chance," she whispers to me calmly, but I can see that she's anything but calm on the inside. I know my mother.

"What it all boils down to," the guidance counselor says when it's his turn to speak, "is that we don't see how Cory can possibly make up what he missed in the fall semester while he's taking on new work in the current term. Up to now there's been some... difficulty just keeping up with the regular work—not that he hasn't tried," he adds in a feeble attempt to be kind. "Plus, let's be honest, there's very little time left in the term. It would be a lot to ask of anyone."

"Not for me," I blurt out before I can check myself.

Mom throws me a cautionary look, and I go quiet.

That seems to be the end of the speeches. After a lull, everyone turns to my mother to listen politely to anything she could possibly have to say, to get it over with and then leave. Up until now Mom has let them get more and more negative without arguing, but I know that she won't leave without a fight.

But it takes me off guard when I look at her and see that the unexpected gang-up seems to have been too much, even for her. Her eyes are brimming with tears.

And that's when I can't take it anymore. Suddenly the issue is no longer what's going to happen to me.

"How can you do this to my mother?"

I stand up. "Look what you're doing to her. You've made her cry."

Her grip on my wrist tightens, really tightens.

"Don't worry, Mom," I tell her softly. "It isn't worth it. I'll do anything they want me to. I can do it if I have to."

For a long moment, my mother sits there, collecting herself. I can see she's exhausted, not just from this but from a lifetime of helping me survive an endless number of crises. At last she's come to one that she doesn't have a chance of solving. This is the end of the line, the end of her energy, and I can't blame her for giving up. Too much pain. Too much work. Too many years.

I scan the room again. In the end, not a single teacher has really stepped up to fight the decision that's already been made.

Chapter 69

For what seems like a long time, the group is silent, as if a blanket has been thrown over the room. Then my mother clears her throat and takes a deep breath. It startles me to see that she's undergone a change from just a few minutes earlier.

In place of tears I can see composure, and something more. As I've said before, since the day my head started shaking, Mom has given up her own publishing business, her studies in music, her vacations, and pretty much her life to help me. But one good thing has come out of it. All the time she's invested in me has made her very smart, not only about my situation but also about dealing with doctors, hospitals, and entire school systems. In a way, she's been getting ready for this moment for a long, long time.

When she starts to speak, she's totally in command. And she's my guardian angel all over again.

"Last semester was the hardest Cory has ever had," she begins. "You all know that. His Tourette's and OCD were so out of control he couldn't get to school as much as he'd wanted. He was on a shortened day and was put in the most basic classes just so that he could try to get through junior year.

"There was a time early on when it got too hard for him to walk, and he came to school in a wheelchair just so he wouldn't miss his work. Believe me, that wasn't easy for him. He used to play football and . . ."

She falters briefly but gathers herself again quickly. My mom just won't quit.

"Cory fought harder than you can imagine to stay in this school, and when that wasn't enough, he took a leave of absence to rehabilitate himself. You know where he went and what he did. Wilderness camp. Sleeping in the snow and freezing cold for a month. And he did it, and came out a survivor. All his counselors agreed on that."

A few heads bob up and down in support. At least they're still listening.

"After that he went to one of the best and hardest OCD hospitals in the world, and he started to turn his life around, a day at a time. It was amazing, and also heroic. And now you're telling him that all this, all his efforts, are just going to be thrown away? *That they don't count for anything?*"

She lets the thought settle in. Her energy and passion are building by the second.

"If you make Cory repeat junior year, you'll be hurting him so much more than helping, and it will cancel out the unbelievable efforts he's made. It will stop his progress cold."

My history teacher starts to lift her hand off the table as if to object, but it's tentative, like she's a student herself, unsure of an answer.

Mom continues without acknowledging her. "But I know you have to go on what he needs to learn. And the rules. So let's talk about the learning he's done that you may not have thought about. Let's talk about that hospital he was in, the Wellington Neurological Center. Do you know that a substantial part of every single day was spent on classroom time, in all subjects? Cory was a star student while he was there. Is that anywhere in your records? It's in *ours.*"

She plucks some loose pages from a file and drops them on the table. A couple of the teachers look surprised. This is definitely new information that they're not ready to deal with.

"You all know how innately intelligent Cory is, and about his auditory gift. Whatever he hears in classes, he retains. I know that he's picked up as much knowledge just from sitting in class as most kids do taking notes and doing lessons. Did he miss some things? Yes. Do other kids miss some things?"

She lets the challenge hang in the air. No one interrupts with a rebuttal.

"The Devorough School that Cory

went to is an advanced college prep school with a highly accelerated schedule. He was there for only about a month, but I know he learned a lot more than a month's worth of history. And the same goes for chemistry. As a matter of fact, he's already had a good bit of Chemistry II," she adds, training her eyes on Mrs. Hanover, "even when he didn't have the basics of Chemistry I. How? By working seven days a week and staying up late at night studying until he caught up to everyone else. He could do that with algebra, too—in fact, he already started at the Devorough School with some work in Algebra II."

I'm not sure, but I think I can sense a shift of mood in the room. Everybody, even Mrs. Hanover, is listening hard.

"Did you know that Cory has also done work in areas other students haven't even been exposed to? Last summer, while his friends were playing ball and hanging around, Cory took a seventy-hour course on Web site design. It dealt with designing home pages on the Internet. And this wasn't just any course—it was a course for *college-level students and professionals.* Cory was the youngest one there by far.

"At first they thought he was too young to attend. But in the end, he not only earned their certificate, he was asked to come back to lecture on Internet marketing because of what he knew that they didn't. I understand that he could have been given some credits for that here in high school, but we never asked for them. Now we're asking!"

The guidance counselor perks up at this. He's always encouraged students to learn things outside of school as a way to earn extra credit. This is exactly the kind of stuff he talks about.

"The same goes for the thousands of hours—and I mean thousands—he's spent becoming an expert on the computer at home, studying marketing, taking dozens of courses from experts, publishing articles on Internet marketing, starting five small Internet businesses all by himself. I didn't think to ask for credit for that, but I know credit is given for all kinds of extracurricular learning. I have friends in town who've gotten it for their kids . . . with letters of recommendation from some of you."

It's amazing to watch and listen to my mother. I never thought about how all the things I've learned on the computer could relate to a high school education, and hearing it all at once, I think it sounds pretty impressive. Even so, my history teacher still isn't making eye contact with my mother and me. She's a tough one.

But Mom has already picked up on her stubbornness. "History? Well, that's not as easy to defend, except I'll tell you this: Cory may not know exactly when the Battle of Waterloo occurred, but his father and I talk about current events all the time. He probably knows as much about what's going on in the world today as any of the other students. And not just the facts but *why* things are happening—the concepts. I guess in this area you could call that homeschooling."

"That's all well and good," the history teacher interrupts, "but there are specific lessons that have to be completed. Assignments to be done that weren't."

"Yes, I understand that," my mother answers, "and I'm glad you brought it up. As far as all the assignments he's missed, not only in history but in math and English, I want you to see what I found in his backpack at the end of last term."

Mom opens a large manila folder and takes out a stack of papers more than an inch thick.

"These are all homework assignments Cory did on the nights he was able to work. All subjects. It took him a long time to do each of them, and in the end he was exhausted. But no matter how many times I reminded him to turn them in the next day, he usually didn't remember."

"May I?" the history teacher asks suspiciously.

My mother pushes them over to her without comment.

"There are close to sixty assignments here, including fifteen just in history. He did the work; he just didn't get the credit. There was no one at school to remind him to hand them in."

The history teacher inspects the papers and has nothing to say about this latest shocker. Clearly she's starting to lose the basis of her argument.

"But he still didn't take the tests, the midterms," she says anyway.

There is no answer for this. "That's true," my mother admits. Then she continues, "Now, someone mentioned physical education before. So let's talk about eight-mile hikes in deep snow every day for weeks at wilderness camp. What about working on survival skills in twenty-below temperatures? What about losing sixty pounds and quitting smoking and getting incredibly healthy? What have your other students done in physical-education classes this year? How many of them can even come close to Cory's record in gym class?"

With her questions still echoing in the air, she finally takes a moment to catch her breath. We've been in the room for less than an hour, but it's one of the longest meetings of my life.

"Let's be honest," she says, her voice suddenly more relaxed but still serious. "You all know that this isn't about only rules or the number of hours Cory has physically sat in classes. You have enough reason to help him keep going if you want to. That's what it really comes down to. Taking what he has been able to do here so far, thinking about all the amazing things he's achieved out of school, and helping him to build on them, helping him to keep going, like you always have before. You've always been on his side. Most of you have been wonderful to him. Why turn your backs on him now?"

Nearing the end of her talk, my mom looks at me tenderly. Her face is glowing. She looks so beautiful I can't begin to describe it.

"This is one amazing kid," she says to the room. "Don't ever give up on him. He'll always surprise you and come through for you."

After a long silence, there's another voice in the room. It's that of my English teacher, speaking her true thoughts for the first time.

"Cory is my best student," she starts quietly, then her voice rises. "By far my best. His ideas get the other students excited to learn."

The room is quiet again. Outside in the hallway, there are kids rushing somewhere. The English teacher's compliment feels great, but one voice is probably not enough. If the group is beginning to change its mind, it's impossible to tell.

The caseworker turns to me and asks if there's anything I want to say. Before I can respond, the history teacher demands to know how I can possibly do all the work now when I couldn't get it done before. Amazingly, she isn't giving up. After what my mother has told her, I really don't know what else I can say, so I just tell them all how I feel.

"Things have always been harder for me," I say simply. "But that's never stopped me, and it never will."

Miracle Days

Chapter 70

It seemed to happen to me when I wasn't even aware of it. Or maybe it occurred over a few days, or even weeks. You would think that if I'd known the *exact* moment of anything that's ever happened in my life, it would be this.

It's the last period of the school day toward the end of my junior year, and I'm doing pretty well. I still can't believe that I sat through all eight periods again today. One reason may be that I'm not on most of the drugs that used to make me feel so out of it.

In history class the Civil War is coming alive for me. It's as if I'm living back in that time, and the teacher likes my answers. The history teacher likes my answers! *The history teacher—how about that!* As usual, my hand has been shooting up in the air a lot, but only with questions and answers, not with my usual middle-finger salute.

When the period ends, I leave the room feeling that something important has changed, but I'm not sure what. I have an unusual sense of well-being, as if the electric current that usually races around my body has suddenly been turned way down, as though it's on a dimmer.

At the exit I push open the door and step into bright sunshine. The puffy clouds in the sky are so interesting that I stop for a while to study them.

The clouds are lit from behind by the sun, which is highlighting their wispy edges and making them glow as if a great artist has painted them. There was a sky something like this in the mountains of Wyoming not so long ago.

I take a few more moments to watch the sky. There's no hurry. I feel like I have all the time in the world.

Finally I walk toward the end of the

parking lot, where my car is parked. On the way I pass the handicapped spots that I was told I could use for my dirt bike and that I always refused.

Walking to my car, I realize that I have an unusual amount of energy and concentration, plus I'm light on my feet.

Normally at this time of day I'd be totally exhausted and on edge, ready to go home and rest from my classes. My new feelings puzzle me. I play back the day in my mind and am happy to recall that none of my classes turned out to be a problem.

The realization comes over me, not like a bolt of lightning, as people say, but like a calm breeze that creeps into my mind and spreads a peaceful blanket of serenity.

I'm not ticcing. I'm not ticcing at all.

Chapter 71

The thought is so miraculous, so *impossible,* that I automatically dismiss it. I can't actually remember if it's been this way all day, but I feel weak at the knees from the possibility that it might be true. I'm just standing there as other kids are passing by and noticing me, a few saying hello.

Out of habit I wait for familiar urges to come back—the need to contort my face, to hop or lurch forward, to dip to one side or bend at the waist. I count the seconds until my arm will undoubtedly shoot out three times in front of me to punch the air, or my neck will tilt up to the sky.

And what's happening is *nothing.*

A different kind of panicky feeling begins to take hold of me, the fear that this is going to end any second.

I need to divert myself from thinking about ticcing because that's what always brings it on.

In a little while, when the movements still aren't happening, I test them by challenging myself to tic. Deliberately I jerk my hand in front of my chest, but I have no compulsion to complete the ritual with the usual two more thrusts.

I still think this is all a bizarre mistake, a miscalculation my brain has made that will soon be corrected.

Or maybe I'm dreaming the whole thing. I've dreamed it so many times before, but this seems real. Even if it's crazy or is a temporary mistake or only lasts a short time, at least I know that it's possible.

I travel the rest of the way to my car without a single hop and with a sense of wonder.

On the ten-minute drive home, my foot is steady on the gas pedal and I don't have the involuntary stiffening of my leg that makes me speed up. I don't jerk the wheel to the right or left, not even once. I don't jack up the volume on the radio before turning it on.

When my mother greets me at the door, I'm too afraid to tell her what's going on. Raising her hopes only to have them crushed again would be an unbearably unkind act, and it's still too early to risk it.

Jessie is in the living room, and she flashes me a gentle smile. As I've gotten better, we've gotten closer again. I know she's proud of how far I've come. As a senior, Jessie applied to six colleges and got accepted to five of them. She's going after the degree in special ed that she's always wanted. The thought of not having her around saddens me, but I have something else to think about today.

An hour later, the tics still haven't returned, and I have to at least allow for the possibility that something has really changed.

By eight o'clock I've finished my homework in record time and I'm sitting at the computer, playing with some new ideas for an Internet marketing business.

My hands are unbelievably steady on the keys, and I feel no need to pound the table after every few words like I used to. My eyes and mouth are still.

This really is happening, isn't it?

The doctors have said that Tourette's symptoms improve over time for some people, but not all. Have I turned out to be one of the lucky ones?

If my parents have noticed a change, they aren't saying anything, probably for the same reason I'm not. They're conditioned not to mention my physical habits unless I do, but I know they're always watching out of the corner of their eyes, praying to see exactly what's happening now. *Nothing at all.*

Later, I head for bed in a state of total wonder but also apprehension. On the way up the stairs, I catch my mother looking at me.

"I know," I tell her. "Don't say anything."

Chapter 72

The next morning I lie in bed, afraid to get up and see that I'm the same person I always was.

I can't tell yet if anything's changed because the best time for me is usually when I first wake up. I know I should be incredibly excited at the prospect of a day of being like everyone else, but excitement is always my enemy, and the fear that today I will return to the *old me* is almost paralyzing. I honestly don't know if I could take the fall.

Still, I stand up, and I test myself.

Leaving my room for the shower, I remember that doorways can make me do a compulsive little triple shuffle step before I can pass through.

This time I sail through without anything happening.

Soon my body is enveloped in hot water and steam, and I'm sinking into a deep state of relaxation. I look down at the busted floor tiles . . . and wonder if I'm really done breaking them.

I get to the kitchen smoothly, letting the idea of a miracle sink in. The quiet feeling is with me again today, as though I'm under anesthesia but have remained awake and alert.

I want to shout my sudden happiness at the top of my lungs, to wake the world and say, *Look at me,* but I still don't dare to assume that this is real.

I go to school feeling good but worried that this is where it will end. But even the stress of another day of sitting in the confined space of my classrooms isn't changing me back. Today is starting like yesterday ended, completely calm.

My classes are easier than they've ever been, and I can't stop myself from participating. Maybe I'm participating too much; one of my teachers asks me to give the other students a chance to share with the class. Fair enough. I can do that.

In between periods I walk down the halls like everyone else. It's amazing to me what a luxury, what a gift, normal walking is. I'm not sure, but I think the kids are looking at me differently. They're not avoiding my eyes like they do when I stumble or make a noise. A few of them greet me warmly as I pass by. I'm fascinated by the thought that today might be the first day I don't get any strange looks or hear muffled laughter after I leave a hallway or room.

After school I walk the streets of my hometown as if for the very first time. In a way, it is.

The early-spring breeze feels good on my skin as I come to the pizza place where a lot of kids from the high school hang out. This is the same restaurant where a customer once called the police because she thought I was having seizures.

I talk to some kids I know—without

twitching. I'm in full control. I have a new urge now, but it's a good one—to be with everyone I've ever known and let them see me as I suddenly am. Now they can judge me for what I say and do, not how I move.

Chapter 73

Later that night, when my family's asleep, an idea takes shape that's been rumbling around in my mind for hours, or maybe years. I sneak out of bed and hurry down the hallway stairs without making a sound.

I gently pry open the front door and leave the house.

The night is warm as I step up to my dirt bike and straddle the seat. I put it in neutral and walk the heavy machine out to the end of the driveway so the engine won't wake anyone in our house.

Once I'm out on the street, the bike comes alive under me, and when I start moving, I look back at my home, my eyes filling with tears. For more than a decade, this has been my refuge and my prison. Most of the time I've been afraid to leave. But not tonight.

The engine sputters once when I rev it and shift into higher gear. Then it smooths to a purr. In a way, this is like what's just happened to me. *Sputtering, missing, then running smooth.*

For the next few hours, I ride the streets of our town in darkness and anonymity, my bike and I in perfect harmony for the first time. The road, the whole world, is empty. Yet for me it's never been so full of promise and hope.

I shift into third gear, give it the gas, and take off, laughing.

I am alive.

I am free.

I am flying with the wind.

I am me.

A Father's Epilogue

In January 2002, my son lay in the darkened basement of our house in a downward spiral of depression, alcohol addiction, and hopelessness, and he made the decision to change. *He did it himself.* Roughly three months later, he began to reclaim his life with astonishing new strength and an irrepressible determination to beat the overwhelming odds against him.

It had taken years of debilitating neurological problems to bring Cory close to his breaking point. He suffered from one of the most complex cases of OCD, Tourette's syndrome, and anxiety disorder his doctors had ever seen. Even though our family lived through each and every moment of his resurrection, we could hardly believe that his recovery had happened. It was a miracle.

When the members of the high school

administration decided to allow Cory to complete his junior year, they laid out a daunting number of requirements. In addition to having to take the new midterms, he had to make up some past midterm exams, including the history test, on which he received an A. Several weeks later, he took the final history exam for the fall semester, which he also aced. These accomplishments were achieved in major part by his studying hundreds of three-by-five note cards prepared and gone over time and again by his mother. Maybe a hundred hours' worth.

Cory's English teacher waived all the past smaller assignments and asked only for the junior-year formal paper. He completed this task as well, a phenomenal essay on Walt Whitman for which he also got an A.

After that spectacular show of what he could do, and because most of the teachers and administrators really were on his side, they had no choice but to pass him on to the next semester.

After that, Cory had only one surprising request, a very revealing one: that he be allowed to take a few advanced courses instead of just basic ones. He had won his chance to prove himself, and that's what he set out to do.

During the remainder of that school year, teachers and students alike were astonished to see what the boy who once came to only a few basic-level classes a day—and for a while in a wheelchair—was capable of.

In the little time left in the spring term, Cory completed practically *two* terms at once without missing a single day. In the end he satisfied all of the school's criteria, passed every exam, and earned an A average. His teachers voted him the most-improved student in a high school of seven hundred.

In his senior year, Cory's progress continued just as dramatically.

That spring his name was called at the graduation ceremony on the same field where he'd once thrilled the crowd with his football play. On that fateful day the tears flowed freely, and not just from our family.

The main credit, of course, goes to

Cory himself and his irrepressible spirit; also to one very special therapist who never left us even after she moved away; and to a few wonderful champions he had in our school system.

It also helped, we believe, that Cory was always told—and therefore always assumed—there was nothing in life he couldn't accomplish, no matter what the obstacles.

Cory's mother, his true angel, never faltered in that arena. Not once did I ever see my wife, Sophia, let up under pressure or give in to despair. She has always been, and remains, an endlessly loving, unselfish, and giving human being with no other agenda than her family's well-being. I am certain beyond a doubt that her strength has become Cory's, not to mention mine.

During his senior year, Cory applied to a number of colleges with the rest of his classmates. His résumé was unlike any of theirs, however. To offset gaps in his formal education caused by absences, he created a unique portfolio that presented an unusual record of achievements outside the classroom. This included his experience on the computer, his place of refuge during years of isolation from friends.

One day in April 2003, a little more than a year after he walked out of the wilderness camp, Cory opened a letter that informed him that, against all odds, he'd been accepted into the School of Information Studies at Syracuse University. This was a moment for Cory and the rest of our family that was simply impossible to describe.

At Syracuse, Cory's professors were so impressed with his computer marketing knowledge that he was offered his own office in the Information Studies School, one of only six, and he was even asked to lecture at one of their classes. He became the lead singer in a band and performed in front of hundreds of students, once receiving a cheering ovation from the same basketball team that had won a national championship.

As of this writing, some of Cory's physical symptoms still return, but they are nowhere near as severe as they used to be. He is on very little medicine, and he's not taking anything that coincided with a worsening of his symptoms in the past. Our family is convinced that his most extreme symptoms were caused by medications prescribed in good faith but with unhappy results, almost without exception. Cory's battle to control OCD has been more successful, as he brings to bear his hard-won coping skills from Wellington. His optimism knows no bounds.

A complete cure for Tourette's remains elusive. Within the past few years, however, a young man with a vastly more extreme movement disorder had a pioneering operation at the Cleveland Clinic. From reports we've heard, it stopped all of his symptoms instantly.

Since then a number of operations involving Tourette's patients have been performed at this clinic and at other hospitals around the world. Exact information on their success is difficult to obtain, as official clearance is still pending, but we have heard that the results are promising, and there will be more trials.

Today, Cory is deeply involved in Internet marketing and has created a number of fledgling businesses of his own. He frequently makes trips to New York City to sing at karaoke clubs and is a lead singer in a really good band in New Jersey that's just formed. As always, no obstacle seems too great for him.

Over the thirteen long, hard years that this story covers, Cory had dreams that some people would consider modest. He wanted to go to school, play sports, have friends, and be treated with respect. These are things a normal childhood provides, but they were not often Cory's to enjoy. Yet despite his complex problems and many cruel setbacks, he always clung to the belief that he would survive his travails and achieve a happier life. And over time, this belief has only strengthened.

He has been to the bottom of the abyss, but he has been to the top of the mountain as well.

Appendix

Records and Medicines

New Zoloft { 1 pill
3½ Respardal

I never did have the courage to take Cory off all Respardal. He has been on 3–4 mg since the beginning of school year. Academically, with lots of support & continous contact w. school ie: writing homework down, typing his work and in-class support w/ math, reading & lang. arts) he has done fairly well – A's & B's.

Socially – We are at an all-time low. No one has called him for months!!.

Tics – has suffered with numerous tics, particularly internal stomach tics and shoulder tic. These have produced pain!

Vocal bantering – terrible – always has need to provoke!!!.

Sample of extensive medical records detailing medicines, side effects, and behavior from September 29, 1999, through January 4, 2000.

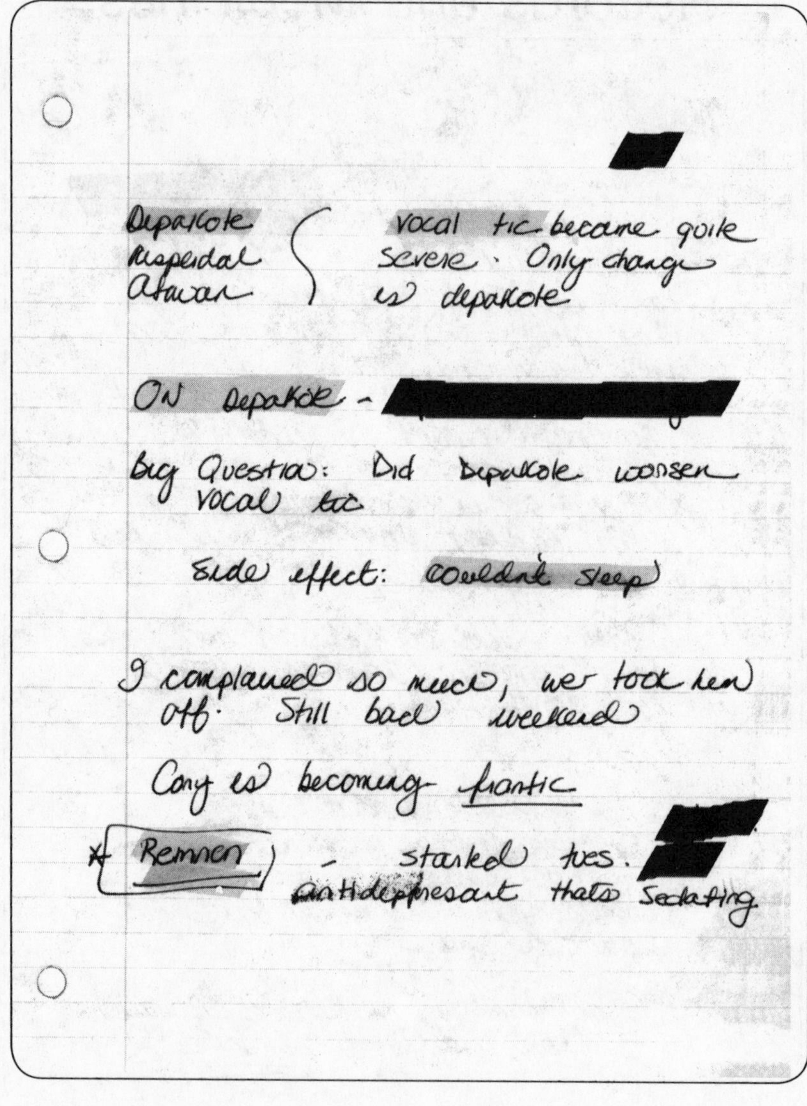

Depakote
Risperdal
Ativan
} vocal tic became quite severe. Only change is depakote

ON Depakote -

Big Question: Did Depakote worsen vocal tic

Side effect: couldn't sleep

I complained so much, we took him off. Still bad weekend

Cory is becoming frantic

* Remeron - started tues. antidepressant thats sedating.

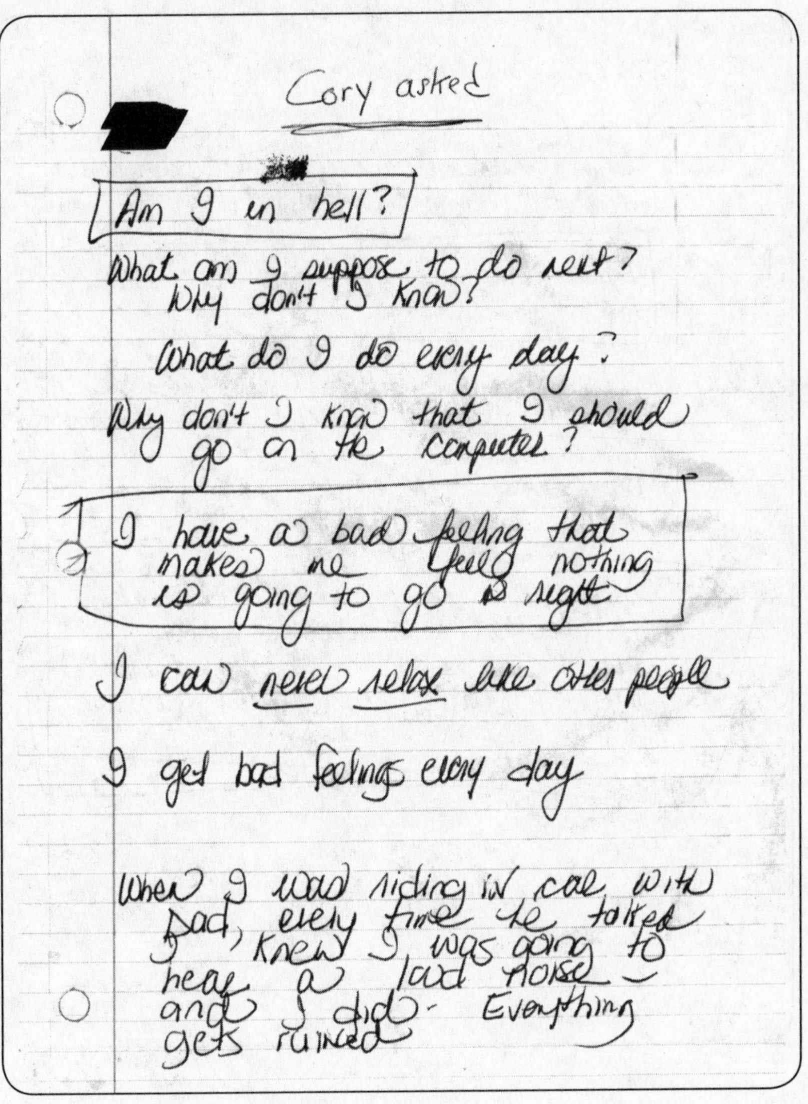

Cory asked

Am I in hell?

What am I suppose to do next?
Why don't I know?

What do I do every day?

Why don't I know that I should
go on the computer?

I have a bad feeling that
makes me feel nothing
is going to go right

I can never relax like other people

I get bad feelings every day

When I was riding in car with
Dad, every time he talked
I knew I was going to
hear a loud noise -
and I did - Everything
gets ruined

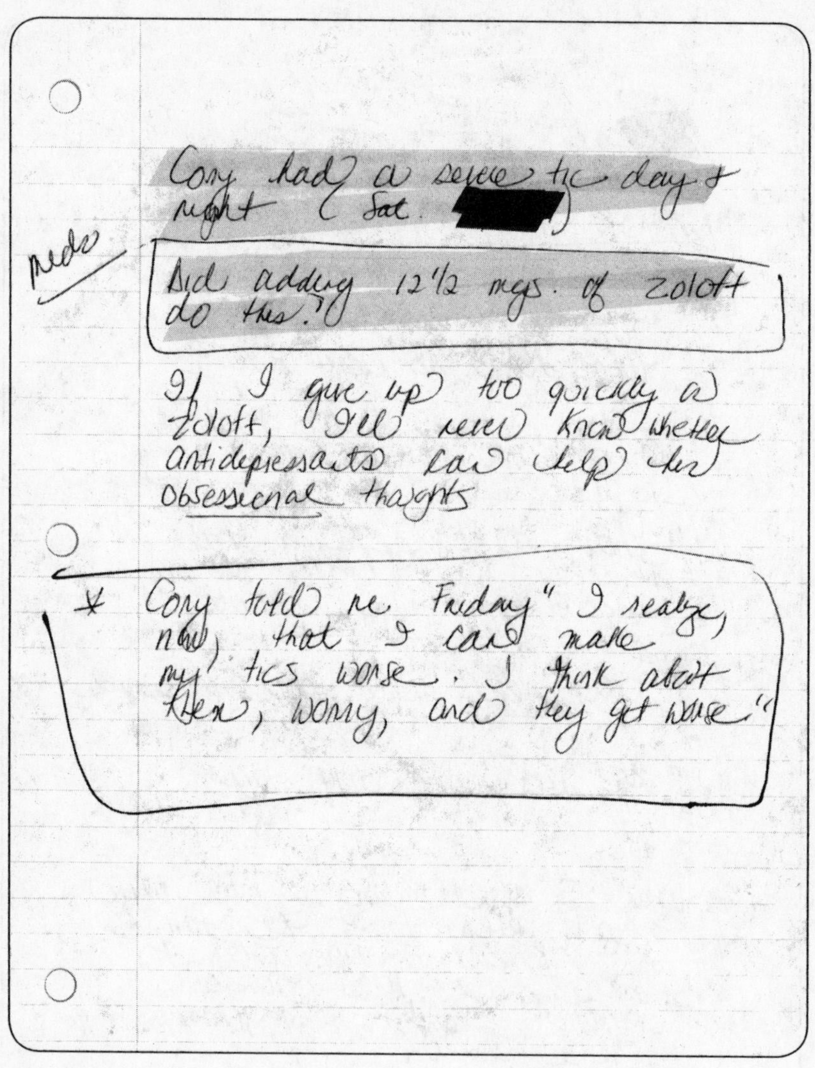

Cory had a severe tic day & night (Sat. ■■■)

meds

Did adding 12½ mgs. of Zoloft do this?

If I give up too quickly on Zoloft, I'll never know whether antidepressants can help her obsessional thoughts

* Cory told me Friday "I realize, now, that I can make my tics worse. I think about them, worry, and they get worse."

Buspar - 15 mg 3x day
Risperdal 1 1/2 mg - bedtime
→ Tenex - 1 1/2 pills - (divided AM + PM)
Ativan - 5 pills (AM, After - bed)
→ * Celexa - 20 mg (AM)

Most Prominent Tic - leg shuffle - quite severe - esp. going in + out of doors

Compulsions - touch people (v. annoying to friends)

Changes

→ Zoloft - Didn't work out - teachers complained he was v. agitated

(*) Celexa - 1st antidepressant he is tolerating. Seems calmer, able to watch some TV (couldn't before)

→

Cory went to school in wheelchair — leg tic too severe

Raising Celexa — Did increase make tic worse? Or going back to school.

I want to stay course to see.

Improvement

V. marked change — able to watch TV & movies.

Hasn't for years. Must be Celexa.

Longer fuse

Checked [redacted] 1cw – 100/60

Horrendous night – Tics have been keeping him from sleeping. Cory asked to go to hospital for injection to "put him to sleep"

We are at a frightening point – Cory is at his worst and we seem to have run out of drugs.

Risperdal
Zyprexia
Ativan
√ Buspar
√ Tenex
√ Clonidine
Zoloft
Prozac
Celexa
Neurontin
Depakote

Orap
Tetrabenazine

Aricept
Remeron

!

Hopefully, aricept, if it exacerbate things, will leave his system today

1½ Risp
Buspar 15 3x day
Ativan 4–6 per day
Tenex– ½ AM 1½ PM
Celexa ↓ 1 pill

Despite the fact that Corey's attention to TV has improved, his leg tic is horrendous – got him out of wheelchair but I honestly don't know how he is doing it. He shuffles backwards violently. Has fallen a few times. I lowered Celexa in last few days from 1¾ to 1

Restless
hot
Complaining of tics (v. pronounced when his mind is not engaged – sitting & doing nothing)

Unfortunately, besides computer, there

2 mg Risperdal
Ativan (as per needed, plus 2 2mg at
bedtime)

Seizing whole body
leg tic
assorted small tics
} very bad shape

Again - We took a trip, this time
to Florida

Except for new "seizing" tic, we have
a basic repeat of last year:

tics so bad, he's now not able
to be at school.

Neurologist [redacted] wants to rule
out seizures. EEG 4/4/10

Traditional Allergist - next week

→

Medicines Prescribed for Various Symptoms and Taken over a Thirteen-Year Period

Neuroleptic/ Antipsychotic	*Antidepressants*	*Blood Pressure/ Agitation*
Geodon	Anafranil	clonidine
Haldol	Celexa	Tenex
Orap	Effexor	
Risperdal	fluvoxamine	*Muscle Relaxer*
Seroquel	Paxil	baclofen
tetrabenazine	Remeron	
Zyprexa	trazodone	
	Wellbutrin	
	Zoloft	

Antidyskinetic	*ADHD*	*Antinausea*
Cogentin	Ritalin	Zofran

Anxiety/ Sedation	*Anticonvulsants/ Mood Stabilizers*	*Beta-Blocker*
Ativan (lorazepam)	Aricept	Inderal (propranolol)
Benadryl	Depakote	
BuSpar	Lamictal	
Klonopin	Neurontin	
Valium	nicotine patch	
Xanax	Tegretol	
	Topamax	

Vitamins and Minerals

(All taken daily for approximately six weeks, in addition to prescription medicines)

---

beta-carotene
calcium
fish oil
glutathione
grape seed extract
inositol
lecithin
magnesium
pantothenic acid
para-aminobenzoic acid (PABA)
selenium
vitamin B_1
vitamin B_2
vitamin B_3
vitamin B_6
vitamin B_{12}
vitamin C
vitamin E
zinc

About the Authors

James Patterson published his first thriller in 1976 and since then has become one of the best-known and bestselling writers of all time, with more than 140 million copies of his books sold worldwide. He is the author of the two most popular detective series of the past decade, featuring Alex Cross and the Women's Murder Club, and he has written numerous other #1 bestsellers. He has won an Edgar Award—the mystery world's highest honor—and his novels *Kiss the Girls* and *Along Came a Spider* were made into feature films starring Morgan Freeman. His charity, the James

Patterson PageTurner Awards, has given hundreds of thousands of dollars to individuals and groups that promote the excitement of books and reading. He lives in Florida.

Hal Friedman has published five works of fiction. He lives with his wife, Sophia, at the edge of a forest in northern New Jersey.

The Novels of James Patterson

FEATURING ALEX CROSS

Double Cross
Cross
Mary, Mary
London Bridges
The Big Bad Wolf
Four Blind Mice
Violets Are Blue
Roses Are Red
Pop Goes the Weasel
Cat & Mouse
Jack & Jill
Kiss the Girls
Along Came a Spider

THE WOMEN'S MURDER CLUB

7th Heaven (coauthor Maxine Paetro)
The 6th Target (Maxine Paetro)
The 5th Horseman (Maxine Paetro)
4th of July (Maxine Paetro)
3rd Degree (Andrew Gross)
2nd Chance (Andrew Gross)
1st to Die

THE JAMES PATTERSON PAGETURNERS

The Dangerous Days of Daniel X
The Final Warning: A Maximum Ride Novel
Maximum Ride: Saving the World and Other Extreme Sports
Maximum Ride: School's Out—Forever
Maximum Ride: The Angel Experiment

OTHER BOOKS

Against Medical Advice: A True Story (coauthor Hal Friedman)

Sail (Howard Roughan)
Sundays at Tiffany's
You've Been Warned (Howard Roughan)
The Quickie (Michael Ledwidge)
Step on a Crack (Michael Ledwidge)
Judge & Jury (Andrew Gross)
Beach Road (Peter de Jonge)
Lifeguard (Andrew Gross)
Honeymoon (Howard Roughan)
SantaKid
Sam's Letters to Jennifer
The Lake House
The Jester (Andrew Gross)
The Beach House (Peter de Jonge)
Suzanne's Diary for Nicholas
Cradle and All
When the Wind Blows
Miracle on the 17th Green (Peter de Jonge)
Hide & Seek
The Midnight Club
Black Friday (originally published as *Black Market*)
See How They Run (originally published as *The Jericho Commandment*)
Season of the Machete
The Thomas Berryman Number

For previews of upcoming books by James Patterson and more information about the author, visit www.JamesPatterson.com.